# TWENTY THOUSAND
# STREETS UNDER THE SKY

Patrick Anthony Hamilton was born in 1904 in West
Sussex, his father a comic actor, mediocre writer and
intermittent soldier, his mother a singer and expert
copier of oil paintings. He was sent to commercial school
in London, and for a time trained as an actor, before
realising that his talents lay in literature instead. His first
novel, *Monday Morning*, was published when he was
only nineteen, and two more followed in quick succession, as he began to be admired and widely read. In 1927
he fell disastrously in love with a prostitute, and started
to drink heavily – experiences brilliantly transmuted into
his trilogy of novels, *Twenty Thousand Streets Under the
Sky*. In 1929 he turned to the theatre, writing *Rope*, a
tense thriller staged at the Ambassadors Theatre to huge
success and later filmed by Hitchcock. The resulting
adulation and financial ease was followed by his
marriage, in 1930, to Lois Martin. Then in January
1932, Hamilton was knocked down by a car and lay
seriously ill for many months. It took two years before
he was able to start another book, yet he went on to
write novels, including *Hangover Square* and *Slaves of
Solitude*, radio dramas and plays, several of which were
filmed, including *Gaslight*, starring Ingrid Bergman and
Charles Boyer. His first marriage failed, and in 1954 he
married again, this time Lady Ursula Winifred Stewart.
When he died in 1962, after a long illness, *The Times*
obituary paid tribute to him as 'a genuine minor poet
(to use the term in its broad, modern sense) of the loneliness, purposelessness, and frustration of contemporary
urban life'.

Patrick Hamilton

# TWENTY THOUSAND STREETS UNDER THE SKY

A London Trilogy

WITH AN INTRODUCTION BY
Michael Holroyd

VINTAGE

To
D. H.
L. M. H.
M. S.
*and*
C. R. M.

Published by Vintage 1998

2 4 6 8 10 9 7 5 3 1

First published in Great Britain in 1935 by
Constable and Co. Ltd
Hogarth Edition published in Great Britain in 1987

Vintage
Random House, 20 Vauxhall Bridge Road,
London SW1V 2SA

Random House Australia (Pty) Limited
20 Alfred Street, Milsons Point, Sydney
New South Wales 2061, Australia

Random House New Zealand Limited
18 Poland Road, Glenfield, Auckland 10,
New Zealand

Random House South Africa (Pty) Limited
Endulini, 5A Jubilee Road, Parktown 2193,
South Africa

Random House UK Limited Reg. No. 954009

A CIP catalogue record for this book
is available from the British Library

ISBN 0 09 928865 6

Papers used by Random House UK Ltd are natural, recyclable
products made from wood grown in sustainable forests. The
manufacturing processes conform to the environmental regulations of the country of origin

Printed and bound in Great Britain by
Cox & Wyman, Reading, Berkshire

# CONTENTS

NEW INTRODUCTION BY MICHAEL HOLROYD
*page vii*

THE MIDNIGHT BELL
BOB
*page 11*

THE SIEGE OF PLEASURE
JENNY
*page 222*

THE PLAINS OF CEMENT
ELLA
*page 333*

# INTRODUCTION

Patrick Hamilton wrote this London trilogy when in his middle and late twenties. *The Midnight Bell, The Siege of Pleasure* and *The Plains of Cement* are each self-contained and were first published separately before being collected in 1935 under the title *Twenty Thousand Streets Under the Sky*. *The Midnight Bell*, which appeared in 1929 when the author was still twenty-four, is by far the most autobiographical of the three books. The tension of the narrative rises and in the last pages breaks through the structure of the novel, involving us in the emotional wreckage of Patrick Hamilton's life.

The controlling figure in his life was his father. Bernard Hamilton had been given little affection as a child and grew up without much self-esteem or self-knowledge. "What a low comedian you would have made!" Henry Irving had complimented him after he had been speaking at great length on the principles of religion. But Bernard Hamilton could never get his act together. He was a comedian equipped with a monocle but no sense of humour, a chameleon-like figure given to self-dramatization who nevertheless drank to be rid of himself. His children found it impossible to form a consistent or friendly relationship with him and would await with trepidation his return from various trips abroad. From Italy he came back a conscript father with a dash of Mussolini; from France he returned with an ineffable Gallic accent; Spain gave him an air of grave courtesy and a grandee's dignity; alighting at Euston Station very Scotch and drunk after a journey north, he told Patrick, "My boy, if ever it comes to war between England and Scotland, you and I will cross the border."

Though often absent from home, and despite violent scenes with his wife, Bernard took a solemn view of his parental duties and, having been granted a commission in the Royal Horse Artillery, would address his children in parade-ground language and have them up for military-style inspections.

Patrick grew up a silent, observant child, fretted by anxieties, and longing for some creed of certainty – which he was eventually to find in Marxism. From his father he could win no support for his wish to be a writer, although this wish reflected Patrick's need to feel closer to him. For Bernard, when acting the novelist, published several historical novels of which he appeared to think rather well ("As a puff preliminary," he advised his publisher, "you may say that this is the greatest novel ever written – which indeed it is"). His disinclination to help may have come from the suspicion that his son was naturally more gifted as a writer. Instead, he sent him to a commercial school near Holborn with a marvellous letter of instruction:

On Sabbath mornings you will sit, regularly, under the minister of the Scots Presbyterian Church near St Pancas. This is a *parade*. You will then proceed to Chiswick, reporting for Dinner at one-thirty, military time – i.e. five minutes early . . . You will bring with you a weekly report on conduct and progress from your tutors, endorsed by the Principal. If any difficulty should arise, you are to say that, I, your father, the author and barrister, require this.

You will make enquiries as to membership of the City Volunteer or Cadet companies; I believe such bodies still exist. Understand this is an *order*; excuses will have no more avail with me than the preachments of Mormon missionaries.

For exercise I recommend rowing. Ascertain the conditions of membership of the London or Thames Boat Clubs – you cannot hope for Leander.

Patrick did not remain long at this school, but while there he first fell in love. "His surrender was instant, absolute and agonizing," his brother Bruce Hamilton remembered. "I could see that her mere appearance made him almost faint with longing." More damaging was a love affair which began in 1927 with Lily, a West End prostitute. This must have seemed an escape from the respectable middle-class world of his parents into the world of London's defeated classes – the insignificant, the needy, the homeless and the ostracized – that populate his novels. But it also followed the pattern of his father's first marriage to a prostitute he had met in the promenade of the Empire Theatre, which ended when she threw herself under a train. The affair with Lily seemed both a copy of, and perhaps an exculpation for, that marriage – for here it is the prostitute who educates and takes revenge on the gentleman. By moving into a lower social sphere, Patrick Hamilton did not shed the insecurities implanted by his upbringing: his emotional vulnerability helped to make him one of the chronically dissolute and distressed who wander the dingy London streets and find refuge in its pubs and dosshouses.

*The Midnight Bell* (1930) is an account – in places almost a transcription – of Patrick Hamilton's disastrous romance with Lily. When first published it had the subtitle "A Love Story". But the word love, though desperately repeated in the many blurred conversations, loses all particular meaning and becomes a vague shorthand for what the characters imagine they want – the possession of beauty, money or security: in short, the possession of the unattainable.

*The Midnight Bell* is a study of infatuation. We are spared none of its detailed tortures or griefs, betrayals and deceits, in this anatomy of humiliation that brings us to the frontiers of Patrick Hamilton's famous psychological thrillers for the stage, *Rope* and *Gaslight*, and his classic murder novel *Hangover Square*. "Her perfect cruelty and egotism appalled him . . . He would kill her." But there are to be no murders in this trilogy, for it is the endurance of ordinary life that we are being shown. What *The Midnight Bell* loses in detachment, it gains in intensity. The appalling monster-bores of this pub are excruciatingly observed and intimately known. As we follow the intricately plotted inanities of their tales, which divert us by driving the other characters to distraction, we do not overhear them from a distance, but are brought into their very presence.

*The Siege of Pleasure* (1932) is the story of Jenny Maple's first step down from respectable servant girl towards prostitution. "Jever hear of Bernard Shaw? . . . He wrote a book called

*Mrs Warren's Profession* – an' showed it was all economics," Bob, the waiter of "The Midnight Bell", tells her – to which she replies: "I guess he was just about *right*." The economic point is well made in *The Siege of Pleasure*, which portrays the meagre and pleasureless conditions of her servant life as a form of socially acceptable, class-regimented prostitution. By describing as the place of her employment his own suburban home in Chiswick, and giving portraits of his nerveless mother and eccentric aunt as her employers, together with a fearful silhouette of his father (pathetically fallen away after a stroke and the unwelcome double success of *Rope* and *The Midnight Bell*), he aligns his own escape with Jenny's to make it all the more comprehensible.

Jenny is a shallow character – her shallowness makes all the more remarkable the power of her beauty which so profoundly impresses Bob. "He decided he would really die for such beauty." This sexual-aesthetic longing, and a longing for the freedom of financial security, are the two motivating forces in all these novels. Jenny herself has no eye for beauty and is even blind to her own looks, believing Bob is "a bit mad" to be so "crazily in love" with her. It is one of the ironies of the trilogy that the prostitute is sexless and the barmaid, Ella, does not drink. Both have little understanding of their clients, though a good deal of professonal expertise. As a servant, Jenny has been "arduously trained in the practice of pleasing strangers" and it is this skill she has taken on to the streets. Her own pleasure comes through drink which gives her access to wonderful sensations and the feeling of being in harmony with her environment. "She never believed it was possible to be so happy." For Jenny, drink is the replacement for everything that her existence itself has prevented her from enjoying naturally. "Love, of which some spoke, was a closed book to her, and she honestly believed it would remain a closed book all her life. It was a closed book which she had no desire to open."

But love seems an open book to Bob and as real as his literary aspirations. When, intoxicated by her murderous beauty, he puts his arms round Jenny and wills himself to believe that she loves him, happiness feels very close. Led into a hell by this alluring and irresistible pilot, he comes to use drink as a way of forgetting a "vile and disappointing planet", where such promised happiness is only a mirage.

Between the writing of *The Midnight Bell* and *The Siege of Pleasure*, Patrick Hamilton managed to free himself from his debilitating passion for Lily. He was helped in bringing his life under control by a sensible, if passionless, marriage in 1930 to a woman who was also in retreat from an unsatisfactory romance. Having reduced his drinking, he was in good spirits when, in January 1932, walking along Earl's Court Road with his wife and sister, he was knocked down and critically injured by a car. For a time his life was in danger, but after some months he made the best recovery possible, though he was left with a withered arm and, despite plastic surgery, marks and scars on his face, particularly his nose, which had been almost torn off. He added the accident to his final draft of *The Siege of Pleasure*, equating those who had done him emotional damage with those who had damaged him physically.

For almost two years following the completion of *The Siege of Pleasure*, he was unable to write anything new. Then, in a sudden concentration of creative energy, he completed the trilogy with a wonderfully balanced and accomplished novel developing a subsidiary plot from *The Midnight Bell*. Also centred in the pub, *The Plains of Cement* (1934) is Ella the barmaid's story, which complements Bob's story and brings a deeper perspective to the themes of *Twenty Thousand Streets Under the Sky*. Although apparently disinherited from the privileges of romance by her plain looks and financially disadvantaged by her background of lower-class poverty, this sensible girl is not without her dreams of a better emotional and economic life. But, unlike Bob and Jenny, she struggles to keep these tempting fantasies under control. She is secretly in love with Bob but endeavours to keep this a secret even from herself. She has it in her to feel for him what he feels for Jenny, for although "a placid and efficient girl, she also worshipped at the shrine of pure beauty and romance". Knowing nothing of Jenny, she believes that "any girl with eyes in her head would be after" Bob, but schools herself to accept that she can never hope to attract his attention. "She was, she found, incapable of inspiring his tenderness."

Because of the social divisions between men and women and the incompatibilities of male and female sexuality, there is truth in Ella's sober assessment. To Bob's mind, Jenny, with her ingenuous expression and clear blue eyes, is a heavenly creature who "with the child's weight of her body" seems magically uncontaminated by the world; while the humming buoyant figure of Ella, his frank and admirable companion in toil, who really *is* uncontaminated, appears no more than "a jolly good sort". Jenny is the child who must be owned, and Ella the mother who is taken for granted and eventually will be left. His intelligence tells him that this is false; but we do not act through intelligence, reserving it for commentary on our actions:

Particularly did he feel he was betraying Ella. She so deserved his respect, but all his homage went to another. Poor Ella. He watched her as she moved about merrily (in the cap which became her so), and gave back chaff for chaff in the crowded Christmassy bar. She had only one sin: she was without beauty. But she had all the heart-breaking desires, and you could see them there, in her charming face, as she laughingly and maternally answered – a creature eternally maternal, eternally fruitless – the insincere compliments of the men.

Ella uses her intelligence more than most, but she is "for ever seeking little reassurances and excuses for optimism". As a means of overcoming her sorrowful intuitions she is determined to see the best in everyone – even her horrifying suitor, Mr. Ernest Eccles. It is her fate to have one of the most dreadful admirers in English literature. As a besieging lover with all the propaganda of youth, the fifty-two-year-old Mr. Eccles is a sinister as well as an idiotic man. He presents himself as a romantic figure but appears in Ella's eyes merely as an old man with "something put by" which could buy her comfort and stability in life.

Money seems more likely than love to change Ella's life, and she is pressured by her circumstances to think of men as Jenny has regarded them – "appendages, curiously willing providers, attendants, flatterers of an indolent mood, footers of bills and payers of 'bus fares' ''. She is horrified to find herself calculating that if she inherits money from the death of her stepfather – a bully who carries overtones of Bernard Hamilton – she will evade marriage to Mr. Eccles, which would be a living death. "I can't stand cruelty," says Jenny. But everyone is destined to be cruel to someone in these novels: Jenny irresponsibly torments Bob; Bob unwittingly wounds Ella; Ella hurts Mr. Eccles, who in turn ill-treats her whenever he gets the chance.

The fact that all this should not depress the reader is a tribute to the power of Patrick Hamilton's storytelling and the exhilaration of his humour. In the earlier pages there are signs of immaturity – some passages of overdeliberation, moments of facetiousness, and an anxious reliance on what J. B. Priestley called Komic Kapitals. But as the book progresses, wonderfully comic scenes proliferate. Mr. Eccles, in particular, is a character of Dickensian proportions – Mr. Eccles who lives so intensely through his new hat that "it cost him sharp torture even to put it on his head, where he could not see it", who when looking for his visiting card is "not unlike a parrot diving into its feathers", who creates a "private cloakroom for his innumerable accessories whenever he sits down", who polishes his dignity on a lurching bus "by peering and looking back in a critical way out of the window, rather as though London was being partially managed by him, and he had to see that the buildings were in their right places". But though Mr. Eccles hardly ever fails to utter the most subtle drivel, he is no one-dimensional character. Touchy, crippled by shyness, desperately lonely and absurd, he too has his dreams of redemption. We feel compassion for anyone who meets him, but are also made to feel compassion for the man himself. He is used to give retrospective detachment to *The Midnight Bell*, for his wooing of Ella is another version of Bob's pursuit of Jenny, and it provokes a similar reaction: "We all have to take these risks."

Patrick Hamilton treats the pub as a theatre, describing its exits and entrances, laying down its decor and stage directions ("On your right was the bar itself, in all its bottly glitter, and on your left was a row of tables . . ."), taking us "behind-scenes just before the show" and up to the attic rooms where Bob and Ella pass their "endless procession of solitary nights after senseless working days". Performing against the lurid illumination of the saloon bar, his cast of ordinary habitués is magnified into a troupe of crazed misfits, and the conventions of English life reveal themselves as dramatically foolish.

Patrick Hamilton is an expert guide to English social distinctions, with all their snobbish mimicry and fortified non-communication. He describes wonderfully well how the hyphenated upper classes, yelling at their dogs, splashing in their baths like captured seals, and writing their aloof letters in the third person (like broadcasters recounting an athletic event), remain so mysterious to the lesser breeds. Taking us out of the pub into the swarming streets of London, he gives us a social map of this malignant city as it was in the harsh commercial era of the 1920s and the early 1930s. His Marxism became a method of distinguishing between the avoidable and the unavoidable suffering of people, and, in so far as literature can change social conditions, such a vivid facsimile in fiction may have helped to do so. Since it has been out of print for thirty years, this is a good opportunity to recommend it to a new generation of readers. While the narrative drives you forward, you will absorb the authentic atmosphere of what it was like to live in England between the two world wars.

*Michael Holroyd, London 1986*

# THE MIDNIGHT BELL

## BOB

## CHAPTER I

SLEEPING, just before five, on a dark October's afternoon, he had a singularly vivid and audible dream. He dreamed that he was on a ship, which was bound upon some far, lovely, and momentous voyage, but which had left the coast less than an hour ago. The coast, implicitly and strangely, was that of Spain. He was leaning over the side and peacefully savouring the phase of the journey—a phase which he knew well. It was that curiously dreamlike and uninspiring phase in which the familiarity and proximity of the coast yet steals all venturesomeness from the undertaking, and in which the climax of departure is dying down, to the level tune of winds and waves and motion, into the throbbing humdrum of voyage. That throbbing would continue for weeks and weeks. . . . A strong wind was blowing, buffeting his ears, roaring over the green waves, and rendering utterly silent and unreal the land he had just left. He was extraordinarily cold, and a trifle sick. But he did not want to move—indeed he could not move. He was lulled by the mighty swish of the water beneath him, as it went seething out into the wake, and he could not, under any circumstances, move. . . .

He awoke, with jarring abruptness, into the obliterating darkness of his own room. The swishing was his own breath, and the disinclination to move traceable to his snuggled, though cold and stiff position, on the bed. His dream sickness was a waking sickness. The thundering of the wind in his dream was the passing of a lorry in the Euston Road outside.

The burden of cold and ever-recurring existence weighed down his spirit. Here he was again.

He took stock of his miserable predicament. He was in his little hovel of a room—on his bed. He was not in bed, though.

Save for his coat and shoes he was fully dressed, and he was protected from the cold by his rough quilt alone. He apprehended that his clothes were wrinkled and frowsy from his heavy recumbence. . . .

It was pitch dark—but it was not yet five o'clock. His alarm would have gone, if it had been. He need not yet stir. There were no sounds of life in the house below.

Why had he slept? He remembered coming up here, a happy man, at half-past three. It had been bright daylight then. Now the dark was uncanny.

He turned over with a sigh and a fresh spasm of sickness swept over him. He waited motionlessly and submissively until it passed. Then he cursed himself softly and vindictively. He faced facts. He had got drunk at lunch again.

At last he sprang from bed and lit the gas.

He poured out all the water from his jug into his basin, and plunged in his head, holding his breath and keeping down. He gasped into his towel and rubbed madly.

Braced by the friction he returned to normal and all but unrepentant humanity again. Horror fled. For a moment he had been a racked soul contemplating itself in a pitch-dark and irrevocable Universe. Now he was reinstated as the waiter of " The Midnight Bell " dressing in his room a quarter of an hour before opening time.

Nevertheless, the gas-lit walls and objects around him were heavy with his own depression—the depression of one who awakes from the excess in the late afternoon. Only at dawn should a man awake from excess—at dawn agleam with red and sorrowful resolve. The late, dark afternoon, with an evening's toil ahead, affords no such palliation.

In the house below—" The Midnight Bell "—the silence was creepy. Creepy in a perfectly literal sense—the silence of things creeping. It was the silence of malignant things lurking in passages, and softly creeping up a little, and lurking again. . . .

There came, however, the welcome and dispelling sound of light women's footsteps on the bare wooden stairs : and a humming, buoyant body swept past his door, and slammed itself into the room adjoining his.

That was Ella—his pert companion in toil—the barmaid of
" The Midnight Bell."

She always hummed when she passed his door. In some
respects, he reflected, she was a very self-conscious girl. He
believed also that the brusque bumpings, the lively jug-and-
basin sounds, which now came through the wall, were similarly
subtly challenging and alluding to himself. A rather mystifying
creature, of whom he knew, really, nothing—for all their chaff
and friendliness. Her afternoon had been spent in goodness.
She had been over to see her sick " Auntie " (as she so naïvely
and characteristically called her) at Clapham.

By and by she called out to him, through the wall, chanting
his name in two distinct syllables.

" Bo—ob ! "

" Ullo ! "

" What's the time, Bob ? "

" Five To ! "

Ella's retort was a mumble and a bump.

" *What ?* "

" *Nuth*—thing ! "

Silence.

They had five more minutes. They did not speak again. The
hush in the house beneath them once more asserted itself. It
was the hush of behind-scenes just before the show. These
two, high up here, quietly preparing and making themselves
decent, were aware of the part they played, and of their shared
distinction from the besieging many.

He was now all but ready. He put on his white coat, and
fixed his white apron. He then went over to his mirror, in front
of which he crouched eagerly to brush his hair—a soothing
and reviving operation in itself.

His own reflection gave little dissatisfaction. The clear,
clean skin ; the clear, clean teeth ; the firm clean-shaven
features ; the nous, efficiency, and yet frankness of his face ;
the dark, well-kept hair ; the dark brown eyes, set rather far
back—all these collectively were as bracing to a remorseful
spirit as you could wish. He was, however, not an Englishman.
His American and Irish parentage gleamed from him—most
particularly his American. His father had been (and it was his

proudest boast) an American " Cop." But he had never seen his father, and his mother had died in London when he was sixteen and at sea. He had spent all his early life at sea, and England was the country of his adoption. He spoke with a Cockney accent. He was now twenty-five, but looked any age between twenty and thirty. He was an acquisition to " The Midnight Bell," and a favourite everywhere.

As he brushed his hair, Ella came out and knocked at his door. Without leaving the mirror he cried " Come in," and she entered. She was a dark, plain girl, with shingled hair and a trim figure. She was clean, practical, virtuous, and not without admirers. The slightly mocking and non-committal demeanour which she employed as her professional manner towards those who leered and laughed at her across the bar was carried into ordinary life, and was never so emphasized as when she was in the presence of Bob, whom she loved. She had loved him ever since meeting him, five months ago, when he had first come to " The Midnight Bell." He had twice taken her out to tea, and once to the pictures. She had nerved herself for a not inconceivable romance. There, however, the thing had ended. She was, she found, incapable of inspiring his tenderness. Where another might have pined and sickened at this, she, in the efficiency and resource of her healthy character, had automatically mastered and diverted her emotions, and now, without languor or jealousy, bore him nothing but good will. She was about twenty-seven. She stood looking at him, in the doorway.

" Well, ' *Bob*,' " she said, disparagingly.

She always put her " Bob " in inverted commas, as though he were not really Bob at all, and his assumption of being so, along with all his other pretensions, were pure impostures which *she* had tumbled to a long while ago. This was the convention of their flirtation, and he replied in the same spirit.

" Well, ' Ella,' " he said, and did not look up from the mirror.

" Brushing his precious ' *hair*,' " said Ella. . . . His having hair was impudence, in itself.

" How's Clapham ? " he asked.

" Oh. All right. What *you* been doing all the afternoon ? "

" Me ? . . . Stayed in."

" Sleeping—*I* bet."

" Oh well. . . ."

" And I should think so too," said Ella, " after all them drinks."

" What drinks ? " asked Bob.

But Ella ignored this

" If this was my place," she said, " I'd've sent you out of the bar."

" I wasn't drunk."

" Well, you weren't far. I thought you said you was giving up drink, Bob ? "

" Well, _I_ can't help it, if they give 'em to me."

" Oh _yes_," said Ella, with profound sarcasm. " The Penalties of Popularity, I suppose."

He had left his hair and was rubbing his shoes with a rag.

" If they gave me tips instead," he said. " It'd be talking. . . ."

There was a pause. She looked at him ironically, and around the room.

" You and your old John O' London's Weekly," she said. . . .

This was referring to a bundle of eleven or twelve numbers of this periodical, which lay on the little wicker table by his bed.

" What's wrong with my John O' London's Weekly ? "

" Nothing, Bob. Glad to know you've got such littery tastes."

He said nothing. The secret, jealously guarded inner craving, which was responsible for those papers lying there, was not a thing he could elucidate to Ella.

She, on the other hand, was intrigued by, and a little glad of, his reticence in this connection—giving him full credit for experience in realms she secretly revered. She became more serious.

" You're a great Reader, ain't you, Bob ? " she said, and picked up a little green volume that also lay on the table.

" My word ! " she said. " _The History of the Decline an' Fall of the Roman Empire—by Edward Gibbon._ Do you wade all through this, Bob ? "

Bob became a little nervous.

" That's only Volume One. They're seven in all. I'm getting 'em one by one."

" My word ! " said Ella, scanning the pages. " What did he want to write all that for, Bob ? "

This was a stupid query, and almost impossible to answer at random. His reply, however, revealed his innate courtesy.

" I couldn't tell you, Ella," he said, and rubbed his shoes.

" Well, I'll Decline and Fall downstairs," said Ella, with sudden decision. " So long, Bob."

" So long, Ella."

She went out, and he heard her footsteps receding down the hollow wooden stairs. He looked at himself once more in the glass, turned off the gas, and followed her.

## CHAPTER II

THOSE entering the Saloon Bar of " The Midnight Bell " from the street came through a large door with a fancifully frosted glass pane, a handle like a dumb-bell, a brass inscription " *Saloon Bar and Lounge*," and a brass adjuration to Push. Anyone temperamentally so wilful, careless, or incredulous as to ignore this friendly admonition was instantly snubbed, for this door actually would only succumb to Pushing. Nevertheless hundreds of temperamental people nightly argued with this door and got the worst of it.

Given proper treatment, however, it swung back in the most accomplished way, and announced you to the Saloon Bar with a welcoming creak. The Saloon Bar was narrow and about thirty feet in length. On your right was the bar itself, in all its bottly glitter, and on your left was a row of tables set against a comfortable and continuous leather seat which went the whole length of the bar. At the far end the Saloon Bar opened out into the Saloon Lounge. This was a large, square room, filled with a dozen or so small, round, copper-covered tables. Around each table were three or four white wicker armchairs, and on each table there lay a large stone ash-tray supplied by a Whisky firm. The walls were lined with a series of prints depicting moustached cavalrymen in a variety of brilliant uniforms ; there was a fireplace with a well-provided fire ; the floor was of chessboard oil-cloth, broken by an occasional mat, and the whole atmosphere was spotless, tidy, bright, and a little chilly. This was no scene for the brawler, but rather for the principled and restrained drinker, with his wife. In here and in the Saloon Bar " The Midnight Bell " did most of its business—the two other bars (the Public and the Private) being dreary, seatless, bareboarded structures wherein drunkenness was dispensed in coarser tumblers and at a cheaper rate to a mostly collarless and frankly downtrodden stratum of society. The Public Bar could nevertheless be glimpsed by a customer in the Saloon Bar, and as the evening wore on it provided the latter with an acoustic background of deep mumbling and excited talk without which its whole atmosphere would have been lost—without which, indeed, the nightly drama of the Saloon Bar would have been rather like a cinematograph drama without music. . . .

When Bob came down to this, Ella was already at her post, in casual conversation with Freda, her companion barmaid, who had only arrived at " The Midnight Bell " a few weeks ago, who did not sleep in, and with whom Bob had but the lightest acquaintanceship. The Governor, too, was in evidence ; and so was the Governor's Wife. And the Governor's Wife's Sister was somewhere about.

Of this trio of administrators, two—the Governor and his wife—made no attempt at divergence from type. They were as benign as they were bloated. It was pretty obvious to everybody that they might both burst at any moment, but this fact seemed to contribute towards rather than detract from their unvarying benevolence. Indeed, swathed round and round with their own tissue, they appeared to be numbed and protected from the general apprehensiveness which besets ordinary humanity. Instead, the rare qualities of warmth, geniality, fair-mindedness, and complete tranquillity had been given opportunity to flourish. Above all, complete tranquillity. The Governor and his wife would burst all in good time, and when they thought proper ; and the same principle would apply to everything else concerning them. They were both about fifty. The Governor wore a large blonde moustache on a round, flat face : the Governor's Wife had her hair peroxided and bobbed. You would have judged her a woman of vivid, and even lurid experience, and rightly. But this would have belonged to her youth, and that would have been cast behind when the Governor married her eighteen years ago. She was not legally married to the Governor, for she had a husband living ; but no one knew this. At night she wore black, semi-evening dress. The Governor remained in his grey suit. This was a terribly tight fit (possibly because no tailor in the world could be made fully to credit the proportions demanded), and he never made any attempt to button the coat. The spectacle of his waistcoat, and all it contained, was doubtless an indecent spectacle to snobs, but a pure delight to the naïve. It was the same shape as the world, but a little smaller. The Governor, as he walked about, was a kind of original Atlas. He took the burden not on his shoulders, like the mythological figure, but in the middle. You could positively find yourself trying to spot the continents on the Governor's waistcoat. His legs were surprisingly small for such a burden—tapering down from the waist to feet of little more than normal size. His wife's legs and feet were the same. It was for this reason that the shape of both of them could be said to resemble less that of the pig than that of the tadpole—a much more agreeable comparison. And the kindest comparison was welcome in the case of these two, who were, in the last analysis, as charming human beings as could be found. They possessed, between them, over half a dozen chins.

The Governor's Wife's Sister was a different proposition altogether. She was, to begin with, thin. She was also dark, and tall, and bony, and ugly, and her dark brown eyes were the quick eyes of one who has been trapped at last and is looking about for a cunning escape. She was intensely unpopular amongst her subordinates, and, in fact, something of a blot upon the house. She was, however, all-powerful—the true ruler and organizer of " The Midnight Bell." She had, it was widely known, a Head for Business. As the Governor's Wife's Sister her status was disputable ; and this made her ascendancy all the more bitter. " Who does she think *she* is, anyway ? " Ella would ask, and Bob would ask the same. The Governor, they said, was the one they took orders from. They were employed by the *Governor* weren't they ? Or were they not ? One day they were going to tell her off. In the meantime they obeyed her commands, which were peremptory, and bore her quibbles, which were continuous, without demur. But one day they were going to tell her off. In that faith they survived.


## CHAPTER III

AS Bob came down to the bar, the large round clock, fixed high on the wall above the opening leading from the bar to the lounge, stood at five past five. It did not do this because the time was five past five, or even because anybody thought it was. The house was due to open at five, and would do so. The clock was five minutes fast—a naïve ruse employed by this trade for the purpose of ejecting, with greater facility, its lingering and incredulous customers at closing time.

One minute before opening time. . . . A faint bustle of preparation in the other bars, but deep silence in the Saloon. . . . Bob switched on the lights in the Lounge (this was his routine) and went in and poked the fire into a crackling blaze. . . . He came back and encountered the Governor lifting the flap of the bar, and coming out to unbolt the door. The Governor almost invariably opened his own house. He carried the *Evening News* in his hand, and he gave it to Bob. This was also routine.

" That there Prince of Wales again," said the Governor.

" What ?—fallen off ? " asked Bob, scanning the head-lines.

The Governor grunted an affirmative, and moved on towards the door.

" He'll break his neck—one of these days," said Ella, patting her hair in a bottle-surrounded little mirror she had secreted near the till. " That boy. . . ."

" He will," said Bob. . . .

The Governor had now reached the door. He slid back the upper bolt ; and he slid back the middle bolt. He was now faced by the lower bolt—a different matter. A breath was taken ; and he stood a little further away. Then, with infinite precaution, the world-shape was let slowly down. A sharp click, a grunt of achievement, and " The Midnight Bell " was open. The

Governor came waddling back, again lifted the flap, passed through without a word, and disappeared.

" The Midnight Bell " was open. The public was at liberty to enter " The Midnight Bell." No sudden eruption, no announcing sound, proclaimed the fact. Only the click of sliding bolts, and the steady burning of electric light behind a door which might be Pushed.

But who was going to Push ? A deeper silence fell. Bob, with his right foot on the rail, and his newspaper on the bar, continued to read. . . . Ella, leaning over the bar with her hands clasped, stared into the distance and listened to London. . . . A grim, yet burdened and plaintive sound—the dim roar of traffic in the Tottenham Court Road—the far thunder of trams where the Hampstead Road began—the yelling of children in Warren Street near by. . . . And still no one Pushed. Bob's newspaper rattled as he turned a page. . . .

" Seems as though they've all gone and signed it to-night," said Bob. . . .

He was alluding to an obscurely conceived document spoken of as the Pledge.

Ella murmured assent, and again referred herself to her little mirror. She was always glancing at herself in the glass. This was not the result of vanity, but rather of a general despondence for ever seeking little reassurances and excuses for optimism.

Bob turned over another rattling page. Ella began to hum.

But humming was no good, and the row upon row of labelled, glittering bottles, standing in military order and with military submissive stiffness upon the shelves, told her as much. . . .

A lorry smashed by in the Euston Road, and faded away in the distance. . . .

What if no one ever came ? What if all the customers of " The Midnight Bell " had decided against it for the future ? What if some fatal misadventure had occurred in the dark streets outside—some vast and unknown cataclysm to which the whole of London was rushing in mad haste ? . . . The rows of uncanny bottles, in all their vigilant and eavesdropping stillness under the electric light, were more than susceptible to such morbid conceptions. . . .

The Governor's Wife came down to fetch something. " Quiet to-night," she said, and went upstairs again. . . .

But saying it was Quiet, like that, did not make it any less quiet. On the contrary it made it rather more so. . . .

Firm footsteps rang on the pavement outside, and the door swung briskly open with its habitual creak.

## CHAPTER IV

ONLY Mr. Sounder, certainly ; but there was nothing more to worry about. Fear flew back to its evil haunts and the house respired again.

" Ah—good evening," said Mr. Sounder, pacing up to the bar, and fishing in his pocket without ado.

" Good evening, Mr. Sounder," returned Ella and Bob— Ella with her professional sauciness, Bob with a hint of coolness, and barely glancing up from his paper.

Mr. Sounder was not a particularly welcome figure at " The Midnight Bell." He was an habitué. " The Midnight Bell " without Mr. Sounder would not quite have been " The Midnight Bell." It would have been deprived, to begin with, of thousands of words every night—millions of words every year. He generally arrived at about this time, and he would stay, if he was lucky, until closing time. But if he was unlucky, and no one came in to pay his expenses, he would go out and come in again at half-past nine. His first beer was in the nature of an investment.

His appearance was eccentric. Though of short stature he wore a thick beard and moustache which (though they did not in fact decrease his height) created an illusion of dwarfishness. This impression was augmented by the hair on his head, which went back in a thick mane magnificent for his age, which was something over fifty. But then Mr. Sounder went in greatly for hair. Apart from that already mentioned, he had a great deal of hair upon his hands, and a great deal of hair between his eyebrows, and a great deal of hair in his ears, and rather more hair coming in two exact little sprouts from his nostrils than modern fashion allows or nicety dictates.

He wore, and had worn for years without interruption, a thick tweed suit, a soft collar, and a heavy bow tie. But sometimes his tie was a piece of black ribbon tied into a bow. How he lived nobody knew—but one imagined by the application of the same principles as won him his nightly beer. He had, and had had for years, a small upper room in the seedy environs of Osnaburgh Terrace, and he was never in evidence until the evening. He had been to Oxford University, and was a man of letters—mostly to the papers. He wrote articles and short stories for the press, which were very occasionally accepted. He called this Turning Out Little Things from Time to Time. An enormous Thing perpetually in progress was postulated but left in the dark.

" I'll have a half of Burton," said Mr. Sounder.

" Half of Burton ? " repeated Ella (she automatically repeated every order), and drew it for him.

There was a clink of coins—a smash from the till—and a pause in which Mr. Sounder took his first sip. . . .

The door swung open in the Public Bar round the corner, and a morose, heavy-booted customer came forward—a postman.

Bob went on with his paper and no one spoke. . . . The postman, in the silence, could be discerned swallowing beer, with a forlorn and suspended expression, from a pint glass. . . . There was no life in the place.

Footsteps again rang on the pavement outside ; the door was flung back, and there entered a tall, violent gentleman with a long nose and wearing a bowler hat. A complete stranger. He ordered a small " Black and White " and splash. He drank it in two gulps, and instantly paced out again, leaving " The Midnight Bell " in the precise predicament in which he had found it.

One apprehended for the millionth time that it was indeed a very queer life. Silence again reigned. . . .

" Is that the *Star* you've got there, Bob ? " asked Mr. Sounder at last.

" No, Mr. Sounder. *Evening News*."

" Oh," said Mr. Sounder, heavily, and took another sip. As he put the tumbler down there was observable in his eyes a faint but glassy gleam.

To those (such as Bob and Ella) instructed in Mr. Sounder's ways, there was no mistaking that gleam—or what it portended. It was the gleam of a man who has not long ago Turned Out a Little Thing. They offered him no assistance, however.

" I thought perhaps you'd seen my own little contribution," tried Mr. Sounder.

" What—have you written something in the *Star* ? " asked Ella.

Mr. Sounder returned that he could not deny the soft impeachment.

" Let's have a look," said Ella, kindly, and took his own copy from him.

" Only a letter. I think you'll find it on page five." Mr. Sounder lit a cigarette, and puffed gracefully into the air. Ella searched. " Here we are," she said, and read it through.

Mr. Sounder's letter dealt in a manly but rather vituperative style with the topic of woman's hair. He personally liked it long. That much was clear from the start. Having asked to be allowed to " concur most heartily with M.B.L." (a previous enthusiast), he proceeded with sundry allusions to such themes as " woman's crowning glory," " these days of close-shaven tresses," " the would-be modern young Miss," and " her Grandmother," which bespoke alike his fervour and irony. He also mentioned cocktails and night clubs. He thunderously signed himself " Harold B. Sounder " and the bolt fell from " Osnaburgh Terrace, N.W.I."

" Very Good, isn't it ? " said the amiable Ella. " Seen that, Bob ? "

It was given to Bob. He read it through. He also thought it was Very Good. . . .

The favourable decision, however, was followed by a slightly awkward pause. (Two women had entered the Public Bar, and the murmur of their voices was audible.)

" I fear you don't hold with my views yourself, Ella," said Mr. Sounder, looking at her shingled head.

" Ah—you'd like a lot of Lady Godivas knocking about, wouldn't you, Mr. Sounder ? "

Mr. Sounder smiled, but was at a loss for a reply.

" And I guess you'd be the Peeping Tom, wouldn't you ?" she added, looking at him with the mock knowingness of the barmaid.

" Ah—that would depend on the Lady Godiva, Ella," said Mr. Sounder. Another gleam portended gallantry. " Now if *you*, for instance. . . ." Mr. Sounder could only conclude with a flourish of the hand.

" Not me," said Ella. " Too cold."

" Ah—but your hair would keep you warm. Why don't you grow it, like a sensible girl, Ella ? I can assure you that it would increase your charms a thousandfold."

" Oh yes. I'm sure."

" Not that any increase is required," added Mr. Sounder, with a nice little leer.

There was a pause.

" Oh well—I don't know," said Ella, staring dreamily into the distance, and relapsing, in a curious, and rather sweet way she had, from raillery into frankness. " We all have to keep up with the Fashion, don't we ? "

There was heard a murmur of voices outside, and the door opened to a middle-aged couple, who did not go through to the lounge, but sat down at a table in the bar. Being seated they were within Bob's province. He took his tray, went over to them, and met their eyes. The lady was doubtful, but at last decided on Guinness, and the gentleman wanted a Gin and It. Ella, hearing the order, got to work without Bob's repeating it. Bob returned with the drinks on his tray, placed them on the table, took a half crown from the man, gave the change and received no tip. He had expected none, and returned to his newspaper. The lady, apparently, knew Ella.

" Rather quiet to-night, aren't you ? " she said.

" Yes, we are, ain't we ? " said Ella. " 'Spect they'll be in soon, though."

Mr. Sounder stood quietly observing the couple—possibly with an eye to getting off with them. His first investment was almost swallowed, and things were looking bad.

But the door again creaked open, and a brisk man of fifty entered. This was Mr. Brooks—another habitué—the owner

of a nondescript hardware store near by—a seller of pots, and
pans, and kitchen accessories, and screws—particularly screws.
He had a terrible squint. It was as though the screws had somehow gone to his brain, and his eyes were twisted in fanatical
endeavours to follow their obscure gyrations. He looked
intently at your left ear as he spoke to you, as though you had
left some soap in it. But he gave Mr. Sounder a warm " Good
evening," and spotted the soap and asked him what he would
have simultaneously. Mr. Sounder would have another Burton,
he thought. He caught Ella's eye rather shamefacedly as he said
so, and Ella pulled her levers with a touch of irony.

At the same time three rough males had entered the Public
Bar, and were talking in loud voices, and the Saloon door again
creaked open, and another couple entered and went straight
through into the lounge and sat down. They were followed
by two men, who came and stood at the bar. With a sudden
burst the place was awake.


## CHAPTER V

BOB'S nightly aspiration was five shillings. He was a young
man who kept a keen eye upon his finances, and a pound
a week in tips he regarded as a peremptory necessity.

It may be supposed that the amounts he received were de
pendent upon chance : but Bob did not believe this to be the
case. He believed it possible, by energy, subtlety, and dexterity,
to manipulate and augment the largesse of his customers. The
great thing was always to have plenty of coppers. Sixpence
change from two shillings, for instance, should almost invariably
be proffered in this form. And they should not be put down in a
lump, but counted out slowly one by one, so as to give the
recipient full time in which to make his decision and expel a
magnificent twopence, or even threepence, for the waiter. Bob,
as a point of honour, would never hover. He took his defeats
in the same spirit as his successes—with " Thankyouvery-
muchsir " and instant withdrawal.

Not that sixpence change from two shillings should invariably be submitted in the form of coppers. Sometimes it was wise to employ the silver coin, and here Bob gambled with human psychology. He risked getting nothing (few people know how often waiters get nothing when there are no coppers to hand) and it lay with him to make lightning interpretations of situation and character—to divine on what occasions it was worth the risk. In the case of a well-disposed or slightly intoxicated customer, it was obviously worth the risk : the same thing applied to any young man on not too familiar terms with the young woman accompanying him. The first would not care, the second would not dare, to leave the waiter nothing. But it was up to Bob to gauge with precision how well disposed the customer was or how familiar the young man with the young woman. It was also up to him to keep a perpetual supply of coppers, sixpences, and shillings readily available in separate pockets. For besides the one just mentioned, there were infinite other subtle combinations of change in relation to character and situation, all of which depended upon a smooth-working supply. He tormented Ella with his pleas for different coins.

Like most waiters Bob had an unmistakable, unhesitating, and carefully cultivated style, wherewith to uphold his dignity. In his case it centred around his tray. Bob without his tray would have been like an excitable writer without dashes—he would hardly have been able to carry on. On going up to any table he held his tray lightly in the fingers of both hands, and, balancing it perpendicularly upon the table, said either " Yessir " or " Goodeveningsir " according to the case. In resting the tray thus upon the table he was able to achieve a minute bow. Without the tray he could not have bowed, would not have known what to do with his hands, and could only have stood there looking limp and inadequate. Similarly, in the indecisive conversation which invariably followed amongst those he served, the tray was a barrier, a counter, a thing behind which he could resolutely stand and wait, deferent and official.

He now employed these tactics with his first couple in the lounge. He took their order, returned to the bar, and repeated it briskly to Ella. She put the drinks on his tray ; he paid her ; went back, and achieved twopence. Two other couples entered almost at once. " The Midnight Bell," once started, seemed to gather force from its own impetus, and in the next half hour he served over a dozen tables.

By this time, too, the bar itself was filling, and Ella also was very busy. She was, however, in spite of this, in conversation with a young man in plus fours. That is to say, there was a young man in plus fours at one end of the bar to whom Ella, after each fitful and furious outburst of energy, would return. When she returned she would continue the conversation where it had been left off. But if she had forgotten the previous conversation she would all the same return to the young man, face him, with one elbow on the bar, and look about her and hum quietly to herself until they could think of something else to talk about. The young man would sometimes hum as well. The young man, in fact, was temporarily hers; and it was a case of the young man and herself against the bar. Her work was merely parenthetic in this amiable and slightly diffident relationship.

Ella, at this phase of the evening, was seldom without someone to come back and hum to; and Bob also, at this time, generally had a friend during lulls. Already to-night he was himself in conversation with a young man of his own. This young man was connected with motors in Great Portland Street, and came into " The Midnight Bell " every other night. He had much in common with Bob, and he always bought him a drink at the bar. Bob returned to him in the same way as Ella returned to her own young man, though, having a stronger personality, he did not have to hum when the conversation ran dry. Bob was never quite sure as to whether he was allowed to accept drinks from customers in this way, but it was always being done. He was very popular. Sometimes, towards the close of a busy evening, he would have as many as three friends, with an equal amount of drinks, all awaiting his company along the bar.

Because of his excess in the morning Bob had resolved to drink nothing to-night : the evening was to be penal. But now, with his first drink, his spirits rose and he believed he was going to enjoy himself. The place was filling : he had already made one and six : he experienced spiritual and physical elasticity.

Moreover, although he had time for conversation, in those intermittent spurts of exertion to which his duties compelled him he was filled with all the gladness of a man who has a little too much to do at one time but is serenely conscious of being able to do it. He called out the orders in an authoritative voice to Ella, and snapped up empty glasses to return to the bar with the verve and rapidity of a performer.

## CHAPTER VI

A ND so the evening wore on. Eight o'clock came, and crept to a quarter past. The Lounge was filled with couples : the Bar was packed with men. People were already making remarks about Sardines, and the whole house was filled with the level ebullience of tongues. The Governor and his wife were down in their bar, the former in conversation with a customer, the latter emulating Ella in the performance of that infinitely rapid sequence of wobbling and insecure dexterities with bottle and glass which falls to the lot of the barmaid when the house is full.

And behind all this blurred noise and fuss, and distinct from it, and as though it were some kind of accompaniment to it, came the continual crash of the till, and the blithe creaking of the door as each newcomer entered.

No one could have said how, or by what stages it had happened ; but the atmosphere now prevailing was as different from what it was when the place first opened as a prayer meeting is different from a naval action. A similar metamorphosis had taken place in Mr. Sounder. He was now at a table in the lounge, and with the aid of five beers he had spilled words upon three different acquaintances since entering. His present acquaintance was at this moment looking at a letter in *The Star*. Mr. Sounder was leaning back and puffing out his cigarette smoke as one who would infer it was a very moderate effort, though, regarded purely as a Little Thing Turned Out from Time to Time, he rather thought it would pass. . . .

His acquaintance, so far as Bob could see, was evidently going one further, and thinking it was Very Good. . . . Mr. Sounder's attitude towards the house and Bob was now completely altered. They were his very own. He rapped on the table with his glass when his friend desired to give an order, and he chaffed Bob good-humouredly for his laziness.

In the occasional breaks between toil which Bob still managed to hew out for himself, the creaking of the door served him well. In that it announced every invasion before it took place, he was able to look up and see whether his services would be required. It was his business, in fact, to listen to that door. For besides serving his customers, it was his duty to protect them from the importunities of all those husky-voiced social miscarriages who, entering furtively and hoping not to be seen, endeavoured to sell as many confidential bootlaces, studs, watches, buttons, *Daily Liars*, or necklaces as they possibly could before he dismissed them with a curt " Not this side, please ! " Only one sort of mendicant was allowed in the Saloon—those from the Salvation Army, who seldom profited by less than two shillings nightly.

Nor was Bob the only one to listen to that door. Widely apart in life as were the different groups along the bar, there was sufficient of a collective festal spirit amongst them to cause a faint and obscure suspicion, or even resentment, to arise against the newcomer. Each newcomer, at least, had to submit to a very brief, perhaps even unconscious, inspection before immediate loss of identity in the crowd. And it was for this reason that every creak of the door was coincident with a minute pause, a barely noticeable modification of noise, as the interloper came forward to the bar or sat down at a table.

Now so far, apart from the fact that business was exceptionally good, the demeanour of the evening had presented no irregularities, and did not appear to be about to do so. But now, at twenty minutes past nine, there occurred a trivial event, which was far from being unique, but which was at the same time a little out of the common. While the noise was at its height the door creaked open again and two figures entered—a young woman and a young girl—passing straight through the bar and sitting down at a table in the lounge.

Now this passing through was accomplished in less than

fifteen seconds, but there was something which subtly distinguished it from any other such intrusion. To begin with, that minute pause and modification of noise which greeted every newcomer was in this case tremendously emphasized. Indeed, if you had magnified it a dozen times you would have had a positive hush. It was almost as though someone had suddenly shouted too loudly, or as though a bottle had been smashed. Nearly all eyes were turned upon the couple ; many people ceased speaking ; and the loudest speakers tempered their tones.

This was all very brief, ceasing immediately, and as though with a breath of relief, directly the couple was seated ; and its origin lay, of course, in the appearance and demeanour of the couple. But what it was about these two that caused their so singular reception was not perhaps susceptible to immediate analysis. It was a confusion of many things.

It was not a question simply of good looks—though the heavy dark handsomeness of the elder and the blonde prettiness of the younger might well have excited scrutiny on their own account. It was not because these good looks had, in themselves, an air of being assumed, of being painted on, of being made self-conscious, and over distinct, and too explicit by the lavish use of cosmetics. It was not even the phenomenon ot their bold unescortedness, or rather of their own quaint chaperonage. It was not the discrepancy between the comparative costliness of their finery and what must surely have been their original station in society. It was not the strange blending of their isolation with a certain hard and unrelenting self-sufficiency. But it was a mixture of all these things which, stirring the imagination of the crowd in " The Midnight Bell " revealed them for what they were—revealed the fact that these two were beyond the reach of society because they evaded its burdens : that these two were born to toil but did not toil : that these two were for that reason bold, lazy, ruthless, and insensitive : that they were women of the street.

The brief hush and hiatus, then, which marked their entrance into good society as represented by " The Midnight Bell," was easily explained and derived from a natural feeling—the feeling, that is, which the unthinkingly upright citizen cannot help

experiencing when face to face with the delinquent—a feeling
which is partly curiosity and partly disgust. And as those two
walked through to the lounge, under the eyes of the crowd,
there took place in little what takes place on a larger scale when
a pickpocket is carried smouldering through the streets between
two policemen. Though modified past all reckoning in this
case, the same sensation of pity and horror, of shock and weird
fascination, was present.

But this only lasted for a few seconds ; and directly they
were seated the place was as noisy as before—noisier than
before. Bob took his tray, and went over to serve them.


## CHAPTER VII

HE classified them mentally as the dark one and the fair
one. " Yes, Miss," he said, and smiled at the dark one.
        His social instincts yet forbade the more cordial welcome
of " Good evening, Miss," but his smile was an atonement.

" I'll have a Bass," she said. " What're you havin', Jenny ? "
Jenny, the fair one, replied, in a sickly voice, that she thought
she'd just have a tonic water.

" Come on, dear. '*Ave* something ! " urged the other, and
looked at her friend with a kind of angry concern.

" My Friend's not very well," she explained to Bob. . . .

" Oh," said Bob, and looked in a friendly way at the invalid,
who smiled up at him.

" Indigestion ? " he hazarded, rather commonly. But he
was always rather common when he was embarrassed.

" Yes. That's right," she replied, in a naïve, clear, and
unexpectedly childish voice, and their smile to each other
conveyed a wonderful common comprehension of all the horrors
and ramifications of the illness. He observed that she was much
prettier than he had thought at first, and really might not be a
day more than seventeen.

" Why not have a Gin and Peppermint ? " he suggested.

" That's very good, isn't it ? " she asked, in the same naïve, indolent tone.

" Nothing like it." It was part of his duty to the house to prescribe Gin and Peppermint for the afflicted.

" Well, I'll have a Gin and Peppermint, then."

A vague and slightly pleasurable sensation, that he had made rather a hit with the fair one, overcame him.

" A Gin and Pep and a Bass ? "

" That's right."

He returned to the bar, and gave the order to Ella, who remarked, as she filled the tumbler with the Bass, that she was Glad he Liked his new customers. The remark was characteristic of Ella, and his reply was equally inane.

" What do you mean ? I don't like 'em," he said. But in the very moment of saying so it quaintly dawned upon him that he rather did. He was rather intrigued by his new customers.

" Don't you tell *me*," said Ella, put the drinks on his tray, gave him his change, and went off.

He returned to the ladies. The three beers he had had—all this time plotting their subtle loosenings along his brain—now had a sudden piece of luck and managed to release his next remark before he was ready for it. " There," he said. " That'll do you all the good in the world."

" Sincerely hope so," said the invalid, and they smiled again —she with forlorn languor, he as though to brace her with his own energy. He fumbled in his pocket for the change.

" Don't suppose you're ever ill, are you, waiter ? " asked the dark one.

" Oh no. I keep pretty all right." He put down the change, and she expelled sixpence without a word. " Thank you very much," he said, and was about to leave.

" Looks well enough, anyhow," said the invalid.

He balanced his tray on the table, and smiled down on them, committed to conversation.

" Don't always feel it," he said.

Everybody smiled, all round, and there was a difficult pause.

" Tell you who 'e looks like, Jenny," said the dark one, glancing appraisingly at Bob. " That man we saw on the pictures the other night—what's 'is name ? "

" I know," said Jenny. " Antonio Moreno."

" Yes. That's right. He ain't half like him, ain't he ? "

" Only not so soppy," qualified Jenny.

The three of them laughed.

" What—me like Antonio Moreno ? I've never been told that before ! " But the compliment enriched his soul, as he stood there.

" You are, though," said Jenny, gazing at him with a sudden dreamy seriousness which accorded only too well with her ingenuous face and clear blue eyes.

" He is, though," affirmed the dark one. " Ain't he ? "

" Yes," said Jenny. " He is."

It appeared that he was. For a moment he did not quite know what to do about it. They looked at him.

" Wish I had some of his money, anyway," he achieved at last.

" He's a Spaniard, isn't he ? " asked the dark one.

" Italian, I think," said Bob. " Not sure, though."

There was another pause. He looked round to see if he was neglecting the house, and decided he was not.

" You're not a Talian, are you ? " asked Jenny, with the same slow, indolent, ingenuous, blue-eyed seriousness as before.

" Me ? No. I suppose I'm an American—strickly speaking. American father an' Irish mother."

" You don't speak like an American," was Jenny's comment.

" No. I came over here when I was five, you see. Don't remember nothing about it. Don't remember my father even—not properly." His difficulty with his negatives betrayed that he was flustered, as it always did.

" Don't you really ? " asked the dark one.

" No," said Bob, and then added, with even greater self-consciousness : " He was an American ' Cop.' "

" My word ! " said the dark one, inclined to titter, and the news did not seem to have made a great impression upon either of the ladies. He was not wounded, however. Quite impossible for them, after all ! Impossible for them to know of a clear and shining ideal—of a tall, sturdy figure in a trim uniform—a figure that swung a baton, and helped little children across roads, and was good, and strong, and authoritative, and kind, and brave, and his father. It was asking too much.

Jenny, however, suddenly and surprisingly, caught on to the idea.

"Like what you see on the films," she said.

"That's right," he said, and his eyes spoke his gratitude for her thoughtfulness and sympathy.

"I wonder *you* don't go on the films, waiter," said the dark one.

"*Me ?*—" He realized that his duties, articulate in the noise of coins and tumblers being banged on tables, were calling him. "I must go. There're three tables waiting." He left them.

Ella, as she served him, was ironic and reserved.

"I'm surprised at *you*, Bob," said Ella.

"Surprised at me ? What's up ? "

But she preferred mystery. "I'm surprised at *you*, Bob," she reaffirmed, and left him.

He now worked for ten minutes unremittingly. The time was twenty to ten; and the place was still filling up. He had made four and ninepence already. He looked over in the direction of his new acquaintances and observed that the dark one had vanished. The other was sitting alone, staring absently, but at the same time inconsolably, in front of her. The combined unconsciousness, unhappiness, and harmlessness of her bearing, awoke his sympathy. He could not resist going over.

"Well," he said. "How's the Gin and Pep ? "

She withdrew from dreams with a smile.

"Oh—very nice, thanks. I'm feelin' much better already."

"Doing its work ? "

"That's right. I'm very glad you recommended it."

He smiled, drummed on his tray with his fingers, looked about him, and wondered how he could excuse himself.

"Don't know what's the matter with *me*," she said. "I'm always gettin' these funny attacks."

You would hardly credit, to listen to her, that she was a dreadfully wicked young woman.

"Ah—that's because you don't get enough exercise," he said and smiled again.

"Exercise ? Physical jerks in the morning, I suppose you mean ? "

" Well. Don't know about that. But you ought to go in for good long walks or something."

She looked along the bar, with a little smile to herself.

" Get enough walking," she said. " One way and another."

There was a pause.

" Oh well—" he began.

" An' I guess I've got to do some more to-night," she said——

" Oh—how's that ? "

" How's that ? " She smiled again. " You ask my landlady. She'll tell you ' How's that.' "

" What—short with the rent ? "

" You bet."

" That's bad," said Bob, and there was a silence.

She smiled sadly at him. The sorrows of her existence descended upon them both, drawing them closer, flowing through each of them—as though they had joined hands affectionately.

" Well—grumbling won't help," she said . . . and both of them looked sideways at different objects. . . .

" S'pose I shouldn't have come in here drinking," she added, and looked at her wrist-watch. " What's the time ? I ought to be off."

" Only ten to ten."

All at once she sat up stiffly.

" Oh lord—I don't half feel bad," she said. " Really."

" I guess you ought to be in bed," he said, not quite knowing what to say.

" You bet." She drew her lips into a little sneer, not at him, but with him, against existence.

" What about another Gin and Pep ? "

She nodded. " Yes. That first one did me good, didn't it ? " She was clearly in pain.

" Yes. Go on. I'll get you one."

" Right you are. A Gin and Pep."

She smiled again, conveying her appreciation, and he returned to the bar.

Here the noise was tremendous, and Ella was off her head with work. " Well, what do *you* want, Bob ? " she asked, as she poured out drinks for somebody else.

" I want a Gin and Peppermint, please, Ella."

" I'm surprised at *you*, Bob," she said, as she served him.

" Heard that somewhere before. What's the worry ? "

Ella glanced at him reproachfully, and explained herself. " Talking to those *Pros*titutes," said Ella. . . .

Her violent stress upon the first syllable of this word implied a differentiation between a large class of almost venial Titutes, and another branch of the same class, designated as Pros, and beyond the pale.

" What's wrong with 'em ? " asked Bob.

" What's *wrong* with 'em ! " said Ella. " The *creatures*."

" Ladies must live," hazarded Bob, a little insecurely.

" Don't you tell *me*," said Ella, and left him.

Her illness and isolation glowed all the stronger for Ella's derision, as he placed the drink upon her table and she fumbled in her bag and produced a two shilling piece. He gave her the change, and she tried to pass him another sixpence.

" No," he said, smiling, and slipping it back. " I guess that's the sort of thing you're wanting."

" No. Go on. Don't be silly."

A sudden intimation that people near by were watching them, and that he, a self-respecting waiter in a decent house, could not stand there arguing about change with a woman of the streets, compelled him to accept it. He picked it up quickly.

" Well," he said. " I only wish I could do something, that's all."

Her reply was another weary smile.

He stood there, with his tray balanced on the table, looking around as though to see if anyone needed serving. . . .

" And it's only a question of eight and sixpence too," she said. . . .

" What ?—" He spotted a customer. " I must go and work." He left her for five minutes.

He returned with a soul expanded.

" That's not much," he said.

" Too much for me, at any rate."

" Why not let me give it to you."

" What ? You ? Likely ! I bet you've got a lot to throw away."

" No. Go on. You can pay it back, if you like."

" Don't be silly."

" No. Go on. It's not silly."

" Don't be silly. I wouldn't think of it, an' that's flat."

" But what's wrong, if you pay me back ? "

There was a pause. She looked into the distance. " I'd certainly do that," she said. . . .

" Well come on. I'll give it you. An' then you can go to bed."

She still looked into the distance. " Come on," he said. . . . She was very pretty. It was almost as though he were making love to her. . . .

" Well—if I pay it back to-morrow. . . ."

" Just when you like."

" All right then." She met his eyes. " And you know how grateful I am, don't you ? "

" No cause for that."

" Well, there is, an' that's a fact."

" Tell you what though. Don't want 'em to see me giving it you in here. You finish that drink and then go out an' wait outside. An' then I'll slip out an' give it you. That's the best way, isn't it ? "

" That'll do fine. Shall I go now ? " She sat up again.

" No. Wait a bit. I've got to serve some people. I'll spot you as you go out, and then I'll follow. Don't mind if I keep you waiting a bit. Well—good-bye for the present." He smiled and again left her.

In the next few minutes he threw himself into his work with tremendous bounce, once or twice looking over in her direction, and catching her eye, and smiling. And then he saw her rising, with a mock-serious and self-conscious little look (which was a kind of wink to him), and passing through the bar, and going out.

Some three or four minutes passed before he was again released. Then he went audaciously to the door, and out into the street.

She was not just outside, as he had expected she would be, but about twenty yards away, looking into the window of a little sweet-and-newspaper shop which was closed. He went owards her and she came towards him. The night was cold and serene in the light of a clear, buoyant moon. After the fuddled thick noise of the house it was as though he stepped from orgy into spirituality. He spoke low, out of deference to the atmosphere, and so did she.

" Here's the doings," he said, and proffered a ten shilling note.

" Oh—but I don't want all that. It's only eight and six."

" Oh, that don't matter. Go on."

" All right, I will then," she conceded, and put it in her bag, and snapped it close, without ado. Then she looked up at him, speaking rather like one who has been punished unjustly. " An' I hope you know how grateful I am—'cos I am."

He held out his hand. " Not a bit. Only too glad to help where I can."

" An' I'll come in an' pay it back to-morrow. I will, honest."

" No need for that. Just when you like."

Their hands were still joined. " And whenever *you* want any help, I'll give it to *you*," she said, in the same punished tone. " I will, truly."

" Let's hope I won't."

It was all rather awkward. She released her hand, smilingly bending her head sideways to make the withdrawal gracious and tender. " Well—good-night," she said.

" Good night. Sleep well."

" You bet. Good night."

" Good night."

He watched her going down the street. As she reached the corner she waved and vanished. He stood at the door of " The Midnight Bell " for a few moments, with his hands on his hips, looking each way, savouring the night ; then went inside.

## CHAPTER VIII

THE clock stood at five to ten, and he at once perceived that the climax of the evening had been reached.

Apart from a few at the back of the lounge, there were

now no women in the place, and it seemed as though their disappearance had relaxed the last bonds of equability and restraint.

A horrible excitement was upon everybody and everything. Indeed, to one unacquainted with the feverish magic that alcohol can work there could have been only one way of accounting for the scene. This house must have been the theatre of some tremendous conference, in which some tremendous crisis had arisen at the moment of adjournment, and the individuals had gathered into frightened but loquacious groups to discuss the bombshell. (But some of them were in fits of laughter about it.) In such circumstances alone might the ordinary despondence and lethargy of man have been galvanized into such potency of discourse, such keenness of confidence, such an air of released honour-brightness and getting down to the essentials of life as was apparent everywhere here.

Men! They thrust their hats back on their heads; they put their feet firmly on the rail; they looked you straight in the eye; they beat their palms with their fists, and they swilled largely and cried for more. Their arguments were top-heavy with the swagger of their altruism. They appealed passionately to the laws of logic and honesty. Life, just for to-night, was miraculously clarified into simple and dramatic issues. It was the last five minutes of the evening, and they were drunk.

And they were in every phase of drunkenness conceivable. They were talking drunk, and confidential drunk, and laughing drunk, and beautifully drunk, and leering drunk, and secretive drunk, and dignified drunk, and admittedly drunk, and fighting drunk, and even rolling drunk. One gentleman, Bob observed, was patently blind drunk. Only one stage off dead drunk, that is—in which event he would not be able to leave the place unassisted.

And over all this ranting scene Ella, bright and pert and neat and industrious, held her barmaid's sway. She was the recipient of half the confidences, and half the jokes, and half the leers. Because she symbolized, in her sober but smiling figure, all those restraints and righteous inhibitions which had been gloriously cast behind to-night, she was made the butt of their friendly irony and arrogance. And she accepted the challenge, and adopted one good-humoured, non-committal and chiding attitude to all. Furthermore she was never at a loss for a reply to throw over her shoulder as she swept away to fulfil the next order.

It seemed to Bob that he never admired Ella so much as at this time of night. Her naïve goodness, and innate decency never glowed out so strongly as when she gave tit for tat amid this maudlin and besetting pack. But there was something even more than this. There was the fact of her femininity and the charm of her infinite tolerance. And these things, added to her wonderful equability and efficiency, transformed her into something quite maternal and irresistible. She became, in fact, scarcely a barmaid at all, but rather the little mother of the bar, and everyone was made just naughty and innocent in the radiance of her forgiveness.

But Bob was in that sort of mood to-night. He had only just come in from under the stars—stars in whose tender light he had proffered aid to a fallen human being. And one who has just done that sort of thing feels he wants to forgive and love everything.

He apprehended the enormous gulf that separated Ella from the little wretch (the rather pretty little wretch) he had just assisted. He apprehended the gulf, but bridged it with his magnanimity. Ella, the sweet and upright Ella, did as she should in designating her as a " Creature "—but he also did as he should in bestowing his compassion upon a " creature "—if only for the very reason that she was a " creature," and in need. For he was in that mood when he loved all human creatures. He loved Ella because she was a good woman, and he loved the other because she was a bad woman. It was a good world.

In brief, because he had given ten shillings to a young prostitute without expecting the usual thing in return he was dreadfully conceited. He was so innocent as to believe the transaction was almost unique. He little suspected cunning mankind's general awareness of the charms of chivalry. He was in love with himself.

And a man successfully in love desires above all things to sing. And the fates were so propitious to Bob to-night that no

sooner was the desire formulated than he was given the chance
to do so.  The deceitful clock pointed to ten o'clock, and it was
time to cry " All Out ! "


The Governor began it.  His voice was scarcely heard above
the din.  " Now then, gentlemen please ! " he cried.  " Last
orders, please ! "  And he looked over at Bob.

Bob, serving in the lounge, waited a few moments.  Then
" Last orders, please, gentlemen !  Time please ! " he cried, in
sternly expressionless tones.

Bob did not suppose that this would cause any modification
in the great, grumbling growl of talk around him, and it did
not.  Possibly, in the far recesses of vinous brains, the dark
admonition was heard by a few.  Possibly this manifested itself
(in the persons of those few) in a sudden vague unease, a glancing
round, a barely observable drop of the countenance. . . . But
the infamy (or rather the absurdity) could obviously never gain
popular credit.  And it was, of course, an absolute absurdity,
for the people in " The Midnight Bell " were only just beginning
to enjoy themselves.

He began again, more loudly, and more reproachfully.

" Now then gentlemen !  *Time*, please ! "

But they did not hear that, either.  He paced to the door,
flung it back, fastened it back, and opened his lungs.

" NOW then, gentlemen !  TIME, please ! "

They had got that all right.  He went to the tables in the
bar, snapped up empty glasses, shoved his way through to the
counter, and slammed them ferociously down.

" TIME please, gentlemen !  ALL OUT please ! "

And now a kind of panic and babel fell upon " The Midnight
Bell."  A searching draught swept in from the open door, and
suddenly the Governor lowered all the lights save one above the
bar.  At this a few realized that the game was up, and left the
place abruptly :  others besieged Ella madly for last orders.
Some of the groups dispersed with bawled farewells :  others
drew closer protectively, and argued the louder and more
earnestly for the assault that was being made upon their happiness.

" NOW then, gentlemen, please !  LONG PAST TIME ! "

He rushed about the place, filling his fingers with empty glasses, and banging them down on the counter. He was, for the moment, a bully and a braggart. And his miserable, huddled victims knew it and resented it.

But they knew also that they had to go. Suddenly one of the groups—a group of five men—broke up and filed out. It was instantly apparent that they had been responsible for the greater part of the din. There were not more than half a dozen left. A hush fell, and he had no further need to shout. His voice became quiet and full of expression.

"Now then, gentlemen, please. It's long past time, you know."

A minute later, and only three remained—two drunk gentlemen, and the blind drunk gentleman. The Public Bar round the corner was empty and in darkness. The two drunk gentlemen were talking drunkenly to Ella, and the blind drunk gentleman was talking drunkenly to the air. Bob went up to him.

"This way out, sir."

"S'all righ', wair," said the blind drunk gentleman. "S'all-righ'. Wonnarseyousuth!"

"What's that, sir?"

"All ee sigh God?—Nod all ee sigh God?"

"Sight of God, sir? Yes, sir, all equal sir. It's time you made for home though, isn't it, sir?"

"Then why," said the blind drunk gentleman, grasping Bob's coat with one fist, and making his point with the other, "then why . . . then why. . . ."

"Why what, sir?"

"Wize everybody s'znobbish?"

"Couldn't say, sir. Way of the world, I suppose, sir. No sir—this way, sir."

"Z'damznobbish. . . . Z'damznobbish. . . . Z'damznobbish," murmured the blind drunk gentleman, and, so protesting, groped his staggering way into the night.

He was followed by the two drunk gentlemen, who walked out with that too balanced strut peculiar to drunk gentlemen knowing themselves to be nothing of the sort.

"Good night, waiter."

"Good night, sir. Good night."

He went out with them, and gazed again at the cool and temperate heavens.

The blind drunk gentleman, lingering darkly, at once connected with the two drunk gentlemen, and a short conversation ensued. Unanimity was instant. Three crusaders against Snobbery, arm in arm and full of faith, staggered down towards the south side of Oxford Street, where drinks might yet be obtained and the world awaited conversion.

He came in again. Ella, about to retire, was patting her hair for the last time in her little bottle-surrounded mirror. The one light feebly lit the bar, and the silence was that ultra-silence, at once sad, and terrifying, and beautiful, of a banquet ended, of people gone. They were both highly susceptible to it.

He bolted the door. " Well," he said. " How's everything ? "

" I'm surprised at you, Bob," said Ella, and went upstairs.


## CHAPTER IX

THE less spectacular side of Bob's employment revealed itself every morning. The Brass was his care, and by half-past eight he was up and rubbing. He also replaced an old with a new fire in the Lounge, but did not put a match to it until the place opened at eleven o'clock. For these activities he dispensed with his coat and collar, rolled up his shirt sleeves, and wore professional trousers of unknown age and origin. Ella called him (accurately) a Sight.

But he exchanged few words with Ella at this time of day, drawing into himself and soothing his soul with rubbing, humming, intermittent whistling, and a tacit understanding with the dog.

For " The Midnight Bell " ran to a dog. It was a belonging of the Governor's Wife and known as Jim. It trotted placidly about with its head held high, and its brown eyes were filled with a chilling and noble aloofness. " Well, what do *you* want ? " Ella asked it every other five minutes, but it clearly did not want anything. And it wouldn't ask you for it if it did.

It was surprising, indeed, that its pure and passionless detachment from her did not finally repel Ella. But it did not needless to say. She took snub after snub all the morning, and had a profound love for the animal.

At eleven o'clock " The Midnight Bell " opened. Bob resumed decent clothes and his white coat, and a few people came in. But business was very slack until about half-past twelve, when the place filled up with a sober crowd. Ham sandwiches, beef sandwiches, arrowroot biscuits and cheese, sardines or prawns on toast—all these were in constant demand and allayed the fumes of bravery. But these were mostly taken at the bar, and Bob had very little to do. The dog, by this time rather weary, came down to earth so far as to go round smelling everybody in turn (without apparent pleasure), and to trot away and occasionally get a biscuit, which it consumed in the manner of dogs—that is, by having almost to throw it out and catch it again in order to achieve a bite, and then moving its nose despondently amongst the crumbs. Bob was offered drinks, but, remembering yesterday, withheld. In the Public Bar round the corner there were corduroys, pint glasses of beer, hunks of bread and cheese, and arguments—all about as thick as they could possibly be. When, at three o'clock, it was time to turn them all out, there was no need for shouting.

He then ran upstairs, changed into clean linen and his best clothes, and made himself very spruce altogether. For this was Thursday, his Day Off, and he had not only the whole afternoon, but the whole evening as well, to spend as he wished.


It was a clear, sunny, winter's day, and he decided first to relish his liberty in Regent's Park. This was in accordance with a now almost regular Thursday afternoon routine. Regent's Park, tea in the West End, a visit to the Capitol or Plaza, dinner at Lyons' Corner House, a walk, and home.

Ella could never make out what Bob did with his Thursday afternoons. She suspected adventures. The truth, that he took them and revelled in them alone, was beyond the comprehension of so unambitious and sociable a being as herself.

Ella often thought that Bob must have, secretly, a Girl. His youth, neatness, and personableness cried out for such an assumption. She little suspected that perhaps these very qualities themselves accounted for Bob's not having a Girl. Bob was not unaware of his advantages, and fully alive to a certain recurrent tenderness, shyness, and flexibility of Girls in his company. He was, for this reason, supremely sure of being able to get a girl when he wanted one, and so (because Providence has arranged that we may sometimes get what we want but never want what we get) he did not really want a girl. There would be a Girl one day, but at present he walked, on his Thursday afternoons, with far richer and more tremulous absorptions—those of his youth, and his aspiration, and his eighty pounds.

Most particularly his eighty pounds. Indeed, these little preliminary strolls in Regent's Park he knew to be nothing but little eighty-pound strolls—a thing which gave him more pleasure than anything else in the world. His eighty pounds resided at the Midland Bank in the Tottenham Court Road. It had once been only forty-seven pounds, which had come to him on his mother's death seven years ago. It had only been within the last two years or so that he had begun properly to save. He could still remember the calm satisfaction with which he had brought it up to fifty : the self-applause caused by its reaching sixty : the elation and sheer priggish conceit of seventy —and now it was eighty—eighty exactly. Having, like most of us, a congenitally decimal mind, he always enjoyed his money most when the sum was exactly divisible by ten. Eighty-three, for instance, would be quite a bore—just a depressingly distant halting-place on the road to ninety.

Not that Bob had any greed for money itself, or had any formulated intentions towards his own. It merely stood between him and the dire need to toil, and made a man of him. And he needed this fortification more than others. For he knew now that he was a dreamer. Dreams were his life, were becoming more and more his life, and he worshipped at the shrine of dreams. Furthermore, he proposed to go on dreaming, and the solidity and mathematically appraisable achievement represented by those eighty pounds gave him exactly the reassurance he required.

Bob believed that one day his dreams would come true.

This was an enormous assumption for one such as Bob, for his dreams amounted to little less than this—to govern his own life, to subdue the terrific disadvantages to which he had been born, and to become eminent amongst men. Nothing less. This was Bob's secret—his inner life—the derivation of all those queer reticences and mysteries which so puzzled Ella when she saw volumes of Gibbon, or copies of *John O' London's Weekly*, lying on his bedroom table.

It was Bob's naïve ambition, in fact, to become a great writer. He was the first to apprehend his own naïveté. Hence his secrecy—a secrecy which arose not from pride but from fear of ridicule. Ella, as a matter of fact, if he had told her, would not have thought the ambition naïve, but rather fine and plausible. But Bob was wiser than Ella, and knew it to be naïve  But he knew also how dear it was to him : and because it was a secret, and his own, he took it to his bosom like a lover, and walked with it on his walks.

Bob had not at present essayed much in the way of writing. He was in his twenty-sixth year, but still very young in spirit. He had, in abundance, that quality which perhaps most clearly characterizes youth—namely, a marvellous, unreasoning conviction that the highest and noblest things in life must, of some hidden but automatic necessity, come its way—a perfect assurance of good about to befall. And this feeling still spread a pleasant mist around the actual exigencies and spade-work of ambition.

Nor was it certain that Bob's love of literature was absolutely pure. It had began, many years ago, with an admiration for the works of Conan Doyle. The simplicity, skill, and intelligence of this lovable and rather childish writer had captured his heart. He thought at one time, indeed, that this was the only author that he cared to read ; but later he took to Scott. *Quentin Durward* and *The Fair Maid of Perth* were books he could read again and again. And then came Dumas, and *The Cloister and the Hearth*—and then, strangely enough, Washington Irving, who, with his *Mahomet* and *Columbus* and *Conquest of Granada* was still perhaps Bob's favourite author. He was, to Bob, so lucid, learned, clever, sincere, and serene—a sort of sublimated Conan Doyle.

And then came Wells, whose *Outline of History* supplied his most poignant requirements, and then there was a great deal of miscellaneous and modern reading; and then came *John O' London's Weekly*.

Until this time Bob's devotion had been natural, personal and unaffected. But with *John O' London's Weekly* he fell a victim, in some measure, to popularized great literature. He even began to read tabulated outlines of it and to acquire what may be called the Great-Short-Story-Of-The-World mentality. Like an idle playgoer with the drama, he became, with literature, even more interested in the names and picturesque personalities than in the actual achievements thereof. He familiarized himself with the Love Stories (rather than the greatness) of the Great.

And then he began to write short stories, and to send them in to magazines, and to have them sent back. And then he gave up doing that, and took to dreaming again—dreaming about a great novel that he would one day write. This would take the form mostly employed by young novelists who have never written any novels. That is to say, it would hardly be a novel at all, but all novels in one, life itself—its mystery, its beauty, its grotesquerie, its humour, its sadness, its terror. And it would take, possibly, years and years to write, and it would put you in a class with Hugo, Tolstoy, and Dreiser.

## CHAPTER X

THIS, then, was Bob's secret, which he took, this cold, sunny afternoon, first of all into Regent's Park by the South entrance, and then up and all along by the Zoological Gardens, and at last out again by Camden Town. And then he went down Mount Street, and took it to tea with him at a small and crowded Lyons in the Hampstead Road.

He spent over an hour in here, smoking three cigarettes, and strangely enjoying the electric-lit, spoon-clinking liveliness of the place; and when he came out the world was transfigured by dusk. Bob identified and adored this transfiguratioh. All day long the Hampstead Road is a thing of sluggish grey litter and rumbling trams. But at dusk it glitters. Glitters, and gleams, and twinkles, and is phosphorescent—and the very noises of the trams are like romantic thunders from the hoofs of approaching night. In exultant spirits he strolled down towards the West End.

It was half-past five by the time he reached the Charing Cross Road, and he spent half an hour amongst the books. He then had a drink at a corner near the Palace Theatre, and came out, and strolled along Shaftesbury Avenue.

There was a little red yet in the high clouds of the glowing sky, and in this inspiring light, and amid the winking illuminations of a mauve metropolis, Bob's high spirits reached a peak of pure contentment and peace. The scene was, for indescribable reasons, so magnificent, and life was so indescribably fine. Or at least life could be so indescribably fine, and he was going to make it so.

Bob was not susceptible to the faintest glimmering of the fact that the people he was passing in the street really existed. He observed their faces, he even caught their eyes, but he had no notion of their entity other than as inexplicable objects moving about in that vast disporting-place of his own soul—London. It is doubtful, of course, whether anybody, save in rare divining and emotional moments, suspects the true existence of the souls of anybody else : but Bob to-night, in his vainglory, exceeded this human rule.

And because he was so happy he went and had another drink at a bar at the corner of Wardour Street, where the lights were bright and they were already doing a brisk trade. And because the barmaid was affable, and because he had a kind of beautiful pity for the barmaid for not existing, and not being about to make her life indescribably fine, but being affable all the same, he had an extraordinary pleasant and forgiving chat with her about nothing in particular. And then he came out and walked down Wardour Street.

And then, because his heart was, after all, youthful and frivolous, and this was his evening off, he cast his high thoughts aside (or rather tucked them deliciously away on his person, knowing that he might resume them whenever he willed) and began to interest himself in the shops, and the sights, and the shoplit people, and to wonder what to do with his evening. He decided to go and have a look at the Capitol, and a look at the Plaza, and choose which to go to after he had had his meal at the Corner House. This he now did, and decided on the Plaza.

But even after this it was still a little too early to go and eat, and anyway the streets were far too fascinating to leave. He again entered Wardour Street, and walked up towards Shaftesbury Avenue.

Bob was always diverted by Wardour Street, because it was the principal resort of the women of the town. To him, as with most young men, of whatever class, the poisonous horror of their bearing yet bore the glamour and beauty of the macabre, even if he prided himself that he was superior to adventure of this kind. Or rather that he had now finished with adventure of this kind; for Bob had been to sea, and his behaviour had been neither eccentric nor snobbish in foreign ports.

This evening, too, passing these women and girls, as they lurked solitary in shop doorways, or aimlessly crossed the road, or came down the street in couples absorbed by that frantic garrulity and backbiting which rend their kind—this evening, remembering yesterday evening, and the chivalrous episode it contained, he experienced a new interest.

Indeed, his mood of vaingloriousness transferred itself to this. He again felt glowingly different from other men—and particularly those, of course, whom he now saw lingering in search of those contacts towards which he himself had adopted so austere and magnificent an attitude.

In fact, before long a bemused Bob had reached a phase of overweening spiritual swagger such as is granted to despairing humans seldom, and he had just bought a paper, and was strolling along Shaftesbury Avenue again, when he saw, coming in his direction, and on his side of the pavement, two of these women; in one of whom he thought he recognized the girl herself.

A few paces revealed that this was so. He was at once too flustered to know whether he intended to speak to her; and she, talking to her friend, did not notice him until he had nearly passed. But suddenly her face lit into a smile and she stopped.

" Hullo !—how are *you* ? " she said, and offered her hand.

" Hullo ! " he said, and smiled down upon her.

Her friend (it was a different friend from that of last night) moved on tactfully and looked in a shop window about five yards away.

" What're *you* doin' up this end ? " she asked. She seemed very cheerful.

" Oh—just strollin'."

" Well—come and have a drink with me."

" Right you are. Where shall we go ? "

" Good night, Bet," she cried.

" Good night, Jen ! " returned her friend, and moved away.

They were walking together towards Piccadilly. He looked at her face. He was profoundly impressed by her prettiness and smartness of attire. She really didn't look like one. He saw people looking at them—rather enviously, it seemed to him. His entire evening was altered. He was enjoying himself tremendously.

## CHAPTER XI

" I'M glad I met *you* to-night," she said.

" Oh—why's that ? " But he knew the answer.

" So's I can give you back that money what you gave me," she said.

His spirits expanded.

" Oh no. That's forgotten. How'd' you get on when I left you ? "

" Fine, thanks," she said, briefly and cheerfully.

For a moment he was a little thrown out by this unsentimental retort. Also by the way in which she had gaily slid over the fact that he had (with his " That's forgotten ") just presented her with the money. After all, it was ten shillings gone west. In his next remark he sort to connect with her again, to reinstate himself once more as her hero.

" Were you coming back, as you said you were ? "

" Sure," she said with a continued airiness of manner which considerably piqued him. But he would not give in.

" I bet you weren't," he said, chaffingly.

" *Sure*," she said. " I *was*." And she met his eyes as much as to ask him what it was all about.

He had to be content with that. It was no use ragging her.

" I say—where are we going ? " he said.

By this time they were half way down Wardour Street. She led him into a little alleyway leading therefrom, and into a little public house situated therein. They went up into a little room on the first floor, where there was a bar, tables, chairs and sofas, some people on them, and an automatic piano sort of instrument, which was susceptible to pennies, but brief in its susceptibility, and dumb at the time of their arrival.

She sat down on one of the sofas (she was extraordinarily pretty) and he asked her what she would have. She asked for a sherry, and he went to the bar to get it.

He observed in passing, quite uncritically, that whereas she had invited him to, he was paying for, the drinks ; and when he came back to her she had already bribed, with a penny, the piano, which responded with a brisk rendering of " So Blue "— which clamoured uproariously in the ears of all present, many of whom (including himself) would have eagerly given it a penny (or even sixpence) to have done nothing of the sort.

They smiled at each other once or twice while this lasted, and sipped their drinks.

Then, when it was over, " I Like Music," she said. " Don't you ? "

Bob said that he did.

" Specially them waltzes," she added, " an' all those Sad ones. Don't you ? "

" Yes. I do. I think the waltz is the best of the lot."

" You know what I mean." She was in great travail to make herself clear. " I ain't *sloppy*, but I think I got a taste for Good Music, like. *You* know what I mean."

He comprehended only too well what she was at such pains to express, and it abruptly occurred to him that the evening was going to be rather a bore. He reflected, however, that it would hardly be fair to expect presentable conversation from her, and since she was desirous of his sympathy, he endeavoured to descend to her level.

" Get's you thinking of the Past," he tried. . . .

But this was descending even lower than he had intended, and there was a pause. Nevertheless she took it up.

" Don't want to get thinkin' of *that*," she said.

" Oh—why's that ? " This was more hopeful. He believed they were verging on confessions, which would at any rate not be dull.

" Well—can't you imagine ? "

They were positively verging on confessions.

" Oh—I dunno," he said. " Future's the important thing I guess."

At this someone else put a penny into the piano, and confessions were perforce abandoned in a wild flood of tintinnabulation.

Amid the noise she began to fumble in her bag. " I must give you that ten shillings now," she said.

Then she had not calmly accepted it as he had supposed ? She was rather a dear.

" Ten shillings ? What ten shillings ? Put it away. Go on. Put it away."

" No," she said. " Go on."

" No," he said. " Go on."

" No—go on," she said.

" You put that away," he said.

She did so, adopting the injured tone with which he was familiar. " Well I will then," she said. " But I'm sure I don't know how to thank you."

" Ain't nothing."

The music abruptly ceased.

" An' I don't know *why* you're so good to me," she said, without looking at him. . . .

" Oh well. . . ."

There was a long, and undeniably rather delicious pause. . . .

" Do you dance at all ? " she said, changing the subject with an ingenuous self-consciousness.

" Oh—a bit. Not much good, though."

" Oh, go on. I expect you're fine."

"I'm not. Really. Do you dance a lot, then?"

"Oh—fair amount. When I get the chance."

"Where d'you go?"

"Oh—I generally go down to the 'Globe'—just round here. You can get the drinks till twelve there."

"Oh yes. I know it. Leicester Square way."

"That's right."

There was another silence. She sipped her drink. He watched her. She was awfully pretty. Whatever her sins, he and she were both young. . . . He saw a man, at a near table, looking at her. She really didn't look like one—in here and in the company of a man. Last night he was her deliverer. He felt unaccountably proud and satisfied.

"Couldn't we go round there?" he said.

"What—the 'Globe'?"

"Yes."

"Well, we *could*. They don't start dancin' till eleven, though."

"Well, we'll go there when the time comes. What about it?"

"Fine," she said.

She was a bit of a puzzle. She had a way of suddenly taking things rather for granted. His mind fled darkly and rapidly into a contemplation of his own resources. He should get out of the 'Globe' on ten shillings, and five shillings should cover the drinks etc., before that. Fifteen shillings. Apart from a little loose change, he had two pounds on him, both of which were to have been deposited at the Midland Bank on Monday. But, he reflected, you only lived once, and not long at that.

## CHAPTER XII

"WE'LL go along, then," he said, and seeing that she had finished her drink—"what are you going to have now?"

"No. You ain't going to pay for any more. I'll pay for this one."

Three drinks were already inside him, and now they announced their occupation.

" You kindly do as you're told," he said. " What're you havin' ? "

She was entirely responsive.

" Shan't do as I'm told. An' I'm goin' to pay for them, so there ! "

He rose. " You'll have another sherry," he said, and strode magnificently to the bar.

When he came back another tune from the piano had begun, and the whole conduct of the evening was altered—pitched to a light and frothy gaiety. He beamed upon her and she beamed upon him.

" Never seems I c'n stop bein' a waiter," he said as he put the drinks on the table and sat down. But she smiled and ignored the remark.

" I'd like to know what your Girl would think of *you*," she said. " If she saw you in here."

The naïve reasoning that led her to believe that he must have a " girl," or that, having one, he would be so two-faced and irresolute as to be sitting in here with her, amused him.

" I ain't got no girl," he said, but rather as though he had, really.

" Oo ! I bet ! "

" No, I ain't—*really*."

" Oo, I bet you have ! An' I 'speck she's just the opposite of me."

She was wonderfully cheeky—taking to herself sufficient of consequence to place herself in contradistinction to this hypothetical girl. But he liked it.

" Just the opposite of you ? " he said, feeding her.

" Yes. Just the opposite. Dark—an' brown-eyed—an' nice straight nose, an' all."

" Why—ain't your nose nice an' straight ? "

" Mine ! Why, it's turned up just like a little button ! "

He saw that while she disparaged her own nose, she secretly fancied it ; and he felt the same about it.

" So much the better," he said.

" Not like your girl's," she said. " She's lovely, ain't she ? "

" There isn't one, I keep on tellin' you."

" You tell that somewhere else. An' I 'speck she's more

than a nice straight nose. I 'speck she's a nice straight *girl*, too."

"Why—aren't you nice an' straight?"

She paused and smiled.

"Well," she said. "I hardly give that impression, do I, dear?"

He noted the spontaneous and characteristic "dear' of the courtesan.

"Why—what's wrong with you?" he asked courteously.

"Heaps of things, dear—— An' you'll marry her, an' settle down, an' she'll look after you. That's it, ain't it?"

"Darn socks an' things," suggested Bob.

"That's right. Sweet li'l wife. You won't be able to see any more of me then. She'd scratch my eyes out."

"So you're on'y my tempor'y girl?"

"That's right."

"M'm," said Bob, ruminating. . . .

"Ain't never not much more than tempor'y," she said. "I guess. . . ."

He was slightly baffled by these constant, and it seemed almost conscientious, allusions to her own profession. Also they struck him as being rather wistful and pathetic. Was she seeking his commiseration?

"And who are *you* goin' to marry?" he asked.

"Me? Oo—my dear! The Prince of Wales. Haven't you heard?"

"Oh yes," said Bob. "I did hear something to that effect. . . ."

And so on. The evening was off, with a flying start. They had two more rounds of drinks, and they sat on for an hour and a half. They laughed, and chatted, and she told him, in her indolent, friendly way, a good deal about herself. In fact she did most of the talking.

Only at half-past nine, just before they got up to go, did a slight cloud come to darken the calm and sunny contentment of his mood.

She was giving him proofs of the prevailing, the almost singular honesty of her temperament.

"An' I'll tell you what," she said. "I once knew a man what used to give me four pounds a week—see?"

Bob, who had been Seeing continuously throughout the evening, saw.

" Only it was only just until I got a job. It wasn't *For* anything, like—see ? "

Bob nodded.

" 'Cos he used to say he was *sorry* for us, see ? He used to
say he was sorry for us girls—an' that we wasn't the real ones
to blame. An' he used to go on givin' me this money till I
got a job, like—see ? "

Bob saw.

" Well, one day," she continued, settling down comfortably
into her story, " I was walking about—just not far from here
—when Up comes a Lady to speak to me. Oo—an' she was a
lady, too ! all lovely fur coat'n everything. An' she asks if she
can speak to me, as she's somethin' private to say, like. An' she
takes me round the corner, like, an' she says, ' Now I want you
to tell me,' she says, ' what Relationship you Bear to my husband,' she says. She says, ' You an' I understand all about that
sort of thing,' she says, ' an' I simply want you to tell me quite
straight,' she says. ' An' I'll make it Worth your While,' she
says, ' you needn't worry about that.' See ? "

Bob saw.

" So I said ' Well,' I said. ' There's no need to give me any
money,' I said, ' an' I wouldn't take it. Your husband's just a
straight an' honourable gentleman,' I said, ' an' there's never
been nothing of that kind between us.' An' she tried to offer me
money, but I wouldn't take it."

There was a pause.

" Must've been a very nice fellow," said Bob.

" Oo—he was ! An' he used to say it wasn't us girls' fault.
He used to say it was *Conditions*. He used to say if only girls
over here was paid decently, as they was in America, there
wouldn't be none of us on the street. An' *he* ought to have
known, 'cos he was in Business. Oo—he was ever such a big
man. He was in Cotton, 's' matter of fact. I mean he understood
all about it. He was a big man in Cotton."

" M'm," said Bob, and there was another pause. Her implicit
faith in Cotton as a product almost identical with economic
erudition he could afford to take lightly. But for the rest, his
happiness had flown.

He frankly resented this intruder in Cotton. He knew the

economic side of the situation just as well as him, and he disliked
him as much for having exceeded, as for having preceded, him
in chivalry. Four pounds a week! The sum astonished and
enraged him. How meagre was his own ten shillings now!
And his eighty pounds at the bank, scraped together with such
self-denial and rapture! It was a disgusting world, in which
some people had everything, and others, for no reason, nothing.
And labour, ideals, and honesty were sheer waste of time. He
would show them, though. He would show them.

And because he now suddenly saw her as the object of this
extravagant and fatuous liberality—because the little man in
Cotton had got in years before him and done the thing on an
infinitely larger scale—because there had probably been, or even
were, quantities of other little munificent men in her life—and
because, therefore, his own ten shillings was a paltry trifle, and
she positively magnanimous in giving him so much attention
in return for it—because of all these things, she now suddenly
seemed to draw away from him, to become more remote and
self-contained. She had, after all, a life of her own, and had no
need to bother with him.

Not that he wanted her to bother with him. It only was that,
by reason of this detachment, her prettiness was transformed
into something much less approachable, and because less
approachable perhaps more desirable. And this irritated him.

He was her hero no more. He had, in fact, come down a peg
or two.


## CHAPTER XIII

AS they came out into Wardour Street again she took his
arm. He felt reassured.

A passer-by would not have thought twice about either
of them. He would have observed a fair, full-mouthed, pretty,
and possibly rather fast young woman, arm in arm with a common but nicely dressed young man—probably her fiancé.
They came out into Coventry Street, and walked along by the

Corner House, wending their way through a thick, lingering mass of people lit by a garish shop-light.

There were millions and millions of people, millions and millions of winking lights, and millions and millions of cars, taxis, and buses. And the people themselves were as silent and placid as the machinery was blustering, resolute, and violent. It was a horrible scene, and Bob wondered what the world was coming to.

She still held his arm, and they did not speak much. It might be well (he thought) to possess, in this tumultuous chaos, one thing at least of your own, one human and comprehending organism of your own. He sought sympathy and solace from the vast ramifications of civilization around him, and could almost imagine he had found it, in her light arm snuggled up gladly in his. . . . He wondered what *she* was thinking about it all.

She took him to another little house off the Haymarket, where they had sandwiches and continued to drink and talk, and whence they were at last ejected, at eleven o'clock, with the rest of imbibing London, on to the cold and still crowded streets.

It was indeed very cold ; but then they were now very well filled, and they hurried along in great spirits to the " Globe." They might have known each other for years. It occurred to him that he was having a queer night, and that he had better be careful, for he had to be up working in the morning. She, of course, was not under that obligation.

The " Globe " is in the vicinity of Leicester Square. On the ground floor there is a long spacious bar, with ample seating accommodation, to which the scum of the earth, or the cream of the West End underworld (as you wish it) nightly repairs. Everybody is drunk by half-past ten. By this time there are still remaining one or two boisterous young men from second-rate public schools and respectable business men having a night out, but the place is distinguished by an enormous prevalence of harlots, and their clientèle. Which includes American Sailors, crooks, thriving little Jew furriers and hairdressers, and non-descripts of all sorts—all with a great deal of ugly money to scatter about. At eleven o'clock they are all turned out, but those who wish may go downstairs. Here there is a band of four, a floor for dancing, and about forty odd tables with white cloths, at which you may have food and drink till twelve. But the law forbids you to drink unless you make a pretence of eating as well, so you have to order a sandwich which you never touch. In this manner great profit accrues to the owners of the " Globe."

When they arrived here, there was a thick crowd on the stairs going down, and it seemed rather doubtful whether they would get in. They did so, however—entering into the blare of the band, the shuffle of the crowded floor, and that confusion of blazing light, people, talk, and smoke almost inseparable from the pursuit of nightly pleasure. They found a seat at the back, and could barely hear each other talk. He ordered drinks as in a dream, and asked her to dance.

She danced, not to his surprise, beautifully. She snuggled up, as though with a gesture, in his arms. A lot of people looked at them, and he was very proud. He could hold his own with any of them. He held the prettiest woman in the room in his arms, and he could hold his own with any of them. He was convinced that she was the prettiest woman in the room. He was proud to be seen with her. He was having a great night.

The dance ended, they smiled and clapped, and they went back to their table. Here drinks were waiting for them, and at last the alcohol began to mount to Bob's brain in real earnest. Everything became excited and confused. Another tune began. Somebody came up and asked her to dance. She appealed for permission, he gave it, and she went. He watched her dancing. He danced with her again. He came back and ordered more drinks. Someone else came up and asked her to dance (this was apparently customary at the " Globe ") ; and he again watched her.

As she danced with others he could not take his eyes off her. The prettiest thing in the room. He observed her body, embraced by another, as he had embraced it, swaying to the tune. A kind of jealous sense of ownership prompted him to smile at her nearly every time she came round. She never failed him. She was phenomenally desirable, and he was proud of her. He had never had such a delightful evening. He was drunk.

And now everything grew more and more confused. He was talking gaily with her at the tables ; he was dancing with

her; he was talking with her again. The place was beginning
to reel; she was speaking with amused disparagement of her
other partners; he was finding himself strangely gratified by the
disparagement, and trying to order some more drinks. They
were getting on famously. And all at once there was a strange
pause, and she was looking at him in a new way.

" Ain't you really got a girl ? " she said.

He looked at her—in a queer, exalted moment—and then
replied:

" No," he said. " I said I hadn't. . . ."

" Honest ? "

" Yes. Honest. Why ? "

" Oh—only just wondered." She stuck out her cigarette
on the plate. " Come on. Let's dance this one. It's the last."

They went on to the floor. It was, as she had said, the last
dance, and the band took it at a terrific rate, ending up with a
kind of jig. It then carefully played precisely one half of " God
Save the King." At this the spirit of loyalty, not to say Im-
perialism, filled the " Globe " (the gentlemen standing impres-
sively to attention, and the ladies looking respectfully at a loss)
—but only for the duration of the tune. In a few minutes they
were all out in the air.

" Well, where are you going now ? " she asked.

" Well. S'pose I ought to go home. What're you doing ? "

" Me ? Oh—I suppose I got to hang about. . . ."

" Oh. . . ."

" Tell you what. I'll walk up some of the way with you."

She took his arm, and walked up with him, through Soho,
as far as Oxford Street. They were cheerful, sprightly in retort,
and very friendly.

" Well—when do I see you again ? " he said, taking her
hand, as they came to the point of departure.

" Well—tell you what. I'll come in and see you one evening.
I'll come in to-morrow."

" Will you ? "

" Yes. I will. I'll be in about seven. That's right. About
seven."

" All right. An' I'll expect you, mind you. About seven.
Then if I'm not workin' too hard I'll come over and talk to you."

" That's right. . . . I'll be in all right. Good night, then, dear."

" Good night."

He smiled down at her smile, and left her.

He paced down the silent and lamp-lit spaciousness of Great Portland Street. Gleaming motors crouched in the darkness behind shimmering show windows. Couples of policemen were at deserted corners. It was almost one o'clock. It had been a great evening.

Out of two pounds he had seven shillings left. It was hard to credit that you could spend all that on so innocent an evening. She could hardly have extracted more from him if she had been a harpy.

It occurred to him that she had never thanked him. He supposed it was implied. For one moment a vision of his lost evening—a quiet evening at the pictures with himself and his ambitions (and his two pounds intact), awoke a suspicion of a regret. But he cast it away. A little nonsense now and then was relished by the wisest men.

And her? Arranging to meet her to-morrow. . . . What was this queer alliance, and what was she herself thinking about it all ?

All that talk about his not having a " girl." . . . It was rather appalling. Was it possible that she herself desired to be his " girl " ? No, she was a sensible girl, and plainly saw that this was beyond reason.

But the thing must have crossed her mind. He had respected her and treated her with unexampled tenderness ; he was quite personable ; they were, in the beginning, of the same class. Was it not indeed plausible to hazard that she was already in love with him ?

He sincerely hoped not. It was all rather sad. He would never forget her asking him, like that, if he had a girl. Did that type of girl fall in love ? They needed such consolation, surely, more than others. Their love, if once given, might indeed be blind and devastating.

For that reason they would never allow themselves to enter into it unless they were sure of their ground, unless sincere advances had been made to them. He remembered her own half-humorous insistence upon her ineligibility as his " girl."

He was therefore quite safe. He had made no advances, and even if the idea had entered her head she would keep it as something quite impractical and apart.

He would have to be a little careful, though. It must not go any further. It would never do to start breaking anybody's heart.

## CHAPTER XIV

HE went to bed with a rich and glorious evening, and he awoke at seven to find that it had gone bad overnight, as it were (like milk), and was in his mouth—bitter and sickly. He had been fooled. He had not, after all, had a great time : he had merely been drinking again. All the exalted expansiveness of the night before was transformed into the ranting ebullition of intoxication. He had been fooling about the West End with a woman of the streets. He had spent two pounds. He had, in fact, done it again : and he was becoming, according to his own standards, totally dissolute.

He washed and dressed, and swallowed some breakfast, and began on the Brass.

Ella was glowing with her own perky healthfulness.

" And what was *you* gettin' up to last night, Bob ? " she asked.

" Me ? Oh—I knocked about the West End a bit."

" Oh yes," said Ella. " Don't you tell me ! "

" Go on," said Bob. " Say it."

" Say what ? "

" You're surprised at me."

" Well. So I *am*," retorted Ella, in an indignant tone.

There was a rubbing pause.

" Meet any of your lovely ladies ? " she asked. . . .

She somehow vaguely guessed what he had been up to, he reflected. But how ? What on earth induced her to make these long shots, and how did she always manage to bring them off ? There was something uncanny about these plain, really good women. You could no more fool them than you could your

own conscience. She could not know for certain, however, and
he would not give in.

"Don't know what you mean about lovely ladies," he said.
"I spent a nice quiet evening at the pictures—if that's what you
want to know."

"Yes," said Ella, with equanimity. "I've heard that one
before."

There was a silence. Bob rubbed away.

"You'll be gettin' entangled with one of them creatures—
one of these days," said Ella. "You mark my words."

There you were! Another long shot! Not quite on the mark,
certainly, but horribly near. Her femininity was beyond him.

"All right, I'll mark 'em," he said, and the subject was
dropped.


Bob had nothing to drink at lunch time, and had a good
walk in the afternoon. By the time "The Midnight Bell"
opened in the evening, he had quite pulled round from his
excess of the night before. So much so that he was really looking
forward to seven o'clock, and was confident of being able to
handle the acquaintanceship with the required delicacy and
firmness.

The first to enter the Saloon Bar that night was Mr. Wall.
This was a very sprightly little man, and another habitué. He
had a red face, fair hair, twinkling blue eyes, a comic little
moustache, and a bowler hat. He was obscurely connected
with motors in Great Portland Street, and incorrigible. His
incorrigibility was his charm. Indeed, he kept his company
perpetually diverted. But this was not because his jokes and
innuendoes were good, but because they were so terribly,
terribly bad. You couldn't believe that anyone could behave
so badly and awfully, and you loved to hear him exceed himself.
Against all your sense of propriety you were obscurely tickled
—simply because he was at it again. There was no doing anything with him.

His jokes, like all bad jokes, were mostly tomfooleries with
the language. To call, for instance, "The Four Horsemen of the
Apocalypse" "The Four Horsemen of the Eucalyptus" was,

to him, quite tremendous in its sly and impudent irony. But he was not always as subtle as this. Having a wonderful comic susceptibility to words, and particularly those with as many as, or more than, four syllables in them, he could hardly let any hopeful ones go by without raillery. Thus, if in the course of conversation you happened innocently to employ the word "Vocabulary" he would instantly cry out "Oh my word—let's take a Cab!" or something like that, and repeat it until you had fully registered it. Or if you said that something was Identical with something else, he would say that So long as there wasn't a Dent in it, we would be all right. Or if you said that things looked rather Ominous, he would declare that So long as we weren't all run over by an Omnibus we would be all right. Or if you were so priggishly erudite as to allude to Metaphysics, he would first of all ask you, in a complaining tone, Met What? —and then add consolingly that So long as we Met it Half Way it would be all right. It was a kind of patter in the conditional. Similarly, in his own peculiar idiom, Martyrs were associated with Tomatoes, Waiters with Hot Potatoes, Cribbage with Cabbage, Salary with Celery (the entire vegetable world was ineffably droll), Suits with Suet, Fiascoes with Fiancées, and the popular wireless genius with Macaroni. He was, perhaps, practically off his head.

"Well, Bob, my boy," he said, rallyingly, as he came in. "How're you? B an' B, please, oalgirl."

He employed the popular abbreviation for Bitter and Burton mixed, and Ella gave it him, primly and deprecatingly, and took his money.

"How are you, Mr. Wall?" she said. "We haven't seen you lately."

"Oh—I'm all right. Wotyavin, Bob?"

"I won't have nothing to-night, thank you, Mr. Wall."

"What—You on the Wagon?"

"Pro Tem," said Bob.

"'Bout time he was," said Ella.

At this the door creaked open, and Mr. Sounder entered.

"Ah Ha!" said Mr. Sounder. "The worthy Mr. Wall!"

"Oh ho!" said Mr. Wall. "The good Mr. Sounder!"

But the two gentlemen looked at each other with a kind of

glassy gleam which belied this broad and amicable opening. Indeed, these two were notoriously incapable of hitting it off, and the thwarted condescension of the one, together with the invulnerable impudence of the other, were features of " The Midnight Bell " in the evening.

" Been writin' any more letters to those there papers of yours, Mr. Sounder ? " asked Mr. Wall.

" Not *my* papers—alas—Mr. Wall.  Bitter I think, please, Ella."

" Wish I owned a paper, 'tanyrate," said Ella, trying to keep the peace, and she gave him his beer.

" No. . . ." said Mr. Sounder.  " As a matter of Absolute Fact, within the last hour I have been in the Throes of Composition."

" So long as it ain't a *false* position," said Mr. Wall.  " It's all right."

Here both Bob and Ella were seized by that irritating and inexplicable desire to giggle, and showed it on their shamefaced faces : but Mr. Sounder ignored the interruption.

" I have, in fact, brought forth a Sonnet," he said.

" A Sonnet ? " said Bob.

" Oh," said Mr. Wall.  " Didn't know you wore a Bonnet. Glad to hear it."

" What's the subject ? " asked Bob.

(" You might lend it to me," said Mr. Wall.)

" The subject is Evensong In Westminster Abbey," said Mr. Sounder, suavely, and looked portentously at his beer.

" Brought it with you ? " asked Ella, coming straight to the point.

" Well—I have it with me, Ella.  But I doubt if it's quite in your line."

" Why not ? " said Ella.  " I like Poetry."

" So do I," said Mr. Wall.  " I'm a poet, if you'd only know it.  There you are !

                    ' I'm a poet,
                    If you'd only know it ! '
There you are !  That's Poetry, ain't it ? "

" Hardly," said Mr. Sounder.

" No !" cried Mr. Wall, becoming perfectly violent in his endeavour to convince.  " That's Poetry.

'I'm a poet,
If you'd only know it!'
That's Poetry all right! That's Poetry!"

"Of a Somewhat Crude Kind, I fear," said Mr. Sounder, reflectively.

"No. That's Poetry!" complained a tortured Mr. Wall. "That's *good* Poetry, that is!"

"Can't we see the sonnet?" asked Bob.

"Certainly," said Mr. Sounder, "if you like." And bringing from his pocket a folded sheet of quarto typewriting paper, he handed it to Bob. "It is done on the Petrarchan model," he benignly added.

"On the Model? My word!" said Mr. Wall. "Well—so long as she wasn't *naked*——"

But Bob was already looking at the thing, and the remark passed unheeded.

"I says so long as the model's not *naked*, I don't mind," said Mr. Wall, for he did not like you to miss his points. "But this ain't no artist's studio, you know."

Ella told him not to be silly.

"The Petrarchan," said Bob. "That's different from the Shakespearean, isn't it, Mr. Sounder?"

Mr. Sounder, very much taken aback, said that it was—yes.

"In the Petrarchan," continued Bob, already beginning to blush, "you get eight lines to begin with, an' then six to follow. An' in the Shakespearean you get four quatrains an' then a couplet. Ain't that right?"

"But my dear Bob! Whence this erudition?"

"Oh, he's like that," said Ella. "You don't know him."

"Astonishing," said Mr. Sounder, encouragingly, but he obviously didn't like it very much.

Bob's blush at last subsided. "I'm just interested—that's all," he said.

"He reads the *Decline an' Fall of the Roman Empire*," said Ella, mouthing the words. "Doesn't he?"

Mr. Wall hoped it got up again all right, and at this the door creaked open and a man entered. He was tall, with a bowler hat, yellow gloves, and a silver-knobbed black stick. He wore an expensive, shapely grey overcoat—rather too shapely: and

he had large, handsome features—rather too large and hand-
home. His eyes were blue and fine. His voice was rich, deep,
patrician—authentically beautiful. With all this there was an
elusive shabbiness and meretriciousness about the man. In a
word—an actor.

He had been quite a regular client of " The Midnight Bell "
within the last few months. His name was Gerald Loame, and
he had been known to bring in friends of his own calling.

" Good evening, sir," said the Governor, who had also
entered from behind the bar.

" Good evening," he said, and ordered a Black and White
and Splash.

The conversation was rather dashed. Mr. Sounder, who had
more than once, in the past, tried to get off with this fellow
member of the arts, looked rather awkwardly at his beer.

" I have been telling your friends," he said, ostensibly to the
Governor, but actually to the object of his designs, " that I
have only lately emerged from the throes of Composition."

" Oh," said the Governor. " Reely ? "

" Yes," said Bob. " I've got it here."

" You're a long time readin' that, Bob," said Ella. " I want
to have a look at it myself."

" All right," said Bob, and while the others talked, did his
best to read it. This, however, in view of the distraction of their
voices, was not an easy thing to do conscientiously. Nevertheless, knowing the subject, he was able to get a pretty fair picture
of Mr. Sounder sitting in the Abbey and enjoying the scenery
and organ.

Beginning with an impassioned apostrophe to the " fretted
lights and tall, aspiring *nave*," Mr. Sounder went straight
ahead to describe the music, which was coming in " wave on
*wave*," and which in so doing (as we might have known) his
" soul did *lave* " in all sorts of mystic feelings. Sometimes, he
continued, the effect was so tremulous and delicate as to remind
him of nothing so much as " wind in forest *tree*," while at certain
notable moments there was a " very *sea* " of sound—indeed
it caused him to " well-nigh *rave*." Which fluctuations were
replaced, when the thing left off, by an even more breath-taking
silence—" as of *grave* " in fact.

He then testified to the fullness of his own soul—which was
full to the " *brim* "—and fancied he could positively catch, from
a limitless distance, " echoes of angel's *choir*." Surely, he declared, this service was being conducted not under human
agency, but rather in the glorious and invisible presence of
" some stray Cheru*bim* "—some spiritual being, anyhow, who
knew how to " touch the heavenly *wire* " in a manner unexampled. But this was only supposition. *He* did not know—
*he* did not dare *enquire*. His tears fell fast, his eyes were weak
and *dim*. On that line Mr. Sounder's sonnet concluded.

The courteous Bob rushed through Mr. Sounder's soul-
lavings with a grave but rather abbreviated sympathy, which
was incommoded firstly by the fact that they were all waiting
for him to give it back with some comment, and secondly by
the fact that a couple had entered the lounge and was already
banging on the table with a sprightly but justifiable disregard of
Westminster Abbey.

" Yes. That's very good, ain't it ? " he said, handing it to
Ella, and went about his duties.

Another couple came in immediately afterwards, and with
them " The Midnight Bell " lost its personal atmosphere and
became a public place once more.

In an hour the house was quite full ; he had made one and
seven in tips, he had had nothing to drink, and it was a quarter
to seven.

A quarter to seven. She had said about seven. He had his
first drink.

Now what did About Seven mean ? Did it mean a quarter to
seven ? Or seven ? Or a quarter past ? You couldn't tell.

Five minutes to seven came. It evidently meant Seven.

But it did not apparently mean that, either. For five past
seven came, and still she had not entered. He had his second
drink. Perhaps it meant a quarter past. . . .

By twenty minutes past he was looking up at every creak of
the door, surprised at a curious perturbation in himself. If
things went on like this he would have to develop, protectively,
a Half-Past theory.

By five and twenty past he had developed, and was confident
in, a Half-Past theory.

But unjustifiably confident, as twenty to eight boldly demonstrated. Meanwhile the door had been continuously creaking, and people who were not her continuously entering—entering with a unique, and, it seemed to him, almost churlish opaqueness to the fact that they were not her. . . .

He wondered whether she was Ill.

By a quarter to eight he had lost his temper and was telling himself that anyway it was nothing to do with him. He didn't care, anyway. And she probably had to earn her living, the poor little wretch.

He then verged upon an Eight O'clock theory. . . .

But this fell through also, and after a time he cast it from his mind. He entered whole-heartedly into his work, and made a good deal of money.


## CHAPTER XV

SHE did not come in throughout the entire next week, and he told himself (prompted by a minute but unforeseen malice) that it was just as well.

All the same, intermittently, and at odd moments of the day, the thing occupied and irritated him. She had not kept her word. He could not credit that it was sheer perfidy : he guessed that it was due to some contingency in her life of which he had no knowledge. A week, however, should have covered this, and she should have been in, if only for a moment. And in the event of her having slighted him of her own free will, he desired vaguely, to get his revenge—to meet her once more, even, in order to get his revenge. He had spent over thirty shillings on her the other evening. At least he could not tolerate rough edges, and wanted to round the thing off.

The only little advantage was that it gave Ella what she deserved. She was too clever by half.


" None of your friends in to-night, Bob," she had said,

working on some mystic divinations of her own, on that first evening of his disappointment. And she had clearly expected them to come sooner or later.

But they had not done so, for a whole week, and possibly would never do so again. Ella was therefore mistaken. Ella had been very properly snubbed for being right when she had no right to be—the most intolerable of all advantages.

But on Thursday evening (his next night off) Bob was again in the West End. He had bought a book in the Charing Cross Road, paid an early visit to the " Capitol," and then gone on to the Corner House for a meal. He came out of this at about half-past nine, and found himself in Shaftesbury Avenue.

It occurred to him that this was where he had met her before, and that he might very easily run into her now. Such an encounter, he decided, would give him indisputable pleasure— the pleasure of hearing her excuses and observing her bearing. Furthermore, he was detachedly interested in what had actually become of her.

For these reasons, on reaching the end of Shaftesbury Avenue, he turned again and strolled back. If he knew anything of her habits, she was certain to be somewhere about. He was not looking for her. He was submitting himself to the possibility of encounter. The night air was fine and he had nothing better to do than stroll around.

But she was not in Shaftesbury Avenue, and he turned down Wardour Street. The place was alive with them—old and young. He made a complete circle, round by the Pavilion to the top of Wardour Street again. He then once more walked along Shaftesbury Avenue towards the Palace.

Now there is an extraordinary allure in walking around, or hanging about the streets, in the vague hope of catching (and so justifying your rather bold speculations) one who has no thought of meeting you. You may, after a while, have lost all desire to see the individual in question, but at the same time you find a peculiar difficulty in behaving like a man and cutting

a loss. Having gone to the trouble of trailing up and down six
or seven streets, you are loth to lose your point for a ha'porth of
obstinacy, and are almost convinced that the very street providence has selected for you is the eighth. You therefore go up it.
Then your eighth will probably bring you to some short cut,
or other topographically excusable ninth, and unless you are
very careful you will find yourself before long calmly attacking
your nineteenth. Meanwhile your obstinacy has hardened almost
to the pitch of impregnability. You go round and round.
Indeed, unless there is definitely something else to be done,
only the strongest minds can ever tear themselves away from
this diversion.

Half an hour later found Bob somewhere near the Hippo-
drome. . . .

She would certainly feel honoured, he reflected, if she knew
what he was doing. He went in and had a drink.

He came out, walked into Leicester Square, and again up by
Wardour Street into Shaftesbury Avenue—for the last time, he
swore before Heaven (but he had already sworn before it)—
and was just passing the Shaftesbury Theatre, when he discerned,
on the other side of the street (just a few yards up Dean Street,
in fact) a man in conversation with a woman. It was her.

The two, so far as he could see, were just about to part.
He stopped, retraced his footsteps, crossed the road, and strolled
up again in her direction. He was delighted with himself for
having found her, and was not going to let her go now.

When he reached Dean Street again, the two were a yard away
from each other, and obviously having their final words. The
man apparently intended to go up Dean Street, and she was
coming down in Bob's direction. Bob hesitated, and then
stopped at the corner—waiting for her.

All at once, however, the two joined again, to discuss something else. Bob stayed where he was, lit a cigarette, and looked
self-consciously about him.

Many people passed him, looking at him disinterestedly. A
minute passed. The two were still in conversation.

He suddenly perceived that he had been trailing the streets for
an hour for this girl, and was now awaiting her pleasure. It gave
him rather a shock. He could not understand his own motives.

The two broke away, and she came down towards him. She was smiling, and, it seemed to him, breathlessly pretty. There was no doubt about that. He knew it already.

" Saw you standin' there," she said.


## CHAPTER XVI

HE was at a loss, and anxious to maintain his dignity. He smiled and took her hand.

" Yes," he said. " Saw you standin' there, an' thought I might's'well wait. Fancy meetin' you, of all people ! "

They were walking down towards the Palace. He saw, from her silence, that his assumed detachment had not quite washed, and waited for an opportunity to rectify matters. She wanted putting in her place. Seeing that she had not been in to see him, she had, really, no right to be alive—let alone calmly at large like this.

" 'Spect you're wondering why I haven't been in," she said, in her amiable drawl.

" Oh no," he said. " Never noticed it, as a matter of fact."

Now he had gone and overdone it. He had been deliberately rude.

" Why weren't you in, anyway ? " he asked, trying to pull himself out.

" Don't know, dear. Couldn't get away, I suppose."

She was angry. Unwarrantably and ungratefully angry, in view of all he had done for her, but there you were. He wasn't going to have any of her cheek, though. With him she had no right to be anything but submissive. He saw that the whole thing would probably end here.

" I been busy, too," he said. . . .

They walked on in silence until they reached the Palace. There she suddenly stopped.

" Well," she said. " I got to be going somewhere now, I'm afraid."

He had never thought she would go as far as this, and he was

staggered by her impudence.  Apparently he had been right.
It *was* going to end here.  All the little excitement of it, and
intrigue, and fun, and sentimental stimulation, was over.
Henceforward his life would be exactly as it was before—something uninspired by this little diversion.  He would never see her
again.  She was a breathlessly pretty young woman, and he was
letting her slip out into the night.  He could not do it.  He gave
in.

" Oh," he said.  " Must you ? "

" 'Fraid I must," she drawled.

Bob's fate hung in the balance.  Could he submit to this second
affront ?  She had managed to strike him down with her first
talk of departure :  now she had kicked him.  He had either to
grovel, or come up and settle with her once and for all.  He
decided to grovel.

" Oh—must you ? " he said.  " Can't you just come an' have
one with me ? "

She was looking at the passing people.

" Well—I might stay just for one," she said. . . .

" Right you are," he said.  "Let's go that little place what
we went before."  His grammar was in pieces.

" No," she said.  " Don't want to go there. . . ."

" Why not ? " he asked, observing her use of the word
" want," and marvelling at its implications.

" Had a bit of a bust up in there—the other night," she
fortunately added.

" Well what about this one, over the road—here ? "

" Yes—that's all right," she said. . . .

They walked on.  He thought that they had, perhaps, better
try and be cheerful.

" I was sorry you didn't come in, you know," he said.  " I
thought you'd be along."

" Well, I'm sorry, too," she said, confessing, in her tone,
that they had just had a row, but that she was as willing as him
to patch it up.  " I'm *very* sorry.  But you don't know the life I
lead—really you don't.  It's all one thing after another."

" Oh, I dunno," he said.  " 'Spect I can imagine it."  He was
almost enjoying himself in the old manner.

" Well, *you* may," she said.  " But others don't. . . ."

He, then, was something without precise parallel in her life. . . . They were perfect friends again.

The house he had indicated was at the corner. The main bar was large, with partitions along the wall containing tables and padded seats. The floor was of chequered oil-cloth. It was rather crowded. She went straight to a table : he obtained drinks at the bar, and brought them to her in silence. They were friends again, but there was a difference. She made no attempt to thank him for the drinks, but took her first sip at once, slightly constricting her face as it went down. Then, holding her glass and with her legs crossed, she looked casually around at the people without talking.

He looked at her, and had himself nothing to say. It seemed, as he looked at her, that the tables were queerly turned. The little creature to whom he had given ten shillings a week ago was a quite different little creature from the one whom he was now privileged, after considerable obstruction, to be fortifying with drink.

And this, he realized, was the second of his Thursday evenings off that he was spending in this strange manner. He was puzzled. His own life was becoming unfamiliar to him. . . .

" So you haven't had a very bright time of it since I saw you last ? " he tried.

" No," she said. " Not very."

She was listless and inattentive. She was, as a matter of fact, interested in a garrulous little man who was holding forth at the bar. . . . There was a long silence, which he eagerly sought, but did not know how, to break.

" Funny you meetin' me like that," she said suddenly, and smiling. " That man I was with thought you was trying to get off with me."

" Oh—did he ? "

" Yes." She giggled. (She was a vulgar little bitch.) There was a pause.

" Who's he, then ? " asked Bob, in as off-hand a manner as possible, and taking a gulp at his beer.

" Him ? Oh, I've known him a long time. He's been very good to me, 's'matter of fact."

" Oh—has he ? "

" Yes."

Silence.

" Took me out in his car last Sunday. We went down to Maidenhead. Do you know Maidenhead ? "

" No. Never been there," said Bob, and took another gulp.

His mind was in a turmoil. Car ? Maidenhead ? What was this ? She had, then, friends—and powerful friends—on an equality. " *Do you know Maidenhead ?*" It was the off-hand remark of a lady to a gentleman in a drawing-room. So far from being his wistful little protégée, she was his equal and more. Did she not comprehend her own degradation—the fact that she was an outcast ?

" It's very nice down there, really," she said.

" Yes," said Bob. " I expect it is."

A meaningless reply, to fill in time, and he knew it at once. He decided to steal her thunder. She should not think she could surprise him. He would show her that this was all very natural, and that he knew all about his Maidenhead.

" Went on the river, I suppose ? " he said, lighting a cigarette.

" No," she said. " Not this time of year. . . ."

She had not only held her own : she had made him look a fool. He was losing his nerve, and she was getting the best of it all along the line. There was a silence.

He again thought it would be better if they were cheerful.

He had heard that you could generally win their hearts by noting or belauding their attire.

" That's ever such a nice sort of dress you've got on," he said.

Apparently it had worked. She brightened at once.

" Oh—do you like it ? " she said, fingering the sleeve. " It ain't half bad, is it ? "

He forged ahead. " Darned fine," he said. " Suits you like anything."

" My ! What a price though ! " she said. And, magically, she was sitting up and entering into the conversation. You could hardly credit their vanity and susceptibility.

" Well, you'll never get nothin' to suit you like that," said Bob. " So it's well worth it, whatever it was."

She was beaming upon him. His soul strangely rejoiced.

" M'm," she said. " Came from Paris."

"Gay Paree, eh?" he said, instantly deploring his own vulgarity.

"Yes," she returned, brightly. "I been to Paris."

"*Been to Paris?*" It shot out of Bob before he could stop himself.

"Yes. I spent two weeks there."

She said this with a kind of naïve proudness which saved his own pride; but it was a terrible blow. Maidenhead was a trifle compared to this. It was too great a blow to contemplate even, and he would have to put it away and think about it afterwards.

"Really?" he said. "You're a lucky one if you like. How did you manage it?"

"Oh," she said, and smiled a kind of self-reproachful and disillusioned smile. "Chap took me. . . ."

He was grateful for that smile, and the humility it contained. She possibly realized it was a blow, and was doing her best to soften it for him. He smiled back, and was friendly.

"How did you like it?" he asked.

"Oh, very well, really," she said. "Had a fine time." And there was another pause. . . .

"Oo!—but they don't half jabber over there!" she added suddenly. . . .

"Do they?" asked Bob, amiably.

"Oo, don't they half! Jabber, jabber, jabber all the time . . . . I can't understand their lingo."

"Yes, they do seem to go fast," said Bob, and there was yet another pause.

"Course—I don't expect they're *really* goin' fast," she conceded, with an air of explaining something to herself as well as him. "I expect it only *seems* they do, like. 'Spect if they heard us, they would think *we* was fast. 'Spect it's on'y the *lingo*, like. . . ."

Bob did not think that this was any great subtlety, but agreed with it as though it were. There was another pause.

"Oo," she said. "An' they don't half treat their horses badly!"

"Really?"

"M'm," she said. "That Crool. . . ."

Bob nodded.

" I can't stand Cruelty," she said. " Can you ? "

" No. Awful."

" That's one of the things I *can't* stand," she said.

" Go to any shows ? " he asked.

" Shows ? " She looked meaningly at him. " Oo. I should say I did ! "

He smiled.

" There's a big place they got there," she went on. " It's called the Casino Der Paree."

" Oh yes. I heard of that."

" Oo, it's a big fine place ! An' it ain't half funny inside. An' you never saw such shows ! All them girls coming on half naked. I call it shocking. I do."

He was baffled by what appeared to be her strangely discrepant standards, but felt elatedly indulgent towards her ingenuousness.

" They do," she insisted, as though he wasn't going to swallow it too easily. " They come on half naked. Breasts an' all. . . ."

" Sure of it," said Bob.

" An' when you get the programme from the girl," she threw out, with grave irrelevance, " you have to give her a tip."

" M'm," said Bob. . . .

There was another pause. It was felt that Paris had been succinctly described.

" But what I really didn't like was the Cruelty," she added. " Them whipping those poor horses like that. You know, I don't really *like* them foreigners, say what you like. An' I always used to say so, even when I was there."

" Shouldn't call 'em foreigners," offered Bob, amiably. " Not when you're in their own country."

But this was too much for her. She looked at him.

" Well," she said with sweet reasonableness. " They *are*— aren't they ? "

He decided not to cope with her logic. " Well—what about another drink ? " he said.

" Oh no," she said. " I don't think so. Not now."

## CHAPTER XVII

"OH—surely you can stay just for another quick one?"
"No—can't, I'm afraid—really." She looked at him.
"Sorry. . . ."

So it had really come to this. She was being positively tender
with him! She was "sorry." He marvelled at himself and at
her.

"Well, if you can't you can't, I suppose," he said, with the
friendly air of a man who grins and bears it. "Where've you
got to be now?"

"Oh—I got to go down Leicester Square way."

"Oh."

He noticed that she made no attempt to tell him what her
business was, and that quite inexplicably he did not quite dare
to ask her. This wasn't such a nice evening as the other one, was
it?

"Well. . ." he said, and they rose, and went out into the air.

It was a quarter to eleven. His evening, evidently, was at an
end. A futile thing, petering out here—an unrounded and
incomplete evening—without the stamp either of having spent
it with her or without her. But her own evening, apparently,
was ahead of her : she had merely had him in parentheses. He
felt like a child being suddenly banished, at a crucial moment,
to bed ; and was filled with every kind of dissatisfaction and
irritation.

"Can I walk down with you, then?" he said. It was all he
could say.

"Yes," she said. "Certainly."

*Certainly!* But she had broken him in now. He was only
grateful. All that mattered was that he had prolonged his
evening by five or six minutes. They walked on in silence. He
watched her face, as she looked at the traffic, and was reminded
once more of her desirability. He again saw people looking at
them.

They were nearing Leicester Square. Like the child being
banished to bed, he tried to get a sweet before going. He would

regard a sweet as full compensation.   He asked for it.

" So you haven't had a very bright time since I saw you last ? " he asked, in a sympathetic voice, endeavouring, in the little time he had, to beat up their original tender understanding.

But there were no sweets for him.   She smiled. " No," she said.  " You asked me that before, didn't you ? "

She did not say it insolently, but she had made a complete fool of him.  Also it dawned upon him, for the first time, that she was no fool.  She had a clear memory, and a perfect apprehension of situation.  Had she meant deliberately to be unkind, or was she just putting him in his place for conversational fatuousness ?  He was hurt, but past the desire for revenge.  He wanted his sweet.

" Yes," he said, making it clear that she had hurt him. " But I only wanted to know."

She relented.  " Well, anyway," she said, " you're quite right. I've never had such a rotten time."

He put his sweet in his mouth and relished it.

" Oh well, it's a funny life," he tried. . . .

" It is," she said.   " An' my landlady's a funny landlady, too. . . ."

" Rent again ? "

She smiled an affirmative.  " I got to get two pounds somewhere before to-morrow night," she said.

" Oh dear.  That's bad."

It was now all rather strained.  They were both conscious, perhaps, of the fact that he was having his sweet—that these confidences were now almost mechanical.  They were entering Leicester Square.

" Well," he said.  " When'll I be seeing you again ? "

" Any time you like, dear."

That was better.

" I'll tell you what," she said.  " I've got a 'phone where I'm staying now.  Or I can use it, anyway.  It's downstairs. Why don't you ring me up one day ? "

He breathed a vast relief.  She had a 'phone.  At any rate she was now at his mercy.  At any rate she could not elude him. She was accessible at the end of a line, and he could indulge his whim and pleasure in the matter of ringing her up.  She could not now stampede him into an undesirable meeting. He had her just where he wanted her. It was a lovely and satisfactory evening after all.

" A 'phone ? " he said. " Oh—that's fine. What's the best time for getting you ? "

" Oh—any time, really. In the morning's best perhaps. Will you ring me up one day then ? "

" Certainly I will." (It was his turn to do some Certainly-ing now.) " I'll tell you what—I'll ring you early next week, shall I ? What about Monday ? P'raps you might come in an' see me before then, though."

" Well. I *might*. . . . But it'd be best if you rang me—in case I couldn't. I don't want to *Say*, like—when I couldn't—like I did before—do I ? "

" No. That's right. Come in if you can, but anyway I'll 'phone you Monday. Who do I ask for ? "

She smiled again. " You ask for Miss Jennie Maple," she said. " I'll give you the number." She stopped and commenced to fumble in her bag.

(Maple ! He had never conceived of her as a thing possessing a surname. Who and what were her progenitors—Mr. and Mrs. Maple ? An unimaginable family.)

" Here you are," she said, and handed him a slip of paper with her address and 'phone number. The address was in Doughty Street. They walked on.

" Oh, I know that," he said. " That's just off Theobald's Road, isn't it ? "

" That's right. So you'll 'phone me on Monday, will you ? "

" That's right." They were the soul of cordiality. The memory of their quibblings earlier in the evening had faded from the minds of both. She was completely captivating, he thought—completely captivating, and accessible by 'phone. What more could he ask for ?

And all at once, in the gladness of his new security, he was inspired with a project which arose partly from a pure resurrection of his old feelings of pity and generosity, but mostly, perhaps, from a desire to make assurance doubly sure, as it were, and to rivet again what was already so firmly riveted. He offered her some more money.

"And what about this rent of yours?" he said. "Can't help you with that?"

They were still walking along. "Oh, don't be silly," she said. "*You* haven't got the money."

"Yes I have. Or I can manage it anyway. Come on. I'll give you a pound to help pay it off with."

"You won't do nothin' of the sort," she said. "I can *get* the money—if I take the trouble. It's *my* mess I'm in—not yours."

"Yes. But it's not exactly a pleasant way of gettin' it."

("It's certainly *not*," she admitted. . . .)

"An' so you might just as well let me give it you. Just this time. Come along now."

She was silent, as they walked along. They were now in Coventry Street. He looked at her face. She was so damned pretty. She was looking ahead with a kind of contemplative wretchedness. . . .

"Come on," he urged. . . . He felt the same strange thrill he had felt before. It was almost as though he were making love. . . .

"Well, I'll tell you what," she said. "Have you got one an' threepence?"

"Yes. Why?"

"Well you give me that. Then I can get some lunch for certain in the morning. I can get fish an' chips for that. An' some for my friend, too. It's just one an' threepence. You give me that."

They had now reached Rupert Street, and were walking up it in sheer inadvertency. He stopped.

"All right," he said. "I'll give you one and threepence."

He felt in his trouser pocket, and at the same time in the inner pocket of his coat.

"Here you are," he said. "Here's your one and threepence. An' here's something to wrap the fish an' chips in."

It was a pound note. He put it into her hand, and she did not resist him.

"Oh, you mustn't," she said, and looked up at him. . . .

"Go on. That's all right. And I'm goin' to 'phone you up on Monday morning. About eleven. That all fixed?"

" Yes." She was still looking up at him. " An' I don't know why you're so good to me."

" I'm not good." He felt a bit of an ass, and took her hand in departure. " Only helping where I can. Eleven o'clock, then —Monday. Good-bye."

" Good-bye," she said, still holding his hand. " Eleven o'clock."

And then, all at once, out of the blue—out of the blueness of her round, concerned eyes looking up into his, she hesitated, as though not knowing in what spirit it would be taken. . . . The next instant she had kissed him, lightly and briefly, and yet with an extraordinary trueness and tenderness, full upon the mouth, and was hurrying away—simply tearing away, and not looking back. . . .

He was stupefied and inexplicably happy. He walked up Rupert Street.

The absolute naïveté of the thing—the childish artlessness and directness—the freshness and chastity of it ! Was it supposed to be a reward ? And did she suppose he had desired it ? He could well believe it. Such a thing would only enhance its glorious ingenuousness. Or was it just impulsive and sexless affection ? He could well believe that, too. . . . Or was it, perhaps, love ? . . . Whatever the answer, her simplicity remained to baffle and delight him.

The kiss of a wicked woman—the kiss of Sin. . . . The sweet, brief, virginal kiss of Sin ! A miraculous and exhilarating contradiction ! It remained on his mouth like a touch of violets. There had never been such a kiss in the history of the world.

Expanded again with yet another of those moods of terrible soul-conceit and self-congratulation to which he was so subject, Bob went straight in to have another drink before closing time. . . .

There was a large and rather turbulent crowd in the house he chose, and after a while he cooled down a bit. Nevertheless, over his beer he reviewed the whole evening with glowing satisfaction. He had snatched it from despondency, at the last moment, and made it a triumph.

Why he was so taken up with all this, and what his next move was in this so original and bewitching relationship, he did not know. And, since the telephone had entered into it, he had no need to know at present. He had her at the end of a line, and could think it all over during the week-end.

The way she got money out of him, of course, was simply staggering. To-night he had spent another pound. But he did not grudge a penny of it. It was as cement. With it he had made the already secure ground of her obligation to him doubly secure. He had now no apprehensiveness.

But what apprehensiveness could he have? None surely— since the girl meant nothing to him. It was, then, a pound greedily, almost sybaritically, spent—just to fortify his soul with rampart after rampart against the invasion of those insignificant little distresses he had experienced earlier in the evening.

Now, he honestly believed, he had won her heart for good and all. Not that he had any desire to win her heart. Doing so was merely a little acquired luxury, but one which he was finding difficult to do without. The thing, frankly, was diverting him.

And her virgin's kiss. . . . Oh yes—it was a pound well spent all right. That kiss would have been worth five pounds. Indeed, it was priceless.

## CHAPTER XVIII

NEXT morning, full of well-being and on the Brass, Bob came to a new theory of Money. He was shrewd enough to see that his eighty pounds was not really lying at the Bank. Long ago embraced in oceans of money and credit, it existed merely in his mind and that of the Midland—had no reality. The whole thing being, then, purely arithmetical and immaterial, if he drew from the sum he would not be subtracting anything from a lump of money, but simply changing his mind about what he possessed—revising his mental attitude towards his own wealth. This he was willingly prepared to do. He was prepared, for instance, henceforward to regard himself as a man with seventy-five pounds behind him instead of eighty.

That all this was great sophistry he was aware, but that would be instantly compensated for by his having in his hands, in crisp notes—five pounds to do whatever he liked with. Since his youth at sea, he had never had such a sensation, and he was stimulated beyond measure by the idea. He would go down and draw it this afternoon.

That this caprice was inspired by the prospect of his ' phone call on Monday he was also aware. He wanted enough money when he saw her next. But why did he ? What was going to happen when he did ring her ? He had, as yet, no idea.

That night, at peace with all the world, and with five pounds in his pocket, he spoke rallyingly to Ella across the crowded bar.

" I see your Friend's at the pictures this week ? " he said.

" My Friend ? " said Ella. " Who's my Friend ? "

" Richard," said Bob.

" Richard," said Ella. " Who's Richard ? " But she knew perfectly. He was alluding to Richard Dix. And indeed, Richard Dix was her Friend—if that was a proper epithet to use in connection with her romantic and aesthetic responses towards this actor. At night Ella dreamed submissive dreams of Richard Dix. For although Ella, in her heart of hearts, was a placid and efficient girl, she also worshipped at the shrine of pure beauty and romance. And in Richard Dix both these forces were incarnate.

" Richard Dix," said Bob.

" Oh," said Ella. " *Him*." And wiped a tumbler.

" I thought you might like to go and see him to-morrow."

" Can't afford such luxuries," said Ella.

" Oh well—I'll afford it."

" You ? "

" Yes. I'll take you there."

Ella, putting down the tumbler and meeting his eyes, relapsed into that sincere and gentle unaffectedness which was her true self.

" What—will you take me to the pictures, Bob ? " She was quite overcome.

How abundantly and enchantingly dependent all these women were, thought a rather glowing Bob, his mind going back to the night before. You could win their hearts with the merest courtesy. He found the world more and more charming every day.

" If you'll honour me," he replied.  " You're free all right to-morrow afternoon, aren't you ? "

" I should say I *am*," said Ella. . . .

" Well—that's fixed, then.  An' you might oblige me now with a Gin and French."

" Gin and French ? "  She went to get it for him.

But it was still on her mind when she came back.

" You come into a Gold Mine, Bob ? " she asked, exultantly . . . . It was her barmaid's way of saying Thank you.

## CHAPTER XIX

THE two-dimensional ghost of Mr. Dix was performing at the new Cinema now included in the building of Madame Tussaud.  Bob and Ella left " The Midnight Bell " the next afternoon at five past three, and had not much time in which to enjoy themselves.  Therefore, at Marylebone Church, Bob insisted that they should take a bus along.  Ella cried out against this, as being extravagant, but Bob would not hear her. Ella was enormously chatty and sprightly, and so neatly attired as to seem almost dressed for the occasion.  This, in fact, she was.

There was further extravagance at the entrance.  He asked for two two-and-fours, and Ella could take it or leave it.  She being at the time under the eyes of a tall, vigilant, and rather inquisitive attendant in uniform, took it.  Whereat the attendant, satisfied of their honesty, pulled back the door, and the waiter and barmaid went through into an atmosphere of dim, shaded lights and heavy carpets.  Here they were met by two voluptuous but doll-like young creatures wearing pert brown dresses and enormous bows in their hair, and the whole thing was decidedly Eastern.  With profound and charming veneration one of these seductresses put forth a nail-glinting and powdered hand, gathered Bob's tickets, and with a pleasant manner at once ushered himself and Ella down the centre gangway.  Which savoured more than ever of the East and was testimony to the theory that money may buy anything.

The gangway was dark and insecurely defined. They gropingly selected a row. Seated people, and peopled seats, were maddeningly where they were. " Here we are," said Bob. But it was the blind leading the blind.

At last they were settled. In a few moments they were a part of the audience. That is to say their faces had abandoned every trace of the sensibility and character they had borne outside, and had taken on instead the blank, calm, inhuman stare of the picturegoer—an expression which would observe the wrecking of ships, the burning of cities, the fall of empires, the projection of pies, and the flooding of countries with an unchanging and grave equanimity.

They were lucky in coming in just at the end of " Eve's Film Review," and the next picture was " The Gay Defender " —featuring Richard Dix. Ella and Bob watched all this through practically without a word. Only when there was something to laugh at did Ella turn to Bob, saying " Silly ! " and desiring him to endorse and share her sense of its preposterousness ; and Bob smiled back. His sense of humour was not the same as Ella's but he felt, towards her, the courtesies encumbent upon a host.

" That was very *good*, wasn't it ? " said Ella, when it had faded, and Bob agreed that it was. They then watched some topical events, which were followed by the leading feature of the programme—a German film called " The Spy." But already time was pressing, and they could not hope to see it all through. Certainly not, if they proposed to have tea before going back. Providentially unwitting of their own wistfulness they agreed to see " five and twenty minutes of it." But knowing that they could not watch the thing artistically, and as a whole, they were unable to take it seriously and were more flippant and talkative. " This is *your* type, ain't it, Bob ? " said Ella at the appearance of the leading lady.

It was true. It was his type—a large-eyed, slim and shingled blonde. In calm and loveliness she eclipsed even the little beauty to whom he had given a pound two nights ago. What madly adorable things women could be, thought Bob. They took your breath away with a radiant and inexhaustible perfection. Did such women as the one he saw now really exist ?

Certainly not for him. For the rich, then? But it was obvious that the flabbiness and dissipation of wealth was unfitted to cope with such masterwork of vitality and loveliness. They required a Siegfried, or Launcelot—or, in the last resort, himself. He at any rate could adore comprehendingly. The music played tenderly, and Bob's soul was filled with adoration.

This was quite a new discovery. He had forgotten that women were miraculous. He had known it in early youth and now it was coming back to him. He was very pleased with himself, and glanced at Ella. You either had it or not. She had not. Did she know she belonged to the neuter gender? Probably not. She probably thought that she belonged to the same sex as the enravishing thing upon the screen. She probably thought that she had lesser charm, but the same potentialities—an infamous but comprehensible assumption.

At the appointed time they forced themselves out of their seats by the employment of will-power. The dolls and uniforms had no further interest in them, as they passed out, and they were in the cold, turbulent thoroughfare, lit by the first lamps of evening. Bob took Ella's arm, and led her to a little restaurant over the road. Ella submitted that this was again wasteful, and that they should go to a Lyons or A.B.C., but he would not listen to her.

"You're gettin' Extravagant, Bob. That's what's the matter with you," she said. "What you want is a wife to look after you."

He replied nothing, but wondered whether this was true. Did she mean a thing of joy for ever (such as he had just seen) for his own—a divinity domesticated? In that case he certainly did. He also suspected that Ella was disseminating, vaguely, the air of a candidate.

The little restaurant was very nearly empty, and they took a table in a corner. Tea was brought, and bread and butter, and jam. Despite pressure, Ella would not hear of anything more confectional and luxurious. "I'll be Mother," she said, and poured out the tea. He experienced further subtle knowledge of disseminations.

"By the way, Bob," she said, as she gave him his cup, "I haven't told you something yet."

"Oh—what's that?"

" You may be losin' me before long."

" Losin' you ?   What's happened ? "

She was rather flustered.   " Well—you won't tell no one—will you ? "

" No."

" Honest ? "

" No—solemn."

" Well—I got a job."

" Gawd—what kind ? "

" I'm goin' to look after kids.   Nursemaid.   I may be goin' to India."

" India ! "

" Yes.   It's my Auntie's done it for me.   It's a couple that lives in St. John's Wood—with two kids.   They're ever such a nice couple. . . ."

" That sounds fine."

" 'Course, it didn't look well—comin' from a pub, like—but they was ever so nice."

" That's great."

" 'Tain't half bad."

" Is it all fixed—kind of ? "

" Well—not quite—no.   There was another girl they was wantin' first—an' they still don't know if she can come, like. Of course, if she can, then they'll *have* to have her, like.   But otherwise they want me.   They said so."

Bob at once perceived that Ella would never reach India. So did Ella really, but her bravery and belief in life were transcending her sorrowful intuitions.

" An' I love kids, too," she brightly added.

" Fine," said Bob.   " When do you expect to know ? . . ."

" Oh—they're going to write to me."   She sought his approval and advice.   " I think it's *best*, Bob, don't you ?   'Course it wouldn't be as *bright* as this business, but I think it'd be *better*, don't you ? "

" Oh—all the time.   An' goin' to India, too.   Just fancy."

" Yes.   It ain't half bad, is it ?   An' she's a real lady, too—the one I saw."

There was a silence.   The subject, really, was at an end.

" What's a real lady ? " asked Bob, lighting a cigarette.

" A real lady ? . . . Why ? . . . A Real Lady, of course."

" Like yourself ? " he suggested.

Ella paused, a little insecure, looking at him. " Yes," she said. " Oh—I see."

He knew exactly what was coming, and it came.

" Being a Lady," said Ella, " isn't in what you *are*. It's in how you *act*."

" I wonder," said Bob, and there was a silence.

" Don't be so silly, Bob," said Ella. " Money doesn't bring happiness, anyhow."

He wanted to explain to her that it was not exactly a question of money and happiness, but remained silent.

" I'm just as much a lady as *some* of those, anyway," said Ella. " With the way they go on."

" Who are ' those,' then ? "

" Why ? . . . Those that *are*, I suppose. . . ."

" Oh, then there is a *real* kind of real lady ? "

" Oh, don't talk such *nonsense*, Bob," she said, and he succumbed.

" Well," he said. " I'm ever so glad about this job of yours, anyway."

" Yes. It'll be grand—if it comes off. But *you* won't miss me, Bob, will you ? "

" You bet I will."

" Oh no, you won't. You've got all your Girls to think about."

" There you go again. Where do you get all these ideas ? "

" Oh, well," Ella conceded. " I may be wrong. . . ."

She had given in, he saw, just at the wrong moment. He *wouldn't* miss her for the very reason that he *did* have his " girls " to think about—if " girls " was a suitable epithet to cover his recent emotions. If Ella had only (instead of being so optimistically and irritatingly neuter) been capable of qualifying as a " girl " herself, then he might have missed her.

" I expect you'll have one," added Ella. " One day. . . ."

" I wonder," said Bob, but it occurred to him that perhaps he had one already. Could he not, by a stretch of the imagination regard the little beauty awaiting his 'phone call on Monday as his " girl."

To have a girl.  To have, exclusively to yourself, a girl.  To own a girl—the humanity and inexhaustible loveliness thereof.  It was a tremendous idea.

And could he not be said to have a girl already ?  If mere loveliness was asked for she certainly filled the bill as a " girl." He had from the first admitted that she was, in her way, a beauty.

Of course it was all absurd, but—just as a fancy—a conceit —might he not call her his " girl "?  She had kissed him with her virgin's kiss, and was already, he believed, half in love with him.  How, situated as they were, could she really be anything else ?  Poor little wretch.  Poor blue-eyed, fair-haired, large-mouthed lovely little wretch. . . .

Yes—he had a girl.  He insisted upon the fancy.  He was never so pleased in his life.  Ella's prophecies had been gloriously fulfilled.

" I dare say I will—one day," he said, and Ella returned that she was sure of it.


## CHAPTER XX

MONDAY dawned, but it was not Monday at all.  A dense brown fog obliterated the Universe ; and it was a day outside ordinary human computation.

You were cold to the marrow of your bones.  Garish lights were lit everywhere inside ;  your breathing made perpetual little white fogs.  The roll of the traffic was hushed and torpid.  Fog signals went off like distant tyres bursting.

Bob began on the brass as usual, and Ella came down a little later.  Her nose was very pink, and her first news was in accordance with the general atmosphere of the day.  India was Off.  She had had a letter only that morning.

She took it well, but it had an effect upon Bob as well as herself.  A fog obliterated the Universe, and India was Off.  The imprisoning and inescapable factors of existence made themselves felt.  India was Off.  Would anything ever be On gain ?

Also, Bob was a little ashamed of himself in conversation with Ella. The truth was that he had his own private little line of escape from a pea-soup Universe in which India was Off—the telephone of eleven o'clock. Ella had no such little treat. Nor did she have any idea that he had. She believed him to be a fellow prisoner in a Universe in which India was Off, but actually he wasn't. He felt he was taking a rather mean advantage of her.

Though, as a matter of fact, he wasn't quite sure that it was a treat. Now that he was only half an hour away from it (and the day being so unfamiliar), he was feeling unaccountably nervous. He supposed that she would be waiting for him just the same, in a fog, but he somehow felt that they had not reckoned with this when they had made the appointment. Then again—the 'phoning itself—that was not so uncomplicated an operation as it had looked. He could not, of course, 'phone from the house itself. The instrument was only just behind the bar, and within easy earshot of Ella and everybody. He would have to go out to a box. That, in itself, was not difficult. At eleven o'clock there was nothing for him to do, and there was no danger of his being missed. Indeed, quite frequently he had gone out for a paper at this time.

But there was a difference between vanishing innocently like that, and going out with secret intent to 'phone a woman; and the fog, in some way or another, bestowed upon the whole thing a darker, and more deceptive, and even underhand quality.

However, when the clock pointed to five to eleven, he ran upstairs for his hat and coat, and came down and left the place without a word.

He was going to use the box at Great Portland Street Station. The walk would take him about three and a half minutes, and he calculated to connect with her on the stroke of eleven.

As he walked along he noticed that the fog was really very dense indeed—almost a record, he imagined. That meant that in the *Evening News* there would be ghostly pictures of darkened policemen and flares. He knew all their tricks.

He wondered vaguely why he was doing this, and what it was all about. She, he supposed, was now sitting somewhere, in a room, waiting for his ring. Queer. But he would not dispense with this little intrigue for worlds. He was 'phoning his " girl." She was waiting for him. She had great beauty and was already half in love with him. What more perfect redemption from a foggy day could you obtain ? The fact that she was only poetically speaking his " girl," and could never be so (he supposed) in actual fact, did not concern him.

He entered the box. He saw with annoyance that it was one of those new ones, with Press Button " A " and " B," and a lot of instructions. He had to read them all over again. He had only used one of these once before, and he didn't like them. He put in his two pennies and lifted the receiver. There was a pause. There was a click, and a shrill, quick " *Nummerpease ? * "

" Holborn," said Bob, " X143."

" Holborn X143 ? "

" Please."

The owner of the voice knew nothing about having girls, nor the subtleties and inexplicable thrills thereof. There was a long pause in which the owner of the voice was presumably, but not apparently, doing her business.

" 'Ullo," came another female voice.

He pressed button " A " in a panic. The pennies fell in with a clang. " Hullo ! " he said. " Hullo ! "

" 'Ullo ? " said the female voice, that of an elderly woman it seemed.

" Hullo," said Bob. " Is that Holborn X143 ? "

" Yes."

" Is there a Miss Jenny Maple there, please ? "

" Yes. Don't know if she's in. Will you 'old the line, please."

" Thank you very much."

There was a silence. Who was this ? The landlady, he supposed. " *Didn't know if she was in.* " Rather off-hand, wasn't it ? But there was no reason why a landlady *should* know if she was in. She also did not understand the thrills of having a girl. But she *was* in, and the landlady would be put in her place for her ignorance and aloofness. He had expended a pound sterling on her being in. He disliked the landlady already.

" 'Ullo," came the same drawling voice. " Are you there ? "

" Yes."

" No—she ain't in."

" Oh—ain't she ? " said Bob.   The words leapt from his mouth before he had time even to feel the blow.

" No.  She's Out."

" Can you tell me at all when she'll be back ? "

" Can't, I'm afraid," the loathsome woman returned.  Her little victory over him had been complete, and he was filled with hatred of her.

" Haven't you any idea ? " he asked, showing a little irritation.

" No.  Afraid I haven't."

She couldn't even say " No " properly.  She was saying " Now."  " *Now—afraid I haven't !* " He wanted to pull a face and mimic her.

" You don't know at all, then ? "

" *Now*.  Afraid I don't. . . ."

" Very well," he said curtly.  " I'll ring again."   And he thrust down the receiver.

He came out into the fog.  So he was not after all to have his little treat.  He was really angry.  What on earth had happened to her ?  Where was she now ?  Was she trying to play the fool with him ?  This was the second time she had let him down.  Did she think she could try and play the fool with him ?  He'd show her if she did. . . .  Possibly she had an excuse this time too, but it would have to be very subtle or powerful to gain his forgiveness.  And why had she left no message ? . . .

But he had been a fool to have been so rude to that woman.  He would have to 'phone again, and now he had made an enemy.  And suppose she were not the landlady ?  Suppose she were Jenny's " friend " ?  On second thoughts she sounded like a " friend "—one of those hideous women that pretty women of her class were in the habit of dragging around with them.  Good lord, suppose he had gone and put up her " friend's " back ? . . .

But what did it matter to him, anyway ?  He wasn't going to get messed up with the little bitches. . . .  He re-entered " The Midnight Bell."

Ella was drawing beer for the first few customers.  India

was Off, but she had accepted it resignedly. His own treat was off, and he had to do the same. He was now on Ella's plane and he resented coming down to it.

" They've been *lookin'* for you, Bob," said Ella. " There's some trouble in the cellar."

" Is there ? " said Bob, " Well, it can wait."

" My word ! " said Ella.

He went upstairs to remove his hat and coat, and went down to the cellar to see what it was all about. The Governor's Wife's Sister was down there. As he had foreseen, there wasn't the minutest trouble—merely the Governor's Wife's Sister was at it again. He would murder her one day.

" I've been lookin' for you all this time," she said. " Where'd you get to ? "

" Oh—I just dropped out for a moment."

When he returned to the bar, both Mr. Sounder and Mr. Wall had entered. Mr. Sounder was making scholastic references to the " *Tenebrous* Condition of the Firmament," and Mr. Wall interpolating that if you gave *him* a tenner, he wouldn't mind. A fiver would do, in fact. Mr. Wall also declared that it was a good thing that he (Mr. Wall) had a Red Nose, so as he could see his way about in all this blinkin' fog. This little piece of self-congratulation being tactfully but totally neglected by the others, he waited a moment, and then repeated that So Long as one had a Red Nose it didn't matter.

Ella politely tittered. But Bob was in no mood for the man. He ordered a bitter for himself and drank it gravely.

At three that afternoon Bob went out alone. He was in a wild mood and meant to go to the pictures again. The money he would have spent on her he proposed spending on himself.

He went to Tussaud's Cinema, took a one and threepenny seat, and had no pleasure. There was a fog even in the cinema. He was wrought up and could concentrate on nothing save his own disappointment. He came out, had tea at Lyons, and wished to heaven that he had never got this " girl " business into his head.

But it was in now, and he was going to 'phone her again

before returning to work—at five to five that was. He calculated that that was a likely time. From what he knew of her habits she did not usually descend upon the West End until about half-past six, and she'd probably be back there for tea before going out.

Nerve-racking things, 'phones, Bob thought, as he stepped into the same box as before and put his pennies in. He gave the number and, when the moment came, pressed button " A."

" 'Ullo ? " came the same drawling voice.

" Hullo. Is that Holborn X143 ? "

" Yes."

He was carefully propitiatory.

" Could you tell me if Miss Jenny Maple's there yet, please ? "

" *Now*. She's not in yet, I'm afraid."

He saw that the woman, whoever she was, was enervated rather than uncivil.

" She *is* staying there, isn't she ? "

" Ow, yes. She's staying here."

" I suppose you couldn't tell me when she might be in ? I'm very sorry to trouble you like this, but I'm rather anxious to catch her."

" *Now*—that's quite all right. Only I don't know, you see."

He was making peace in this quarter, at any rate.

" Oh. Well I'll have to ring up again to-morrow. Thank you very much."

" Not at all."

" Sorry to trouble you," he repeated, as a kind of final bouquet, but she had put the receiver down.

The fog was thinning as he walked back to " The Midnight Bell," but it was still bitterly cold. He had not really expected her to be there, he told himself. Now he would have to wait until to-morrow, that was all. Where on earth *was* she ?

He had patched up that little squabble with the woman. That was something.

The Governor had already opened the house, and he was only just in time when he came down to the bar.

The Governor handed him the *Evening News*. There, sure enough, on the front page, was a ghostly picture of darkened policemen and flares. It had been an odd day.

## CHAPTER XXI

IT had rained during the night, and when Bob woke next morning he looked at the window and noticed with relief that the Universe had returned.

By ten o'clock he was rubbing away briskly and regarding yesterday as a kind of nightmare. It had been the fog. He had been frightened of the dark, and had lost his nerve. In familiar weather everything was all right again. He would 'phone her this morning at eleven—probably without results. In that case he did not know what he would do—but it did not matter very much.

By the way, that pound had gone west absolutely for nothing, hadn't it ?

Again, at five to eleven, he left the house. The sky was blue, the wind was blowing, the sun was shining. " Fresh " was the word that Ella had applied to the day, and there could have been no more apt and lovely epithet. Drains ran, the reflecting mud on the pavements was bright blue, bicycles were skidding, the wind smelt keen and bashed you in the face, slates glistened, and everything was washed and beginning again. It all wafted him along to the 'phone box without the slightest morbid introspection.

But once inside, with the door closed tightly, and with the sound of the traffic deadened, and with the bracing wind merely a surrounding and moaning old enemy, and with the stale smell and heat of the box, he was up against something different. He was face to face with his problems.

His two pennies fell, and he had to wait a long while until they attended to him.

" Holborn," he said. " X143."

" Holborn X143 ? "

" Please."

A long silence. . . .

" 'Ullo."

Button " A " and his pennies falling.

" Hullo, Hullo ! "

" 'Ullo."

" Is that Holborn X143 ? "

" Yes."

" Could you tell me if Miss Jenny Maple's there yet, please?"

" Yes. She's upstairs. Will you 'old the line a moment, please ? "

" Oh. Thanks very much."

Then he had got her. She was coming down to him—now. He was going to speak to her. " She is coming, my own, my sweet ! " That was Tennyson. Perfectly inapplicable. How did it go on ? " Were it ever so airy a tread. . . ." He couldn't remember. She'd have excuses, and he would forgive her, of course. She was coming. He could hardly believe it.

" Hullo, are you there ? " The voice was merely surly and enquiring.

" Hullo. Is that Miss Jenny Maple ? "

" Yes."

" Hullo. Miss Maple."

" Hullo. Who's that ? "

" Can't you guess ? "

" No. 'Fraid I can't."

" This is ' Bob,' " he said, putting himself in inverted commas.

Her whole tone changed to a bright and welcoming gladness.

" Oh—is that you, Bob ? " she said. " I'm so glad you rang up. How are you ? "

He noticed that she had removed the inverted commas from " Bob "—uttered it quite spontaneously, in fact—and he was singularly appeased.

" Question is how are _you_ ? " he said. " What's been happenin' to you ? "

" Oh, I've had to go out of town. I'll tell you all about it when I see you. I do hope you ain't been put out, Bob."

Bob again. Complete and vivacious spontaneity. It made him go all funny with pleasure. Rather check, too—bless her. As though he were an old friend—as though there were really something between them.

" No, that's all right. I 'phoned up once or twice, but I thought something must've 'appened."

Elation invariably deprived him of his aitches.

"Oh well, that's all right," she said.    "But I hope you weren't put out."

"No, not a bit.  Now when am I goin' to see you ? "

"Well.  Whenever you like."

"M'm.  Well, let's think. . . .  Well, I'll tell you what, Jenny——"

"Yes, Bob ? "

This was getting absurd. She was all over him. But he could do with it, after all he had suffered in the fog yesterday.

"Our trouble is," he continued, "that the only time I can get off is in the afternoon."

"Well, what's wrong with the afternoon, dear ? "

"*Dear !* " It seemed she regarded him as her own.  Cheek again—but tremendously bracing.  Perhaps this *was* an affair, after all.  Dare he return it ?

"Well, dear," he said (he had !), " it's all right if you can get away."

"Yes.  I can get away all right.  You just say the time'n I'll meet you."

And this clear, bright, sweet childish voice of hers. It was naïve and pure and friendly as the virgin's kiss she had bestowed. It came into his ears like siren's music, at once soothing and exciting, wrapping him round with fervid delights. She was certainly, in her strange way, a marvellous girl.

"I'll tell you what though," she continued, "I'm supposed to be going out with a girl friend of mine this afternoon. What about to-morrow ? "

That, he said, would do finely.  They arranged to meet at three fifteen outside " The Green Man," opposite Great Portland Street Station.  That would be most convenient for him, and she could easily get up there in time.  They might go to the pictures.

"Well then," said Bob, " good-bye."

"Good-bye, dear," she said, and rang off.

He came out into the freshness of the air.

Well, that was that, he told himself, as he walked briskly back to " The Midnight Bell."  Nothing much to it, now he had got the matter cleared up.  She was a queer kid. He was quite indifferent, of course, really.

Mr. Sounder was already in the bar when he returned.

"Ah—ha," said Mr. Sounder. "Our Literary Servitor! Where have *you* been?"

"Me? I've been for a stroll."

"It's nice and fine outside, isn't it?" said Ella, making conversation.

Yes, it was all really a matter of indifference now: but "You're right," he said emphatically, in reply to Ella. "Glorious!"

And it was as though he was jovially slapping her on the back about the day.

"Any more letters in the paper, Mr. Sounder?" he asked, with a kind of rich, chaffing humour, and another metaphorical slap.

"No," said Mr. Sounder, "nothing lately."

"Oh well," said Bob consolingly, "I expect there will be soon."

Mr. Sounder, slightly taken aback, looked curiously at Bob.

"Your constitutional," said Ella, "seems to have done you *good*."

She had again hit the mark.

## CHAPTER XXII

THE next day was grey, threatening rain. He was there at seven minutes past three. The clock on the church over the way pointed to it. They had arranged to meet at three fifteen. Therefore, if she had been there when he came, she would have been eight minutes before her time. But, very sensibly, she was not there eight minutes before her time.

Nor was there any reason why she should be there eight minutes before her time. Nor yet five minutes before her time. Nor yet four, three, or two minutes before her time. And she was not. He applauded her discretion.

At a quarter past, however, he had a right to expect her. She had not come. But that didn't matter, as it was part of a

woman's business to be late. Five minutes late at least. During
the next five minutes she scrupulously obeyed the laws of her
femininity. But by five and twenty past he was growing disturbed. It seemed that only five minutes stood between him
and an almost unthinkable dilemma. For at half past he would
have to give up hope. His mind and soul concentrated on the
hands of the clock, trying to stay their movement. In walking
up and down he was careful to look at the dial only when
farthest to the right of it. In that way you gained, by the angle,
about half a minute.

But there came a time when no angle could mitigate the facts
of the case. It was half-past three. He would now wait as a
formality until four.

There was a voice behind him. " Hullo, Bob," it said.

It was Ella—confound her. She was going to her " Auntie,"
and was rather dressed up.

" Who are *you* waiting for ? " she asked.

" Oh," said Bob, " pal of mine."

She didn't seem to doubt him. " Well, it's going to *rain*
in a minute," she said. " Ta, ta."

" Ta, ta."

He watched her crossing the road and disappearing down
Great Portland Street Station. Going to her " Auntie." He
envied her her plainness and goodness. . . . It was a facile
mode of life, and he wished his own temperament was the same.

At five to four he went into the box and 'phoned up. He tried
to pretend he was someone else. Was Miss Maple there by any
chance ? *Now*, she wasn't in.

Seeing nothing, Bob walked straight down towards the West
End.

He might find her there. Where else could she be ? He had
found her there twice already.

What would he say to her if he did find her ? He had no idea.
He was beyond responding to the situation. He must find her,
that was all.

He began on Shaftesbury Avenue. When arrived there he
realized that he had pinned his hopes upon the corner of Dean
Street where he had last discovered her talking to that man.
She was, of course, not there. It was beginning to rain, but

ere were still many of her kind about. It was half-past four.
He walked down Shaftesbury Avenue, down Wardour
Street, round by the Corner House, up Rupert Street, round by
the Pavilion and back to Wardour Street again. It was raining
quite hard and growing dark. They lurked everywhere in shop
doorways.

The approach of love is something as stealthy and imperceptible as the catching of a cold. A man of spirit never knows
he has it until the last moment. He experiences a little dryness
in the throat or a slight thickness in the head, but these symptoms
are nothing. They have frequently visited him before without
leading to anything more serious. Moreover, they seem to be
passing off during the day. Dozens of his friends about him
have colds, but he, owing to some special dispensation, is going
to escape. The symptoms return. His throat seems sore. He
swallows nothing continually to see how sore it is. He sincerely
believes that it is very mildly sore. Also he knows that you can
easily have a sore throat without having a cold. Nevertheless,
as all these colds are about he had better take something. He
knows that prevention is better than cure, and he is a great
believer in taking these things at the very first sign—however
morbid and fantastic doing so may seem. He takes something.
His throat is no better, but decidedly worse, and he is a little
thicker in the head. But he has no cold. Those around him
who have colds (poor devils) are in one class, he is in another.
Then, one night in bed, he realizes that his breathing is causing
him pain and that he is in something like a fever. He is no worse
than he was before, but suddenly he changes his whole attitude.
A minute ago he had no cold : this minute he succumbs. He
has an appalling cold, and he is one of the poor devils.

Round and round again, down Wardour Street, round by the
Corner House, up Rupert Street, round by the Pavilion, and
back to Wardour Street again. And the traffic hooting, and
the mud splashing, and the rain coming finely down from a
despondent sky, on a darkening winter's afternoon.

At last he boarded a bus and was driven northwards, in the
gloaming, to his evening duties.

## CHAPTER XXIII

A T about ten o'clock next morning, and while Bob was busy polishing the handle of the door, the Governor came through into the bar and spoke across to him.

" Something for you 'ere, Bob," he said.

Bob was not feeling very well at the time, for he had had too much to drink the night before. It was a beautiful morning, with the sun pouring down and flooding everything.

" Something for me ? " he said, and went to the bar with a dirty rag and a bottle-shaped tin of " Blue-bell " in his hand.

" Yes," said the Governor, in a rather curious tone, and handed it over.

Ella, about a yard away, was watching the transaction.

Bob at once perceived why the Governor had not called it a letter (which it was), but Something. The envelope was of cheap mauve material, and in a giddy and sickening moment his eyes ran over the address :

" Bob "
    the Midnight bell public House
      " Off " Euston road
        London.

He did not think he blushed. " Oh," he said, " I know what that is." And put it straight in his pocket and went back to the door.

He had saved his face. By saying in that unruffled way that he knew what it was, he had cleverly intimated to the Governor and Ella that the apparent humiliation of his receiving such a missive was deliberate and with some inner meaning.

He rubbed away at the door handle. So wrought up was he, by the little crisis, that for quite a few moments he totally overlooked the fact that the envelope contained something for him to read.

An apology, he supposed. Well, it was needed : but he could not deny that he was pleased, flattered, and excited. When would he read it ? Not until the house opened, he thought. Then he would run up to his bedroom and open it.

For an hour he kept the thing, a delicious torment, in his pocket. Then, at eleven o'clock, he ran up to his room and shut the door.

It was on cheap, ruled paper, from a Woolworth's writing block, and it was written in pencil. The handwriting was rounded, stupid, but conscientious. The " i's " were dotted with a jab and twirl :

" Dear Bob

" No doubt by now you are through with me as I did not turn up today but Bob it was not my fault dear. You must excuse pensil as I have no pen Well dear you must understand it was not my fault as I was out all that night before and did not get in till half past 4 in the morning and overslept myself untill it was too late to meet you And I have not had anything to eat all day dear as I have no money.

" Well Bob it was not my fault and if you are not through with me perhaps you will meet me on Friday Bob will you I will be at the Green man at 3 and hope you come along there I will be there erlier if you like I hope you will let me hear.

" Please excuse pensil and not turning up
                        " yours truly
                              " Jenny Maple."

Bob read this through three or four times, fully unravelled her constructions, and finally decided she had made handsome amends—more handsome than he would have credited. All his troubles, in fact, were at an end. He came downstairs, obtained a bitter from Ella and, while engaged on various duties, gave himself up to thought.

It was, of course, simply overwhelmingly pathetic. She was, after all, merely the poor little misery he had always thought her. And yet she was an alluring and prettily mannered little misery, and he fancied he could detect her coquetry transcending even her unhappiness and frailty. " No doubt by now you are through with me. . . . And if you are not through with me perhaps you will meet me on Friday." Her naïve humility in reiterating the condition combined with her delightful inner assurance of his complete forgiveness, made him smile and feel indulgent towards her. Loving towards her, even. And then again : " and I have not had anything to eat all day dear as I have no money." That, perhaps, was a bit too " broad," too deliberately and self-consciously pathetic.    But was it not pathetic that she should even try to be pathetic ?  And might it not be true that she had had nothing to eat ?  They led a grim and precarious life, these women—he knew that.  Perhaps he had been unwarrantably harsh in thinking her so heavily to blame.  Perhaps, so far from behaving loosely and inconsequently with him, she had been making every attempt to meet him that her unfortunate circumstances would allow.  He must learn to make allowances for other people besides himself.

Indeed, this was a new line of thought.  He realized that, living as she did, she was as inaccessible, almost, as a princess.  Her appointments meant food.  It was marvellous, really, that she had conceded him so much.  For what was he to her ?  It was not as though he was providing for her, or had any intention of doing so.  She was doing it purely for the sake of a friendship quite profitless to her.  And here he had a humble, sweet, illiterate letter from her begging his forgiveness. He had been an atrocious egoist.  He finished his drink, attended to some people in the lounge, made five pence, and glowed with his own unfairness and egotism.  Bob generally managed to glow about something, sooner or later.

But what was he going to do about it ?    After that walk in the rain yesterday evening, he had to admit that the girl had some sort of morbid fascination over him.  Now that he had got her letter, and all was well again, he was prepared to admit it.  But what was he going to do ?

He knew the advice of the man of the world.  Have her and done with it.  But was he, really, a man of the world, and did he desire her in that way ?  Besides, men of the world were never rewarded with virgin kisses of that kind, and it was not in him to turn its memory sour.  That kiss beautified but made hopelessly intricate the situation. . . .

Was he in love with her, then ?  That, surely, was impossible. You couldn't be in love with a woman like that.  The convention was that directly you began to think you would go mad.  But would you ?  It was all very strange.  He had better send her a line saying he would be there at a quarter past three on Friday.

But why not make it two o'clock and get the whole afternoon off from the Governor. He could easily make an excuse; and the Governor was very amenable about that sort of thing. Then he would have at least three hours with her, and find out what he really felt. If this weather held, he could take her up to Hampstead for a walk. Probably she did not know what fresh air was. It would be his pleasure to introduce her to it.

He would not send a letter—but a wire. He didn't want the fag of telling her she was forgiven by letter. Besides, a wire would put more of the fear of God into her, give greater gravity to the meeting and so make it doubly sure that she would be there. He still had more than three pounds left out of that five.

And the wire? . . .

"Many thanks letter. Meet Green Man two o'clock Friday."

No. He had been an atrocious egotist.

"Many thanks letter. Will be Green Man two o'clock Friday. Try best meet. Bob."

He despatched it that afternoon.

## CHAPTER XXIV

HE was there ten minutes before the time, but she was not. Restraining himself, he went for a walk and came back one minute before the time.

He looked down the Euston Road, and saw her coming in the distance. She waved to him and he went towards her.

His relaxed tension was a thing in which he bathed. He had no cares. The sun was shining brilliantly, and all the afternoon was ahead. They smiled.

"Hullo," she said. "How are you?"

"I'm all right. How are you?"

He was leading her along towards Tottenham Court Road. They talked brightly.

"It's such a lovely afternoon," he said. "I thought we might go up to Hampstead, and have a walk."

" A walk ? " she said, suddenly looking rather doubtfully in front of her. For an instant he thought he detected, coming into her eyes, something of that strange, pettish adamance which he had encountered when he had tried to be domineering with her the other night. He decided to beg for mercy while he could.

" Not if you don't like," he said quickly. " But it'd be awfully nice if you could manage it. Do come."

He informed himself that he was not so insanely anxious to get her on this walk because he was in any way in love with her. It was simply because he had to find out whether he was or not—to see where he was. All the same the fact remained that, whatever the cause, he was insanely anxious to get this delicious object by his side to come for a walk with him. Did it not all amount to the same thing ?

" All right," she said, after a pause, and with good grace. " I'll come."

" Oh—that's great," he said. " Tell you what. We'll go by Warren Street Tube an' then get out at Hampstead. That all right ? "

She could not help dimly smiling, and letting him see her smile, at his unaffected pleasure. Pleased with her power, she embellished the gift.

" I expect it'll be lovely up there to-day," she said, " too."

" That's what I thought," he said, and took her arm as they crossed the road. " Well—what you been doin' with yourself all this time ? "

She accepted his arm with just a slight, inviting pressure. Warmly enclosed, his hand sensed the delicious pulses of her being.

" Oh," she said. " I been havin' my usual hetkick—hecktickt——

" Heck Tick," prompted Bob, smiling upon her. (Where on earth did she get such words ?)

" My usual—Heck Tick—time. How've you been doin' ? "

" Oh—I've been hectic, too." He could not stop himself. " Mostly about you, I guess."

" Well," she said. " That's not nothin' much to get excited about."

He caught her full-lipped and half-smiling face in a fresh and

enravishing pose. He decided that he would readily die for
such beauty.

"*Is* it ? . . ." she added, with a more emphatic coquetry. . . .

She had overdone it—been too acutely aware of her charms.
All at once, and in one of those inexplicable transitions which
may at any time occur in the affliction from which Bob was
suffering, the whole thing fell dead. . . .

"Oh. I don't know," he said, and a little while afterwards
released his hand.

She, however, remained cheerful. They went into Warren
Street Station and entered the lift.

They did not talk much on their way to Hampstead, but
smiled at each other in the noise of the train. He wondered
what the other passengers discerned of them and their relationship. Very little, certainly, since he himself could not have
proffered any information.

They emerged at Hampstead Tube Station, and began to
climb the hill. She talked cheerfully, and rather pantingly, all
the way as they went up, telling him artless tales about her
mother, who was dead, and of whom she thought highly.

"Oo, an' she *was* pretty when she was younger," she said.
"She had a lovely Olive Complexion, an' brown eyes, an' all.
She was more a Southern Type, like. She wasn't a bit like me—
'cos I'm fair. That's funny, ain't it ? "

"Very successful, anyway," said Bob.

"No—it *is* funny, though, ain't it ? 'Cos it's not as though
I was dyed. I got real natural fair hair. I *have*."

"I know you have," said Bob. (And real natural blue eyes
to match, he silently reflected.)

"An' not many people have that, do they ? But it wasn't like
my mother. She was dark, an' ever so pretty."

"Well—ain't you pretty, too ? "

"No. I ain't pretty. I'm better than I was, though. You
should have seen me when I was a kid. I wasn't half ugly. I
was. I got better as I grew up like. I 'member I was in Service
at the time, an' the lady says to me, she says ' I didn't think
much of you at first, Jenny,' she says, ' but I believe you're goin'
to be pretty after all.' I'ze about fifteen, then. . . . That wasn't
half a funny Place. . . ."

They had now reached the top of the hill.

" Oo ! " she said.  " Look at the pond ! "

She was delighted.  The sun shone down, with hard brilliance, on the heath all round.  London was out of sight, and out of mind—far behind and far below.

It was cold and quiet up here, and a few children were playing with boats at the edge of the water.  Bob and Jenny tempered their voices with a kind of reverence for the placidity of the scene, and stopped by the children to watch, with an absorption at once intent and indolent, the hazards and successes of the little voyages.  A light wind rippled the water.

## CHAPTER XXV

"I WISH I had a little boat like that," she said, at last.  " And I'd sail right away."

" Oh—where'd you sail to ? "  He led her on in the direction of The Spaniards.

" Oo—just anywhere."

" Have you ever been up here before ? " he asked.

" Oh yes.  I've often been up."

He was instantly dejected.  He had almost hoped that he was giving her her first introduction to fresh air.  And who had had the privilege of taking her up before ?  He looked at her again.  She was very lovely, and it was a privilege. . . .

" I've been an' had dinner at the ' Ole Bull and Bush,' " she said :  " That's where all them costers go on Bank Holiday.  It's not far from here.  Do you know it ? "

" Yes.  I know it."

" I been to the ' Spaniards ' too."  She put one little foot precisely before the other as she walked along, taking two paces for every one of his, and there was no stopping her chatter.  " And—oo—" she continued, " do you know what they got there ?  They got all them pistols hangin' up on the walls, what the highwaymen used to use."

" Really," said Bob.

" And do you know what those highwaymen used to do ?
They used to hold up a carriage like, and take the money, an'
be ever so polite, an' have a dance with the lady before goin'
on. They did. They'd dance in the middle of the road. That's
what they used to do. They did."

" Really," said Bob, " did they ? "

They had now branched off to the left.

" I always think," she said unaffectedly, " that there's a
Lot of Romance—don't you ? "

" I certainly do."

" In History, like, and all that—you know what I mean ? "

He did. She kept up the same chatter for the next ten minutes.
They approached green and rather pathetically countrified
spaces. To their right was a steep green slope, and they were
walking by a little stream, with trees leaning over the water,
beneath it.

" Oo," she said, " I ain't half glad you brought me up here.
You might be right in the country, mightn't you ? "

" Never been *this* part before then ? "

" No. I never been this part," she said, quietly. She seemed
subtly to realize that the news would please him. It did. He
was enormously happy.

They climbed the hill. At one point she tripped up, and he
saved her with his hand. He retained the hand, and they went
on together, speaking less.

" Ain't that lovely ? " she said, when they reached the top.

" Yes. Ain't it," said Bob.

It was not very lovely really. Far below them were factory
chimneys, works, and suburban villas, interspersed with green
—merely a thin distant outpost of the glimmering and smoky
town. It was about half-past three. It was very warm, but the
sun was already reddening in its decline.

" Well—let's sit down," he said. They did so. They were
propped up comfortably against a bank of turf. She took off her hat.

They did not speak, but listened to the wind, and sensed
their own solitariness. He was in an easy attitude and chewing
a bit of grass.

" Did you get my wire all right, yesterday ? " he said.

" Yes. I got it. And did you get my letter ? "

" Yes."

He looked at her and thought of her sins. She was not think-ing of him. She was looking out into the distance, with her hands clasped over her knees, as though concentrating upon some problem—possibly that of her own life. The wind ruffled her yellow hair. For all her youth and freshness he could discern faint lines of sorrow and dissipation. She perpetually looked as though she might have been crying an hour ago. She could not be more than twenty-one, but she was a woman of the town—of the streets. He was filled with pity.

She caught him looking at her and smiled at him.

This was a new Jenny.

" You shouldn't eat that grass like that," she said, " you'll catch something."

She suddenly changed her position, and sat up facing him, her legs beneath her. She pulled a long blade of grass herself and began deliberately consuming it, looking down at it after each little bite. He laughed.

" An' then I'll have to take you to Hospital," she said.

He did not answer.

" *Won't I?* " she added, dreamingly, and leaned over to pull a little yellow flower by his feet. " There you are. There's a pretty little buttercup." She fondled it.

" That's not a buttercup," he said.

" Yes it is," she said. " Come on. Let's see if you like butter."

" How do you do that? " But he knew.

" Come on," she said.

He drew nearer to her, and she to him. She made him hold up his chin, and held the little flower under it, scrutinizing the results carefully. " Yes," she said, " you like butter."

" How do you know? "

" 'Cos there's a little reflection. That means that you like butter."

" No, it don't," he said.

They looked at each other. Her face, radiant in its young and sorrowful beauty, had never been so close to his before. He was overcome.

" Yes, it does," she repeated gravely, " that means that you like butter."

He looked at her for another moment, and then, with the utmost simplicity, kissed her, and looked at her.

It was as though she was frightened. She did nothing. Her blue eyes were merely fixed upon him. The little flower was held out absurdly in her right hand. He thought of all the kisses she must have known—she, the courtesan, who traded in the whole bad trade of kisses. He was appalled by his own innocence and hers—with her blue eyes and the flower held out.

She was innocent. His own purity made her pure. He took her hand. He kissed that. His emotion arose. He could not understand the way she was taking it. Was it surprise, fright, gladness, or mere submission to a familiar importunity—an importunity which she had learnt not to expect from him?

Then he had her in his arms, and she was looking up at him. She neither rejected nor invited him, but merely looked up at him.

" Oh, I do love you, Jenny," he said.

She put her head down. " No you don't," she said, " you couldn't love *me*. . . ."

He passed his lips along her cheek, and she drew up nearer to him. Her warm, living being, seeking his own being for consolation—the little wanton with her wanton charms, tacitly confessing all and awaiting a child's absolution. And obtaining it, too, for he knew now that he had always adored her. He knew that all other moments and attitudes were as nothing compared to this moment. He knew that, in fact, he held heaven within his arms.

" Why couldn't I love you ? " he said.

She did not look up. " No," she said, " you couldn't love *me*."

" But I do. I do ! " he said, and held her closer. " Why couldn't I love you ? "

" You couldn't love me," she said, " 'cos I'm what I am."

" Well, *what* are you ? "

" You know what I am all right. You wouldn't have helped me if I hadn't been what I am."

" But I love you—I love you. It don't matter I tell you. It don't matter ! "

" Oh, yes it do. You couldn't love *me*, 'cos I'm a prostitute.

That's what I am. You couldn't love one of them, could you Bob ? "

" Oh—you're not, you're not, dear ! " he said absurdly. He was astonished beyond measure, and bizarrely amused, by her employment of this term. He never thought she would have heard of the epithet, let alone level it against herself.

" But I am one, all the same, ain't I ? "

" Look here, Jenny. Do you love me ? "

" Oh yes. I love you all right." She looked at him " You're real straight, ain't you, Bob ? "

" D'you only love me 'cos I'm straight ? "

" Oh, no," she said, and put her head down and began to fondle his hand. " I love you in all sorts of ways."

His eyes were misty with tears. He caught her up and kissed her and kissed her again. Her head fell once more. He kissed her hair. Her real natural fair hair. She drew closer to him. " You're my straight Bob," she said.

There was a long silence.

" Did you always love me, Jenny ? From the first ? "

She paused to deliberate, still playing with his hand.

" Yes. I always loved you," she said, at last. " Not 'cos you helped me—but 'cos you respected me."

He held closer still the child's weight of her body, and looked out upon the scene. Now the red sun was setting over the works and villas. Lights were peeping out, and smoke was rising into a smoky sunset.

" An' I'll *always* respect you, Jenny," he said.

And he knew he was speaking the truth. He loved her. He could hardly bear his happiness. He was filled with a calm and overflowing happiness.

This, then, was what life had held in store for him. Life—all these marvels and mysteries—the smoky sunset, and the ancient night above, and the living being in his arms—it was too much. But it was reality. And she had real natural fair hair. He touched it. His own dear Jenny. Life. He was thankful, so thankful for gift of life. He could have prayed with thankfulness and happiness.

## CHAPTER XXVI

"LOOK, Bob," she said, "the sun's goin' down."
      "I know, dear. . . . Jenny, dear ? "
      "Yes."
"You understand, dear, don't you ? I love you, dear."
She did not reply.
"Don't you, dear ? "
"No," she said. "I don't 'speck you really love me. I 'speck
you only 'magine you love me. I don't see how you could love
me."
      "But I do, dear. I do, I tell you I do ! "
      "No. I 'speck you just think I'm pretty."
      "No. It ain't that, dear. It ain't that."
      "Not that I am," she added. " 'Cos I'm ugly."
      "Oh, you aren't, Jenny. You aren't. You're lovely ! You
know you are."
      "You ain't half been good to me, Bob," she said. "Ain't
you ? " She looked up at him, and was kissed again. There
was a long silence, as she took his hand again in hers. . . .
      "Well. I guess you got a girl, now, ain't you, Bob ? "
      "Yes. I got a girl. But she don't love me as much as I love
her."
      "Oh, yes, she does. She loves you more than what you do."
      "Does she ? "
      "Yes. An' she won't let you go now she's got you. You're
my Bob now, ain't you ? "
      "Yes, Jenny." He was so happy. Her Bob. His Jenny.
His ! His living Jenny in his arms ! The perils of the future
were obliterated by her warm consoling presence and reality.
He would love her for ever.
      "Oh, I'm so lucky and happy ! " he said.
      "Well, I hope you will be," she said. " 'Cos I won't let you
go. Not never."
      A long silence followed. She would never let him go. He
believed her. He gloried in his sentence. He took stock of his
delicious and inescapable possession. Not only the real natural

fair hair—not only the real natural blue eyes—but the mouth, and the hands, and the sweet limbs, and all the fabrics and silks containing them and made magic by them. Her shoes. Her stockings. The bangle on her wrist. Every little appurtenance. A complete and golden girl! His girl. She would never let him go. Oh, indeed, his doom was sweet!—and she had pronounced it. He asked no more of life.

All at once she drew away from him and sat up. " Oo, ain't it gettin' cold? " she said. And with her legs beneath her she began to adjust her hair.

Her skirt fell above her knees, and one garter, ornate and trim, was revealed. Another accessory! Another little article, as it were, which he had forgotten to include in the heavenly inventory! Where would it all stop?

She produced a little comb—(another still!)—and ran it through her hair. He asked if he might do it for her.

" No, it's all right," she said, " finished now."

He childishly felt rebuffed. She would not let him do her hair. What if all this was not his own? What if this ravishing organism preserved its aloofness and independence—was merely something to be admired and adored, by others as well as himself? What if she did not love him? But no. She had said that she would never let him go. You couldn't expect her to " take on " (as she would put it) all the time. She had made him mad and greedy.

" It's about time we went," he said. . . .

" I know," she said, and commenced fumbling in her bag. She closed it with a snap, and began putting on her hat. . . . The episode was over.

He rose, and gave her his hand to help her up. She stood, and he kissed her again. For a brief moment the episode was renewed and he felt securer and more deeply happy than ever. Then they began to walk back.

On the heights of Hampstead the lamps were already lit. A crescent moon was out. Dead leaves rustled beneath their feet. The sensuous fervours of his passion had fled, but the charm remained, and quiet Nature conspired tender scenery for their romance. They hardly spoke.

When they reached the road between Jack Straw's Castle and

the Spaniards, however, the high atmosphere was different.
" Oo—ain't it jes' cold ! " she said ; and it was. Bitterly
cold—and windy, and dark. He took her arm. It was too cold
and windy and dark even for romance. They hurried along.

They descended the hill towards the station, and were
back again with people and unchanged reality. He had burned
his emotions out, and was glad to speak of other things.

In the lift at Hampstead Station the strong light glared upon
her powdered but faultless skin. He saw that she was tired, and
so was he. The noise of the train obliterated—or at least suspended—any feeling of any kind.

Where was she going to-night ? To earn her living ? Unthinkable thoughts. The situation was really ghastly. He would have
to think it all out before he saw her next. At present he was a
little too tired to think or even care about anything.

She came out with him at Warren Street Station, and walked
along the Euston Road with him.

" Well, Jenny dear," he said, " have you had a nice afternoon ? "

She smiled, but did not reply.

" And you're not to worry about things," he said. " 'Cos
I'm going to do a lot of hard thinkin', and get everything
straight. By the way, how much money have you got ? "

" I got three shillings—why ? "

He had three of his five pounds left. He now offered her two.
After a little argument she accepted them. She looked at him
as though she thought him too wonderful for words, and he
rather agreed with her. They had stopped at a corner.

" Well, when am I goin' to see you again ? " he said brightly.

" Whenever you like, dear."

" Well—why not come in and see me ? To-night. 'Bout
nine."

" Certainly, dear."

They arranged that she should come in by herself, go along
to the table at which she had first met him, and wait for him to
come along and attend to her.

" Only you will be there, dear, won't you ? " he said. " 'Cos
something always seems to go wrong with our meetings."

" Yes, I swear I will."

" Swear solemnly ? "

" Yes. Honest I will. Look. I swear on my Liberty—there."

He wondered what exactly she meant by her Liberty, but she seemed to attach great importance to the oath, and he was satisfied.

" Well, good-bye, dear," he said.

" Good-bye, dear."

She put up her face for a brief and final embrace. He gave it to her. The gesture was as spontaneous and respectable as the most conscientious citizen might require. But, coming from her, it had wonderful piquancy.

" Good-bye."

" Good-bye."

She smiled again, and was gone. He walked to " The Midnight Bell."

" Liberty " dawned upon him. He had never thought that the little sinner had ever been locked up. But she had, of course —must have.

She would never let him go.

Oh lord—he was rather letting himself in for something, wasn't he ?

Well—it was done now.


CHAPTER XXVII

NEVERTHELESS, he was in great spirits as he entered the bar for his evening duties, and again slapped Ella metaphorically on the back. He no longer envied, but rather pitied, her goodness.

Mr. Sounder was the first in as usual, and was soon joined by Mr. Wall and also by Mr. Loame, the actor. With the latter Mr. Sounder had now got beautifully off—even to the extent of having Little Things in—ah—Mr. Loame's line—dramatic sketches, to be blunt—which he thought Mr. Loame might just like to cast his eye over. But he had only Turned them Out every now and again and was quite willing to admit that the dramatic craft was very different from the literary one. That was where Mr. Loame came in. He would Know. He would doubtless be able to Put him Right on countless little points. . . . Thus worked the silver tongue of flattery. Production was imminent; and the proceeds would of course be halved. In the meantime if Mr. Loame had anything in the *literary* line (and he had confessed to short stories) very possibly Mr. Sounder could Put *him* Right. In fact they were both going to put each other right. They had both been more or less in the dark all their lives, and it was a decidedly fortunate encounter. Mr. Loame (perhaps a little more doubtful than the other) paid for the drinks.

Also " The Midnight Bell " was to-night visited by the Illegal Operation.

This young man's actual name was MacDonald. But this was transcended by his reputation. As an Illegal Operation (and as nothing else) he drank his whiskies, leered across his bar, and inhaled his endless cigarettes before the world. For he never told you his name, but when he had had more whisky than was good for him he invariably began to swagger confidentially about his Illegal Operation. By performing one of these (successfully), it appeared, he had abruptly terminated his career as a medical student, and served six months in prison. This was his tragedy, and he was famous for it in " The Midnight Bell." He was now about thirty-two, and wore old grey flannel trousers, a sports coat, rather dirty shirts, and knitted ties. He had sandy hair, rather closely cropped (as though he had acquired the habit in prison and rather fancied the style) and grey eyes. He had enormous ears, and a long nose with a rather bashed-in appearance—an illegal nose, in fact— and a full mouth and a large chin. Every now and again he tried to commit suicide, but could never manage to bring it off. Despite all these things, he really wouldn't have hurt a fly and was quite a good fellow if you didn't rub him up the wrong way. He lived in Fitzroy Square.

To-night he was perfectly inebriated even before entering. But this was not surprising, since he was known to take bottles of whisky back to his own room. Ella gave him his whisky before he asked for it, and he smiled at her.

He then, without getting out his money, gazed at Ella steadily, rather as though he thought *she* wouldn't be at all a bad subject for an illegal operation, either. Or at least so it seemed to Ella, who looked foolish, and asked him what he wanted.

" Li'l Splash," he said, with the same transfixing and decidedly operative eye upon her.

She produced the syphon, and took his glass to fill it, but he snatched it away from her.

" *Oh no !* " he said, " Oh, *dear* me no ! "

" What's the matter ? " asked Ella.

Making no attempt to enlighten her he held out his hand dramatically for the syphon. She gave it to him. " Oh, *dear* no," he repeated, but although he was so mysterious, all he wanted to do, apparently, was to fill it himself.

For this, however, an Illegal Operation was too staggeringly drunk to be fully qualified. Instead of causing the soda to flow peacefully into the whisky, there quietly to commingle and effervesce with it, he preferred his own lax measures. That is to say, he jabbed down the lever with rude and sudden pressure, and did exactly what he didn't want to do—the entire amount of the whisky being shot out gracefully on to the floor, and a sparkling glass of soda water elegantly replacing it. Which, of course, was rather dullish, and very inconvenient. Bob fetched a rag. This was quite a characteristic opening with the Illegal Operation, and Bob was in no way perturbed. Nor was the Illegal Operation, for that matter. He grinned at Ella and asked for another.

" I should have thought you'd had enough," said Ella, as she gave it to him.

" Nevadnuf," said the Illegal Operation, and espied Bob at his feet. " Hullo, Bob, how're you ? "

Bob, who could never quite make up his mind whether it was quite in order for an Illegal Operation to address the waiter as Bob, replied rather coolly that he was very well. He then went away, and served some people in the lounge.

" The Midnight Bell " was doing heavy business to-night, and by seven o'clock the place was well filled. By eight o'clock it was crowded, and by half-past eight packed. Bob was kept working at lightning pace, had made four and twopence, and had the greatest difficulty in forcing his way through the crowd at the bar to give Ella his orders. But he was agile and authoritative, and felt the captain of his own soul. He had two little squabbles with Ella, one about change, and the other about what constituted a liqueur glass and what did not (she trying to bemuse his customers with outrageous and unfamiliar shapes); but forgave her both times because she was only good and plain and had never been, and could never go, up to Hampstead Heath and know what love was.

He had not bargained with this crowd, and as he looked at the clock and saw that it was a quarter to nine, he rather regretted his invitation. He had got everything exactly where he wanted it, and he ought to have given it a rest. Having her round tonight was perhaps overdoing it. But you couldn't overdo it really, and he would give her a drink and make her very welcome secretly. A delicious secret. He hoped that she would behave tactfully.

Mr. Sounder, meanwhile, had firmly established himself at a table in the bar with Mr. Loame, and Bob was having to serve them constantly. Mr. Sounder had already rough diagrams of scenery placed upon the table for debate, and wanted to know if various things could be Managed. Mr. Loame would Know. . . . Mr. Loame certainly thought so—yes. . . . Mr. Sounder was glad. Mr. Loame Knew—*he* didn't. . . . Then again, said Mr. Loame, you might play the whole thing just in Tabs. Mr. Sounder replied with an intent, glassy look which was a mixture between a respectful " Might you ? " and a slight ache to be told what Tabs, precisely, were. Mr. Loame explained himself . . . . Ah-ha, now that wasn't at all a bad idea. There you were again, you see. Mr. Loame Knew.

The Illegal Operation also still remained, having allied himself, in all the garrulous crowd, with Mr. Wall, who was expounding a heated argument. Mr. Wall, was, alas, quite as drunk as the Illegal Operation. Indeed, in a strange (and rather illegal) manner the latter often sobered up later in the evening. They were discussing Women, and the Illegal Operation, when listening to the other (which took place very seldom) was being studiedly impudent.

" Now what *I* want to know," Mr. Wall was saying, beating

his fist on the bar, " is is Woman *Woman* or ain't she ?  That's all.  Is Woman Woman, or ain't she ? "

The Illegal Operation couldn't say.

" Now look at my eldest brother's wife," commanded Mr. Wall.

" Shooden like do that," murmured the Illegal Operation, but Mr. Wall was too carried away to observe the offensiveness of the remark.

" Now look at her !  She'd try to Wear the Trousers, if she could ! "

" Jussfassy," said the Illegal Operation, " Juss *Fassy* ! "

" She would !  That's a fact !  She'd try to Wear the Trousers ! But it ain't right, *I* say !  *I* say is Woman Woman or ain't she ? "

Bob coming up at this moment, to give an order to Ella, Mr. Wall appealed to him.

" 'Ere y'are Bob !  'Ere's what I'm asking !  Is Woman Woman or ain't she ? "

Bob hazarded that, so far as he knew, she probably was—and shouted to Ella for two Black and White.

" But it's more than that," cried Mr. Wall, going deeper, " Is Love *Love*, or ain't it ? "

That was certainly more subtle, but Bob had always believed it to be—and went back with his whiskies on a tray.  Reassured, Mr. Wall turned again to a slightly bewildered Illegal Operation, and they both looked fiercely at his eldest brother's wife—the brother-in-law with righteous anger, the Operation with a staggering endeavour properly to concentrate.

It was now five past nine, and she had not come in.  The possibility of her not coming flashed across Bob's mind.  The strange thing was that he really felt that he wouldn't care.  He could almost find it in himself to hope that she wouldn't come. The mere thought was, of course, a betrayal of her, and her trust in him—but there you were.  It was human nature, he supposed.  He had got her in his pocket, and he was no longer mad about her.  He could even conceive of her as an inconvenience. . . .

Then what about all that stuff about having a girl of your own ?  Oh yes—it would never do not to have her there.  But having a girl was, somehow, rather a bore to-night.

He was enjoying his work to-night—enjoying humanity What poor, ranting fools they all were—Sounder, and Loame, and Mr. Wall and the Illegal Operation, and all the crew of bowler-hatted gossips along the bar, and all the valiant couples and trios in the lounge, hatching schemes, discussing events, and summoning the waiter with deep-chested and haughty nonchalance.

It was an amazing life—and a quarter past nine. She had not come in. He began to listen to the creaking door. It would be too absurd if she didn't come, but he had an idea that she wouldn't.

Twenty past nine. What sort of trick did she think she was playing on him ? But he didn't care—that was the funny thing. It would serve her jolly well right if he never got into touch with her again—if he used this as an excuse to get out of the affair. Did he want to get out of it ? No. But he really wouldn't care.

For his own welfare, the wisdom of escaping now would be profound. But he supposed he couldn't. She loved him. She almost certainly would have a perfect excuse, and he would have to give her the chance. There would be another letter in the morning, he imagined. . . .

In fact he was tied up to her now. . . . Good heavens ! tied up to a street walker—something only just removed from a crook. . . .

What would Ella think, if she knew ? . . .

What would the Governor, everybody, think if they knew ? . . .

Half-past nine. She was certainly not coming now. Not only did he not care ; he was glad.

Yes. Glad.


## CHAPTER XXVIII

THE next morning, rather to his surprise, his mood held. No letter had come. Now was his chance, if he cared, to escape. At least, so long as she did not write to him or pay him a visit at " The Midnight Bell " it was. But suppose

she never *did* write, or pay him a visit at " The Midnight Bell " ?
Would it not be an intolerable slight ? Her character was so
odd that he could quite believe it of her. And could he put up
with such a thing ? Never. At least he would have to have
the last word—to take some sort of revenge.

It was therefore purely for the sake of revenge, for the sake
of bringing the business abruptly to a clean cut understanding
or termination that he was going to 'phone her up this morning.
He was, after all, an orderly man.

Conscience whispered that if he was a man at all he would
leave it where it was. He replied that he could not do that.
Conscience returned that a man could do anything. He merely
rejoined that he didn't happen to be going to, anyway, so it
might as well shut up. A knock on the head like that will
temporarily stun, though it will never finally destroy, conscience.
In this case it did the former. He was in the telephone box at
eleven o'clock.

" 'Ullo ? "

" Hullo. Is Miss Jenny Maple there, please ? "

" Yes, will you 'old the line a moment, please ? "

" Thank you very much."

This was excellent. It would have been the devil if she had
not been there. He was glad he had taken this step—it had fully
justified itself. He proposed being decidedly cool.

" 'Ullo. . . ."

" Hullo. . . . Who's that ? Is that—? "

" Miss Maple's in bed. She wants to know if that's ' Mr.
Bob ' speaking ? "

Of all the stupidity and vulgarity. " *Mr. Bob.*" What a fool
she was making of him in front of this blasted woman. •And
why in heaven's name couldn't she come down ?

" Yes, it is. Why ? "

" She says will you meet her in Piccadilly, please, as she's in
bed and doesn't want to come down."

*Piccadilly !* Where on earth did she mean by that ? He was
dealing with imbeciles.

" Do you know what part of Piccadilly ? " he asked.

" *Now.* I don't know."

" Well, would you ask ? Perhaps she'll come down herself."

" Yes.  Will you hold on ? "

" Yes."

He waited.

" 'Ullo."

" Yes."

" She says in the Station, at five thirty."

*The Station !*  He would go mad.

" Could you tell me what part of the station ? "

" *Now.*  I don't know."

" Well, would you tell her I'll be standing outside the bookstall
in the entrance from the Haymarket at five thirty.  You might
go and tell me if that's all right.  I'll hold on."

He waited.  If this was what dealing with women involved
he wished he had never started dealing with women.

" Are you there ? "

" Yes."

" Yes.  She says that'll be all right."

" Oh—thank you very much."  He rang off, and came out.

She, Miss Maple, in bed at eleven o'clock—when everybody
else was working (the lazy little beast)—granted him an interview at five thirty.  Not a single word about her default of
yesterday.  And " Mr. Bob " (her suddenly rather importunate
and ridiculous suitor), because he was so fortunate as to have
one whole evening in the week in which he escaped from toil,
was able to take advantage of her offer.  He was fed up.

## CHAPTER XXIX

A ND she should know that he was fed up, he decided that
afternoon, as he left " The Midnight Bell."  He had until
   five thirty, and was going for a walk in Regent's Park.

It was about time that he got this thing straight.  He doubted
whether he loved her.  How the whole thing had come upon
him was beyond his comprehension.  From the first moment
he had met her, to the last time he had seen her, he had never
made one conscious move towards either wooing or winning

her. Indeed, he had done nothing but retreat. And yet here he was stuck with her—fully committed. Agencies beyond him had been at work.

And was she not, technically, a criminal ?—or at least a delinquent, a member of the underworld, a breaker of the laws, liable to arrests, fines, and detention—marked by the police, and at their arbitrary mercy ? A fine associate for one who proposed to make his mark in the world ! " You'll be gettin' into *trouble* with one of them girls," Ella had said, and she was, as usual, right.

The situation was fantastic. He was seeing things clearly at last. He would either have to cut it out, or keep his head. He supposed he wanted to go on with it. Her extraordinary prettiness and attractiveness atoned, he imagined, for the trouble to which he would be put. But the trouble would be enormous, and now it was going to have his attention.

To begin with, if she desired to go on with him, she would have to submit absolutely to himself as master. It would be for her own good, and she would have to realize the fact.

Next, she would have to get a job. Until she was working and supporting herself decently, he wanted none of her—his pride and decency forbade him to be anything but hypothetically in love with her. That was obvious, and he did not know how it was that her attractions had made him overlook the fact. When she had fought her way back to the normal level of humanity, then he would forgive and forget. To know all is to forgive all. She should become his " girl.". . .

And then ? . . . Marriage ? . . . Jenny would not expect that. . . . Anyway, the future was all dark, and that would be a later problem which would depend upon a thousand other circumstances. . . .

Unfortunately he was a man who proposed to make his mark upon the world. . . . At any rate, whatever happened, an association with him would be elevating her standards and he could be doing her no wrong.

But now there was to be no more tomfoolery. She had to get a job straight away, and he would tell her so this evening. He would help her, if he could ; and were not all things possible to love ?

What were the actual prospects ? That would be coolly and carefully discussed this evening. This evening she would learn that he was master of the situation. If she would not submit, he was through—*and* glad of it.

And if she thought she was going on breaking her appointments like this, she was very much mistaken. And he would tell her so.

It was *funny*, that was what it was, *funny*. And he would tell her so. It was funny enough that he, seeing her degradation, should have ever made the smallest human advances to her. But that she, in that degradation, should think that she could play about with him like this, breaking arrangements overnight and sending down fool messages from bed the next morning, was too funny for words. And, quite dispassionately, he would tell her so.

Oh yes—there was going to be a great clearance and adjustment this evening.

At four thirty Bob entered the Lyons opposite Great Portland Street Station, and had a boiled egg for tea. He glowed with his own angry and resolute lucidity.

At five thirty Bob was waiting in the entrance to the Piccadilly tube from the Haymarket. He looked at the novels on the bookstall. He might have one of his own here, one day. It occurred to him that his present appointment accorded ill with the manner of life proper for realizing such an ambition. But he would win out all right.

Ten minutes later he was scampering round to the other entrances, to see if she was there. . . .

At ten to six she came. She was walking quietly along, looking, not frantically, at the meeting place, but, inadvertently, at the traffic.

Had she forgotten yesterday—Hampstead Heath ? She looked more than ever like one—terribly like one—but admittedly a very attractive one.

" Hullo," they said, and smiled, and shook hands. They walked up towards the Circus.

" You're a bit on the late side, aren't you ? " he ventured.

She knew he was angry. She did not look at him, but absently at a passer-by.

"Didn't think I'd be able to get here at all," she said, "'s'matter of fact."

Evidently she was going to be angry back. Not a very promising opening, he thought, for an evening of clearance and laboured adjustment. He would leave her stone cold, if he had any more impudence.

Perhaps, however, she only wanted talking to. And the night was young.

## CHAPTER XXX

"OH—how's that?" he said, and took her arm as they crossed the road.

"Oo—ain't it cold!" she said, and touched his hand with hers, as though to discover if he was as frozen. A compliment, he supposed. But no answer to his query. Well, let her have it. She was "in for it" all right before the night was done.

He agreed that it was cold, and they walked on in silence. They made for the little house where they had first sat together (the one with the room upstairs, and the piano instrument susceptible to pennies). After a while they began to talk, in a casually agreeable way, but could not, somehow, get properly going. He had something up his sleeve, and she sensed the fact. But so far from being concerned, she was rather inclined to be resentful. It seemed to him that the whole affair was exactly where it was before. There might have been no Hampstead episode, and he was simply back to where he was that night when he had found her at the corner of Dean Street. A fatal night, that. If he hadn't found her, he wouldn't have been here now.

They took a table near the piano instrument, and he bought her drinks. There were a few people at other tables, including a trio who were making a lot of noise. She looked at them while Bob talked to her, and answered him in a very off-hand way.

Something had completely altered her. There was no doubt about that. Perhaps this was her manner of taking him for granted. Well, he would wait until they were in their second drink before he began. It would probably be a different story when she learnt that she was in danger of losing him.

" What'll you have ? " he asked. " Same again ? "

" That's right."

He got up and brought them to her. They came to one and eight—a good hour's work at " The Midnight Bell." " Ta, dear," she said. It was marvellous the way this little criminal accepted his money and homage.

He sat down. " Well, look here, Jenny. I've got a lot to talk to you about."

She sipped at the drink, spilt a little, and wiped her skirt with her hand.

" Really, dear ? What's that ? "

There was no shirking the fact. She was in a simply filthy temper. How dared she be in a temper with him ? How dared she have the impertinence to resent his righteous resentment ?

" Well, to begin with, why didn't you turn up last night ? "

" S'pose I couldn't get away, dear, that's all," she said, and began to fumble in the recesses of her bag.

He watched her doing this, vaguely hoping that she was about to furnish therefrom some documented evidence of the cause of her last night's absence and her present behaviour. She produced, however, her powder puff.

" Well, *why* couldn't you get away ? "

" S'pose I had a previous engagement, dear, that's all," she said. And bringing her mirror out too, she began to powder her face.

What did this mean ? What was the *matter* with her ? What had happened ? Was she, perhaps, demented ? Could anything else account for these fluctuations in her manner towards him ? Perhaps the lot of them were demented. Perhaps they could never do what they did, unless they were. He had better clear out as soon as he could. He was getting involved in Bedlam.

At this point someone came over and put a penny in the piano. " My Blue Heaven " began, dinning and clanging on the ears, like something demented itself. He was drowned in " My Blue Heaven " and a general dementia of the Universe. . . .

But perhaps she was not demented. She looked rather tired.

Perhaps she was ill. Also, he knew from experience that she was incapable of tolerating the slightest criticism of her behaviour. It was one of her fads. And being ill, should she be blamed? The slightest thing would upset a woman. She was ill. He would try that.

" Aren't you feeling well to-night, Jenny? " he asked, as tenderly as possible, and in defiance of " My Blue Heaven."

" No. I'm very well, thank you."

Miraculous—the way he would come up for punishment— and get it. He might as well have some more.

" Jenny," he said, " do you love me? "

She looked at him, for once.

" Well, I've *said* so, ain't I? "

" Well—you don't act as though you do."

" I don't know what's the matter with you to-night," she said. " Why are you naggin' at me? I shouldn't be here if I didn't, would I? "

" You love me, then? "

" Sure. I told you I do."

The moment, he thought, had come.

" Well, I don't want to be hard, Jenny : but if you go on like this you'll be darned near losin' me, an' that's flat."

" My Blue Heaven " came to an abrupt end. She did not answer, but looked sulkily at her glass.

" I got a lot to talk about," he continued, in lower tones. " You an' I've got to come to an understanding. As things are, they're *funny*."

" What's funny? "

" Well, it's funny enough me making love to you at all. But it's funnier still the way you go on."

" So I'm funny, am I? "

" No. Not you. But things are."

He looked at her. There was a long pause. . . .

" I suppose you think I love you," she said, at last, " just 'cos I got soft with you up on Hampstead Heath. That it? "

He was smitten dumb. The brutality, the low-down servant-girl meanness of her. He would never forgive her. She had betrayed and humiliated him. He thought of leaving her on the spot. His look was far from pleasant, and she relented.

"Well—I'm sorry I said that. But you get me angry some-times."

"So it didn't mean nothing up there, then?"

"Yes, it did. I said I'm sorry, ain't I? What was you wantin' to say?"

"Oh—nothing."

"No. Go on. What was you goin' to say? I'm listenin'."

"No. I'm too fed up to go on now."

There was a silence.

"Well," she said, "I ain't got all the evening to waste, you know."

"Well, I'll tell you what I want to say, if you must hear it."

"What?"

"It's just this. I'm willin' to go on with you, but if you can't bother to keep your dates, I'm not goin' to go trailin' round after prostitutes. That's all."

"Oh—so I'm a prostitute, am I?" She snapped her bag to, and began to drink her drink hurriedly.

The little idiot wasn't going to leave him, was she? He was not going to let her scare him, anyway.

"Well—what do you think you are?"

She finished her drink and put it down.

"Oh, that's quite all right. I just wanted to know, that's all. That's very satisfactory. Good-bye."

She rose and went out without looking back.

The thing had happened. She had " walked out " on him, as the saying went. This was a Scene. Everybody in the room, he believed, had observed it. By the blessed grace of providence there was a newspaper under the table. He picked it up and opened it. . . .

What now? He was through with her. That was one thing. But it was only seven o'clock. He was beautifully calm, but his evening was spoiled. He couldn't go to the pictures after this. It would have been much better to have kept the peace and gone to the pictures with her.

He was through. He was never going to see her again. He shouldn't, of course, have called her that. She had always naïvely admitted to it; and it was cruel of him. Perhaps she was genuinely hurt. . . .

His imagination worked apace. . . . A little, lonely, ill-used wanton, told what she was and walking out with her last poor shreds of pride. . . . Walking out on to the streets—the cold streets she knew so well. . . .

Oh God. He ought to apologize to her. After all, he *had* been nagging at her ever since they had met (he, who was supposed to love her). And his own infamy had exceeded her own—that remark about Hampstead for which she had apologized.

Did she love him, or did she not ? She had no earthly reason for saying she did, if she didn't. If only he knew, he would be satisfied. If he could find her and apologize, he might find out.

At any rate, this was not the point at which he could break with her. He had been too much in the wrong for that. He would have to choose a time when she had been in the wrong.

Ten minutes later he was out on Wardour Street. He was in luck's way. There she was, coming down. Probably looking for him—poor little wretch. He stopped to light a cigarette, and walked towards her.

" Hullo Jenny," he said, with a silly smile, and raised his hat. She passed him by, quickening her pace.

He turned round and followed her, touching her arm. She shook his hand off.

" I'm ever so sorry, Jenny. Don't be angry. I want to apologize."

" You leave me alone."

" Don't be silly, Jenny." He was hurrying along by her side like a mendicant. " I been fairly good to you. You might forgive me now."

He tried to take her arm again. Again she shook it off. People were observing them in passing. He was humiliating himself unspeakably : he did not know why he went on. But he was dizzy with a strange incredulousness. Abasing himself like this, it was not in human nature for her to turn him down.

" Please, Jenny. Don't be angry."

And he touched her arm again.

She stopped.

" I'll tell you what'll happen to *you*," she said.

" What ? "

" If you go on Annoyin' me, you'll get put in *charge*."

" Oh, very well.  Good evening."

" Good evening."

*In charge !  Annoying her !*  He walked up the street, his giddy
and blazing humiliation carrying him along.

And to him!  Her deliverer!  The man who proposed to
make his mark upon the world accused of accosting in Wardour
Street !

It was his own fault.  Fancy, at his age, imagining there was a
resemblance between a harlot and a human being !  He had
deserved all he had got. . . .

There were many of her kind about. . . .  " Hullo, dear,"
said one of them. . . .

What a filthy crew.  They were all the same.  But retribution
fell on them.

Yes, they got what was coming to them.  There was, after all,
a God.  They rotted in their own sins and diseases.  God was
just and good.  He loved God.  He was on the side of God.
They rotted in their own sins and diseases.

In the meanwhile, it would be best to get drunk.

He did so.

## CHAPTER XXXI

AT half-past three next morning Bob awoke in the darkness
of his little room.  He had only slept two hours.  He had
come in, reeling drunk, at half-past one, and fallen straight
into a whirling oblivion.  Now he was awake.  His head was like
a midnight mill, grinding out his problems.  About him and
around him the night was awfully still.  He knew this drunkard's
interlude.  He would be sick and heavy in the morning ;  now
he was giddy but horribly lucid.  Sleep was out of the question.
He lit a cigarette.

He had got drunk again.  The truth was that he was letting
himself go.  He was becoming debauched.  This girl was playing
hell with him.  Fiction informed you that girls could do that,
but he had never credited fiction.

The fact was that he *wanted* that little devil. He had better admit it. And he wanted no other little devil.

It was no good telling him that there were other fish in the sea—no good telling him that he might win a better and prettier and decent " girl " for his own. It wasn't true. He knew nobody. He had no money. He had no friends. She was the loveliest thing he had ever met, and the only girl he *knew*.

He *wanted* her.

Half-past three ! . . . She was now probably sleeping in Bloomsbury—only a few miles away on the plains of London . . . . There, the living organism which he desired so completely, was sleeping and untouched. . . . A little vulgar soul with a little white body, that walked about the West End and sold itself. . . . But he wanted her. She was all the mystery and beauty of woman, and he wanted her.

Moreover, because she affected him so strangely, she robbed all mystery and beauty from every other woman. He wanted no one else, for the simple reason that no one else was her. He was, in fact, in love with her.

Furthermore, on her own terms, she was accessible. She was keeping nothing from him. Only his rudeness had alienated her. He must now regard this in a more practical way.

Already he had a plan. He could not, of course, humiliate himself any further, but he would have a gamble. He did not know what had come over him lately—he had been getting wild. Let him have one last fling, and then succumb. He would have a gamble—something which would settle things one way or another—which, if it failed, would force him back into the familiar paths of righteousness.

To-morrow he would go and get five more pounds out of the bank. He would send a wire to her, asking for forgiveness. He would name a time and place, asking her to meet him. It would be her last chance. If she did not meet him, that was the end. In this way the matter would be taken out of his hands. That was all he wanted.

If she met him, he would treat her differently. He would not reproach, he would not nag at her. He would give her a good time—take her to dance—something like that. Surely, after all his goodness, she must develop some sort of feeling towards him

He could not get that day at Hampstead out of his mind—
the day when he had believed that all that loveliness, with all
its accessories, was his very own. If he wooed her rightly,
might it not be his own again? Or if it never had been his
own, might it not become so? She couldn't hold out against his
goodness much longer.

A gamble. That was the thing. To-morrow. He would go
to the Governor and get the evening off. He would say his stepmother was ill. Stepmother was absurd, but they knew he had
no mother or father; grandmothers consorted ridiculously
with cup-finals and office boys, and Ella had used up the aunts.
He would get to-morrow evening off. The prospect of this—
the thought that he was, in a manner, reprieved—was the only
thing to get him off to sleep now. He had better try to. . . .

How hungry he was! The false hunger of the drunkard.
He could eat and eat. Turkish Delight. He could eat pounds
and pounds of Turkish Delight. A blind soul, surrounded
by the darkness of the infinity of the cosmos, lay throbbing with
orgiastic desire for Turkish Delight! What a life!

Or bread and cheese. A white loaf, crust, butter, cheese.
He couldn't go to sleep unless he ate. Why not creep downstairs and find some? He would.

He sprung out of bed and put on his overcoat. He took his
matches and crept downstairs in the darkness. He passed the
Governor's room with excessive caution. He found all he
wanted in a cupboard in the bar. It cost him six matches. He
began to creep upstairs again.

He heard a creak outside the Governor's door. He hesitated.
There was a footstep, and a torch was flashed in his face.

In the pallid light behind the torch the Governor glared at
him with fright and surprise.

" All right, Governor. Only me."

" Oh—is that you, Bob ? "

The Governor could not remove his eyes from him. Bob
returned the stare. It was three o'clock in the morning, and he
was glaring into the eyes of the man to whom, to-morrow
morning, he would invent fictions regarding his stepmother.
. . . Life grew ever more and more involved.

" I didn't have no dinner to-night," said Bob. " And I got

so hungry I thought I'd come down for bread and cheese."

" Oh, that's all right, Bob. You gave me quite a fright."

The Governor returned to his doorway. Bob observed that the Mrs. was up, in an atmosphere of candles and perturbation.

" Good night, Governor."

" Good night, Bob."

Bob returned to his room. He was sorry for the episode. It was a queer thing to do—to wander about the place at night like that. The Governor must have seen he had been drinking. And to-morrow he was going to ask for an afternoon off. He would be losing his reputation, as well as his money, over this little fiend, if he wasn't careful. He gobbled at his bread and cheese, and went to sleep.


## CHAPTER XXXII

THE next morning he was even more ill than he had supposed he was going to be. He was too ill and tired to think, and he proposed to fulfil his resolution of last night as an instruction from a source he was too weak to appraise. He had lost interest in everything.

He was clever with the Governor. He apologized for the night before, explained that he had been distressed and sleepless, and so led on gracefully to Stepmother.

The Governor was cordial. He also mentioned Bob's holiday. Bob was owed six days, and it would be better if he took them after Christmas—beginning on Boxing Day.

Bob had never thought of his holiday in connection with his present preoccupation. He now saw that there were astonishing potentialities in the idea. At eleven o'clock he sent his wire : " *Sincerely sorry do please forgive and meet five o'clock same place this evening.*" It was his last throw, thank God.

In the afternoon he went to the bank, and drew another five pounds. He still had seventy left.

Between three and five he had nothing to do. He went for a walk, and, not to his surprise, found himself in Bloomsbury. He looked for Doughty Street, and found it.

Doughty Street ! It dawned on him ! This was where Dickens
lived—where the Museum was.

And her house (which he found) only about two hundred
yards away ! Quite a decent house, in its dilapidated way.
Probably she had a top room. Jenny and Dickens ! The association was grotesque—and yet how like London. Dickens—
with his blacking factory, and his waistcoats, and his Miss
Beadnell, and his Pickwick. . . . Jenny, who sold her body
upon the streets. . . . It was a wicked old town.

And yet he felt, somehow, that something auspicious had
occurred. In chasing an ill-omened phantom he had arrived at
Dickens' house—at the abode of the greatest exemplar of what
industry might create from nothing. Surely it was a sign. He
needed so badly a sign.

Anyway, he would take it as one. He didn't think the girl
would turn up this evening, and he was through now. Here-
after he would concentrate upon his future. It had been an
experience.

He was honestly anxious that she should not turn up. He had
tea at a Lyons in Theobald's Road and walked down to Piccadilly with refreshed spirit. He was going to start all over again.

As he entered the Haymarket he saw that he was three minutes
before his time.

She was standing there, waiting for him.


CHAPTER XXXIII

IT was such an extraordinary thing, to see her waiting there—
so out of character, as it were—that it seemed possible that
she loved him.

" Hullo," he said, " I'm not late, am I ? "

" No. It's me that's early."

He took her arm and they walked in the same direction as the
night before.

" How are you to-night ? " he said.

" Well," she answered, " I'm not very well, s'matter of fact."

" Oh dear. What's the matter ? "

" I got a pain in my side. It ain't half bad."

" Oh dear. Well, we'll get you something for it."

He was sure she loved him. She was in pain, and she came naturally to him . . . waiting trustfully three minutes before the time of the appointment. He couldn't think what all the fuss had been about—why he had got raging drunk on her account the night before. He had merely been insultingly rude to her, and they had quarrelled. Now she came quietly back to him—as to reality.

There was nothing very thrilling about it. He foresaw a dull evening. But he was glad to have her back, and to hold her arm, and be seen with her. So elusive had she always been that he had developed towards her the passion almost of a collector rather than a lover. And this evening was a prize.

He took her to the same little place, glad to demonstrate to the people there that they were still friends—that if they thought she had walked out on him last night they had never made such a mistake in their lives. They chose the same table ; he brought her Gin and Peppermint, and beer for himself.

" Well," he said. " I want to apologize for what I said last night."

" No," she admitted, " you shouldn't have said that. But I was just as bad."

" No, you weren't. I should never have said that."

She looked at him and smiled at the memory.

" I said I'd put you in charge, didn't I ? "

" Yes. That's what you said."

" Did you think I would ? "

" Didn't know."

" Well, you ought to have known I wouldn't. Fancy thinkin' I'd've done a thing like that."

" Well, you might have done anything—after what I called you."

" Well—I *am* one, ain't I ? "

" Maybe. But that ain't your fault."

" Who's fault is it then ? "

" Oh, I dunno. Just circumstances, I suppose."

" Well, you don't know how right you are. It ain't nothin' else."

" I know it."

" I tell you, I been at the stage where I had to go in to an A.B.C. an' have one stale bun for lunch. You try some of that an' see what you do."

" I know, dear. It's all economic, anyway. Jever hear of Bernard Shaw ? "

" Yes. I've heard of him. He's one of them Great Writers, ain't he ? "

" Yes. Well, he wrote a book called *Mrs. Warren's Profession* —an' showed it was all economics." . . .

There was a pause.

" Well," said Jenny, with emphasis, " I guess he was just about *right*." . . .

And there was another pause as she sipped her drink.

" How are you feelin' ? " asked Bob.

" I'm better now, dear. I like this drink."

There was another pause.

" D'you read much, Jenny ? "

" No. Not much. Only the cheap stuff. You know. The threepenny stuff. It's ever so silly. It's only written for factory girls really—ain't it ? "

" Yes. I suppose it is."

There was a silence as he meditated upon her curiously subtle and involved relegations of class.

" I should like to read that book by Bernard Shaw, though," said Jenny.

" Would you, Jenny ? I'll get it for you if you like."

" Oh—it ain't worth that. I should like to read it, though. Them writers are interested in us, aren't they ? "

" Are they ? "

" Yes, they are. 'Cos prostitution's been goin' on for ever, ain't it ? "

" Has it ? " Her detached and diffident interest in this topic was, as usual, disconcerting.

" Yes, it has. We're mentioned in the Bible."

" Are you ? "

" Yes. Didn't you know that ? We're mentioned in the Bible. There's a part where God's goin' to destroy a big city, 'cos they haven't done what he told them to, an' there's this prostitute there, an' she's the only one that's spared. 'Cos she did what God told her to. And she's a prostitute."

" Thasso ? . . ."

" Yes. An' God's always speaking about us, all over the Bible. There's another part, too, where all the people are throwin' stones at one of 'em—see ? . . ."

" Yes."

" An' God comes along an' says, ' You shouldn't do that '— see ? He says, ' Don't cast the first stone,' he says, 'cos ' Who is without sin amongst you ? ' he says. An' that's not the only case. He is always goin' on about us."

Bob nodded.

" An' that's 'cos God knows that there'll always be prostitutes so long as the world goes on. There always was an' there always will be. 'Cos there's always men, and they always want 'em. You can't get rid of us."

" Have another drink ? " said Bob.

" Thank you," said Jenny, " I will."

" Tell me, Jenny," he said, when he returned with them, " would you come away with me for a holiday ? "

" Course I will, dear. Why ? "

" Well, I got six days after Christmas. I thought we might go away together."

" That'd be fine. Where'd we go ? "

" We might go to Brighton."

" That'd be lovely, dear."

Nothing, apparently, would go wrong to-night.

" I love you, Jenny. That's what's the matter with me."

" An' I love you, Bob, too. Don't I ? "

" Do you ? " he said.

" Yes. You don't know how much I love you. I c'n tell you."

He was very happy. He didn't think he would have any more trouble with her. She was a simple soul, and it had all been his own fault.

He knew, of course, that she was not always as placid as now. He knew that she had endless and intricate powers of riling and maddening him. Indeed the affair, hitherto, had been nothing but torture. But the blame resided not in her—rather in himself

and in the circumstances. Her character was dawning on him.
He believed it was of the utmost simplicity and tragedy.
Beautiful, ill-educated, foolish, weak, miserable, well-meaning,
her beauty had been her downfall. If, occasionally, she was
irritable and inconstant, how could he blame her ? It was a
marvel that she was not worse.

When you worked it out his only complaint against her was
that she did not stand by her arrangements. But what did he
know of her other life—the tortures and exactions of the
streets.

And she looked so tired, sitting there. And yet so lovely.
And only twenty-one. A child and a woman. He loved her
to distraction. He could be so happy with her—merely to look
at her and own her. It would compensate for all the bitterness
of life.

Why not marry her ? If only he had no future to consider,
he would. But might not his future bear it ? Might he not be
great enough to carry Jenny on his own shoulders ? She might
rise with him, or be his secret girl. There was no precedent for
it, but might he not create from herself and himself a romance
undreamed of ?

And he wanted her so badly—and he wanted her perpetual
and exclusive kindness so badly. And the future was dark
and here was a young, living, palpitating, enravishing thing
which he might have for his own.

He would marry her ! From this instant he would concentrate upon marrying her. It was always what he had wanted to
do ; and now the decision was made he could have peace of
mind. It was the only thing for him to do. How on earth had
he expected to carry on the affair like this ? She—poor, submitting thing—must have known how silly it was. And yet
she had made no complaint, but suffered his insults gladly, and
snatched every moment from her hideous existence to come
and be with him.

He thought of all these things as he was talking to her.
Every gesture, every answer she made, confirmed his new theory.

" Jenny," he said, at last.

" Yes, Bob ? "

" Do you think we might be married one day ? "

She looked at him.

" What, Bob—would you *marry* me ? "

She was staring at him.

" 'Course, I would.  I love you, don't I ? "

" After all what I done ? "  She was still staring at him.

" I don't mind what you done.  If you'll get a job, I'll marry you straight away.  Why are you looking at me like that ? "

There was a pause.  She still looked at him.

" What's the matter ? " asked Bob.

" Look, Bob.  I got somethin' to tell you."

He knew what was coming.  Incredible !  Incredible !  Incredible !

" What, Jenny ? " he said.

" It's a bit of a shock, Bob."

He might have known !  He might have known !

" What is it, Jenny ? "

" Well—I'm married."

" Oh God," said Bob.

There was a long silence.  She put her hand out consolingly on to his.  He was appalled by its white sweetness and beauty. He hoped people wouldn't see.  It didn't look well—being tenderly consoled by a prostitute in a public place.


CHAPTER XXXIV

IT was not jealousy : he was beyond that.  It was the snub. The perfect snub to his generosity and originality.  He had thrown away the world for her, merely to discover that another had thrown it away before.  After this he was prostrate before her.  She had got him beaten.  He loved her.  He adored her.  The touch of her hand, as it lay on his, sent excruciating currents of her being into his own.  Another, before him, had known the same.  They were both beggars for her kindness. Was there some magic in her ?  He looked at her.  Yes, assuredly she was magic.  She seemed transcended with an unholy beauty. He stared miserably in front of him.

" What's the matter, Bob ? You ain't upset, are you ? " she said, and withdrew her hand.

" Don't take your hand away, Jenny."

It came back at once.

" What's the matter, Bob ? It don't affect you, do it ? "

He concentrated all his thoughts upon her hand. It soothed, excited, appeased, maddened, thrilled. It was slim, and white, and delicate, and weighted with the soft weight of paradise. He wanted to kiss it. He would have to kiss it.

On one of the forefingers there was a little freckle. He would certainly have to kiss that. He desired to kiss her hand in token of his defeat. He would be making a damn fool of himself in a moment.

" God. It's awful, Jenny."

" What's awful, dear ? "

" I love you so."

" Nothin' awful in that. Go on. Drink your drink."

She took her hand away and put the glass nearer to him.

" Who is he, Jenny ? "

" Oh. *He's* not very interestin'. I shouldn't worry about *him*."

" Do you love him ? "

" Love *him ?* My word, no."

" Who is he ? What does he do ? "

" He works in a bicycle shop."

Bicycle shop consoled him. He was a common man—like himself. Also he could discern a faint aura of ridiculousness attached to bicycles. Perhaps he might even be able to pity this newcomer—this interloper—her husband.

" Does he love you ? "

" Yes. He thinks he does."

" But you don't love him ? "

" No."

" Why not ? "

" 'Cos I don't, I suppose. That's all."

This was horrible. The man loved her, but she did not love him. Her favours, then, were arbitrary and selective. (And he had once thought he could win her with a ten shilling note !)

" Do you love me, Jenny ? "

" Sure. I've said I do."

" But *do* you ? "

" Yes. Don't be so silly."

" He doesn't love you as much as I do, *does* he ? "

" Don't know, I'm sure."

" But he *doesn't !* "

" All right. He doesn't."

" Oh, Jenny, do be merciful. Can't you see I adore you ? I'd die for you, Jenny."

" All right, Bob. Why are you takin' on so ? " She gave him her hand again.

" He couldn't love you—not if he lets you do what you do now."

" Oh—I'm not livin' with him. I've left him a long while ago."

" Why did you leave him ? "

" Oh, he's a big brute. He used to knock me about."

Joy ! He had knocked her about ! A lyric thankfulness to the man arose in Bob. He had put himself beyond the pale. He had knocked her about. (He didn't blame him, by God!)

" Why did you marry him ? "

" Oh. I dunno. He was kind to me. I used to know him when I was only seventeen, when I was straight, like. An' then he found me afterwards and asked me to marry him, that's all. An' after all I'd been through I thought I liked him enough, and I *did*. That's all."

" How long ago was all this ? "

" He married me about two years ago. We was never compatible, and never will be."

Compatible ? What words she got hold of ! Would then, he, Bob, be compatible ? He was physically sick with longing for her.

" Lord, I don't half feel bad. . . ."

" What's the matter, Bob ? Don't be so silly. I'll marry *you*, if you like."

For a brief instant he could not resist a droll comparison of his state now with what it had been. That she should have brought him to this—that he should be aspiring to her hand ! But it was the case.

" How can you marry me, if you're married ? "

" Well, he can divorce me, can't he ? "

" Will he ? "

" Yes. He'll do anything I tell him. He loves me, really, in his funny way."

Then he was to rob another of this strange and terrible prize ? He could not do such a thing. He must hear some more about this knocking about.

" But how can he love you if he knocks you about ? "

" Well—p'raps that's just his way of showin' his love."

There was no outlet. She crushed him everywhere. He had better run away and never come back.

She finished her drink.

" Well, Bob," she said, " it's about time I was movin'."

" What do you mean ? "

" Well, I got to go out to-night, ain't I ? "

" What do you mean—' go out ' ? "

" Well—' go out '—you know what I mean."

" Oh, don't do that, for Christ's sake."

" Well, I can't help it, can I ? I got to get some money."

" How much do you want ? "

"I want thirty shillin's, really. But I got to get a pound at least."

" I'll give it you. I'll give you thirty shillin's."

" Well, a pound'd be enough. But you can't afford it."

" Yes I can. Don't talk any more." He was irritated by the continuance of this grotesque aside.

" Well, I'm very grateful. I wouldn't take it—only I'm not feelin' very well myself to-night."

" Ain't you feeling well ? "

" No. That pain's comin' on again."

" Well, I'll see you home. May I see you home—to Doughty Street ? "

" All right. And you need only give me a pound. That'll be quite enough."

He need only give her a pound ! Another ironic instant ! But he was thankful, at the price. He was going to take his loved one back to her abode.

" Oh, I do love you, Jenny," he said, " can't we do something about it ? "

" Oh yes.  We can do somethin' I 'spect.  Well, let's go—
shall we ? "

She didn't care.  She expected something could be done, and
wanted to go.  " Yes," he said, and rose in despair.

He was following her out like a dog.  It was obvious that
she was sexless.  She had bewitched him.

They came out into the air and Wardour Street.  He took her
arm.

" Oo, look ! " she said, " it's snowing ! "

And it was.  Quite hard.  Tiny flakes, whirling and scampering
down, as though in terror or ecstasy, from the hidden night
above.  A myriad host of minute invaders, coming to fill, with
their delicate but excited concerns, the gloomy plains of electric-
lit London.  A pleasant surprise—a visitation !  One little flake
fell on her young cheek and stayed there.  She put her blue eyes
up to the sky.  She was delighted.

" Oo !" she said.  " It ain't half coming down ! "

They walked on.  There were many of her calling lurking
about.  She smiled at one of them, in passing, in an amiable way.

## CHAPTER XXXV

HE had never had before the slightest intimation that he
loved her like this.

"I *love* you, Jenny, dear," he said, " I love you.  I'd die
for you ! "

" Well," she said, smiling faintly, " there wouldn't be much
sense in *that*. . . ."

She was plainly gratified by the new turn of affairs—gratified
in a quiet and rather greedy way—in the way that a cat is gratified when it has at last consumed the canary.

" *Would* there ? . . ."  she added.  And, with their arms
interlocked, she slipped her hand into his.  The cat lay down on
the rug before the fire.

" Oh, Jenny, dear, I'll work for you.  I will.  I'll work till
I get you, Jenny ! "

She did not answer, but gave his hand a little pressure. They were by now in Shaftesbury Avenue.

" How old is he ? " asked Bob.

" What—my husband ? "

" Yes."

" Oh. 'Bout thirty-two."

She could speak of him so coolly now. Her monstrous and prolonged deceitfulness in not telling him before dawned upon him. But he was beyond complaining.

" Oh, Jenny. I do love you !"

" All right, Bob. I know you do. You mustn't take on so."

" Jenny, dear ? "

" Yes."

" You're coming away with me, aren't you ? For a holiday. After Christmas."

" Yes. All right. I'll come away with you."

She was taking advantages already. Before, the idea of going away for a holiday had been " lovely." Now, graciously, she was conceding it.

" I'll give you a lovely holiday, Jenny. We'll go to Brighton."

" All right."

(All right !)

" Where do you get all your money from, Bob ? "

" I ain't got any. That's the funny part. I got seventy pounds —what I saved. I had eighty. I only got seventy now."

" You shouldn't be so extravagant," said Jenny.

" I guess you're an extravagant article, Jenny."

" No, I'm not. I'm ever so thrifty, if you knew me. I'd make ever such a good wife. I would. Honest. I know how to save, 'cos I've learnt the need of it."

" Oh Jenny. Why ain't you *my* wife ? "

" Well, p'raps I will be one day."

" Oh Jenny. I'll get you. I will. . . . An' maybe I'll have a lot of money one day."

" What—have you got rich relatives, or somethin' ? "

" No. I ain't got no rich relatives. But I may make some money, all the same."

" How's that ? "

" Oh. I 'spect you'd only laugh if I told you."

"No. I wouldn't. Go on."

"No. I won't tell you."

"No. Go on, Bob."

"Well—remember our talk about writers?"

He had never spoken of this to another soul in the world. All things flowed irresistibly from him into her loveliness.

"What?" said Jenny. "Are you goin' to be an Author?"

"Yes. Sounds silly. But I got my ideas. . . ."

There was a pause. He was breathlessly anxious for her answer.

"*I'll* write a book one of these days," said Jenny, and smiled to herself.

Her perfect cruelty and egotism appalled him. He had told her his most secret secret, revealed his anguished, dearest hope. And she had turned it off lightly, to afford a pretty conceit for herself.

"I could tell 'em somethin'," said Jenny, "couldn't I?"

"No, Jenny. I'm serious. I'm *goin'* to write a book one day. You don't understand. I know ever such a lot about it."

"Do you, Bob?"

"Yes. I'm goin' to write a novel."

"Are you? An' I 'spect you'll make me your heroine, won't you?"

She was vulgar, ignorant, detestable. And vain into the bargain. He could kill her.

No, no. He was merely maddened. She was artless, innocuous, innocent. "*You'll make me your heroine.*" A charming and tentative observation. She supposed, because he loved her, that he would make her his "heroine." After all, what right had he to expect any intelligence from her?

"They don't have 'heroines' in books, nowadays, Jenny."

"Yes they do," said Jenny. (She was perfectly secure on the point.) "An' they have heroes, too."

"No, they don't, Jenny. 'Heroines' are out of date."

"Don't be so silly, Bob. 'Course they have heroines. You got to have a girl, what goes through it all, haven't you?"

"Yes, but you don't make them 'heroines' any longer."

"Don't be silly, Bob. 'Course you do."

"But you *don't*, Jenny."

" All right, then. You don't. You know more about it than me.' '

" You might have protagonists," compromised Bob. . . .

" Pro*whatt*onists ? "

" Protagonists."

" Well," said Jenny, " *that's* a good thing." But she was speaking satirically.

At this point they had reached Oxford Street, and were opposite Mudie's. Their way to Doughty Street lay to the right. With a vague hope of fooling her into prolonging the walk, he tried to lead her up in the direction of the Museum. But she would have none of it. " No, this way, dear," she said. The snow was already settling on the ground.

" You and your old pro Whatsiznames," she said. . . They walked on in silence. She began to hum.

" An author *gave* me a book of his once," she said. . . .

An author ! His blood ran cold. This was too much. She had been to Paris. A languishing husband loved her hopelessly. Now authors gave her books. Authors. She had smitten him where he could bear it least.

" Oh—how's that ? "

" Oh, he met me one night, an' took me back to his flat. There wasn't nothing in it. He gave me a drink, an' asked me to tell him my story."

" Did you ? "

" Oh, yes. I told him something. He said I was oo young he wanted to know how I got started. Then he gave me his book, and said I'd find myself in it—or somethin' like that. It was only *me*, under another name, he said. . . ."

" What a damned fool," said Bob.

" He wasn't a damned fool at all," she said. " He was very nice." (He had offended her now, Heaven help him.)

" I am sorry. Perhaps he wasn't."

" I think you're jealous, aren't you ? "

" Yes. I am. Some people get all the best of it."

" Well, you needn't be jealous of him, 'cos he wasn't interested in *me*."

" Oh, Jenny, I love you too much. That's what's the matter."

" Well, don't be so silly." And she pressed his hand again forgivingly.

And how could he complain? Languishing husbands might love her to distraction; authors might give her books. She might go to Paris. But she was here now, forgiving him with little pressures—his " girl." She had said she loved him.

" Oh, Jenny, dear. Won't you get a job? "

" Yes. I'll get a job—if you can find me one. 'S'matter of fact I'm after one now."

" Oh—what's that? "

" It's as a dancing instructress. I'm quite good at dancin'. I've been in a chorus, you know."

" Have you? "

He had now to deal with an actress. Would it ever end?

" Yes. Well, this job's as a dancin' instructress in a place in Soho. I got it through my friend. I got a letter saying Will you please come along next Tuesday in evening dress, an' we will give you your instructions. That's what they said. That looks as though I got it, don't it? "

" Yes. It looks like it."

They had now entered Theobald's Road, and were not far from their destination.

" Only I haven't got an evening dress. That's the trouble."

" How much is an evening dress? "

" Oh—I could get one down Berwick Street for three guineas, I expect."

" Do you think you'll get the job? "

" Oh yes. I think I'll get it all right. My friend says I've got it already, for sure."

" I'll give it you."

" What—will you give me an evening dress? "

" Yes. I'll bring the money next time."

She assumed a simple-hearted detachment.

" Well, I'll tell you what. That ain't such a bad idea as it sounds. I wouldn't take it—not in the ordinary way—— "

(She would never, he perceived, under any circumstances take anything; and she never, under any circumstances, failed to take everything.)

" . . . Not in the ordinary way I wouldn't. But this would be an Investment. Wouldn't it? It's like an Investment—ain't it? "

" I'll bring it along next time," he said.

" No. It would be an investment, *wouldn't* it ? " But her voice was insecure with inward glee.

" I hope so, Jenny. I only want you to get a job, that's all." She snuggled up to him.

" You ain't half good, Bob, ain't you ? An' I'll wear it when we go away together, shall I ? "

She intertwined her fingers in his. " I'll wear it for my Bob. How's that ? "

" That's right."

" I'll be kissin' you in the street one of these days, Bob, you know—jes' by accident."

A more perfect demonstration of cupboard love he could not have imagined possible. She was flagrant, intemperate.

" Accidents will happen," he said, wearily.

" They *will*," she said. . . .

" Hullo, here we are," he said. " Here's your Doughty Street."

" Yes. Here we are. My word. Ain't it just snowin' ! "

It was snowing in Doughty Street, and the remaining moments with the woman he loved might be counted. The pavement was already covered with a white carpet, glistening and sound-deadening.

" Did you know you lived in the same Street as Dickens, Jenny ? "

" What—do I ? "

" Yes. That's his house over the way."

" Was that where he lived, then ? "

" Yes."

" I guess he was a silly old man—wasn't he, Bob ? "

" Was he ? "

" Yes," said Jenny. She was secure on this point too. " He was a silly old man with a beard."

They walked on in silence.

" Well, when am I goin' to see you again, Jenny ? "

" Whenever you like, darling."

" Oh—I must give you that pound." He gave it her. " And I'll bring those three guineas along next time."

" Thanks ever so much, dear." She pressed his hand, still

intertwined with her own. "And then we'll go away, after Christmas, shall we?"

"Yes, dear. . . . Well, when shall I see you? I can't have any more evenings off till next Thursday. I had to make up stories to get this one."

"What—did you make up stories?"

"Yes. I think it'd be better if we gave it a rest for a bit. How about next Monday?"

"Do you want a rest from me, then, Bob?"

"Yes. You're better in small doses, Jenny."

And it was true. She had worn him out. He was, in a manner, dead weary of her.

"Well—this is me, dear," she said, and smiled and stopped. He retained her hand.

"What a fine house, Jenny. Which is your room?"

"Oh. Your poor little Jenny's right up at the top."

"Well—what about Monday, Jenny—3.30—same place?"

"Monday, 3.30? Right you are, dear. I'll be there."

"You're *sure* you'll be there, Jenny?"

"Yes. I promise I will."

"Promise solemnly?"

"Yes. I promise solemnly. Look. I promise on my Mother's Life. There."

What was this? Her Mother's Life? Was this a greater concession than her Liberty? Her Mother's Life. Perhaps he had stumbled upon a formula. It was worth looking into.

"But your Mother's dead," he said, "isn't she?"

"Well. I promise on my Mother's Grave, then. I wouldn't do *that*, would I?"

Her Mother's Grave. It sounded almost as if it would do the trick. "Well, go on. Promise."

"I promise on my Mother's Grave," said Jenny, "that I'll meet you."

(At any rate she is promising me, thought Bob, on her Evening Dress, that she will meet me.)

"And name the time," he demanded.

"I promise on my Mother's Grave," said Jenny, "that I'll meet you at 2.30."

"Three-thirty! Three-thirty!"

Her inconsequence was awful. Her Mother's Grave would have been wasted on thin air.

" Sorry," said Jenny, " I promise on my——"

" All right, dear, all right. 3.30—same place."

" Right you are, dear."

" Good-bye, Jenny."

" Good-bye, Bob."

She put up her face so that he might kiss her. He kissed her. He put his arms around her, and surrounded his desires. The snow fell. His own Jenny. From her mouth he accepted intimations of her tender relenting being along his own. In love, he was her invalid : she was sustenance, assuagement, calm. Briefly he was clinging to violets and paradise. It was over.

" Good-bye, dear," she said.

" Good-bye." He clung to her hand as she moved away. " Oh, Jenny—Don't go ! Kiss me again."

" Very well, dear."

The assuagement was renewed. She soothed, she appeased, she intoxicated. She cured. She inspired with sweetness his remotest nerves. She was Jenny, that was all—Jenny—his only draught to summon the gardens of forgetfulness. And she was giving him her best. . . .

" There," she said. . . .

" Oh, Jenny, I do want you so. I'm dyin' for you. I am ! "

" Well, Bob—you can't say I am not Nice to you, can you ? "

" No."

" Well—good-bye, dear."

" Good-bye."

He watched her, broken-hearted, as she let herself in with a key. She waved and smiled at him. The door closed : she was gone to her secrets.

He was trudging up Doughty Street again in the snow. It snowed, in heavy, luscious, rapid, even flakes.

## CHAPTER XXXVI

THERE was a great deal of freakishness and fantasia in the world next morning.

To begin with, it was colder than you could ever remember it having been in the course of your life. Ella, making up the sandwiches for the bar, accidentally spilt some mustard on to her fingers. She drew her hand away as though she had been burnt. It was as cold as that.

Then the snow, which had apparently not ceased falling through the night, was thick upon the ground and the roofs, and was still falling. If you looked out of the window, and watched it falling, you could hypnotically and giddily imagine that you were going up, up, up—as though in some universal elevator. . . . Fantastic enough in itself. Then there was the unfamiliar light. Ella, with her usual unconscious genius, described it perfectly : " It ain't half a bad light, ain't it ?" she said. It was bad. It wasevil. It weighed on the soul, and played every kind of trick. Things that you thought were clean, were dirty, and things that you thought were white were not. Sugar was a despondent grey, and bread was the colour of mud.

Then, when the house opened, you could hear nothing of the first few arrivals until the door creaked open and they were in with you. Their arrival was in itself an achievement, which they emanated in white steam. Also they left brittle cakes and oddments of muddy snow on the floor—messes which Bob would have to clear away.

He and Ella were a little reserved with each other. He had been absent last night and she must have heard the story of his stepmother. You could not hope to fool Ella (that dexterous interpreter of his soul) with stepmothers. She said nothing, but you could see what she thought. " *You* and your stepmothers ! " But she said nothing, because she could not take the risk. By some impossible fluke Bob might actually have had a stepmother who was ill. If that was so, then it was a question of family relationships. And, in Ella's unquestioning mentality, any sort

of family relationship involved, axiomatically and unhesitatingly
Love. Therefore, if by any chance she was mistaken, to make fun,
of it would not be " kind." From love and kindness her good
soul was constructed.

Her nose, this morning, was dreadfully red. She did not
know it was red : Bob did not object to it being red : but it was.
Why, in the cold weather, were plain women's noses always red,
while beautiful women's weren't ? You would have thought
the atmosphere would have afflicted them all alike. But no :
it was a law of nature. Unto those who have, it shall be given :
unto those who have not, it shall be taken away. Ella was
born plain, so her nose went red when it was chilly.

As for Bob, this morning, his mind was diverted in a curious
way. He had suddenly decided to buy himself a dark blue suit,
and literally could think of nothing else.

Jenny was too much for him. At the moment, what he required (he believed) was *morale*. There was no *morale* so great
as that conferred by a good suit. He was going to get the real
article this time. He would surprise himself and Jenny with it.
He would astonish Ella with it. He would appal " The Midnight
Bell " with it. He was going to Moss's for it.

Of the last five pounds he had drawn, he had three pounds
ten left. That had to go for her evening dress. He would
draw another ten pounds. Six on the suit, and four to spend on
Jenny. . . . Only sixty pounds left. He had eighty once.
Was he going to the devil ? Damn it, there was precisely one
thing now which could provide him with tangible pleasure in
life. A suit. He would go this afternoon and she would see
him wearing it on Monday. Life had its compensations.

## CHAPTER XXXVII

THE cashier did not so much as glance at Bob as he slipped
across the ten pounds that afternoon. Bob wondered
whether the cashier had any idea of what was happening.
Twenty pounds in little over two weeks was heavy going.

He walked down to Moss's. It was well to be out in the
streets. The snow still fell thickly, and on the ground it was
frozen. It had been cleared away from the main thoroughfares,
but in the side streets it was shocking. You continually found
yourself walking without advancing and making an exhibition
of yourself. This was in direct contrast to all the little children
abroad in the streets, whose sole pleasure it was to run like the
devil in order to experience, for one brief instant, the joys of
advancing without walking.

Wonderful transitions befell London. Bob felt that this
snow was an interlude. Life could not be properly resumed,
as it were, until it thawed.

The premises of Messrs. Moss are at the top of Bedford
Street. He walked down Bedford Street a little way. He was a
bit scared. After all, it was a swell place. Swell. He mustn't
use words like that, even in thought. They betrayed his com-
monness. To the true swell, nothing was swell. Besides, Moss's
was not a swell place. By the highest standards, certainly not.
It was merely swell to him.

He entered. The atmosphere was dark. There were mounds
of cloth, and one or two assistants. The latter took no notice
of him. The astonishing fancy that they knew he was a waiter,
and were going to have nothing to do with him at all, flashed
across his mind. He went up to one of them.

" Yes, sir ? "

" I want a suit."

It sounded so inadequate and bald. But what, in like circum-
stance, would your true swell have said ?

" (Yes, sir.) Here !"

Assistant called to assistant. Moss's was set in motion for
him. " This way, sir," said another assistant.

He was led down some stairs, and found himself in a little
cubicle surrounded by mirrors. The assistant deserted him.
Other people were being Tried On each side of him. He could
hear them talking, and grunting into their trousers.

He examined his profile. He was rottenly dressed. But he
wasn't bad looking, if you gave him a chance. He wasn't half
bad looking really. Half. There you were again. As bad as
" swell."

Another assistant entered, and attacked the matter in a brighter spirit.

" Yes, sir. What kind of suit would you like, sir ? "

" Well, I want a blue one, really. Double breasted."

Why had he said he wanted one " really " ? Why had he *apologized* for wanting a suit ?

" Yes, sir."

The assistant vanished. He returned, a few minutes later, with three blue suits. Without comment he helped Bob on with the coat of one of them. It was horrible—about the same blue that you see in the sky. Was this suit business, after all, going to be a failure ? Bob looked at himself.

" No," said Bob. " I don't think I quite like that pattern. . ."

" Very well, sir," said the assistant, but Bob was afraid .he was wounded.

On went the next. The assistant was wasting no time. Bob looked at himself. The assistant looked at him.

" M'm . . . ." said Bob.

" That's beautiful across the shoulders, sir," said the assistant.

" Let's have a look at the other," said Bob.

Another lightning change. The assistant caressed Bob's back.

" Ah—that's your suit, sir," he said tenderly.

And, indeed, it appeared to be.

" Yes. . . ." said Bob. And looked at himself.

Now the tragedy and evil of buying a ready-made suit is this —that it ends, just like that, in " Yes. . . ." You think it would be a good idea if you bought a suit ; you delightedly resolve to buy a suit ; you work yourself up into a heavenly climax about a suit—and then suddenly it is all over and you are merely saying " Yes. . . ." You stare at it. You pat the pockets ; you turn round and look at yourself sideways ; you see what it would look like if it wasn't buttoned. But whatever you do, there is nothing else to be said. " Yes. . . ." You look at the cuffs—but they're no help to you—they're excellent. You examine the lining—it couldn't be better. Perhaps it is too tight under the arms. But it is not. It is no good. You are faced by the depressing fact that you are going to buy it.

" Yes," said Bob. . . .

"I don't see you could do much better than that, sir," said the assistant. . . .

"Yes," said Bob. . . .

The assistant stared at it. Bob stared at it. A hopeless eternity stretched before them both—an eternity in which the assistant stared approvingly and Bob went on murmuring "Yes. . . ." There was no hope.

"Yes," said Bob. . . .

Inspiration seized the assistant.

"How about slipping on the trousers, sir?"

The trousers! Of course! They returned to life.

For the trying on of the trousers the assistant left the cubicle. This was possibly on behalf of modesty and possibly on behalf of the firm; and he returned a few minutes later.

The trousers were flawless. . . .    Another, and trouser eternity threatened, but was skilfully diverted by a question touching the price, from Bob. It was six and a half guineas.

Bob agreed to it: the hostilities of transaction were over, and they were the best of friends. Bob began to take it off.

"Now will you have that sent, sir?"

This was an awkward moment. One son of toil faced another, and both were aware of the fact. But the laws governing clothes are, and have ever been, subject to weird conventions, reticences, and mystifications. Bob would have liked to have had it sent, but he could not bring himself to give the address of a pub. It would look as though he were a mere son of toil.

"No," he said, "I think I might as well take it with me."

"Very well, sir. That's the quickest service after all, ain't it, sir?"

And they both thought this tremendously sardonic, and laughed together.

Mere pelf, of course, after this, was a little degrading: but between two personal friends anything may be carried off with tolerable dignity, and soon Bob had his receipt. It occurred to him briefly, as he watched the parcel being eagerly and dexterously tied, that you encountered very little snobbishness when it came to your spending money in London (indeed, people were most affable about it)—but he smothered the thought.

The assistant made a critical comment on the weather, to

which Bob made an agreeable reply, and they elaborated the theme with the same slightly hysterical unanimity. Then the parcel was in Bob's hands, and the assistant, still talking, was leading him out.

They reached the door. The modern fashion forbade them to embrace : they might not even shake hands : but eyes and voice may do what gesture may not.

" *Good* afternoon, sir."

" *Good* afternoon."

And he was out in the snow again. His life was consoled and warmed. She would get a shock, if you liked.

## CHAPTER XXXVIII

HE put it on first on Sunday afternoon. He wore also a clean shirt, with a collar to match, and his best shoes. Ella, knocking at his door and coming in to reclaim a shoe-rag he had borrowed, saw it on him. He was brushing his hair carefully.

" My word, Bob," she said, " who's that for ? "

" Who's what for ? "

" All that Get-up."

" What ' Get-up' ? "

He would not show it, but she had wounded him dreadfully. Was he, after all, merely making a fool of himself—showing off ? Was it, perhaps, " common," in one of his class, to wear a first-class suit ? Or was it Ella's " ignorance " ?

Ella, alive, as ever, to the minutest alarms in the realm of sentiment, made hasty amends.

" You look fine in it," she said. " Dark blue suits you, don't it ? "

" Do you like it ? "

" Yes. It doesn't half suit you. She won't know you in that, will she, Bob ? "

" Who won't ? "

" Oo ! " said Ella, and left the room.

He was beginning to grow rather fond of Ella's absurd long shots. It was something to have someone interested in you, if only to that extent. Lacking any one to talk to about Jenny, these little passages with Ella were the nearest approaches to confidences he could get. Ella was a jolly good sort, there was no getting out of that.

On Monday afternoon he left the house at ten past three, and had just time to walk down to the appointed place.

He had no idea what he was going to do with her this afternoon. Just take her to tea somewhere, he supposed. At present he could not argue with her any more, nor face his problems. Besides, the snow was still falling, in flicking, sparse, and irritating little flakes under a leaden sky, and was thick and frozen upon the roofs and ground. London's garish interlude was maintained, and their meeting this afternoon could be nothing but garish interlude. A man in love drifts, and is hopelessly susceptible to scenery. . . .

How had it all come upon him ? How had she done it ? How had she gained this hypnotic ascendancy over him—how, from being a rather pretty and piteous little wretch, had she subtly developed into an erotic and deadly drug now utterly indispensable alike to his spiritual and nervous system ? And she was nothing else. He could weep with wanting her and her kindness.

But how had it got started ? He went back over all the times he had met her—from the first night at " The Midnight Bell "—up to the Hampstead episode (that was where the poison had really gripped his blood)—and on to last night—when she had told him that she was married. He all at once perceived that, so often had she failed him, that he had actually met her only six times. Good God !—he had only met her six times ! Shocking discovery ! Six times only, and she had remained so calm, while his own soul had been the theatre for a drama so horrid and ruinous ! He thought he had met her fifty times at least.

He was, in fact, at her mercy. To meet her, now, was boon in itself. His will had gone. She could lead him to the devil. And where else could he expect one of her kind to lead him ?

Where would it all end ? It was consoling, and not uninteresting, to reflect that, in the course of nature, some positive conclusion of some kind had to be reached. One day, however distant, he would know exactly where he stood. The fates could not deny him ultimate certainty—he would get her or he wouldn't, and he would know.

No indication of the fates' intentions, however, was granted Bob this afternoon. He waited, for an hour and a quarter, at the appointed place ; but she made no appearance.

Eventually, in his new blue suit, he walked back to " The Midnight Bell."

## CHAPTER XXXIX

BOB honestly believed he would get a letter. Unless she were a fiend of darkness he would get a letter.

He would never get it, of course, but he would wait until Thursday for it. Perhaps, by Thursday, he would be calmer, and anyway his not taking any notice of her till then might give her a lesson. After that, there was always the 'phone.

Where would he have been without that 'phone ? At least he ought to be thankful for small mercies.

Tuesday and Wednesday. . . . The snow was still upon the ground. . . . Everybody was sick to death of it. What had started as a charming and friendly fantasy had ended as a muddy disgrace. It was still bitterly cold.

On Thursday morning the postman (whose heavy feet came clumping upon a waiter's very nerves) was given his last opportunity of delivering anything other than lifeless and stupid simulations of correspondence at " The Midnight Bell," and failed. At eleven o'clock Bob left the house.

Above all, Bob was going to keep his head. In 'phoning Jenny, there were two fundamental precepts to be observed—firstly, not to quarrel with, or endeavour to mimic, even in thought, the whining negatives of the landlady—secondly (and if you were so lucky as to speak to the little goddess herself), not to criticize, nor to lament, nor do anything but personally apologize for her latest deceptions and shortcomings.

She could not bear criticism, and she might easily ring off. Obey these two rules and you were fairly safe.

The door of the box closed upon Bob. Enclosed from the rush and noise of a vital and still visible world, he faced in silence, communion with his own problems. Here he was again. His hand trembled. His two pennies fell.

He was soon through.

" 'Ullo ? "

" Hullo. Is that Holborn X143 ? "

" Yes."

" May I speak to Miss Jenny Maple, please ? "

" Now. She's not here."

" Could you tell me when she might be in, please ? "

" Now. She's not here."

He saw it all. There was no misinterpreting the woman's blunt tone. Jenny had arranged not to be " in " to him. But he was not going to lose his nerve. He had done well to fortify himself beforehand.

" I know," he said, equably. " But I thought you might know when she'd be back ? "

" But she ain't here. She's run away."

" Run away ? "

" Yes. She's run away without payin' her rent."

" Oh," said Bob. . . .

Then, blindly and automatically pursuing his precepts : " Thank you very much. So sorry to have troubled you."

" Thank you."

He was out in the noisy air.

So he had lost her. He had no idea where on earth she was, and had absolutely lost her. He might have known something like this would have happened. He was strangely calm. Was it relief ? Was this his chance of escape—that actual conclusion which he had thought so remote yesterday ?

What an abysmal fool he had been to let the thing hang over until Thursday. If he had only 'phoned her before, he would not be in this mess. It was his punishment. She always got him —everywhere.

So the halcyon days of 'phoning were over. He was too weary to think about it. Two facts, unpretentiously, but insistently, presented themselves to him. To-day he had his evening off. And he knew where, in the evenings, she walked.


## CHAPTER XL

BOB was too afraid of not meeting her to allow that, having had his tea that afternoon up at Camden Town as usual, he afterwards descended upon the West End in search of Jenny. But he discovered himself in that quarter, as he invariably did on Thursday evenings, and was willing to submit to fate and accident.

There is, of course, no sharp dividing line between a man, indolently, throwing himself open to accident, and a man, wearily, hunting round and round for the object of his adoration. And one who throws himself open to accident, in a confined and specified region, with continued zest, between the hours of five thirty and seven, and never dreams of going to the pictures, is difficult to classify.

By seven o'clock no accident had befallen Bob, and he went into the Corner House for a meal. He then came out to place himself further at the disposal of the elusive gods.

The West End was very crowded. By ten thirty he had passed, on the pavements, at least fifty thousand people. Shortly after ten thirty he found her.

She passed clean by him outside the Pavilion. She was with another girl, and did not see him. With profound and wearied calm he turned round and followed her.

He tried, before addressing her, to pull himself together, to appraise the situation, so that he might make the most of it. But he was too tired. He caught her up.

" Hullo, Jenny."

" Hullo, dear ! " she at once and calmly replied, turning round and stopping, and looking up at him with a kind of giddy and smiling impudence : " you turned up again ? "

There was something strange about her.

" Oo ! " said her friend. " Don't be so rude, Jenny."

" This is my friend," said Jenny, in the same impervious tone.

" How do you do," said Bob.

" Pleased to meet you," said her friend.

They shook hands and smiled.

" My friend's name's Prunella," said Jenny, and laughed. The three walked on.

They were each side of him. A dignified situation, in the West End! So, in this manner, he met his love for the seventh time!

" You mustn't mind Jenny to-night," said Prunella, looking over and chaffing the other. " She's gone and got blotto."

" So I see," said Bob.

The culprit smiled faintly, but made no comment.

" Can't help it, poor girl," added Prunella. . . .

Prunella was a dark, handsome, flashy girl, who looked as though she had seen the inside of jails. And, indeed, had. Bob rather liked her.

" Well," said Bob, " where are we going ? "

" Well, I'm goin' to have a drink," said Jenny. " Don't know about you."

" Go on, Jenny," said Prunella. " You've had enough."

" Well, let's go and sit somewhere, shall we ? " said Bob.

" Tell you what," said Prunella, " you two want to be together. I'll hop it."

" No," Jenny commanded. " You ain't to hop it."

" No. That's all right. You two want to be together. I'll hop it."

His admiration for Prunella went up by leaps and bounds.

Jenny stopped in the street.

" If my friend don't go with me, I don't go. That's all. There."

" Don't be silly, Jenny. Why can't I hop it ? "

" 'Cos you ain't to hop it, that's all ! "

They walked on.

" And what I say," added Jenny, with irresistible emphasis, " I say."

" You're a naughty girl, Jenny, to go and get tight like this," said Prunella. " I don't know what your friend'll think of you." She exchanged a glance with Bob.

Prunella was enchanting. She was, however, not to be allowed to Hop it. That much was clear.

" Well, let's go in he e," said Bob. They were outside the " Globe."

They went in. The long bar was very crowded, but they were lucky enough to get a table in one of the partitioned recesses. The heat and light and noise confused the mind. Jenny, like a fractious child, sat between her friend and Bob, and drinks were brought by a waiter.

On the arrival of these, Jenny brightened a little.

" Well—here's how," she said, and drank. . . .

" I'm livin' up in *your* part of the world now, Bob," she added, more kindly, as she put the glass down.

" Oh—are you ? "

He spoke with deliberate brusquerie. After all she had done to him, she had the effrontery to imagine that it was still in her power to give him sweets. She thought she could wipe out all the torments of the last few days with a friendly word. He almost thought he was through with her now. She was only a little drunken harlot after all. He would show her for once.

" Yes," she said, not comprehending the change, and even more graciously. " I'm in Bolsover Street, now. It's only a few doors away from you."

" Oh. That so ? Why didn't you meet me the last time ? "

She looked at him in surprise. She was having no nonsense of that sort.

" Didn't want to, I suppose, dear," she said, and took another sip.

In the infinite perversity of human nature, his dejection was immediate. He loved her. He looked at her and her beauty and knew that he could not bear her disfavour.

" But why didn't you ? " he said. But now it was too late.

" I really don't know, darling," she said, " do you ? "

She was tight, of course. He had to make allowances for that.

" I waited ever such a long time for you."

" Really, dear ! How very annoying."

This was hopeless—an *impasse*. There was a silence. There was nothing more to be said. His seventh meeting with Jenny was, perhaps, the fatal one.

" You're blotto, Jen," said Prunella. " That's what's the matter with you."

" No ? Not really, dear ? "

" She's ever so silly," said Prunella to Bob. " She's the sweetest little girl when she ain't been drinkin'—ain't she ? "

" I know," said Bob.

" *And* the prettiest," said Prunella. " She's the prettiest little girl in the West End."

Bob's heart sank. Any testimonies to her beauty, from an extraneous source, crucified him—augmenting, as they did, her preciousness and remoteness. He had always vaguely hoped it was merely his own private madness.

" I ain't pretty," said Jenny.

" Yes, she is, an' all," said Prunella. " I always say she's the prettiest little girl in the West End."

" Well, I'm goin' to have another drink," said Jenny.

" No, you're not, Jen," said Prunella. " Don't be so silly." Jenny turned to Bob.

" Go on. Go and buy me another drink."

" All right. Wait till the waiter comes."

" Waiter ! " cried Jenny.

She was quite mad. Why did he remain ?

" Say, Jen," said Prunella. " See that chap over there ? "

Jenny stared at a peculiarly seedy, indeed an almost originally seedy young man of about thirty-five, sitting at a table not far away, and looking over in their direction. " What about him ? "

" I believe he wants me. Shall I go ? "

" Just as you like, dear."

They sat in silence, as Prunella hesitated. " I think I'd better go," she said. . . .

" Do what you like, dear."

Prunella rose, addressing Bob. " You won't think it rude me leavin' you, will you, dear ?" said Prunella. " But this is business."

Bob signified amiable comprehension. Prunella went off, and, settling down beside it, submitted her virile charms to seediness.

Between Jenny and Bob there was a long silence.

" Well, Jenny. How are you ? "

" You've asked me that before, dear—ain't you ? Waiter ! "

"Oh, Jenny. Don't go like this. I love you."

"So I gather, my dear."

Why, seeing that she was temporarily unbalanced, did he still pursue her with soft words? He could not restrain himself. Her murderous beauty held him enthralled.

"Jenny. What's happened? You're not nearly as nice to me as you used to be."

He had no sooner said this than he saw how untrue it was. All at once it seemed that he divined her whole character. She had never once been nice to him—throughout. She had never kept her appointments, unless it had suited her: she had fooled him about her husband, and in every other way: and in their meetings she had tolerated him just so long as he flattered her, and no longer. At the slightest criticism of herself she had been ready to dispense with him. Only when he had given her money had she briefly sweetened and softened towards him, and he had been giving her money all along. She had " played him up " throughout—that was all. And it was natural enough too. He was a poor damned waiter, and she was " the prettiest little girl in the West End." Others had described her so. He would cry soon, he needed her so.

"Waiter!" she shouted.

The waiter came and she ordered the drink herself.

"My garter's hurting me," she said.

"Is it?"

"Yes. Look." In the vulgarity of her inebriation she revealed it. She began to slip it down the leg. Wild and unforeseen lusts momentarily beset Bob. She took it off and handed it to him. "You can have that," she said, "if it's any use to you." He took it.

"How'll you keep your stocking up?"

"That's all right. They're suspended."

"Oh."

"They are in a state of suspense, dear!" she added, and laughed her drunken laugh.

Were there any lower circles, he wondered, to which he might descend in hell?

## CHAPTER XLI

ALL at once Prunella returned. He had hoped, in her absence, to make things right with Jenny. That hope must now be finally abandoned.

" Well, dear ? " asked Jenny.

Prunella's ironic glance, as she sat down, betrayed her opinion of mankind.

" Ten bob, my dear ! " she said. " And he wanted me to take him back with me."

" God's Truth," said Jenny. " What did you tell him ? "

" I told him he wanted to go to Woolworth's," said Prunella, despondently.

" Should think so, too," said Jenny. " Penny bazaar, more like. . . ."

" An' I told him if he wanted my white body he could pay for it," said Prunella, more vindictively, and there was a silence of approbation. Bob felt a trifle embarrassed.

" Will you have another drink," he said.

" Ta," said Prunella. " You're a sport."

Another drink was ordered and they talked of other things. But the young man's seediness of mind, as well as body, had rather damped the occasion.

" Did you ever do anything about that job, Jenny ? " asked Bob at last.

" No, dear," said Jenny. " I didn't."

So that was the end of that.

He was not going to worry. It was all right. She was not responsible for what she was saying.

" What's been happening ? I rang you up this morning, and they said you weren't there."

" No, dear. I ran away."

" Why was that ? "

" Because I hadn't any money, I suppose, dear."

" Yes," said Prunella. " Jenny's been in trouble. An' she's owed five pounds, too."

" Who owes her five pounds ? "

" Oh—a girl friend.  She got taken up.  Dirty plain clothes man got a grudge on her.  And Jenny paid her fine."

" I'll kill that man one day," said Jenny.  " And he doesn't like *me*, either. . . ."

" That man," said Prunella, " makes *thirty pounds a week*—takin' his wages off us girls."

" Really ? "

" Any may God strike me dead," said Prunella, " if I'm not speakin' the truth."

God did not strike Prunella dead.  (He never does this.) So Bob supposed she was speaking the truth.  It also occurred to him that God, by diverse methods, had probably stricken Prunella enough already.

" Of course, it don't matter to a millionaire like Bob," said Jenny.

" Why.  Has he got some money ? "

" He's got fifty pounds."

" Go on," said Prunella.

" He has," said Jenny.

" Go on," said Prunella.

" Ain't he," said Jenny. . . .

" Go on," said Prunella.  " Why don't you lend Jenny a fiver ? "

" I offered to lend her one, for an evening dress.  But now that's off, apparently."

" No.  Go on," said Prunella.  " You lend Jenny a fiver. She'll pay you back.  She's goin' to get it back all right—an' I'll see that she gives it you.  She's livin' with me now.  I'll guarantee to give it you myself if she doesn't.  But she's goin' to get it back all right, an' she'll just hand it over."

" I'd give her the money," said Bob, " if she'd go for the job."

" Well, you'll go for the job, won't you, Jenny ? "

" Yes, I'll go for the job."  She had softened again already.

" Well, we'll see about it," said Bob, " next time I see you." To begin with, he would be damned if he gave her another penny.  But apart from that, and since he would have, of course, to give it to her, he was going to drive the best bargain he could.  He couldn't possibly go on spending like this.

" When'll that be ? " asked Prunella.

" Well, what about to-morrow ? "

" That's all right," said Jenny. " An' you can come up, if you like."

" What ? To your room ? "

" Yes."

Ever so slightly the skies seemed to be clearing. Her room. The thought was strangely enticing. What might not occur in Jenny's room ? If he could only get Jenny alone again, and talk to her, something might yet be done.

They now arranged to meet outside " The Green Man " at ten past three. She would then take him back with her.

" Well, Jen," said Prunella, " we'd best be goin' if we're goin' to meet Bill."

" Who's Bill ? " asked Bob.

" Bill ? Oh, he's my boy," said Prunella. " He's going to take us to dance."

Her boy. How in Heaven's name did these women get hold of men ? Were they not utterly outcast—beyond the pale ? They didn't seem to think themselves so. He recalled the episode with the seedy young man, and wondered what it felt like, being Prunella's boy. . . . But what, then, was his own relationship to Jenny ? . . .

" Well, don't let me keep you," he said. " I'll stay on. See you to-morrow. Ten past three."

" Right you are, dear." They arose. " Ta-ta ! "

Jenny smiled at him, and had clearly forgiven him all.

Only as he saw her vanishing through the door, to revelries he could not share, did he realize that she had made no excuse (nor attempted to make any) for not having met him on Monday.

## CHAPTER XLII

THE first thing he did the next morning was to slip down to the bank and draw another ten pounds. These subtractions were becoming, of course, really terrifying, but at this juncture it was necessary. Also he skilfully exempted himself from the charge of extravagance and weakness by yet another new theory of money. He would now have exactly fifty pounds left—a round and sensible sum—a half century. Any savings he had ever had over and above that sum had been merely poetic extras. He had been indulging in unparalleled wildness of late, and the extras had gone. That was all.

Besides, after this, he would never spend a penny over and above his salary.

And then again, he honestly believed that a new era was opening in this affair. She now had an address near by : he was allowed to visit her : he could talk to her alone and in peace, and some sort of an arrangement or conclusion could be hammered out. Hitherto he had been baffled, not so much by herself as by his sheer inability to meet her—surely a quite unique obstacle—though natural enough if you took into consideration her manner of living. Yes—Bob honestly believed a new era was dawning.

At ten past three he was outside " The Green Man." She was not there. Nor was she at twenty past. But at five and twenty past he saw Prunella coming towards him.

" Hullo, dear," she said. " Waiting for Jenny ? " She smiled.

" That's right."

" Well, she's got a bit of toothache, an' stayed in bed all the morning. She told me to ask you if you'd get her somethin' to eat, like, and then go along up."

He was greatly relieved. " Right you are. What am I to get ? "

" Oh—there's a place just along here. I'll take you round there before we go up."

Prunella was coming up, too, then ? They walked along the Euston Road in silence. What on earth would happen if Ella came out and saw him ? Nothing was more likely. Jenny might have passed, but there was no mistaking Prunella. . . . Such were the hazards of this wicked and uncanny adventure.

" Jenny ain't half been goin' on about *you*," said Prunella, " this morning."

" Oh—really ? "

" Ain't she half ? She wouldn't never leave off about you. She said you were the straightest boy she'd ever met."

" Did she ? " Bob laughed nervously.

"Yes, she said you were the straightest and nicest boy she'd
ever met. And I wouldn't Say that, would I?"

By which Prunella meant that she would not Say what she
had said if she did not mean it, or if it were not true.

"No," said Bob.

"An' she said she ain't half treated you bad, but you always
stood by her. She said she ain't half led you a dance, but you was
a boy worth stickin' to. She did. Honest. An' there ain't any
Object, is there?"

By which Prunella meant that there was no Object in her
saying what she had said, if she did not mean it, or if it were
not true.

"Of course not," said Bob. . . . (Was this appreciation at
last?)

"She didn't half go on about you—reely," continued
Prunella. "It'd have made your ears burn if you'd heard all
she said."

Bob again laughed nervously.

"An' I haven't any Cause," said Prunella. "Have I?"

By which Prunella meant that she had no Cause to say what
she was saying except in so far as she meant it, and it was true.

"No," said Bob. "Rather not."

At this point they reached the small and rather grubby little
delicatessen shop which Prunella had in mind. After looking
briefly in the window, she decided upon one of those terrible,
meretricious, castellated round objects which are so crusty and
alluring to the eye, so wearying, ugly, and stodgy to the tongue
and digestion—a pork pie. Potato salad was Bob's idea, and
accepted. He paid for both; they came out and walked back
again.

She was evidently a born matchmaker, and having sung his
own, now began to sing Jenny's praises.

"Oh—she ain't half a sweet little girl," she said.

"I know," said Bob. (But he lied.)

"There ain't no one I'm so fond of as Jen. We just hit it off
lovely. I think we must have very sim'lar temper'ments, you
know."

Bob nodded.

"I mean it—reely. And I haven't any Reason, have I?"

"Rather not."

"Of course, I don't think Jen's quite as well as she ought to be, you know."

"Don't you?"

"No," said Prunella, critically. "She's *thin*, don't you think so?"

"Yes. Perhaps she is."

He perceived that she expected Jenny's "boy" to be naturally and fixedly interested in such a topic, and though in some measure pleased and flattered, could not help wondering what in heaven's name he was letting himself in for.

"What *she* wants," said Prunella, "is more Nourishing Food."

"M'm," said Bob.

"I'm trying to get her to take Phosferine," said Prunella, "but I can't make her do it regular. She's a silly girl. She wants lookin' after. She's impulsive, you know." She was interpreting her character like a friend of the family with an engaged couple.

At this point they reached Bolsover Street. This starts off with tall and newly erected buildings, but soon dwindles down into the drab and decayed slum which actually it is. She took him to a door not far down. The house was of four stories, and seemed to be untenanted. At least, you could only hope that that was what accounted for the evil and deliberate stagnation with which it confronted the world. She let herself in with a large key, and they found themselves in a dark passage which chilled Bob's soul, but which had no such effect upon Prunella, whose dainty high heels went clock-clocking up the bare wooden stairs. He followed. On each landing three different doors led into three different rooms containing three different families. All the doors were closed, but the awful belligerence of the poor was to be heard and sensed. On the first floor a man was reviling a woman, and a child, in another room, screaming. It did this not as though it was being beaten (which it possibly was) but as though it was being put to death. On the second floor someone was playing a harmonica, but in the front room an old woman groaned. You could not imagine what at, unless it was the harmonica. On the third floor two other children were being put to death. You could hardly

believe that three children were being put to death, simultaneously, in the same house, at the precise time of your arrival,
but there you were. Bob hoped that he would not have to go
any higher than the third floor, but was disappointed. The
heels clocked untiringly ahead of him. The bower of love was
reserved, romantically, for the top. Here there were no noises.
Prunella opened the door.

Jenny stood before the fire, combing her hair in the mirror
above the mantelpiece.

" Here's your boy," said Prunella. " I've brought him back."

## CHAPTER XLIII

A BEDROOM for two. In the confined, crowded, low-
ceilinged space you could hardly move. The window was
small, and, inexplicably, barred. Outside was the fog of the
late afternoon, and the shapes of things glowed strangely in its
murky dusk. Only in certain lights could you see each other's
faces.

There were two arm-chairs—threadbare, down at castors, and
bursting. There was a plain deal table in the centre, with a
coloured check cloth at least a decade old. There was a large
double bed, whose sheets were grey. There was a deal cupboard,
with shelves above for plates. There was a washing stand with
a jug and basin—a source of cleanliness, no doubt, but easily
the dirtiest thing in the room. A towel, attached to it by a line
of string, was several grades greyer than the sheets. Propped
up everywhere were framed portraits of men. The favoured
gentlemen were mostly taken in their hats and grinned their
signed compliments in a sidelong way. An affable army of
Boys. . . .

At first Bob thought that these, perhaps, were all Jenny's
current admirers, and the thought made him sick. But later
he saw that they belonged to a past, that this room had been
occupied by generations of harlots, who had left old relics of
the profession of love. This was, doubtless, down in Wardour

Street, an exchanged and popular address. Its atmosphere and character were unmistakable, and could only have been acquired through years. Disease and delinquency were in the air : no one had ever cleaned it out, for no toiler had ever inhabited it. Only those who had fled from toil—only unemployed servant girls, and the spoiled beauties of the slums, had filled it with the lotus odour of their indolence and unhappiness. The mantel-piece was crowded out with old medicine bottles—a pathetic testimony to past sufferings, and an unenquiring faith in the efficacy of Science. More " Mixtures," more Bovril, more Cod-liver Oil, more Ovaltine, more Veno's Lightning Cough Cure, more Iron Jelloids, more Beecham's Pills, more Proven Remedies are consumed by these bemused and felonious souls than in any other section of the community.

" Come right in, dear," said Jenny, warmly, and from the first moment they made it clear that the atmosphere was purely social, and that he was to be treated with the courtesies due to a guest. He was at once offered the best arm-chair, and before ten minutes had passed Jenny had finished what she could eat of her pie (which was very little), and they were all seated round the fire, and talking in an affable way.

So many things had happened to Bob within the last few weeks, and so filled was he with a sense of everything being nothing but a kind of nightmare interlude, that he could make absolutely no response to his present situation. All he could do was to enter, with as much spirit as possible, into the con-versation.

This at once took a highly moral and genteel course, opening with a fine discourse from Prunella on the topic of Swearing. For Jenny having discovered a ladder in her stocking, Let Go a Bad Word, and Prunella, as her mentor, brought her to book. It was not that Prunella was Religious : it was not that Prunella was Stuck Up : but she simply thought it let a girl down, if she didn't keep her talk clean. A man, said Prunella, always thought much more of a girl if she knew how to behave. Didn't Bob think so ?

He did.

" What I always say," said Prunella, " is that it doesn't matter whether you've been *well* brought up, or whether you've been *badly* brought up—you can always refrain from usin' them words. Ain't that so ? "

" It is," said Bob, and there was a silence.

" An' I just *happen* to have been well brought up," said Prunella, parenthetically. " Not that there's anything in it. . . ."

Bob did not dream of disputing this openly, but in private thought of jails.

" An' me too," said Jenny. " Not that there's anything in it. . . ."

There being nothing in it, the observation being, in fact, so exquisitely and purely ornamental, Bob did not think it worth while laying claim to these advantages himself. Also he doubted whether he could do so in good faith. The topic was concluded, and there was a silence.

Prunella now struck a romantic note.

" I love a Fire, don't you ? " she said, looking into it. " I always say there's nothin' like a fire. . . ."

" No," said Bob, " there ain't."

" I can Just Gaze into one for hours," said Prunella. " Can't you ? "

" M'm," said Bob, " M'm."

Jenny, having sternly pursued Prunella in the matter of Bringing Up, was not going to let her get away with sensibility, either.

" So can I," she said, and there was a silence. . . .

" Just seeing Pictures," said Prunella. . . .

Just Seeing (Bob's affirmative nod seemed to endorse) Pictures. . . .

And there was yet another silence.

" Castles in the Air," tried Prunella. . . .

Castles, undoubtedly, in the Air. . . .

But the subject, also undoubtedly, was wearing thin.

" Expect Sammy'll be here soon," said Prunella.

" Who's Sammy ? " asked Bob.

" Sammy ? Oh, she's our girl friend. She's with us here. It's her room really."

Three ! Bob's thoughts fled sickeningly to the double bed behind.

" She ain't half got hold of a funny man, either," said Jenny.

" Why—who is he ? "

" My dear," said Prunella. " 'E's Dark. Indian or something."

" Merhommerdan," said Jenny, wishing to be more precise. . . .
But it remained for Prunella to hit upon the *mot juste*. " A
real native, anyway," she said.

There was a pause.

" Do them Indians believe in God ? " asked Jenny.

It was Prunella's turn to instruct.

" Course they do, my dear. They believe in God. They got a
Creed of their own. They believe in their *own* God."

" But that ain't God," said Jenny.

" Yes it is. That's God all right." Prunella appealed to
Bob. " Ain't it ? "

" That's right," said Bob.

" Well, *I* don't call it God," said Jenny. " Anyway."

And against this there was no appeal.

" And I don't believe," added Jenny, sternly, " that the Races
should Intermix."

" No," said Prunella. " You're right there. I say white's
white an' black's black, an' that holds whatever you say. Don't
you think so ? "

" M'm," said Bob.

" It's not that I ain't Broadminded," Prunella continued,
" 'cos I am. And I know that some of them dark chaps can be
Great Gentlemen. It's just they shouldn't Mingle, that's all."

" No," said Bob. . . .

" Sammy says this one's very well Educated," said Jenny.
" Speaks languages."

" Oh, yes," said Prunella. " They're great Students too."

And they all looked into the fire.

" I once had a boy," said Prunella, " what could speak four
languages : French—German—Spanish—an' English."

" Really," said Bob.

But as with Education, and as with Sensibility, so now, with
Tongues, Jenny was not to be ousted.

" I once had a boy who knew a lot," she said, " too."

" Which were they ? " asked Bob, coming in on the side of
Prunella.

" Oh," said Jenny. " All different kinds "

"I could speak French a little," said Prunella, "when I was at school."

"Oo—" said Jenny.  "I can't half speak French!"

"But I gone and forgotten it all now," said Prunella, ignoring the interruption.  "It's dreadful how one forgets, isn't it."

"*Cooshay avec ma sirswar!*" said Jenny.  "That's French."

"What?"

"*Cooshay—avec—*" repeated Jenny slowly, "*ma—sirswar.*"

"What does that mean, Jen?" asked Prunella.

"That means 'Where are you goin', deary?'—or 'Hullo, darling'—or somethin' like that."

"No it don't," said Bob.

"Yes it do," said Jenny.  "That's what it means. 'Where are you goin', deary?'"

"No," said Bob, "not literally."

"Well, what do it mean, then?"

"It means 'Sleep with me to-night,'" said Bob, "literally."

"Well, that's the same, ain't it?"

"Yes," said Bob, "I suppose it is."

"Only a bit more business-like," said Prunella.  And the matter was dropped.

All this time the darkness of evening, with its secret, busy, but imperceptible machinations, had mobilized in the room behind them; and the fire, now in the full explosive summer of its redness and brightness, arrayed distorted shadows upon the walls and ceiling, which, positively exultant in their own wickedness and ugliness, danced. . . .

Down the foggy streets could be heard the bell of a muffin man.  Long pauses beset the conversation. . . .

Jenny's face was lit in a blaze of glory.  She sat quite still, with her hands limp upon the arms of the chair, like a blue-eyed princess, enthroned and brooding.

Her golden and friendly loveliness, seen, for just this brief interlude, in repose, afforded him an unusual and relenting calm.  The moment was filled, not with wild torments of his obsession, but with the dignity of both their sorrows.  The firelight and the solemnity of the hour revealed much.  She was four years younger than himself, but had suffered, probably, more.

## CHAPTER XLIV

ALL at once the door burst open and Sammy entered.
"Ah, here she is—like a breath from the country!" said
Prunella, and though it was uttered humorously, there
was a certain vague rightness about the metaphor.

Like a breath, if not from the country, at least from the
lower depths of an underground railway, Sammy's pungent
personality filled the room.

Her character and history having been roughly sketched to
Bob before her arrival, there was no difficulty now in ascertaining
the cause of Sammy's downfall. Possessing some beauty, but
born to extreme poverty, she had left home at an early age
owing to the evening recreations of her father. These, having
great variety, but including, recurrently, the practice of beating
his children to unconsciousness with wire, as well as the application of red-hot pokers to their limbs, had been too much for a
character congenitally unstable. Philanthropic societies might
photograph and display her physical misadventures, but they
could not redeem such inauspicious beginnings. Subject to
epileptic fits, she was about thirty-four, with a red mop of
hair, and the glazed blue eyes of a carefree kleptomaniac—in a
word, completely "dotty."

Not that this impaired her ordinary conversation, which was
ripe with disillusionment and wisdom. She was, moreover, full
of vitality and happiness. On introduction she took Bob's hand
with extraordinary violence, said "Pleased to meet you," cried
for tea, filled a kettle, and slammed it on the fire. She then drew
up another chair, and joined the party as its leading spirit.

"Well—what have *you* been up to?" asked Prunella.

"*Me?* I ain't half had a time, dear. I been Seducin' Youth.
I'd tell you, if it wasn't for your friend."

"Oh, Bob doesn't mind," said Jenny. "Does he?"

Bob signified that he didn't.

"He's one of us," said Prunella, and Bob felt a little sick
again.

"Well," said Sammy. "I been havin' my soul saved. You

know that corner where Lisle Street joins Wardour Street ? "

The company did.

" Well, there was a boy standin' there—see ? "

The company did.

" He couldn't've been more than seventeen or eighteen—it's just about three o'clock, an' 'e was sort of standin' about. See? "

The company did.

" Well, so I goes up to him, like, you see, an' I says, ' Where do you come from,' I says, ' Eton or 'Arrow ' ? See ? "

The company did, and tittered.

" So he don't say nothin'. 'E just sort of Tugs at 'is collar. . . . So I says ' Do you want me ? ' I says. So 'e says ' Oh—Ah—' he says, ' Oh—Ah—I don't know—ah—weallay,' he says. So I says ' Well, for God's sake make up your mind, boy, 'cos I can't stand about here all night !' So he goes on like that, till at last I says ' Well, you'd better come along, hadn't you, and see what you feel like later.' So we goes along together. See ? "

The company did.

" Well—we was just goin' in, when he says ' Oh—Ah,' he says, ' I don't think—ah—I want to do this—ah—weallay,' he says. So I says ' Well, what in hell *do* you want to do, boy ? ' So he says ' Well—ah—won't you come along—ah—and have a drink with me.' So I says ' Certainly, if you'll make it worth my while.' So he says he will—so we goes to a bar near by. See ? . . . .

" So we goes into a bar, an' then he starts sayin' how Sorry he is for me (see ?) an' all us girls. . . . So I finishes my drink quickly and says, ' Well, there's nobody so sorry as me, kid, but what about what you said you was goin' to give me ? ' So he says ' Well, I think I'd better be goin',' he says. So I says, ' Oh no, not at all,' I says—' you don't want a row, do you ? ' " Sammy appealed to her friends. " That's right, ain't it ? "

Sammy could not have done better.

" Well—so he says ' How much do you want,' he says. So I says ' You've wasted a fine lot of my time—how much have you got ? ' So he says ' Would ten shillings do ? ' so I says ' No it would *not* do—and you don't want me to Create in here, do you ? ' "

By which Sammy had meant that the young man would not

have wanted her to Create a brawl, or trouble, in the public eye.

"So he's as meek as a lamb, my dears. So he says 'No, I don't want that,' he says. 'How much do you want?'... So I says 'Well, you give me three pounds, an' I'll let you go.' So he says he hasn't got that much. So I says 'Well, you give me two pounds ten,' I says, 'an' be quick about it.' So he says 'If I do that,' he says, 'I won't be able to pay my fare home.' So I asks where he lives, an' he says Bedford. So I says 'Well, if you give me two pounds ten,' I says, 'I'll give you back your fare.' So he wasn't half scared, so he says 'Will you promise to?' he says, so I says 'Course I will! I'm Honest, ain't I?' So he says 'The fare's three and eight,' an' he gives me the two pounds ten. So I takes it an' I says 'What class do you travel?' I says. So he says 'Well—I'll have to go third.' So I says 'Well —here's five bob,' I says, 'and you can go first.' An' I gave it him out of my bag. No—" Sammy broke off to appeal again to her audience. "That's Honest, ain't it?"

Murmurs applauded the perfection of Sammy's code.

"What happened then?" asked Jenny.

"Well—so I gives it to him, and he says 'Thank you very much,' he says. An' I says 'Not at all. Pleased to have met you, dear.' So he says 'Well, I'll be going,' so I shakes his hand and says 'By all means, dear.' 'And' I says 'In future, dear,' I says, 'don't hang about tryin' to save prostitutes' souls.' So he says 'No, I won't.' So I says 'They ain't got none, dear. They're a rough lot. You run along.' An' he doesn't half do a bunk out of that place."

(Saving prostitutes' souls. "*They ain't got none.*" Here was a tip from the horse's mouth! Had he not better admit, finally, that he himself was trying precisely to do this? Was he not, and with less excuse, infinitely more gullible and ingenuous than the young man? Was it not for him, more than any other, to take Sammy's lesson to heart?)

The story was at an end. "No," said Sammy. "That was Honest, wasn't it? I gave him his first-class ticket. That was Honest, wasn't it?"

The company obviously thought it was, but this was not enough for Sammy.

" What I *say* I'll do," said Sammy, bullyingly. " I do. Don't I ? "

The company clearly knew she did, but this wasn't enough, either.

" And you know that, don't you ? " she said, in the same aggressive tone.

" Yes," said Prunella. " And that's like me. When I give my word I keep it."

" *And* me," said Jenny. . . .

" No," said Sammy, bitterly. " I'm not like the other sort. . . ."

" What Don't," said Prunella. . . .

And, in the silence that followed, the air was filled with that adamant and terrible honesty characteristic of their kind. Bob thought of Jenny's Mother's Grave. . . .

" They ain't half funny," said Jenny, " when they want to save your soul."

Bob sat up. " Why, have you ever had your soul saved, Jenny ? "

" Me ? I should say I have. I got four pounds off a man who saved it, once."

" What did he give you four pounds for ? "

" Oh," said Jenny, " he didn't know it had gone."

There was silence.

He could not even recoil from the shock. Now, at last, he was done for. He might have known it. On his eighth meeting with his beloved, he found that she was a thief. A mean, common thief. He must get out of here.

" Not till afterwards," she added, with a smile, twisting round the knife. . . .

" You *stole* it, then ? " he said.

She sensed his altered tone.

" Yes. What's wrong ? "

" I didn't know you took money," he said. " That's all."

Prunella and Sammy both looked a trifle embarrassed, but he did not care.

" I wouldn't take money off a friend," said Jenny. " Not off nobody I knew. I wouldn't take money off *you*."

" I don't see that that enters in," said Bob. . . .

Prunella came to the rescue with a clever euphemism.

"A lot of things happen," she said, "when you get a man in a generous mood."

"And I happened to make this one," said Jenny, again smiling, "a bit more generous than he meant to be."

And they all three laughed.

In that guffaw his hatred for her was vitriolic and without limit. This was the end. He must get out of this filthy den.

"I'm afraid your boy," said Prunella, "don't quite approve."

## CHAPTER XLV

PRUNELLA got up and lit the gas.

This was of a nightmare green brightness, and as well as reintroducing to the mind the wild filth and disorder of the room, brought to a nervous consciousness a little clock on the mantelpiece, which, after brief debate, and comparison with harlots' wrist-watches, was ascertained to be Right, and which informed Bob that he was due at "The Midnight Bell" in twenty minutes.

He said he must be going. But Jenny would have none of this, saying that he could wait and have tea, after which she would come down with him. He said that he had not the time. She replied that he was not to be so silly.

And, indeed, he was glad to let her take it out of his hands. For the horror of having to leave her in this green and malignant den—of having to part, before her friends, with no conclusion come to, with no protest made, with no reassurance given, nor even rupture brought about, was too much for him. He had to speak to her alone.

Tea was soon ready, and they again settled around the fire—Sammy going off into another long story relating to a Postman, her dealings with him, and the singular passions from which an innocent bag and blue uniform commonly diverts the public's attention. Sammy concluded by saying that she would Publish a Book, one of these fine days, on the topic.

Whereupon Jenny asked Bob when he was going to Publish his own Book.

"What do you mean?" said Bob, going rather white.

"Why?" she said. "You're writin' a book, ain't you?"

"No," said Bob, but it was too late.

"What?" said Prunella. "Is your Boy writin' a book?"

She spared him no wretchedness. To have revealed this secret even to the good and trustworthy Ella would have been shameful enough, and he had never done so. Now he had revealed it to her, and she calmly spread it amongst her friends. A strange port for the brave little ship of his aspirations— a gang of prostitutes in an upper room! But he told himself again what he had told himself a thousand times before—he was beyond bitterness. He would not be surprised to find she had done murder next.

"He always said he was writin' a book," said Jenny.

"Well," said Bob, "I ain't."

"No—you *should* write a book," said Prunella, "and then you can dedicate it to Jenny."

"*Whattycate?*" asked Jenny.

"Dedicate," said Sammy, gulping her tea. "That means when it's To a person."

"I don't expect he wants to," said Jenny, who was now rather hurt at his denials. "I expect he wants to whattsizname it to that there Girl of his."

"Which girl?" asked Bob.

"That girl in that there bar of yours."

"Oh," said Bob. "You mean Ella."

"Is that her name—Ella?"

He instantly repented having given as much as the name away. He would be betraying Ella, as well as himself, in a moment.

"That's right," he said.

"And who's that other one?" she asked. "The fat one with the peroxide hair?"

"Oh—that's the Mrs. The Governor's Wife."

"*She* don't look quite all that she should be," said Jenny. "Neither."

"She isn't," said Bob, too quickly to stop himself. She got

everything out of him. Now he was betraying the poor, dear, fat Mrs., as well. Needless to say, Jenny chose this moment to be interested.

" Isn't she ? " she pursued.

" Well. There's nothing wrong with her now," he said. But she wouldn't leave it alone.

" What—was she a prostitute at one time ? "

" It's only the rumour," said Bob. " I don't expect it's true."

" You shouldn't talk of prostitutes," said Sammy, still gulping. " You're one yourself, dear."

" Yes," said Jenny, " but I ain't Glaring—not like that old woman."

" She's a very good sort, anyway," said Bob, and remarked again that he must be going. He was again told not to be silly.

But a little later, seeing that he had only seven minutes in which to reach " The Midnight Bell," he put down his cup and rose.

" Go on," said Sammy. " Let the boy go. You go on down with him."

Jenny rose, grumbling ; put on her hat, powdered her nose, brushed her clothes, and put on her coat. He shook hands with Sammy and Prunella, who expressed a courteous, but obviously insincere desire that he would call again. He left the room with Jenny, shutting the door.

In the absolute darkness of the passage outside, he took the hand of his love, the thief, who guided him warily downstairs.

## CHAPTER XLVI

THERE was no light on any of the floors. The old woman was still groaning though the harmonica had ceased. Another child was being put to death, but in a slightly more merciful way. In the hall a dim light burned. At the door, with her hand on the latch, she put up her mouth, in a liberal and indolent way, to be kissed. . . .

They were out in the raw night air, walking towards Euston

Road. She slipped her arm, as though seeking protection from the cold, into his.

" Oh, Jenny," he said. . . .

" M'm ? " she murmured, with a kind of tender and questioning friendliness, and snuggled up closer.

He perceived that at this very moment—the moment when her bland admissions had appalled him most—when she had confessed herself a pure criminal and he was half terrified by mere proximity to her—at this precise moment he was in good favour with her—in better favour than he had ever been. She was quiet, pliable, responsive. She loved him.

" Oh, Jenny," he said. " Don't tell me you're a thief ! "

" Don't be so silly, Bob," she said, and drew nearer still to him. Nothing, plainly, could disturb the new softness of her mood.

" But it ain't silly ! It means everything ! How can I go on with you, if you're a thief ? "

" Don't be so silly, Bob. I'm not a thief."

" But you said you took money ! "

" Well—that ain't being a thief. Besides, I ain't done it often."

" Haven't you ? How often ? "

She paused.

" I don't remember any time," she said. " Besides that."

He clutched at the straw.

" Is that true ? "

She was clearly out to please him, and his eagerness had been too manifest.

" Yes. Honest. That's the only time I've ever done it."

He saw that she was clearly out to please him, and that his eagerness had been too manifest. He saw, therefore, that her reassurance meant nothing.

" But, Jenny, I can't believe you. You tell me such lies."

" Very well, then," she said, beginning to sulk, " I tell you lies."

Her telling him like that (he reflected) that she told him lies, did not mitigate or conceal, for an instant, the simple fact that she told him lies.

" But you do, Jenny ! "

" Very well, then. I do. I'm just a cheat and liar."

Her telling him that she was a cheat and liar did not mitigate or conceal, for a single instant, the fact that she was a cheat and liar.

" But you *know* how you fool me, Jenny ! "

" Very well, I do. I ain't no good to you."

How could he explain to her that she wasn't !—that by self-impeachment she was not acquitted ! He gave in.

" Jenny. Will you promise me that you'll never steal again."

" Yes. I promise. I only done it once, an' I'll never do it again. There."

He felt a little better. He had gained something, however insecure, to which he might cling—or (knowing his own genius at it) at least something with which he might later trick himself into his usual fool's paradise. . . .

" Besides," she added, nestling even closer, " when you and I are married I'll never do anything like that."

Married to her ? In his late ordeal he had lost not only all hope, but all thought, of that far and improbable consummation, and now she herself reminded him of it. Instantly, the thought of ultimately possessing her, of having this warm, living, elusive organism for his own, worked its old magic and he was begging.

" Oh, Jenny—*will* you marry me ? "

" Course I will, dear. I love you."

" Do you ? "

" Course I love you. Shouldn't be here if I didn't—would I ? "

He was sick to death of this testimony—she never had any other. To this moment he had not the remotest conception whether she loved him or not.

He tried to call her bluff.

" Well—will you get a job ? "

There was a pause.

" Yes. I'll get a job."

If only she would say she wouldn't !—Anything but this fatuous equability.

By this time they were nearing " The Midnight Bell " and he led her down a side street. He had only three minutes more.

" What happened about that other job ? "

" Nothing. I didn't go. I haven't got a dress."

" Well, look here, Jenny, I've got ten pounds in my pocket I promised you five for the dress yesterday evening : if you can land that job I'll give you the ten.  Do you think it's too late ? "

" No.  I don't expect it's too late."

" Well, will you go down there to-night ? "

" Yes.  But if you give me that ten, I'll pay it all back—when I get it back from my friend."

She had already presumed she was going to get the ten. " It's not the money that matters—it's the job.  Will you go down there to-night ? "

" Yes.  But I'm goin' to pay that money back."

He wanted to tell her that she hadn't got it yet.  At any rate he was damned if he would give it her before she had promised. He stopped in the street.

" Will you go for that job *to-night* ? "

" Yes.  All right.  I'll do somethin'."

What did she think she meant by that ?

" Will you go round there *now* ? "

" Well.  I can't go round without a dress."

" Oh, Jenny.  Don't stand there like that.  I got to go.  I'm late already.  Will you *'phone* them ? "

" Yes.  I'll 'phone them."

She would drive him fighting mad.

" Do you know their *number* ? "

" No.  But my friend does."

" Well, can you *find* your friend ? "

" Yes.  I can find her easy."

" Jenny.  I've got to go.  When will I see you next ? "

" Any time you like, dear."

" I got to go.  Here's the money."  It was too late to argue and he handed it to her.  " Let me see you to-morrow.  Three thirty.  Down in the Haymarket.  Same place.  See your friend, 'phone about the job, meet me to-morrow, three thirty same place, and tell me what happened.  Can you do all that—for ten pounds ? "

He was instantly sorry for this last irony, for she at once began to sulk, and there was positively no time for sulking.

" I'm not doin' it for the ten pounds," she said.  " And you can have your old money, if you want it."

" I'm sorry, Jenny. Forgive me. I didn't mean it. I got to
go. Will you do all that ? "

" Not if you speak like that."

" Oh, I'm *sorry*, Jenny ! I got to go ! Will you do all that ? "

" Yes. I'll do all that. I'll see you to-morrow three thirty."

" Promise ? "

" Yes. Solemn."

With which should he reinforce the oath—her Mother's
Grave or her Liberty ? After her recent disclosures he rather
favoured her Liberty.

" On your Liberty ? "

" Yes. On my Liberty."

" Good-bye, dearest. I do love you so."

" Good-bye, darling."

They embraced.


## CHAPTER XLVII

IT is astonishing with what abruptness the entire quality and
atmosphere of life can be rendered unfamiliar, and never was
the transition so sudden as at " The Midnight Bell " the next
morning. It went to bed in all innocence on Friday, and awoke
on Saturday to a new world and the fact that Christmas was
upon it. Not Christmas Day, of course (that was not until next
Tuesday) but Christmas in general.

At midnight on Friday, unknown to all, the Governor and
his wife had decorated the bar, and the result in the morning
was spectacular ! Everybody had known for weeks, of course,
that the thing was coming, but it was none the less a surprise
when it came. Even Bob's spirits responded to the little diversion, wondering what he could give Jenny for a present ; and
Ella, of course, was perter, and neater, and happier than ever.

Mr. Sounder, however, was a little heavy about His Majesty's
illness. For by now " the poor old king " (as Ella, with a compassion sincere but slightly disrespectful, invariably called him)
had been in danger for over three weeks, and Mr. Sounder said

that our Festive Season could be Hardly Joyous with that Looming over us.

The other opinions and reactions were varied. Ella asked for news from every customer, and maintained firmly that he would pull through : Bob (selfish as ever) said nothing but secretly wondered whether he (Bob) would be more successful as an Edwardian than as a Georgian, and hoped so. The Governor had got it into his head that the Prince of Wales would Never Come to the Throne, but that the Duke of York would be Elected instead (a fantastic and unconstitutional theory from which he would not budge an inch, but which was listened to with forced respect because the Governor was the Governor) : the Governor's Wife said that if Anybody had done their Job *he* had. The Illegal Operation said that it was all a damn lot of humbug (but what precisely he meant by that nobody knew, and he was drunk when he said it anyway) : and Mr. Wall had just one thing to say on the matter, and one only, and one continuously :—it was only Science what was Keeping Him Alive.

This Saturday morning Mr. Sounder was even heavier than usual. He spoke across the bar to the Governor.

" According to *Inside* Information," he said, " he's never going to get well. . . ."

" Yes," said the Governor, and looked reflective as he puffed at his pipe. . . .

This, of course, was the incorrect reply. The correct reply was " Ah-ha ! So you have *inside* information ? You are in the know. Come along. Tell us all about it." Instead of which, the tactless Governor puffed at his pipe and merely replied " Yes. . . ."

" That's according to *Inside* Information," said Mr. Sounder, trying again. . . .

To which the Governor, once more, replied " Yes. . . ."

The afternoon was dark and foggy. He was at the appointed place at the appointed time, and five minutes later she came strolling along. This was the second appointment she had not broken, and, seeing her smiling on him again, he could almost believe that she was beginning to take this affair in earnest.

" Where shall we go ? " he said, in the noise of the Haymarket traffic.

She explained that she wished to meet a girl friend in Soho and that they could have tea in a little place she knew. . . . Having no idea of what kind of place this was, and being naturally interested in her backgrounds, he consented. She took his arm, and they walked along in silence.

"I'm afraid I ain't got that job," she said. . . .

He had expected nothing else, and found himself grateful, even, that she had regarded the matter so seriously as to bring it up for discussion so early.

"I didn't think you would."

"I'm ever so sorry," she said.

"Yes. It is a nuisance. Not your fault, though."

"I 'phoned them up, just as you said, an' they said it had gone."

They were walking up Wardour Street.

"I'll have to give you back that ten pounds," she said, " now."

"Ohno. No need for that."

"Ohyes there is."

"No, there ain't. Perhaps you'll get another job soon."

"Well, I'll try. I'd do anything for you, Bob. You know that—don't you?"

What was this? She had never volunteered anything quite like that before. Was it possible that, after all his great travail, his reward was coming? Could it be that he had won through, that he had earned, by persistence, her love? It almost looked like it. Twice running she had kept her appointments. Twice running she had relented thus.

"I wonder," he said.

"Well, I would, so there," she said. " And you *know* I love you—don't you?—you know I love you *now*. . . ."

Now! The word was charged with breathless potentialities. It endorsed his new hypothesis : it at last gave realism to her declarations ! Never before (and he had known it only too well) —but *now*, perhaps !

"Only now?" he said.

"P'raps so," she said. " Can't you see it?"

"Oh, darling," he said, foolishly, and felt for her hand. Immediately it was intertwined with his own. " Silly old Bob," she said, and he bathed in a roseate and all-surrounding happiness. He forgot all else, and for the moment there was no alloy. He recognized the scene : he had seen it on the stage, read of it in books—the wearied lover at last rewarded, the wayward girl at last succumbing.

" Oh, darling ! " he said, again, and pressed her hand.

" It's you that's the darling," she said. " And I'll darling you all right when we go away."

" Are we going away ? "

" Well, you said we were.   You said we was going after Christmas."

" Oh, Jenny—we can !  If you'll come !  An' do you realize it's only next Wednesday, Boxing Day.  I've got a week from then."

" That's right.  An' where're you going to take me ? "

" Well—anything wrong with Brighton ? "

" Oo !—I'm not so sure about Brighton."

" Why not, Jenny ? "

" Too many girls at Brighton. I don't think I'd have my Bob safe enough."

" Oh, Jenny.  I'm safe anywhere with you."

" If any girl comes along," said Jenny, solemnly, " an' tries to steal my Bob, I'd tear her eyes out."

" Oh, Jenny.  They couldn't."

" Well," said Jenny, " they'd better not try."

This was growing absurd. To think, that in one brief walk, from the Haymarket to Soho, he could be lifted from an inferno into heaven ! He had not a care in the world ! She loved him at last ! This was the final climax of all.

" You haven't reckoned with me," said Jenny, exceeding excess in her bestowal of bliss. " I've got a very jealous nature."

" Oh, Jenny.  I'm willing to take it on."

" An' you don't know what you're takin' on, Bob, I can tell you.  I hope you won't regret it."

It had come to that. She was dubious of the future. All the barriers were down. They were as good as wedded. They were reckoning with their temperaments.

" Oh, Jenny—tell me you love me."

" I love you a whole lot too much, that's what's the matter with me. And you'll know it, all right."

So had the tables turned, that he became almost afraid. Perhaps, one day, this dreadful flower of the underworld actually would tear other girls' eyes out. Perhaps he would be unable to cope with her violence. He remembered Prunella and Sammy. To what was he committing himself?

These vague misgivings were not decreased as she stopped outside a little curtained window (inscribed " Coffee Bar ") in Soho—told him that this was them, and led him through a door to what he immediately recognized as something perfectly typical of her own haunts—to wit, a thieves' den, and full of thieves.

## CHAPTER XLVIII

A NARROW, long, dreary, bareboarded, and resounding little den, with marble-topped tables each side, and one gas mantle at the back, lit against the fog and darkness of the afternoon. On Jenny's entrance there was a kind of ironic cheer of welcome.

" Seen Petal ? " she asked, but was answered with guffaws. Of Bob, an interloper, no kind of notice was taken.

At the back, under the light, was a bar, and on it two silver urns, steaming with coffee and tea—also cheese cakes, sandwiches, and a bowl of sugar.

Little could be seen of the bar, however, it being temporarily under the dominance of that noisiest of the criminal elements —a gang of lusty young Jews, who boasted, laughed, postured, Charlestoned, and scrapped humorously amongst themselves in their habitual high-spirited manner. Wearing breathlessly tight suits, silken (but far from spotless) shirts, and soft collars (with perpendicular stripes) to match, they were juvenile and as yet more or less amateur—the type that aspires to Cars, but is making do at present with fur coats, brooches, scarves, watches, and is not above an occasional umbrella. All this was done, however, rather in the ebullience of youth than in any studied and intentioned felony : they were young brigands rather than crooks, and would probably end, not in jail, but business.

The rest were seated at the tables.  There was a painted young woman of about fifty-two, with a figure about three times the size of that of the ordinary woman, and such as only the impecunious taxi driver could love : there were one or two young things as slim and fresh as Jenny, though more Glaring (as she would say) : and the men varied accordingly, and were of all classes.  There were paper sellers, unemployed mechanics, pickpockets, Jews, a gentleman resembling a bruiser, and two or three nondescript down-and-outs.  In the corner was a clean-shaven, neatly dressed little man in a bowler hat, described later by Jenny as a Confidence Man, and now talking (confidentially) to a sly youth of about thirty who looked as though he lived upon the immoral earnings of women, and did.

" Petal," for whom Jenny had asked, was not there, but there was a table vacant, and Jenny asked Bob if he minded staying, as she wanted to see her bad about a dress.  He went to the bar, and brought her tea.  They could hardly hear each other in all the noise but she endeavoured to entertain him.

" This place is called ' *Billy's*,' " she said.  " I often come in here."

" Really ? "

" Yes.  Rather a Rough Crowd, I'm afraid.  But that's the sort of life I lead."

He answered courteously, but secretly wondered whether any crowd, outside a jail, could be rougher.  It had already cast the old gloom over his soul, and the old, old question beset him.  Would this ever end ?  It seemed as though she were some alluring and irresistible pilot, leading him on and downwards (for his sins and weakness) through every circle of hell—to atmospheres which formed her own sorrowful lot, but in which he could hardly breathe.

Why had he pitted himself against all the accepted facts ? Any fledgeling could have told him from the first what he was now learning with such cost and pain—that women of the streets were of and for the streets, and that love of such was inconceivable—unnegotiable—mere despair and degradation. She had even told him so herself when he first knew her.  And yet, like a child of eighteen, he had thought that in his own case it would be different.

But had he not been justified ? She had promised to be his, and his alone. But what did that mean ? The briefest analysis revealed the unreality of it all. *When* was she going to be his— and how ? What intentions, prospects, had either of them ? It was a foggy afternoon, and in an hour he would have to return to work. . . . She sat there so calmly. . . . What on earth were they both doing in this place ?

The same old thoughts—on and on—round and round.

" Oh, Jenny," he said, suddenly. " Can't we get out of here ? I hate it."

" What—don't you like it ? "

" No. Jenny. I don't."

" All right, then. We'll go. Come along."

And, to his infinite astonishment, she rose.


## CHAPTER XLIX

"I WANTED to do some shopping in any case," she said, and again took his arm. They walked on in the direction of Berwick Street.

" I want to get you away from all that sort of thing, Jenny," he said. " I want to take you right away."

" I know, dear. An' you're goin' to—aren't you ? "

" Yes. An' we're goin' away next week, aren't we ? "

" That's right, dear."

" Just for one week. An' I'm goin' to make you real happy. You see if I don't."

" Are you ? "

" Yes. Just to show what it might be. I don't mind how much money I spend—so long as you're happy. An' after that you'll come back, an' get a job, an' everything'll be different."

" I won't let you spend too much money," said Jenny.

" I will, though. This holiday means everything. We'll be all alone, an' together, an' we can talk it all out. We don't know each other yet, Jenny. But we will when we've done."

" I know quite enough about my Bob already."

" Darling. . . ." His own words had expanded him. This holiday idea was tremendous. It was near and real—credible. It offered a week's calm—haven from the rough storms of his passion. But it was more than that—it might very well be the salvation of the situation. He would be with her constantly, and they could survey themselves, talk it out.

And there was more than that, too. Jenny herself—his own sweet drug, his lovely and tantalizing poison—transcended every other consideration. For a week she would be his—his own. He could barely think about it.

" Oh, Jenny, dear."

" Yes, dear ? "

" I don't know what'll happen when I get you to myself."

" Don't you ? "

And she drew up closer to him, with sweet promise of herself.

They had reached Berwick Street. In love there are few things more tender, pleasant, and intimate than to go shopping with the one you love. " I ain't half got a lot of things to get," said Jenny (who had a list), and the words thrilled him. To be thus taken behind the scenes, to follow her round in shop after shop, to be made to carry her flippant purchases (for nothing that so pretty a woman could buy could be anything but flippant) ; to have revealed, in so confidential a way, all her unimagined and yet so ordinary requirements—it was all exhilarating beyond measure. It was an excursion into a new side of her personality.

And, indeed, this was a new Jenny. She was methodical but civil, economic but affable, precise in manner but radiant in beauty. There was Cocoa, Apples, Oranges, Stamps, to Call for Prunella's Jumper, and Notepaper. Nobody could play any tricks on her, but nobody could desire to. She knew what she wanted, and in what order she wanted it, but looked for a long while in windows, and deferred to Bob on knotty points. And all the shopkeepers saw how lovely she was, but she was his. By the time she was done, Bob was laden with parcels (the very chains and weights of pure domesticity) and with a clearer and more healthful soul than he had had for months.

By this time, also, he had only twenty minutes more, but

they were going to walk together up to " The Midnight Bell."
She took his arm, carried some of the parcels, displayed every
conceivable charm, and suddenly told him that Christmas Eve
was her birthday.

" What—Christmas Eve ? "

" Yes."

" Oh, Jenny. I'll have to get you something great for that."

" No," she said. " You're not to get me anything. You've
got to save your money now."

" I'll get you something, all the same."

" No you won't. Listen to me—if you go and get me something I'll throw it away. There."

" You won't."

" Yes. I will."

" No you won't."

" Yes I will."

" I'll tell you what," said Bob. " They're giving me Christmas
Eve off. I'll take you out for a birthday party, shall I ? We'll go
somewhere real nice."

" Oo—where'll you take me, Bob ? "

" Never mind," said Bob. " It'll be a real surprise. An' then
we'll go on an' dance. What about that ? "

" Fine. Only you're not to spend too much money."

And walking along Bob honestly believed that the dawn had
come.



## CHAPTER I.

AT six thirty, on Christmas Eve, Bob dressed in his little
room.

Christmas Eve—the anniversary of an apparently meaningless, wicked, and obscure event—Jenny's birth in the world !

But only so apparently, for love, which achieves all things,
had mended her ills. In his love for her, and her love for him
(thought Bob) she was redeemed. She had been born, not to
sin and death, but to light and console, with the brightness of
her beauty, and the gentleness of her being, the existence of

another. He redeemed her, and she redeemed him : and she
was his own dear Jenny.

He had only this afternoon been down to the bank and
cashed a cheque for twenty-five pounds. A hideous amount, he
knew—but he did not regret a penny of the expenditure. For
a week life was to be his, and there were going to be no mistakes.
He rejoiced in his expenditure.

The future was filled with roses. After infinite obstacles and
despairs he had gained what he wanted—the woman he loved.
And what more might any man gain ? He saw that, after all,
his life was to be crowned with success. Now he could look
back and applaud his courage and persistency—qualities which
others would not have shown, and, in not showing, lost the
highest reward of life.

He was, in brief, something better than his fellow men.
To that conviction Bob inevitably returned.

He was meeting her at seven in the Haymarket. On his way
out he had to pass through the bar, which contained a few
customers and Ella. . . .

" My *word* ! " said Ella as he passed. . . .

She was alluding, in the spirit of satire, to his apparel, his
exquisiteness, his demeanour. She had seen the blue suit before,
but (perceiving all things), she perceived, in the brief moment of
his passing, that there was something over and above the blue
suit. She perceived that he was making a night of it, that he
glowed with the fires of health and hope. And knowing how
foolish it was to glow about anything on this vile and disappointing planet (and not having anything to glow about
herself), she could not resist taking him down a peg or two.
And so she said, in the spirit of satire—" My *word* ! "

## CHAPTER LI

ANY lingering doubts as to the perfection and reality of
her love for him were serenely dispelled as he came along
to the Haymarket, five minutes before the time, and saw
her waiting for him.

" I'm not late, am I ? " he asked, eagerly.

" No, you're not late. . . ." She smiled up at him, and they walked along.

" Well," said Bob. " Many happy returns of the day, Jenny."

She smiled again, but her reply produced the faintest of faint chills.

" Don't want so many—myself," she said. . . . In the disillusionment it bespoke it was not quite the remark he could have desired from one who, having found love, should properly require nothing save immortality on earth with her lover. . . .

" Why not ? " he said, a little aggrieved.

" Had about enough, I should say."

Again depressing. But he had better leave it alone. He was not going to quarrel about *that*.

" Well, Jenny—how've you been since I saw you ? "

" Quite all right, thanks," she said, as they crossed the road. " 'S'matter of fact I've got some news."

The problem of evading the traffic, in the middle of Coventry Street, temporarily diverted an optimistic consciousness from the problem of what the devil this might mean. It did, however, just flash across Bob's mind that perhaps all the old torture was going to begin again.

" Good or bad ? " he asked, brightly, as they reached the other side.

" Well—half an' half."

" What's it about ? "

There was a pause.

" Well," said Jenny. " It's about that holiday of ours."

This time, he decided, he was not going to lose his head.

" Is it off ? " he asked, as though he were not very interested. But the world was swimming about him.

" No—it ain't off. I'll tell you when we're sittin' down."

" Where are we going ? "

" Well—let's go and have a drink."

" All right. But I wanted to take you somewhere nice to-night."

" Well—we'll go there later. I'll tell you everything when we're sittin' down."

They walked along to the " Globe," which was almost

deserted, and sat down at a table. Drinks were brought them by a waiter.

" Well ? " said Bob.

" There's nothing to tell, really. I won't be able to come away Not all the time, that's all."

" Oh—why's that ? "

" Just can't, dear—that's all."

" But why not ? . . . Don't be afraid to tell me, Jenny." He was not going to lose his head.

" I've got to go away—that's all."

" Who with ? " He was not going to lose his head.

" It don't matter who with. I've got to go for the week-end, that's all."

He was not going to lose his head.

" Do tell me who with, Jenny ? "

" I don't see no need for that. . . ."

" Do tell me who with, Jenny ? "

" Well. If you must know. . . ."

" Yes ? "

" It's a Chap, that's all."

He was not going to lose his head.

" And you've promised to go with him for the week-end ? "

" Yes."

" Where are you going ? "

" Well—funny enough—I'm going to Brighton. I'll meet you afterwards, though—after the week-end. I will, really."

There was a pause.

" Jenny ? "

" Yes."

" If you love me you won't go."

" It's not love that enters in."

" Do you love me ? "

" I said I do—ain't I ? "

" But *do* you ? "

" Yes. I do."

But Bob would not take Yes for an answer.

" Oh, for God's sake say if you don't ! "

" But I do. I said so. Ain't I ? "

" Then if you love me, you won't go."

"It's not love at all. He's goin' to give me So Much, if I go with him for the week-end, and I can't afford to throw it away—that's all."

"How much is he going to give you?"

There was a pause. This was a crucial moment. He saw that she intended to go. He saw that she knew he was going to offer to pay the sum himself. He saw her mind working—calculating an appropriate falsehood. If she made it too little he would pay it himself—if she made it too much he would not believe her. He saw, finally, that she did not love him, and that all the world was lost.

"Twenty pounds," said Jenny.

It was a clever appraisement of the situation. He would have chosen the same amount himself—something beyond his purse but just credible.

But why was she lying to him? Why did she desire to put this man before him?

"Who is he?"

"Oh—I've known him a long time."

"Where did you meet him?"

"Oh—about here."

"Picked him up, you mean?"

"Yes, if you want to put it that way."

There was a silence.

"He's a Gentleman," said Jenny. "'S'matter of fact."

"What do you mean—'gentleman'?"

"Well—you know what I mean. A Proper gentleman. He's very nice."

"Is he?"

"Yes. He's teachin' me how to talk Educated."

This was too much, and his malice leapt out.

"But not with a great success," he said.

He had never known before, in this affair, what jealousy meant. A gentleman. What he was not—what he might never be. This was the unkindest cut of all. What would he himself not give to have a gentleman teach him to talk Educated! How often had he hoped, from his little eminence, to undertake Jenny's education himself. And here was a gentleman to come and do it instead of him.

And to steal Jenny into the bargain. He felt that he could never rise now. It was all too unfair. He was mocked. Jenny and her Gentleman—" the prettiest little girl in the West End " and her gentleman lover—passed on to higher spheres—two cold and remote figures, forsaking him—leaving him to his own and perpetual degradation. He had always known she was too much for him.

" There's no need to be sarcastic," said Jenny. " You're not too great yourself."

But she could hurt him no further.

" No," he said, submissively. " I'm not."

## CHAPTER LII

" YOU seem to have forgotten it's my birthday," said Jenny.
        " I'm sorry, Jenny."
        " Why don't you cheer up ? "
" I can't. I love you too much."
" Well, I love you, too, don't I ? "
Now, in his hopelessness, he felt almost tenderly towards her.
" No, dear, you don't. I love you, but you don't love me. An' I'll never get you. That's all there is to it."
" Are you upset about this Man ? "
He was grateful, with a faint, ill gratefulness, for " Man "—for the omission of the horrid prefix and the disparaging " this."
" Yes, Jenny, I am."
" Well, there's no need to, dear. After all, having someone like that's better for *me*, ain't it ? "
" What's better ? "
" Well—it's better than me walkin' about the streets, ain't it ? "
He saw the point of this. In this obsession, for long periods he would totally forget her manner of life. A single man—and a gentleman—certainly was better than walking about the streets. If only for a week-end. He made no answer.

" And I'm only playing 'im up for what he's worth. He's
ever such a fool, really."

He discovered, to his surprise, that it was still in her power
to make him happy.

" Is he ? " he said, smiling up with a kind of wearied appeal.

" Yes. An' I'll tell you what. If I play my cards right—"
Jenny tossed off the rest of her drink.

" Yes ? " He was feeling almost convalescent.

" If I play them right I can get a lot out of him. For you as
well as me. There's a lot of money there."

" Is there ? "

What was she making him now ? A *souteneur* ?—one who
lived on the immoral earnings of women ?

" Yes," said Jenny. " There's a lot of money in that quarter."

He had not the energy to reproach her. She was trying to
console him, and he was merely grateful to her for trying.

" What does he do ? " he asked.

" He's a journalist," said Jenny. " 'S'matter of fact."

He did not know whether this was good news or bad. At
least the man earned his own living. Apparently he was not
the most fatal kind of gentleman.

" He's married," said Jenny, " too. . . ."

" Well—can I have the four days after the week-end ? " asked
Bob.

" Yes, of course you can. That's what I was sayin'. If you
could have your holiday later, you could have the whole week."

" I can't do that. It's all arranged, and they've got another
man. Couldn't you manage to put him off, Jenny ? "

" No, dear—I can't do that. But you'll have me after the
week-end. It's only halving it."

He dared not threaten her new tenderness with more pleading.

" What day are you going down ? "

" Boxing Day. Wednesday."

" And what day are you coming up ? "

" Monday, I suppose."

" What's the use of coming up ? Couldn't I meet you down
there ? "

" Yes. I suppose you could."

" But *will* you ? "

TWENTY THOUSAND STREETS UNDER THE SKY

" Yes. I will."

Her accursed pliability again !

" *Where* could I meet you ? "

" Wherever you like, dear."

" Could I meet you at Brighton Station ? "

" Yes. Meet me at Brighton Station."

" But what *part* of Brighton Station ? Is there a clock ? "

" Yes. Meet me under the clock."

" But *is* there a clock ? "

" Well, there must be."

" Oh, Jenny, you'll drive me mad ! "

" What am I doin' now ? "

" Can't you be more helpful ? "

" Well, I'm being helpful, ain't I ? "

He began again—laboriously—lucidly.

" Will you meet me at Brighton Station, under the clock, at six o'clock—on Monday night ? "

" Yes."

" Are you sure you can manage it ? "

" Yes."

" Can I write you before ? Do you know where you're staying ? "

" Yes. We're staying in rooms."

" What's the address."

" I can't remember."

" Can't you try and remember, Jenny ? "

" Yes. I remember. It's Dunville Road, or something like that."

" Dunville Road ? "

" Yes. Dunville Road. That's right."

" What number ? "

" I can't remember what number. But it's Dunville Road."

" And you'll be in rooms there ? "

" Yes."

A sensation of sheer physical sickness overtook Bob, and he paused until it was allayed.

" That'll be romantic, won't it ? " he said.

" What'll be romantic ? "

" Me gettin' you straight from him like that."

" Oh—don't be silly. It ain't my fault."

The sensation of sickness returned, with redoubled power, and he again waited until it was allayed. But this time it showed no sign of going, and he was silent for almost a minute.

" What's the matter ? " she asked.

" I'm feeling ill—sick."

" About all this ? "

" No. Really bad. Half a moment. . . ."

There was a long silence as she watched him. . . .

" Are you goin' to *Be* Sick ? " asked Jenny. . . . And there was another silence as she watched him.

" Half a moment," said Bob. . . .

" 'Cos you'd better go outside," said Jenny. . . . Her voice came from a distance.

" Half a jiffy," he said. . . .

" Come on. Come on out. You'll only look silly. . . ."

He rose. Jenny, a remote being, guided him through the bar, and out into the street. He was a remote being to himself. He leant against the wall. He met the casually curious eyes of hurrying passers-by. . . .

" I'll be all right. . . . I'm sorry. . . . It's your birthday . . . . I'll be all right."

" You've been Eatin' Somethin'," said Jenny, " that Disagreed with you. . . ."

" I'd better go home," he said. " I'm sorry. . . ."

" All right. I'll get a taxi for you. Shall I ? "

" Will you come in it ? " His brain could still function to that extent.

" Yes. I'll come in it. You stay here, an' I'll get you one. Are you all right ? "

" Yes."

She had vanished. He quite expected her not to come back. He was having a curious Christmas Eve. It was a curious existence altogether. He wondered whether the crowds and crowds of people passing him were enjoying themselves. . . .

Miraculously she had returned—and with a taxi.

" Come on," she said. . . .

He was in the padded darkness of a taxi, whirring along in

unknown directions. He had lost all sense of direction. But
she was by his side.

" Sorry," he said, and took her hand.

" You didn't half Come Over," said Jenny. " Are you better
now ? "

" Yes. I'm a bit better. Where are we going ? "

" We're going up to your place."

After a while he felt a little better, and looked out of the
window. They were entering Oxford Street from the Charing
Cross Road. The journey could not last much longer than five
minutes.

" Oh God. When am I going to see you next ? Can I see you
to-morrow ? "

" Well," said Jenny. " It's Christmas to-morrow. I don't
think I can. I'm going out with some friends."

He was too unwell, there was no time, for argument.

" And you're going away Boxing Day ? "

" Yes."

" Then I shalln't see you until next Monday at Brighton ? "

" 'Fraid you won't."

" But I must, Jenny, I must ! "

" But how can you, dear ? "

The taxi was swinging round, and whizzing up Great
Portland Street.

" But will you *meet* me at Brighton ? Will you swear on your
life you'll *meet* me there ? "

" Yes. I swear on my life."

" Oh, Jenny—this is absurd. You'll never be there. You'll
never be there ! "

" Yes I will."

" You won't, Jenny, you won't. . . . You can't *go*. You
can't *go* ! "

" But I must go."

" But I won't let you go, Jenny, I won't let you go ! "

" Don't be silly, dear. I got to go."

" I'll give you the money, rather. I'll give you the money ! "

" What ? Twenty pounds ? "

" Yes. Twenty pounds. I will ! "

## CHAPTER LIII

SHE was obviously taken aback, and he enjoyed a brief moment of pure triumph.

" You can't do that," she said.

" Yes I can. An' I got the money on me."

" What ? Twenty pounds ? "

" Yes. Twenty pounds. What he said he'd give you."

" You can't afford all that," she said. . . .

" Yes I can. I'll give it you now, an' you can write an' tell him you ain't coming. You're comin' on this trip, if I die gettin' you ! "

" I might just as well get it from him instead of you. Why can't you wait—just for the week-end."

" 'Cos I've waited too long—that's why ! It's all been waitin' ! An' I'm goin' to get you, this time ! "

There was a silence.

" Besides," said Jenny, " He promised to buy me dresses, an' all. . . ."

" Did he ? Well, I'll buy you dresses. . . ."

" You can't do that. . . ."

" Look here, Jenny. I've twenty-five pounds here what I drew this afternoon. You can take the lot. That'll cover the dresses."

" Oh don't be so silly. I don't know why you talk like this."

" I mean it, I tell you. I mean it ! "

" So you're goin' to give me twenty-five pounds ? "

(So she had slipped it up to twenty-five !)

" Yes. Right now. If you'll promise to come away on Boxing Day as we arranged. Right now."

She did not answer.

" Come on, Jenny. Is that a bargain ? "

She did not answer.

" Is it a bargain, Jenny ? "

There was a pause.

" All right," said Jenny. . . .

" Right," said Bob, and handed her the notes at once from his wallet. She put them in her bag.

" That'll be your birthday present," said Bob.

" I still think you're silly," said Jenny. . . .

" No. Not silly. I just mean to have my way this time. I don't care what happens after."

" All right, then. When am I to meet you ? "

" It's Victoria. I've worked out all the trains. It's six fifteen it leaves. Shall I call for you at your room, or will you meet me down there."

" Better meet me down there. Don't want Prunella to see us. . . ."

" Why not ? " At this the taxi drew up at the kerb. The abominable man had found " The Midnight Bell " of his own accord and they were directly outside it. " Tell him to drive on ! " said Bob. " Tell him to drive on ! " He never dreamed, in his hysterical state, of telling him to do so himself.

" No," said Jenny. " Don't be silly. You go in an' go to bed. I'll be there. Six o'clock. Victoria Station, day after to-morrow—Boxing Day. Go on. You go on in."

In a state of stupor he opened the door, and stepped out on to the kerb.

" Is that fixed, then ? "

" Yes. All fixed."

At any moment Ella, the Governor, the Governor's Wife might come out and find him here.

" Under the clock—Victoria Station—day after to-morrow—Boxing Day—you promise ? "

" Yes. I promise."

" What time ? "

" Six o'clock."

" You swear on your life ? "

" Yes. I swear on my life."

There was nothing more he could do. " Where do you want to go now ? "

" Tell him to take me down to Oxford Street again."

He did so, came back and shut the door and looked through the window.

" Promise again, Jenny. I'll give you such a good time, if you'll come. I've got a lot more money."

" I promise on my life."

"Do you love me, Jenny?"

"Yes. You know I love you. Don't be such a silly old Bob."

"Good-bye, then."

"Good-bye, dear."

The taxi moved off, passed round a corner, and was gone. How had all this come upon him? Why was he not spending the evening with her? He was feeling quite well. His attack of illness had gone ten minutes ago. That was what she did to him —stampeded him into frantic and inexplicable behaviours.

It was only nine o'clock. He did not go into "The Midnight Bell." He walked into the Euston Road, and along to "The Green Man."

Here he stayed, drinking by himself, until closing time. He then went for a long walk.

When, shortly before twelve, and Christmas Day, he returned to his little room, he discerned something on his pillow. It was an elegant silk handkerchief.

It was wrapped around a box of twenty cigarettes, and was a Christmas present from Ella.


# CHAPTER LIV

THEY had a splendid Christmas Day at "The Midnight Bell." They all decided that it could not have been better. Work had to go on just the same, of course, but there was not a great crowd of people in the morning (they had it bottled at home); and when the place closed in the afternoon Bob and Ella were invited upstairs to a stupendous Christmas dinner given by the Governor.

The cellar had been plundered for unimaginable wines : there was a turkey : there were crackers, almonds and raisins, silver nut-crackers, and everything appropriate.

The Governor presided, and was seen in a new light—as quite a wit in fact. Indeed, the wine flowed and everything was seen in a new light. Even the Governor's Wife's Sister was seen in a new light. She was perfectly affable. You could not help feeling, in fact, that she had been a little misjudged. Bob and Ella would not have admitted this to each other for an instant—it would have been a betrayal of their favourite unanimity and grouse—but it was what they thought in secret.

Caps were put on (the best, they said, was the Governor's Wife's) : tea was had in the gloaming, and then they all went down to their evening duties, but in an unserious spirit. At the Governor's express permission (nay, command) the caps were kept on, and the joke was much appreciated by the customers. Ella's cap was green, and, in a strange way, it made her look quite beautiful. You might, even, have misjudged Ella's possibilities. . . .

Bob was not of course happy, but at the same time he was not unhappy : he was excited, rather. He was in an hysterical state and for long periods managed to forget his own preoccupation.

The only snag was that he had to get the Governor to cash, or get cashed, a cheque for him. In view of the sum, this was a great undertaking, and he was doubtful of its results. He could not go down to the bank to-morrow, because it would be Boxing Day. He would have to have enough for a whole week's holiday for two, and he had decided to take all the rest of his money out—twenty-five pounds. He would never spend all this, but he was going to have a week's happiness at least, and he wanted to leave a broad margin and feel secure. It was awful to think that it was the last of his money, but he just wouldn't think about it. He was in an hysterical state, and admitted it.

The Governor was obviously a little surprised when Bob took him aside and asked him for the sum in exchange for his cheque ; but Bob explained that he had to have enough money for his holiday, that he had forgotten to cash it before, and that it was now too late to get it at the bank. Also he luckily had his pass-book, which he showed to the Governor. Also the Governor knew about Bob's money, and they both employed the same branch of the Midland Bank. Nevertheless, the Governor was a little hesitant, and called the Mrs. in. . . . The Mrs. (who also knew about Bob's savings) was very good, and said at once that that would be quite all right. Certainly

Bob should have the money. She was, perhaps, also a bit surprised at the amount : but the matter was very soon all cleared up—they heard that he was going to Brighton—they thought that the weather was going to hold—and they wished him the best of luck. . . .

This took place just before the house opened in the evening, and he was so relieved that he really quite enjoyed himself that night.

The Governor and the Mrs. had been so good and trusting— so eager to show their trust in him—and everybody, on this Christmas Day, was being so good to everybody else. He really wished that they were not all so good and open—while he was so weak, and underhand, and bad. He felt almost that he was betraying them.

Particularly did he feel that he was betraying Ella. She so deserved his respect, but all the homage went to another. Poor Ella. He watched her as she moved about merrily (in the cap which became her so), and gave back chaff for chaff in the crowded Christmassy bar. She had only one sin : she was without beauty. But she had all the heart-breaking desires, and you could see them there, on her charming face, as she laughingly and maternally answered—a creature eternally maternal, eternally fruitless—the insincere compliments of the men. . . .

That night he slept quite peacefully.


The next morning he was very impatient, hardly knowing what he was doing. It was the first day of his holidays, he had no work to do, he could eat hardly any lunch, and walked aimlessly about the streets. . . .

But five o'clock came at last, and he packed his bag, and managed to leave " The Midnight Bell " without being seen.

He rode, on the top of a bus, in the dusk, down to Victoria Station.

London ! It was half-past five and he knew the dusky hour well. It was the hour when London glistened—when the lights came forth—when people were going home—when pleasure was just beginning—when, in the ordinary way, Jenny, and her honest but intemperate companions, arrayed themselves in dusky dishevelled rooms, and came glowing down upon the lit West End. . . .

He was glad he had not started too early. He would be there only a quarter of an hour before the time, and thus would spare himself torture. She might not turn up. But he thought she would. He also thought (touch wood) that she would be there early. He had spent a dreadful lot of money, and she would not let him down this time.

He arrived at Victoria Station. He went straight to the clock, carrying his suit case. She was not there. There was no reason why she should be.

Six o'clock came. She had a right to be late—a woman's right to be late. And she had been late before—many times.

Five past six.

A quarter past six.

Bob was quite calm. He sat on his suit case under the clock and was calm.

He was the calmest and most submissive individual in an atmosphere of singular perturbation and aggression. Engines hissed, trucks rolled, echoes rang. Luggage was labelled, indicators were altered, whistles screamed, people were told to mind their backs. But Bob was calm. He had a whole week's holiday in which to act, and he was not going to hurry it, or do anything foolish. He sat there quietly contemplating his own drama.

Jenny did not come. At last he rose, dragged his bag to the cloakroom, received a slip in exchange for it, and went into the Buffet. He ordered a double whisky. That step was obvious. He drank it rather theatrically and rather theatrically ordered another. For the moment he could regard himself theatrically. He was, perhaps, almost enjoying himself.

## CHAPTER LV

THERE are few motives so dangerous as theatricality and
no wildness is so futile as deliberate wildness. Bob conceived it his duty to get wildly drunk and do mad things.
He had no authentic craving to do so : he merely objectivized
himself as an abused and terrible character, and surrendered to
the explicit demands of drama. The motivation of popular
fiction in behaviour—the susceptibility of mankind to poetic
precedents—are subjects which will one day be treated with
the gravity they deserve. In deciding to get wildly drunk and
do mad things, Bob believed he was achieving something of
vague magnificence and import, redeeming and magnifying
himself—cutting a figure before himself and the world. The
fact that, in deliberately attempting to get wildly drunk and do
mad things, he might actually get wildly drunk, and actually do
mad things, completely eluded him.

The age of necromancy has surely not expired, for in whisky
there are possessing devils such as the Middle Ages might not
have conceived, and you may yet buy the potion of raging madness with a few shillings. No irredeemable lunatic, beating at
the walls of his padded cell, has a more passionate and lucid
conviction of the truth of his words, and the necessity of his
objects, than a man, with a dozen or so whiskies inside him,
being ejected from a saloon. The spirit is upon them both :
they are both equally entranced, inspired, possessed—seers of
things denied of others. They are frantically incredulous of the
world's unbelief. This is not mania, cries the maniac : I am not
drunk, cries the drunkard. And for all we know they may be
right. But they are both, in this workaday world, locked up.

Bob, afterwards, remembered very little of that night, and
that disjointedly. He remembered leaving Victoria, with four
double whiskies to his credit, and riding in a bus to Piccadilly.
He remembered arriving at Knightsbridge (for it was in that
direction that the bus, contrary to his airy suppositions, was
going) and entering a pub and having two more.

This, he remembered, was at eight o'clock, and he remem-

bered nothing more until nine, when he found himself in the
Irish House in Piccadilly, talking to a seedy little Jew, who was
rolling drunk but believed firmly in God. . . . You could prove
the existence of God, said the seedy little Jew, by the Principle
of Mathematics. Bob said you couldn't. The seedy little Jew
said, *Oh* yes you could. Bob asked him to do it. The seedy little
Jew drew himself up and looked sternly at Bob. What, he asked,
did two and two make ? Four, said Bob, or did when he was a
kid. Well, said the seedy little Jew, there you were. Bob asked
where he was. *There*, said the seedy little Jew. Where ? asked
Bob. The seedy little Jew, with infinite patience, began again.
Did two and two make four, or did they *not*. They did. Well,
what was Bob arguing about ? Bob did not know and they had
another drink. . . .

After this there was another blank, and his next memory was
of staggering along Shaftesbury Avenue in search of Jenny,
and not finding her. . . .

After this the world never ceased, for one moment, to swim
around Bob. He remembered that he had another drink near
the Palace—that he smashed a glass there—that he was made
to put sixpence in a charity box for smashing it—that on coming
out he was instantly accosted by two harlots, of the most revolt-
ing nature, and that they dragged him along to the " Globe."

He remembered that they talked across him and made a great
fuss of him and asked him if his intentions were (from their own
point of view) honourable. He remembered having no intentions at all, but asking how much they wanted. He remembered
they asked for a fiver, and he remembered replying that he had
never heard of such a thing. He remembered offering them
with embittered impudence, sixpence. He remembered that
they were much too greedy to be affronted, and obviously
thought that he was drunk and easy game. He remembered
delighting in the thought that they thought him drunk, and
taking enormous pleasure in fooling them. He remembered
this going on for an hour—their patience being inexhaustible.
He remembered them at last asking him what he was going to
do for wasting their time. He remembered coming out, and
their clinging to his arms each side. He remembered at last
giving them a pound—ten shillings each—to be rid of them.

By this time he had lost all sense of money. Only the conviction that he was not yet drunk and abandoned, and that he
must at all costs become so—only the diabolic fancy that to-
night he was saying good-bye to his past life—that he must
spend and spite himself without stint or regret, obsessed him.

He remembered, almost immediately afterwards, falling in
with another woman, of a more superior character, and she
took him down below the Criterion. He remembered that she
said she came from America (though she was true Irish really
and was all for Fairness. . . . Life wasn't Fair. It wasn't Fair,
for instance, that when she was trying to come to England with
some other girls—and there was questions about them getting
in—it wasn't Fair that *she* should be let through—and none of
the others—just because she was a doctor's daughter. . . . It
wasn't Fair, was it ? Those girls were as good as *her*—weren't
they ? Just because she was a doctor's daughter, it wasn't
Fair, was it ? No, said Bob, it wasn't Fair. . . . And an unfair
world, full of unfair people, with unfair waiters rushing around
between unfair tables, swam about Bob. . . .

She somehow passed from his life (for ever), and his next
memory was of sitting in the little Café bar in Soho. It was the
one to which Jenny had brought him, a week ago, and he had
come here in search of her. The Jew gang was still at the bar,
as though it had never moved, and its leader was in conversation
with him. He was feeling vaguely flattered. . . . The light-
suited and virulent young men breathed beer over him, and
were showing him a trick with a knife. . . . One of them had
his arm round his shoulder, and was entreating him, in ecstatic
tones to watch. . . . It was a real Beaut, he said, " See that
side ? " said the conjuror. " Yes," said Bob. " An' see that
side ? " " Yes." Lightning twists took place. . . . " An' you
see that side. . . ." " An' you see that side. . . ." Bob's head
fell forward in a giddy universe of knife sides and Jew boys. . . .
" Very good," he said at last, and stumbled out. . . .

And then, miraculously, he had met Prunella (of all people)
and was giving her a drink at a bar. . . . But he could hardly
see her to talk to, and could hardly pronounce any of his words.
He kept on trying to murmur something about Jenny, but he
either could not hear, or could not piece together, the sense of

her replies. . . . She was saying something about Jenny—about her having been blind drunk ever since coming into twenty-five pounds. . . . But he did not know what she meant. How had she come into twenty-five pounds ? . . .

Also Prunella kept on telling him, with an idiotic irrelevance, that he was drunk himself, and that he had better go home. He knew that, fundamentally, he was in full possession of his senses, and could not understand why she kept on bringing it up, dragging it in. . . . He thought it was probably because she was drunk herself.

And then he was calling for more drinks. . . . And then, for some obscure cause, they could not get any more drinks—because of some failing on his part. . . . And then suddenly he was out in the street again, and Prunella was growing absurdly insistent about something else. . . . She was staring into his face and talking about his money.

Money. Money. Money. . . . She wouldn't leave it alone. " You're money mad," he said. . . . She was asking how much he had brought out with him. She wouldn't leave him alone. " Twenty-five pounds," he said. " Twenty-five pounds . . . ." And still she wouldn't leave him alone. . . .

And then another harlot had appeared on the scene, and a queer little man who looked like a paper seller, and they were all conferring about him under a lamp-post. " It's them Jew boys," he heard the other harlot saying. " That's what it is. It's them Jews." And they all went on talking. Jews. Jews. Jews. Money. Money. Money. They were all mad. He wanted to go to sleep, and tried to. . . .

And then he felt himself being punched on the back, and pinched in the arm, and he heard them crying : " Wake up, wake up, there's a copper ! A copper, kid, a copper ! Wake up ! " And he could only think of some dreadful kind of Penny, and wondered what it was all about.

And all at once he was looking into the level grey eyes of a policeman, with a yellow moustache. . . .

And he suddenly realized that he was drunk, and stood up, supported by Prunella, and faced the level grey eyes and the yellow moustache. . . .

And then the policeman had gone on, and they were all

saying that he was better now, and he was wondering why they were all being so kind to him. . . . And then they were all standing at a corner, and Prunella was giving him five shillings—putting it into his waistcoat pocket. He could not make out why. . . .

And then he was alone with the little paper man, and he asked where he was being taken. . . . And he was told he was being taken to bed. . . . And he suddenly thought it would be a good idea to go to Brighton, and asked if they couldn't both go down . . . and the little man, with a kind of unnecessary and relentless terseness, said that they couldn't. . . .

And then all at once, he was in a bare place with wooden passages, and facing a queer man seen through an aperture, at a pay desk . . . . And his companion was removing one of the half crowns which Prunella had given him, and putting it down for him. . . . And he was picking up his change, together with a slip of yellow paper. . . .

And then he was walking up some wooden stairs, and was in a bare, square, wooden room, lit by one hanging electric bulb in the centre. . . . And up against the walls, all around this room, about a yard distant from each other, were narrow beds. . . .

And he was taking off his clothes, by one of these beds, and so was the little man. . . .

And then he was in bed. . . . Very comfortable, though the sheets were rather damp. . . . And the light was still on, and he wondered why it was. And he wondered what on earth it could all be. . . .

And nearly all the other beds were occupied. And some of the people in them were snoring, and some, every now and again, were murmuring in their sleep. . . . And one man cried out in his sleep, and was silent. . . .

And then the light suddenly went out (he saw that it must be worked from below) and he was in complete darkness. . . .

And then, after about a quarter of an hour, the light suddenly went on again. And he heard footsteps coming up the stairs.

And there entered a dirty old man, with no collar, and bursting boots, and a matted grey beard—of the type that stands in the gutter and says " God bless you, Sir," whether you have given him anything or not. . . .

And then the truth dawned upon Bob.

The old man got into bed. There was a pause of a few minutes. . . . The light again went out. . . .

In the darkness he saw it all. He had got drunk. All his money had been stolen. Prunella had lent him five shillings. He had been brought to a doss house to sleep. Jenny did not love him, and this was the first day of his holidays.

Glad to know, he went to sleep.

## CHAPTER LVI

POSSIBLY one of the most peculiarly depressing situations in the world is this : to be a waiter who has once had eighty pounds, to have fallen incontinently in love with a blue-eyed young prostitute of twenty-one, to have arranged to meet her at Victoria so as to go away on a holiday with her, to have waited for an hour for her without result, to have decided to get wildly drunk, to have succeeded, to have had every penny of the last of your money stolen by a gang of Jews, to have been got to bed by the charity of another prostitute and a friendly paper seller—and, finally, to wake up, trembling with cold, in a doss house, at the black bitter hour of half-past five, and slowly divine that all this has occurred. Indeed, this situation is almost without parallel in its power to inflict unhappiness.

And when, in addition to all this, this situation is aggravated by the fact that your mouth resembles sand paper of the most vindictive nature, that your ears are singing, that you are dying of thirst in the darkness, and that you dare not move your head an inch for fear of being sick, the situation is so hard as to be almost unbearable, and if only there were an instrument of death at hand it would not be borne.

This was at half-past five. Hoping obscurely (and he knew not why) for the dawn, Bob maintained one position, put his hands to his head—as though praying—as though indicted by life for his sins and folly—and submitted to the passing of an hour. . . .

At last, in the blackness of his darkness, his ears sang no more, and he listened to the unearthly functionings of existence near by. . . . Outside, in what seemed to be a mews below, a lorry was being loaded. In the darkness men, every now and again, cried to each other; heavy boots rang on hollow pavements, thudding packages were dropped. . . .

Someone, eventually, began to use a hose. . . . Pails clanked amid a cool and intermittent hiss. . . . Two men argued with each other, for a long while, in low and grumbling tones. . . . This was London at half-past five in the morning, and the occupations and ways of men were indeed unfathomable. . . .

Within the room London's defeated slept. . . . Slept and snored, in an extraordinarily violent way, as though grasping angrily at oblivion. . . . One groaned. . . . Another began, with quiet, clear, yet unintelligible articulation, to express himself. . . . Another's breath was a recurrent whistle. . . . Nearly all snored, and the only one awake banged ferociously at his pillow. . . . The peace of despair was here unknown: sleep revealed the truth, and the angry souls of the downtrodden complained and raged in dreams. . . .

At last dawn, through a window opposite Bob, gave intimations of her approach—the dark and patient staging of herself. He lay on his back and watched—as patiently. . . .

Half an hour passed, and at last a sign was given—a little rent of silver light torn in the stormy blueness of the heavens. There after she advanced, or rather imperceptibly occurred, before the patient Bob. She occurred fixedly, calmly, aloofly—a reminder of all the dawns, and the hopeless fate of man. A sight appalling in its silence and grief. . . .

All sounds below suddenly ceased. . . . Even the dreamers made less noise, and, for the first time, London really seemed asleep.

Tears of sorrow and dissipation filled Bob's eyes. . . . Reading his own fate in the sky, he sensed something too vast, profound, and inconsolable to be malignant; and the tears, half of self pity, half of dissipation, flowed.

He honestly believed he was glad. For it was all over now. There was no doubt about that.

Chimney-pots, of the glowing blackness of soot, stood like

a comic, defeated army of soldiers, fantastically caparisoned, before the horizon. . . .

Another pail clanked. . . . A window shrieked open. . . . Somebody began to beat a mat. . . . One of the sleepers woke, punched his pillow, and subsided again greedily. . . . It was day.

What now? He could go to "The Midnight Bell," he supposed. They would always welcome him there. Ella, the Governor, the Governor's Wife. They had always been so good and friendly, and he had played them so false. With his inner passion, his secret life, he had thought to deceive them —but they would take him back. He would have to get the Governor to advance him some money. There was no doubt that he'd get it. If possible, he would start work again at once. . . .

What story could he tell them—how account for his return? He would have to tell them something near the truth. The thought gave him relief. He so sorely needed confession. "I'm afraid I've got in with a bad lot lately," he would say, and they would forgive and understand.

These thoughts flowed through an unmoving head that watched the dawn. . . . At last he sat up, and looked at the bed on his left. The little paper seller slept peacefully. Over the little paper-seller's bed was spread his heavy but threadbare overcoat, his coat and trousers—to give him warmth. . . . Bob looked for his own clothes--and found them spread similarly over his own bed. That must have been done for him last night. He had no memory of it. There was a great deal of rough tenderness about. . . .

Under his pillow he found the change from the five shillings Prunella had given him. . . . Under his pillow, as a precaution against robbery—another service. He would have liked to thank the little man, but he didn't want to wake him. . . .

He must get out of here.

His head reeling, he got out of bed and shivered into his clothes. He found that he was still wearing his shirt, collar, and tie. He was glad of this, and soon ready. . . .

The streets were darker than he had supposed, and very cold. He did not know where he was, except that he was in Soho, but soon found Old Compton Street. He passed the little café

bar, where he supposed he had been robbed, and saw that it
was shut. . . . He entered Shaftesbury Avenue, and made for
Lyons' Corner House, where he might get some breakfast.

The streets were glittering and empty. Glittering with rain
that had fallen, and empty with an emptiness which a few
taxis, a policeman or so, and an occasional passer-by served to
emphasize rather than lessen. . . .

He counted Prunella's money. He had exactly four and
twopence. He would have to spend it carefully. He could not
return to " The Midnight Bell " until he had washed and made
himself presentable—until he had had one or two drinks—got
himself right. The pubs didn't open till eleven. It was now
seven. Four hours to wait. He would have to save some
money for some drinks. He might return to " The Midnight
Bell " about lunch time. But he would have to have some
drinks. He was light-headed and scarcely knew what he was
doing.

He didn't believe he had sinned enough to deserve this. He
must get some cigarettes. But he hadn't sixpence to put into a
machine. Could one ask a policeman for change ? Why not take
a taxi and return to " The Midnight Bell " ? No, he couldn't
face them until he was more presentable. He must have some
cigarettes.

He entered the Coventry Street Corner House. On the ground
floor breakfasts were being served to a few people—either
remnants of the night, like himself, or the lucky ones beginning
the day. He smelt bacon, and the fearful false hunger of alcohol
filled him.

He ordered an egg and bacon, and coffee. He could not
eat the egg and the bacon. It cost him one and five. The warming coffee made him want to sleep. He could hardly keep his
eyes open. He watched the waitress clearing his things away.
He seized a chance to go suddenly without leaving a tip.

He walked down the Haymarket, and across Trafalgar
Square, making quite naturally (bit again in unconscious
obedience to dramatic precedent) for the river. He began to
feel better, and his mind cleared. He supposed, if he had any
sense, he would go to the police about that money. But he
would never do it. That all belonged to a terrible nightmare

past from which he only desired to flee. Any more travail and suspense would finish him. He desired nothing to mar the perfection and peace of his despair.

He reached the embankment and walked along to Westminster Bridge. It was a fine, fresh morning : he had never seen a finer or fresher. It made the soul feel fine and fresh and forgiving.

It could never have been otherwise. He had merely essayed the impossible and failed. He believed it was not her fault. Existence had abused her and made her what she was : poverty had crushed him and made him unable to help her. He knew that he had never made any impression on her, and never would have done so. He knew that it all had come from him, and only the obssession and hysteria of his pursuit had given a weak semblance of reciprocation. He knew that his gesticulations had never disturbed, for one instant, the calm equability of her degradation. She had not, really, fooled him : she had been too passive and indolent for that. He had only fooled himself.

It was a healing thought. He reached Westminster Bridge.

Big Ben pointed to a quarter to eight. The glorious sun smote the astonished day. Not a cloud was in the sky. The river, full to the brim, sped quickly by, wallowing in its liquid and twinkling plenitude—flowing out to the sea—flowing out to the sea. . . .

The sea ! The sea ! What of the sea ?

The sea !

The solution—salvation ! The sea ! Why not ? He would go back, like the great river, to the sea ! To the sea of his early youth—the mighty and motherly sea—that rolled over and around the earth !

Why had he not thought of it before ? Dear God, he had been a landsman too long !

Now ! He had his papers intact at " The Midnight Bell." Now ! No time to waste. He had wasted enough time. He would go down to the docks now, and see what was doing. Now ! Now ! Now !

And here, curiously and abruptly, is the end of Bob's story, or at any rate of his love story. Bob went to sea : but this story cannot be concerned with his adventures thereon, nor with what befell him afterwards. It is much more concerned with the mere fact that, after all he had suffered, and after all he had lost, Bob was yet able to glow in this manner and resolve to go to sea.

For because of this power of glowing and resolving, and straining still to rise, Bob, weak as he was, revealed, perhaps, something which was far greater than and embraced himself— something which he shared, perhaps, with the whole race of men of which he was so insignificant, needy, and distressed a member.

For there is this about men. You can embitter and torment them from birth. You can make them waiters and sailors (like Bob) when they want to be authors. You can make them (as Bob and most of them were made) servants of their passions— weak— timorous — querulous — vain — egotistic — puny and afraid. Then, having made them so, you can trick them and mock them with all the implements of fate—lead them on, as Bob was led on, only to betray them, obsess them with hopeless dreams, punish them with senseless accidents, and harass them with wretched fears. You can buffet them, bait them, enrage them—load upon them all evils and follies in this vale of obstruction and tears. But, even at that, there is yet one thing that you cannot do. You can never make them, under any provocation, say die. And therein lies their acquittal.

# THE SIEGE OF PLEASURE

## JENNY

### PROLOGUE

JENNY MAPLE, a girl of the West End streets, was walking in the vicinity of Shaftesbury Avenue, Piccadilly Circus, and Great Windmill Street at about eleven o'clock one night, when she became aware that she had attracted the glances of a seedy, furtive little man wearing a white silk muffler and a soft hat.

As a business proposition she did not altogether like his appearance; he looked sly, inelegant, and grasping. But she thought it best to give him what encouragement she could, as she was desperately hard up at the moment, and " in trouble " (as she put it).

She was " in trouble " for two reasons. First, she believed that she was at any moment liable to arrest. A " plain-clothesman " (whom she knew well by sight and who had always, she imagined, " had his knife into her ") had only last night arrested her girl friend, and was clearly out to get her too if she didn't take the very greatest care : and apart from all the worry and humiliation of appearing before a magistrate, she simply had no idea where she could get the money for her fine.

The other trouble arose more from her own fault. A week ago a young man named Bob (he was a young waiter in a pub called " The Midnight Bell " off the Euston Road) had given her, for various reasons, twenty-five pounds in order to make it worth her while to go away with him to Brighton for a week. It had been a fantastic thing to do, and she had known all the time that he had only done it because he had been crazily in love with her. He was a bit mad. All the same she had promised to go to Brighton and to meet him at Victoria with that end in view. Well, she had not. The twenty-five pounds in a lump sum had been too much for her. She had got drunk and spent all the money instead. She knew she was wrong there, and her conscience smote her somewhat. But even more than by her conscience she was smitten by the fear of what he might do. It was quite likely that he was wandering round looking for her now (he had often done that sort of thing before) and if they met she dreaded to think of the scene he might make.

So being thus doubly in trouble, she was much too anxious merely to get off the streets to pick and choose, and she decided that if this little man in the silk muffler would only make up his mind and speak to her, she would be glad enough.

That he was having a great struggle in this matter of making up his mind about her she could see plainly, and she was doing all she could to help him. That is to say that she was walking regularly and methodically round the London Pavilion : at one moment she was in Shaftesbury Avenue, at the next she was in Piccadilly Circus, at the next in Great Windmill Street, and then in Shaftesbury Avenue again, and so on round. This procedure, while avoiding frightening him by stopping still, gave him certain knowledge of her movements and every opportunity to look at her in passing and make his decision without committing himself. She really could not do fairer.

He, however, was in an appalling state of doubt and nerves. So far from showing the same method as herself, and waiting to meet her regularly as the circle came round, he was dodging all over the place. He was at one moment lurking behind her, at the next walking rapidly ahead of her and trying to get a look at her sideways, then hurrying round the whole circle to get behind her again, then lurking in a doorway pretending not to notice her, then boldly coming down the street to look at her fairly and squarely as though he had never seen her in his life before, then dashing over the road to get an opinion in safety from the other side—in fact, behaving idiotically and despicably.

At last it wore down even her own endurance. She decided to put the tormented connoisseur out of his pain. He had stopped in another doorway, and she was bearing down upon him. She went up to him.

" Good evening, dearie," she said, smiling. " Do you want me ?"

He took the cigarette out of his mouth and grinned, revealing the gaps in his yellow teeth.

"What?" he said, grinningly taken aback, and almost shaking with fright.

"I think you want me—don't you?" she said. "You've been hanging about ever such a long while."

There was a pause in which he looked down the street.

"Depends how much you want," he said. He had now regained his repose a little.

"Well, that depends on you, doesn't it, dear?" She spoke with sweet reasonableness. "I haven't got a flat, so we'd have to go to a hotel. Would you like to spend the whole night?"

"Well—depends on what it would come to."

"Well, if I spent the whole night I'd want a fiver—to make it worth my while. But if it was just for a little while it would come cheaper, like—wouldn't it?"

He thought for a moment, and then adopted a business-like tone.

"What about the whole night for four quid?"

Secretly she thought this a good bargain in her present state of distress, but of course she was not going to let him see that.

"Haven't you got a fiver?" she asked.

"No. I can only spare four pounds. Afraid it's that or nothing. I ain't *got* the money."

She pretended to hesitate.

"Very well," she said. "I'm very hard up, so I suppose I'll have to."

"Right you are," he said. "Let's go and have a drink first, shall we?"

She saw how badly he needed a drink, and marvelled, as she always did, at these little men, to whom an evening of delight, apart from the money they paid for it, entailed such strenuous mental suffering. You would have thought he hated the sight of her—instead of loving the look of her—which his four pounds definitely demonstrated that he did in some sort of way. "All right," she said. "There's just time before they close."

She conducted him to a little public house off Rupert Street. They went into the Saloon Bar. This was filled with a crowd of people swallowing as much drink as they could before closing

time, but they were lucky enough to find an unoccupied table
in a corner. He asked her what she would have ; she asked for
a port, and sat down and waited while he shoved his way through
to the bar to get it for her. A minute later he returned with it ;
together with a large whisky and soda for himself. He offered
her a cigarette, which she took, and he lit a match wherewith
he lighted her cigarette and his own.

At such moments as these Jenny always tried to establish a
calm and companionable feeling.

" Well, dear," she said, having taken a sip at her port. " What
sort of business are *you* in ?"

" Me ?" He puffed at his cigarette and looked quizzingly at
her. " What do you think ?"

" I can't say. You look as though you're in business
though."

Experience had taught her that her clients were generally
flattered by being told that they looked as though they were in
business.

" Well, I suppose I am. I'm in Motors as it happens."

" Oh yes ? That must be very interestin'."

" Oh yes. Interestin' enough. . . . Not quite as interestin'
as certain others though." And he brought his head humorously
a little nearer to her, in order to reinforce the double meaning,
and almost as if to remind her of the objects with which they had
met.

Seeing him look at her like that, it occurred to her, for a
moment, that she had seen this unpleasant little person somewhere before, but she could not for the life of her remember
where.

" I believe I've seen you somewhere before," she said.

" Oh ! Have you ?" he replied. " Well, I hope we'll see a
lot more of each other."

Intending a double meaning again, he had the lighthearted
air of a man who obviously did not give the notion the slightest
credit, and she herself was not sufficiently interested to pursue
the matter. A few minutes later half the lights went down in the
pub ; they finished their drinks rapidly and went out into the
street. He stopped a passing taxi, and Jenny stepped into it.

" Where to ?" he asked Jenny.

"The **** Hotel, Paddington," she said. "I expect he knows it."

"The **** Hotel, Paddington," he repeated briskly to the driver, who gave a gloomy nod, and bent down his meter.

As she had foreseen, the taxi had scarcely started before he took her arm and cajolingly drew up near to her.

"You're a bad little girl, ain't you?" he said waggishly. "How did you get that way?"

"Oo," she said, in the same burlesquing spirit. "I Took the Wrong Turning, my dear. I Took to Drink."

"You did—eh?"

"That's right, my dear," she went on in the same way. "All through a Glass of Port."

She was speaking without the slightest seriousness at the moment, but a little later, thinking of odd things as she humoured him and his kisses and the taxi curved and sped through the mauve-lit London streets, she wondered whether she had not accidentally hit upon the truth. At the same time she remembered where it was that she had met this little man before.

"All through a glass of port." Fantastic as the notion was, she believed it reflected, in an amusing way, one aspect of the whole truth. And her mind fled back (while she still humoured him and saw Paddington and their destination for the night approach) to the now barely imaginable days when, greenly innocent of drink and all else, she partook of that single glass.

What follows is the story of that glass of port, and those days.

# I

## THE TREASURE

IT seems that the tragic predicament of the aged is that, having no further desire for their bodies, they have little left to do in life but concentrate upon the exacting and meaningless problem of living in them. Paradoxically, at no time of life is existence so intensely physical as in old age. Youth, in the careless working of its bodily perfection, may well attend to things of the spirit and mind : but senility, whose every corporal faculty is decaying and working arbitrarily, awaits on the body as all in all. Incessant organic events and misadventures, occupying the vigilant mind to the exclusion of all else, are observed, prophesied, and medicinally forestalled and mitigated. In the majority of cases it is not with beauty and seemly abstractions, but with pills and digestive expedients, that the superannuated await release in death.

In a middle-sized residence in the suburb of Chiswick, five or six years ago, there lived three people in this intensely physical state. There were two old ladies—Miss Chingford and Mrs. Rodgers, who were sisters and both over seventy—and their brother Dr. Chingford, who was eighty-three.

The three were figures in the neighbourhood, with which they had very few dealings. Sometimes the old man was taken for a walk, and the old ladies went shopping together pretty regularly every morning.

These two were not particularly welcome or liked abroad. Tradesmen, as they served them, winked or glanced meaningly at the next customer, and the latter could barely resist returning the same kind of glance as they shuffled out of the shop. They really were so old, and ugly, and silly to look at.

Tradesmen and others, of course, were unable to divine that they were not being old and ugly and silly on purpose

They were seen as hideous old women without past or future, and it was imagined that they were this because they had somehow decided to be so. For all that was thought about it, they might have been born hideous old women. At any rate they had now taken a resolute and unrepentant stand upon it, and people resented such a peculiar taste.

Nothing actually was further from their minds. But, being totally unaware that they were the victims of this injustice, they did nothing to remedy the matter. Indeed, as you saw them coming down the street—the tall, parrot-like, red-eyed, fussy, fatuously hatted Miss Chingford—the small, thin-lipped, anæmic, bowed, wrinkled Mrs. Rodgers, with her enlarging pince-nez stuck with slight but maddening lopsidedness on her little nose—as they came down the street they had about them, in their old legs and person, a kind of formidable, bull-dog like waddle which well might make you think they were being positively arrogant about themselves. Also, being old, and having lost their nerve, and not being able to see or think quickly and properly, they were always getting into panics, and talking too loud, and peering at things too long, and holding people up, and waving umbrellas at bus-drivers, and fiddling in their bags, and obstinately refusing to be " done," in a manner which was really exasperating even to those who were wise enough to perceive that they were afflicted rather than contumacious.

They differed from each other in that the elder, Miss Chingford, was practically a full-blown eccentric and useless everywhere, whereas Mrs. Rodgers, by comparison and within the limits of age and illness, was tolerably complacent, and ran the house at Chiswick.

From Dr. Chingford, whose wife had died some thirty years ago, they both greatly differed. He, when he went abroad, caused no resentment in the neighbourhood. This was because he made no fuss, and was not ugly. On the contrary he was an extraordinarily tall and handsome man, wearing a white beard, and he was incapable of making any fuss, owing to his deafness, which removed him from common affairs. Only by shouting wildly at him, for some time, could you produce any imitation of responding language from him .and then you had miserably to

translate whatever sounds had emerged as well as you could.
For this reason he was practically an unknown quantity in life,
through which he appeared to float like little more than an
apparition. All the same, with regard to him, people made the
same error as they made with his sisters—that of assuming
that he had adopted extreme old age and deafness as a career.

It happened that these three old people, who were far from
well off as regards money, required a new servant. For the
last six months they had been making do with a woman called
Mrs. Brackett, whose business it was to come in daily. The
arrival of Mrs. Brackett's little boy, with a meagre and illiterate
note explaining Mrs. Brackett's inability to appear herself was,
however, a constant occurrence, and the daily suspense endured
by Miss Chingford and Mrs. Rodgers round about eight o'clock
was fast growing unendurable. It might, though, have been
endured a great deal longer had not Mrs. Rodgers one afternoon
been visited by a servant once in her employ, who came for a
reference.

This girl, whose name was Kate and who had left Mrs.
Rodgers two years ago to get married, still sometimes came
in to help, and was on very friendly terms with her old " mistress." Mrs. Rodgers gave her a cup of tea on this occasion, and
afterwards they had a chat. In the course of their conversation
Kate asked Mrs. Rodgers whether she " happened " to require
a new servant. She knew, she said, of the very thing if she did.

A young girl, a vague connection of hers by marriage, was
in need of employment. She had not actually been in service
before, but was perfectly trained in domestic usage, an excellent
plain cook, and extremely willing. She desired, if possible, to
" sleep in," though she would not exact this.

Mrs. Rodgers was taken with the idea, and, unknown to
Mrs. Brackett, the girl was given an interview. This took place
in the drawing-room. Only Mrs. Rodgers saw her, and she
came out in two minds.

She pronounced the girl neat, capable-looking, and respectful.
She could, in fact, in view of Kate's recommendation, actually
furnish no excuse for rejecting her, save perhaps that of her
age, which was only eighteen. The sum of years accumulated
by the three upon whom she would minister amounting to over

two hundred and twenty-five, the arrangement seemed ill-balanced. But Miss Chingford, an avid optimist and restless enthusiast for change, perceived no disadvantage in this, and after sleeping on the matter her sister came round to the same point of view.

There was, all the same, just one dim objection and foreboding at the back of Mrs. Rodger's mind, which she could not define clearly either to her sister or herself. It arose from the extraordinary prettiness of the girl.

From what she had seen at the time, and as far as she could remember now, the girl was not ordinarily, but extraordinarily pretty. During the brief interview this perfectly inconsequent and unacknowledgeable little matter had impinged itself upon the consciousness, it seemed of both, in a meek but peculiarly nettling way.

A second interview took place, and this time Mrs. Rodgers decided, but not with an entirely clean conscience, that perhaps she was not so pretty after all. She engaged her. She was to begin work on Thursday, coming in to work on that evening, and for the day on Friday, and then she was to bring her " box " (a purely mythical and traditional container) on Saturday, when she would take up residence in her own room at the top of the house.

Her name was Jane Taylor. During this interview Mrs. Rodgers learned that she had once worked in a factory. This, in combination with her prettiness, again worked a minute disturbance in the heart of Mrs. Rodgers. Was it conceivable that she was about to lodge in her house not a new servant, but a pretty factory girl ? She could have swallowed an ordinary factory girl converted to domestic service, but was not a pretty factory girl (however deeply rooted her change of heart) a little too much of a good thing ?

She confessed her trepidations to her sister. But Miss Chingford, who had still not seen the girl but was dead set on her, knew no fear of factories in her soul. Her faith infected Mrs. Rodgers, and the next afternoon Kate and the newcomer both came round for an hour or so to go over the house—the former expounding in detail to the latter the domestic geography, traditions, drawers, cupboards and utensils in relation to each other. This went off very well, with gaiety indeed, and that evening both Mrs. Rodgers and Miss Chingford were highly pleased with themselves.

At this juncture a curious thing occurred. Mrs. Brackett, now to be dismissed, underwent a horrible metamorphosis. From a respectable though rather trying and inconsistent " daily," she was converted, overnight, into a black monster of every evil. It seemed that they had never in their hearts liked her, but not until now, at the rising of a new dawn, did they apprehend how dark their household night had been. Filth, unpunctuality, insolence, cunning, scandal-mongering, smashing, lying—all these qualities in Mrs. Brackett stood out clear in the illumination of the coming change. Thieving, in fact, was the sole misdemeanour not positively attributable to Mrs. Brackett, but even here shrewd and exultant suspicions enlivened the mind. Mrs. Brackett was given no knowledge of this lightning plunge from grace, and departed peacefully with presents.

*      *      *      *

Dr. Chingford, Mrs. Rodgers, and Miss Chingford, who were known respectively within their own precincts as Robert, Marion, and Bella, took a large lunch in the middle of the day. Afterwards they all felt dazed and rather ill. Robert then retired to his " study," wherein he studied exclusively slumber, with whose every department he was majestically acquainted : Marion went to her bedroom ; and Bella stayed down in an armchair before the fire.

The two ladies generally read for some time, finally letting fall both their literature and their lower jaws, and swimming off into a fuddled coma until tea time. Then Marion took the initiative, came quietly down the creaking stairs, and in a tense zero period put on the kettle for tea.

A cup was taken up to Robert, and spirits slowly revived. Then the two ladies generally went out for a walk. After this it commonly occurred that one or both of them suffered from some slight indisposition or other—a headache, giddiness, indigestion or mere fatigue—and they again parted to recuperate alone.

It therefore chanced, on Thursday evening at six o'clock, when the new girl arrived, that Bella was alone downstairs in the dining-room armchair, while Marion was up in her bedroom.

Though it was a sunny evening, a bright fire burned in the grate, and Bella had fallen into another doze. The girl's single knock—the timid and barely audible knock of her class—startled Bella extremely, and threw her into a mental state bordering upon panic. All door-opening was left to Marion, Bella being unused and constitutionally unsuited to the task.

She therefore sprang up, took a hurried glimpse through the window curtain, confirmed her worst fears, went out into the hall, and, standing to listen, prayed in her craven soul that Marion had heard.

Marion had not heard. Instead, a sepulchral silence reigned upstairs and all over the house. On one side of the front door the new maid diffidently awaited promised admission, on the other an old lady stood disconcerted.

But at last, taking her courage into both hands, Bella went to the door and opened it.

" Ah ! . . . You're . . ."

Bella did not describe, but smiled and nodded a welcoming comprehension of what the young person was.

" Yes, madam," said the girl shyly, and smiled, and came in.

Bella went to the bottom of the stairs. " Marion !" she cried.

Marion shouted something from a distance, and Bella, smiling sweetly once more, went into the dining room, leaving the door open.

Marion made no further sign, and oceans of silence descended again upon the house. The girl remained standing in the hall ; Bella remained standing in the dining-room. Each was agonizingly aware of the other's creaking proximity, and the moment was charged with awkwardness and ulterior significance. They were both in their hearts conscious of the near, one might say intimate nature of the relationship about to come into being between them, and yet were dismayed by each other's strangeness. They had never set eyes on each other before, and yet out of the blue they were in the same house and about to participate

closely in the same personal things—from the cooking and
eating of food down to the handling of personal linen.

Marion coming downstairs made things a great deal easier.
She greeted the girl apparently without introspection or misgiving of any sort, and conducted her to the kitchen.

The kitchen was on the ground floor, and communicable
with the dining-room by means of a sliding hatch situate in a
dark passage between the two. If the bell remained unheard
you thrust your head out of the hatch and shouted to the kitchen.
The hatch, also, was a reputed means to the end of the eaves-
dropper, and was often winked and nodded at when the ladies
thought they were speaking too loudly.

Marion now stayed for some time in the kitchen talking to
the newcomer, and returning, every now and again, to the
dining-room. On each occasion she returned she found her
sister, for no obvious reason, standing up. Nothing was said,
but Marion was irritated by this symptom and confession of
restlessness over what she desired to regard as a perfectly
commonplace event—the installation of a new maid.

Finally Marion went upstairs again, and five minutes later the
girl knocked on the door and entered. Bella, now in an armchair,
peered over her newspaper and her spectacles and smirked
affably again. The girl smiled back, and at once proceeded
primly and methodically to lay the table.

Bella began slyly to take stock of her, and her first reflex
was one of alarm. She now saw the girl for the first time without
her hat, and was staggered by her prettiness. The fact that
Marion had said she was very pretty was in an instant submerged
and lost to the mind for ever in the overwhelming phenomenon
of her actual prettiness. Bella, in fact, strongly suspected that
she was lovely. Her very fair hair—her rather full mouth—her
clear wide blue eyes—her slim figure and white arms—who was
this that had come to share her privacy in her old age? She was
so pretty that, with her quiet erect gait, she gave a mischievous
impression of playing, like a theatrical doll, at laying the table.

She now accidentally dropped a fork, and they smiled at
each other again.

"Did you find your way here all right?" asked the old
lady, and in the manner common to those who are slightly

deaf and imagine others equally stricken, repeated the question.
" Did you find your way here ?"

" Oh yes, madam. It was quite easy."

This was the first time Bella had heard a full-blown " madam "
uttered in the house since the war. It gratified her, but she was
unable entirely to rid herself of the impression that it was
merely in keeping with the solemn game being played by this
little thing.

" I came by the 27 'bus," she added.

" Oh yes. Let me see now—you live up at Hackney, don't
you ?"

" No. Camden Town, madam."

" Oh yes. Camden Town. How silly of me."

" Yes. It's just a threepenny ride, madam."

" Oh yes. But then you're coming in to live with us on
Saturday, aren't you ?"

" Yes, madam. That's right."

She left the room, returning a few moments later. She herself
next volunteered a remark.

" It's over a pet animal shop, madam—where we live," she
said, in naïve, clear, and peculiarly childish accents. She was
clearly delighted and diverted by the uniqueness of her own
habitation.

" Oh yes ?" Bella was surprised by the girl's simplicity.
" That must be very interesting."

" Yes madam. They're interesting to look at—some
times."

There was then a silence, and Bella again looked at her.
What on earth did it all mean—this prettiness, this neatness,
this humility, this grave courtesy, this perfect charm and complacency ? She had an air of being much too good to be true.

The wild dogs of optimism in Bella's heart leaped to the
occasion. What if the problem was as clear as day ? What if
the good, for once, had come true ? What if this child were a
treasure ? Why not ? She looked at her again and was convinced she was.

At this moment Marion came into the room. Rendered self-
conscious by the presence of the other two, she went to poke the
fire.

" Jane's been telling me about where she lives," said Bella. " We must start calling you *Jane* now, mustn't we ?"

" Yes, we must, mustn't we ?" said Marion. " Is that what they call you at home ?"

" Yes, madam. Though a lot call me Jenny."

" Oh. Jenny. That's very pretty."

" Though you couldn't hardly say it's for short, could you, madam ?"

All three laughed nervously at this truism and said " No !"

" Yes," said Marion. " I think that's *very* pretty. We'll call you that . . . *Jenny*. . . ."

Jenny, without blushing, here assumed the countenance of one who blushes, and a moment afterwards left the room, closing the door softly behind her.

" Well, what do you think of *that* ?" whispered Bella.

" Don't know at present. What do you ?"

Bella here mumbled a few words culminating, as had been ant'cipated by Marion, in the word Treasure.

" M'm," said Marion severely. " New brooms sweep clean."

But there was an unhabitual gleam of exultation in her voice, and she did not look at her sister as she brushed the fireplace.

Jenny had been advised to beat the gong five minutes before actually laying the supper on the table. This was a crude estimate of the time it should take the " Doctor " to bring himself downstairs. The beating of the gong was supplemented by a stentorian visit from Marion, and the old man got to work at once. With his mouth agape, and gazing fixedly ahead, he achieved the journey in a series of methodical advances from one stair to another—remaining a full period upon each, it seemed less with the object of recuperation than of appraising and exhausting its responsive creaks. With experience a maid might well boil an egg from observation of his progress.

Jenny's first glimpse of the Doctor was when he was on the seventh stair from the bottom. She was moving rapidly in and out between the dining-room and the kitchen, and she caught the straight beam of his steady but alarming eye. She imagined he would be in the dining-room by the time she returned. He was, however, still in serious occupation merely of the next

TWENTY THOUSAND STREETS UNDER THE SKY     236

stair further down. Indeed, so far as she knew he had remained
quite stationary. He again caught her eye, looking at her
without embarrassment, pleasure, or disgust. She kept on
coming in and out, and he continued to look at her. It struck
her (but not apparently him) as being a singular mode of making
an acquaintance.

His journey was ultimately brought to a successful close
in a chair on the fire side of the table, and all was in readiness
for the evening repast. This was always of a sparse nature,
consisting most often of boiled eggs and a little ham or tongue,
in conjunction with brown bread and butter. In fairness to his
waistcoat, which would otherwise have shared his supper, it
was necessary to tie a large napkin around the Doctor's neck.
His beard, left out in the cold, but no more immune, was wipe-
able by another napkin which was tenderly placed on his lap.

Apart from such infinitesimally shamefaced details, the
presence of this remarkable old dodderer in the room worked
an austere and bracing effect upon the service. Voices were
deferentially lowered, and it was felt that, whereas all confabula-
tions between Marion and the girl had hitherto been conducted
as it were behind-scenes, now the curtain was up. " Very well,"
she whispered, nodding and smiling. " We'll ring when we
want you, Jenny."

The removal of the dish cover was a little sensation. The girl
had done them omelettes. " She said she wanted to," said
Marion. " So I let her."

Bella was the first to taste hers, and she pronounced it next
thing to a miracle of cooking. And the *sauté* potatoes (an
unforeseen embellishment) were deemed as good. Both ladies
munched away, taking more salt, deciding a little pepper would
be the thing, passing it affably, and in general betraying a highly
self-conscious approach to their food.

This did not apply to the Doctor, upon whose drooping mouth
and forsaken look, omelettes, like new maids (and, one might
be sure, floods and earthquakes) were impotent to make any
impression.

" Looks as though we may be able to live decently at last,"
said Marion, and Bella agreed.

The faith that they were certain to live decently in the near future had furnished these two women with the self-respect they needed for ages—ever since, in fact, old age, advancing poverty, and an acuter servant problem had set them going down the steep decline leading to Mrs. Brackett. The true realization that they had not been living decently in the near past, however, only assailed them on occasions such as these. They then faced the truth frankly and fearlessly, and with the exaltation of spirit of all converts.

"When I *think* of that woman . . ." said Bella.

"Don't talk about her," said Marion. But she did not mean this. She loved to talk about Mrs. Brackett. As a saved sinner loves to talk of his sins, she loved to talk about her.

"No. We *won't*," said Bella, rigidly. But she did not mean it, either.

When Marion rang the bell, Jenny immediately appeared, and in perfect silence began to collect the plates. Obviously a morsel of Praise must be doled out at this juncture, but the timing and execution thereof was left to Marion. Everything was left to Marion, and in the manipulation of Praise, as in all else, she was an adept. She restrained herself until Jenny had gone out with the tray and returned again with the cheese.

"I thought those omelettes were beautifully done, Jenny," she said, smiling up at her.

Jenny, again without blushing, again assumed the countenance of one who blushes. "Were they, madam," she said. "They make a nice Change, don't they?"

This rejoinder was in the best traditions of a cook's modesty. It engendered a feeling that variety alone had been aimed at, and drew the attention away from the cleverness of the performance itself.

"Yes," said Marion. "I don't know where you learnt to cook like that, I'm sure."

"It was my aunt—taught me most, madam," replied Jenny, and left the room.

"And so *pretty*!" whispered Bella.

"I know," said Marion. "That's what's so strange."

Shortly afterwards they rang again, and Jenny entered to clear away. The old gentleman was tactfully released from his napkin by Marion, and rose, not without assistance. The door was opened for him, and he paused. Then slowly he set out upon the long expedition—the last of the day. Later Marion would go up and help him into bed.

The curtains were now drawn, and the electric light was switched on. They plied the girl with sundry questions concerning herself as she cleared away. She answered in the same modest, naïve, pleased tones—amiably expansive and yet never garrulous—and an atmosphere of bright accord grew and flowered apace. It was obvious that they liked her, and that she liked them, and if there was any evidence to show that this girl was not, as had been instinctively foreseen, a Treasure, it had yet to reveal itself. At last a peak of intimacy and cheerfulness was reached.

" I expect *you* have some young man eating his heart out for you, haven't you, Jenny ?" asked Bella.

Jenny looked at the table-cloth with a faint smile as she cleared the things.

" No, madam. Not just at present, madam."

" Oh well. I expect there will be soon."

" I daresay, madam. But I always think there's plenty of time for that, don't you, madam ?"

The ladies laughed at this and prophesied that it would not be long. Jenny left the room.

If that was not a Treasure's way of looking at things, what was ? Indeed, was it not the remark not merely of a Treasure, but of an adorned Treasure—might they not even dare to aver an Old Fashioned Treasure ? In low tones they debated the delicious mystery of the girl.

At last a foreboding that she was tempting Providence (an ever-vigilant and revengeful monster of whom she lived in nervous dread) beset Marion.

" We'll have to see what to-morrow brings forth," she said, and casually took up the newspaper and began to read, as though striving not to attract Providence's attention to what she had already let fall. Bella did the same with her book.

They were not aided in this nonchalant pastime, however, by innumerable clinking testimonies to fervid industry floating through the hatch from the kitchen. After Mrs. Brackett, the newcomer's air of irresistible thoroughness simply cried out for notice.

She gave at least twenty minutes more to the kitchen than
Mrs. Brackett had ever given, and then was heard mounting
the stairs. She was evidently going to straighten the bedrooms
and turn down the coverlets. During the long reign of Mrs.
Brackett and her daily forerunners, this service had dropped
out of use and been practically forgotten.

"Did you ask her ?" whispered Bella, and Marion confessed
that she had not.

"My *dear* !" said Bella, and even Marion was moved.
Positively, instead of they shaming the child, the child had
shamed them !

The pleasure they felt at this gratuitous assumption of a duty
coincided, however, with a slightly hunted look upon the faces
of both—a look brought into being by a fear of exposure
derived from an automatic misgiving that they had " left something out." But a moment of rapid mental retrospection
relieved their souls, and soon after Jenny came downstairs and
was safely in the kitchen again. Rather curiously, complete
silence fell.

Bella provided the solution. " Putting on her hat and coat,"
she said. . . .

This, after another period of silence, proved to be the case.
A knock came, and she stood in the doorway dressed for the
streets. Broad smiles and a kind of sitting at attention occurred
within the room.

" Going now ?" asked Marion.

"' Yes, madam. Half-past eight to-morrow then, madam ?"

" That's right, Jenny. Good-night."

" Good-night, madam."

" Good-night, Jenny." Bella was not going to be left out.

" Good-night, madam." Jenny had no intention of leaving
her out.

A moment later the front door closed with a click which in
itself contrived to be modest and retiring, and then rapid
footsteps hastened down the street into the distances of the dark.

Having seen her in her hat and coat, and hearing those
receding footsteps, there dawned upon the two old women,
for the first time, a faint realization that the girl actually had
being, and pursued activities, apart from them. But it lingered

for but the briefest of instants, nor did they say a word about it.

"See how she's left her kitchen," murmured Marion, and went out.

Bella could not resist following her, and they stumbled along the dark passage, one after the other.

There was only gas laid on in the kitchen. It was black and chill out here, and a tap hissed and dripped. They groped their way towards the matches. "Here we are," said Marion. . . .

The weak gas lit with a pop, and in its frigid, aquarium illumination was revealed the zeal of a saintly and scrupulous personality. With a single stroke a kitchen Cromwell had subdued the insidious advances of dirt and derangement, and retrieved from anarchy the miserable pass into which Mrs. Brackett's slovenly reign had brought all things. Clean and suspended pots, cups, and pans, a brushed floor, a shining oven, a scrubbed sink, spread sheets of newspaper, hanging cloths—all displayed an air of symmetry and meticulous method. Countless little details and tokens of ingenuity refreshed the eye. And in one corner the child's neat working shoes—dainty reminders of the departed genius, and prim promise of her return.

In the throaty noise made by the gas the old ladies cast round their eyes in awe. At last Bella could restrain herself no more.

"My dear," she said. "We've got a *Treasure*."

They returned as it were dramatically to the dining-room, and made ready to go to bed. It was of no avail : neither could hold out any longer. They could discern no flaw in the pattern of the evening : their content in their servant was ripe and unblemished.

And because of this, and because this problem of a servant had lately filled their anxious minds to the exclusion of all else, to these old women all life itself, at this instant, was flawless, and a thing of joy.

\*    \*    \*    \*

In briefly suspecting that the girl had being, and pursued activities, apart from them, Marion and Bella had been right.

She did. In point of fact Jenny was unmistakably drinking at the fount of her own life within a minute and a half of her departure from the house.

It had been stated in the dining-room that no young man was eating out his heart for Jenny. But waiting for Jenny in the darkness, at the corner of the road, there was one who did nothing less than this. He was a young, pale electrician, with thin features and a consumptive look, of the name of Tom Lockyer.

In justice to Jenny's integrity it should be said that although he was eating his heart out for her, she neither allowed, acknowledged, nor even fully credited that he was doing any such thing. The passion of love had not as yet awakened in Jenny's immature breast, and those who know not love in themselves, know it not in others.

The fierceness with which this pale young man was gnawing at his own vitals was indicated by the fact that he had come all the way from Camden Town, where he lived near to Jenny, solely in order to escort her back and have a little more time with her during the evening.

She smiled graciously upon him as she came up, and he perceived that she was in a good mood.

" You been waitin' long ?" she said.

" No. 'Bout ten minutes," he replied. There was no other acknowledgment of his having come over all this way to fetch her, which had been arranged previously, and was now taken for granted. She was young and hard. They walked immediately, and at a good pace, up towards the High Road.

" Well, 'ow d'you get on, Jen ?"

Jenny was not the sort to provide information of this kind without being asked first, but she was perfectly well aware that he would ask her.

" Oo—ever so well," she replied with genuine enthusiasm. " They ain't half nice old people."

Being insanely and hatefully in love with her, the fires of jealousy leaped up in Tom at hearing this. In his heart he had hoped that it might have been otherwise; that things might have somehow gone ill with her; that some failure or disappointment might have come to break her perpetual composure, and so have made her turn to him for compassion or aid. But he had foreseen the pleasure she would take in her new employment. Behind his love for her, he knew enough of her character to have diagnosed her talent—her fostered and unique talent—of pleasing and being pleased at first sight, and, insignificant a person as he was, he could have enlightened Marion and Bella in many ways. She always pleased : she took pleasure in pleasing. She had ensnared him and originally raised his hopes purely by the devilish and undirected exercising of this gift. And now she continued to please everyone, but had discontinued, for no reason, apparently, save that he loved her, attempting to please him.

He knew this only at the back of his mind. In the forefront thereof, remembering the brief perfection of the time when it had pleased her to please him, he adored and believed in her. The only obstacle, he imagined, was that she did not love him " in that way." She had admitted as much, while as frequently testifying to her knowledge of the excellence of his character and affections.

" Oh—that's good," he said. He dissimulated : but to please Jenny herself was now his sole aim in life. " S'pect it'll be a bit of all right, then," he added.

" Yes. Looks like it, certainly. They're ever such nice old girls."

The surging spirits of Marion and Bella, who were at this moment gazing at their treasure's handiwork in the kitchen, might have been a little curbed had they known that they were being called " old girls," in the street outside to a strange young man.

" An' it looks as though they like me, too," she added, brightly though modestly.

" You ain't half a good little girl, ain't you, Jen," said Tom, quietly, and with the minutest pinch of sarcasm in his voice.

" What do you mean by that ?" she returned, in the same light spirit.

" Oh—nothin'."

And actually Tom did not quite know what he had meant. All the same there were worlds of significance behind the remark, and the way in which he had uttered it. It was, in fact, a perfect expression of the peculiarly insidious and tricky quality of her character.

She was as unaware as himself of anything having come to light like this, and went on cheerfully.

" Oo—and he isn't half a funny old Boy, either," she said. " All with a grey beard, like Bernard Shaw."

All wearers of beards, young or old, in Jenny's blithe classification, resembled Bernard Shaw.

" He's ever such a fine looking old chap, though," she added. " I like him."

Tom now brought up the question of how they were going to dispose of the evening.

" Well," said Jenny, in a kind of naïve, detached tone, which habitually crept in when she was about to seek favours. " I feel I could do with a little something to eat."

This was all against the notions of Tom, who longed to take her to the pictures. At the pictures Jenny softened, and allowed him to hold her hand.

" Oh," he said. " I thought we might go to the pictures."

" Well—we could go to the pictures after—if you liked."

Tom thought painfully of the expense involved by this double programme. His salary, which was three pounds ten a week, had once resembled great riches, but now it was but a despicable little army of funds wherewith to pursue his present campaign. But as in bodily disease a man will spend all the money he has to work a cure, regarding health as a thing transcending base economy, so Tom poured out all he had for the sake of love. He had become, in fact, a pastmaster in the art of spending money he did not have. All the same, he was not going to give in without a struggle.

" It'd be too late for the Pictures—wouldn't it ?" he said.

" Not for the Big picture," said Jenny, and there was no further appeal.

They therefore made their way to the Lyons in the High Road. This had lately been enlarged and refurbished in the modern manner, with a large show window piled with gelatinous sweets, a soda fountain, and white glazed tiles in the ceiling.

To Jenny these Lyons' establishments were almost as great a pleasure as the pictures. They appeased her social cravings, they provided her with entertainment (she was enormously interested in people), and what was more they furnished a setting for herself. Indeed she was something of a Langtry in these places, her extraordinary prettiness never failing to excite glances, stares, and all manner of looks, furtive and admiring, or gallant and lighthearted, from the rather pawky young men of the district. With her usual gift for pleasing at first sight she was always on delightful terms of friendship with the staff, with whom she conversed agreeably in their slack moments. Having given her order she would look around her with the air of one definitely alive. She missed nothing, and the assortment around her of " old boys " and " old girls," whose clothes and features were singled out for her satire and ridicule, filled the conversation to the exclusion of almost all else.

She knew her way extremely well about the menu, and was in the habit of demanding rather outlandish dishes unknown to customers with less initiative. But to-night she was frustrated by the majority of these being " off," and so made do with two fillets of fish, and fried potatoes—that is to say, " chips." But she did not call them " chips," for there was much that was genteel in Jenny. Tom made do with a cup of coffee.

" I love you, Jen—that's what's the matter with me," said Tom, when the food had come, and he was watching her delicate little teeth at work upon it.

" Don't be so silly, Tom," she said, looking modestly at her plate. She naturally felt that it was rather inconsiderate to go on calmly filling her face after such a declaration, but common sense protested that there was no earthly use in stopping. So she continued to lift her fork to her mouth, though in a rather wriggling and self-effacing way.

" Don't look," she said, suddenly bending forward with a sly glance.

" What ? "

" There's ever such a funny old thing sitting behind you. Don't look."

The admonition not to look was of course an irresistible temptation (after a methodic pause) by degrees and unconcernedly to turn the head, and in this way the attention was diverted from the problem of unrequited love.

The rest of the meal was largely a repetition of this, there being many other unconscious (and indeed conscious) objects of derision or flippant criticism within the restaurant, which catered for the sad and failing income.

After a roll and butter and some St. Ivel cheese, which Jenny again, in a naïve abstract spirit, " thought " she would have, she had finished. They rose and went to the door.

In their journey from the table to the door Jenny said nothing about Turkish Delight. In fact, she was scrupulously careful not even to *look* Turkish Delight—possibly too careful. At any rate, in Tom's imagination, it seemed that if he did not get Turkish Delight the entire evening was endangered. For it was an axiom that, amid all the varied delights that generous nature showered, to Turkish Delight Jenny was most consistently faithful.

He therefore purchased Turkish Delight with the money he did not have, and they went out into the air. They had decided upon a small picture house in the neighbourhood of Camden Town, and they boarded a 'bus to take them there. She was very cheerful upon the 'bus—already allowing him to hold her hand, and even returning his pressures and intertwining her fingers with his. Turkish Delight after food was to Jenny like a cigar crowning a banquet ; and she seldom failed to mellow under its influence.

Most of it, however, was held over until they were in the cinema. Then, all at once, a delicious, almost salacious little rattle took place in the darkness, and Tom knew that she had begun. The bag was passed to him, but he fortunately desired only one lump, and said as much. Apart from this Jenny despatched a quarter of a pound in the same fraction of an hour. A pound an hour was Jenny's usual speed with Turkish Delight.

They were in the shilling seats, and as she had foreseen they were just in time for the Big picture. As far as Jenny was concerned, sensuousness advanced little beyond the realms of Turkish Delight during the showing of this, though she still allowed him to hold her hand. She concentrated fully upon the pictures; he thought only of herself and her hand. She did not as a rule like being "touched." But an exception was always made at the pictures, and he was happy because, though she in no way surrendered to him, she was placid and acquiescent. Her attention being elsewhere, she did not speak, and so could not contradict or damp him. Accordingly he was beguiled into a state of mind wherein he could almost imagine that she was his own, and that the cold world was paradise.

How erroneous such a state of mind was became clear enough when the show was over and they were out in the chilly street. She set out at a brisk pace towards her home, to which he was accorded the brief privilege of escorting her. Panic seized him. He had to make use of this period to wrangle with her about when he was going to see her next—a matter upon which she was always very arbitrary and doubtful.

To-night he managed to exact a promise from her that she would meet him to-morrow evening—that was if he did not mind her coming an hour later and bringing with her Violet, a friend of hers known to him, whom she was meeting first.

"Well," she said, as they came into sight of the corner at which she always made him leave her. "That's been a very enjoyable evening." She slackened her pace relentlessly.

She never failed to express her gratitude in this way, but it did not in the slightest manner appease him. His sole thought was to sidle her up against the railings and delay her with words of love.

He generally managed to achieve this. She looked along the street as he spoke soft, burning words, and passers-by imagined that they were lovers.

To-night, much as usual, she promised him a kiss if he in his turn would guarantee to "go after it." He agreed, and she at once disconcertingly forced the pace by putting up her face. She gave him quite good measure while it lasted. Then, with a cool "So long, then," she left him.

As he walked away it was as clear as day that she had no use in the world for him. He had brought off nothing: got not an inch further with her. The evening had cost him, altogether, five shillings and threepence—a soul-searing sum. He was wretchedly unhappy but could lodge no specific complaint against her.

Throughout the whole evening she had merely been perfectly herself.

Tom had a long walk back, but Jenny only a few paces to go. She lived with some people called Molden, who occupied rooms above the pet animal shop she had spoken of, in a little street branching off Park Street. Both street and shop were in an equally dejected and decayed state. The shop sported a large sign outside, which, with the aid of cages and bowls containing living captive things brought out into the front in the day time, served to attract the attention of the populace in Park Street itself. Nevertheless it remained an enigma how Mr. Jefferies, the proprietor, contrived to keep either himself or his animals alive. No light was thrown upon the miracle by Mr. Jefferies himself, who had given up marvelling, talking to his fellow beings, and shaving regularly. The animals were brought in at night time, and huddled into a confined space, wherein they formed a perplexed company—a number of canaries, rabbits, parrots, guinea-pigs, lizards and goldfish being left alone, throughout the still hours of the night, in the presence of the mystery of their unnatural contiguity and without clue to the obscure part they played in Mr. Jefferies' and cosmic existence.

Jenny was in no way related to the Moldens. She had been a close friend of Ada Molden, the daughter, and she now stayed with them. Her mother had died when she was fourteen, and she had first of all lived with her uncle and aunt—the Taylors. The Taylors were a slovenly pair, whose quarrels were a theme in the neighbourhood, and her sojourn with them had never been a success. So soon as she had obtained work in the factory she had begun to drift away from them, gaining new friends, new ideas, and new tastes in a slightly higher though more flashy stratum of Camden Town society. Finally there was an outburst in which Jenny was arraigned for being " above herself," and imagining herself " too good for them." Peaceful relations were resumed, but when a little later Jenny had suggested going to live with Ada Molden, with whom at that time she was thicker than ever before or afterwards, they raised no objection and were indeed glad to be rid of her. Occasionally she visited them, but this was becoming rarer and rarer, and otherwise she had dropped completely out of their lives. She appeared in fine raiment when she did appear, and when she had gone they forebode darkly of her future.

She paid the Moldens a portion of her weekly salary in return for odd meals and a room at the top of the house. Ada, not long ago, had departed, but Jenny stayed on. Ada had gone into service in Cheltenham, whence she wrote glowing accounts of her life to Jenny.

The Moldens' door was closed when she came in to-night, and she went straight up to her room.

Jenny's room was barely furnished with a small bed, a few mats, a deal chest of drawers with a mirror, and a washing stand. Bare and chill as it was, it was her nest, enclosing her virginal plots and secrets.

There were no pictures on the walls save one—a portrait of Rudolph Valentino taken from a picture magazine and stuck to the wall with a single drawing pin. The charmer's drooping lids and sensuously ominous gaze followed her around the room; but it was impossible to conjecture in what frame of mind she had put this up, and for the rest the room was singularly characterless.

It is doubtful whether Jenny could be said to be the owner either of a character or conscience. Though not frequently inspired with true generosity, she had no active evil in her soul, and her gift of pleasing was as yet an invaluable discipline upon her conduct. It often happens that to make people good it is advisable not to tell them to be good, but to tell them that they are good. If Jenny desired to continue pleasing (and she desired) this keenly, since pleasing people was by now almost her hobby, she had to live up to her reputation. Many people, particularly women, believed her to be the epitome of unselfishness, sweetness, and modesty.

All the same, these virtues were imposed from without rather than flowing naturally from within, and Jenny was, in fact, beginning to find their exactions a little confining. Also the unreliable nature of this self-imposed discipline was revealed by its complete disappearance when for some reason she no longer desired to please, or found herself able to please by merely existing in any state, as in the case of Tom.

But such people as Tom were exceptions, and to the rest of the world she was as good as her word. As she undressed to-night Tom had vanished from her mind (he had very little place in it at any time) and she was thinking solely of her new employment.

If Marion and Bella had been able to get inside her mind at this moment, they might have found much to surprise and alarm them, but search as they might they would have been unable to come across the minutest resemblance of dishonesty in her attitude and intentions towards them. They thought her a treasure; and that was the impression she had laboured with all her might to give. But that did not mean that she did not propose being a treasure. She had been acting a part, certainly but it was a part she fully intended to go on acting, and so, in reality, to live.

There was perhaps even a touch of chivalry in her feelings towards them. Like most apparently simple-minded people, Jenny had, in her heart, a perfect apprehension of the subtleties of situation and character, and it had not taken her long to realize that the old people were indeed old, and being weak and ill, were neurotically anxious to retain and placate a decent servant. She therefore saw that no really rigid discipline could ever be exercised over her: that she had, on the whole, the upper hand already; and that it would be in her power to " take advantage," if she cared.

But this flattering knowledge of power filled Jenny merely with a warmth of heart, and a serene resolution to give full measure in return for her board and wages. The evening, in fact, presented to her mind exactly the same flawless pattern it had presented to Marion and Bella: and, having snuffed out her candle, she in two minutes relapsed sweetly into oblivion of those two, Tom, all-surrounding London, the far-stretching and unknown future, the entire world and its temptations.

*       *       *       *

At half-past eight to the moment next morning, another just audible knock upon the front door proclaimed to Marion and Bella that last night had been no dream, and that the delightful turn of events set in motion then was to survive and continue in the sober light of day.

It was, all the same, day time, and the atmosphere was charged less with emotion as Marion came down and let Jenny in. After an affable but curtailed greeting, for she was in her dressing gown and the passage was cold, Marion went up to her room again. Jenny went straight through into the kitchen, and in two minutes' time the day's work was in normal progress. An hour later breakfast was ready.

Breakfast, to Marion and Bella, was a critical and dangerous period. If it passed off well there were some hopes of a reasonably cheerful day ahead, but if the opposite was the case things generally went from bad to worse. As at all other times of the day the nerves of both were agonizingly on edge, but the greatest weight rested upon Marion, who suffered from insomnia. Silence and heroism did not alter this fact, and there are many subtle methods of self-expression open to the stoic.

In fact, it would not be much of an exaggeration to say that at moments Bella suffered from Marion's insomnia almost as much as Marion, and that there were certain breakfast times when she would have given a great deal to have slept badly herself. Disconcertingly in this respect, she invariably slept like a log.

" Well—what sort of a night ? . . ." was Bella's first and necessary query each morning, as Marion handed her her tea : and though she did not show it, she waited with racked apprehension for the reply.

Because she did all the work and was responsible for the running of the house, Marion was at times inclined to snub and intimidate her foolish and impractical sister, adopting towards her something of the attitude of a nursemaid with her charge, and being goaded into administering little mental smackings from time to time.

If there were any smackings coming, this question about sleep was the habitual opening for them. If Marion was not in a good temper, a deep breath and suffering expression, signifying that she was not likely to survive the day on her feet, would be her only reply.

This placed Bella in a miserable pass. If she suspected Marion of exaggeration, it was impossible to voice that suspicion : and if Marion had indeed slept as badly as she had indicated, the

suffering expression was natural enough. She was in the hideous
predicament of having to try and assess the real amount of
insomnia endured by Marion and diagnose whether it was in
fair proportion to the petulance displayed. But as there is no
conceivable criterion of pain, and degrees of which can be
estimated only personally and arbitrarily by the sufferer, Bella
was hopelessly nettled, and at Marion's mercy.

Her only means of defence, indeed, was an attack of her own.
And she had, of late, years, when occasion or temperament
called for it, taken to going into the enemy's camp of a morning
with a Strange Weight on the Head. As a rival to insomnia, this
Strange Weight never quite came off, but it was at any rate some
sort of reprisal. Marion had perforce to show outward deference
to the visitations of the weight, and was inwardly driven mad
(as Bella with the insomnia) by being hopelessly in the dark as to
how strange, and how heavy it was in comparison to Bella's
despondency.

All this does not mean that Marion did not sleep badly, or
that Bella did not suffer in her head : it merely was that neither
knew quite how far the other was playing the game according
to the rules. The trouble with both was that they never had a
resounding quarrel and made peace afterwards ; but went on
year after year, and day after day, and hour after hour, in their
tardy progress to the grave, adjusting their little differences in
this petty manner. They differed neither in their habits nor on
any larger issue, and when they woke up each morning they
bore no grudge and were perfectly unaware that anything but
perfect harmony was to ensue. They were merely on each other's
nerves.

This morning, however, the sun shone, and there was a new
servant to divert the mind from malady and counter-malady.
Marion was down first, and Bella followed just as the girl was
coming in with the tea.

" Good-morning, madam," she said, with her bright, warm
smile, and in the clear light of day Bella perceived the same
brilliant paragon that had dawned upon her life last night—the
same neatness, air of competence, ravishing prettiness, humility
and cheerfulness.

And Jenny, in her soul, was, and felt the same. That she had, since she last saw them, substantiated with living deeds and flesh-and-blood reality that fugitive conception of their treasure's life apart which had visited Marion and Bella last night as they heard her going down the street and away from them : that she had been taken and fed by her frantic adorer : that she had freely alluded to both those in the room with her now as " old girls," and the masculine god upstairs as a " funny old boy " : that the omelette-maker had partaken of crude quantities of Turkish Delight in the cinema—all these things were of no account, had already been dispelled for ever, like the night itself, in the sober propriety and business of the morning.

" Good-morning, Jenny," Bella returned.    " Colder this morning, isn't it ?"

" Yes, madam," said Jenny.    " I'm afraid we've seen the last of the warm weather now."

And having gracefully fixed the cosy well over the pot, she slid erectly from the room.

" Such an *old-fashioned* little thing !" murmured Bella, in the tone of sheer incredulousness she had employed ever since yesterday evening, and then she put the fatal question about sleep.

To her joy Marion conceded that she could not complain. In these pleasant circumstances no enquiry was made, nor testimony furnished, concerning the Strange Weight, and they went on to consume their food practically without speaking.

But now it was Marion's turn to suffer.    At this period she gritted her teeth for what was perhaps the main ordeal of her day—Bella's " eating."

At what period Bella's eating had begun slowly to take on its present intolerable character, or at which period Marion's nerves had at first become aware of what was taking place, it was impossible to say.    Now it was beyond remedy, and Bella seemed to go from bad to worse.

It was too horrible for words.    She clattered : she licked : she smacked.    She seemed to lean over her plate with a peculiar gloating and concentrated expression : she savoured all with senile relish of its succulence : she gathered in the remotest morsels and made no pause : she was unaware that aught was amiss.    Electric drills, rending glass, screams of burning victims —none of these could have so pierced and torn at Marion's

sensibilities as those little sharp sounds, not so loud as the
chirrup of a sparrow, coming across the dining-room table three
times a day. And never, never could she protest, or " say "
anything. For some reason this matter was sacred to the unconscious perpetrator, and to remark upon it, with whatever subtlety
or diplomacy, would be to commit a blushing and unforgettable
affront, and violate the inner sanctuaries of personal pride.

Breakfast over, another torment impended—this time one
which they shared equally. It was now necessary to decide what
they were going to have for lunch.

Since they had only this moment finished breakfast, and were
filled out and weighed down with the load of that repast, there
could have been no more perfectly loathsome moment to set
aside for grappling with this theme. Nevertheless, experience
had never taught them to arrange things otherwise.

Marion always complained of Bella that she never " helped."
But why should she help ? So far as she knew at present, she
never intended to eat again. After seventy-eight years' eating
experience, she was once more disillusioned by food.

Marion, if the truth were known, was in like case, and she
generally ended by enlisting the aid of the servant, in the hope
that the latter had not overeaten herself, and might be in a
condition sincerely to exercise her critical and selective faculties.

Accordingly, when Jenny came in, Marion asked her what
she thought might be nice for lunch.

Jenny, who was also full to the brim, paused and replied
" Well—there were a lot of things, weren't there ?"—and added
that calves' liver and bacon made " a very nice change." Jenny
conceived of food almost exclusively in terms of mutation.

As this dish had not been seen or smelt in the house for a long
time, and so carried no near memories wherewith to make more
wan the wan imagination, it was instantly acclaimed as an
excellent idea.

" Yes. I think that would be very nice," said Marion, and
Bella was even more enthusiastic. And, to look at them and hear
them, an illusion was created that the insides of all three were
not doing what actually they were doing—turning over in
nauseated repugnance at the thought of one o'clock.

They then got ready for shopping.

Before they got out there was a great deal of losing, and running up, and finding and shouting down, and general commerce from room to room, but at last they were in the hallway putting on their gloves and taking their last apprehensive survey of things before departure.

Then the front door closed, and Jenny realized that she was alone in the house. She then realized that she was not alone, of course, for the Doctor was upstairs wrapped in mystery. Jenny did not quite know how she stood in regard to him. " Then, of course, the Doctor's always upstairs in his room," Marion had said, with a rather ambiguous glance, while giving her instructions on another head, and Jenny did not fully understand whether she was looking after him or he was looking after her—which was supposed to be likely to get into mischief.

It mattered not to Jenny, who had weighty work on hand—that is not to say weighty in the figurative sense of the term—but work which involved hauling out mighty bedsteads so as to get round and make the bed, dragging out monstrous furniture so as to dust behind it, emptying vast Edwardian basins of their brimming soap-grey lakes, lifting enormous and replenished jugs and lowering them at arm's length slowly lest they smashed the massive crockery, transporting wabbling pails, as heavy as children but not so tractable, down stairs and along passages, and carrying piled trays about in a world wherein practically everything was breakable, and only terrific muscular exertion and an agonized striving after balance could avert the impending crash—in brief, " woman's work."

All these activities were subject to incessant interruptions from the bell below, which exacted immediate and breathless attention, whatever was taking place. When Marion and Bella returned, which was at about half-past eleven, Jenny was nowhere near the end of her work. And by twelve o'clock it was time to think about lunch.

For while all this was taking place, the gastric juices within, unknown and in secret but just as busily, had been at their unending toil of assimilating what had come their way in the body, which now worked yet another change of opinion in the mind, which now perceived that lunch, after all, was a credible occurrence in the future. If only the gastric juices had not done this there would have been no trouble—no deciding, no shopping, no tradesmen, no cooking, no digestion, no indigestion —in fact no bother whatever in the long run, since the old ladies would have starved and so achieved the only thing they really in their heart of hearts desired to achieve—death. But there is no controlling or stopping gastric juices.

Jenny did wonders with the calves' liver and bacon—the Doctor making his pilgrimage downstairs in order to partake of it. Then, as usual, each departed to sleep in private; and Jenny, having washed up the lunch things, spent the afternoon clearing out and making ready the room at the top of the house which she would occupy to-morrow.

She then made tea for them, and afterwards Marion sent her out to do some odd shopping. She was out about three-quarters of an hour, and when she came back she knocked softly upon the door. It was just on six (the same time as that at which she had arrived last night) and Bella, in the same manner, rose from her chair and let her in.

In this way the wheel of day and night had, uneventfully and insensibly, completed a single revolution, and now appeared to be running smoothly. Jenny was less of a ravishing stranger, more of an ordinary servant. A perfect joy, a treasure, a paragon but all the same it was becoming less impossible for the mind to divert to other mundane matters.

As for supper, how could one do better than another omelette ? It had really been such a treat last night. Jenny did another.

It was again perfection, though of course it had not just that added gusto of novelty which distinguished it last night, and Marion did not see fit to yield any further instalment of Praise from the store she so zealously hoarded for use on more appropriate occasions.

Jenny, it was noticed (but not openly remarked), did not take quite so long over her washing-up as she had taken last night : but then supper had come in a little later. She entered the dining-room, as she had done last night, to pay her respects before going. She did not look exactly the same as she looked last night, but she was not a whit less affable and respectful.

" Good-night, then, madam."

" Good-night, Jenny."

" Good-night, madam."

And she was gone. Wherein, exactly, her appearance to-night differed from her appearance last night, they were unable at first to fix in their minds ; and Bella, oddly enough, was the first to tumble to it.

" Makes up, of course," said Bella.

" Yes," said Marion. " I noticed that." And there was a pause.

" But then they all do, nowadays," added Marion, and Bella agreed without hesitation.

" *Including absolutely perfect treasures ?*" was the sudden query which leaped up in the minds of both old ladies. But it was not voiced, and fled instantly away.

## II

## A GLASS OF PORT

JENNY had been fully aware that her face was made up a little more lavishly than it was last night, and she had purposely let it be seen. It was necessary, sooner or later, to break them in to the fact that she did make up. She saw no sin in the use of cosmetics, and she doubted whether they did. Marion's rather disparaging " They all do nowadays," however, did not convey Jenny's way of looking at the matter. As Jenny saw it, it was " the fashion," and she suspected the old ladies, 'n their suburban retreat, of being " old-fashioned." Such was her calm estimate, and Marion and Bella would have been surprised if they could have realized that she had in this manner coolly turned the tables on them.

In Jenny's mind, there were, of course, degrees and varieties of the practice. There was a great difference between being " made up " and being " dolled up," and it was possible to be

made up in a " common " way.  Jenny tolerated nothing even
savouring of the " common."

When Tom, last night, had asked Jenny whether he might
have her company for to-night, she had at last consented provided she arrived an hour late, bringing with her her friend
Violet, whom she was meeting at Hammersmith.  She was
therefore now on her way to the Broadway.

That Jenny should have bothered little about her make-up
when meeting Tom, but have taken some pains in the case of
Violet, was an apparent contradiction of feminine tendency.
The explanation was to be found in the character of Violet herself.
Violet was always made up to the nines, and she expected the
same thing from her friends.

Actually Jenny had some doubts as to the wisdom of coming
out with Violet to-night, and, indeed, of continuing the friendship at all.  To begin with Violet was a perfect example of one
beyond all dispute " common."  Jenny had first become
acquainted with her at the factory, whence, in Jenny's time, she
had been dismissed for impudence to her immediate superior.
She was a violent, frank, disconcertingly outspoken girl,
obsessed by one topic alone—Boys.  By these she contrived not
to be entirely neglected, less by virtue of her appearance (her
face, though painted and powdered, was quite hideous) than
by sheer high spirits, personality, cheerfulness, and the practice
of raillery.  She acted, indeed, as a tonic upon those who had
the nerves to stand her, and if you shared her enthusiasm for
Boys, there was no reason why you should not hit it off very
well with her, for she had great experience, method, and initiative in that matter.

In Jenny's mentality, however, Boys were relegated to a much
more reasonable and proportionate niche, and she had long ago
decided, for her own good, to " give Violet up."  Whatever
might have taken place in the past, Violet was certainly not the
sort of friend she desired now in her new employment.

Jenny told herself, in fact, that she would not be meeting
Violet to-night had that employment properly begun.  But it
did not properly begin until to-morrow, Saturday, when she
was to sleep in.  So long as she was sleeping out, she felt, she
yet belonged to the world outside, and might, without damage

to her conscience, have final commerce with associations and things that were, before definitely launching upon the things that were to be.

Violet's faults did not embrace unpunctuality—she was much too anxious to be out on any sort of spree to be a moment late for it—and when Jenny came in to the Arcade entrance to Hammersmith Underground Station, where they had arranged to meet, she was already standing there.

Jenny had not seen her friend for a few months, and she was not prepared for what she now witnessed. " Common," she had always known Violet to be. But to-night, so it seemed, she was more than common. Jenny was not certain that she was not " glaring "—the final epithet of impeachment in Jenny's genteel vocabulary.

Violet was in a black lustre coat : she wore cheap, gaudy silk stockings of a reddish-brown colour, a small black hat and a skirt up to her knees. Her face, with its long nose, resembled rich confectionery.

Quite unaware of the impression she gave, she welcomed Jenny with fervour, and affably comparing notes as to how each had got there, they wandered aimlessly up in the direction of Baron's Court, where the crowd was less dense.

But it did not take long for Violet to abandon small talk and enter upon the theme which dominated her.

" Well—I don't know why we're walkin' up here," she said. " There's no Boys up this end."

Subtlety, or a delicate sense of approach, were means unknown to Violet. This announcement rendered transparent at once her unambiguous conception of the evening they were to spend.

" Ain't there ?" was all Jenny was able to reply.

" No. They don't come up this way," said Violet, with the kindly, shrewd air of an old campaigner in this particular neighbourhood. " Let's go back."

And they turned round.

Jenny was filled with shame for her friend, and reproach against herself for having allowed this meeting to come to pass. But she knew how impossible it was to convey her feelings to the inno- cent and cheerful Violet, and so she tried to change the subject.

" That's a nice brooch you got in your hat, Vi," she said. " I ain't seen that before."

" Yes, it is nice, ain't it ?" said Violet. " A Boy gave it to me."

Thus Jenny's lead was serenely countered, and there was another silence as they walked along.

" By the way," said Violet, " What's happened to that pale Boy you was walkin' out with ?"

Violet never minced matters. A pale boy to her was a pale boy.

" What pale boy ?" said Jenny. " Who do you mean ?"

" You know," said Violet. " That pale boy."

And Jenny did know. Violet meant Tom. But there could be few things more perfectly calculated to throw a proud young girl out of countenance than the bland allegation that she is walking out with a pale boy, and Jenny was exasperated with Violet for dragging her into this despicably " common " topic, and forcing her to defend herself.

" No," said Jenny, persistently. " What pale boy ?"

" You know," returned Violet. " That *pale* boy."

She seemed to think that the more she underlined his pallor, the easier it would be for Jenny to identify him. But actually this was aggravating the affront.

" You don't mean *Tom*, do you," said Jenny. " By any chance ?"

" That's the Boy," said Violet. " Tom."

" What !" cried Jenny. " Me walking out with Tom ! I should like to see myself."

" Oh, I thought perhaps you might be. I knew you went about with him."

" Well, I might go about with him sometimes," Jenny allowed. " But that ain't walkin' out."

Their idiom required no further comment to illustrate the vast distance between these two procedures, and Violet said she was sorry for making the mistake.

" He's in consumption, ain't he ?" she casually added.

" What ? Tom in consumption ? I've never heard of it. Who told you that ?"

" Oh, I may be wrong," said Violet. " I thought I heard he was inclined that way, though. He looks it, anyway."

It was typical of Violet to throw out a fantastic rumour in this inconsequent way, and Jenny knew that she was talking nonsense. All the same, she did briefly wonder whether Tom's ill look derived from unsuspected disease. Also she began to wonder how she was to explain to Violet that she had already arranged to meet the pale boy himself to-night. In fact she was trying to think of some excuse whereby she could get away without telling her at all, when Violet cut into her thoughts.

"I know those two," she said suddenly, having turned her head round in continuation of a self-conscious and mocking glance she had bestowed upon a passing couple. "But they ain't no good. Specially that soppy one with a moustache."

"That so?" was all Jenny could say, and there was another silence.

All at once Violet cheerfully espied a fresh problem.

"Do you like moustaches on Boys?" she said. "Some girls don't."

*Moustaches on Boys!* Really, Violet was nauseating.

"I don't know anything about 'em," said Jenny.

"I like 'em myself," said Violet. "So long as they're not too Prickly."

*Prickly!* This was really intolerable. Jenny felt she must make some sort of stand about it.

"Well, where are we goin', Vi," she said. "We don't seem to be movin' nowhere at present."

"Going? Where d'you want to go, then, Jen?"

"Well, I thought we might go an' have a cup of coffee at Lyons or something."

A puzzled look came over Violet's face.

"What—do you want to go into Lyons, Jen?"

"Yes. Why not?"

"Go on," said Violet. "You don't want to go stuffin' yourself up in Lyons a lovely fine night like this. You want to get the air while you can."

This deceitful and transparent attempt to identify herself with the cause of pure hygiene would have beguiled not a soul in the world. Environed by Boys, the depths of the Black Hole of Calcutta would have awakened few misgivings in Violet.

" I'll tell you what your trouble is, Vi," said Jenny. " You can't think of nothing but boys."

" Oo—Jenny, what a thing and a half to say ! I never think about them."

" Yes, you do. You know you do."

" No, I don't. And you ain't the one to talk, anyway."

" What do you mean ?"

" Well, other girls ain't got much chance with you hangin' around."

" What do you mean ?" said Jenny.

" If I had a part of *your* looks," continued Violet. " I shouldn't be worrying."

" Don't be so silly," said Jenny. " You're pretty enough yourself, ain't you ?"

" No I ain't," said Violet. " I'm as ugly as the devil. It's a wonder what I do—with what I got to work on."

In her odd way she had hit the nail on the head.

" Don't be so silly," said Jenny.

" But you're different. You're lovely. You're as pretty as a Picture. Yes you are. You're a real *Picture.*"

There returned to Jenny a glimmering of what she had once had in common with Violet.

" Come on, Vi," she said, cajolingly. " Let's go to Lyons."

" Well, what's the sense of going to Lyons," said Violet, " if you can get taken ?"

" You mean you want to get off ?"

" No. I don't want to get off. But you never know what might happen."

" Well, I don't want to. It's too near where I Am."

" What's the matter with that ?"

" Well—I might be seen. And in any case I don't want to."

" Come on, Jen. Let's hang about a bit," said Violet, and at this moment a startling thing occurred.

" *Pardonnay mwa* !" came a masculine voice from behind, and they turned round.

" My word !" said Violet. " You didn't half give me a turn."

\*        \*        \*        \*

Jenny and Violet confronted two figures. One seemed little more than a perky boy of about nineteen ; the other was a fully grown man of stunted stature. The boy's gawky and countrified figure was garbed in a blue suit of navy serge surmounted by a double-breasted blue overcoat : he wore a trilby hat (which was at the moment still held humorously in the air in Gallic manner after his " Pardonnay-mwa ") ; his complexion was red and fresh, his eyes were blue, and though he was neat and clean he obviously had no pretensions as regards style.

His companion presented a completely different picture. Over thirty, and resembling, in his wan face, gait, and figure, a dismissed stable-boy, he was yet dressed in obedience to the highest and latest caprices of Hammersmith mode. A light brown overcoat of velvety material (taken well in at the waist and prodigiously buttoned and banded) matched a brown hat, a brown suit, and brown shoes, and was set off by a brilliant white knitted scarf, which poured like a waterfall down from his chin, and which he kept on touching and adjusting in a self-conscious manner. In this waterfall his chin like a rock was permanently embedded ; since he did not shift it even when he turned to speak, but reared his shoulders round in a choked way, and gave a sidelong glance. But then he spoke very little ; indeed he quite evidently took pride in taciturnity and pithiness. Also his companion did all the talking that was necessary and more.

The latter now followed up his opening with " Was you going anywhere by any chance ?" and an awkward grin. His gusto and diffidence were at present at strife inwardly with each other.

" No—we ain't goin' nowhere," said Violet. " Are you ?"

" No. I ain't. Ain't I met you before somewhere ?"

" Can't say I remember it," said Violet, fully mistress of the situation. " Glad to meet you, though. Meet my friend."

" Good-evening."

" Good-evening," said Jenny, smiling as pleasantly as her feelings allowed.

" And meet *my* chum. Andy's 'is name."

" Good-evening, Andy," said Violet, smiling brightly upon him. His age and weedy appearance were nothing to Violet, who had, in this respect, a heart like that of a Madonna, in whose broad and undistinguishing robe all of his sex, whatever their age or uncouthness, might find welcome and shelter simply as " boys."

Andy, however, merely gave a brief smile and nod, and then looked away at the traffic and twitched the waterfall. This made things rather awkward for everybody concerned, for it looked as though he took no interest in the proceedings at all, and was inclined to be rude. There was a pause.

" And mine's Reginald," said his junior. " Commonly known as Rex."

"Good-evening Rex," said Violet, and there was another pause.

" Well, what do you two girls say to a little liquid refreshment ?" suggested Rex, rubbing his hands together.

" All for it," said Violet. " Where do you suggest ?"

" Well, what's wrong with the King's Head down here, where we can sit down ?"

" Well, I don't mind," said Violet. " Don't know about my friend, though."

" Go on ? She doesn't mind a pub, does she ?"

" I think she's a teetotaller—ain't you, Jen ?"

" Go on ?" said Rex.

" Don't be so silly, Vi," said Jenny. " Of course I ain't." And she blushed.

" Well, that's a blessing," said Rex. " You nearly gave me heart failure."

There was general laughter at this and the four began to walk in the direction he had indicated. But inwardly Jenny was resolving that this was the last time she came out with Violet. She would never forgive her for letting her into this scandalous escapade. Going into a Hammersmith " pub " with a painted thing like Violet and two casual " pick-ups " ! She was too flabbergasted at the moment to think of an excuse to get away, but that she was going to get away, and that in time to meet Tom in three-quarters of an hour's time at Camden Town, as she had arranged, was clear in her mind.

It was impossible to walk four abreast on the crowded pavement, and Jenny found herself alongside Andy in the throng, with Violet and the other talking busily ahead. She had no intention of being the first to speak, and neither had he, apparently. Fortunately, however, they reached the King's Head in less than a minute.

This was a large and respectable house in the most crowded section of King Street. They went through a door marked " Saloon Lounge " into a spacious room with chocolate-coloured wood panelling, and copper-covered tables all round. There was a bar at one end, and one or two shining specimens of old-time armour in the corners. It was fully and brilliantly lit, though it was not yet completely dark outside and few of the tables were engaged.

" This is ever such a nice place," said Violet, as they sat down, and Jenny herself was agreeably surprised. In point of fact, and although in her present company this would have been the last thing she would have openly granted, she was impressed. The truth was that she had never been in a public house in her life before, and she had a preconceived horror of them derived from glimpses of habitués lurching from low-class bars into the street. She was aware, however, that " times were changed," and that many of her more " common " and " fast " acquaintances frequented them regularly with their boy friends : and now that she saw this spacious, clean, and well-ordered lounge she felt that she might very soon have to re-adjust her views herself. All the same, she would have much preferred a Lyons.

" Well," said Rex. " What are you takin' ? "

Here, for Jenny, was a quandary. She knew as little about alcoholic drinks as she did about public houses. At Christmas times she had had sherry and white wine, and once or twice she had partaken of a glass of Guinness in sedate company. She thought she had better ask for a Guinness now. Guinness she knew to be " the ladies' drink," a fair compromise with the devil, a legitimate " pick-me-up." Even Doctors advised a Guinness " now and again." Its prime and avowed object was to " nourish," its accidental operation to intoxicate. But outside the realms of Guinness and festive occasions, Jenny had inherited from her mother what her mother called " a horror of drink." She knew that so soon as a " taste " was acquired, ruin followed in clearly discernible stages. The danger lay in once starting : a single drink had been known to lead to ruin. On the other hand she had no desire to be fanatical, and for one in full control of herself a " nice glass " of something, before or after a meal, could do no harm. She now decided to follow Violet's lead.

" I don't know I'm sure," said Violet. " What are *you* havin' Jenny ?"

" I don't know," said Jenny. " What are you ?"

" Come along now," said Rex. " Make up your minds."

" Well then," said Jenny. " I think I'll have a Guinness."

" What ?" exclaimed Rex, looking at her curiously. " Did I hear you say Guinness ?"

" My word !" said Violet. " You *are* going the pace, aren't you ?"

" Why—what's wrong with Guinness ?" returned Jenny. But, without knowing exactly where her mistake lay, she knew that she had made a *faux-pas*. Here was a fine state of affairs ! The tables were turned, and these " common " people whom she despised, were making herself look cheap ! Her resentment against Violet glowed stronger than ever.

" Well, I'm going to have something shorter," said Violet. " I'm going to have a port."

" Same here," said Rex. " You going to have a port, Andy ?" Andy nodded curtly in the waterfall.

" Sure you won't change your mind," said Rex to Jenny.

" Well, I might have something shorter, then," she said, having quickly perceived that this was the line to take. " Perhaps I will."

The waiter had already appeared.

" Four Ports, Please," said Rex.

" Tens or one and twos ?" asked the waiter, a brief and rather disapproving man.

" One and twos," said Rex. " And you might bring some biscuits." And having thus dominated and dismissed the surly son of toil, he was pleased with himself, and hitched his trousers. He then turned to the ladies with an airy " What was you sayin' ?"

" Wasn't saying anything," said Violet. " This is ever such a nice place, isn't it ?"

" Yes, it ain't bad, is it ?" said Jenny. " Not for Hammersmith."

This was a thrust.

" No. Not for Hammersmith," said Rex, carefully simulating her reserve.

" All got up Historical, ain't it ?" said Violet, looking around with the air of a period-critic.

" Yes," said Jenny. " That's right."

All at once Andy entered the conversation, sudden humour prompting his reserved and enigmatic character.

" When Knights were Bold !" he exclaimed, and embedding his chin even further into the waterfall he shook with a sudden wheezing laughter, which drew hideous and hypnotic attention to the gaps and calamities of his teeth. All the same, they all contrived to surmount his teeth and laugh with him.

" More likely they were bowled over !" said Rex, and amid further laughter the drinks arrived and there was an air of release.

" Well—here's wishing you," said Rex, holding up his glass, and they all took a sip.

" We're goin' on to dance after this," he added. " So you'd better not get blotto."

" Oh—are we ?" said Violet. " That's what you says."

" Why—any objections ? "

" No. I ain't any objections."

" Well, I have," said Jenny. " I've got to go."

" You ain't," said Rex. " Don't be so silly."

" Yes, I have. I promised to be in Camden Town by half-past eight."

" You 'ave ?" put in Andy, taking an unforeseen interest in life and her concerns which should have flattered her.

" You ain't, Jenny," said Violet, " 'Ave you ?"

" Yes, I have," said Jenny, firmly. " I'll have to get off direckly I've finished this." She was relieved to have got this out, and had not the slightest intention of changing her mind.

" Don't be so silly, Jenny," said Violet, speaking more earnestly, and sincerely believing that her friend was dissembling in order to get away. " You ain't got to be anywhere."

" Yes, I have. I got to be somewhere at half-past eight."

"Who is it, then?" persisted Violet, by now a little angered, for her own evening was endangered by this backsliding.

But, after what had passed, how could Jenny own up to the pale boy?

"Never you mind," she said.

This convinced Violet for good and all that Jenny was lying.

"Coo," she said. "Some people are funny."

"Yes, they are," returned Jenny, at a loss for a better reply, and there was a very nasty, daggered silence.

Rex, aware of the situation, tried to smooth matters.

"Well, you drink that up and see what you feel like," he said. "We don't like to lose you, you know." He then took out his handkerchief, and loudly blew his nose. "'Scuse my nasal organ," he said. "It's like Charley's Aunt. Know why?"

To this there was no reply.

"I said it's like Charley's Aunt," he said.

"Is it?" said Violet. "Why?"

"Still Runnin'," said Rex, and causing his cheek to protrude with his tongue, he put his handkerchief jauntily away again.

At this vulgarism Violet went off into shrill laughter, and Jenny forced a pale smile : Andy's countenance remained unmoved. Jenny decided that of the two she preferred Andy.

All this time the lounge had been slowly filling with people, and a hum of conversation had come into being all round. Outside in the tram-shaken street Hammersmith roared and swirled on its own furious and meaningless course. As meaningless and obscurely motivated as that crowd and chaos surrounding them were the relationships of these four respectively to each other : yet to the onlooker, who heard them laugh, they gave a perfect impression of unity and exclusiveness, of close friendship even, at any rate of having raised the banner of their common personality against a critical and watchful world. Many glances and stares were excited by Jenny's prettiness and freshness, and the males were envied as if they were her possessors. So erring are the fleeting judgments made in public places.

*        *        *        *

As might have been foreseen, Rex, though fancying Jenny,

naturally paired in conversation with Violet, and soon, while those two bantered each other, Jenny and Andy, who were seated next to each other a little apart from them, were left out in silence. Jenny was quite content that this should be so. She was going to get up and go directly she had finished her port, half of which she had now swallowed. She had her eye on the clock in the distance over the bar. It pointed now, to five to eight. If she left at eight o'clock she would have good time to catch a 'bus and reach Camden Town in time for Tom at half-past eight. She would then make him take her to Lyons, and she would leave him and go to bed directly after. It would be too late to go to the pictures, and she was not going to walk about the streets with Tom all night. She was in a bad temper, and distantly aware that she was going to take it out of Tom.

These ruminations were cut into by Andy, who in perfect silence thrust a beautiful silver cigarette case in front of her. She extracted a cigarette therefrom, and thanked him. She did not in the ordinary way approve of young women smoking in public, which she thought was a way of " making an exhibition," but she was anxious not again to appear unfamiliar with the manners and ways of her present company. " I'll just have time for one," she said, and again looked at the clock.

Andy did not answer this, but again in perfect silence produced a beautiful cigarette lighter, and flicking it neatly open into a flame, held it in front of her cigarette.

" 'Scuse my dirty hands," he said.

" They're not dirty," she said politely.

" You get 'em covered all over with dirt—doing what I've been doing," he added.

She saw plainly enough that this was an invitation to ask him what he had been doing, but was not good-humoured enough to accept it.

" Muckin' about with one's car all the afternoon," he explained, lighting a cigarette of his own.

Jenny started. Had she heard correctly ? Had he not said Car—" one's car ?" Car ? The funny little man didn't have a car. Get away with him.

" Yes, it's a dirty job, I know," she said, as though she had

frequently experienced nausea in the same task. (He probably
worked in a garage, or it was his employer's car.)

"It is and all," he replied. " And it seems my car collects all
the dirt there is in London."

"Have you got a car, then ?" It simply leaped out of her
before she could stop herself.

"Of course I have. What do you think ?"

"Oh—I just wondered. . . ." She blushed again. She
was deeply chagrined by the blush and by herself. She had
allowed him to see that she was hopelessly impressed at his
having a car. It was simply incredible—the way these people,
these base inferiors, were getting the better of her. But could
car-owners be called inferiors ? Perhaps she herself was " out
of it." Perhaps Violet was right, and there was more to this
" getting off " than she had imagined. But how on earth did he
come to have a car ?

" I'm always deciding to get rid of it," he went on. " But
somehow I never bring myself to do it. You get attached to a
thing you've had for a long time, don't you ?"

" Yes," she said. " You do."

Glancing at the clock she saw that it was practically eight
o'clock, and took another sip at her port, judging that she could
finish the rest at one go in a moment, and then depart.

" I could get a good price for it, too," he continued. " There's
an old friend of mine—an old boy I know down at Brighton—
old Major Rogers—he's always wantin' to take it off my hands,
but I'm blessed if I can let it go."

*Major !* What was this ? It was on the tip of her tongue
to say " Do you know a Major, then ?" But luckily she controlled herself in time. An old friend of his ? Things were
going from bad to worse.

" Yes," she said. " One feels like that."

Who the devil did this apeish little man think he was ? If
such a one owned a car and consorted with Majors, what were
the standards of to-day ? She knew how odd the protest was,
coming from one in her own lowly situation, but she was
unable to curb it. Jenny's soul, if she but knew it, was charged
through and through with a vigilant snobbery and awareness
of class, and now it rebelled hotly against so uncouth an off-

shoot of democracy.  One thing she did perceive, however.
He was, though not without delicacy, showing off.  He had the
makings of a " swank-pot."

" Fond of Motoring ?" he asked.

" Yes.  I'm very fond of it, really," she replied.  " 'Specially
in the summer months."

Jenny would have spoken more honestly had she said that she
was fond of the prospect of Motoring in the summer months, for
she had never been in a motor-car in her life.  Hitherto an occasional pillion had formed the sum of her experience in this direction.

" I must take you out," he said.  " One of these fine days."

" I should like to," said Jenny, and there was a silence.

Jenny looked about her, and idly wondering whether she
would really like to go out with Andy in a car, and in what
manner he would behave in such an event, fell into a sort of
dream.  Looking at the clock again, she saw that it was two
minutes past eight—time she finished up her port and went.
Though, of course, she could easily wait until five past, or ten
past, if it came to that.  Strictly speaking she could make it
easily in twenty minutes ;  she had only said she must go at
eight o'clock in order to get away.

She all at once realized that now she was in here, in the warm
fuggy air, she was somewhat loth to move.  The thought of a
'bus ride was like the thought of a cold bath ; physically speaking, she would like to stay on here indefinitely.  Laziness.  Or
was it the port ?  She had heard that drink made you sleepy.
She sipped at it again.

Suddenly Andy drained off his glass, and banged it down on
the table.

" We'll have some more of these," he said.  " Waiter !"

" Here," said Jenny.  " Not for me."

But the waiter was already above them.

" Four more ports, please, waiter," said Andy.

" Four one and twos ?"  The man had vanished.

" I *ain't* goin' to have another," she said.

" Go on," said Andy derisively.

" I *ain't*," she repeated, but all Andy did was to look at her
in a mocking way.

Quite evidently his soul was not ruffled by the slightest

intimation that she was serious, and she did not see what form
of protest she could make against such a glance. In fact, there
was no protest. All she could do now, if she really wished to
go, was to get up and briefly and discourteously depart. But
to one so long and arduously trained in the practice of pleasing
strangers, to one so wary of her genteel dignity, so morbidly
fearful of participating in the minutest dimension of a Scene,
such a line of action was a practical impossibility. It looked as
though she must stay.

Over and above this, however, she found that half of her
honestly desired to stay. As well as the courage, she lacked the
pure inclination to go which she had felt a few moments ago.
A new sensation had replaced it. A permeating coma, a warm
haze of noises and conversation, wrapped her comfortably
around—together with something more. What that something
more was she did not quite know. She sat there and let it flow
through her. It was a glow, and a kind of premonition. It was
certainly a spiritual, but much more emphatically a physical,
premonition of good about to befall. It was like the effect on the
body of good news, without the good news—a delicious short
cut to that inconstant elation which was so arduously won by
virtue from the everyday world. It engendered the desire to
celebrate nothing for no reason.

She asked herself whether this was intoxication. She decided
that at any rate it was a foretaste of it, and in a flash understood
what had been a closed book to her until now—the temptations
and perils of alcohol. She decided that she was growing up—
that yet another of the veiled mysteries of the world had been
illuminated by experience. Experience—that was the thing.
Sitting there, she exulted in experience.

There still remained the problem of whether she would
drink this second port which was coming. She could easily
refuse it and content herself with sitting on in the warmth for a
little. She decided to leave this matter over until it came. It
was now five past eight. She would leave at twenty past. She
reckoned that that would make her only five minutes late for
Tom at the most.

The waiter returned. Andy paid for the drinks and at once
raised his glass. "Well—here we go," he said.

Without thinking Jenny lifted her responding glass along with the others, and drank. The thoughtless and mechanic movement solved her problem for her. Without sophistry of any kind, she now felt herself committed to the whole glass. Two ports !—she was surprised and diverted by her daring. " I shall come to a bad end," was what she very nearly humorously said, but she luckily restrained herself from again betraying her *gaucherie* in this company. And that she lacked tact and experience, that they had slightly the better of her, she was now almost ready to admit. She was now anxious to maintain an equal status rather than a superior eminence.

The fresh round of drinks re-established a communal sense in the four of them.

" Well—what part of the world do you two girls come from ?" asked Rex.

" I live round here," said Violet, and nodding at Jenny added.  " She's over at Chiswick."

" You live at Chiswick ?" said Andy.  " That's where I used to live."

" Well—I shall be shortly," said Jenny.

" Oh yes ?" said Andy, and paused.  " Are you in—er—business over there, then ?"

" No—not exactly in business.  I'm with two old ladies."

Jenny thought this a rather deft escape from the bald acknow-ledgment that she was a humble servant girl.  But Violet had no fear of the truth.

" In other words she's in service," she said.  " I don't know how she sticks it."

" Oh well," said Rex.  " Everyone to their taste."  But Andy gave no sign of what he felt.

Jenny felt that she could have torn Violet's eyes out.  Not only had she taken it on herself to state the unvarnished facts : she had revealed Jenny ignominiously trying to escape from them.

After a pause, the talk circulated again, and before long Andy and Jenny were again left out in silence.  Jenny felt she had lost ground which she could scarcely recover now.  Were they in the right ?  Was there something mean and debasing in being " in service," in being a " skivvy "?  Well—there was in a way :

she knew that. But she was "born to that class," and that was that.

To what class, then, did these three imagine they belonged, that they should look down upon her occupation ? Surely they did not esteem themselves above her : their accents and manners precluded that : and she was the better of Violet any day. But if they were all of the same class, why did she not think as they did ? Suppose she herself was in error. Suppose she had not rightly appraised her own quality ; suppose " skivvys," in the ordinary way, were extracted from a stratum lower than her own ? Suppose she ought to seek, as her due, something better ?

This was a new line of thought—not without allurement. *Ought* she to remain a servant girl ? By merely detachedly propounding such a question, she felt that she was in a manner betraying her kind present employers—the two old women at Chiswick a few miles away—the " ever such nice old people." But if it came to that, she was letting them down outrageously by being in here at all. Were these dangerous speculations—the insidious promptings of alcohol ? If so, she had better stop drinking at once. She took another sip.

At this point Andy leaned over to her, and spoke in a confidential way.

" Pretty girl like you don't want to be in service," he said.

Not displeased by the compliment, of which she had been the recipient often enough from strangers, but which on this occasion had been in a rather mortifying interval delayed, she smiled.

" What's wrong with it ?" she said, taking another sip at her port. " You got to live, ain't you ?"

She looked again at the clock and saw that it was a quarter past. She had only five minutes more.

" Oh yes—you got to live," said Andy. " But that ain't the way for a beautiful girl like you."

Beautiful ! He wasn't half going it, wasn't he ?

" I don't see what that's got to do with it," she said, and added, in an awkward way " even if I was," and nearly blushed again.

There was a pause.

" Oh no," said Andy, sternly repeating himself. " Not for a

beautiful girl like you." He was evidently anxious to thrust
the compliment home, and Jenny suspected that very soon
others would be following on its heels, that, in fact, a new feeling
was in the air and he had (as she put it to herself ) " commenced
operations."

" What would you suggest, then ?" she said, allowing a
note of responsive raillery to creep into her voice, though she
in no way savoured the idea of a flirtation with such an oddity
as Andy.

" What do I suggest for you ?" he said, getting a little further
away from her and looking at her appraisingly.

" Well—what ?"

" You ? . . ." said Andy, looking her up and down in the
same way. " You ought to be a mannequin by the look of you."

" Oo !" said Jenny, and smiling self-consciously, took another
sip at her port.

" Yes, you ought. A Mannequin. That's what you ought to
be."

" Well," she said. " You find me the job, an' I'll take it."

" I'll find you the job all right," was his rather unexpected
reply.

She made no reply, but fingered her glass, and looked mock-
ingly at it.

" I bet !" she said, and there was a prolonged silence, in which
she was aware that he was looking at her.

" Don't you believe me ?" he said.

" No," said Jenny. " I don't."

" Don't you, though. Then I'll tell you this," said Andy.
" I've only got to send you along to my friend Ned Hall, an'
he'd give you one like a shot."

His friend Ned Hall ? Give her one like a shot ? Who was
this funny little man ? Was he to be taken, by any wild stretch
of the imagination, seriously ?

" Go on," she said. " I'll bet he would."

" That he would," said Andy. " He'd give it to you as soon
as look at you, if I sent you along. He's the oldest pal I got.
I've known Ned since he was in knickerbockers."

" Go on," said Jenny. " Who is he, then ?"

" What ? Ned ? Ned Hall ? He's got four or five shops

round here, and two in the West End. I've known him since
he was in knickerbockers."

He seemed to set great store by his friend's knickerbockers,
which actually did not strike Jenny's imagination so vividly as
his shops.

"Go on," she said. "Has he? What sort of shops?"

"Ladies' Wear," said Andy briefly, as though she ought
to have known.

"Well," said Jenny. "I shall have to think about it."

"You certainly should. That's what you ought to be. A
Mannequin. You're cut out for the job."

There was another pause while Andy lit a fresh cigarette
from the old one. Jenny took another sip at her port.

A Mannequin. Cut out for the job. Was there any truth in
that? She felt the port trickling down inside, and it seemed
that a kind of light fell upon her. Was it not abundantly clear
that she *was* cut out for the job?

A Mannequin. To what other end had this singular and as
yet unexploited endowment—her much-debated prettiness—
been destined? And she was definitely pretty. Everybody said
she was pretty. Even those two old girls could not forbear
saying how pretty she was. Violet said she was pretty—lovely.
He himself had said she was beautiful. A Mannequin. This
was really a revelation.

And he had said he would get her the job. Did he mean it?
But she had only just got a job. She was going too fast. She
must pull up a bit. She believed she had had a bit too much to
drink. She looked at the clock. In a minute it would be twenty
past, and at twenty past she had decided to go.

"Go on," said Andy. "Don't keep on looking at that clock.
You know you don't want to go."

It was a rather more diffident Jenny that repelled the suggestion.

"Afraid I've got to," she said. "In a moment."

"Go on," said Andy. "He ain't as important as all that, is
he?"

"Oh, no. He ain't very important," said Jenny.

Her mind fled to Tom—the pale boy. If she knew anything
of his ways, he was probably waiting for her in the street at this

very moment. He was always about half an hour before his time when meeting her. The vision itself revealed the truth of what she had said—his supreme unimportance—his wraith-like quality—his " soppiness."

Why on earth had she promised to meet him ? A scorn of him, no longer passive, filled her. She half-consciously resolved that she would " give it him " to-night, when she saw him.

She was sick of his moping. She wanted some Life. She believed she was living at the moment. And yet just for him she had to forsake this vital atmosphere—this company of real people. She would turn up late at any rate. She was going to hear some more about this job.

" Well—stay and have another then," said Andy.

" I'm afraid I promised" she said, and then, seeing that he was not going to reply to this, she added, in clear, naïve tones. " Do you really mean you would get me a job as a Mannequin ? "

" Well, I couldn't not unless you stay and have another," he said archly.

She smiled at him. " Very well," she said. " I will."

It was out of her before she knew what she was saying, but she at once set about the task of acquitting herself inwardly. In the ordinary way, she told herself, she would never have dreamed of letting him order another. But this was different. This was Policy. If it was true that he had the powers he claimed, this talk might lead to a great deal. Indeed, it might make " all the difference " to her. It was her business to " keep on the right side of him, " to " butter him up " even.

That she was now certain to be very late for Tom she looked upon as an advantage. It was twenty past now. She betted he was waiting already. Well, let him wait.

Three ports. It was a lot, and she believed it had gone to her head a bit already. Well—what was wrong there ? You have to be merry once in a while.

" There's a good girl," said Andy. " Waiter ! "

\*   \*   \*   \*

A complete severance from Violet and Rex (who were at this point enrapturedly returning This One for This One in low tones in each other's ears, and shrieking with mirth at what they heard) had now been established. So much was this so, in fact, that when the waiter appeared Andy did not see fit to interrupt and include them in his order of port, and merely asked for two more.

" Here goes," he said, when they came, and she lifted her glass along with him, and drank. He then offered her another cigarette, which she took.

" Well," she said, rather awkwardly, when he had lit it for her. " What about that job ? "

He needn't think he was going to get out of it—and since she could not keep Tom waiting for ever, it was imperative to get down to the matter at once.

" This is darned good port, ain't it ? " said Andy, suddenly speaking from his heart, and it looked for a moment as though his enthusiasm for his wine had ridden over his obligation to reply to her question. Fortunately, however, he added : " What did you say ? Job ? Well—what about it ? "

Jenny did not quite like his tone. " Well," she said. " That's for you to say. Didn't you say your friend could get me one ? "

" 'Course he can. Certainly he can. Tell you what. What are you doin' to-morrow ? "

Fortified with a few ports, Andy was a different man. Indeed, they seemed to have affected him even more than her.

" Nothing particular I know of," she said. " Bar work."

" Well—you meet me at eleven in the morning an' I'll take you along."

At once Jenny took fright. She hadn't meant anything like this. She had wanted him to come to earth, certainly, but he had come to earth with too great a bump. She had only meant to talk about it. What !—go after another job when she had only been a day in the one she had ! The notion was monstrous. It wasn't as though she wasn't happy with those two old girls.

But on second thoughts, was she so happy with them ? Looking back on the day behind her, from a rosy indolence of mind and limb in this crowded, giddy place, she was beset by doubt as to that. The thought of her work, with its tyrannical call on her to-morrow morning, was indeed remote in here, but not too remote to stand between her and the perfection of happiness of which she now, for some reason, felt capable.

Making beds, washing up, cooking—was that her destiny to-morrow and all her life? She almost wished she hadn't come in here. It had all upset her.

" I couldn't get out in the morning," she said.

" Go on," said Andy. " You could give 'em the chuck just for one morning, couldn't you ? "

" No. I couldn't do that. I could get Saturday afternoon off, though."

" Very good. Saturday afternoon. Day after to-morrow. I'll take you round myself. I'll 'phone him up and fix it up to-morrow. There."

" Here," said Jenny. " Are you serious ? "

" Serious. 'Course I am. What do you think ? I haven't any reason, have I ? "

She did not answer.

" Eh ? " said Andy.

" No, you ain't got no reason," said Jenny. " It's very good of you."

" I guarantee you'll get that job as soon as he sets eyes on you. He's crying for girls like you."

" Perhaps he mightn't like the look of me."

" Don't talk silly. Besides, he's got other reasons for doing as I ask him."

" Has he ? "

She was impressed by this. It looked as though she was dealing with fellow magnates.

"Yes," said Andy, rather ominously. " He's got other reasons for doing as I ask him. He's my partner in another little show."

Partner ? What more could she have asked ? Was this really true, or was she dreaming ? Was it not morbid to doubt any further ? They were partners. She was dealing direct with the gods. She had as good as got the job, if she wanted it. A sudden vibration of joy and release overtook her. What if her true fate had overtaken her—at this hour, of this day, of this year ! What if, after all, she was not constrained to return to the gloomy round awaiting her to-morrow morning. A Manne-quin. What would Violet, who had mocked at her, think of that ? What would Tom think, what would her friend Ada Molden think, what would everybody think ? And to what might it not lead ? A Mannequin was the next thing to a chorus girl. Endless vistas were opened. Not that she had fully decided to take the job. She merely revelled in her potency to take or leave it. She thought she would take it, though, for all that. Gee, she wasn't half feeling all right. She must be careful, though. She believed she was a bit " on " already.

"What would the work consist of, like ? " she asked.

" Just wearin' dresses, that's all. Get there at ten, leave at six. Of course, you'd probably have to look after the customers a bit—but you wouldn't mind that, would you ? "

" No," said Jenny. " I shouldn't mind that."

A tremor of joy, quite beyond control, crept into her voice as she answered. Mind looking after the customers ! Get there at ten and leave at six ! Wearing dresses ! She could hardly believe her ears !

" And good screw, too," said Andy. " I don't know exactly what he pays—but it's something between three and four."

Between three and four ! And at Chiswick she was to be immured for fifteen shillings ! She had made up her mind. Yes—she had made up her mind.

" Well, it's certainly very kind of you," she said. " I should like to go along and see him."

" That's right. We'll go along on Saturday. Here's to it." Andy lifted his glass.

Jenny lifted hers, and they drank.

" It's very kind of you, indeed," she said, as she put it down. " It is truly."

" And what are you goin' to do for me in return," said Andy in a quizzing way. " Eh ? "

She took alarm. Had he, after all, ulterior intentions, in pursuit of which he was going to wield his power over her ? Was this the " old story " of which she had so often heard and read ?

" Oo, I don't know," she said, deciding that it was up to her to "manage " him. " What do you want ? "

" It's not what I want," he said. " It's what you got to give."

She had no idea what he meant by this, and her reply was equally obscure.

" Ah," she said. " That depends."

"It does," said Andy pithily, and it was felt that worlds had been said.

"Tell you what you *can* do for me, though," said Andy.

"What's that?"

"You can have another and stay on and spend the evening."

"Well," she said. "That's not so difficult."

"Ah—there's a good girl," said Andy, and, rising, he began to take off his overcoat.

Was she mad? To what had she committed herself? Was she going to throw over Tom? She glanced at the clock again, and saw that it was half past. By rights she should be with him at this moment. She couldn't do such a thing—surely she could not. She had never done such a thing in her life. He was waiting there for her. And to "have another" too. Four ports! It was out of the question. She had to make some excuse before it was too late.

But what excuse was there? Andy had asked her to stay, and how could she refuse without "offending" him. And if she "offended" him, where was her new job? It was, then, a choice between the all-powerful and visible Andy, and the pale and distant Tom—nay, more—between her whole future and the keeping of a thoughtless promise. She could decide but in one way. She would have to give Tom a miss.

She was relieved by having made the decision, and breathed a clearer air. It was a bit "mean"—with him waiting there—but there you were. And wouldn't he "take on" when he saw her next! She was sick of his misery. It might be a jolly good chance to throw him over. That was an idea. Who was he, anyway? Violet was quite right. He was a pretty poor specimen to be seen about with. If she became a Mannequin, it would be pretty odd, wouldn't it?—being seen about with a boy like Tom. Tom would have to go. She had been meaning to get rid of him for a long while. Now she had decided.

In the meantime she had the whole evening to spend as she wished. She felt grand at the moment, but she had got to be careful. If she didn't look out, she'd be drunk. Could she risk another after this, as Andy desired? She would have to wait and see when the time came.

The crowd in here was awful. You could hardly see through the smoke, and hardly hear yourself speak. But she revelled in it. It was all new to her, and she revelled in it. And to think she might have been in a Lyons now!

"What was we saying?" said Andy, sitting down again. He had removed his hat and scarf along with his overcoat, and in his spick and span brown suit was a transformed being. She noticed that his hair was so thin on top that he practically might be called bald, but so far from seeing this as a drawback, she thought it lent him distinction. He really was quite a passable little thing.

"You was saying I was a good girl," she said, reopening the gates to flirtation.

"Well, so you are—ain't you?"

"Don't know about that. Seems more like I'm a bad one—sitting in here drinkin'."

"Don't know about bad," said Andy. "Naughty though, I guess. Just a hot little baby straight from Paris. Eh?"

"Oo!" she said. "What an idea!"

All the same she was rather struck by the image. A hot little baby straight from Paris. She had never thought of herself in that light before, but her vanity had no difficulty in summoning up such a vision of herself, and gazing, Narcissus-like, upon it.

"Made for Love," said Andy, seeing he had made an impression, and elaborating the image. "All tied up in pink ribbon." She was astonished by his delightful gift of expression.

"Oo," she said. "Don't be so silly." But she could not help letting him see that she was pleased. She could listen to him indefinitely in this strain.

"I should like to have you with me in Paris, anyway," he said.

"I bet," she said. Was he "making suggestions"? Nobody had ever "made suggestions" to Jenny in her life before. It was the sort of thing, she knew, which inevitably befell "fast" girls who went into pubs. But was she not in a pub herself, and had she not within the last hour awakened to new things, stepped forth from the limited apparel of prudery? Andy's manly virtues glowed all the stronger for having made her her first "suggestion."

" Who's the lucky customer—eh ? " he asked.

" What do you mean ? "

" Go on. You know what I mean. Who is he ? "

" There ain't none," said Jenny. " Not at present."

" Oh—ain't there ? Well—what about yours truly ? "

" You ? "

" Yes. Me. Ain't I eligible ? "

" I'll think about it," said Jenny.

" You might do worse. And suppose you begin by calling me Andy ? What about that ? "

" All right. I'll think about it."

So the magnate wanted her to call him Andy ! She was surprised at herself—encouraging him like this. It was all very well to " butter him up " for her own purposes, but she mustn't go too far.

" That's better," he said. " You and I are going to know each other a whole lot better, believe me."

" Just as you say, Andy."

She was again amazed at herself. Why was she leading him on ? Was it just because she was in such tremendous spirits ? The idea of Andy as a being " eligible "—of Andy as her " boy "—was fantastic.

But on second thoughts, was it ? Why when you came to think about it, should *she* trouble about a boy's age and appearance ? Love, of which some spoke, was a closed book to her, and she honestly believed it would remain a closed book all her life. It was a closed book which she had no desire to open. She had never, if she looked facts in the face, regarded " boys " as anything more or other than mere base appendages, curiously willing providers, attendants, flatterers for an indolent mood, footers of bills and payers of 'bus-fares. And wherein was Andy ineligible on these heads ?

In fact, was he not superbly eligible ? He was no common " pick-up." He was the owner of a car ; he consorted with the retired military ; and all his talk went to prove that he was " in a good way." It she played her cards right, there was no end of what she might get out of him. She had him round her little finger already.

She took another sip at her port, and felt it running down,

filling her again with that prodigious sense of well-being. Why not ? She was hanged if she wouldn't take him on !

She saw it all. She had made a " find " ! Without seeking it, she had stumbled to-night upon a rich man ! And she jolly well wasn't going to let him go. She could play him up all right. He wouldn't get much change out of her. She could be a " gold-digger " with the rest. Why not ? She rather fancied the rôle. Was it not, in fact, the destined part of a hot little baby straight from Paris ?

Gee, what had happened to her to-night ? She had found a job, and she had found a " boy "!—an influential little man round her little finger ! Was that not the crown of every girl's true desire ? Gee—what more could she ask ? Was she dreaming—or had she had too much to drink ? She took another sip.

At this point Andy drained off the remains of his glass.

" Come on," he said. " We'll have another."

" Oo," she said. " I don't think I ought to have another."

" Come on now. Just to celebrate our meeting. Let's make a night of it."

Make a night of it ? To celebrate ? That was a new way of looking at it. Why not ? Was not this the one and perfect occasion for celebration. What if she had had a bit too much to drink—what if this was a wild piece of folly, and she had to go back to her dreary routine in the morning what of it ? She was happy, she was immensely and wildly happy, that was all that mattered. You had to enjoy yourself once in a while didn't you ? Besides, she had got the job all right. There was not a shadow of doubt about it. A Mannequin. A new era had dawned for her. She was born again. And a rich man round her little finger ! If she didn't celebrate to-night she never would, she might write herself down a little prude for ever. Of course she'd have another drink. She liked drink. She'd have as many more as she wanted. At last she was abandoned. She was going to have some pleasure for once. Pleasure—that was the thing —pleasure for once !

" All right," she said. " Ta."

*        *        *        *

"Oh dear me no," Andy was saying. "You don't want to go on working for those two old fossils. . . ."

Nearly half an hour had passed. It had seemed like less than five minutes, and wine had taken Jenny at her word.

She had never believed it was possible to be so happy. She sat there, amid the multitudinous mumble and tumult of a busy bar, a being enthroned in lucid joy. Each tortuous knot of her experience and endeavour had been unravelled at a magic touch; she gazed bright-eyed into the risen and revealed sun of her future.

"Two old fossils. . . ." How could they have been described with greater clarity or skill? All was now so perfectly and meticulously clear. Two old fossils—two old withered antiques —two old museum pieces. And only a few hours ago she had been resigned to dissipating her whole youth and beauty on such. Not that she had any grudge against them. They were nice old things in their way.

And to think that they were over at Chiswick now, only a few miles away, confidently awaiting her return to-morrow to the vile and ridiculous servitude they offered.

"You're just about right," she said. "You're just about right."

"I'll show you how to live," said Andy. "I'll show you how to live. I'll show you life with a capital L. I'm a pastmaster of the art."

"I'll bet you are," she said.

Andy had been going on in this strain for some time now, and it was quite clear to Jenny that he had had too much to drink. She thought this was strange, seeing that he had had no more than her, and that she, though elevated, had never felt more beautifully composed in her life.

From Violet and Rex they were now completely cut off. Once Violet had cried over to them in a mocking way, "Well—what are you two love-birds talkin' about?" and Jenny had told her to mind her own business. Whereat, veiled behind raillery, a pronounced bitterness and jealousy pervaded the air between the two pairs—they were both getting on a little bit too "famously" for each other's liking.

She did not know how many drinks she had had since making her decision to stay, but she knew that more than once their empty glasses had been snapped away like lightning, and that replenished ones had replaced them, and there was ever such a mess upon the table.

" Treat me the right way," Andy went on, " and you can get anything out of me. All I want is a Pal."

Jenny returned that that was all she wanted.

That was the way to speak. That was the way to speak. No sooner had he clapped eyes on her than he knew she was the girl for him. No sooner had he clapped eyes on her.

And no sooner, said Jenny, had she clapped eyes on him than she felt the same.

That was the way to speak. All Andy wanted was Sympathy. Sympathy, that was all. There was some girls would take anything from a man—hard-hearted, scheming bitches, that's what they were—he wouldn't have nothing to do with 'em—he wouldn't not so much as waste two minutes of his time on them. Sympathy was what he wanted—that was all—just sympathy. Didn't Jenny agree ?

What was the sense of anything without Sympathy—without Understanding ? What Andy wanted was a Mate—that was what he wanted in a girl—he wanted her to be a Mate. A Girl ought to be a Chap's Chum—she ought to be his little Pal— she ought to be his *Mate*—that was the word.

" She certainly ought," said Jenny.

She ought to Share his Joys, and Share his Troubles. What was the use of life without a Mate ? One was one, and two was two, weren't they ?

Emphatically Jenny returned that they were.

What he wanted was a Mate. Didn't all Nature have Mates ? Didn't the little Birds have Mates—didn't the Animals have Mates ? That was Nature, wasn't it ? And there wasn't nothing unnatural in that, was there ?

There was *not*.

That was Science all right, wasn't it ? If that wasn't Biology he'd like to know what was.

Quite right, said Jenny. Evolution, that was what it was.

She was quite right. Then why shouldn't he have a Mate ? He might be a quiet little chap to look at, but he'd thought things out on the q.t. He'd got his own Philosophy. And that wasn't learnt from the Greek, neither. Nor the Latin. He didn't pretend to be an Aristotle. He'd tell Jenny what he *ought* to have been, though. He ought to have been a Preacher. Yes, he ought. Here you were. Here was a bit of Preaching.

> " Dearly beloved Brethren,
> Is it not a Sin,
> When you peel potatoes,
> To throw away the Skin ! "

Eh ? What about that. That was Preaching all right, wasn't it ? . . . Andy threw back his head and revealed the gaps in his teeth in mirthless drunken laughter.

That'd be a good thing to Preach 'em in the Pulpit, wouldn't it ?

No—he wasn't joking. He wanted Sympathy. That was why he liked Jenny—she was Sympathetic.

Jenny said that she always tried to be.

That was right. He knew she did. He had summed her up all right. He summed people up in a moment. He happened to have a nasty little talent for it. She was different. She wasn't like some people he could mention.

" I certainly hope I'm not," said Jenny.

No, said Andy, she wasn't like some people. Some people that weren't too far away either. It might even be that they weren't more than three yards away. He wasn't going to say anything against her girl friend. . . .

" Don't see why you shouldn't," said Jenny. " She ain't no one anyway."

Ah—he was glad to hear it. He was glad to hear it. He knew it all right, he knew it. He'd summed that girl up so soon as he had clapped eyes on her. He didn't want to speak against her girl friend—but he'd tell her what she was. She wasn't no more than an Oar, that girl—she wasn't no more than an Oar.

" You're just about right," said Jenny. " She ain't no friend of mine."

He was glad to hear her say it. He'd summed her up all right. She'd end up as an Oar—that girl would. . . . Well, what about another of these, and then they would go on somewhere else. . . .

Like lightning the waiter had appeared : like lightning the
glasses had been snapped up ; like lightning the new drinks
had appeared.

" Ignorance—that's all it is," said Jenny, glorying, she knew
not why, in this sudden vilification and betrayal of Violet.
" It's just Ignorance."

But Andy thought the case worse than this. She was an Oar,
that girl was. She had the ways of an Oar. She had the look of
an Oar. He could tell an Oar when he saw one.

Oar. . . . Now Andy had got hold of the word he couldn't
leave it alone. It was as though he had got hold of an authentic
Oar, such as is used in boats, and was lustily rowing down the
yielding tide of obfuscation.

Jenny let him do all the rowing, and reclining blissfully on
that full stream, hardly listened to him.

And to think that she was supposed to be up in the morning
and working ! She presumed she would have to go. She
didn't mind. It would be fun doing the job—now she hadn't
got to, now she had got another. How she'd laugh at those two
old fossils in the morning. Silly old things—they had thought
they were doing her a favour by engaging her. Favour indeed !
—she'd show 'em. She was as good as them any day. She
betted Andy had got as much money as them any day, and
what mattered in these days save money ? What were class
distinctions nowadays ? Relics of the past. She'd show 'em.
She'd show everybody.


Thus Andy discoursed, and thus Jenny brooded in sullen
joy, and without her knowing it her empty glass had vanished
again, and again a full one had replaced it. In the fumes and
wild noise about her she had lost all count and all caring to
count. The din grew more and more terrific every minute, and
she couldn't properly hear what Andy was saying, even if she
cared to listen. Without actually being further away in space,
he seemed like a being at a great distance—though his voice,
like the voice of all the crowd present, was doubly loud and
urgent in her ears.

And then all at once, and by what means she had not observed, she found that Andy had reopened communications with Rex and the Oar, and that the two, forgiven, were now seated at their own table. And in a few moments she had forgiven them herself, and was talking like mad with them.

" Come on ! " Rex was shouting. " Who's going to paint this ruddy old town red ? "

" We are ! " cried Violet, banging her fist on the table, and " We are ! " echoed Jenny, doing the same.

And then Rex was putting his arm round Andy, and trying to kiss him. " Poor little Handy Andy, then," he was saying. " Won't 'e kiss 'is Mum ?—won't 'e kiss 'is poor old Mum ? " —and Violet and she were in fits at the sight.

" Go on—kiss your mum, Andy ! " yelled Violet, and " Go on, Andy ! " cried Jenny. And she looked about her and saw that all the people around were smiling at them, and was filled with uncanny pleasure at thus holding the stage before so many eyes. " Go on, Andy," she cried, desiring to call all the attention to herself. " Give 'im a kiss ! " And she saw them all smiling again. . . .

And then, the next thing she knew, they were all going out— Rex going ahead, and, with one hand poised high in the air and the other on his waist, swaying his hips and mincing along like an affected woman. And while going to the door she tripped up by accident, and would have fallen if Violet hadn't caught her. And " Are you all right, Jen ? " Violet was saying. " Are you all right ? " And she was surprised at her earnest tone, and said " Me all right ? Of course I'm all right. What do you think ? "

And then she and Violet were out in the cold night air of King Street, and the two boys had mysteriously vanished. But Violet didn't seem to be worrying about this, and was talking rather violently at her.

" You keep in with that boy Andy," she was saying. " You keep in with 'im. I've been 'earing all about him. 'E's got pots of money, my dear—pots ! 'E's got a garage at Twickenham, and 'e's made it all this year. You keep in with 'im. You take my advice. I'm givin' you the tip."

" I will," said Jenny. " I knew 'e had some."

" I'm giving you the tip—that's all," said Violet. " I'm giving you the tip. I'm your pal." And then, as suddenly as they had vanished, the two boys had returned, and they were all walking and singing down King Street.

And then, just as they had reached a side-street, she looked around for Andy, and saw that he had fallen behind and was signalling to her, with avid and conspiratorial wavings, to join him where he stood. And so she went back to him and asked what was the matter.

Whereat he took her by the arm, and still making furious winks and signs, as though he thought the others, who were at least thirty yards away, might yet be in earshot, said : " Come on, let's go on the Common, shall we ? " " Common," she said, " what Common ? " " Barnes Common," he returned, plainly enough. " Barnes Common ? " she said, " what do you want to go to Barnes Common for ? " " Come on," he said, " let's go on Barnes Common. There's nowhere else to go." " But what for ? " she pleaded. " Go on," he said. " You know what for."

At last getting a glimmering of his meaning she replied : " Here—what do you take me for ? " To which he replied : " Come on. Let's go to Barnes Common. You want to get that job—don't you ? " and he put his arm round her.

At which despicable and indelicate attempt to wield his power over her, she felt a slight revulsion arising, and might very well have let him see it, had not Rex and Violet arrived at this very moment and asked them why they delayed.

And then they were all walking along the street again, and Andy was holding her arm in complete forgetfulness of Barnes Common. And then they were all in another pub—a small one this time—standing up at a small bar drinking port as usual.

And then she was finding herself not listening to the conversation around her, but taking prodigious interest in a man behind the bar. He had a red face and a white drooping moustache, and was evidently the landlord. What particularly interested her about him was that he had two red faces, and two white drooping moustaches, and two morose expressions exactly similar. He was in fact, two landlords. Tradition told her that her seeing him like this was evidence of her own intoxication, and she did her best to pull herself together and only see one of him. But it was quite beyond her powers—she could only see two. And it was quite impossible to tell which was the right one.

And then she had forgotten about the landlord, and was talking wildly with her friends again, and then, as they were moving to the door once more, she did not know what happened, but as she moved forwards she felt herself falling backwards, and she couldn't stop herself and fell down.

And as she wasn't hurt she simply wanted to laugh. But everybody was around her making a dreadful fuss—including the man with the red face and drooping moustache.

They were leaning over her, and discussing her, and arguing about her. They helped her to her feet, and she leaned on Violet. " Are you all right ? " said Violet, and " She's all right," said Rex, and " Of course I'm all right," she said. And the next moment they were out in the street.

She felt a little funny on her feet, coming out into the air, but she leaned on Violet, and soon felt herself again.

" Come on," she said. " Let's have another drink."

At this they all laughed at her. " Well, that's the spirit," said Rex. " There's just time for one more."

She knew they thought, because she had accidentally tumbled over, that she had had too much to drink, but clearly as she knew they were mistaken, she could not be bothered to argue with them. Indeed, she rather liked them thinking it, as it gave her great pleasure to prove what a daredevil she was, and how little she cared.

" Here we are," said Rex, and they had gone through another door into another public house, and were shouldering their way, amid a thick crowd of people, towards the bar. " We're just on time," said Rex, and shoved his way ahead.

All at once Jenny heard a voice behind her.

" Jenny."

She turned round, and saw Tom at her side.

\*      \*      \*      \*

For one moment the furious pace of her evening was checked, and she stared at him, in that perfervid and voluble atmosphere, without a word. The sight of his pale, frightened face, and staring eyes; the sheer unexpectedness of the meeting; the overpowering mystery of how he came to be there; the knowledge that she had wronged him and had been found out—all combined, for a brief instant, to alarm and sober her.

"Hullo, Jenny," he said, and she saw that he trembled with fear and love.

"Hullo," she said. "What are you doing here?"

"Come on, Jenny," he said. "You got to get out of here."

"How did *you* get in here?" she said. She was recovering already.

"Come on, Jen. You must come out."

"How did *you* get here?" she repeated, feeling a not unpleasing resentment rising in her voice and soul.

"I followed you," he said. "I came over here to try and find you, and saw you walking in the street."

"Oh—so you followed me—did you?" With grim delight she saw the case against him, and how she could thrust it home. "You been sneakin' on me—have you?"

"No—I ain't been sneakin' on you, Jenny. I——"

"What are you tremblin' for?"

"Jenny. I ain't tremblin'. Jenny——"

"Yes, you are. Go on. What are you tremblin' for? Seen a ghost or something?"

It gave her extraordinary pleasure to torture and make Tom look a fool in this manner. This was what she called "giving it him." She recalled making up her mind earlier in the evening to "give it him" and get rid of him once and for all

"Jenny. You got to come back. You *got* to." He put his hand on her arm.

"Leave go of me, will you?" she said. "Do you want to make a scene in 'ere?"

"But Jenny. It's for your *good*."

She looked round quickly to see if her friends were watching. She heard Violet's shrill cackle, and saw them some distance away in the crowd, standing at the bar and talking to each other. Any moment they might see her, and she would be disgraced. Was this not the pale boy himself?

"Here. Come on out," she said. "I'll soon see what you want."

They pushed their way through the crowd, and he opened the door for her.

" Jenny ! " he said, when they were outside, but she did not answer him until they were round a corner, and out of sight of the pub.

" Now," she said. " What is it ? Eh ? "

" Jenny ! " he said. " Don't take on so. I love you."

" Go on. I've heard that one. You love me enough to come sneakin' on me—that it ? "

" Jenny. It's for your *good*. It's for your *good* ! You're drunk, Jenny. You know you are. You're drunk."

Again Tom's exceeding wild look almost pulled her up. There was something mad about him. He had the air of a prophet, an inspired mystic—a seer of things beyond her own vision and sphere. And, indeed, this was the case, since he saw with agonized clarity the one thing concerning which light was now denied her—that she was drunk.

" Oh, so I'm drunk, am I ? So that's what you say to the girl you love, is it ? "

" But you *are*, Jenny. You *are*. You got——" He touched her arm again.

" How *dare* you say such a thing ! " She flung his hand away. " How *dare* you !—eh ? "

" But Jenny. You got to listen. You got to be up in the morning. *You got to be up in the morning !* "

" Oh, have I, indeed ? And who said I had ? Supposing I haven't ! What then ! "

" But Jenny—it's for your good. You'll lose your job. *You'll lose your job !* "

" And suppose I don't want my job—eh ? What then ? Suppose I don't want the dirty job ! Suppose I got a better one ? "

" Jenny—— "

" I'll tell you something. I don't want your dirty jobs—see ? I wouldn't defile my 'ands with 'em—see ? You thought you was dealin' with a skivvy—didn't you ? "

" Jenny—— "

." And I don't want you neither—see ? I don't want to see your funny pale face again. I'm sick of the sight of it. And

I'll tell you where you ought to be. You ought to be in 'ospital
—see? You're infectious!"

For one moment Tom drew himself up, and his face worked
with distraught and sickly rage. He looked as though he could
kill her.

But now Jenny had taken this line, like one who is stamping
out the life of an insect which still maddeningly writhes, she was
blind and uncontrolled : and the thought that he might be about
to show fight merely impelled her to strike and strike again.

" Jenny. . . ." he said.

" You're in *consumption*—that's what's the matter with you—
*see*? You got T.B.—that's your trouble—T.B.! An' I don't
want the likes of you hangin' round *me*—see? An' that's final.
An' if you don't shove off now, I'll go in there and set my friends
on you—got that! They'll soon give you what you want!"

They looked into each other's eyes. There was no motion
in his face or body.

" All right, Jenny," he said, and still did not move.

She walked away.

*          *          *          *

Gee, she had been mad! Gee, she had given him a piece
of her mind! Gee, she never knew she had a temper like that!
She'd " dressed him down " all right!

She flung back the swing door, and was in the crowd and
smoke once more. Lord—what a crush! Where were they?
She discerned them at the far end of the room seated at a table.

" Hooray!" cried Rex, and they all cried " Hooray," and
made room for her to sit down.

There now appeared to be an addition to the party. Andy
was in drunken argument with a rather good-looking young
man, anything between thirty and forty, wearing a military
moustache, and speaking with the affected (though now inebriated) accents of a " gentleman."

" Here you are," said Violet, and she made room for Jenny
between herself and the stranger. " Where've you been all this
time ? "

" Where've I been ? " she said. " I just happen to have had a bit of an argument with someone, that's all. Come on. Let's have a drink."

There was a drink in readiness for her, and she gulped almost half of it down at one go. "That's better," she said. "Gee— I ain't half a little spitfire when I get going." And she sat there glorying in the part.

Rex and Violet asked her who it was, but she wouldn't say. "Never you mind," she said. "Never you mind. Never you mind."

"Never you mind," she added, a moment later. She knew, in a dizzy way, that she had said "Never you mind" too often, and that she was behaving wildly and hysterically, but she didn't care any more. It was at this moment that, if there was any final inhibition dwelling in Jenny to restrain her, it took its flight along with the others.

It was just on closing time in Hammersmith, and all she said and did in the remaining minutes in that place she hardly knew at the time, and never remembered afterwards.

She had scarcely been sitting down a moment before the moustached "gentleman" stranger next to her had put his arm round her.

"Well, my little one—how are we?" he began, and she said *she* was all right—what about him?

"Passing well, passing well, passing well," he said, but Alas and Alack, he was no longer what he was. He had fallen into the sere and yellow leaf. Shakespeare. Act one. Scene Three. . . . Well, said Jenny, that sounded all right, but was he quite sure it wasn't Hamlet? . . .

No, he said, it wasn't. It was Milton. The Greatest of the Puritans. Did she read Milton? . . . No, said Jenny, she didn't. The only sort of Milton *she* read was the disinfectant. . . . "Quite true," he said. "Quite true. Only one in five escapes deadly pyorrhœa. . ." But she ought to read Milton. All the lower classes ought to read Milton. Not that she was a member of the lower classes—though, of course, she *was*, wasn't she? . . .

And then Andy was cutting in and saying *he* knew some Milton—what about this?—There was a Young Lady of Tring. . . . And having recited the bawdy limerick in full, he asked whether Milton could beat *that*. . . .

Whereat Rex joined in with another Limerick, and Violet with another, and Jenny tried to think of one herself; but her mind wandered away and she noted with renewed interest that she was seeing double again. . . .

When she next listened to them they were all talking about a Bet. . . . It was Bet. . . . Bet. . . . Bet. . . . " I'll bet *you*," Andy was saying to the young man, and the young man was saying, " Excuse me, sir, you will *not*. I will bet *you*. . . ."

It seemed they were talking about a Car. . . . " My dear sir," said the young man, " I will take you in that Car and bloody well demonstrate *now*." " No, you won't," said Andy. " I'll bloody well take you in mine." " Done ! " said the young man. " Done ! " said Andy.

And then suddenly half the lights had gone down, and there was a sound of glasses being briskly and harshly snapped up in all directions, and a man's voice crying " Now then, gentlemen, please ! *Time* please, ladies and gennelmen ! ALL OUT THERE !"

And with Andy and the young man still arguing, and Rex trying to shout them both down in passionate argument against the folly of argument, they all got up.

And walking towards the door, with all of them arguing around her and over her, Jenny felt decidedly giddy. Everything kept on going round and round, and then rather horribly stopping, and then going round and round again. . . .

And for a moment it did just occur to Jenny that she had, after all, to be up and working in the morning, and she wondered how on earth she was going to do it, and what was going to happen now. But the thought didn't trouble her, and passed away at once.

And then they were out in the street, with a dumb and darkened house being savagely bolted behind them, and the next thing she was aware of was the moustached stranger, who was again embracing her, and at the same time yodelling to the skies—displaying with great virtuosity an astonishing falsetto voice. " Yo-ah-ah-eye-atee !" he went. " Yo-ah-ah-eye-atee ! " and she noticed that people on the other side of the street were standing in couples and trios and looking at them.

And then they had all gone down a corner, and he was doling out whisky to them, in turn, from a little thermos cup. . . . And then they were moving on again, and the young man was again embracing her, and again yodelling. " Yo-ah-ah-eye-atee !" he went. " Yo-ah-ah-eye-atee ! " And by now it didn't seem in the slightest way odd.

And then they were passing over the Broadway, and then they had gone down a side-street, and were outside a large garage, with " ALL NIGHT GARAGE " on a large electric sign outside.

And then Andy was telling them all to stay where they were, and not to behave silly or they wouldn't let him take the car out. . . . And then he had vanished and Jenny realized that they were all going out for a car ride. . . .

She was delighted at this, as she had never been in a car in her life. " Where's he taking us ? " she asked. " Where's he taking us ? " But nobody seemed to answer. Instead the young man again put his arm round her and said " Well, little one—are you coming home with Daddy to-night ? " " What for ? " she said. "To sleep, my angel," he said. . . .

And then Andy had drawn up to the pavement in a lovely big car, and they were all clambering in. · " I'm by the driver ! " cried Jenny. " I'm by the driver ! " And she pushed Violet out of the way. " Here—who're you pushin' ? " said Violet. " Go on. Get on out," said Jenny, " you take a back seat." " No," said Violet, " you're Rough." " Oh, shut your row," said Jenny, and " No," said Violet. " You're Rough." " Yo-ah-ah-eye-atee ! " went the young man, and he embraced Violet in the back seat.

And then the car had started, and she felt the wind on her face. Gee, this was fun ! And to think she'd never been in a car before ! Gee, this was just what she was wanting to clear her head.

They were back in the Broadway in less than a minute, and flying along King Street in the direction of Chiswick.

" Where are we going ? " cried Jenny, against the speed and wind. But no one answered her. The young man was yodelling, and Rex and Violet were cuddling each other with raucous laughter behind ; and Andy, now wrapped in the authoritative taciturnity of the driver, did not see fit to answer.

Gosh—he was getting up a pace ! . . . Ravenscourt Park. . . . Stamford Brook. . . . She knew the route well enough—she had come that way earlier in the evening by tram. . . . She supposed it was safe—going at this pace. There were very few vehicles on the road, but he was overtaking them all. She supposed it seemed risky to her because she had never been in a car before. . . .

Here they were !—scouring along the Chiswick High Road itself ! Chiswick ! As they whizzed past the Green she looked over towards the home of the two old fossils. And to think of them sleeping peacefully in bed, and she out here. It must be pretty well midnight. Gee, what a life !

And now they had passed Gunnersbury, and had turned up to the right, and were ripping up the wide, smooth, deserted spaces of the Great West Road. . . . Gee !—it was like a racing track—no wonder he put on speed. It was like being in an aeroplane !

" Go on. Let her rip ! " cried Rex from behind, and " Yo-ah-ah-eye-atee ! " yodelled the young man.

Gosh—they must have gone about two miles on this road already. They were leaving London behind. Andy, whose face was set, was clearly out for nothing but speed now.

" Go on—step on 'er. Step on 'er ! " screamed Violet from behind.

" That's right. Step on 'er ! Step on 'er ! " echoed Jenny, and Andy's face grew more and more set.

And then, intoxicated with wine and speed together, and with the wind tearing at her face and round her ears, an insane and uncontrollable impulse surged into Jenny's soul. She stood up like a fury. She screamed.

" Step on 'er ! " she screamed. " Step on 'er ! *Step on 'er ! *"

And then " Look out for the bike ! *Look out for the bike ! *"

But it was too late. With a grating noise and a thud, a man and his bicycle were hurled helplessly against the side of the car, and left behind in the darkness.

She heard Violet scream piercingly, and she looked back.

" You've hit him ! " Violet yelled. " You've hit him. *Stop !*"

"Yo-ah-ah-eye-atee ! " went the young man from the comfortable depths of the back seat. " Stop, you dirty swine ! " yelled Violet. " You've killed 'im ! Will you stop ! "

Andy slowed down a little and Jenny watched his face. It was like something made of stone, with false glass eyes. Putting his tongue carefully out of his mouth, he swerved round and entered a quiet lane to their right.

" Yo-ah-ah-eye-atee ! " went the young man, and Violet emitted another piercing scream. " Stop ! Stop ! *Will you stop, you dirty rotter ! Will you stop !*"

It was slightly up-hill, and Andy changed his gear. The car gathered pace. The headlights shone dazzlingly on to leafy hedges.

" Stop ! Stop ! Will you stop ! "

Jenny sank back into her seat. She felt and heard a singing in her ears, and she was aware of a crawling numbness rising in her legs. She tried by will-power to check its advance up into her body—but she could not. She began to sweat in her endeavour to stop it. Great black blotches sprawled and floundered over her eyes. Her stomach turned over, and rose up. She was going to be sick. She was going to faint.

" *Will you stop !* " she heard Violet yelling, and then, at a great distance, the sound of Violet's passionate and resigned weeping. After that she knew nothing else.

<br>

III

# THE MORNING AFTER

PROJECTED from an urgent and resounding dream, Jenny opened her eyes in silent darkness, her head buried between unfamiliar sheets.

She had slept a long while, but apprehended that it was still night in the world without. That the sheets were unfamiliar she

sensed, but was not at present consciously aware. Also she heard
the sound of a Venetian blind spasmodically crack-cracking
against a window in the draught, but she did not realize that that
sound was unfamiliar. . . .

A shot of pain careered through her head, and left it hideously
throbbing, and a feeling of bile spread up and over her. She
closed her eyes until it allayed itself a little. Something had
happened. That was all she could take in at the moment. Something had happened.

What was it? What was the time? Where was she? What
had she done? She heard her trembling breath coming and
going in a roar in the sheets. Yes. She remembered. She had
got drunk. (Couldn't she stop her trembling?) She had got drunk.

Last night she had got drunk. She had gone into that pub,
and got drunk. It was in Hammersmith, with those three. It
wasn't fair—them making her drunk like that. Violet, and those
two common " boys."

Where were they now? What had they all done? Oh God
—she was in trouble. She was in trouble all right this time.

What was it she had done? Tom. . . . Tom was in it somewhere. . . . Yes—she had gone outside that pub, and heaped
vile words on him. She had been mad. She had been drunk, and
he had told her so. She had been drunk all over Hammersmith.
Oh God—what had she said and what had she done?
Oh God—she was in trouble. In fearful crescendo her memories
flocked back upon her.

Then they had all gone in that car. Andy had been driving,
and she had been beside him. And the other three shouting and
drinking behind. It wasn't fair—that dirty crowd making her
drunk like that. Where had they all gone? Past Chiswick and
out on the Great West Road. . . .

The accident! The bike! " *Look out for the bike. Look out
for the bike !* " She heard herself screaming it now. That vibrat-
ing thud against the side ! They had knocked a poor man over.
And she had been in the car with that drunken lot ; she had
been the drunkest of the lot ! They had killed a man ! Oh
God—she was in a scrape this time all right.

Had they been found out? What had happened? Andy had
driven on. Had they escaped?

Where was she? These sheets—they weren't hers. That blind rattling—this wasn't her room. Someone had brought her somewhere. Oh God—what had they done with her, and where was she? She sprang up in bed and stared in horror and silence at the window.

She was in a narrow slip of a room, with the window facing her a few yards from the end of the bed. Through the open slats of the Venetian blind she perceived that the window was open at the bottom, and she at once knew what manner of day it was outside. Though the dawn had risen, the world was hidden in sombre brown darkness. It was one of those night-days, familiar to Londoners, wherein visibility below is not obscured, but the upper air is occupied by that dense black fog which glows purple when reflecting the lights of a city.

Beyond the window, through the slats of the blind, she saw the laced outline of a denuded tree, and, listening intently, she heard the faint, miserable chirrup of a sparrow. The blind went " clack . . . clack " gently—stirred by an insensible draught.

She gazed ahead without motion, and tried to think in what room, under whose shelter, in what part of London, she might be.

Then delayed panic struck. Where was she? Had she been kidnapped? Someone had kidnapped her. Where *was* she? What horror was this? She jumped out of bed, and was rushing to the window, but stopped. She was in her underclothes. She looked down on herself. *She was in her underclothes!* In that sombre fog-light she felt hideously, terrifyingly denuded —stripped! Where was her dress? Oh—where was her dress? It was nowhere. They had taken it. There was a man—there were men in this somewhere. Where was she?

*Oh, where was she, where was she, where was she!* She flew over in a blind frenzy to the window. She grasped madly at the cord of the blind, cutting her finger on the nail round which it was wound. She pulled it up with a mighty rattle, and tied the cord furiously and carelessly round the nail. The whole thing fell down again, flying down upon her like a giant angry bat, and striking her forehead. Once again she pulled it up, and firmly tied the cord.

She looked out of the window.

The house she was in had three stories, and she was on the second. In the eerie quiet of the night-day, she saw on each side a succession of walled suburban garden plots. There were two rows of them, and behind them rose the backs of another row of houses. Some of these plots were neatly kept, others were rank with weeds. Wireless poles abounded. To her left, about a hundred yards away, was a road, down which she heard a cart rattling in a business-like way.

What was the time ? Judging by the sound of that cart, and the general look of the sky, she judged it was about seven o'clock. What part of the world this might be she could not guess, but she experienced a very faint relief at its apparently respectable air.

The biting cold caught her bare arms, and she shiveringly tried to close the window. But it would not close. She put her whole weight on it, but it would not close. Oh God—she'd catch her death. Where was her dress ? She came back into the room. *Where was her dress ! She'd catch her death !*

She jumped back into the bed, and drawing the clothes up around her, stared once more at the window. Where was she ? She had got to do some thinking—some quick thinking. She was so sick and giddy she could hardly think. She had got to get out of here. She must think. Sitting up in bed, staring at the window, her teeth chattering, Jenny thought.

She had got to get out. The door was behind her. She would have to go out and see where she was. Not yet. She was too cold.

Oh—what had God done to her ? This was God's doing. She had been " bad," and now she was stricken. This was her " punishment." She had been told that God did that sort of thing. Why had she not listened ? The very darkness of the day bespoke God's wrath and gloom against her.

Would she ever be forgiven now ? What had she done that was so terrible ? The accident !—that was it—she had almost forgotten it in her panic. They had killed a man. He must have been killed. Remembering Violet's screams she could not doubt it.

Somewhere, under this awful sky, that man lay dead. It was no dream. Somewhere, at this moment a crowd of people knew of the crime and were clamouring for knowledge of the guilty party. Had they already succeeded in finding it? Would they succeed? What would aid them? The police! By now it was in the hands of the police! The police were after her! Oh, worse than God—the police! She wished she was dead.

Where on earth was she? She must go and see. If only she wasn't feeling so sick she might have contended with this.

She got out of bed, and wrapped the counterpane round herself. She turned the handle of the door. Was it locked? No. She opened it a little way. The counterpane fell off her. Without troubling to put it on again, she opened the door a little wider. She perceived a light. It shone from a door ajar just over the way. Who was it that burned electricity at this hour, in this house, in these circumstances?

· She heard the sound of heavy regular breathing from within the room. Although the light was on, someone was asleep. What was this? Who was it?

She could bear it no longer. She advanced to the door. She knocked timidly upon it.

" Excuse me," she said.

There was no answer.

" Excuse me," she said.

There was a grunt from within.

She knocked again. " Excuse me," she said.

" Hullo? " It was a man's voice, sleepy and uncertain.

" Excuse me——" she began, but the voice interrupted her.

" Hullo," it said. " Come in."

She put her head round the door. Sitting up in bed, in pyjamas, was one whom she had no difficulty in recognizing. It was the yodeller of the night before.

\*       \*       \*       \*

They glared in a frightened way into each other's eyes.

" Oh—hullo. . . ." he said.

Realizing that she was not dressed she dodged behind the door again. There was a pause.

" Do you know where my dress is, please? " she asked from behind the door.

" No. Haven't you got it? "

He spoke with a perfect calm, a stupefaction from sleep, which a little reassured her.

" No, I haven't," she said.

" Well, it must be somewhere. Can't you find it ? "

" No, I'm afraid I can't. Can you tell me where I am, please ? "

" What ? . . . You're *here*," he said protestingly.

" Yes—but can you tell me where, please ? "

" This is my flat. This is Richmond."

Richmond. She felt a certain relief at knowing.

" How did I get here ? " she asked. " I was drunk, wasn't I ? "

" Yes."

" Was I brought in, then ? "

" Yes." He had the querulous and slightly bored manner of a man who desired to go on sleeping. He evidently was not in an immediate panic about anything.

" There was an accident—wasn't there ? "

" Yes. I believe there was."

Did he take nothing seriously ?

" Was anyone hurt ? "

" I don't know. We were too drunk to go back."

" But oughtn't we to have ? "

" Yes. I suppose we ought."

" But won't there be some trouble ? "

" I hope not."

What was the use of going on like this ? She might just as well be talking to herself. She was freezing with cold out here, too.

" Don't you know where my dress is ? "

" No. It must be somewhere. That girl got you to bed. I'll come and look in a moment."

" All right. Will you bring it to me ? "

" Yes. All right."

" Will you leave it outside my door ? "

" Yes. All right."

She went back to her room, and shutting the door got into bed and again tried to warm herself. Her heart was beating like mad, sending shots of pain up into her head. It was as dark as ever outside, and the temporary relief she had felt at knowing where she was forsook her as she waited for him to come. What was the time ? She had forgotten to ask him. What was she going to do now ?

Her job. In all her panic her job had never been out of her mind, and she knew that her only hope lay in somehow getting back to it in time. Was it too late ? She was supposed to be there at eight. It must be well past seven already. She heard the hoot of motors in the distance, proclaiming a risen world. Perhaps she could be a bit late, and make an excuse. She could say the fog held up the train. Richmond to Chiswick. It wasn't far. But had she any money ? Where w as her bag ? With her dress, she supposed. Why didn't he come ?

Who was he—this casual male ? So this was his flat. He was a " gentleman " obviously. She could tell that from his voice and looks. In other circumstances she might have been flattered by the acquaintanceship. Why didn't he come ? He didn't care. He was a " gentleman "—he had no work to do—no job to go to.

How long did it take to get from Richmond to Chiswick ? Half an hour—it shouldn't take more. What excuse could she make if she was late ? If she could only think of a good excuse, she could turn up half an hour late—an hour even. Suppose she said she had had an accident. Or that her aunt had had an accident, and had been taken to hospital. That was an idea. She must think out the details. She must think out the details . . . . She couldn't bear this pain in her head.

Oh, God had no mercy. She hadn't deserved all this. Gazing at the window, Jenny could not believe that for so brief and tempestuous a pleasure there could be exacted so dolorous a penance.

There he was—she heard him flopping about on the oil-cloth floor in his loose carpet slippers. He had knocked.

" Hullo," she said.

" Here's your dress," he said from behind the door. " You're going to stay to breakfast, aren't you ? "

Breakfast ? She hadn't thought of that.

" I've got to get to my job," she said.

" Oh—have you ? . . . Surely you can stay for something to eat ? "

Something to eat. Yes—she ought to have something to eat —it might make her less faint. She had had nothing to eat last night. And she could do with a cup of tea. Lord—she could do with a cup of tea!

" All right, then, thank you. But I've got to get over to Chiswick."

" Chiswick? Oh, that's all right. That's where my bank is. I can take you in the car."

Car? That sounded better. That sounded feasible. She might be able to make it in decent time after all.

" Oh, thank you," she said. " That'd be very useful."

She heard him flopping away again. (What a noise those slippers of his made!) She rose, opened the door a little way, and pulled in her dress. She closed the door and began to put it on. Car—that was better. If she could only get over to Chiswick in time she might yet be saved. What was that sound of running water? What was he up to out there? If she once got to Chiswick, she didn't see how they could find her out. She would be immured there—she would lie low. She was supposed to be sleeping in there to-night. She could sneak over to Camden Town for her baggage, and vanish from everyone she knew. No one knew her address at Chiswick. But the police found out everything. They were like God—they knew everything and punished all. Oh Lord—this might end in prison yet. Chiswick. That was her only chance.

She heard him flopping towards her door again. He knocked.

" Hullo? " she said.

" I've turned on your bath," he said blandly. " It'll be ready in about five minutes."

Good God!—*Bath!* What had he done now?

" Oh, thank you." She could think of nothing else to say.

" Will you go along, then? "

" Yes. Thank you."

He flopped away again.

Bath! She was going to prison, and he expected her to have a bath! She had, as she guessed, about half an hour in which to get to her job, and he had told her her bath would be ready in

five minutes ! This because he was a " gentleman." " Gentlemen " took baths every morning of their lives. He had taken it
for granted. How could she explain to him that she was not his
counterpart—a " lady "—that she loathed the idea of a bath—
that she was a servant girl with her work to go to.

It was beyond her. His broad and unsuspecting gentility
admitted of no challenge. She would have to have the beastly thing.

She was hanged if she would, though. She would have a bit
of a wash, and splash the water about a bit, and let it out. She
needed a wash, but nothing on earth would make her have his
blasted bath.

She heard him flopping about a great deal, and listened till
she thought he was in his room. Then she came out, and guided
by the sound of running water, found the bathroom.

A decrepit geyser was pouring forth a hot bubbling stream
into a half-filled bath, and the whole confined space was filled
with white vapour. The walls and window dripped with
heavy, oozing dew. She shut the door.

Gee—it was warm. But she could not turn the geyser off yet.
He would hear it stop running, and know that she wasn't having
a proper bath.    Strange—that even in this predicament she
should allow a false point of pride to influence her, but there it
was. She had better undress—she would only get her clothes
damp in all this steam.

She took everything off, and put one foot in the water. Oo !
—it was hot ! She turned on the cold water. She put her foot
in again. It was just bearable. She brought her other foot in.
She turned the cold water off. She was afraid she had made it too
cold now. It was nice—this warmth. Why not have a bath ?
It wouldn't take more than five minutes, and it would warm
her up proper. She would. She turned off the geyser.

The water ceased pouring, and a heavy dripping silence fell.
She sank into the bath. It was lovely and hot, and she wished
she could stay in it. She looked at the window and saw that the
sky was growing a little lighter.

There he was—flop-flopping about again. Lord !—she
hadn't locked the door ! He was coming in—he was coming
in ! She sprang up in the bath.

" Here ! " she cried. " Don't come in ! "

" What ? " he said vaguely.

" Oh, I'm sorry. I thought you was coming in."

" Oh." He was flopping away again.

No, he wasn't. He was flopping back.

" What'll you have for breakfast ? " he said. " Will a boiled egg do you ? "

" Yes—thank you."

" One ? Or two ? "

" One, please. Thank you."

" I've got to get the breakfast myself," he explained. " The blasted skivvy's down with 'flu."

" Oh—I see."

He flopped away again. So he had a " skivvy "—did he ? It didn't even cross his mind that she herself might be a " skivvy." His " blasted skivvy. . . ." So that was the way her kind were talked of. He was mistaking her for a " lady " apparently—an equal at any rate. By rights, she supposed, she ought to be calling him " Sir " and getting his breakfast for him. Yet here he was, giving her the use of his bath, and getting her breakfast for her. A wicked pass and paradox indeed—that in falling so low from her own mean grace she should be elevated to so spurious and insecure a level.

There he was again—flopping about. What was he up to now ? He seemed to be in a dream. She must get out of this bath. Where was the towel ?

The towel ! There wasn't one ! Would her tortures never cease ? She stood up in the bath distraught. She heard him passing, and cried, " Excuse me ! "

" Hullo ? "

" Have you a towel, please ? "

" Oh, I'm sorry. I'll get one. I'm rather vague this morning."

Rather vague ! She should think he was. But she could understand it, if he was feeling anything like herself. And she supposed he must be, after all that drink.

" Here you are," he said. " Shall I heave it in ? "

" Will you leave it outside, please ? "

But, ignoring this, he opened the door a few inches, and flung it in.

" Thank you," she said.

" Are you out of your bath ? " he cried.

" Yes. Why ? "

She knew what was coming !

" You might turn mine on—would you ? Can you work the geyser thing ? "

" Yes. All right."

" Ta," he said, and flopped away again.

This was the last straw. He was going to have a bath himself. Her own bath water had not run out yet. She dried herself in mad haste, and began to put on her clothes. Had he no realization of her situation ? How could they get to Chiswick in time now ? What *was* the time ? The sky was rapidly growing lighter, and it might be any time.

She was so *thirsty* she didn't know what to do. Oh—she was being punished all right.

He was flopping past the door again.

" Do you know the time, please ? " she cried.

" No. I'll tell you in a jiffy."

She was putting on her stockings now. She heard him flopping back again, and waited in agonized suspense for his answer.

" It's just five to nine," he said.

" Oh Lord ! "

It couldn't be true ! Then she was an hour late already ! It couldn't be true.

" What's the matter ? " he asked.

" I'm late. That's what's the matter."

" Oh."

That was all he said. He flopped away again. How cruel he was. Could she instil no sense of urgency into him ? He seemed without care. Why didn't he offer to forgo his bath ? Suppose she asked him to ? She must ask him. But how ? How dared she interpose her " skivvy's " will between a " gentleman " and his bath ? All things concerning their " dip " she knew were the holy of holies to gentlefolk. They were Spartans on the matter. She could not " give herself away " by asking him such a thing.

The last of the dirty water ran out with a gurgle. She seized the matches and lit the geyser.

*　　　*　　　*　　　*

Half an hour later he joined her in the dining-room. He had been twenty minutes in his bath, splashing, and washing, and scrubbing, and slooshing as though he had never had a bath in his life before. He had been like a freshly captured seal in there. In the meantime she had found her hat and coat, and dusted her shoes, and combed her hair with his comb, and under his bellowed directions cooked the breakfast and laid the table. She had now realized that she could not be at Chiswick till ten, and all the time she had been beating up her mind for some excuse to make when she arrived there. She had practically decided on an accident. " Oo, madam, I'm ever so sorry I'm late "—these were going to be her first words—" did you get my wire ? " Then she was going to be mystified because they hadn't got the wire, and then go on to say that her aunt had had an accident—run over by a car. . .

Her host entered the dining-room with an assumed brightness, and on seeing that the table was laid and that everything was ready, murmured, " Ha. Excellent," and rubbed his hands.

She took stock of him properly for the first time. He wore a glue double-breasted suit, and he was about thirty-five, with a virile appearance. A thick black moustache, neatly cropped, braced a full and sensual mouth. His dark hair was thick and somewhat wavy, and if allowance were made for the promise of corpulence and a wholly dissipated look, he might have been described as handsome. There was no doubt that he was a " gentleman " all right, Jenny decided. She divined that he had been an " officer " in the war, ever since which, with money of his own, he had devoted himself in a singleminded way to drunkenness. Subsequent conversation proved her surmise to be roughly correct.

As he cracked open his egg, she saw that his hand trembled and that he was suffering physically almost as much as herself from the effects of the night before. He did not speak, but began to eat with an appetite—every now and again giving a sort of sidelong glance at her plate to see how she was getting on.

" How long do you expect it'll take to get to Chiswick ? " she asked at last.

" Oh—not long," he said, and went on munching.

Had he nothing to say ? Had he no explanation to give or

apology to make? She hated this worn and callous air of his.

"We didn't half go it last night—didn't we?" she tried.

"Yes. We did. I'm feeling foul, aren't you?"

"I should say I am. I ain't ever done anything like *that* before."

She was glad to have had the opportunity of making this clear to him, but he made no answer. Instead he filled his mouth with egg, and went on munching.

"Have *you*?" she said.

"Yes. I have. As a matter of fact."

Nothing more. He had as much conversation in him as a stone.

"I'm afraid to say . . ." he added, and took a gulp at his tea. The cup trembled at his lips.

"It was awful about that accident, wasn't it?" she said. She wanted to talk it out—to try and get some comfort from him.

"Yes. It was. Ghastly."

"Do you think that man was—*hurt*?" she said. She could not bring herself to utter the real word.

"Must have been. I'm afraid. . . ."

"You don't think he was killed, do you?" She did not know how she had brought it out, and she felt quite sick as she waited for him to reply.

"Hope not," he said. "You can't say."

All this time she had been trying to eat her egg. At this point, she knew that she did not want it, that she could never eat it, and that it was so much sickly embryo immeasurably repellent in her mouth.

"We ought to have gone back—oughtn't we?"

"Yes. We ought. If I hadn't been so drunk I'd have tried to. It's done now, though."

"Do you think they'll find out?"

"Hope not. They may, of course."

What was he saying! She pushed the plate blindly away from her. She was feeling faint again, and she believed she was going to be sick. She couldn't trouble to pretend to eat any more.

"Aren't you going to eat that egg?"

"No."

"Go on. Can't you eat it?"

"No, thank you."

" May I have it, then. I'm rather ravenous this morning."

" Yes."

She feebly pushed the plate towards him. He at once seized the egg, and began on it.

" What'll happen if they find out ? " she said.

" That's the trouble. You can get jailed for that sort of thing nowadays."

*Jailed !* The word rang through her like a wild peal of bells. She was going to faint. Those black smudges were coming again. . . . She was going to faint. . . .

" Here," she heard him saying. " Are you all right ? . . ."

She looked at the window, and the smudges danced in front of her. He had risen now, and was standing over her.

" I'll be all right," she managed to murmur.

" Sure ? "

" Yes."

" I'll get you some water, shall I ? "

" Ta."

He left the room. She was better now. Jailed ! Oh—she wished she was dead—she wished she was dead and out of it.

He returned with the water. She took it and sipped at it.

" Sorry to trouble you," she said.

" Not a bit. One feels like that after a binge like last night." And he returned to his egg.

" I shouldn't worry about that accident," he said, a few moments later. " We weren't driving after all."

" No. We weren't. They couldn't do much to us if we weren't driving, could they ? "

" No. I don't expect so."

He didn't expect so ! A fat lot of comfort he was. Was he not affected by the prospect of jail ?

" You don't seem to be taking on much," she said.

" Oh—one's got to be philosophical. I'm feeling pretty bloody myself."

She was surprised by his language. He didn't sound much like a gentleman. Tom would never have dreamed of using such a word in front of her. Tom. Where was Tom now ? If only she were with Tom now—instead of this hard, cold-mannered "gentleman." She hated him and his class. She had it in her heart to love Tom now, she felt.

"We'll have a good stiff whisky and soda when we go out," he said. "It's the only thing."

Whisky and soda? What a strange idea. Did he imagine she was going to drink any more, after all she had had? He must be a confirmed and hopeless drunkard to think of such a thing. And couldn't he get it into his head that she had got to go to work?

"I've got to go to work," she said.

"Oh, you can be a bit late, can't you? What sort of a job is it?"

"I'm with two old ladies," she said, remembering the evasion of the night before.

"Well, that doesn't sound very fearsome."

"I'm a servant," she said, suddenly feeling savage. But she repented having said it a moment after, and burned with humiliation. Remembering all her talk of being a mannequin, all her castles-in-the-air of the night before, it was as painful as if she had admitted she was a thief.

"Oh," was his expressionless comment. But she could see that he despised her. There was a pause.

"There may be something about it in the papers this morning," he said. "We'll see when we go out."

The papers! She had never thought of that. Oh God—was there to be no end to her miseries? Then this was an affair for the public—she was to be disgraced before the whole world! She would die—that's what she would do—she would die.

He gulped down the rest of his tea noisily, and rose.

"Well—let's get going," he said.

\*       \*       \*       \*

"Let's get going." The words horrified her. She rose with him, and at once a panic transcending all her other panics seized her. "Let's get going!" Her hour was upon her! Action called, and now she was to be put to the test. "Oo, madam, I'm ever so sorry I'm late—did you get my wire?" She'd never do it—she'd never do it! He went briskly out of the room (he could move sharply enough when she didn't want him to) and she followed him.

She went into the bedroom, and, distraught with outward trembling and intestinal excitement, put on her coat and hat. She looked at herself in the little mirror. She was ready. She came out again into the passage.

" Ready ? " he said.

" Yes."

He motioned her to precede him downstairs. At the bottom of the stairs a small white door with a Yale lock faced her. She opened it, and they were in a dark passage. They went down an ill-lit stairway with other little doors on each landing.

No one was about, and the front door of the house was open. In this manner was concluded Jenny's first night with a gentleman friend.

They emerged into a quiet, ordinary suburban road, with trees. The sun was now shining in a blue sky, and everything bore the easy-going countenance of tradesmen's ten o'clock. A few carts were stationed outside the houses, and a woman called to her delaying child down the street.

" Is the garage far ? " she asked.

" No. It's just round here."

They did not speak as they walked along. They turned round a corner, and came upon some shops. She thought she saw a garage in the distance.

" Is that it ? " she said.

" Yes. That's it."

She hoped it was a closed car. When they reached Chiswick she would make him drop her just at the corner. No—there were infinite perils to that. They might be out of doors, and see her getting out. Suppose they saw her getting out of a " gentleman's " car ! She must make him drop her a good way away.

Here was the garage—a vast, stone-floored place, with a few cars scattered about, but no sign of human life. He blew a horn belonging to one of the cars—but nothing happened. He blew it again, and a little man came forth from within. He was within five yards of them when he was hailed from a small office right at the back. He went back again.

" Ain't he coming ? " she asked.

" Oh—he'll be along," he said, and looked vaguely at a car near by.

Was the whole world in a conspiracy to delay her this morning ? He went on as though she had the whole morning to waste. She dared not guess how long past ten it was now.

The little man came out again.

" Good morning, Mr. Perry."

" Good morning, Joe."

So her friend's name was Perry. She wondered what his Christian name was. They were moving leisurely towards a car at the back.

" I believe your back tyre's down, Mr. Perry."

" Oh. Is it ? "

They came up to the car.

" Yes," said Joe, touching the tyre affectionately, and smiling. " Flat as your hat."

" M'm . . ." said her friend, and they looked at it critically. Joe went away.

" What does that mean ? " she said. " Can't we go ? "

" Oh no. It only wants some air."

Joe came back with an instrument, and attached it to the valve. A moment later a horrible roaring noise began.

" I've left my gloves behind ! " shouted Mr. Perry, through this noise. " If you'll sit in the car I'll be back in a moment ! "

He had gone. He had left her, in this nerve-tearing noise, to battle alone with the world ! His unthinking cruelty knew no limits. She climbed into the throbbing car. It was an open one, needless to say. She sat by the driver's seat.

The noise ceased, and Joe detached the instrument. " That'll last for a little anyway," he said, and smiled.

She smiled back. " I hope so," she said. " Do you know what the time is ? "

" Yes." He walked backwards in order to look up at a clock. " It's just five and twenty past."

Five and twenty past ! Then she wouldn't be there till something like eleven ! And he had gone to fetch his gloves !

Ah—here he was. He had been quick—she had to admit that. He looked briefly at the tyre, jumped into his seat, and banged the door after him.

He pushed a knob, but nothing happened, save a little cough from the engine. He pushed it again. Another little cough—no more. He pushed it again. . . .

" Here, Joe ! " he cried.

Silence reigned in the garage.

" Joe ! "

Joe came out.

" Give her a swing, will you, Joe ? "

It was all right, apparently. It only wanted a swing, whatever that was.

" She's cold, is she ? " said Joe.

" Yes."

Joe went to the handle, and gave it a jerk. Then another. The engine hesitated : then caught. A terrifying and overwhelming roar ensued, and Joe walked away. The roar died down. The car began to move. At last they were off.


He turned round to the left outside the garage, and, changing his gear, went snarling straight up a long incline with houses each side. At the top he turned to the right, and they were going down hill. She at once knew where she was. They were on the steep road leading from Richmond Park down into the town. He said nothing, but concentrated on his driving.

Here she was in another car, then ! She was familiar with cars now. How grim and overwhelming had been her sudden commerce with these fearful machines—these relentless, man-killing inventions of man ! And only last night she had fancied the prospect of Motoring. Oh—all that was changed now. In one night her whole life had been changed.

They had passed Richmond Bridge on their left, and were coming into the thick of the town. She saw a few people on the pavement glancing at them as they passed—but without interest. She might have been a " lady " taking a drive. If they only knew how far she was from that.

There was a policeman down there—in the middle of the road. The arm of the law ! He couldn't know who they were. But suppose he did ? They were magic—the police. They knew everything. No one knew how they knew it.

He was clean-shaven, with a red face. Just as they approached him, he came forward and put up his hand. She met his eyes. It was all right—it was only a hold-up of the traffic—but her heart had missed a beat.

He had his back to them now. He was less than three yards away, and she shuddered at the sight of him. What would he do—that red-necked, tall, hard policeman—if he knew who were behind him now? She was in the very jaws of destruction.

The policeman dropped his hand, and again caught her eye as he motioned them forward. They sped ahead. Any moment, she felt, there might be a sudden call from behind, and they would be after her.

" I'm so scared," she said, " that even a policeman frightens me."

" Yes," he said. " I got rather a funny feeling, too."

If only he hadn't said that! If only he would try to reassure her! But how could he? There was no reassurance. They were a pair of criminals driving exposed through the town.

Now they were flying along the Richmond Road, by the high wall of Kew Gardens.

" If you see a paper man, we'll stop," he said. " There may be something in."

If only he wouldn't keep on reminding her! The idea of the papers—of public exposure of this event—frightened her most of all. Oh, what had happened to her in one night?

She wished he wouldn't go so fast—she was beginning to feel sick again. She was cold, too.

Here they were—going over Kew Bridge. And there was another policeman. Was he going to stop them, too? No. He had let them go by. It was astounding—the way the whole world was letting them go by. . . .

She wished he wouldn't turn so sharp—she had come all over sick again. . . . And cold. . . . She was freezing cold.

Here they were, passing the Great West Road. The Great West Road! Only a few miles up there it had happened! Why weren't they arrested here and now? She was so cold and sick she would faint. She was going all giddy! She must control herself—control herself! And in a few minutes' time they would be at Chiswick! . . . " Oo—I'm ever so sorry, madam. . . ."

She could never do it ! Her teeth were chattering with cold and fright. She'd die of cold. She could never do it !

" Where do you turn off ? " he asked.

" At the Green," she said. " It's just ahead."

He put on speed. In another moment they would be practically opposite the Green. But there was a tram ahead of them now—lumberingly barring their progress.

" Here we are, aren't we ? " he said, indicating the road to the right by the Church.

" Oo—I'm *ever so sorry, madam.* . . ." She couldn't—she couldn't ! She had got to have time to collect herself a bit.

" Yes," she said. " But drive on a bit, will you ? I'm feeling too queer to go in at the moment."

" Right you are. We'll go on to my Bank, shall we ? It's just along here in the High Road."

" Yes," she said.

" Have you *got* to go back to these weird people ? " he asked.

" Yes. I'm afraid I have."

What an extraordinary attitude he took. . . . They still could not get ahead of the tram, and they were going at a snail's pace. The High Road was massed with traffic on the road and people on the pavement. What if she were seen ? What if one of those old women were out shopping and saw her ? It would be all up then. She ought to have had the courage to go in at once.

Here they were—here was the Bank. . . . Oh Lord—he was going to stop in front of everybody ! . . .

He got out and slammed the door of the car. " I shan't be a moment," he said. " We'll have a drink after this." He had gone.

Another drink ? Did he imagine she was ever going to touch another drop of alcohol again ? She had got to get in, and get in quick.

Everybody was looking at her now. He could have chosen no more perfect way of exposing her to the multitude. She had never seen such a crowd. It was the thickest moment of the shopping hour. It seemed that thousands of women were passing her every moment—and each one staring at her. Fancy, —sitting in a car, outside a bank, with a gentleman friend at eleven o'clock, in the very neighbourhood wherein she should

three hours ago have been making beds and scrubbing dishes !
Fine goings on for a " skivvy " ! And all these women knew
it, too—or they looked as though they did.

" Oo, madam, I'm ever so sorry. . . ." She'd never do it.
Why hadn't she thought out a proper excuse in detail ? She had
meant to. She had had two hours in which to think one out,
and yet somehow she hadn't. She was too cold to think now.
He would be out any moment. She was too cold to think.

A stiff whisky and soda, he had said at breakfast. Would that
warm her ? She had heard that whisky warmed you. Perhaps
he was right. And if she sat down in the warm a minute she
would have time to collect herself and think. It was too late to
worry about being late now. Here he was.

He came out into the road, jumped in, slammed the door,
and began to put on his gloves.

" They're open by now," he said. " We'll go and have one,
shall we ? "

" All right," she said. " I don't see one would do any harm."

\* \* \* \*

They moved on, behind another tram, about five hundred
yards, and then slowed down before a large public house on the
left, facing the Chiswick Market on the other side of the road.
He turned round to the left and pulled up before its side entrance.

She was too cold and silly to open the door of the car for
herself, and he came round to do it for her. As soon as she
touched the ground she found that her legs were barely supporting her. They moved forward to a heavy swing door, which
he held back for her, and they went in.

All was darkness and silence within. The place had just
opened. A public house, which is normally blazing with electricity, is at its gloomiest in the morning, when there are few
customers to be pleased and its thrifty proprietors are making
use of whatever sunlight may shine through its spare apertures.
They passed through a bare-boarded, deserted public bar, and
through another door into the lounge.

This was a large, echoing, dismal room, with oilcloth on the
floor, tables and chairs all about, and a low jutting fire, upon
which a man was at this moment pouring coals. On one side

was the bar, and at the opposite end a decayed fountain not in use set in a despondent nook, whose stone and trellis work caught the oblique light of day from an invisible skylight above.

So here she was in another pub ! Her introduction to these haunts of destruction had been as melancholy and overpowering as her introduction to the motoring world, and she felt used to them already.

The man, who was dressed in rough working costume, looked at them as they came in, and then went away with his scuttle. They took a table in front of the fire.

" What'll you have ? " he said, speaking in a low voice, as though in deference to the tenantless gloom of the place. " Whisky and soda ? "

" Yes, please," she said.

" What brand ? "

" I don't know."

" Black and White, White Label, Johnny, White Horse, what ? "

" I think I'll have a Johnny," she said, snatching at a familiar name, and visioning a dreadfully robust figure striding prodigiously through summer landscapes. That was not the symbol of her own impression of the effects of alcohol.

He went to the bar, and she drew up a little nearer to the fire. She was grateful enough for the warmth. If she could only get warm she might be able to face her fate.

He returned with two small tumblers filled to the brim, and he sat down. " You'll feel better when you've had that," he said, and splitting open a freshly bought packet of cigarettes, he offered her one.

She hesitated. It would never do to go in smelling of smoke. But then she would be smelling of alcohol ! She had better smoke to take that away. She shouldn't have come in here. She took the cigarette, and he lit it for her.

She looked at her drink. It looked like ginger ale to her. She had no faith in its efficacy. She took a sip.

" That's a strong one, ain't it ? " she said.

" Yes," he said. " It's a double double. It's the only thing on occasions like this."

She had never tasted whisky before. It was horrid. It was

like wood or cork gone rotten. But the sharp taste of the soda cleansed her mouth. He had drunk half his already.

" Oo, madam, I'm ever so sorry I'm late. . . ." She still hadn't thought of a decent excuse. And if they accepted what she said, she would have to set to and do the housework ! It was too dreadful to think about. She took another sip. This drink was cleaning her mouth at any rate. And this fire was lovely. She could stay by it for ever.

" Have you really got to go to these weird people ? " he asked.

" Of course, I have. What do you think ? "

" Can't you telephone them or something ? "

" They ain't on the telephone."

" Well—can't you send them a wire or something ? "

" Saying what ? " she said.

" Oh—you can make some excuse—can't you ? "

" Yes—I can if I want to be out of a job."

" Is it as good a job as all that ? "

He would never understand. He was just a " gentleman "— an idler without knowledge of the laws governing workers. She took another sip, and looked wretchedly at the decayed, wanly lit fountain. She ought to have gone by now. But she couldn't leave this fire just for a moment.

" You don't seem to realize what trouble I'm in," she said.

" I don't see that you're in any trouble," he said.

She believed this whisky was going to her head already. A strange feeling of lightheadedness had come over her, and remained as she looked at the fountain. It was not sickness— but lightheadedness. It couldn't be drunkenness—she had had nothing. She took another sip.

" Well, I should like to know what trouble is, then," she answered.

" Oh—surely it's not as bad as all that."

This lightheadedness—it was the whisky. And it was something besides lightheadedness—a faint warming and enlivening feeling about the heart. It made her feel a little better. She took another sip.

" I should say it's bad enough," she said, " with that accident and all."

"No," he said. "I don't see why. We can't do anything now."

He seemed to be changing his mind a bit now. He hadn't taken that attitude before. Was it possible that she had exaggerated the horror of what had occurred? It might be so. This lightheaded feeling. . . . She didn't seem to be able to think about anything. She was feeling better, though, inside and altogether. He was right about the whisky. It was picking her up.

"I hope you're right," she said, and took another sip.

There it went again. It seemed to trickle down and heat and awaken every little cell and channel with its brisk medicining. It was like what she had felt last night—a little nicer if anything. Last night it had been like the feeling of good news without the good news. Now it was like the news that her bad news was not such bad news after all.

"Of course I'm right," he said. "Do you think we're going to be behind prison bars or something?"

What was this? He was taking a different line now. Had she read too much into his odd remarks about jails and the papers this morning? She rather thought she had.

She was feeling better. It was this whisky. She took another sip. It was wonderful stuff as a reviver —there was no doubt about that. Nothing he could say, no mental comforting could so brace her as this inward corporal reassurance, this physical information, of good things descending on her. She was still lightheaded, but she felt worlds better.

"Well," she said, "I hope you're right."

He had drained off his glass. "Of course I am," he said. "There's nothing to get a wind up about. Let's have another, shall we?"

"Lord, no! I've got to go. I haven't finished this one."

"Well—do you mind if I do?"

"No."

He had left her. The door opened, and two men came in, laughing and talking with each other. They went to the bar, and in an instant had enlivened the whole atmosphere.

"Nothing to get the wind up about. . . ." She wondered whether he was right. He had been calm like that all the time.

It had been she alone that had got the wind up. She took another sip.

What, after all, had she done ? She had been with a party in a car, and there had been an accident. What was wrong with that ? *She* hadn't been driving. It wasn't her fault. She had exaggerated this out of all proportion.

He had returned. " Sure you won't have another ? " he said, as he sat down.

" No thanks," she said. " It's ever so good, though, this whisky, ain't it ? "

What had happened to her ? She had been tricked into speaking almost with hilarity.

" Yes, it is," he said, and added, " I say—why don't you cut these people out and spend the day with me ? "

" Oo—I can't," she said.

To spend the day with him ? What an idea. . . . Gee—she was hot. It was this fire. And lightheaded, too. She wasn't in a fit state to go and work. Spend the day with him. . . . She took a gulp at her whisky.

" Why not ? " he said. " We could go and have lunch at the Clarendon."

The Clarendon ! That swell place at Hammersmith ! Gee she was with a " gentleman " all right this time—and he seemed to have money to spend. This was something a cut above Andy —if you liked. Lunch at the Clarendon. That would be something to tell 'em. What would Violet think of that ? And gee ! —wasn't she just hungry !

" But I couldn't," she said. " I'd lose my job."

" Well, you can find another, can't you ? "

Find another ? She had not seen it in that light. It sounded plausible enough.

" But I ain't got no money," she said.

" Well, I let you have some. How much do you want ? "

" Oh, I couldn't take money," she said. " Thank you very much."

" Yes you could. You can't go back in this state. I feel responsible in a way. Would ten pounds be any good ? "

Was she dreaming ? Ten pounds ! She could live for weeks on ten pounds—for an indefinite period !

She must control herself. To accept ten pounds from a gentleman friend? This way led to destruction. She must exercise her will and get away.

"Come on," he said. "We'll lunch at the Clarendon, and then go and rest our weary heads at the pictures. What about it?"

The Clarendon—and then to the pictures with a gentleman friend!

And the alternative to go back, and plead lying excuses, and wash dirty dishes, and make beds, and cook!

"Come on," he said. "Why not?"

Why not! Wild fiends of joy knocked at the gates of her will. How could she resist them? This was ruin—she was getting drunk again. This was the turning point of her life. If she lost her will now she had lost all. Yet why not? With one word of assent she could be lifted from undreamed of woe to undreamed of bliss—step out from her deep unhappiness as from a garment. She could be free of all care. She could have a grand time. She had insanely exaggerated the horrors of last night. Once again she could laugh at those two—see them pityingly as "two old fossils."

"Well, I might think about it," she said.

She had only opened the gate a little way, but the fiends had surged in and captured the citadel in a moment. She would! She was free again! She was going to the Clarendon with her gentleman friend! Those two old fossils could wait for her!

They were nothing but old fossils. She had always known it. They could wait for her. Serve them right! She'd find another job all right. She'd find a better one. Why had she wanted to stick to that silly job? She had been mad—distraught with absurd depression. But the mists had disappeared now—simply vanished like magic! She had awakened. She had become herself once more!

"That's better," he said. "Will you have another now?"

"All right," she said. "Ta."

## IV

## MARION AND BELLA

A ND so Marion and Bella never saw their treasure again. That was a black morning over at Chiswick. Like a plague, Jenny's guilt infected others as well as herself, contorted them equally with pain, and brought them, for the time being at any rate, as low.

At five past eight, that is to say when Jenny was five minutes late, Marion knocked at Bella's bedroom door and went in. She found Bella up and awake, combing her hair in front of the mirror of the dressing-table. She went to a cupboard they both used, and rearranged some clothes.

Having adroitly prefaced the query with general remarks on the weather and their health, " Has the girl come yet ? " asked Bella.

" Not yet," said Marion, calmly. " It's only just on eight." And she left the room.

She knew what Bella was feeling, but she rather despised her for giving way to herself so early and readily. She was not going to let Bella's nervousness and morbidity stimulate her own. So often had Marion doubted and feared concerning such matters, and so often had her doubts and fears been proved foolish, that she felt she at least had enough control of herself now, not to start worrying when the girl was less than ten minutes late. All the same, the sheer effort of control (like all other efforts) was a little painful, and she could not help wishing that the girl would come, so that she might be released merely from that effort.

When it was twenty minutes past eight, that is to say when the girl was twenty minutes late, Bella came and knocked at Marion's door.

" Come in," said Marion, and Bella entered.

Marion was now combing her own hair.

" Here's that paper you were wanting," said Bella, and she laid a copy of *The Daily Express* (which Marion had asked for yesterday) on the dressing-table beside Marion. She then went to the window, without a word, and looked out.

Seeing that the girl was twenty minutes late, Marion now thought that it was rather absurd, and in itself symptomatic of acute nervousness, to say nothing and pretend that nothing had happened. So she said, quite firmly and coolly :

" She's twenty minutes late. I wonder what's happened."

This made Bella think that this was an opportunity to show self-control.

" Oh," she said, " She's just a little late. I shouldn't worry, if I were you."

This annoyed Marion, because she knew that it was only Bella that was worrying. So she said, rather tartly :

" *I'm* not worrying."

This annoyed Bella, because it implied that she (Bella) was the one that was worrying, whereas exactly the opposite was the case. So, being annoyed, she said :

" Well, you seem to be, Marion."

This annoyed Marion extremely, because it was directly provocative, and she did think that Bella might have refrained from bringing personal feeling into a crisis like this. And so she said :

" Really, Bella, I'm not going to quarrel with you, you know. You'd better leave me alone, hadn't you ? "

This quite enraged Bella, because it looked as though she were being ordered out of the room. And so she said :

" Really, Marion, how dare you speak to me like that ? "

And so in this way the wretched little servant girl, who had gone and got drunk and was at this very moment having a bath in a strange gentleman's flat at Richmond, had unwittingly brought about a prodigious event at Chiswick—a full blown quarrel between the two old women. So widespread and capsizing is the wash of the barge of sin.

There was no doubt about its being a quarrel.

" Oh, shut up, shut up—can't you ! " cried Marion. " You'll drive me mad ! "

" Mad ! I like that ! " cried Bella. " Mad, indeed ! It's you that's mad ! "

" Well, get on out—can't you ! Get on out ! Leave me alone ! "

" Leave you alone ! I'll leave you alone all right ! I'll——"

" Where *is* the girl ! " cried Marion. " Where *is* the girl ! That's what I want to know ! "

" Ah, that's what I want to know," said Bella, quietly, and because they had now stumbled upon the true origin and fount of their trouble, they both lost in a moment all their rage against each other and were quite calm.

" We're getting worried about this girl," said Marion, after a pause, " that's all."

No further apology was needed.

" Yes," said Bella. " You're quite right. We must keep calm."

" That's right," said Marion. " We must keep calm."

Keep calm. From that moment " Keep calm " was their standard and watchword. But how could they keep calm when the situation contained not the ingredients of calm ?— when they had rapidly to decide what was to be done ?—when a thousand alternatives of action clamoured for their due ?

What were they to do ? Were they to get breakfast themselves ? If so, were they to get it at once, or wait till the half-past and see if the girl turned up ? Should they get Robert a cup of tea to go on with ? Should they tell Robert ? Should they beguile Robert ? Should they go out and send a wire to the girl's address ? Should Bella go out and send the wire, and Marion get the breakfast ? Or should Marion go out and send the wire, and Bella get the breakfast ? Should they cease bothering about the girl, and do all the housework themselves ? Should they go out and try and get Mrs. Brackett to come in for an hour or two ? Was it wise to have that awful woman in the house again ? Was it not unwise to turn from possible aid in a crisis ? Should Bella go out for Mrs. Brackett while Marion got the breakfast ? Or should Marion go out for Mrs. Brackett while Bella got the breakfast ? Would Mrs. Brackett come ? Hadn't

they better go to the Registry Office for a new servant altogether ?
But wasn't Mrs. Brackett better than a new servant at this jucture
because she was familiar with the house ? Hadn't they better
see if the girl turned up ? . . .

In other words, what in God's name *were* they going to do ?
Running about the kitchen and the house, and looking out of
the windows down the street, and putting on the kettle, and
finishing their dressing, their minds and conversation revolved
around the crisis, and they swore that they would keep calm.

From this turmoil a line of action finally evolved. They
prepared Robert a reasonable breakfast, and Marion took it
up to his room. She yelled at him that the girl was delayed, but
would be coming later. His grave eyes gave no intimation as
to whether he had been deceived by the semi-falsehood or was
resigned to the truth, and she left it at that. Then she got ready
to go out for Mrs. Brackett.

At the front door she departed from Bella with a kiss, like a
last messenger to the lines from a beleaguered outpost, and
Bella was left in charge. It was then half-past ten.

An hour later Marion returned. Bella had only to look at her
to see that she was transfigured with important tidings.

" Well ? " she said.

" She's coming at five o'clock," said Marion.

" Well, that's something," said Bella. The moment was too
great for any further display of relief.

" Now I must lie down," said Marion. " I've been hurrying
too much."

Bella did what housework she could, and when Marion rose
they began to get lunch together.

As there was no proper food in the house, and so the questions
arose as to whether they should go out to buy food, what
manner of food they should go out to buy, which of them should
go out for it, whether there was not enough in the house after
all, whether there was *time* to go out for it in any case, why
Marion had not got some while she was out before, and so on
and so forth—the getting of lunch had as wearing effect upon
the nerves as the pursuit of Mrs. Brackett. At the very last
moment they decided not to go out for any food, and they
poached some eggs.

And so it went on all day. At five Mrs. Brackett, true to her word, came. She cooked the man evening meal, she cleared up the house, she re-established order in every way, and she promised to come to-morrow, and continue exactly as before the change.

Much as they disliked her, and inferior as she was to the little treasure they had for some mysterious reason lost, they had to admit that she had turned up trumps on this occasion.

And then, three or four days later, as they were sitting talking peacefully just before going to bed, a curious thing occurred. Jenny underwent a horrible metamorphosis. From a perfect little treasure of a girl who for some reason (probably illness) had failed to return, she was converted, in a moment, into a black scheming little devil of all evil. As they talked they discovered that in their hearts they had never liked her, but not until now, when they had returned to the solid Mrs. Brackett, did they realize what danger they had been in, and how insane they had been to engage such a painted, saucy, specious, common little factory thing like that. How could they be surprised that she had run away ? It was a good thing she had not taken anything with her, and they might very well find that she had when they looked things over. Indeed, it was more than likely that she belonged to some gang of thieves, and had been sent by them to look over the house. They could hardly credit that they had not seen through her. However, it was no use regretting anything now. They had Mrs. Brackett back, after all. They had every admiration for Mrs. Brackett. She might have her faults, but you could *rely* on Mrs. Brackett. And what more could you ask, in these days, than a servant to rely on ?

Thus they talked, and flattered themselves with hopeful thoughts, and went to bed once more unconscious of their long-drawn-out sorrow and helplessness. And so they would go on and on, day after day, and perhaps year after year, in the same tormented way—and never, oddly enough, have anything but a kind of horror of the thought of the day when they would not be able to get up and go on, but would have perforce to lie and be patient, and then, of a sudden, while all the world moved and suffered around them, become startling waxen images which did not move or suffer.

# CONCLUSION

"ALL through a glass of port," Jenny, the girl of the streets, had said. She had said it in jest, but who shall decline to surmise that she had stumbled upon the literal truth? If Jenny had not taken that first glass she would not have taken the second, and if she had not taken the second she would not have taken the third, and if she had not taken the third she would not then and there have resolved to abandon herself to the pleasures and perils of drink. And if she had not done that, she would not have become involved in the events which lost her her job, and set her going down the paths of destruction.

Probably there was never any doubt of Jenny's social destiny, but can it not at least be said that that glass of port unlocked her destiny? Her ignorance, her shallowness, her scheming self-absorption, her vanity, her callousness, her unscrupulousness—all these qualities—in combination with her extreme prettiness and her utter lack of harmony with her environment—were merely waiting and accumulating in heavy suspense in the realms of respectability to be plunged down into the realms where they rightly belonged: and a single storm, lasting no longer than six hours, achieved this.

From the sheer nervous wear and tear of that calamitous and climactic night Jenny never survived. Being what she was, how could she? Her story, from her brief moment of revival in whisky that morning, is another story altogether, but it deviated, as has been seen, in no way from that which the sardonic world in general (hearing of a run-away servant girl spending the night and drinking whisky and having lunch with a strange gentleman friend) would have predicted.

At half-past eight that morning, at the **** Hotel, Paddington, there was a knock at their bedroom door, and a stout woman, incongruously dressed as a maid, brought in a large breakfast tray for two, and laid it on the bed without a word.

Jenny, lying over on her side, was very sleepy, and for a moment actually could not recall where she was or with whom she had spent the night. She succeeded in remembering, however, without opening her eyes to look. " You pour it out," she said.

After a while she sat up, and, taking her first sip at the tea, began to revive. She even had a little toast and marmalade.

He was in a wretched state of depression, and could eat nothing. She could see that he repented last night's dissipation, and she had suffered too much in that way herself not to feel sorry for him. He gulped and gasped at the hot tea, and looked ahead of him.

" You're feeling sorry now," she said, smiling. " Aren't you ? "

She always rather enjoyed this moment of the morning, after she had spent the night with a man. Being able to lie on in bed, without regrets of any sort, while he, full of remorse and with passion spent, had to rush off back to his work, filled her with an indolently indulgent, one might almost say a maternal feeling towards him.

" Oh—I'm all right," he said.

There was a pause as she buttered her roll.

" Have you got to get back to business ? " she asked.

" Yes. I got to be there at half-past nine."

" Married ? " she said.

" Ah ! . . ."

" I'll bet you'll tell *her* a fine story when you get back, won't you ? "

He grinned, revealing the gaps in his yellowed teeth.

A moment later he gulped off the rest of his tea, and got out of bed. He was a simply dreadful sight in his shirt, and she tactfully lay back and looked at the ceiling.

" You know I said last night I'd seen you somewhere before ? . . ." she said.

" Yes ? " He was washing his face in cold water at the washing stand now.

" I've remembered where it was."

" Oh ? " He went on washing his face.

" I know your name."

" What ? "   He turned round and looked at her with his face dripping. This had clearly alarmed him.

" I said I know your name. Your Christian name at any rate."

" I bet," he said, hiding his nervousness by drying his face. " Go on. What is it ? "

" It's Andy," she said. " Isn't it ? "

She saw how afraid he was, and she despised him for it.

" Eh ? " she said.

" How do you know that ? " he said, now drying his hands.

" You were in a car accident with me, weren't you ? " she said.

He stopped drying his hands, and looked at her, for an awe-stricken moment, in the face. Then he went on drying.

" Well—what about it ? "

" We ran over a man on a bike—didn't we ? "

" Well—what about it ? "

" And you drove on—didn't you ? "

" Well—what about it ? "

" Oh—nothing. Bit funny meeting you again like this, though."

" Yes. I suppose it is."

What a funk he was in ! Why did these little men always imagine they were going to be blackmailed when they went with women ? It would serve him right if he was. In fact, on second thoughts, that was rather a good idea. She had never tried blackmail.

" Did the police ever get on to that accident ? " she said.

" No. Why do you ask ? "

" I expect they'd still give a lot to know, wouldn't they ? "

" What do you mean by that ? "

" Oh—nothing."

There was a silence as he began to climb into his trousers.

" You're not trying to blackmail me by any chance, are you ? " he said.

" Oh no," she said.   " But I do think you might give me that extra quid—to make up the fiver. I know you've got it on you.'

" Well, you can get it out of your mind—see ? I'll bring in a policeman here, if you're not careful."

" So's I can tell them about that accident ? "

He did not answer. He was trembling all over.

" You're getting rather excited, aren't you ? " she said.

He went on dressing in silence. As he put on his waistcoat he took out a pound note and flung it on the bed.

" There," he said. " That do you ? "

" Very nicely. Ta."

She thought him a pitiable fool to have lost his nerve to the extent of giving in to her demand, but she was pleased with the success of her little ruse, and felt nothing but kindly indulgence towards him again. Poor little wretch. How oddly had she got the better of him in the long run of years !

He had now got on his hat and coat, and was looking round the room to see whether he had left anything behind.

" Ain't you going to kiss me ? " she said.

" I'm in a hurry, I'm afraid."

" Come on," she said. " Come and kiss me good-bye."

With an air of impatience he strode over to the bed, and kissed her.

" Thank you," said Jenny, smiling at his childishness. " I only hope you've enjoyed yourself, dear."

He went straight out of the room, and a moment later, as she picked up the pound note, she heard his brisk footsteps receding down the pavement outside. Then the sound was lost in the roar of a passing 'bus, and he was swallowed up for ever in the great world of London.

# THE PLAINS OF CEMENT

## ELLA

### CHAPTER I

AT five o'clock in the afternoon, when the turbulent and desperate traffic, coursing through the veins of the West End, announces the climax of London's daily fever, a thing occurs in Oxford Street, which, though unknown to the great majority, and barely perceptible by the senses of anyone in that overwhelming noise, is all the same of great ulterior significance. The bolts on the inner sides of the doors of the public-houses are slid back, and any member of the public is at liberty to enter and drink.

In most cases advantage is not at once taken of this liberty. Indeed, it may be said that only the chronically dissolute are instantaneously alive to the opportunity; and the places generally remain gloomy and empty for at least a quarter of an hour. All the same, there they are open.

By a curious instruction of the law, Oxford Street does not receive impartial treatment at five o'clock. On one side of the street only—the north side—may the houses open their doors. On the other side they must remain dumb and lifeless until half-past five. And the same dispensation applies not only to the buildings on either side of the road but to the entire districts north and south of Oxford Street. Thus it is that Oxford Street, for this area of London at this time of day, constitutes a river of furious traffic dividing an arid from a flowing land—a fact of which an enormous number of its citizens are unconscious, but of the profoundest moment to the chronically dissolute aforementioned.

Among the hundreds upon hundreds of taverns sliding back their bolts in the favoured domain, was " The Midnight Bell "— a small, but bright and cleanly establishment, lying in the vicinity

of the Euston Road and Warren Street. Though it had no wide
reputation, all manner of people frequented "The Midnight
Bell." This was in its nature, of course, since it is notorious that
all manner of people frequent all manner of public-houses—
which in this respect resemble railway stations and mad-houses.
Nevertheless, a student of the streets, conceiving "The Midnight
Bell" as the nucleus of a London zone less than half a mile in
diameter, could not have failed to have been impressed by the
stupendous variety of humanity huddled within the region thus
isolated by the mind's eye. The respectable, residential precincts
of Regent's Park, the barracks and lodging-houses of Albany
Street, the grim senility of Munster Square, the commercial
fury of the Euston and Tottenham Court Roads, the criminal
patches and Belgian penury of Charlotte and Whitfield Streets,
that vast palace of pain known as the Middlesex Hospital, the
motor-salesman's paradise in Great Portland Street, the august
solemnity of Portland Place itself—all these would crowd in upon
each other in the microcosm thus discriminated—a microcosm
well-nigh as incongruous and grotesque as any that the searcher
might be able to alight upon in the endless plains of cement at
his disposal.

Here, then, stood "The Midnight Bell," and anyone entering
its Saloon Bar of an evening would have found its chief figure,
a young woman of the name of Ella, in charge. She would
either be talking quietly to a customer at one end of the bar, or
moving about busily dispensing those distillations to whose
existence and efficacy the whole building owed its origin and
peculiar design.

Ella had no idea that she was dispensing mental or spiritual
states. She had no knowledge of the potency of drink, which she
personally detested : she had no knowledge that she played a
notable and curious part in the uproar and excitation of civilization : she had no knowledge of the oddity of her station behind
that bar—a virtuous, homely, and simple-minded young woman,
set up for five hours on end to withstand and feed the accumulating strength of the behaviour of scores upon scores of strange
men manifestly out, or going out, of their minds. She did not
even have any conscious knowledge of the nightmare variety
of her geographical surroundings.  "We get all sorts in here,"

she would say, in her slow, amiable way. Or, " Oh yes. They
get ever so fresh, sometimes." Or, " It's a funny business, that's
a fact." And having thus peacefully called upon her wonderful
inner machinery for rendering the abnormal normal without a
qualm, she would not give the matter another thought.

Such was the sovereign blindness which characterized Ella's
attitude towards her own employment and the part she played
north of Oxford Street at five o'clock—a mental state which, in
view of its practical uses, might with greater justice be described
as heaven-sent sagacity. And certainly blindness or stupidity,
in the ordinary sense of the terms, were the last features to be
ascribed to Ella. Indeed, the funny thing about Ella was that
although she perceived and apprehended practically nothing,
she unaccountably perceived and apprehended practically
everything. A liar, or a braggart (and drunkards, whom Ella
coped with as part of her daily task, are most often both) had
only to meet her grey and friendly gaze to be irritatingly aware
of this contradiction. Without knowing it herself she summed up
a person or sensed a situation in a second. Nor was she by any
means inarticulate. The banality of the expressions she employed
in voicing her thoughts was no criterion of those thoughts'
real shrewdness or aptness. Infinitely stale and hackneyed
idioms she certainly used, but this was merely because, having
access to the wisdom of the ages, she used the expressions
sanctified by the ages. Ella always meant what she said. She
breathed life into old forms. Hence, when Ella remarked, say,
that " the longest way round is the shortest way home " she was
not echoing a proverb as a parrot would. On the contrary, after
the continually recurring experience in her everyday life, of the
fact that short, hasty, or violent methods on behalf of any end
generally involve the frustration of the whole endeavour, she
had long sought in her thoughtful mind for some law to cover
the detached instances of this phenomenon, and had at last
alighted, with joy, upon the ready-made aphorism. Similarly
Ella, having observed in some of her friends or customers,
the human but indefensible practice of accusing others of the
very faults from which they themselves most glaringly suffered,
would be heard suggesting, with delightful vividness, that
" people in glass houses should not throw stones " or that

" the pot was calling the kettle black." A poet could have done no better. The sheer force of her sincerity made these stale maxims her own original pronouncements. And she took continuous pleasure in the exercise of this gift, though a super-ficial observer—learning from her lips that still waters run deep, or that you cannot burn the candle at both ends, or that the proof of the pudding is in the eating, or that it is no use crying over spilt milk, or that enough is as good as a feast, or that pride goes before a fall, and innumerable other essences of wisdom—might easily mistake for dullness her genuine love of artistic self-expression.

In appearance Ella was a plain girl—which means that she was incapable of startling. She was neither startlingly attractive, nor startlingly ugly. She could attract no attention at first sight : she could therefore never hope to attract very much attention. This does not mean that she was without admirers. But they were few and far between—so few and far between that in her sadder moments she believed herself to be in some way disinherited from the main privileges and delights of other girls and women. But then something would happen which would surprise her, and instil in her mind a new estimation, possibly a too hopeful and deceptive estimation, of her powers. And then she would be disappointed, and proceed to underestimate herself again. Life thus was very difficult—as it must be for a plain, as distinguished from a downright ugly, or a downright attractive, woman. But difficulties did not disturb Ella very much.

Ella was about twenty-eight years of age, had a good figure, and was always neatly and plainly dressed. Her hair was dark, and, to be " in the fashion " as she put it, she had had it shingled.

On the October evening with which this story commences, a gentleman, entering the Saloon Bar of " The Midnight Bell " about five minutes after the place had opened, caused Ella's heart to flutter, but not with love.

## CHAPTER II

THE Saloon Bar was a narrow apartment about thirty feet long, with a substantial wooden bar going its whole length, and opening out at the inner end into the Saloon Lounge— a bright general room with tables and chairs for the drinker not pressed by time. Ella stood behind the bar, near the till. Thus, on her right, she had a view into the Lounge, wherein Bob, the waiter of " The Midnight Bell," was at this moment pouring coal upon the fire, and poking it up into a blaze.

No other customer had as yet entered, and an air of chilly desolation, like that of an empty theatre before the play, made itself felt amidst the harsh electric light, and labelled, bottly sparkle of Ella and Bob's surroundings. This despondent air was added to by the coldness and darkness of the evening outside— the coldest and darkest yet in the declining year—and the fact that the mind had not yet fully adapted itself to the recent switch over from Summer time—that brutal onslaught upon the nervous rhythm and infinitesimal æsthetic adjustments of the modern Londoner.

The first thing that anybody would notice about the newcomer, who now came forward to the bar with a hearty and yet remotely sinister " Good evening " to Ella, was that he was by no means an old man. That fact was promulgated in his entire demeanour. His bright blue eyes, his decided walk, his quick smile, his erect stature, the nervous turns of his body and movements of his arms, all said the same thing. It might have been argued by some that this intense propaganda of youthfulness in itself made him appear older than he actually was, but that is beside the point. The next thing to be noticed about him was that he was by no means an ugly or utterly insignificant man. Though time (he was fifty-two years old) had whitened his hair and short moustache, though he was of but medium height, though he wore black boots and dressed himself in the conservative collars, ties and garments of a respectable middle-aged clerk, there was yet something about his face, something firm, keen, and comparatively young, which attracted attention. It may have been the sparkling blue of the eyes, it may have been the fine head of wiry white hair, it may have been that thick close-cropped moustache—whatever it was, it was something closely allied to a *military* look, and something which could not pass unnoticed, if only for the reason that he himself was so forcibly conscious of it.

The third and final thing to be noticed at a first glance concerning this newcomer was that he was wearing a new hat. Indeed this feature at the moment enveloped and predominated over all the others. There are new hats and new hats. No man in the history of the world had ever worn a hat quite as gloriously and fervidly new as this. Not that it was a hat which, amidst a crowd of new hats in a hatter's shop, would have in any way been distinguished from its brothers (it was just an ordinary new dove-grey trilby with edges bound with grey silk). It was from its wearer, from its wearer's would-be unconcerned and yet all-pervading self-consciousness of what lay on his head, that it gained its beautiful and vigorous novelty. You could see at a glance that for the time being the man lived in and through his hat. You could see that it cost him sharp torture even to put it on his head, where he could not see it, and it had to take its chance. You could see him searching incessantly for furtive little glimpses of his hat in mirrors, you could see him pathetically reading the fate of his hat in the eyes of strangers, you could see him adjusting his tie as a sort of salute to his hat, as an attempt to live up to his hat. You could see him striving to do none of these things.

It has been said that along with the heartiness of his first "Good Evening" to Ella there was a certain sinister quality. What caused this ? First and foremost, necessarily, his new hat. But there were other, subterranean causes as well. Rigorously as Ella tried to deny it to herself, she inwardly believed that there was something minutely foreboding in his whole demeanour towards her. That was why her heart had fluttered a little as he came in.

"Good evening," she said, courageously smiling, and meeting his eyes. Her next instantaneous impulse was to exclaim "Hullo—you've got a new hat"—but she controlled it. Nor, arduous as the feat of restraint was, did she allow her eyes to convey the same message in the short pause that followed.

" You going to have your usual, Mr. . . . Er . . . ? " she
added.

His " usual " was a half pint of bitter, and she called him
" Mr. . . . Er . . ." because she did not know his name, and
felt that she ought to, since he seemed definitely to have made
up his peculiar mind lately to become a client of " The Midnight
Bell." She was an adept at calling people Mr., Mrs., or even
Miss " . . . Er . . ." It was not a questioning " Er ? "—such
as to ask what *is* the name please. It was the dreamy, cool,
assured " Er " of one who had so intimate a knowledge of the
surname that she did not have to go through the formality of
pronouncing it.

" Yes—I'll have my usual, I think," he said, in his suave
gentlemanly tones, and she had already turned away to get it for
him.

" Isn't it cold, to-night ? " she said, as she tugged at the beer
engine. " I'm half frozen."

" Yes. It is." He seemed a little preoccupied as she put his
beer in front of him, and took his money with her barmaid's
" Ta."

" By the way," he said, with another smile, " I don't think
you *know* my name, yet, do you ? "

" Why, no. I don't believe I do. What is it ? " She replied
thus at once in a smiling and off-hand way, as she busied herself
with putting his money in the till : but secretly she knew that
her worst misgivings had received further nourishment. It was
not that she minded the innocent deceptiveness of her " Er "
being disclosed. It was not that his observation was one which
might easily have cropped up in the give-and-take of conversation across the bar. It was the way in which it was said, and the
grin with which it was accompanied. Moreover the " *yet* "
scared her. " You don't know my name *yet*." What did that
infer ? What else, but that there was some obligation on her
part to know his name in the end, that she had by suggestion
admitted some compact with him wherein the knowing of his
name was a necessary, an immanent step leading to involve-
ments beyond ? She felt entrapped in the meshes of that " *yet*,"
and her spirit strove to escape. How had he established the right
to make this claim on her ? He had only been coming in here

for the last three or four weeks, and she had only spoken to him a dozen times at the most. Had she " encouraged " him ? No. She had been polite ; she had been kind. She was polite and kind to all her customers. It had been he who had singled her out, who, from little casual greetings and remarks on the weather, from little desultory chats about nothing when there were not enough people in the bar to occupy her fully, had step by step led on to the present state of affairs, in which he seemed to have made her his subtle yet consistent objective on entering the bar, and had taken more and more to coming in early, when she was not busy, and conversation might be sustained. And she had respected and returned his growing friendliness. To that extent of course she had " encouraged " him. She had " liked " him. Who, in her place, could have dreamed of being landed with this " *yet* " ? He was an old man. It was true that he was wonderfully " young," but he was an old man. That being so, if the smallest suspicion had ever crossed her mind, she had been justified in dismissing it from her mind as ridiculous introspection. And if it came to that, was all this ridiculous introspection on her part ? Could not his " yet " be interpreted as deriving from a mere desire to establish his adoption of " The Midnight Bell " as his particular public-house in the future ? She wished she could believe so. That, at any rate, was what she must assume in front of him for the time being.

Of all these thoughts Ella gave no sign, as she busied herself with the till, and cheerfully answered " Why no. I don't believe I do. What is it ? "

He did not reply to this at once, but stood there smiling. It was very awkward. She wished to Heaven that Bob would come in from the Lounge (where he appeared to be messing about with an electric switch), and put an end to this *tete-a-tete*. She would have to confide in Bob, and enlist his services in handling this elderly man.

" Go on," she said. " What is it ? " She was compelled by his absurd reticence to speak with a certain archness, and she resented it bitterly.

" Well—as a matter of fact," he said, rummaging in an inner breast pocket, " I believe I've got a card somewhere."

" Oh yes ? . . ." she murmured courteously, and had another

view of his glorious new hat, as he bent his head down, not unlike a parrot diving into its feathers, to rummage more deeply. For a moment she had forgotten the new hat. Now, at the instant it was brought to her attention again, she felt the sudden grip of a hideous suspicion that this new hat itself was somehow aimed at her—that in newness it outshone all worldy new hats by virtue of the very fact that it was aimed at her—that the new hat was yet another manœuvre in some weird strategy going on inside his head. But she dismissed the suspicion again as absurd. After all, why on earth shouldn't the man get a new hat if he wanted to ?

" Ah—here we are," he said, and handed the card across the bar to her.

Were her senses deceiving her in making her believe that his whole frame evidenced a state of suppressed nervousness, that his hand trembled as he gave her the card ? And if his hand trembled, what prompted its trembling ? Love ? And if love, what a perplexing, what an unhappy means of overture—his card. A new hat and a visiting card !

" Ta," she said, and cast her eye over it. *Mr. Ernest Eccles,* she read, and in the corner was his address. " Mr. Ernest Eccles, eh ? " she said in her friendly way. " I'll remember that."

What now ? What was she to do with it ? Was she supposed to give it back, or was it a sort of mad present ? He himself provided no clue to these mysteries. He was standing there, in a shaky silence, lighting a cigarette. She had to take the matter into her own hands.

" I'll keep that," she said, wretchedly attempting to set some sort of facetiousness in motion. " So as I can refer to it." And she stood it up against a bottle on a shelf behind her.

" I certainly hope you will," he said, and he met her eyes in a kind of sustained glare which nettled her beyond measure.

" Oh well . . ." she said, having absolutely nothing to say, and she began to hum, and drum her fingers lightly upon the bar. Oh, *why* didn't Bob come in, and put an end to this ?

" Oh well *what ?* " said Mr. Eccles.

There he went again. He had evidently made up his mind to hound down her every utterance and gesture to-night.

" Oh well *what* ? " And he looked at her quizzingly for an answer. And to what, indeed, had her " Oh well " had reference ? Nothing whatever. It had risen up unsummoned, like a blush, from her prevailing subconscious embarrassment. If she had meant anything, she had meant " Oh well, we really can't go on like this, you know." But how could she tell him that ? She decided to feign denseness to his implications.

" What do you mean ? " she said. " Oh well, what ? "

" Oh, just ' Oh well what,' " said Mr. Eccles, still looking at her.

" I'm afraid," said Ella, smiling, " I don't know what you mean." But although she smiled, there was a slightly nasty look in her eyes—the look of one who, though this presumably was all fun, objected to being made to look a fool in the course of a dalliance she did anything but desire herself.

" You said ' Oh well,' " said Mr. Eccles smiling back with sweet reasonableness, " so I asked you what you were thinking of."

She noticed that there was a decidedly glassy look in his eyes, too. At the same time it dawned upon her that all this bore an astounding resemblance to a quarrel. Worse still—with all its silences and evasions, it bore an astounding resemblance to a lover's quarrel. Hideous thought—but how could she escape it ? The fact was clear that he believed himself to be flirting with her. And what sign had she yet given him that she was not flirting back ? How had he managed to inveigle her thus, and what was she to say now ?

" Oh well," she said, " one often says ' Oh well '—doesn't one ? "

" Does one ? "

He came back at her and followed her up for all the world more like a prosecuting counsel than as a presumable admirer. She could stand it no longer.

" Yes, of course one does," she said, and, with a pretence of indifference she picked up a tumbler, and began to wipe it with a rag. She then called through into the Lounge to Bob.

" What are *you* doing in there, Bob ? " she called.

" Me ? " said Bob, who was still fooling with the switch. " Nothing. What's the matter ? "

" Oh, nothing," said Ella, and went on wiping her tumbler. So there was no help coming from Bob. She brusquely dismissed from her mind the thought that his delay was in some measure intentional, that he entertained the objectionable notion that some sort of tact was required of him here ; Bob would not humiliate her by being so absurd.

A silence followed. She picked up another glass, wiped it, and held it up to the light to see if it was clean. She thus avoided looking at Mr. Eccles, but she had the knowledge that Mr. Eccles was looking at her. She had the knowledge as someone sightless might have the knowledge of being in a Turkish Bath. The silence and Mr. Eccles' unwavering gaze wrapped her around. She felt the warmth of a slow blush all over her body.

How could she put an end to this ? She must pull herself together. She must take a new line. She, at her age, blushing ! Plainly she was making a mountain out of a molehill. If an old gentleman wanted to flirt with the barmaid, why shouldn't he ? Was it not an essential part of her duty to sustain light banter with gentlemen of all kinds ? She was never behindhand in the ordinary way. Why had this particular old gentleman with his ridiculous new hat, thrown her off her stroke ? Her course was plain : she must flirt back. If he wanted to make a fool of himself, it was her business to oblige him. She had, now, then, to find the best way of beginning. His hat ! Obviously his hat !

" You've got a new hat, haven't you ? " said Ella, and, conscious of having used exactly the light tone and vaguely mocking look which the situation demanded, she felt instantaneous relief.

" Ah," said Mr. Eccles, " You notice everything—don't you ? "

That was all right. It looked as though they had got away at last.

" Bit audacious," said Ella. " Isn't it ? " There was a slight pause.

" What ? The Hat ? Or me ? " said Mr. Eccles.

These staccato questions, of course, meant nothing, and did not actually call for an answer. Flirtatious questions and answers were not supposed to mean anything. There was, however, for all his apparent flirtatiousness, a slightly intent look in Mr.

Eccles' eye, and a slightly harsh (or did she imagine it?) note in Mr. Eccles' voice, which made Ella wonder whether she had overstepped the mark. The unfortunate man, undoubtedly, was terribly tender, indeed beyond all description neurotic, concerning anything relating to his hat. And she had called it, or at any rate put herself in a position where he might think she had called it, "audacious." She hastened to extract herself.

"Oh no," she said. "It's ever so nice. I was thinking you were getting too extravagant, though."

"Oh well. You're responsible, you know."

"What?" said Ella. "Me? How?"

But the words were no sooner out of her mouth than she gathered his meaning and knew what was to follow. In a flash she recalled something she had utterly forgotten—something which she had no cause to remember, since it had appeared utterly insignificant at the time. Yes, some nights ago, well over a week ago, nearly a fortnight ago, he *had* commented humorously, in front of her, upon the dilapidated state of his old hat. And she *had* humorously agreed with him. She had said " Yes, you could do with a new one " or " Yes, perhaps it is about time you made a change "—how could she be expected to know the exact words? And here he was, summoning them up, like a magician, from the night of vanished small talk, to use against her. What solemn and sustained brooding on his part this implied she dared not think. Possibly he was a little mad. Or again, possibly (she had to face it), he was enamoured. That, she knew, was the same as being a little mad. At any rate, all the seriousness and awkwardness of the situation, which she had thought to lift into flirtatiousness, returned upon her. What was it she had said a fortnight ago? Had she, after all, " encouraged " him?

Again he had not answered her, and was looking at her in the same way.

"How am I responsible?" she added. "Eh?"

"Well—you told me to get another—didn't you?"

"Me? I didn't!"

"Yes, you did. Surely you remember."

"I *didn't*," said Ella, with a kind of protesting softness on her lips which was agonisingly near to a self-conscious maidenly pout. But what could she do, if he went on flatly contradicting her and she was not to be rude to a customer, but pout self-consciously. And yet what else did such pouting give him signs of but her own willingness to persevere in this awful flirtation ? So far as she could see, he had every right to say that she was " encouraging " him with a vengeance now. At every step, it seemed, he implicated her more deeply, and gave her less opportunity of freeing herself.

" Oh yes, you did," said Mr. Eccles. " Don't you remember telling me I ought to get a new one ? "

" Oh well," said Ella, " ' *Ought* ' . . . that's not telling you."

" Well, *I* thought so. I took it as a command."

Oh, why wouldn't Bob come in, thought Ella.

" It's not for me," she said, " to command you."

" Oh—isn't it ? " said Mr. Eccles in the vague and preoccupied tone of one whose intentions of dalliance with her were now too manifest to be disputed.

Since every answer she made was used as a weapon against her, Ella now thought it best to make no answer. So she went on wiping her tumblers. Even the Turkish Bath sensations of his gaze, she decided, were a lesser evil than the commitments engendered by talking to him. But even this was of no avail. When Mr. Eccles next spoke, which was after a long Turkish Bath pause (in the hottest room), he struck her soul with paralytic alarm.

" Are you interested," said Mr. Eccles, " in the theatre at all ? "

## CHAPTER III

IF Mr. Eccles had seized her hand and kissed it fervently, or rushed round behind the bar to embrace her with a torrent of words, it is doubtful whether he would have caused a more staggering sensation in the breast of the barmaid of " The

Midnight Bell " than by casually asking her if she was interested in the theatre at all.

In an instant she had seen in a blinding, unmistakable light all that she had been unable fully to discern in the mysterious and dangerous dusk of his new hat, his self-consciousness, his quizzing gaze, and enclosing silences. She comprehended his whole tendency; she foresaw exactly what was to come. This was an invitation to go to the theatre with him. He had known he was going to invite her to go to the theatre with him before he had come in. He was probably wearing, had probably waited to wear, his new hat as a means of redoubling his impression and onslaught upon her. This was nothing but an onslaught—a strategic onslaught upon her.

For what did an invitation to go to the theatre mean? An invitation to the theatre played no part in a common flirtation. It belonged to a category of manœuvres in quite another campaign—one which had different objects and which could be adequately expressed in no word save one—" *Advances !* " Flirtation began and ended, and was located, purely in the bar : " Advances " might lead anywhere outside, acknowledged a kind of social equality, suggested permanence and evolution, contained the seeds of all base and transitory, or all honest and stable, proposals. Advances opened up worlds—but what sort of worlds were not revealed. What conceivable worlds had Mr. Eccles in mind, with his new hat, and casual remark about the theatre? Looking at him it was difficult, nay, impossible, to say.

All these thoughts flowed through Ella as she replied " The theatre? Yes—I like to go to the theatre."

And there was another pause. Should she now say " Why do you ask? " or let him get ahead with it himself? And what line was she to take in any case.

"I had a reason in asking," said Mr. Eccles, " as I happened to have two seats given me just lately."

" Oh yes ? " said Ella, as though all this had not the remotest bearing upon herself, and inwardly marvelling at his transparency. He *happened*, did he, to have two seats given him just lately? And yet she could not help admiring, and being a little grateful for, the humility and caution of his approach. To say (and she knew he was lying) that he had had two seats given him, which in any case had to be taken advantage of, was a great deal less bold, less like a lord of creation, than to ask the barmaid off-hand to come to the theatre with him. It bespoke a respect for her, and for subtle formalities, which she in turn respected. But go to the theatre with him! What a terrible idea!

"I was wondering," he said, "whether you might like to come."

"*Me?*" she said, in feigned shocked surprise, and added "I can't afford such luxuries."

She knew now that she was not treating him fairly, that she was purposely misunderstanding him—disingenuously assuming, in blunt fact, that he was trying to sell a seat to her, and that no one could possibly be so disinterested as to offer such a thing free. If he had said "you might like to *go*" there might have been some slight justification for throwing this interpretation on the offer. But he hadn't : he had said "You might like to *come*." Actually, of course, her sole object was to gain time to refuse decently.

"It's not a question of affording," he said. "Here are these two seats going, and so one might as well take advantage of them."

"Well—" said Ella, but Mr. Eccles interrupted her.

"They'll only be wasted otherwise," he said.

"Well," said Ella, "that's ever so kind of you, but I don't see how I can manage it. I can't just take an evening off to go to the theatre, can I?"

"Oh—this isn't at night. This is for the afternoon."

"Oh—is it?"

"Yes It's a matinée."

"Well, as a matter of fact that's not much better, is it? I'm only off from about three to half-past four in the afternoon."

"But isn't Thursday your afternoon off?"

"Oh yes—Thursday is."

"Well—there you are."

"Why?" said Ella. "Are these tickets for Thursday?"

"Yes. Of course they are. That's why I thought you might like it. I knew Thursday was your day off."

What was this man after ? Ella once more was overwhelmed by the terrific detail and firmness of his attack. He had now forced her back to her last line—the weak, wavering line of pure falsehood—a line at which she was least adept.

" Well, on Thursday I've got to go somewhere," she said, " as a matter of fact."

" Oh—have you ? "

" Yes. Thanks ever so much all the same. It's ever so kind of you."

" Can't you put the other thing off ? "

" Well, it'd be rather difficult."

" But not impossible, surely ? "

Fool, thought Ella, for merely saying it would be rather difficult. She ought to have learnt by now that he wedged himself in to the smallest opening she gave him.

" Well . . ." she said, at a loss.

" Don't you want to come ? "

" Oh yes. . . . I *want* to come. . . ."

" Then why not. It's a very good show, I believe. Don't you like the theatre ? "

" Oh yes. I like going all right. . . . There's nothing I like better."

And this was true if all else was lies. Ella did more than like the theatre—she adored the theatre. Perhaps because she went so seldom, going to the theatre was an event of enormous, indeed historical magnitude to Ella. She anticipated it days ahead. As soon as the curtain went up she surrendered to and prostrated herself before its illusions with the freshness and gravity of a child. Plays were neither bad nor good to Ella, merely absorbing, frightening almost, with their terrible power of letting you in through the key-hole at real human beings and passions. After such a stimulus her serious, ruminative soul could think about little else for days afterwards. But, of course, she could hardly ever afford it. When she did, she generally saved up and took someone else.

" Then I would come, if I were you," said Mr. Eccles. " It seems a pity to miss the chance."

And it struck Ella, for the first time, that it did seem a pity to miss the chance. And she was instantly tempted to rationalize her desires, and to argue again that she was absurdly exaggerating the seriousness of all this, that Mr. Eccles was a perfectly harmless and friendly old gentleman who " liked " her, just as she used to think she " liked " him. What would be the harm of going to the theatre with such an old gentleman ? But was he, exactly, old, and was he, in that new hat, harmless ? In his new hat he looked as if he might have all sorts of very funny, though possibly tentative, ideas about himself and his age.

" Oh well," she said, " I don't know, I'm sure. . . ."

That left the door open, and gave him further opportunity for persuasion. She could almost believe she desired to be persuaded. Also it gave her a little more time to think.

" Well, you do what you like," he said, " but here are these two seats going."

With her last line shaken and in dismay, she was saved from immediate capitulation by Bob, the waiter, who now came from the Lounge into the Saloon Bar.

## CHAPTER IV

" GOOD evening, sir," said Bob to Mr. Eccles, in that rather harshly cordial manner he had of greeting customers whom he had not singled out as special favourites. And picking up a copy of *The Evening News*, he glanced his eye over the front page, and then settled down on a high stool near Ella and Mr. Eccles to read it inside. In the ordinary way, when customers were in the bar, Bob never outraged proper deference by allowing himself a stool like this. He evidently did not regard Mr. Eccles as " customers."

" Good evening, Bob," said Mr. Eccles, taking the liberty of using the waiter's Christian name, in somewhat the same convention as that in which public-schoolboys call all the butlers and attendants a generic " George " (or whatever it is) patronizingly, and indiscriminatingly. He thus contrived, without tangible offence, to assume a height and to put Bob in his place. Whether this was delibertate it was not easy to say : but it was quite clear, from his glance, that he liked Bob's looks little, and his present company less.

In appearance Bob was a formidably yet casually attractive young man looking anything between twenty and thirty (he was actually twenty-six). He was tall, with dark well-kept hair, dark brown eyes, set rather far back, and firm efficient clean-shaven features which bespoke his partially American origin. He had been at sea a great part of his early life, he was motherless and fatherless, and he had long adopted England as his country, speaking with a definite London accent and with London idiom. He had a resolute and independent air which to one who understood him, did nothing to mitigate his real transparency. Ella, who understood him, loved him. She loved him largely because after due consideration she had decided that he was divinely good-looking, and largely because after due considera-tion she had decided that he was divinely transparent. Though she did not realize it, her whole daily life centred around Bob—his comings, his goings, his moods, his reticences, his absurdities. That he did not return her love in the smallest measure caused no resentment in her whatever. The superb mechanism of her healthy character enabled her to tie up any package of what was not to be, and to shelve it for good. Not that she could always resist casting wistful eyes upon it on the shelf. When she was unhappy, or run down, or in a nervous state, she found Bob's continual proximity a little painful and disquieting. But no mechanism can function perfectly all the time. In addition to all this Bob dominated her existence purely by virtue of his companionship. Since she was so seldom away from " The Midnight Bell, " and had so few friends whom she cared to meet, or who were accessible, she relied more and more upon Bob. She realized now that when he came to " The Midnight Bell " four or five months ago, something had definitely entered her life. On the score of reciprocation of companionship alone she had nothing to complain of in Bob. He clearly liked and respected her, and they had reached a wonderful intimacy. That this for the greater part took the form of playful rallying and semi-flirtatious non-commitment did not detract from its stability and charm. They often talked seriously. In her heart Ella (the incurably serious-minded) liked best of all to talk seriously, and her serious talks with Bob were a great, and glowing, pleasure. Also, she had her work in common with Bob, and stood with Bob in close conspiracy and muttered rebellion against certain injustices and disorders descending almost daily upon them from a higher quarter in " The Midnight Bell." In fact she often thought she could not do without Bob now.

No wonder, then, that she had a feeling of support and safety, of being on comparatively dry land, now that her friend and loved object, Bob, had entered the bar. Also this abruptly terminated all the air of low-toned clandestinity of her colloquy with Mr. Eccles, and gave her a chance to convey to Bob that no secrets had been in the making. Above all things, she desired to keep no secrets from Bob.

" Well, Bob," she said, " what have *you* been up to ? "

" I've been mending the switch in there," said Bob, without looking up from his paper.

" No, I don't mean just now," said Ella. " I mean this afternoon."

She knew that this frantic attempt to change the subject with the appearance of Bob could avail her nothing, that, unless she intended flatly to insult Mr. Eccles by not mentioning the theatre again, it had to be assumed that she was speaking to Bob purely parenthetically, on the score of politeness to a newcomer. And a brief look on her part at Mr. Eccles—at his half-smiling, glazed, unconsciously almost tigerish side-glance at the reading Bob, revealed that he bore the same fact in mind.

" Oh, this afternoon . . . " said Bob. " I went to the pictures."

" Oh," said Ella, and there was a pause.

" So you have time to go to the *pictures* in the afternoon, do you ? " said Mr. Eccles, smiling upon both of them.

Ella felt that her half-truths were finding her out. And her only weapon of defence now was the half-true, subtle, and involved excuse that the Pictures (as distinguished from the theatre with its fixed matinée) began early, ran continuously, and were split up into different features, thus enabling one to apply all the free time at one's disposal and to witness at least one complete artistic unit of the whole, to say nothing of various possible odds and ends of news-reels, comedies, and beginnings.

Bob, who of course did not understand that Mr. Eccles had made a friendly thrust, looked up and vaguely said " What ? . . ."

In answer Mr. Eccles smiled at Ella, as though to refer Bob to her. Bob looked at her. They both looked at her.

What was she to do now—launch upon that tiresome defence ? She had no heart for it. Also she had to explain matters to Bob.

" Mr. Eccles," she said to Bob, " has just been very kind. . . ."

" Oh yes ? " said Bob, politely. But as the other two were too flustered to say anything, and just looked at each other like a couple of schoolgirls caught doing something they shouldn't in a passage, things were very coy and suspended. . . .

" How's that ? " tried Bob. . . .

Mr. Eccles smiled greenly, but his mouth was shut. It was Ella's funeral.

" He's been asking me," she said, " whether I'd like to go to the theatre."

She wondered why the mere utterance of such a statement cost her such intense humiliation. Was it because the mere conception of going to the theatre with someone like Mr. Eccles was humiliating ? Or was it because the blushing secret of the seriousness of Mr. Eccles' advances was now unmasked before Bob ? Or was it because she was so utterly impotent to convey to Bob that she had played no part in this, and was no part of it now—instead of conveying, as she did, with her talk of Mr. Eccles being " very kind," the glad and unreflecting complacence of a simpleton ?

But Bob had quite a different way of looking at things.

" Oh—really ? " he said warmly. " You're in luck then. What's the show ? "

Was Bob just trying to help her out, or was his enthusiasm genuine ? She honestly believed the latter, and she felt a load rising from her spirit. It was characteristic of Bob, to put her at her ease like this.

" What *is* the show, Mr. Eccles ? " she asked. (She was Mr. Ecclesing him like anything now—quite the new acquaintance !)

" It's called ' The Lost Guard,' I believe," said Mr. Eccles. " At the ' Empress.' "

" Oh yes," said Bob. " I know about that. Got a very good press. That ought to be fine."

She noticed that he not only took it for granted that she had already accepted, but regarded acceptance as an act fully in accordance with nature and all the proprieties. Moreover his keenness on her behalf, which she now was certain was sincere, had instantly infected her. Why should she not regard herself as one in luck—in great luck ? She had few enough chances to go to the theatre, and from her own (and the sane) point of view there was no harm in being taken out by a friendly middle-aged customer. If there had been any harm or humiliation it would have been in reference to the opinion of others—particularly, of course, to the opinion of that supremely, that only momentous arbitrator of her values—Bob. And here was Bob himself giving her his sanction ! She had made a fool of herself. She was always reading things into things, and making a fool of herself.

" The point is," said Mr. Eccles, " are you *coming ?* "

" Well . . . " said Ella, with seeming doubt. But there was a kind of smile on her lips and tremor in her voice which showed that she was about to surrender. And " What's the matter ? " said Bob, in the slightly bewildered way of one to whom the notion that she could be such a fool as to turn such an opportunity down had never occurred.

" I thought I couldn't manage it at first," she said. " But as it's *Thursday* . . ." She paused.

" Yes—that's good," said Bob. " You won't be so rushed, then."

" Yes—that's what I thought," said Mr. Eccles, and he caught Bob's eye fairly for the first time, and spoke in a rich friendly tone which denoted that Bob, in addition to being elevated from his inferior sphere, had been forgiven handsomely, and was in warm favour.

" Well—it's very kind of you indeed," said Ella. " I'll enjoy it very much."

" Not at all," said Mr. Eccles, delightedly. " It'd have been a pity to have wasted the seats in any case."

" Yes, it would really," said Ella, in the same delighted way, and Bob chimed in " It certainly would."

And now that the thing was done, and acknowledgments had been proffered and accepted, an astonishing feeling of gladness, of breathing freely once more after battle, of glowing reconciliation almost, filled the air. And it dawned upon Ella that not something horrible, but something entirely pleasing had occurred to-night. With this she at once realized that she " liked " Mr. Eccles again—" liked " him better than ever, in fact—should never have stopped " liking " him. And he, beyond doubt, " liked " her.

" Is that *next* Thursday ? " asked Bob.

" Yes, that's right," said Mr. Eccles, and there was another pause.

" Do you go to the theatre a lot, then, Mr. Eccles ? " said Ella, resorting happily to that charming privilege of the newly reconciled, that of changing the subject, and entering the realms of sheer detachment.

" No . . ." said Mr. Eccles, rounding his mouth on the negative with a reflective and judicial air in full accordance with the new psychology. " I don't go very often, as a matter of fact. Just now and again when there's a good show."

" It's a question of affording with me," said Bob, scarcely less sensitive than the other two to the spirit of the situation. " With the price they charge these days."

" Yes, it's scandalous," said Mr. Eccles, and " I know—something dreadful," said Ella. (But, of course, people like Mr. Eccles, and the lucky friends they invited out, were not so immediately and painfully subject to such scandals !)

" But then everything's so expensive nowadays," said Mr. Eccles.

" Yes, it is," said Bob, and " You're right," said Ella, both imagining that Mr. Eccles was merely keeping the ball of conversation rolling. Oddly, however, with Mr. Eccles' next observation the ball came to a sudden standstill.

" Unless one's looked to the matter," said Mr. Eccles. . . .

Unless one's looked to the matter. Now what, wondered

Bob and Ella, did that mean ? How might a private person have *looked* to the social matter of the cost of commodities nowadays ? " M'm " murmured Bob, and " Yes " said Ella, feigning comprehension, but both in so obviously feeble and vague a manner that the door was left open for further elucidation—which came the next moment.

" *I've* got something comfortable put by," said Mr. Eccles, italicizing his " I've " in a purely scientific and self-effacing distinction between himself and the poor devils who hadn't. . . .

" Oh yes ? " said Bob politely, having gathered Mr. Eccles' meaning without having gathered his exact object. And Ella did not reply.

There was, therefore, a rather uncomfortable silence in which the Comfortable (and yet slightly mysterious and foreboding) Something which Mr. Eccles had contrived to Put By, permeated the amicable and expectant air.

As for Ella, she had not replied because she (unlike Bob) had caught Mr. Eccles' import as well as his meaning, and had again taken fright. There was something so eccentric, so uncalled-for, so ponderous and inelegant in Mr. Eccles' allusion to what he had put by, that she had not the slightest doubt that he was doing what was known as Getting it In. Or Letting her Know. And that meant Advances again. And she had almost hoped, in the last few minutes, that she had expelled the demon of Advances. So he had something comfortable, had he ? That might mean anything. It would be extremely interesting to know his criterion of comfort.

Still no one spoke, and Ella began to feel that it devolved upon her to start the conversation again, when that happened which, had it happened a little earlier, might have prevented, or at least postponed, the whole series of alternative misgivings and reassurances of which Ella had been the well-meaning vessel in the last quarter of an hour—another customer entered.

And directly after this other customer, another customer entered—and then shortly afterwards another. It was nearly always so—" The Midnight Bell," at a certain instant of the evening, becoming uncommonly like an accident which had just occurred, and upon whose scene people materialized from nowhere in complete dramatic awareness of the event. In ten minutes Ella was working hard.

It would have been doubtful whether Mr. Eccles would have had any further chance to hold any sustained conversation with Ella during the rest of the evening : certainly there was an end to any soft impasses and portentous silences. In any case, Mr. Eccles managed to leave well alone, and after drinking up the rest of his beer, he raised his new hat with a cheerful " Goodnight " and went out. " Good-night, Mr. Eccles," cried Ella, cordially, but she was too busy to experience relief or aught else at his departure.

In this manner, then, an obviously cautious middle-aged gentleman (decidedly young for his age) had invited a rather plain barmaid to go to the theatre with him. The barmaid had given every appearance of willing acceptance. They were going on Thursday. They remained, however, despite the private nature of their common commitment, wrapped in the deepest mystery to each other. So uncanny, grotesquely adjusted, and obscurely motivated are the parisitisms and coalitions formed by the small fish in the weird teeming aquarium of the metropolis.

## CHAPTER V

ELLA had a small bedroom—practically an attic—at the top of " The Midnight Bell." It contained little more than a bed, a washing-stand, and a chest of drawers, and was lit lividly by incandescent gas. To this cold retreat she came directly after her work every night, generally humming softly to herself, being in good spirits both by virtue of her late exertions and her release therefrom.

Once inside, however, with the door shut, she ceased to hum. There is a great deal of the tomb in a bedroom ; all passions, delights, schemings, ambitions, triumphs, must be taken back at night to these caves of cold arbitration. All journeyings and

busy vanity must capitulate before their stationary severity. Ella
undressed as quickly as she could.

A little later Bob would come up to his own cave, which
adjoined hers. Although the wall was thin and they could
easily have called to each other, they never said a word—not
even a cheerful " Good-night." Caves were a serious business.
But they could hear each other moving about and guess each
other's mental concentrations. To Ella, Bob was never so near,
and never so far away as at these few minutes at the end of the
day. She knew every dim bump and clink and splash and thud
of his business-like undressing and washing ; she could trace
and visualize every movement. But where were his mind and
soul disporting themselves ? Somewhere, she knew, in that
region which she could never penetrate in her intercourse with
him, however intimate they became. In other words, he was
grinding out his own private problems, and those she would
never share. She was nothing in his life. The nightly reminder
made her own cave more bleak.

So soon as she was in darkness and the warmth of her sheets,
she would listen to the occasional thunder from late traffic in the
Euston Road near by, and her mind would wander away from
Bob to the monotonous scenery of her own existence.

To-night she realized that the scenery had undergone a minute
and unforeseen change. Last night all had been as before, to-
night all was as before with the addition that she was going to
the theatre on Thursday and had apparently acquired a new
friend. She could not resist a certain feeling of pleasure at the
change—for the thought of going to the theatre could not be
anything but stimulating, and there should always be something
exciting or diverting in a new friend.

She wondered why, in this instance, she felt no sense of diversion or excitement in her new friend. Was it just because he was
middle-aged and undistinguished—or did the causes lie deeper ?
Was it not, possibly, because he was something more than
a friend—a potential admirer—and as such a potential problem
and task ? Again, she wondered why she should not feel
flattered and pleased by the thought of acquiring an admirer,
qua admirer, even if she had the task of making him understand
that he must be repelled. It was not as though she had often

had an admirer of any kind. She ought to be delighted by the novelty. Why instead should she have a peculiar sense of being affronted ? This she definitely did. It probably arose from the very fact that she had had so few admirers in her life—and that now one had appeared on the horizon, he should have such a dull, self-conscious, unattractive, and above all middle-aged exterior. If it was a feather in her cap, what a miserable feather— and was it a token of the only sort of feather she was ever fit to receive ? It seemed so, since she was twenty-eight years of age, and had never yet been presented with a young, bright, attractive feather. Hence her feeling of affront from Mr. Eccles, whom she half suspected of having divined this fact, and of having been emboldened by it, in offering his own shoddy feather. If he was in the mood to admire someone, why had he not gone to someone genuinely pretty and attractive ? She knew she was plain all right : she knew it with such depth and frankness that she could positively find it in her heart to despise his taste ! And if she despised his taste, she must despise the whole situation of which she formed a part. He had set in motion a degrading event.

Was she therefore, in matters of physical affection, doomed to degradation in her own eyes ? No. If someone with a bright and beautiful feather to bestow (like Bob) were to admire her, she would not feel that his taste was at fault. The very brightness and beauty of the feather would be a charter of the immaculacy of its bestower's judgment, and she would accept his homage merely as the delicious intimation that she had been mistaken about her own potentialities. For in spite of Ella's realism concerning herself, she still had hopes that she was mistaken, that she had an authentic, if latent, attraction which might make her an active and full participant in the joys she had read about, and heard spoken of, and imagined for herself.

Bob, without making a move, incited these hopes : Mr. Eccles, by making a direct advance, in a manner distorted and discoloured them. How could she do otherwise than faintly resent Mr. Eccles ?

On the other hand, these introspections were much more profound and morbid than the situation warranted, and it was not Mr. Eccles' fault. It was ridiculous to expect him to see that he was not paying her an unambiguous compliment. He could not know what was going on in her mind. Moreover, since she knew in her heart that she was not really attractive, it was sheer arrogance on her part to put herself on a plane above Mr. Eccles. In fact, the common-sense thing to do, and she prided herself on her common-sense, was to accept her fate, and gain every ounce of comfort she could from what homage she could get. And was it not an acknowledged fact that there were enormous compensatory comforts for those who forsook or had no access to the intemperate ecstasies of beauty and delight ?

That word comfort. He had used it himself. He had made a fool of himself in his pains to make her understand that he was a comfortable man. What lay . behind that ungainly attempt ? The hint, surely, of dim possibilities that she might somehow participate in that comfort, that he might shower that comfort upon her. But in what way ? As his wife ? Or in some other capacity ? She knew she was again rushing ahead of herself, and imagining absurd things, but the man must have had *some* motive, *some* logical object in all his shy but intent manœuvrings.

What if he wanted to marry her ? With nearly all the men with whom she came into contact, Ella, like most women, was in the habit of indulging in the droll and entirely disinterested conception of a state of affairs in which they wanted to marry her and Mr. Eccles had given her an unmistakable stimulus. Well, suppose he wanted to marry her ? A comfortable man would be making a comfortable offer to a practically penniless barmaid who desired comfort and stability above all things else in life.

She again wondered what his standards of relative comfort were, how that occult comfortable Something put by, would present itself to the material eye in the form of £.s.d. per annum. He had given no clue to this, but with a man of his caution (and caution was glaringly his characteristic) she did not believe that he would have committed himself even so far as he had unless he was sure of his ground. Such a man would not have entered his name, as it were, in the Comfort Tournament unless he was pretty certain of distinguishing himself. Indeed she was prepared to believe that he was wealthy—by her standards at any rate. And suppose a wealthy man wanted to marry, and give her all the comforts of life ? It was a well-known fact that these men were continually picking on the plain girls. Naturally Ella's dream of earthly happiness was a home of her own, with the comforts and the permanent orientation thereof ; and she had often thought that she would be prepared to make almost any sacrifice to gain it. Would she, then, be doing her duty by herself if she was always going to be so squeamish and to flee from such opportunities.

Furthermore, would she be doing her duty by her unhappy poverty-stricken mother, whom she was so passionately anxious to Help—whom she already Helped in a wretched way from her own minute salary ? What would all her profession of longing to Help amount to if she lost the chance of wealth itself when it came her way ?

An old, or elderly man. But might not his elderliness (to imagine oneself, since this was all sheer imagination, to be perfectly wicked and unscrupulous) be an ultimate advantage ? For apart from her visualization of a home of her own, Ella had another dream of happiness. This was of the proverbial Cottage in a proverbial but unspecified portion of the Country, with her mother and herself in rose-surrounded residence.

What of an elderly and mortal Mr. Eccles unscrupulously viewed as a route to a Cottage ?

But then she was not unscrupulous, and anyway this was all nonsense. She wondered whether anyone in the world let their imagination run riot as she did. She composed herself to sleep.

## CHAPTER VI

BEFORE the Thursday (by degrees characterized in Ella's mind with gay disparagement as " famous ") Mr. Eccles came into " The Midnight Bell " only once, and that briefly in a busy hour, to fix the definite time and place of meet-

ing. As she was not sure of the exact position of the theatre in
St. Martin's Lane they hit upon St. Martin's Church at 2.15.
Mr. Eccles went out without even having a drink.

In the few days that had intervened Ella had given little
thought to Mr. Eccles, except to note that he had not been near
her, but when the famous Thursday dawned she experienced
a renewal of speculation and vague excitement in her heart.

So soon as she was awake she noticed that it was a rather
famous day itself—sunny, blue and cold, with a brisk thudding
wind driving enormous white bulging growths of clouds. The
universe was saluting an occasion, and she went about her
morning tasks, in the church-like, rapidly-changing shadows
of the closed public-house, with a lighter spirit than usual
not only on account of the coming relaxation, but also of the
conceivable dangers, of the afternoon ahead.

She was more than usually cheerful with the morning customers, some of whom she rather proudly told she was going
to the theatre, and at a quarter to two set forth.

By this time the sky was overcast with uniform grey, and in the
bus going down her mood changed to one of insecurity and
puzzlement at this extraordinary arrangement with a perfect
stranger. This feeling was not decreased by the fact that although,
by walking around she timed her arrival exactly at 2.15 outside
St. Martin's Church, there was no sign of Mr. Eccles.

She had certainly expected to find him waiting there and she
had no idea what to make of it. She was not sure that she was not
a little aggrieved. This did not look much like the new trembling
admirer, the elderly self-conscious gentleman who made strange
allusions to his wealth. He just wasn't there. And a minute
or two passed in which he still wasn't there.

She realized the perversity of human nature in that now that
that conception of the trembling admirer was fading, now that
all her fears and trepidations were therefore being put to rest,
at that very moment she was a little hurt, a little disappointed,
a little sad even, at a little triumph having gone out of her life.
In other words there was one base side of her nature which
relished Mr. Eccles' homage purely as homage—with an utterly
unscrupulous disregard of his possible sufferings. So she did
not even attract Mr. Eccles ! On second thoughts, however, the

better side of her nature was what counted, and she was honestly glad to feel that this load was being taken off her chest.

Anything remaining of honest fear (or dishonest wish) that Mr. Eccles was by way of being in love with Ella, was instantly extinguished by the arrival of Mr. Eccles himself, five minutes after his time.   It was at once clear that he was not sorry for, but in a decided temper about, his own lateness, and flustered about personal matters which had probably caused that lateness and had no concern with her.

Indeed, he had been hurrying, and his face was ashen with irritability.   Not that he intended Ella to notice any of these things.   It was only that he was unable to conceal them from her shrewd eye, as he came hurrying up and raising his new hat in greeting.

"Oh, have you been waiting long?" he said, scarcely smiling.  "I'm a bit after time, I'm afraid."

"No, that's quite all right," said Ella, and without meaning anything she looked up at the clock.

He looked up at it too.

"Oh well, that's not so bad," he said.  "We'll get over that. Let's be getting on, shall we?"

And they started walking up towards St. Martin's Lane in silence.

He was furious, reflected Ella, glancing at him.  But why? It was not her fault that he was late.   Had he been offended because she had looked up at the clock like that?  Had he imagined she had been drawing attention to his default?

"I was a bit late myself," she said, falsifying facts to put him less in the wrong.

"Oh yes?" he said. . . . Just that.  Not another word. And he went on plodding beside her.

She looked at him again, and all at once she understood everything.   He was an old man.   His plodding walk, his grey hair and moustache, the harsh drawn lines of his face—all, in the grey light of the chilly sky above, revealed it.   So different from the flattering artificial light of "The Midnight Bell."   And as an old man he was barely responsible for his rage.   Old men were known and allowed to be irritable and to go into rages about nothing.   Nothings assumed enormous proportions in their eyes. Because they were old there was not exacted from them the same duties of self-control towards their fellow-beings as there was from others. Their chagrin was not mental, but physical—they had no control over them. Poor old man! All flustered, was he? Never mind—it was very nice of him to take her out at all, and she must treat him thoughtfully and kindly—indeed with respect for his grey hairs.

But what a difference!—the Mr. Eccles whom she had thought about in bed as a challenge to her peace of mind—and the little old man (how short he was now, by the way!) fussing beside her now. How eminently respectable and dull was her afternoon to be after all—and how weird. How had it all come about?

Thus she pondered amid the roar of traffic outside the Coliseum, as they crossed the road and walked up the other side. True it was almost too noisy to talk. She tried to make a remark on the weather but he was still monosyllabic. You wouldn't have thought they were going to the theatre together for the first time. You would have imagined he was taking her round to report her somewhere.

" It's that infernal girl of mine that caused the trouble," he said. " She was about half an hour late with the lunch."

" Oh yes ? " said Ella. " What a nuisance. . . ."

So he realized that his behaviour was not quite all it should be, and was trying to excuse himself. And his " infernal girl "—who was she? Where did he live, what was his *ménage*, who was he?

" I can't stand unpunctuality," he said. " Can you ? "

" No," said Ella. " I do think people ought to try and be punctual."

Poor girl, she thought. Anyone might be a little bit late with the lunch every now and again without all this bother. Just imagine being married to Mr. Eccles!

" Which *is* the theatre ? " she said, trying to change the conversation. " I don't think I ever remember seeing the ' Empress'. "

" Oh, it's just up here. We're just coming to it."

" It ought to be a good show," she said. " I read a bit about it in the paper only yesterday."

" Yes. It ought to be all right." He seemed to be cooling

down now. " But of course one can't always go by what the Press says."

" No. That's true," said Ella. But this judicial air was pure fake, as she knew by experience that all shows were gloriously good, and she was, in fact, beginning to perk up again in face of the prospect before her. After all, she had only come out with Mr. Eccles because he had promised to take her to the theatre, so why not set her mind to enjoying it, and stop bothering about him ?

They had now reached the portals of the " Empress " Theatre. Taxis and cars were being drawn up in rapid succession to the pavement outside, ladies were being helped out by smart, blue-uniformed, medalled commissionaires, and in the rich-carpeted foyer, which they entered, there was a tense little queue outside the box-office, a lot of queer people talking and lurking about, and a great air of something terrifically grave and vivid (say a mass execution of traitors, or a declaration of world war) about to take place behind the doors and passages leading to the auditorium.

Ella, who was used to the delay and scramble of the gallery or upper circle, could not help being impressed by this wonderful show of wealth, servility, and pomp. Also she felt sadly out of place, almost as though she had found herself at a party to which she had not been asked, and she felt sure that her clothes must be giving her away. What would they all think if they knew she was a barmaid !

Mr. Eccles, she saw, came rather better out of it—in fact much better. Indeed with his black coat, his dark blue silk scarf, his silver-knobbed stick, and his new hat, he quite looked the part. But then he was not a barmaid—or rather the social equivalent of one.    He was, she supposed one would say, a gentleman—what with his " infernal girl " and one thing and another. She should really feel very honoured at being taken out like this. At any rate she was grateful to be under his wing.

After gazing around him in a rather uncertain way, at the various doors, he now turned to her.

" Just wait here a moment, will you ? " he said. " I shan't be a moment."

" Yes," said Ella. " Certainly."

He left her side. What was he doing now ? Not going to the box-office surely—for he had the seats. He had them nearly a week ago. But he was. There he was queuing up. What did this mean ? Had she dreamed, or had he not expressly stated that night that he then had the seats in his pocket ? Yes—there he was, talking to the man in the office, and slipping over a pound note. The coolness of it ! So, he was really taking her to the theatre in the proper sense of the term ! Why ? With what conceivable object ? Was he after all her admirer, with a secret end towards which he was preparing ? She wished to Heaven she could make up her mind one way or the other about this gentleman. Here he was, coming back.

" Here we are," he said, looking vaguely at doors again. " We're in the dress circle."

An attendant came forward to assist them. They entered rose-lit, heavily-carpeted passages (whose sumptuousness again appalled Ella) and up some stairs into the auditorium. Here they were met by a programme girl, in whom Ella recognized but a gilded and pampered sister in toil, and who guided them to their seats in the second row. For the programme alone sixpence went bang—but Mr. Eccles' financial ears were deaf to the report. With the utmost calm he handed her the pro-gramme as they sat down. She had noticed that he had received practically no change from that pound note, and she marvelled at his wealth. He must be rolling in money. That, or desperately in love. Whatever the answer Mr. Eccles was a man to be reck-oned with. Life was full of excitements after all. She noticed, too, that he was looking quite young again in this light.

Now that they were seated peaceably amid the talkative, feminine throng of the audience, the theatre had lost much of its terror and awe-inspiring character, and it was easy to realize that they had not come to see a mass execution of traitors, or a declaration of world war, but an afternoon play whose scenery was wrapped in a very human and prosaic sort of concealment behind a thin drop curtain, and whose coming was announced by the miserable tuning-up and page-turning of an orchestra which had lately had its lunch. But soon this pulled itself together and burst into a swinging march : and Ella's being throbbed with the joy of expectation.

## CHAPTER VII

ABOUT three hours later, with her entire world transfigured and charged with new meaning, and practically in tears, Ella, scarcely trusting herself to speak, stepped with Mr. Eccles and the rest of the audience out into the street. They turned automatically up towards Cranbourn Street.

" Well—that was pretty good, wasn't it," said Mr. Eccles, not unmoved himself.

" It was *wonderful*," said Ella, in so vibrant a tone, that her own transport surprised herself, and she realized that she must not make a fool of herself. But it had been wonderful—there was no other word for it. She had had no idea that such depths of passion and beauty existed, or that she could respond to them in such a way. She felt as though her whole being had suddenly awakened from its apathy, and she could have cried with thankfulness and happiness at the experience.

" Yes," said Mr. Eccles, after another reflective pause. " That was well worth the trouble."

He, being a man, had naturally to restrain himself, but the way in which he said this left no doubt of the fact that he was wellnigh as impressed as herself. He also, then, understood the meaning of beauty and passion—saw things as she did. Her esteem for him rose at once. Indeed, she felt her flood of universal gratitude being diverted towards him, in that he had invented, coaxed her towards, and given her this pleasure from his own pocket. She had been grossly underestimating his value purely as a friend. She was happy to know him.

" I should think it *was* worth the trouble," she said, " I'm sure I'm ever so grateful to you for taking me."

" Oh—never mind about that," said Mr. Eccles, looking straight ahead. " The question *is*," he added with the little thrust of the practical masculine's chin, " where are we going to have *tea* ? "

She had been so engrossed she had not thought about such a thing. But there could have been no more delightful idea. In her state of exaltation she could do with a cup of tea, and it would be all part of the treat. Besides she would be able to get to know him better.

"Well—that would be nice," she said.

"There's an Express just round the corner here," he said, "Do you mind those places?"

"No. That'll be fine," she said.

"They're all right if you just want a cup of tea," he said, "we'll settle somewhere nice to go to dinner later."

*Dinner!* So he was going to take her to dinner afterwards! And yet she could not say that she was quite unprepared for this —that she had not previously speculated upon what Mr. Eccles had intended to do with her after the show. She had even left her evening free by telling her mother that she might not be along. Nor could she say that she was now in any way dismayed by this turn of events. On the contrary, she was electrified by it, and prepared for anything. The theatre had put her into high spirits which she must work off at all costs. And here was Dinner to hand. *Dinner* mind you—not supper—not poached egg on toast and a cup of cocoa at Lyons—but authentic Dinner with a plutocrat. Express Dairies were mere makeshifts to such people. She wouldn't be a bit surprised if they had *Wine!* So far as she could remember she had never been taken out to dinner in her life. What would Bob think if he knew she was going out to Dinner?

"What?" she said, having nothing else to say. "Are we going to Dinner?"

"Yes. What's the matter? You're free, aren't you?"

"Yes. I suppose I am, really. I never thought of it. But haven't you got to get back?"

"Me? Where should I have to get back?"

"Oh—I don't know. . . ."

"I'm a bachelor gay, you know," said Mr. Eccles. "And there *are* advantages."

"Yes," said Ella, "I suppose there are."

"Not that it's all advantages," said Mr. Eccles. . . .

"Isn't it?" said Ella.

"*Oh* no," said Mr. Eccles, and there was a pause. . . .

"Dear me no," added Mr. Eccles, as an emphatic afterthought. . . .

" Well, I daresay it's not," she said. . . .

Why was he talking about advantages and bachelors ? There was something behind it all. There seemed to be something behind everything he said and did. He had the most ulterior manner of any man she knew. Did he want to put an end to bachelordom ? Did he want to marry *her* ? She was prepared to believe anything of him.

Further musings of this nature were put an end to by their arrival outside the Express Dairy Restaurant in Great Newport Street. " Here we are," he said, and held back the door for her.

## CHAPTER VIII

IT was crowded on the ground floor, and so they went downstairs to the basement. This was quiet and almost deserted by customers, and they sat opposite each other at a marble-topped table for four. Before seating himself Mr. Eccles, with some ceremony, indeed minute ostentation, removed his new hat, his scarf, and his overcoat, and placed them in meticulous order one upon the other on the peg on the wall, joining his gloves together and fitting them snugly into the pocket of his overcoat. In this manner Ella was for the first time introduced to Mr. Eccles in the nakedness of his Suit, which was impressive. Impressive because, although it obviously had not actually been bought yesterday, it looked as though it had lately been infected and moved to emulation by the novelty rage begun by the new hat, and had had a kind of thyroid youth injection in the way of Sponging, Cleaning and Pressing. Or so Ella imagined.

A waitress appeared, and after a brief period of argument, pain, and doubt, it was agreed that all they wanted was a pot of tea for two. The waitress went away.

" Sure you won't have anything else ? " asked Mr. Eccles.

" No thanks—" said Ella. " I can never eat anything with tea—can you ? "

"No, I can't. But I should have thought it'd have been different at your age," said Mr. Eccles looking at her.

"My age?" said Ella, conscious of his look. "Why?"

"Oh, nothing," said Mr. Eccles in a faintly unusual way, thus causing Ella instantly to anticipate that something else was coming. He was a terrific Oh nothinger, and his Oh nothings were certain omens of the utterance of anything but nothings. And his next remark proved her right.

"I always thought," said Mr. Eccles, "that you beautiful young people liked to stuff yourself with pastries."

*Beautiful!* This was the last straw—the last of all the straws which the camel's back of her blindness to his tendency had endured so far! Now, surely, there was no mistaking him. She was almost afraid of him. If he could say such things at tea-time, what was he going to say and do late at night? Would she be called upon to defend herself? Perhaps this was a mere " try-on "—an elderly " Don Juan " whose habit it was to take barmaids out, whose technique was the theatre and dinner, and who wielded his enormous economic power indiscriminately and unscrupulously. If that was so, she would " show " himof course, but it might not be so.

In the meantime, she had been called both young and beautiful, and unless she was to pass it over, thereby mutely establishing immodest concurrence in his opinion, she had to make some protest. She paused, seeking the right words.

"Eh? . . ." said Mr. Eccles. . . .

"Well," she said, " I daresay that *beautiful* young people do." (I.e., *she* was *not* beautiful.)

"What?" said Mr. Eccles, still looking at her. . . .

"*Oh nothing,*" " *Eh?* " " *What?* " " *Eh?* " "*Oh nothing,*" " *What?* " she was getting rather confused with these incessantly recurring yet mystic exclamations from a shy yet enveloping amorousness. She had thought she had made herself clear, but she would have to say it again.

"I said," said Ella, " that no doubt if you *are* beautiful you *do* like eating pastries—but if you're not beautiful it's a different matter." That was clear enough she thought.

"What?" said Mr. Eccles.

Unless she was to go on repeating herself until the cows came home, Ella now had but one course open to her—that was, to look at the table and blush. This she did, colouring slowly and evenly under his gaze. Happily, the waitress here made a timely appearance and human thought was submerged for a moment or two in the brusque clatter of china upon marble and itself.

" Shall I be mother ? " said Ella, and started to pour out the tea. But the episode was not closed.

" What were you saying about beautiful young people ? " asked Mr. Eccles, as the teapot was yet poised in the air over the first cup.

" What ? " said Ella. She could do some Whatting too, if she tried. She added, however, " Do you take sugar ? "

" No, not for me, thanks."

She passed him his cup and began to pour out her own.

" You haven't answered my question yet," said Mr. Eccles, stirring his tea.

" Oh—what's that ? " said Ella, successfully mimicking a young woman at once absent-minded and intent upon the fulfilment of her feminine duties.

" I asked you what you were saying about beautiful young people."

" Oh," said Ella, " *That*. . . ."

She popped two lumps of sugar into her tea, hoping he would help her out by saying something else. But he did not.

" You mean about beautiful young people liking pastries," she said.

" Yes—that's right."

" Well—what about them ? " She sipped at her tea.

" Well—that's what I was asking you." Mr. Eccles sipped at his.

" Well, all I said," said Ella, " was that no doubt beautiful young people like eating pastries—but that if you're not beautiful you don't."

" Then what about the beautiful young people that *don't* like eating pastries ? " asked Mr. Eccles.

" How do you mean ? " asked Ella. Apart from everything else, she reflected, what unutterable *drivel* all this was ! By degrees it had been assumed as an axiom that there was a famous universal law which governed beautiful young people on the one hand,

and pastries on the other—which rendered each (in some obscure way) complementary to the other to all eternity, and which they were now arguing out with the seriousness of theologians.

" I said," said Mr. Eccles, who was never afraid of repeating himself, " what about beautiful young people who *don't* like eating pastries ? "

" Oh, well," said Ella, completely out of her depth. " I don't know about *them*."

" But you must," said Mr. Eccles.

" What ? " said Ella.

" You've just told me that you yourself *don't* like eating pastries."

Of course she knew really what he was leading up to, and she could evade the issue no longer.

" Well," she said, " *I'm* not beautiful." And blushed again.

" Ah," said Mr. Eccles. . . .

That, and no more. Ella was a little disappointed. Having been forced to fish for a compliment, she would have liked to have seen something a little more exciting than " Ah " at the end of her line. However, there was no real doubt of his meaning. Beautiful. She had never dreamed of getting near to being called such a thing in her life. Could he really mean it ? With this man there was no telling.

" That was a wonderful play, wasn't it ? " she said, changing the subject. " I don't know when I've ever enjoyed one so much."

" You liked it, did you ? "

" Liked it ? I should say I did."

" Oh well," said Mr. Eccles. " We'll have a lot of that."

She thought she was inured now to the appalling suggestiveness of his casual remarks, but this last one yet had the power to stimulate her to a fury of speculation. Nevertheless, she successfully concealed this, and again changing the subject by telling him she thought that his tea looked too strong, which led to a disinterested discussion on tea in general, she managed thenceforward to keep the conversation on a disinterested basis, until the waitress gave them their check, and it was time to go.

## CHAPTER IX

" WELL now, let me see . . ." said Mr. Eccles, as soon as
they were outside again. " Which is our best way. . . ."
        They had agreed upon a little walk in the Park as the
next item in their programme ; and there they were to " decide "
where they were going to have dinner. Mr. Eccles had now
resumed all his pieces of clothing one after another, and was
looking more like his old self.
" I think we'd better walk to Piccadilly, and then take a bus
along," said Mr. Eccles, and this they did.
They said little to each other as they made for Piccadilly. The
crowds on the pavements were too thick, and there was too much
traffic to wait hours on end for or dash in front of on the roads.
And they said less in the bus, which they caught at the top of
Waterloo Place, and which was packed inside and out. A seat
was found for Ella, but Mr. Eccles was left strap-hanging. For
this he kept his head low, in case his new hat should collide with
the ceiling, lurched a good deal on the quiet, and put what
polish he could upon his dignity by peering and looking back
in a critical way out of the window, rather as though London
was being partially managed by him, and he had to see that the
buildings were in their right places. Ella pretended that she was
his assistant, and looked roughly where he looked. He only
spoke once, and that was at one of the stops, where a lot of people
got out and in. " A Veritable Sardine Tin," he murmured,
leaning over. But Ella did not catch the words. " Pardon ? "
she said. Mr. Eccles was just about to repeat himself, and had got
as far as Veritable, when he was bumped into by a person. He
looked sharply round at the bumper and Ella, in order to pretend
that nothing had happened, asked him again what he said. " A
Veritable Sardine Tin," repeated Mr. Eccles, but all the spontaneity and gaiety had gone out of the observation. Also he had
that glassy look in his eyes, and after having taken another look
at the offender he murmured something about Some People.
Ella didn't quite catch what, but knew that when people start
calling other people Some, they had nothing nice to say about

them. She therefore nodded in an ambiguous manner, which conveyed sympathy with Mr. Eccles, and anger at the person.

By the time they reached the Park, then, a complete, and not very enjoyable hiatus had been made in the flowering process of their friendship, and as they went in by the Wellington Gate, Ella felt as though they had to start all over again. They were walking alongside Rotten Row at a brisk pace, and he was again monosyllabic. She knew by now that he was a very touchy person, and she could see that the Veritable Sardine Tin casualty was still weighing on his mind. She braced herself to entertain him.

" What part of the world do *you* live in, then, Mr. Eccles ? " she said, glad to call him " Mr. Eccles " thus, and to begin again on a more formal basis, almost as though she had him across the bar.

" Well, I'm living over at Chiswick at the moment. But I don't fancy I shall be there much longer."

" Chiswick, eh ? That's a very nice part, isn't it ? I've never been there myself."

" Oh, yes, it's all right," said Mr. Eccles, and added, in a rather forced way, " I have my sister-in-law staying with me at the moment."

" Oh yes ? " said Ella, and tried to create some mental picture of Mr. Eccles at home. Chiswick, an " infernal girl," and a sister-in-law—there was little enough to go on. And what attitude did (or would) sisters-in-law adopt towards new hats and matinées with barmaids ?

" One's relations can get very trying at times, can't they ? " said Mr. Eccles.

" Yes, I should say they can," said Ella, a little pleased and flattered that he should have taken her into his confidence so far.

" But then these Army people are often like that," said Mr. Eccles, gazing ahead of him in the feeble light of the Park lamps, " so I suppose one shouldn't complain."

" Oh yes ? " said Ella, in an even tone, but knowing inwardly that he had opened the bombardment again with a frightful, devastating shell. Army people ! It was impossible to take in all the implications of those words at once. She didn't quite know what Army People meant : technically privates (like her brother who was killed in the war) were Army people. But from the painful yet unctuous way in which Mr. Eccles had dragged the phrase in, it here obviously covered some remote and haughty area between subalterns and Field Marshals, and left her humbled. So his people were Army People ! She wondered (half ironically) that he condescended to speak to her !

" They can be awful, can't they ? " said Mr. Eccles.

" Yes," said Ella. " I suppose they can."

She could not help wishing that he would refrain from making a fool of himself (and her) by pretending that Army People were all in the day's work, and that she was so wearily familiar with the company and stale goings-on of Army People that she must naturally agree with him that they were " awful." At the same time his pains to impress her were so transparent that she could barely take offence; indeed from one point of view she felt inclined to like and pity him for all this, as being pathetically symptomatic of his homage for herself. And Army People ! It was certainly a feather in his cap, whatever you said. There was a pause as they walked along.

" So your people are Army People, are they, Mr. Eccles ? " she said. . . .

" Oh yes," said Mr. Eccles. " *Old* Army People."

Mr. Eccles brought out the word Old in a manner which put all Young, or New Army People out of the picture for good and all, and Ella, glancing at him, observed that he was striding beside her with the brusque determined air of an Old Army Person himself.

" Were you in the Army, then, Mr. Eccles ? " said Ella, meaning to be polite, but quickly regretting her impulse.

" No . . ." said Mr. Eccles, judicially, " I wasn't. As a matter of *Fact*."

The inference was that he was as a matter of principle, as a matter of opportunity, as a matter of temperament, as a matter of everything, indeed, save as a matter of Fact—Fact being a concern one left to scientists, and other materialists, and didn't bother one's head about while walking through Hyde Park with a young lady.

Ella wished she hadn't brought the subject up, and again changed it.

## CHAPTER X

" A H—but one *does* get lonely—that's the point," said Mr.
Eccles, swallowing the remains of his white wine, and
wiping his mouth with a serviette ; and Ella realized
that yet another Mr. Eccles was coming on the scene, a slightly
wined, loquacious and confiding Mr. Eccles, who might at any
moment accidentally drop some clue as to why he had taken
her out, why they were having dinner together, and what the
whole business was about.

They were seated opposite each other at a table for two on the
basement floor of Lyons' Coventry Street Corner House. The
time was about half-past nine. The orchestra was playing,
drowning Mr. Eccles' voice ; and nearly every table in this vast,
marble, subterranean Versailles for London's hungry and
teeming nondescripts, was engaged. Ella had at first been a little
disappointed that he should have brought her to the Corner
House ; for she had been here before of an evening, and after
the terrific splash he had made at the theatre, and what with
Army people and one thing and another, she had somehow got
it into her head that when he spoke of Dinner he had in mind
somewhere a little more intimate, original and exciting—one
of those little restaurants in Soho, say, which she had so often
wondered about. But she at once reproved herself for greed
in pleasure, and was in a way relieved to be on her own ground,
where she knew how to behave and where she was suitably
dressed. Besides, she was intensely fond of Lyons' Corner
House—with the fondness of all healthy-minded beings for
palaces—and Mr. Eccles took a broad-minded view of the menu
which made her gasp. He ordered two cocktails at once, and
burst into the dizziest soups and lobster extravagances without
turning a hair. He also ordered wine for himself, and persuaded
Ella, much against her will, to take a little. Ella reckoned that
what with the theatre and all the rest he had spent little less than
thirty shillings on this jaunt already ; and as one who seldom
spent more than thirty pence on an outing altogether, she had
a peculiar sense of being wasteful, and wanted to stop him.

At the same time she had a peculiar sense of enjoying herself, of merely physically revelling, for the first time in her life, in the brilliant sunshine of his financial plane, and she wanted to do anything but stop him.

Also he had become a great deal more human and talkative under the influence of his wine and food, and by slow degrees she had swerved round again to the conclusion that she definitely Liked him. In fact, it was at the instant of his remark about loneliness that another thought struck her. Was it not conceivable that he was Possible ? The mere thought filled her with a kind of awe and shame at herself for even entertaining such a notion fleetingly ; she felt she was mentally betraying all her true pride and æsthetic austerity. But he looked so young, just now in this light, and he had such a pathos about him at moments, and he was treating her, with no apparent or immediate object, with such prodigal generosity, that she really did not see why she should not amuse herself with the hypothesis. Not that she thought him Possible. It merely was possible that, at some future date, she might imaginably come to regard him as Possible. And even then he would not be *really* Possible, of course—that is to say, Possible to the point of being acceptable in fact. But he might be Possible enough to be rejected—rejected with dignity and kindly sentiment—in short he might not be so utterly Impossible as she had thought him so far.

" But you don't get lonely, do you ? " she said, speaking with genuine sympathy, for she had suffered much from loneliness herself.

" Me ? " he said, as he passed her a cigarette, which she took. " What do you think ? "

" Well, I shouldn't have thought *you* got lonely."

And she noticed that his hand was trembling as she put her head forward, almost with coquettishness, to have her cigarette lit.

At the same time a strange little thrill of power and exaltation ran through her as she realized that she was, perhaps for the first time in her life, flirting with, " encouraging," and to some extent prostrating a male. But then so many strange things had happened since half-past two in the afternoon, and why should she not have her share of such sensations ?

"Well—why do you think I asked you to come out with me to-day?" asked Mr. Eccles.

There was a moment of confusion, which Mr. Eccles covered by lighting his own cigarette.

"Why did you?" said Ella, but as Mr. Eccles did not answer, but merely blew out the match and put it on the ash-tray with a wry smile, the awful electric atmosphere was maintained, and Ella was emboldened still further. "Go on," she said. "Why did you?"

She knew there was no mistaking her soft and coaxing tone. She was more than "encouraging" him now. She was what they called "vamping" the man! Never had she dreamed that she could play such a rôle—or that she could enjoy it as she was enjoying it.

"I suppose it was because I took to you," said Mr. Eccles, "that's all."

"Did you?" said Ella, in the same dreamy tone, and all at once realized that she must be careful. She would make herself cheap if she went on like this. "I was very pleased to come," she added, in a more formal tone, "anyway."

"Don't you ever suffer from loneliness yourself?" asked Mr. Eccles.

"Me? I should just say I do," said Ella, with an emphasis which was not quite sincere, for, sufferer as she was, she had been, as it happened, remarkably free from attacks of this disease during the last year or so. But she couldn't possibly confuse the issue, or squash the awkwardly yet rapidly flowering bud of his own loneliness, by telling him this.

"Ah—then we're in the same boat," said Mr. Eccles. "It isn't nice, is it?"

She could not help feeling that they had embarked a little prematurely and on insufficient understanding, that he had shoved her into the boat, in fact, and was rowing away with her before she had time to protest; but she did not let him see this, and said, "But surely you've got enough friends?"

"Oh yes. I've got friends. If you'd call them friends."

"Why—aren't they friends?"

"Yes. Friends who want to take advantage of you—that's about all."

"But why should they want to take advantage of you?"

"Oh—I don't know. . . ."

"Go on. Why should they?"

"Well, I suppose if one's got a little something"—Mr. Eccles paused for the exact expression—"*Put By*—they're only too willing to be your friends."

(Hullo, thought Ella, here was her old friend the Little Something Put By cropping up again. She wondered whether any of the outer veils enveloping this mystery were about to be lifted.)

"You mean they take advantage of you because you've got some money?" she said.

"Yes. I'm sure they do."

"Well, I don't think that's right."

"No. I know you don't. That's because you're different. I know *you* wouldn't take advantage, for instance."

Again she thought he was going a little bit too fast. Where, precisely, did he glean his evidence that she would not take advantage? In point of fact had she not taken advantage already? Would she have come out with him at all, if he had not bribed her with shining gold for the theatre? But such introspection was ill-timed.

"I certainly wouldn't," she said, with firmness, and there was a pause. . . .

"Of course," said Mr. Eccles, at random. "It's very nice to be in a Position. . . ."

"Yes," said Ella, "I suppose it is. . . ."

"One's Secure," said Mr. Eccles. . . .

"M'm," murmured Ella.

"And one can Help," said Mr. Eccles. . . .

"Yes," said Ella. "I suppose one can."

"As far as one can. . . ."

"M'm."

"And that's something."

"Yes. It certainly is."

And there was a heavy silence in which Ella, as it were, was united with Mr. Eccles in a Position, and contemplated the weary consolations thereof.

## CHAPTER XI

"YOU should take a bus from here, really," said Ella, but "Oh, no," said Mr. Eccles, "I'll see you back."

They were at Oxford Street, crossing the road and going northwards. Dinner was over, and he was seeing her home. As the night was fine they had decided to walk. Actually Ella would have preferred to have gone home alone, as towards the close of dinner her nervous energy had suddenly collapsed under the accumulated strain of seven successive hours with Mr. Eccles ; she was dog-tired, had sore feet and a splitting headache on the way, and desired nothing save to go to bed.

As they started up Great Portland Street, however, towards "The Midnight Bell," she saw the last lap ahead, and took courage.

"Well—you haven't told me anything about yourself, yet, you know," he said, and at this point he slipped his hand into her arm.

"Well, there's nothing to tell, really," said Ella, with the squirmingly off-hand air of one to whom the hand of Mr. Eccles on her arm might have been a lifelong experience.

"Oh, I'm sure there is," said Mr. Eccles in a warm yet slightly patronizing way (as though he himself didn't really believe there was), and he edged a little closer to her, and gave her arm a decided little pressure, as he slipped his own a little further in.

This, she decided, was getting awkward. As well as putting a ridiculous brake upon her walking action, causing them both to wobble and sway as though they were a little drunk, instead of advancing properly to their destination, this arm-holding set up a great agitation in her mind as to the amount of pressure she should return or refuse. On the one hand she appreciated a friendly action, and did not want to let her arm remain entirely limp. On the other hand she was displeased by the folly of such untimely advances in the street, and did not want to let him think she was freely participating in them.

"No, there isn't," she said. "Really."

"Come now," he said. "Of course there is." And they wobbled again horribly.

Good Lord, thought Ella—supposing Bob, or someone from "The Midnight Bell" saw them now! She must somehow shake him off before they got there, or she would be disgraced for life. But for the time being she could only play the game out.

"Well," she said. "There's very little."

"Really?" said Mr. Eccles. "Come now. No *Affaires de Cœur*?"

My word, thought Ella. French now. He *was* being sprightly. She wasn't quite sure what *Affaires de Cœur* meant, but imagined it was some very Continental and finished way of saying "Love Affairs," and replied "No—not at present."

"Oh, surely you have," said Mr. Eccles. "You must confide in me, you know. We understand each other."

Again she observed that he was taking too much for granted. He might understand her, but she wished to Heaven she understood the first thing about him. What on earth was the man *after*? Was this gay air of camaraderie sincere, and was this apparently disinterested interest in her concerns real or feigned? And if it was real, why did he keep on pressing her arm, and why should he have pounced upon her, of all the millions of other girls in London, as the unique object of his interest? And what staying power he had! If he only knew how tired she was. He must be nearly twice her age, and yet he had theatred, and walked and d ned her off her feet, and was now as cheerful and resilient as a¹ two-year-old.

"No, there isn't," she said. "Honestly." At another time she might have tried to raise her prestige by reservations and fencing with him on thiş matter, but now she was too tired, and told the truth.

"What about that young fellow in that bar of yours," said Mr. Eccles. "What's his name?"

"Who do you mean?" said Ella, knowing quite well whom he meant. "Do you mean Bob?"

"Yes. That's right, Bob."

"Oh," said Ella. "Him." It was strange that his instinct should have led him so near the mark—straight to the mark, in fact. And did she detect a note of concealed curiosity and anxiety in Mr. Eccles' voice. How could he know of her secret madness for Bob?

"He's a good-looking enough young fellow, in any case," said Mr. Eccles.

"Yes, he is good-looking, isn't he?" said Ella, with all the indiscretion of her enthusiasm, in which she resembled a stamp-collector or other zealot with his hobby, and could not hear any detached or extraneous praise of the obsessing object without a warm feeling about the heart. In fact, just for this remark it seemed as though she liked Mr. Eccles more at this moment than she had ever liked him—a sad and ironical pass for Mr. Eccles if he was her admirer.

"But there's nothing between you?"

"Oh no. Bob isn't interested in me."

With the more than reasonable conclusion that could be drawn from this, that she herself was interested in Bob, she knew at once that she had said the wrong, indeed possibly the cruel thing, but it had come out before she could stop herself.

"Oh," said Mr. Eccles, and glancing at his face, which had the ghost of a sickly smile on it, she knew that he had read the very worst into it. She believed she had really offended and wounded him now. What awful muddles she was getting into. But there was not much further to go. They had now branched off to the right into Warren Street, and " The Midnight Bell " was only about five hundred yards away. She had hoped to get rid of him at the corner, but he still had her arm and she had not the courage to stop. He was silent now.

"And I'm not interested in *him*," she said, boldly, disliking the thought of leaving him on such evasive and unsatisfactory terms, and hoping to extricate herself while there was still time.

"Aren't you?"

"Good Heavens, no." She was warming up to her falsehood now she had started. "What do you think?"

"Oh, I don't see why you shouldn't be," he said, but it was clear that his suspicions were allayed, and he slipped his arm a little further in. She was glad to be reconciled, but she wished he would take his arm away. "The Midnight Bell" was prac-tically in sight now, and anyone might see them.

"Then we're just waiting for Mr. Right, I suppose?" said

Mr. Eccles, causing another wobble, and sublimely unconscious of her self-consciousness. " Is that it ? "

" Yes. I suppose it is," said Ella. And here, though there was nothing tangible in his remark, there was a kind of leer in his voice, and a tightening up of his arm, which warned Ella that she was not going to get as lightly out of this parting as she had imagined. She saw a lamp-post twenty yards ahead, and decided that at that point she would stop, whatever the cost.

" Eh ? " said Mr. Eccles. . . .

Ella did not answer. She had an awful premonition that there was going to be a scene. She passed the lamp-post—it was too bright under that—and fixed upon a dark patch by some railings a little further on.

" Eh ? " said Mr. Eccles. " What about Mr. Right. . . ."

" I don't know," said Ella, in confusion, and forcing her courage, she slackened her pace, and stopped. " Well—here we are at last," she said.

In stopping like this, she had imagined that Mr. Eccles must automatically release her arm. To her horror, however, she found that he still had hold of it, and that in turning she had somehow got hedged in against the railings at his mercy.

" What ? " said Mr. Eccles, without exactly knowing what he was saying, and looking hard at her.

Now, she realized, the crisis of the day had come. Was he going to kiss her, or something ? And could she repel him, after all he had done for her ? How many couples had she seen in this posture, in dim lamp-lit patches, murmuring their fervent mysteries against railings, and how little she had dreamed that she would ever be enrolled in that strange corps ! But here she was, as though she had been doing it all her life.

" Well—it's been a lovely day," she said, and pretending that he was not holding her arm, and that she did not know that he was staring at her, she looked along the street.

" Has it ? " said Mr. Eccles.

She dared not look at him, but felt his whole person closing imperceptibly yet unrelentingly in upon her.

" Yes. And I'm sure I'm ever so grateful." She wished to Heaven he would buck up, if he was going to do anything, as she would go mad and run away in a moment.

" What ? " said Mr. Eccles, but apart from coming in a little
nearer, made no further contribution to the situation.

" It was ever so kind of you," she tried, and since she could
shirk it no longer, she turned her head and met his eyes.

" What ? " said Mr. Eccles, gazing at her in a hypnotized,
semi-squinting way, and all at once she felt his arm round her
waist.

His face was now so near to hers that she found herself
squinting back. " I don't know," she said, blindly, in complete
prostration of the intellect.

But this was no answer for Mr. Eccles.

" M'm ? " he said, and then, again, as his hold round her
waist was made firm, " What ? " . . .

" You shouldn't be doing this, you know," said Ella. " Should
you ? "

" M'm ? " said Mr. Eccles. " What ? "

Could the unfortunate murmuring man say nothing but
" What ? " Hysteria would seize her in a moment and she would
start giggling.

" I said you shouldn't be doing this," she said. " Should
you ? "

" What ? " said Mr. Eccles. " What ? " . . .

It was no good. Mr. Eccles was in a trance, and would go on
saying " What " till midnight and beyond if left in peace. She
definitely would have to leave him.

" Well, I really must be going," she said putting her hand on
his arm, as though to release herself.

" What ? " said Mr. Eccles, ignoring this, and pressing her
towards him with such vigour and suddenness that they both
swayed, and righted themselves with the greatest difficulty.
" What ? "

" Well—*what ?* " said Ella, now losing her patience a little.

" M'm ? " said Mr. Eccles. " You Little Devil, you. What ? "

Oh Lord, thought Ella, what a terrible, versatile, unaccountable man ! At the last moment he was piling sheer quizzing
rakishness on top of all else. What was she expected to do now—
stay and be Satanic ? She couldn't do it.

" Well, I really must go," she said writhingly. " Will you come
in and see me again soon ? "

" Aren't you a Little Devil ? " said Mr. Eccles. " What ? "

There was nothing for it—she would have to be firm, and risk offending him. She took hold of his arm with both her hands, and freed herself.

" You come in and talk about it some other time," she said and awkwardly seizing his hand to shake it she added " So long. Thanks ever so much. Good-night," and fled—half running from him in a way which she hoped he would construe as maidenly overcomeness.

" What ? " she heard Mr. Eccles protesting as she fled, but she did not dare look back, and in a few moments she was out of sight.

" The Midnight Bell " was closed to the public, but she let herself in by the side door, and ran upstairs unobserved.

With the sound of Mr. Eccles' " Whats " still ringing in her ears, she undressed hastily, got into bed, and lay pondering in the dark.

" *What ?* " But why should he ask *her* What ? It was she, surely, who should question him. And after hour upon hour of fumbling and advancing and lurking he had thrown not a speck of light on the mystery of his pursuit. Instead of making himself clear when it came to the crises all he could say was " What ? " . . .

What indeed ? What ? What ? *What ?*

She gave the problem up, and slept the dead sleep of exhaustion.

## CHAPTER XII

THE deceptive juice Sleep, while it no doubt actually reconstructed and refreshed Ella's nervous resources, always gave the appearance, first thing in the morning, of having wrecked them. Ella was always at her worst when she woke, and her heart would misgive her fearfully. So soon as she was conscious her mind would go stalking anxiously through the debris of yesterday, certain of signs of calamity and wreckage, and seeking to discover what precise shape they had taken, and for what she was to be indicted by herself. Never did she fail to fix upon something to make the jagged worst of, moved by a hateful yet deliberate impulse. As the day wore on the streams of health and positiveness flowed once more in the dried-up channels, and she was her proper self.

This morning she was not long at a loss for her problem. She turned on the pillow and Mr. Eccles towered up above and around her. Nor was she long in ascertaining which peak in the vast range of that problem she was to single out as the focussing point for self-recrimination. It was the final one— the parting—the querying and hideous clumsiness of the parting. She had as good as run away from him, and she had not the slightest doubt, now, that her rudeness had " put him off." Put him off for good, probably. Not that she was by any means certain that she did not desire to put him off—if she came to think about it later she might decide that that was exactly what she wanted. But that was not the question. She had put him off against her conscious will and by virtue of her own silliness or ineptness ; she was landed resentfully with the fact that she had put him off, and the fiends of her customary early morning mood seized the opportunity to scourge her.

In the flurry of her escape she had not given him a chance to mention a further meeting, and she could not conceive him bothering to come near " The Midnight Bell " again. Well, that was that—she had Put him Off, and she supposed she was relieved in a way. But was not this Putting Off symptomatic of the general miscarriage of her technique and manners ? Was she not always Putting people Off with her childishness and self-consciousness ? Why must she always be so critical, why couldn't she have let Mr. Eccles go on saying " What " and embracing her ? Another girl would have encouraged and put him at his ease. It was always the same with her. Who did she think she was, that she could be so fastidious ? And she proceeded on these heads to loathe and castigate herself.

As she dressed she heard Bob dressing in the next room, and the vigour of his personality seemed to emanate through the wall into her room. How full of confidence and triumph his evenings and mornings seemed. Could a man who bumped about and washed himself like that have any self-castigations or longings ? Maybe he had, but in her general sense of yearning for him and everything she did not have, her imagination could not fly so high as to visualize any.

After breakfast, however, Ella's introspections, as usual, imperceptibly vanished as she busied herself in the bar. By demonstrating her brisk command over one inanimate object after another, she set up a symbolic process which put her soul in countenance, and by ten o'clock she was the despotic marshal of a fiercely trained army of tumblers, and her vital self. Furthermore Mr. Eccles was on the shelf along with the tumblers.

This morning, also, there was a diversion in the bar. Yesterday the Governor's young grandson, whose school had broken up owing to an epidemic, and whose parents were out of London, had come as a treat to stay at " The Midnight Bell." He had done this before during the holidays, and Ella knew him well, as it was his custom to " help " her in the mornings in the bar before the house was opened.

For this healthy yet loathsome little boy, with his green school cap, sturdy body, bare chapped knees, and nauseatingly ruddy complexion, Ella had the greatest affection—or at any rate fondly believed she had. Her feeling, that is to say, was founded purely on the fact that he was a child, or " kid " as she called it, and demanded no basis in behaviour. In Ella's amiable yet curiously conventional mentality, the idea of not " loving " a " kid," of not considering a " kid " to be " great," " wonderful," " lovely," " cute," " plucky," " grand," " fine "—in fact singular and outstanding in all he uttered and accomplished—was unthinkable or practically blasphemous.

" Here's Master Eric come to help you, Ella," the Governor would say, and Ella having expressed delight, he would " help " her all the morning. That is to say he would fetch a few things, carry a few things, hum to himself, moon about, wander out on to the pavement where Bob was cleaning the brass, be called in, be stopped pulling at the beer engine, be found tormenting the dog, cause shrieking oscillations by fooling about with the wireless, or fire off a pea-shooter at the bottles—irregularly punctuating these enjoyments either by standing on his head against the wall and looking as though he was going to choke, or standing up against the bar, kicking at the woodwork in his ennui, and cross-examining Ella on points of technical or athletic knowledge.

Subtly and precociously realizing his position as the youngest heir to the establishment and the apple of the all-powerful Governor's eye, he reserved a special air of arrogance and condescension towards the barmaid, calling her " Ella " in an authoritative and feudal tone, and continually making clear the difference in their social states of grace.

His main delight, however, was to tie Ella up into intellectual knots. Bursting as he was with knowledge, electrical and otherwise, lately imbibed at school, they were both aware in their different ways that he was her intellectual and controversial master, and he might well have afforded to show some tact and forbearance on this head. Nevertheless, he was unable to refrain from seizing any and every opportunity to wipe the floor with her.

Indeed, if the opportunity was not there, he had no hesitation in making it. Thus, this morning, kicking his shoes against the woodwork, and seeing Ella putting some bottles on the shelf, " I wonder what the $H_2O$ Content of those bottles is," he said with an unimpressive air of innocent detachment.

" Yes. I wonder," said Ella, suspecting a trap, and hoping the matter would drop here.

" What do you *think* ? " pursued Master Eric, who had no idea of letting it go like that.

" I really don't know," said Ella.

" Yes—but you must be able to think."

" No," said Ella, with a judicial air. " I really couldn't say." And then she had an inspiration. " What do *you* think ? "

" I was asking you."

" Well, you tell me."

There was a pause in which Master Eric went on spasmodically banging at the woodwork with his feet, and, putting his head on one side, he traced a pattern with his finger on the bar.

" I suppose you know," he said at last, in a steady voice, " what $H_2O$ is ? "

" Yes, of course I do," said Ella, but there was no " of course " about it. True, she had a hazy notion that $H_2O$ was an infinitely recondite (but rather unnecessary) way of alluding to plain drinking water, but she was by no means certain even of this.

" What is it then ? " asked Master Eric.

" Ah " . . . said Ella.

" I don't believe you know," said Master Eric. " Do you ? "

" Of course I do," said Ella, seeing that she would have to burn her boats. " It just means water. Don't it ? "

" Of *course* it means *water*," said Master Eric sharply. " But what does $H_2O$ mean—what do the *letters* mean ? "

" Oh," said Ella, " I don't know about that."

" But you said you knew what $H_2O$ meant."

" Did I ? "

" Yes—didn't you ? "

" Yes. I suppose I did."

" Well—then—you didn't know after all."

Ella did not answer this.

" Did you ? "

" No, I suppose I didn't."

" You are Silly," said Master Eric, coolly pointing to facts. " Aren't you ? "

And because he was a " kid," and could do no wrong in her eyes, instead of doing what she should have done, that is, smacked his head, hit him in the solar-plexus and kicked him out of the bar, Ella merely remarked " Oh well," reflected that he had " caught her out," and hoped he would change the subject.

" As a matter of *fact*," said Master Eric, speaking as one who knew that the information was scarcely worth scattering on to such stony ground, " H *happens* to mean Hydrogen, and O *happens* to mean Oxygen."

" Oh," said Ella. " Really ? "

" And those two *happen* to make up water—that's all."

" Oh."

" Funny—isn't it," said Master Eric with searing sarcasm.

At this moment the Governor entered the bar.

" Well, what are *you* talkin' about, little 'un ? " asked the Governor, but the little one did not reply.

"He's been explaining," said Ella blithely, "all about Hydrogen and Oxygen, and I don't know what."

"My word—you know more than me anyway," said the Governor, and "Yes—he's a bright boy all right," said Ella. . . .

And the Governor winked at Ella, and Ella looked back at the Governor with a confidential pride and joy in the youngster that was boundless.

In this way the morning passed, and at eleven o'clock the house was opened, and Ella was kept hard at work till three, when it closed again. She then went upstairs and put on her hat and mackintosh in order to go out into the rain and visit her mother—a visit which was overdue, since to-day was Friday and she usually went on Thursday, her day off.

## CHAPTER XIII

THE parents of this submissive girl dwelling in Pimlico, she walked along to the top of the Tottenham Court Road for a bus, which went at a good speed down the Tottenham Court Road itself; pulled up and rushed forward in dashes along Oxford Street; lined up in a sort of buses' bread line in Bond Street, advancing inch by inch; sped down Piccadilly by the side of Green Park; whizzed furiously and giddily round the great open spaces of Hyde Park Corner, and landed her in the pouring rain in the vicinity of the Grosvenor Hotel, Victoria, where the rich were leaving for happier climes. For this transportation she contributed threepence to the Company's funds, and had about ten minutes' walk ahead of her, threading her way through the least flourishing quarters of tobacco-cum-sweetshoppy Pimlico, and at length arriving at the corner of a decomposing street, where stood a decomposing house with four floors, a basement, and railings. Here, sandwiched between five or six other grim and doubtful *ménages*, lived Ella's mother and stepfather.

This, in fact, was Ella's home and background. Also, in a manner, it was her secret, for those who saw the neat, beer-pulling, chaffing Ella in the bar of " The Midnight Bell " carried social introspection no further than the epithet " barmaid," and it no more occurred to them to suspect that she had some such human background and spiritual resource, that she carried on a complete life of her own in other words, than it would have occurred to them to suspect her of murder or arson. Not even the Governor or Bob suspected.    Actually, however, Ella looked at the matter from exactly the contrary angle.    To her this was her real life, and wherever her mother was was neces-sarily her home ; and however frequently she might leave it, and lodge apart in order to slave her life out elsewhere, she could never regard such departures as anything but prolonged ventures or enforced excursions launched from this fixed centre in her heart.    Such are the cool misapprehensions of a harsh and disinterested world.

Not that Ella was ever at home more than four hours every week on the average, or that she was what is called " happy " at home.    In fact she never failed to make herself dumbly miserable by going there.    At the very outset there was a jarring note, her mother having some years ago acquired the pre-posterous surname of Prosser, whereas her true surname was the same as Ella's—Dawson.    This infantile homage paid to Registry Office formulas invariably puzzled and annoyed Ella, although she could not dispute the fact that her mother was legally, indeed irremediably, married to Mr. Prosser.

To hear her mother being called Mrs. Prosser—that was to say after a fiend in human shape—was often more than Ella could bear, and she would be on the verge of crying out upon her mother for her responsibility in the error.    Her mother, however, bore such an apologetic and uncomprehending air about the matter, and had obviously so completely forgotten the variety of motives which seven or eight years ago had prompted her to commit the act, that Ella always reproached herself for her resentment, and remained silent.    Indeed, in an embarrassed way, they both tried to keep off the subject alto-

gether in so far as it was possible, Ella giving her tacit consent
to the only comment that her mother was capable of feebly
re-affirming in an effort to justify or mitigate the penalty of her
husband—namely, the negative one that he was not as Bad
as he was Painted.

Whether, actually, Mr. Prosser was, or was not, as Bad as he
was Painted (by Ella at any rate), was another matter. In point
of fact, he was not the sort of man that anybody would think
of Painting at all, in the ordinary way—he being one of the
obscurer Paintings by the Almighty in a modern style, whose
significance and place in the general exhibition were not to be
instantly apprehended and whose soul did not show on the
surface. A more silent and reticent man there never was. He had
a thin body, an ashen face, glowering eyes, and a large grey
moustache. A saddler by trade, he had been, before and just
after the war "in his own way." The laws governing the
benign progress of capital, however, had by slow and painful
methods pinched and thrust him from the ranks of the petty-
bourgeoisie into the ranks of the proletariat, with the result
that, instead of being "in his own way" he was now in almost
everybody's way, and a misery to himself. Always a sour-
tempered man, a staunch conservative in politics, and something
of a snob, instead of having sheltered himself with any form of
philosophical encrustation, his fall from private ownership
obviously yet rankled and gnawed at him day by day, and hour
by hour. There was nothing doing in his line, and he made a
few unhappy shillings every week by cleaning the brass, and
sweeping the floors, and snatching up the empty glasses of the
more fortunate in a large public-house round the corner. A
false and humiliating occupation indeed. There was thus much
to excuse him, but not enough to account for his invincible and
chronic silence and savagery, which he wreaked upon his wife,
and which arose, perhaps, less from sheer distress than from a
vindictive sense of vanished superiority. Ella, uncomprehending
of social causation, saw no excuse.

Mr. and Mrs. Prosser inhabited three rooms on the third
floor of the house Ella now entered, and regarded their quarters
as comparatively spacious. There was a bedroom, a sitting-room,
and a general muddling room containing a washing line and a

gas range. The windows at the back looked out on to the sooty structure and black asphalt yard of a school—and the weighted droning of the class-room, or the murderous yelling and squealing of recreation in the yard, accompanied the occupiers through the tasks of the day.

Though, thanks to her mother, everything was fairly (*fairly*) clean inside, the long and steadfast grip of poverty showed itself everywhere and Ella never came up here without a slight sense of shame at being in such a " good place " and wearing such fine clothes—a sensation from which she got hardly any relief in the fact that out of her weekly salary, which was twenty-two shillings, she kept only twelve, and gave the other ten to her mother.

Ella's mother was a grey-haired, quiet, ill, puzzled woman of about fifty, with some resemblance to Ella, particularly about the eyes, and between them there existed the profoundest understanding and affection.

As soon as Ella had climbed the dark, airless and uncared-for stairway, and opened the door, and called for her mother, she saw at once that calamity, which carried on its campaign incessantly all along the line, had stricken the household at a fresh and unforeseen point, and by means of a fresh weapon of warfare, —uric acid. In other words, she had only to glance at her mother to see that she was suffering from a frightful stiff Neck. This was swathed round and safety-pinned with a piece of flannel which made Mrs. Prosser look extraordinarily miserable, and also, if the truth was told, not a little silly. " It's all right," she said at once, seeing Ella look at her. " I've got a stiff Neck." But why she should say it was all right was not clear, since she was obviously in excruciating agony every time she moved her head, and was thus compelled to move across the room with all the delays and caution of a novice on the tight-rope, and, in turning to look at anything, to move her entire stiffened body round as though she were incarcerated in a block of solid ice. Or, again, it was as though a ghostly surgeon had conveniently arranged to operate upon her while she went about her household tasks, and the operation was still in progress.

Not a very pleasant opening for her visit, but Ella was hardened to such occurrences in this damned abode, and expressing the liveliest sympathy, and after having had a Look it at (as though that was going to do any good) and compelling her mother slowly to transport her stiff neck to the arm-chair in the sitting-room, she herself took over the tasks she had interrupted, and put on the kettle for tea.

Her mother did not remain still for long, but in about twenty minutes' time tea was ready, and they settled down in the sitting-room for their weekly chat. By now the smoky dusk was thickening in the rain outside ; the fire, extravagantly heaped for the occasion, was blazing red and spitting white jets of gas ; and in the suitable gloaming impending, there took place, with the clink of tea-cups, a gentle summing-up and discussion of the week's events. As the dusk grew deeper they saw little more than the shapes of each other, and grew more confiding.

## CHAPTER XIV

STRENUOUSLY as they both tried to evade and shirk it, Ella and her mother were never very long able to keep away from the shamefaced topic which actually dominated their thoughts—to wit, Him. Into whatever realms of description they went, however cheerful or absorbed they became, He was lurking there in the conversational background (in fact they both knew He would be back for his tea before very long), and some chance remark would set them going. " And then, of course, He's been very funny all the time," her mother would say. " Has he ? " said Ella, and after a reluctant pause, the various cats would come out of the bags.

There was, as usual, a long inventory of novel crimes to his name this week. He had been more silent than ever, he had taken to coming in at three o'clock in the morning and cooking himself eggs. He had publicly stormed at the floor above, he had stamped on the floor below, he had taken a resolute and fixed stand against washing himself, he had damned and blasted (and

somethinged) the Stiff Neck, he had got speechlessly drunk (even
for a speechless person) on Saturday night, and Lain On on
Sunday till four in the afternoon. In fact, " You wouldn't
*think* he had had any Education," said Ella's mother, and Ella
could have said more.

At last, however, they drifted away from the subject and Ella
began to wonder whether she would say anything to her mother
about Mr. Eccles. She desperately desired to confide in someone
about this strange happening and slight opening (if it was
an opening) in her life ; and quite apart from her need for advice, she had a sheer childish desire to tell gleefully, and perhaps
a little boastfully, to some understanding person, of the extravagant pleasures to which she had been treated, and the
staggering wealth which had been calmly expended upon her—
for no apparent reason save her *beaux yeux*. On the other hand
she was a little ashamed to speak of her participation in such
reckless expenditure before her mother, whose nagging pains
in penury would have been eased by a fraction of the bill for
that afternoon and evening. And she also doubted whether her
mother would Understand. . . . If it came to that, she did
not understand herself.

But she swallowed these scruples, and finding her mother
listening sympathetically at last let out the whole story with
the utmost relief—the entire story, that is to say, minus the
" Whats " and climax. They then talked round and round the
subject.

" But what does he *want* ? " said her mother at last, in her
simple, striving, slightly scared, yet direct way.

" Well," said Ella, " that's just what I want to know, really."
And in the deepening dusk she sensed exactly what her mother
was thinking. Her mother was thinking of dalliance and sin :
and her mother was thinking of Marriage. Furthermore her
mother did not dare risk an observation on either of these
themes, and was silent.

" He's a Gentleman," hazarded Ella, not quite knowing what
she meant to convey by this, but half wishing to describe his
general quality, and half to reassure her mother under the heading
of dalliance.

" Is he ? " was all her mother could say.

" Oh yes," said Ella. " They're Army People, I believe."

Ella brought this out with intense self-consciousness, and was ashamed at her duplicity with herself—inasmuch as she had been only too acutely ready to despise Mr. Eccles for " dragging in " this advantage at the time, and here was she, dragging it in just as clumsily, and taking it over and using it as a weapon herself.

" Is he really ? " said her mother, in a tone of awe which she was no longer able to conceal.

" Yes," said Ella. " So I understand."

It was odd, she reflected, that whenever she was with Mr. Eccles her mind harped incessantly upon his blemishes and absurdities, whereas now she was discussing him with someone else, she was seeing all those blemishes as advantages and sticking up for him—rather swanking about him in fact.

" Well," said her mother, " I certainly think you ought to keep in with him."

" Yes. I suppose one ought," said Ella, and suspected, in the silence that followed, that her mother's mind had again reverted to that dimly discerned yet irresistible concept of matrimony. Mrs. Prosser's next remark proved Ella's suspicion well-founded.

" Is he Nice Looking," she asked, " at all ? "

" Oh yes. Quite all right," said Ella. " He's Getting On, of course. . . ."

" Well, that's sometimes Better, isn't it ? " said Mrs. Prosser, encouragingly.

What was her mother trying to do ? Encouraging her to over-ride her most precious impulses, and calculatingly sell herself to so impressive a bidder ? What else ? Ella had an instinct to be shocked. She was aware, however, of the peculiar unscrupulousness of the elderly, however deep their love, with regard to the matter of marrying off their daughters, and felt she must allow for this.

" I mean he really *is* Getting On," she said. . . .

" Well," said Mrs. Prosser, " perhaps he's learnt some sense."

It was no good. Ella perceived that her white body had no place in her poor mother's calculations. But again she could not be offended. She understood her mother's feelings too well ; she knew, from the anxious, tentative tone of her voice, how

wretchedly, day and night, she yearned for some turn in their
fortune, to see Ella " settled "—a passion so selfless and intense
that it had come to disregard the very self and emotions of its
object. She could not resist throwing her a little scrap of hope.

" Well," she said, almost significantly. " He's certainly been
very kind."

" He certainly has." And Mrs. Prosser, possibly for the first
time in weeks, was a cheerful woman.

" Well, we shall see," said Ella, and there was a pause.

" He hasn't tried," said Mrs. Prosser, in a funny voice, " to
Carry On at all, I suppose, has he ? "

" Oh no," said Ella, " None of That. . . . "

She realized that it would not be proper, nor indeed in any
way possible to furnish an impression of whatever proportion
of Carrying On was implied in the indescribable " Whats "
against the railings. And this was a pity, since they constituted,
really, the sole crisis of the situation, providing the most
suggestive clue from which any vital interpretation of the situation might be made. But there is more often than not a sad
curse attached to confidences of this nature between mother and
daughter (and friend and friend, if it comes to that), whereby the
one confiding is forced to withhold some essential particular,
and yet foolishly seeks to obtain relief in the sympathy and
opinion of a listener who has been, as it were, betrayed, and is
enlarging upon an entirely false and incomplete hypothesis.

So, making the gulf even wider :   " Oh no," Ella repeated,
" I wouldn't allow that. . . . "

" No . . . " said Mrs. Prosser, in an ambiguous voice, and
Ella was not quite certain that she detected the note of relief
that she had anticipated. In fact she was not sure that her mother
was not a little disappointed. In the shattering lack of principle
to which her selfless passion had brought this normally austere
woman, it was quite possible that a little Carrying On might
have a perfectly decent and suitable place in the picture, as part of
the process of Encouragement and general submissiveness to a
lord of creation.    Ella saw that, near and dear as they were to
each other, they were eternally apart, and thought it would be
well to change the subject, lest her mother's innocence of their
separation should be destroyed.

She had no need to bother herself, for at this moment mounting footsteps on the wooden stairs outside caused Mrs. Prosser tensely to whisper " That's Him ! " and the sound of the outer door being opened announced beyond question that He had Come Back.

No sooner were these sounds heard than the warmth of their contact and the glow of their confidings, were transformed, in an instant, like an asbestos gas fire abruptly turned off at the main, into the ashen pallid coldness of fear and self-defence, and they stiffened their nerves for his entrance.

He spent a few exasperating moments walking and fiddling about in the kitchen, and then threw the door violently open— he had an extraordinary way of even opening a door as though he was slamming it—and seeing Ella, said " Oh—" That, and naught else, was his greeting to her.

" Good evening, uncle," said Ella. (There was a convention originating many years ago whereby she addressed him as " Uncle.")  " How are you ? "

Ever since she had learned to hate him, she always made a point of being scrupulously, even if a little vindictively, polite to him, so that there might be no blot upon the virgin whiteness of her initial advantage in civilized behaviour.

" I'm all right, thanks," he said.  " Ain't you got any light in 'ere ? "

Mr. Prosser was not the sort of man who could appreciate the subtleties and charms of the gloaming. He made the comment however, in a fairly good-tempered way, and it was clear that he was in some measure controlling, for the moment, his natural spleen out of respect for the visitor to the household.

" Yes. It's dark, isn't it ? " said Ella. " I'll put it on." And she got up to do so.

And with the lighting of the gas, the visit, so far as Ella was concerned, was at an end. Mrs. Prosser, who always did her best to be in any room save the one her husband was in, went out at once to get his tea ; and Ella, after trying to make some conversation on the weather, went and pretended to help her. She then brought the tea in herself to him, while her mother lit the gas in the kitchen and got on with some ironing. Thus Ella was left in mid-air with only two alternatives, either to stay and talk with her stepfather, which was practically impossible in view of his conversational stone-walling, or to show her favouritism by joining the other camp in the kitchen. She chose the latter. So chilling and disrupting was the influence of this man, who brought misery upon others not by what he said, but by what he did not say, and the bitter way he did not say it.

The door between the sitting-room and kitchen was left slightly ajar, and as her mother worked, and Ella helped her, they carried on a low-toned, semi-conspiratorial conversation, like the timorous gurgling of a feeble brook, in painful earshot and under the uncanny influence of an invisible Mr. Prosser drinking at his tea and gnawing at his bread and butter within. Her mother always dropped her tones to this level in such circumstances, and Ella was forced to imitate her.

But at last this brook-like murmur became too much for Mr. Prosser's nerves, and getting up from his tea, he pointedly and violently slammed the door which divided them.

" There ! " whispered Mrs. Prosser, staring at Ella, half in horror and faintness at this new provocation she had unwittingly given the monster, and half to signify to Ella that she had not exaggerated his behaviour.

" You mustn't mind," said Ella, feeling at any rate a certain relief on her own part at this crude insulting act, in that it wiped out any obligation on her part to see or speak to him again until next week. " You must treat him as a joke."

" But what have I *done* ? " asked Mrs. Prosser.

" You haven't done anything. You mustn't mind," said Ella, putting her arm round her mother, who took in her breath sharply, and was obviously beginning to cry, while pretending to go on with her ironing.

" I never do anything," she said, and there came another sob.

" Come along, mother—you mustn't cry," said Ella, hoping against hope that her mother would get control of herself in time. " You mustn't let him see you're hurt. Things'll be all right. You mustn't let him see you."

But looking round the wretched kitchen, with its snorting green gas illuminating its never-to-be-righted conglomeration of worn-out clothes and utensils ; and seeing her mother, with her Stiff Neck, ironing and trying not to cry ; and conscious of the savage presence next door, filling the air with its cruelty and discontent; and looking at the clock and seeing that she would be late for her work if she didn't look out; and realizing that, whereas she, Ella, was already relieved at the thought that she was clearing out in a few minutes, her ill mother had to stay and suffer it all to-night and every day and night—a wave of resentment swept over Ella, and she herself succumbed, clenching her fists and saying " *Oh* how I wish I could get you away ! "

" Yes," said Mrs. Prosser, who had now regained control and was ironing as if nothing had happened. " I only wish you could." And there was a kind of placid hopelessness and wistfulness about the remark which wrung Ella's heart.

Always, reflected Ella, when she left her mother it was like this—livid green gas in the window-reflected kitchen, fresh calamity, haste lest she was late for her work, black despair on all sides and nothing decided, nothing advanced, no suggestions or gleam of light for the future.

" Well, mother," she said, " I've got to go." And she started to put on her mackintosh. " Things'll come right, somehow."

" Yes, I daresay," said Mrs. Prosser, in a more comforted tone, and added, " Perhaps you'll be getting married one of these days."

Now what exactly, wondered Ella, did she mean to infer by that ? Was she harking back, and did she mean that Mr. Eccles might be going to marry her ?

" Yes, perhaps I will," she said, doubtfully.

" You never know," pursued her mother. " You should certainly be thinking about it."

Ella saw that this was unmistakable Eccles innuendo, and she took alarm. Was her mother Building ? She hoped that she had not said so much that her mother, when alone, would Build. However, there was no time to correct any impression now, and after prompting her mother with a few stern admonitions as to the proper line of defence with fiends in human shape, she gave her her customary ten-shilling note (which was received with a gloomy shamefaced " You shouldn't," but unconcealable evidences of heavenly relief) kissed her brusquely to cover up her embarrassment, and left her.

And that was that. She was out again in the pouring rain,

glad, yet ashamed of being glad, of having got away from that appalling atmosphere, and grinding round in her head for some means of attack or solution.

Only when she was in the bus taking her back did she recall Mr. Eccles, and her mother's innuendoes. She wondered what the gentlemanly Mr. Eccles would think, if he knew he had been described and viewed in the light of prey in a poverty-ridden room down at Pimlico. She was inclined to reprove herself, but reflected that possibly he had discussed her with someone else. It was strange, how quickly two people's business became public—other people's business, in fact.

In her gloom and dissatisfaction with life, however, she felt kindly towards Mr. Eccles, remembering his generous entertainment of yesterday. After Pimlico, she could hardly credit that she had ever moved, however briefly, on so riotous a plane. And, indeed, in her loneliness, his apparent affection was not untouching. Putting all personal feeling right aside for a moment— suppose her mother was right and Mr. Eccles was the solution she was seeking ? It seemed plausible enough. And if once it was plausible, endless vistas were opened up.

But, of course, it would be unwise to forget that Mr. Eccles held the only vital vote in such schemes for the general welfare. And had she not already decided that she had Put Mr. Eccles Off ? Would she ever see him again ? No. Probably, if she understood his psychology, he would avoid the pub, henceforth, and run like mad if he ever saw her. And since she had made such an ass of him against those railings, who could blame him ? What a fool she had been. Heaven knew what she had gone and lost now. She wished she could see him once more, if only to let him know that she took the Railings all in the day's work, as it were and had had no deliberate intention of Putting him Off. Perhaps he would come in this evening. He might, after all.

But ten o'clock that night—the time at which " The Midnight Bell," after a great deal of noise, barred its doors against its last customers—left Ella's heart finally barren of any such hope.

## CHAPTER XV

"I MENDED two wireless sets the term before last," said Master Eric, practically out of the blue, his arrogant pleasure in his achievements depriving him of any power to lead into a subject gracefully, "which all the other chaps had given up."

"Did you now?" said Ella, possibly with the minutest tinge of sarcasm in her voice. This was next morning—still grey and raining. She had now had three successive mornings of Master Eric's "Helping" in the bar, and possibly the cloak of love in which she indiscriminatingly, and because he was a "kid," wrapped Master E., was beginning to wear a little thin in certain patches under his complacent yet nagging friction. Not that she was conscious of this, or would have admitted it to herself if she had been.

"And one of them belonged to the Science Master," pursued Master Eric. "That was funny, wasn't it?"

"Yes. That was funny."

"You wouldn't have thought that I could have done it when the Science Master couldn't, would you?"

"No. You wouldn't," said Ella, secretly thinking either that there was some mistake or that the Science Master hadn't really tried. But she showed nothing of that.

"It was quite simple," said Master Eric, "too."

"Was it?" said Ella, and at this moment Bob, who had been cleaning the brass outside, passed through the bar on his business. In passing through he gave a curious look at the infant, and another curious, and as it were comprehending look at Ella, which she scrupulously refrained from returning. Bob, in his masculinity, took the most extraordinary attitude towards this little boy. Only this morning, earlier, he had made a staggering reference, out of the blue, to "that awful little brat," and "What do you mean, Bob?" Ella had said. But she could not credit that he really meant anything so shocking. Probably, she guessed, it was mere excess of humorous affection which forced him to express himself in so frightful a manner. Nevertheless, the glance which he now gave her in passing through, did nothing to support that plausible and decent theory, and she looked away quickly.

A minute or two later Bob put his head round the inner door, and made her heart stop.

" Don't you want that letter of yours, Ella ? " he said. " It's been hanging about all morning."

" What letter ? " she said, going pale. Ella hardly ever received a letter, and they always frightened the life out of her. And this morning there were extra reasons for taking alarm. In the first place it had been lying there for three or four hours, a terrifying enough thought in itself for an inexperienced letter-receiver, and in the second place she was filled with a pulsating premonition as to the source from which it had come.

" I'll get it," said Bob, and did so.

" Ta," said Ella, with as much indifference as she could rally, and looking at the cautious handwriting of the address, she had practically no doubt that her instinct had been correct. The postmark from Chiswick finally confirmed her, and she tore it open.

" Strange," commented Master Eric, " that you don't read your own letters when they're waiting for you."

Unlike the good-mannered Bob, who had again vanished, Master Eric had no intention of leaving Ella in privacy with her correspondence, but was clearly going to hang about in as close proximity to her as possible and glean whatever of its contents he could. But Ella ignored him and began hastily to read.

> " 178 Mervyn Avenue,
> Chiswick, W.4.

" My dear ' Ella,'

" I write this to say that if the weather is in any way clement to-morrow—unlike this afternoon, when the heavens are surely somewhat reminiscent of the days of the flood !—I shall probably be up in your part of the world, and wondered whether you would care to ' slip out ' and meet ' yours truly ! '

" On no account put yourself out. It is not worth turning out in this dreadful weather, and I shall stay indoors myself unless there is an improvement. But if it is at all decent I shall be in the *Main Hall (Entrance Coventry Street) of Lyons' Corner*

*House at* 3.45 *p.m. sharp.* I shall not expect you to be there, and will wait five minutes. So decide yourself. I just thought I would make the suggestion as if you were in that part of the world, shopping perhaps, it might be pleasant to have a little tea and a chat. But make no effort as I myself shall not turn out if it continues like this. Au revoir, then, (or do we say *Cheerio !*)

" Yours v. sincerely,

" ERNEST ECCLES."

" Is it from a Lover ? " asked Master Eric, who was growing impatient while Ella deciphered this eagerly from beginning to end.

" Don't be so cheeky, Eric," said Ella putting it back in the envelope with a thousand lines of speculations starting in her head.

" But the point is," said Master Eric, with the same suave impudence, " is it ? "

" You run along and mind your own business," said Ella. But the truth was, of course, that the child had unwittingly put his finger precisely on the mark. *Was* it from a Lover ? Here was the old query up before her again, and what light, if any, was thrown upon it by this missive ? None, that she could see. To begin with, it was a peculiarly non-committal and indeed semi-contradictory letter—in that he had not made it quite clear to her, or apparently to himself, as to whether he had asked her out to tea with him or not. The wording, in fact, took away with one hand what it gave with another. He wanted to see her, so far as she could gather, and he did not. She was amused by the way in which he cleverly sent her out shopping towards the end, also by the odd and rather arbitrary way he had chosen the district for her to do her shopping in. In fact he had shown great skill altogether in getting them both into that part of the world purely by accident, so that he did not have to invite her direct, but was merely accommodating her. And what a baffling letter in other respects ! That " Ella," in inverted commas—what was behind that ? Paternal archness ? Or boldness tempered by reserve, as much as to say they had not actually plunged over the giddy cliff into affectionate Christian names as yet, but could stand on the edge and play with the prospect. And then what an extraordinary blend of old-fashionedness and clumsy pseudo-modernity in his allusion to " the Flood," " Yours truly," and " Cheerio ! " At one moment he was an elderly disinterested gentleman afraid of the rain, at the next betraying a kind of forced sprightliness which might be the omen of incalculable developments.

However, the great thing was that she had not Put him Off, and she saw now how morbid she had been in imagining any such thing. On the contrary he must be pretty Keen, when you came to think about it, writing like that the day after he had left her, and she had a slight feeling of triumph. But what was her immediate line of action ? She must put off all other plans and go this afternoon, of course. But what if it was raining ? It was raining now, she believed. Yes, she could hear it beating in gusts against the window of the Saloon Lounge. He would never come out in this, and was she to undergo the humiliation of trapesing down there for nothing ? Yes. On no account could she risk snubbing his advances or Putting him Off again. She had, as it were, got him back (however little she wanted him), and was not going to have any cause to reproach herself again.

She listened to the rain against the window, in each gust casting gloomy dubiousness over the afternoon, and was surprised to find herself curiously excited about the outcome a few hours hence. Rain often affected her nerves like that, but she might have been in love with him, the way she thought and debated with herself about him. Well, anyway it gave her some sort of interest in life, a secret of her own, something which lifted her on to the hitherto remote plane of those who, as their natural right, always had some such secrets going on behind. Like Bob, for instance. Just as she was thinking this, Bob himself came again into the bar.

" Well," he said, " was it a legacy ? "

" What ? " said Ella.

" The letter," said Bob.

" Oh—that . . . " said Ella. " No. Nothing like that."

Amazing, the interest which her correspondence seemed to be causing all round ! Here was Bob subtly aware that her letter had some kind of significance out of the ordinary rut.

" Just from a friend," added Ella, in a voice which a sensitive listener could interpret as suggesting something a great deal more than a friend, and intended as such, for she enjoyed being the centre of mystery for a change.

## CHAPTER XVI

MR. ECCLES had suggested that she should " slip out," but it was not a question of " slipping out " exactly. It was a question of hanging about in her room, from three o'clock, when she finished work, until it was time to go, nervously watching the rain pouring down, repeatedly and senselessly titivating herself in the grey light, and getting into a state. She had little doubt that she was wasting a useful afternoon, but was determined to stick it out.

In her endeavour not to be too early, she finally misjudged things so that she thought she was going to be too late, and suffered agonies in the bus, remembering his stern warning that he would only wait five minutes. But the clock in the Haymarket, when she reached Coventry Street, informed her that she was five minutes too early, and she entered the Corner House hot but with her mind at rest.

No sooner had she entered the great main hall than she saw him standing there, looking at an imposing display of sausage rolls at the end farthest away from her : and no sooner had she seen him than she saw that he was carrying an enormous bunch of yellow flowers ; and no sooner had she seen that, than she realized, with a small proportion of feminine triumph mixed with a large proportion of social terror, that this affair had not even begun as yet, that the first round on Thursday had been a mere sparring bout, and that in this round, the second, he was going to give her a livelier example of his inexhaustible strength.

*Flowers !* Flowers at this stage ! And at tea-time in the pelting rain, which, according to his letter, was to have precluded the

smallest likelihood of either of them turning up! Only the
infinitesimal possibility that the flowers were not intended for
her enabled her successfully to feign not to notice them as she
greeted him, and so preserve a cool and unembarrassed demeanour.

" Ah—here you are ! " he said, his body coming to attention
and his face lighting as he saw her.  " You're nice and early."

" Yes. I thought I was going to be late for a moment, though."
And she smiled and shook his hand, which he just managed to
release in time from a rather catastrophic muddle between
umbrella, hat and flowers.

" Where shall we go ? " he said.  " Downstairs, as before ? "

" Yes. That'd be very nice." And they walked towards the
marble stairs leading downwards.

They had nothing to say on the way down.  Quite apart from
everything else, both were suffering from that state of baffle-
ment, dumbness and confusion which at first confronts all
persons who meet another with no business in hand or avowed
object other than the shyly confessed one of enjoying his or her
company.  But there was a great deal else to bring awkward
silence on these two.  In the first place their difficulty in starting
polite conversation was rendered no easier by the memory of
their last conversation, which had been (incredible as it might
seem) up against the railings and in a warm quivering proximity
out of the realms of politeness altogether—and in the second
place, as Ella realized, there could be no settling down or peace
of mind until the trembling crisis of the Flowers had been got
over—and that was up to him.  She was on the point of saying
" What lovely flowers you've got there ! " or something like
that, but thought she had better leave it to him, and wished that
he would attack the problem manfully and as soon as possible.

It was not very crowded below to-day, and they found a table
for four in a corner.  They sat opposite each other, and Mr.
Eccles was thus able to create a private cloakroom for his
innumerable accessories out of the chair next door to him, taking
some time, as was his custom, to get everything off and comfortably established.  When it came to the flowers, however,
he paused, as though seeking where to put them, and Ella
braced herself for the fatal moment.

"Why—are these for *me* ? " would be her line, and she felt sure her cue was coming.

But instead "Would you like these over there ? " said Mr. Eccles, non-committally, indicating the chair next door to her.

"Yes. That's right," said Ella, taking them from him in frantic bewilderment as to whether this was her cue or not. On the one hand the words "Would you like " . . . might be taken as implying ownership or quasi-ownership on her part; on the other hand he might be merely politely asking her to accommodate him. She did not herself credit the latter interpretation, but how could she take the risk ? She could, however, help him along.

"What lovely flowers," she said.

"Do you like daffodils ? " said Mr. Eccles.

"Yes. They're beautiful. Aren't they ? " said Ella.

"Yes, I'm fond of daffodils myself," said Mr. Eccles in the tones not of a gallant bestower, but a horticulturist, and leaving her more horribly suspended than ever.

"Specially with these double buds," she said, deciding to throw pure horticulture back at him, until such time as he should master his puerile self-consciousness and stop playing with her. *She* was not going to help him any more.

"Yes. I rather thought you would like them," he said, but the waitress appeared at this moment, and they had to stop to order tea. Thus, when this was done, she had got no nearer to an official confirmation of the gift, and worse (since he was now disingenuously pretending that she had naturally assumed he had given them to her), the whole responsibility was thrown upon her shoulders.

"What were you saying ? " she tried, when the waitress had gone.

"What about ? " said Mr. Eccles, absent-mindedly.

"You were saying something about the flowers, weren't you ? " said Ella, touching them again.

"Oh yes. I was saying I was glad you liked them. I thought you would when I got them."

At last ! Not that even this was properly explicit, but if she didn't take the plunge now they would go on all night.

" Why," she said. " They're not—? " And hesitated with an appropriate vision of heaven dawning in her eyes.

" Not what ? "

" Not for *me*, are they ? "

" Of course they are."

" Why, I never *dreamed*. They're *lovely*,"

" I never dreamed that you thought anything else."

" But they're *lovely*," said Ella. " I think that's sweet of you."

" Do you ? " said Mr. Eccles, laughing shyly, and " I do," said Ella, and there was a very nice atmosphere.

And indeed, now that the flowers were her own, and she could look upon them without embarrassment she saw how lovely (and terribly expensive) they really were, and realized that she adored flowers, and really did think him sweet. And on top of this the orchestra struck up, which softened her heart still more.

" I'm glad you turned up to-day," he said. " As I don't know what I'd have done with them if you hadn't."

" Did you just get them on spec, then ? " she said, almost vaingloriously, and noting among other things how stupendously young he was looking to-day.

" Yes. I thought I would."

" You, shouldn't have, you know. You told me not to come if it was raining."

" Ah. We have to take these risks."

Not only ten years younger, but his approach was so much more graceful. Had she been altogether misjudging this man ? If she wasn't careful she would be thinking of marrying him in a moment—that was to say, not as a remote and ridiculous hypothesis but as a serious and imminent proposition. In fact, why shouldn't she marry him ? He was wealthy, he was kind, he had every appearance of being her slave, he was even good-looking. Girls of her class in the ordinary way, and that included pretty girls, would Jump at him, as the saying went. Then why should she, who was not pretty, put herself on a plane above pretty girls ? She knew by now that she had little enough to expect from life—so what if this man sitting opposite her, by some odd trick of fate was the one destined to make her happy ? She must think about this hard when she was alone.

In the meantime why not set her face steadfastly towards his good points instead of his bad—why not see to it that she Jumped at him herself while the Jumping was good. She passed a resolution to that effect.

But what if he had no idea of marrying anybody? What if he made a practice of taking barmaids out and was a wicked rake?

"Are you so used to it, then?" she said, half to stimulate herself in the process of Jumping by flirting with him, and half to see if she could betray him into throwing any light on the latter query.

"Good heavens, no!" he said. "Sadly the other way, believe me."

"Really?" said Ella, and looking at him, she found herself believing him.

"I'm not at all the sort that hangs around stage doors, I can assure you," said Mr. Eccles. "Do I look it?"

"No, I suppose you don't," said Ella. . . .

"In fact," continued Mr. Eccles, "I've never taken a chorus girl out in my life, so far as I can remember."

"Haven't you?" she said, amused that he should be trying to fool her by pretending casually to glance down the corridors of memory in this matter—for somehow the association of Mr. Eccles with chorus girls and stage doors was too damned silly for words. But she saw that, in his old-fashioned way, he was using chorus girls as mere conventional symbols of dalliance and irregular goings-on, and she was pleased to learn of his austerity.

"Not that I'm not Broadminded," said Mr. Eccles. . . .

"No," said Ella. . . .

"Or that one hasn't had one's *Feelings*. . . ." added Mr. Eccles ambiguously. . . .

"No," said Ella, with a rather sinister sensation of Mr. Eccles' mind expanding sensitively and rather too rapidly in front of her, so that she might have to change her opinion concerning his austerity.

"In one's time," said Mr. Eccles, and she was glad to be back in history.

"Yes," she said.

"But I think the Younger Generation's gone Absolutely Mad. Don't you?"

"Yes. I certainly do," said Ella.

"I mean they stop at nothing, do they?"

"No, they don't," said Ella.

"I came across an appalling case—just the other day."

"Oh yes," said Ella.

"Young Girl . . ." said Mr. Eccles, with a gesture, as though there was no need to say any more.

"Really?" said Ella, as though this *was* bad.

"Well—whatever I *did*," said Mr. Eccles, drawing lines on the table-cloth with a fork, "I'd never be the *first*—like *that* young gentleman."

The way in which Mr. Eccles said this rather suggested that he had spent half his career being the second, third, fourth, etc., all over the globe, and Ella saw that he was at pains to appear in her eyes as a man of the world. For all that, she was unable to believe any such thing of him. On the contrary there was a transparency and inexperience about him which belied it on all sides. In fact she was not sure that, if he but knew it, this was not the principal charm of his character for her—for an ounce of helplessness could win her where a ton of boastfulness might fail, and the more she saw of him the more helpless he seemed to be.

Their tea now came, and they got on to other topics. Before long he asked her what she had been doing with herself since he last saw her, and she told him she had been to see her mother.

"Oh yes?" said Mr. Eccles, rather as though he knew her well, "How's she?"

"Not too well, I'm afraid," said Ella.

"Oh dear. How's that?"

Ella did not feel able to enter into any explanation of the fiend in human shape, so said "Oh just too much to do, I suppose."

"Couldn't we help her in some way?" said Mr. Eccles, with uncanny enthusiasm.

"Well, that's kind of you to suggest it," she said, wondering what on earth he meant. "But I don't see what one can do."

"Well, a little help of a certain sort's worth a pound of pity, isn't it," said Mr. Eccles, and set Ella puzzling again. Whatever was he up to now ? What fresh reserves was he bringing up ? Was she mistaken, or was he suggesting that he should aid her mother financially ? There was something in his tone which scarcely left her in doubt that this was what he meant to convey. And what if things so turned out that he was in a position to do this ? Supposing he married her and she and her mother lived happily ever after ? This was all very bewildering, and had an air of being too good to be true.

" And you wouldn't let any Pride or anything stand in your way, would you ? " said Mr. Eccles.

There was not the slightest doubt of what he meant now, and she was covered with confusion.

" Well, I don't know . . . " she said, and there was a pause.

" Besides," said Mr. Eccles. " I might have the Right, mightn't I ? "

The Right ? Was this a Proposal ? If it was not its equivalent she would like to know what it was ! Had the absurd creature already taken it for granted generally, as with the flowers particularly, that she understood his intentions ? A Proposal after two short meetings ! Unless, of course it was a Suggestion. He might not have matrimony in his mind, in which case it would be a Suggestion. But she had an extraordinary feeling that it was not a Suggestion.

" How do you mean ? " she said, looking at the table-cloth.

" Come now—you know what I mean," said Mr. Eccles, looking at her quizzically.

" No, I don't. Honestly."

" Ah. Come now. You mustn't pretend you don't understand that."

" No, I don't," said Ella, having to look at him and smile utter innocence and opaqueness, " honestly Mr. Eccles."

" Mr. Eccles ? " said Mr. Eccles.

But to this there was no sort of reply whatever, and Ella looked giddily at the tablecloth.

" Eh ? " said Mr. Eccles, and there was no reply to this either.

" Suppose we try Ernest ? " said Mr. Eccles.

Ernest ! She would never bring herself to it ! She had completely overlooked this contingency. She had visualized herself

in almost every conceivable relationship with Mr. Eccles, but
never the preposterous one in which she familiarly called him or
thought of him as " Ernest." He would never be " Ernest "
to her. He was too old ! However she might grow to like him,
grow to love him, even, he was established eternally in her mind
as she first knew him, as Mr. Eccles with his new hat.

" What ? " said Mr. Eccles.

What was she to say ? Did he mean that she had got to say
" Ernest " straight off ? " All right, Ernest " or something
like that ? She shuddered, and was unable to utter anything.

" You'll have to sooner or later, you know," said Mr. Eccles.

" Yes," said Ella. " I suppose I will."

And from the coy, soft, confused way in which she was
forced to say this, she dared not guess what worlds of maidenly
consent Mr. Eccles was reading into her general attitude towards him. That was his way with her. He was always forcing
her into positions like this where she had either to snub him
or behave coyly ; and since she always chose the latter she was
always giving him the impression that she was tremulously
pleased with, if not definitely seeking out, his advances. In fact
as far as her own behaviour went he had every right to conclude
that she had been Encouraging him from the word go, and that
she was his for the asking. But was that not what she wanted
him to think ? For had she not as good as decided that she would
marry him if he would have her ? She would have to think it
all out, but she now believed she had as good as decided that.

" And would you have any objections," said Mr. Eccles,
" if I returned the compliment ? "

" No," said Ella, " I should like you to."

" Ah well, now the air's clearer, isn't it," said Mr. Eccles,
and at this point, as though he had got something off his chest,
deliberately changed the atmosphere by switching off on to
indifferent topics. This rather disappointed Ella, as she would
have given a great deal to have had him in some measure
amplify his astounding allusion to a Right, which now seemed
scarcely credible, and which she thought she had possibly
misheard or misunderstood. But she could not possibly incur
the suspicion of Throwing herself at him by making any move
to bring the subject up again, and very soon she looked at the

clock and saw that it was nearing the time for her to go.

"This tiresome work of yours—we'll have to do something about it soon," was the only other significant or thought-provoking remark he made at this meeting, which petered out rather miserably at the end. For it was still pelting when they got outside, and Mr. Eccles insisted that he should see her home. But Ella insisted that he should not, and Mr. Eccles compromised by seeing her to her bus—which was the other side of Piccadilly Circus. But this made him rather irritable, because he had lost the credit of taking her home, and soon discovered that he simply wanted to get out of the rain. Also he did not like sharing his umbrella very much. Neither did Ella, because he kept on bringing one of the spokes down on her head. This with a sort of regular springy poke every six paces or so— a maddening penalty habitually inflicted by well-meaning umbrella-sharers, and quite impossible to call attention to. And then they had to wait hours for the bus, which Ella thought stopped further up, but which Mr. Eccles was certain stopped down here all right—but Ella was right (which didn't make her too popular) and they had to charge up the pavement together, Mr. Eccles frantically explaining that he would either write or look in in the next two days, and Ella breathlessly welcoming the suggestion but not really concentrating. Then some perfectly meaningless waving, and sign-making through the window, and wondering why the bus didn't start, etc.,—so that by the time it was all through, and Ella was being carried away, instead of savouring the brightening dawn of affection, they might have just had a quarrel with each other.

## CHAPTER XVII

IT was next Thursday evening, in the darkness of a secluded bench in Regent's Park, that Mr. Eccles, with the restrained expenditure of little more than half a dozen Whats, finally planted his standard on the subdued heights of his painful manœuvrings and self-consciousness, and kissed her. From that moment onward Mr. Eccles was no longer, and was never again, the Mr. Eccles he had been, nor was Ella the Ella. To each other they were both new characters, with new confessions and new reserves, and the contest was removed to a different sort of arena altogether.

Little had occurred up to this moment. He had not seen her on the Saturday or the Sunday, but on Monday she had had tea with him, and again on Tuesday. But on these occasions he had uttered practically nothing of an intimate or paralysing nature. They had merely exchanged a few further confidences. This afternoon he had taken her to the pictures at Madame Tussaud's in the Marylebone Road, and afterwards to tea at an A.B.C. in Baker Street. He had then suggested a walk in Regent's Park in the dark. They had no sooner embarked on this than he had mentioned that it was warm enough to sit down, really, and she became fearfully aware that some sort of walk like this had been planned, possibly days ahead, and that she was in for it. His conversation had grown weaker and more pre-occupied every minute as he steered her (without seeming to steer her) in a definite direction of his own in the darkness, until at last, under some trees, and far away from people, he had said "Well, suppose we do sit down?" and "What about here?" and she had said "Right you are—let's," feeling like someone just about to have a tooth drawn and fiercely bracing herself to go through with it.

Having kissed her once, he kissed her again, and got his arm well round her for a bout of indefinite length.

"You mustn't," said Ella.

"What?" said Mr. Eccles, and kissed her again, to which Ella returned "You mustn't," to which Mr. Eccles returned "What?" and kissed her again.

"No, you really mustn't," tried Ella, but the indomitable query came back at her, and the only thing she could do was to wriggle and turn her head the other way.

"Why mustn't I?" said Mr. Eccles.

"You don't *want* to," said Ella, lamely. But lame as it was there was a method and intention behind what she said in the darkness. Profoundly as she had dreaded it, she had known it would have to come to this sooner or later, and she had nerved herself to see it through. But one thing she had decided. She was not going through with it unless she got something out of it in return—unless she forced him to show something of his hand at last, and give her some impression of what he was up to generally. Things had been going on long enough now, and if she could help it she was not going to remain the patient beast of burden for his gradually heaped innuendoes any more. Hence her apparently lame " You don't *want* to," which gave him an opportunity to explain that he did want to, to what extent he wanted to, and possibly, what he was prepared to sacrifice in wanting to. In other words, did he want to marry her ?

But Mr. Eccles was not so obliging. To begin with, he naturally said " What ? " straight off. And then, when she had repeated herself he merely said " But *why* don't I want to ? "

And as this, if the words were to be taken on their surface value, bafflingly implied that he didn't really want to, and that was asking her the reason why, they were no further ahead.

" *I* don't know why you don't want to," said Ella, completely out of her depths, and turning her head away as he resumed the attack.

" But I do want to," said Mr. Eccles.

Well, that was something though indeed not very useful, it being self-evident that he wanted to, since he was doing it.

" But *why* do you want to," said Ella, in a gentle tone, but inwardly determined to stick to her guns till she had made him surrender his secrets.

" Because I want to," said Mr. Eccles, and contrived to kiss her again.

" But *why* ? " said Ella, grimly holding on.

" Well—because—"

" Because what ? " said Ella, still in the same soft, coaxing tone, but seeing to it that she took him up quickly on this vital point, lest he should wander away into his habitual vagueness and mystery.

" Because I love you," said Mr. Eccles, but as she had hardly given him any opportunity to say anything else the technical climax and victory was a hollow one.

However, they were getting ahead slowly.

" You don't," said Ella.

" But I do ! I do ! " said Mr. Eccles, and held her closer.

" But how could you ? " said Ella, almost carried away by his enthusiasm, and finding it harder every moment to abide by her resolution to keep him on the track.

" I don't know," said Mr. Eccles, unintentionally being rather rude, " But I do."

" I don't see how you could."

" But I do. I do," said Mr. Eccles. " Don't you love me ? Couldn't you love me ? "

" I don't know," said Ella. " I don't know you well enough, do I ? "

" But what does that matter—if we love each other ? "

There he went again—blurring the issue with conventional phrases which still told her absolutely nothing. Again she was tempted to succumb to the tremulous yet loose and meaningless atmosphere with which he sought to wrap her, but she stuck fast.

" Yes—but what— ? " she said, and hesitated, not knowing how she could lead into cold facts without appearing calculating and brazen. " But what—"

" What *what* ? " said Mr. Eccles, achieving the startling feat of bringing two whats down with one stone in the fervour of his amorous catapulting.

" What would *Happen* ? " said Ella, painfully.

" What would happen where ? " said Mr. Eccles, becoming logical at an awkward moment.

" What would happen in *general* ? " tried Ella.

" What do you mean ? " said Mr. Eccles. " I love you."

What had the fact that he loved her got to do with what she was asking ? It was no good—she would never get this man out into the open until she had cast off every rag of her pride and reserve. But she would *not* give in. She boldly contrived a fresh opening from which he might be induced to emerge.

" I'm not in your Class," she said, " to begin with."

" But what does that matter ? " said Mr. Eccles.

Ella was a little damped by his lightning (and not immaculately courteous) concurrence with the main substance of her humbly propounded objection, but she knew that he was not clever at expressing himself and was perfectly willing to be put in her place so long as they made some headway.

" But it *does* matter," she said.  " You wouldn't want to—"

" Wouldn't want to what ? "

" Well, it just wouldn't work."

" What wouldn't ? "

" Well—*it* wouldn't."

" What wouldn't ? "

" Well, you wouldn't want me *Seriously*," said Ella.  " Would you ? "

" But I do want you.  I do want you.  I love you.  I can't do without you.  I want to kiss you.  Let me kiss you," said Mr. Eccles, and Ella, letting him kiss her, was taken aback by her first real premonition of the power that was in her hands.

" Yes," she said.  " But it isn't Practicable ? "

" Why isn't it—if I love you ? "

" Well, what would all your People say, for instance ? "

" What do they matter ?  I know what I want.  I've thought it all out."

" Have you ? "  said Ella, believing they were at last coming to something.  " What do you want, then ? "

" I want you," said this Houdini of the world of conversational commitments, and Ella had to take another breath, as it were, and start again.

" Yes," she said.  " But what would we Be ? "

" How do you mean—what would we be ? "

" What would we be to each other ? "

" We'd love each other."

" Yes—but what would other people think ? "

" What does it matter what they think ? "

" I mean, it's not as though we'd be Engaged, or anything like that," said Ella, feeling dreadfully humiliated at being forced to say any such thing, and waiting breathlessly to see how he would get out of it.

" Why couldn't we be Engaged ? "

" But that's absurd," said Ella.  " If you're Engaged it means

you're going to be Married some time, or something like that."
She had not quite the temerity to end the sentence at Married,
where the actual sense ended, but had, in her wretched dilemma,
to try and qualify it and make it less crude by the addition of
" some time " and " something like that."

" Well—what if we were married," said Mr. Eccles, in a tense
and perhaps slightly defiant voice, and then minutely lessened
the shock for a stunned Ella by adding " some time."

" What ? " said Ella. " Would you think of Marrying
*me* ? "

" Yes. Of course I would. I've thought it all out. I've
thought it out." He laid great stress on the fact that he had
thought it out, and this gave the thing a greater air of credibility
to Ella, since she could well conceive what a tremendous battle
he had had with himself.

" But you couldn't," she said, again incredulous.

" But I *could*, I tell you. I could. I know what I want, and I
love you. That's all that matters."

" Good Lord," said Ella, simply and thoughtfully. For she
was genuinely affected, and was unable, for the moment, to
have any ulterior thought or keep up any of her defences.

" You could marry me ? " said Mr. Eccles, eagerly in the
darkness. " Couldn't you ? "

So touched was she, so bewildered by this uncanny turn in her
fortune, so surprised at having brought another human being
to such a pass in regard to her, so anxious, from force of habit, to
gladly meet and oblige anyone who could be so kind and disinterested, that her first instinct was to say " Of course I could."
But she stopped herself in time, and said, " But I don't know
you."

" But you will know me. You'll come to know me. Say you
will. Say you will."

(Say you will know me, she wondered in passing, or say you
will marry me ?) " I don't know what to say," she said.

" But I want you. I must have you. I'm so lonely."

" Are you ? " said Ella gently, and, believing him, realized
that he was not without the power to move her heart.

" You don't think I'm too old, do you ? " he said. " You
don't think that, do you ? "

" Of course you're not too old," said Ella. " What an absurd idea."

And she said this with all the greater conviction and strength because she felt grateful to him, in a manner hard to analyse, for his having himself brought forward this lurking but otherwise unmentionable aspect of the matter—for his having had at once the modesty, sincerity and courage to confess its existence. By doing so he put himself at her willing mercy, and as it were in confession absolved himself from the stain which she had thought must always discolour their relationship—that stain being her subtle feeling of resentment at a middle-aged man making love to her because she was less attractive than others, on the basis that second-best matched second-best. Now that he had owned up, and asked her indulgence, she was only too happy to give it. The affair took on a special character of its own, and need not involve any second-bests anywhere.

" Are you sure ? " he said.

" Yes, of course I'm sure. You mustn't think like that."

" But I can't help it. I'm afraid of losing you. You're so young and beautiful."

" Oh, I'm not," said Ella, again in the simple, self-betraying way she had when she dropped her defences. For, from whatever quarter it came, it was quite impossible to resist feeling richer and happier after such a compliment, which gratified her, not because she believed remotely in its truth, but because of the astounding possibility that *he* might—because, in fact, she believed he did—which was the very next best thing to its being true, and which refreshed her famished soul.

" Oh you are," he said. " You're lovely. You know you are."

Again her heart was unreasonably lifted up, and she wondered what she would be feeling now if it had been the man of her choice saying such things in the darkness. But suppose she allowed him to become the man of her choice, since he was the only one who had ever or who ever would say such things and mean them ? To be truly wanted by one man, surely, was as desirable as being admired by many. She believed he might easily win her if he went on like this. Oddly enough, Mr. Eccles as a besieging lover, much as she had formerly dreaded his assuming the rôle, was an infinitely more attractive Mr. Eccles than he was in any other guise.

" I'm not," she said. . . .

" But you are. You are. Say you love me a little."

" Well—"

" You do—don't you—a little ? "

" Well—I suppose I do," said Ella, too weak, and too much under a weird sense of obligation to him for his incomprehensible enthusiasm for her, to withhold a relenting word, and meanly give him nothing in return. Besides she took refuge behind his " a little," and felt justified in thinking that she had not technically overstepped the truth.

" Then, you're going to be mine, aren't you ? You're going to be mine ? "

" But what would that mean ? " said Ella, compelling herself to one final effort to get matters clear. " Would it mean we would be Engaged ? "

" Of course it would. Of course it would. You will, won't you ? Say you will ! "

And as Ella did not reply he kissed her once more, and there was a silence.

" You must ! " said Mr. Eccles. " You must ! "

And enveloped by the strength of his passion and too feeble to argue any more, Ella was hypnotized into feeling, somehow, that indeed she must, and she again made no attempt to answer, thus implying (to what exactly she still did not know) her consent.

## CHAPTER XVIII

" IT'S wonderful, isn't it," said Mr. Eccles. " Just to be strolling arm-in-arm like this."

They were walking briskly now by the lake in the direction of Clarence Gate, whence they were to emerge for their supper into London, whose lights were now seen glittering, and whose buses and trains could be heard roaring, an entirely furious and disparaging welcome to the surface to divers in its dark parks.

So soon as they had started walking Mr. Eccles had become a different creature—experiencing an influx of all that cheerful sense of manhood and resilience known to overtake gentlemen who have just been kissing young ladies a great deal and for the first time, and holding her arm and becoming loquacious. Ella, having got cold sitting out all that time, was also glad to be moving, and inclined for this reason to reflect his mood in some measure, however doubtful her inner frame of mind.

" Yes—it is," she said, not finding it in her heart to damp his spirits, but her heart sank. It sank firstly because his remark, together with some which had preceded it, were all manifesting a growing air of jubilant proprietorship which, in spite of her late tacit agreement, frightened her more and more every moment ; and secondly because, if she did sincerely consent, and if walking thus with him *was* " wonderful," as he had assured her it was, then she must have a blind spot about wonder in general, and would never know the wonders of love. For all she felt was a feeling of being no more and no less puzzled and ordinary than she was at any other moment of the day.

" It changes everything, doesn't it," said Mr. Eccles. " Love."

By what subtle and indomitable methods was he now trying to land her with the assumption that she had conceded all ? Surely that remark was meant to include her. Did he really believe that she had told him she loved him ? Had she conveyed that ? She did not know. Certainly she had not contradicted him, and perhaps he had the right to interpret her silence thus. She should not have let him kiss her like that. If only she had had the smallest experience of affairs like this, she would understand the conventions better, and know where she was, and be able to handle the situation.

" Yes," she said, still unable to stop being polite. " It does." But that only involved her further. There was a silence as they walked briskly along.

" When did you first Know ? " said Mr. Eccles, suddenly,

pressing her arm, and coming a little closer in fond anticipation.

At first she did not get his meaning.

" Know what, Mr. Eccles ? " she said, innocently.

" What ? " said Mr. Eccles, in a shocked manner.

" Know what ? " she repeated, half panic-stricken, for try as she might, she could not, no she could not, bring herself to say it.

" Know what what ? " said Mr. Eccles, bringing off another clever double, but speaking sternly.

" Know what, *Ernest*," she said, pumping it up and heaving it out as it were from some hydraulic machinery within her.

" Ah, that's better. You can really call me Ernest now, can't you ? "

" Yes," said Ella feebly.

" Call me Ernest in Ernest, eh ! " said Mr. Eccles. " That's rather a good one. I must remember that."

Oh dear, thought Ella, if that was his idea of a good one, it was a poor outlook for the more frothy side of their proposed future as an engaged couple.

" But you haven't answered my question yet," he said, dismaying Ella, who thought he might have forgotten about this. " When did you first Know ? "

" I don't know, really," she said, her voice begging him, if he could but know it, to have mercy on her.

" But you must know. When did you first know I Cared— eh ? "

At this she felt relief, as she had thought at first that he had meant to press her as to when *she* first knew, *i.e.* knew she Cared for him.

" It's hard to say," she said. . . .

" But you must have had a Feeling. When did you have a Feeling ? "

" Perhaps," she said, " that time in the bar when you asked me to go to a theatre."

" What first gave you the Feeling then ? "

Impossible to tell him that it had been his absurd new hat which had given her the " feeling." And was the " feeling " the exact expression ? At that time, alas, she would herself have much more readily described it as " the creeps."

"It must have been the way you looked," she said.

"And when did *you* first begin to know," said Mr. Eccles, with an air of tremulously unfolding her own romance.

"Ah" . . . said Ella. . . .

It had come to this, then? There seemed no doubt now that he had read everything he could read into her silence, and was presuming that she was up to the neck in it with him.

"Go on," he said.

"Perhaps," she said, flying to her own retreat, semi-flirtatiousness, "I didn't ever know."

"Ah—you're playing with me now," said Mr. Eccles. "You love to play with me, don't you?"

She could yet marvel at the blithe effrontery with which he took it on himself to write and produce her entire psychology and rôle in this light drama of bashful love, but she had no weapon with which she could meet him, and thought it best to play the game his way.

"Do I," she said, for all the world as though roguishly confessing that she did.

"Don't you just!" said Mr. Eccles, delightedly expanding her trait. "Nothing gives you so much pleasure."

"Does it?" she said, in the same way, and this was too much for him.

"You little Puss!" said Mr. Eccles. "You make me want to Squeeze you!"

Ella's soul went faint. Puss! Squeeze! If he had searched through the entire awful vocabulary of archness he could not have alighted upon two expressions which nauseated her more. She might have stood Puss by itself—saucy, elephantine, fatuous as it was. But Squeeze! Squeeze in conjunction with Puss! Squeeze—the grossest, pawkiest, most ignominious of all ignominious epithets in the realms of sensuous playfulness! She would have to run away from him in a moment.

"You mustn't," she said, meaning it sincerely, indeed, for she was beside herself with shame.

"Mustn't I?" said Mr. Eccles. "You little Puss!" And instead of taking her protest to mean what it did mean, that he must not use such expressions, he disgustingly interpreted it as a coy injunction not to commit the criminal act of Sqeezing itself.

For she suddenly felt his fingers tightening defiantly around
her arm muscles, and apprehended with anguish that he had
stepped from loathsome fancy to reality—that she was in fact
Being Squeezed!

"What?" said Mr. Eccles. "Mustn't I? What? What?"

"Oo—don't," said Ella. "You'll hurt my arm."

"You little Tease," said Mr. Eccles. "I can be a Tease as well
as you, you know."

Tease! Another horrible expression somehow. The very way
it rhymed with Squeeze seemed to put it in a low category, and
made it contribute to the naughty, nudging atmosphere he was
so assiduous in creating. She felt she must make some sort of
stand.

"You're in a gay mood to-night, aren't you?" she said, and
she had enough courage to allow a definite proportion of irony
to enter her tone.

"Ah—but then I'm a gay fellow," said Mr. Eccles,
swimmingly impervious, Ella noticed, to her irony (he had the
hide of a rhinoceros, among other things); and he added "And
there's been enough to make me gay to-night, hasn't there?"

"Has there?" she said, and seeing with relief that they had
now reached Clarence Gate, and were coming out into the
busy traffic of Baker Street, where it would be impossible to
keep up this excruciating *tête-à-tête*, she relented with "I suppose there was."

"You darling," he said (if only he had made do with that
throughout!) "Do you know what we're going to do now?"

"What?"

"We're going to have a little something to celebrate," he
said.

And because she could read practically every thought going
on in his silly head about five seconds or so before he uttered
it she did not have to hear his dashingly suggestive "I *do* like
Bubbly—don't you?" (as he steered her across the traffic to a
public-house standing conveniently over the way) to be apprized
of the next trick up his sleeve—the fact that they were about
to drink champagne.

## CHAPTER XIX

IT was all very well to talk about celebrating, thought Ella, as they entered a large, bright and rather crowded Saloon Bar—but what exactly were they celebrating? Their Engagement?

As there was no waiter he had himself to go to the bar to get the drinks, and while he was gone she had time to ponder this matter. Was she Engaged to him or not? She still had no idea, and her doubt arose not only from her inability to gather whether she had been understood to have given her consent to such an arrangement, but also from her lack of absolute certainty as to whether he had made any such proposal. " Of course we would," he had said, and " You must !—you must !—" but so far as she could remember the atmosphere had never entirely freed itself from something remotely conditional lurking in those Woulds and Musts, and at no point had the explicit given its charter to the implicit. It never did with Mr. Eccles, but it was awkward to be going about London with a gentleman to whom you did not know whether you were Engaged or not. Awkwarder still if you presumed you were when you weren't.

As he returned, smiling and bright as ever, with two medium-sized glasses of draught champagne she smiled back and decided that she really must get it out of him. But as he now had to take off his hat, his coat, his scarf, and his gloves, in the leisurely and methodical succession to which she had become used (it was rather like watching a surgeon getting ready for an operation), it was some time before the decks were clear for renewed discussion. At last, however, he lifted his glass and she lifted hers.

" Well, here's to—" he began, and paused (maddeningly, for her problem would be solved if he would but tell her to what they were drinking), " What shall we say ? "

" I don't know quite," she said, ostensibly jocular, actually grimly questioning.

" Well, just to both of us in general, then," he said, and they both drank. " I suppose we're not Engaged until I've given you a ring."

Then they *were* Engaged! So taken aback was she by this sudden confirmation and its vast implications, that she again forgot herself.

"But *Mr. Eccles*—" she said, not knowing what she was going to follow it with.

"Mr. Who?"

"*Ernest*," she said, correcting herself again by use of hydraulic machinery, but unable to go any further.

"Ah—I love to hear you say ' *Ernest* '—just like that," said Mr. Eccles, imperturbably mistaking the deep groaning of the machinery for the ringing throb of awakened passion. "Well— what have you to say to your—' *Ernest* ' ? "

"But we can't be just engaged—just like that—can we ? "

"Can't we ? " said Mr. Eccles, taking more wine. "I can. Why can't we ? Are you ashamed of it ? "

"No—it's not I'm ashamed. It's just—"

"I'm not. I want to tell the whole world, myself. And I'm going to."

"What ? " said Ella.

"The whole world," Mr. Eccles went on, "that I'm engaged to the most beautiful girl in the world. How about that ? "

And as Ella's blood was now freezing as she realized that the "whole world" would undoubtedly include "The Midnight Bell," Bob, the Governor and everybody, and that unless she could stop him he would be in the bar in the rôle of her fiancé (fiancé !) blandly broadcasting his and her shame to the whole world (for, however much she had got used to the idea, she was still too near her first emotions not to have a deep underlying sense of shame in this inexplicable affair), and that therefore before she knew where she was she would be being Congratulated (Congratulated !) and committed publicly and aternally to this stranger, and that her mother would Find Out, end so on and so forth—as Ella was realizing all these things at one stroke, she made no attempt to reply, but gazed at him as though fascinated.

"Shout it from the housetops ! " said Mr. Eccles.

"Oh no," said Ella, panic overcoming all else. "I don't think we'd better do that."

And then, seeing that his enthusiasm for publicity was intended with the utmost benevolence, deriving purely from his good-natured desire to " show " her that he was not ashamed to declare generally that a man of his standing and wealth was going to marry a barmaid, she felt that she could not return kindness with affront, and risk Wounding him, and added (fatally, as she saw a moment after), " Let's keep it Secret."

" What ? Keep it secret ? Why should we want to keep it secret ? "

" Oh—I don't know. I'd like it to be a Secret."

" Would you then ? " said Mr. Eccles, suddenly putting out his hand under the table, and touching her knee. " Very well— it shall be a Secret. Our Secret—eh ? "

" Yes—that's right," said Ella, but of course she had really got herself into the soup for good and all now, for in admitting, nay, stressing, the existence of a Secret between them, she had moved from tacit to articulate consent, and had pledged herself beyond honourable recall. Good Heavens !—how had it all happened, and what was she to do now ? She wished he would take his hand away from her knee. His very touch proclaimed a sort of new Secretive sense of ownership.

" Little Ladies like to have their little Secrets, don't they," said Mr. Eccles. " I know all their little ways."

She wished he wouldn't call her a Little Lady. Particularly as she was about twice his size—twice his size, that was to say, as masculine should compare to feminine—actually they were about the same in height and weight. Also she believed that, in his present fondling of her knee, he was by some subconscious process of sensuous symbolism transferring his thoughts and utterances concerning Secrets, to thoughts and utterances concerning Knees, and was getting a trifle lascivious. But she hoped she was mistaken.

" Don't they ? " said Mr. Eccles, and, seeing her look thoughtful, " Well—what's going on in its little head now ? "

" Oh—nothing much," said Ella.

" Nothing much—eh ? Come along, now. What is it ? You mustn't have any secrets from me, you know." And he moved his hand from her knee in order to drink some more champagne.

At last it seemed as though she had an opportunity to voice her reservations, and she rushed to seize it before it went.

" Well . . . " she said, ponderously, toying thoughtfully with her glass.

" Well ? "

" Well, you seem to talk as though our Engagement was all fixed. . . ."

" Well—isn't it ? "

" But it *can't* be. Can it ? "

" And why can't it—little Grey-Eyes-Puzzle-Head ? " said Mr. Eccles, putting his head on one side in a rapture of poetic quizzicality.

" No," said Ella, " I'm Serious. . . ."

" Are you ? I *love* you when you're Serious ! "

She suspected, among other things, that the drink had gone to his head already—there were people like that, she knew from experience in the bar—in which case she would never divert him from this overbearing flippancy.

" No. I am serious," said Ella. " You mustn't mind what I say. . . ."

" I shan't mind. I don't mind what anybody says," said Mr. Eccles, and she was certain he was drunk.

" But it's so Impossible," she said. " It might be all right if I was in your Class. But I'm not."

" Aren't you in my class ? What would that matter, if it's true ? "

" Well, I'm not Educated. I should let you down. We could never be married and Set Up."

" Educated ? What's education. Do you mean Aitches ? " said Mr. Eccles, with surprising, and perhaps slightly painful frankness.

" No—it's not Aitches," said Ella, who, in fact, had always taken great pride in her management of these, " it's other things."

" Grammar ? " suggested Mr. Eccles.

" Yes. Grammar, if you like. And it's not only Grammar that gives you away, is it ? "

" What else does, then ? "

" Well—everything. I'm not a *Lady*—that's what it amounts to," said Ella, glad to have got this out. " And that's all there is to it."

" Don't be so silly," said Mr. Eccles, neither exactly denying

nor exactly confirming this accusation against herself, but just
pooh-poohing her in general.

"But it's true. And when you come to think about it quietly
you'll see it is."

"Will I?"

"And what about all your people?"

"What people?"

"Well, all your Army People, and all that," said Ella, shyly....

"Oh bother my Army people."

"But you can't just bother them. Imagine me being introduced to them at a Tea Party." Not usually an articulate person,
she was now rather pleased with her argumentative power,
and even had a dim hope that she might yet prevail upon him
to grant her some Stay of Engagement, or other concession,
which would give her time to think about it all and discover
some line of escape if necessary.

"But you wouldn't have to be introduced to them."

"But I would, if we were married."

"Yes. I suppose you would," said Mr. Eccles.

"Besides there's *my* people, too," she said, playing her
trump card. "They're only poor people, you know. *They*
haven't got an Aitch to their name."

"Haven't they?"

"No, of course they haven't," she said, feeling justified in
sacrificing her mother in her cause. "And I don't expect you'd
like that."

"But would I have to meet them?" said Mr. Eccles, perhaps
a faint gleam of dismay showing in his eyes.

"Well—that's marriage, isn't it. I don't want to Deceive you
about myself you know—just because I Pass." She knew now
that she was being rather a humbug, and she paid for it instantly.

"Ah—but that's what's so wonderful about you," he said.
"You're so Honest. I can See it."

"Yes, that's all very well . . ." said Ella, but now she had
lost the thread. "You see—"

"Besides, I don't see what you're getting at. If we love each
other what do people matter?"

"Yes—but—"

"Well. What?"

" Well, I think we ought to *think* about it, that's all."

And with those words she knew that she had come to the end of her resources, and as it were bowed her head, looking at her wine glass, and awaiting sentence in the pause that followed.

" You darling," she heard Mr. Eccles saying. " Do you know what'll be happening to you in a moment ? "

" What ? "

" I'll be coming round and kissing you in front of all these people if you're not careful."

She did not answer but looked at her glass.

" Or giving you a good spanking. I don't know which," said Mr. Eccles with indescribable roguishness. " What about some more champagne ? "

So ended Ella's last attempt that evening to break through the walls of his imperturbability and gaiety—her principal concern thenceforward being to see that he did not drink too much and make fools of them both in public—a feat which she accomplished with some success on the strength of her barmaid's experience—eventually leading him to dinner at the Corner House again, and doing her utmost, as he escorted her back, to avoid Railings—at any rate Railings as near " The Midnight Bell " as before. But here she had no success, for he had by now got those Railings, and no others, established in his conservative mind as the fixed and rightful Embracing Station, and manœuvred towards them inexorably.


## CHAPTER XX

NEXT day Ella went over to see her mother. This was Friday. No word ever passed between them as to why she seemed to have taken to coming over on Friday instead of Thursday, her day off, and Ella suspected her mother of suspecting that she was devoting her one stretch of liberty in the week to Mr. Eccles, which of course she was. Ella's mother was a little more cheerful, or less acutely miserable, this week, her Stiff Neck having left her. When asked if it was better, "Oh yes, that's gone," she said, in the peculiarly disinterested and ungrateful tone people have when agonizing inflictions, which they groan under while in progress, have the grace to leave them.

"Well,—how's the Gentleman?" said Ella's mother, the very first moment after they had fixed the tea things to their liking and had settled down in front of the fire for their chat in the gloaming. Thus she unwittingly revealed the main stream of her thought throughout the entire past week, and confirmed Ella's suspicions.

Ella wished that her mother could have chosen some other epithet than "the Gentleman"—there was something half-awed and furtive about it, something respectful yet anticipatory, which put the absurd Mr. Eccles she knew into so utterly false and romantic a light that she felt ashamed both of him and her mother. But then she wished, really, that her mother would not talk about him at all.

"Oh—he's all right," she said, and looked into the fire, knowing that the topic could not drop here.

"Has he taken you to the theatre and dinner again?" asked her mother.

How these poor old people rushed ahead of themselves in their expectations! Had not one theatre and dinner been enough for her? On the one hand so ready to be cast down, on the other they were so intemperate in their hopes, urged by their longing and belief in their children, that no miracle could unduly impress or suffice them.

"No," she said. "Just to the Pictures. . . ."

"Oh well," said Mrs. Prosser, "That's something. . . ."

"And to tea once or twice," said Ella, with all the mixed emotions of one seeing her mother spiritually transformed into a starved dog, and having reluctantly to grant it the bones and scraps which were its due.

"Really," said Mrs. Prosser, "I think he must be Taken—don't you?"

"Yes. I suppose he is," said Ella, "a bit."

" I should say more than a bit," said Mrs. Prosser, " if he takes you out like that. I should say he's *really* Taken."

And the metaphorical lapping-up noise she made over this conclusion, made Ella feel quite abased. And what a meal it was in her power to provide if she cared ! If she only told the whole truth, and confided to her mother the degree in which Mr. Eccles was actually Taken ! But no—at all costs she had to withhold the remotest suspicion of where the land really lay from her mother. If once that came out, and her mother was told that so far from his being merely Taken, they were already Engaged, or as good as Engaged, then, unless she was to break her poor heart later, the door would be shut even further against any of those corridors of escape which she still felt must appear in this unaccountable situation. Not that she really believed she was Engaged, or, being so, that she knew she wanted to escape. All that had happened was that he had succeeded in bringing her to implying that they were Engaged. Beyond that she could look no further at present.

" Well, we'll see," she said, hoping her mother might take a barely perceptible hint to stop questioning her.

" Has it come to Christian names yet ? " asked Mrs. Prosser, evidently meaning to make this the topic of the afternoon.

" Well, I suppose it has, really."

" What *is* his Christian name by the way ? "

" *Ernest*," said Ella, having to use hydraulic pressure even here.

" Ernest, eh ? Well—that's a very nice name."

" Do you think so ? "

" Yes. I do, and let's hope he really *is* in earnest." And Mrs. Prosser gave a weak and awkward little laugh.

She had now given herself away with piteous frankness, and Ella, convulsively putting out her hands as though to warm them over the fire, smiled, shuddered, and was at a loss.

" And if he's a Gentleman, as you say he is," said Mrs. Prosser, " there's no reason why he *shouldn't* be in earnest."

That word Gentleman again. Ella was keenly aware that in using this term her mother was thinking timidly in terms of social strata rather than natural behaviour, and the slavish humility it implied appalled her. She was perfectly ready in her own mind to recognize and appraise the social gulf between Mr.

Eccles and herself, but to hear her mother glibly acknowledging, nay revelling, in it like this, somehow offended what little family pride she had and seemed to lower them both. She had to make some sort of protest.

" Yes," she said with a hint of reproach. " But you mustn't go building castles in the air, you know."

But that, of course, was the wrong thing to have said, suggesting, as it obviously did, that the air was perfectly mature for castles, that she herself was as much for castles as her mother, and that she was merely warning her mother not to tempt Providence too far in the presence of such amazing auspices. And of course she had wanted to convey exactly the opposite. This was like her unintentional admission yesterday of a Secret with Mr. Eccles—she was always getting herself tied up by what she said. What with both of them, she didn't know where they would land her.

" Oh no," said Mrs. Prosser, " I wouldn't do that." But it was quite clear that she delightedly would and did.

When Ella left her mother that evening she reflected that the slow process of years had probably at last turned the scales so that her mother was now, in point of moral wisdom and family experience, going down the decline where she would be less of a mother and resource, than a mental junior whom Ella at last would have to lead. This reflection did anything but improve the bleakness and loneliness of her situation—a depressed sense of which had been upon her all day. On the other hand, what if her mother was in the right? She had no one else to confide in, and it might be well that she was a fool, and a selfish fool, jeopardizing the happiness of others, to turn up her nose (if turning up her nose she was) at the unparalleled Mr. Eccles and all he offered. Always ready to blame herself, she could quite well see this point of view without overcoming a rebellious feeling which at certain moments could almost make her wish that she had not been faced with the dilemma at all. But then she was always in a low, super-analytical frame of mind after leaving her mother.

Another slight shock was awaiting her that night. This occurred in the bar about five minutes after they had opened and were waiting for customers to enter.

" Oh, by the way," said Bob, who was glancing at the evening newspaper on his stool the other side of the bar. " Was that you I saw in Baker Street yesterday evening ? "

" Baker Street ? " said Ella, trying to gain time. It was curiously frightening, at the best of times, to learn that you had been looked upon, unknown to yourself—giving you a sudden defenceless sense of your objectiveness in the eyes of others.

" I was in Baker Street," she said. . . .

" Oh, then it was you. I thought it was. I was on a bus," said Bob, who seemed inclined to drop the matter there.

But this would never suffice Ella. What had he seen ? It must have been while they were going to tea after the Cinema. Did he have hold of her arm then ? Or was it when they came out ? Or didn't he take it till they got inside Regent's Park ?

" What was I doing ? " she said.

" What do you mean—what were you doing ? " said Bob, catching her tone of alarm, and looking up at her in an amused and slightly ironical way. " You were just walking along."

She would have to brave it out.

" Did you see ' Mr. ' ' Eccles ' ? " she said, wrapping him round and round in strenuous inverted commas in her endeavour to disclaim any responsibility for his name or his person, and pretending to wipe the bar.

" No," said Bob. " I thought you were alone. Who's Mr. Eccles ? "

" Oh—didn't you see him ? "

" No—I only saw you in a flash. Who's Mr. Eccles ? "

" Oh—don't you remember Mr. Eccles ? "

" No. Not the slightest."

" He took me to the theatre—don't you remember ? "

" Oh, him. I remember."

" He took me out again yesterday. He's ever so nice," said Ella, speaking as one who enlarges upon the charms of her uncle ; but this did not deceive Bob.

" Oh—so it's come to that, has it ? " he said.

" Come to what ? "

" I thought it would," said Bob. " When I saw you together that night."

She knew he was just fooling with her according to their

convention, but was alarmed to learn that he remembered that
first evening in the bar so clearly.

" Don't be so silly, Bob."

" What's silly ? "

" You don't think—"

" Think what ? "

" You don't think I'd—"

" Why not ? I thought he was very nice."

" Did you ? " (Here was a surprise, if you liked !)

" Yes," said Bob, " nice looking, too."

" Nice looking ? . . . *Him* ? " said Ella. (A funny sort of
way to speak about the man to whom you were betrothed !
But she was so disconcerted, and Bob's view was above all others
of such vital importance to her, that she could not help it.)

" Yes," said Bob, " I thought he was very nice looking."

" *Nice* looking, perhaps," said Ella, meaning that he looked
a nice person—a very different thing, " But not nice looking."

" No," said Bob, " I mean nice looking."

" But, Bob," said Ella, " He's Old. . . ."

" Is he ? I didn't notice it."

Was Bob just trying to be perverse, or had she herself got
an entirely wrong slant on Mr. Eccles ? Looking back, she
could see now that her own opinion at one time had not differed
so very much from Bob's. In those early days she definitely
had thought Mr. Eccles nice looking, for his age, and it had not
occurred to her to think of him as Old. It was only in his
capacity as a practicable marrying proposition that his elderliness had been brought to the fore, and that his relative nice
looks had been therefore discounted. But Bob couldn't know
anything about that.

" Well, he's Getting on," she said. " At any rate."

" So are we all," said Bob.

" Yes. I suppose we are," said Ella, and decided she would
have to think about all this later. Mr. Eccles with the stamp of
Bob's approval was a very different Mr. Eccles. If Bob passed
him, then surely he was passed—in her eyes there could be no
fiercer test. In that case there was no reason why she should
not be able to shed that lurking feeling of something remotely
indecent—yes, indecent, she had to admit it—in Mr. Eccles' ad-

vances, and look him squarely in the face and judge him on his merits.

" Of course," said Bob, " if you've got so many people running after you. . . ."

Was this a conspiracy ? First her mother—now Bob. They clearly thought it was a wonderful idea—and they would throw her into his arms between them. She did not know whether she liked Bob going on like this, or not. On the one hand it had the gratifying result of improving Mr. Eccles' appearance— and therefore the appearance of her entire commitment—a hundredfold in her eyes. On the other hand, it came just at the time when she had been seeking to identify and establish the causes of her inner rebellion, and so put her in further confusion. Also it hammered home yet again Bob's hopeless indifference to her, in his carefree acquiescence in the elderly Mr. Eccles as a partner for her—an acquiescence which she could not help suspecting might be due to certain inner categories and associations in his mind which would have been different had she been a more attractive woman.

" Don't be so silly, Bob," she said, employing her usual method of closing a topic with Bob, and seeing how profitless and possibly painful it would be to go on discussing the man to whom she was engaged with the man she loved.

## CHAPTER XXI

IT was Sunday. By ten o'clock Ella was busy at her tasks in the bar, wondering what it was, breathing in the air, which made it so overpoweringly, all-permeatingly Sunday—so that she would have known it was Sunday morning if all the almanacal evidence in the world had spoken to the contrary.

Was it because she had risen an hour later ? Was it because six million people encircling her had risen an hour later ? Was it the fineness of the weather ? (There had been such a long succession of bright days on Sunday lately that she had got a

queer subconscious impression that that was why it was called
Sunday.) Was it the disquieting way in which this Sunday
sunshine served to intensify rather than remove her depression
of spirits—casting, as it did, churchy beams and shadows into
the poorly lit bar, and making her think of God—a subject
which she still could not get the hang of and which always
dejected her ? Was it the familiar sight of the fat Sunday paper,
with its menu of thick ultrasensationalism on this holy and
paradoxical day ? Was it the diminished, almost stilled, roar
of the traffic in the Euston Road in the distance ? Was it the
sound of the milkman, who alone among tradesmen was left
over from the week, and whose voice yodelled in solitary
mournfulness over the land of streets ? Was it the instinctive
knowledge of the aspect of those streets—empty here, teeming
there with a proletariat arrayed in its collarless Sunday best—
shuttered, littered, despondent ? It was something of all these
well-known Sunday things, taken in conjunction with a well-
known lingering taste in Ella's mouth of the sausages they were
always given for breakfast on Sundays, which made her feel the
day in the intuitive depths of her being.

" Another lovely Sunday," said the Governor, passing
through the bar, and she felt worse than ever.

Yet another cause of her instinctive conviction of the Sabbath
was the fact that she was booked to walk in Regent's Park with
Mr. Eccles in the afternoon. Three weeks or more had now
passed since Mr. Eccles had first dived with her into the darkness of that park with such momentous consequences, and it
had now become a regular practice on Sunday afternoons to
walk therein with " Ernest." Yes—by dint of strenuously and
continuously applied hydraulic pressure, he was almost " Ernest "
to her now, though she did not think she would ever be quite
able to dispel the inverted commas.

It was strange, she reflected, how she had grown into a habit
of mind wherein this walk in the Park, and " Ernest " in general,
had come to be taken for granted as belonging to a natural
order of things. Little more than three weeks had passed, yet
it now seemed as though there had never been a time when the
problem of " Ernest " had not been with her as it was now, like
a hidden anxiety grown almost stale to the perplexed sufferer

—still the focal point of all her waking thoughts and speculations, but seen in the light of day-to-day resignation. You could not keep up the breathless wonderment of those first few meetings for ever. In fact there were moments when " Ernest " was simply a bore.

" Ernest," too, was perhaps not quite the bouncingly enthusiastic creature he had been. Without having made (and she was in a way thankful for it) any further practical allusions to the future or the esoteric meaning of their supposed " Engagement," he had nevertheless succeeded in taking whatever relationship they did bear to each other for granted, and seemed quite content to jog along in their present course indefinitely.

She noticed, too, that everything being apparently settled in his mind, he had lost much of his self-consciousness, and talked less about her and more about himself—his likes and dislikes, his approvals and disapprovals—rather with an air of giving her a Short Course in himself for her present convenience and future reference. In fact, Railings apart, he seemed curiously to have lost interest in her as a human being, and Ella's good-natured attempt to disregard this was in no way aided by her discovery of the fact that he definitely had a Temper. He had a peculiar way, particularly when crossing traffic (which always drove him mad) of going yellow in the face and saying " Come on ! " or " Make up your mind then ! " with uncontrollable spleen. Also he would behave very sharply on entering cinemas when they couldn't find each other and were trying stumblingly to sit on air in the darkness. Indeed there were sometimes whole meetings with him when he bore that yellow look on his countenance, and she had to be careful all the time. But he made up for this with extreme cheerfulness at other moments, and the forbearing Ella respected his seniority in years and for the most part took it all in the day's work.

Their arrangement was, as usual on Sundays, to meet at Great Portland Street Station at five past three. To-day she was there at three minutes past, and found him waiting for her. She was in quite good spirits herself, for she always found that the brooding gloom of the Sabbath could be almost kept at bay in the afternoons as opposed to the hopeless mornings and evenings. But she had only to glance at him to diagnose that it was one of his yellow days.

Not that anyone less sensitive than Ella to his moods would have known this. He raised his hat and smiled, and at once took her arm, as was his habit (though Ella could never quite feel happy about it, or cease to marvel at the fate which had ordained that they should thus be linked in their own eyes and those of the world), and they immediately afterwards launched upon their first skirmish with the traffic in crossing over to Marylebone Church.

This was always one she dreaded, as it was a tricky corner even for those who did not lose their heads, and Mr. Eccles to-day behaved more like someone in a padded cell than some-one in a public thoroughfare, pushing her forward, dragging her back like a shying horse, epileptically clasping her lest she made a move, and finally, when they were over, laying all the blame on her with " It's better really to make up one's mind from the beginning, isn't it ? "

Not a very good start. She tried to be cheerful as they walked along the other side, but he relapsed into monosyllables, as he always did after quarrelling with the traffic. Nor had any real improvement taken place by the time they had entered the Park at York Gate, and were walking up the main avenue towards the Zoo amidst the winter-gripped flower beds and the rippling murmur of a post-prandial Sunday crowd gratefully disporting its undistinguished self in the sun—a sight which always saddened Ella for no exact reason she knew. In fact at last she got so cast down with her silent companion (having had a sudden vision of being married to Mr. Eccles and walking staidly in the Park like this every Sunday afternoon for the rest of her life) that she had the courage to remonstrate.

" You're rather quiet this afternoon," she said, " aren't you ? "

" Am I ? " said Mr. Eccles. " I didn't think so."

" Yes you are. You've been ever so quiet."

" Have I ? " said Mr. Eccles, in the tone of one who intended to go on being as quiet as he wished, which rather enraged Ella.

" Yes. You have," she said. " Is there anything on your mind ? "

To her surprise Mr. Eccles, instead of sinking further into

himself, here took hold of her arm and became companionable.
" Now what should make you think that ? " he said. " Eh ? "
And he gave her arm a little pressure (he would call it a squeeze!).

Did she detect a confessing eagerness in his manner, an
admission that he had been silent, and a desire to confide in her
the real causes thereof ?

" Go on," he said, " what made you think that ? "

She was now certain of his anxiety to get something off his
chest, and felt relief mixed with a not displeasing sense of agitation. What if something was coming to light ? It was about
time, after three weeks of silent evasion of main issues. They
had got to come out into the open sooner or later, and whereas
he was possibly in a state of perturbation, she at the moment
felt triumphantly ready for anything.

" I didn't think," she said, " I knew."

" Ah—you understand me so perfectly—don't you ? " said
Mr. Eccles.

She had never understood any man less in her entire experience
of men, but that was by the way. She gathered that he was
trying to flatter her, which was itself possibly ominous of the
gravity of what was on his mind, and which gave her the hope
that this was going to be anything but a dull Sunday afternoon,
after all.

" Yes. I understand you all right," she said, flattering his
flattery. " Go on. What is it ? "

" Oh—it's nothing."

" Yes it is. Go on."

" No, there isn't anything really."

" Yes, there is," said Ella. " Is it anything about Us ? "

" Now what should make you think that ? " said Mr. Eccles,
renewing his pressure on her arm, and giving the show away.

" Go on. What is it ? "

" Oh, nothing much. . . ."

" Do you want to give it all up ? " said Ella, with a sudden
frankness which surprised herself. But, glancing at him, she
had seen him looking so evasively puzzled and thoughtful, and
she had suddenly felt so bored with his silliness and the whole
thing in general, that so simple and rapid a denouement had
offered itself spontaneously to her mind.

"Oh no," said Mr. Eccles, "I don't think I want to do that. . . ."

Which was an even more surprising answer, and one which, when the shock had passed, she found angering her. *Think*, indeed! Had he been remaining coolly and autocratically undecided all this time, wasting her time and his, and making a fool of her? She was sure she wouldn't mind if he gave it all up, and she had a good mind to tell him so.

"Well," she said, "I should have thought you would have made up your mind by now." And that was actually the first harsh word she had ever spoken to him.

"So I have. . . . I didn't mean that, exactly."

"What did you mean then?" she said, more gently, "go on."

"Well, it's not so much a question of Us, so much, is it?"

"Isn't it?"

"No. You see, it's the other people that make the trouble, isn't it?"

"Is it?" said Ella, smelling sisters-in-law in the air, but saying nothing.

"Yes. But what's the use of talking about it. Let's change the subject."

"Go on. Who is it?"

"No. Let's change the subject."

"No. Go on," said Ella, "is it your sister-in-law?"

"Now, how did you guess that?"

"What has she been saying?" said Ella, feeling very resentful. She might not desire Mr. Eccles herself, but it was not in human nature to like the thought of Mr. Eccles' relations not desiring her, however well she could see their point of view. In fact nothing in the world can be more calculated upon to make any person feel as Good as Anybody Else (or Better) than this sort of thing.

"Oh—there's been a fine old How-d'ye-do," said Mr. Eccles.

"Has there?" said Ella, sternly. "How's that?"

"Well, of course, *They* think I'm making a fool of myself," said Mr. Eccles. "That's all."

And there was in his voice so strong and basely unloverlike a hint that he himself saw and with certain qualifications subscribed to their point of view, that Ella had a notion that this was going to be the last, and fatal, walk with Mr. Eccles, and she got ready for battle. If there was the smallest relaxation on his part, she was only too willing to be rid of him, and she was going to see that she was not humiliated.

" And what do *you* think ? " she said.

" Oh—it's nothing to do with myself. I'm only telling you what *they* think."

" But I'd've thought it was what you think that mattered."

" Are you Angry ? " asked Mr. Eccles.

" No, I'm not a bit Angry. I only want to know."

" You musn't be Angry, you know," said Mr. Eccles, with an air of consoling her. " You mustn't think I want to back out."

The patronage and condescension which this implied—the impudence with which this pursuing little man in his Sunday bowler hat and dark overcoat, dared, from the superior height of his wealth and connections, to turn the tables and play the kindly rôle of the pursued, was too much for Ella.

" Perhaps I might want to Back Out," she said.

" Oh—now you're not being reasonable."

" Well, what's so unreasonable in that ? "

" No," said Mr. Eccles. " Let's talk about it reasonably. I can't help what other people say, can I ? "

" What have they been saying, then ? " asked Ella, moved to curiosity in spite of herself.

" Well, I suppose they don't think it'd be a suitable match. I'm sure I don't know why."

That was more happily put, and Ella relented somewhat.

" Well, perhaps, they're right, you know," she said. " I've always said so, haven't I ? "

" I don't see why they're right. Why do you say they're right ? "

" Well, I'm not—Educated, am I ? What'd you think if one of *your* relations went and married a barmaid ? "

" I wouldn't think anything."

" Oh yes, you would. You would think she was after their money."

" Well, that's absurd. I know you're not after *that*," said Mr. Eccles.

The weird, circuitous, and paradoxical thing about the whole situation, reflected Ella, was that she was after nothing else. Would she have suffered Mr. Eccles so long if he had not been comparatively a millionaire, if she had not resolutely reproached herself for her abnormality and fastidiousness in not jumping at so unexampled a Catch ? Upon what lies and misunderstandings, therefore this affair had its foundation. But how could she explain this to him ?

" I don't know why you're so sure," she said, having to pretend she was speaking half in jest.

" Don't be so silly. Do you think I don't understand you ? "

" Do you ? "

" Of course I do. I know every little thought that's going on in your dear little head," said Mr. Eccles, again pressing her to him, and Ella was too dumbfounded to reply.

" I thought we were getting into the Tantrums for a moment," went on Mr. Eccles, ushering in the reconciliation, " and that would never do—would it ? We've got to discuss these things some time, haven't we ? "

" Yes. I suppose we have."

" You see, I thought we might fix up a meeting sometime, and then she could see for herself—couldn't she ? "

" What ? " said Ella. " Me meet your sister-in-law ? "

" Yes. Suppose you came along to tea one day ? I'm sure she'd like you if she saw you."

" Oh—I don't think that's necessary, do you ? " said Ella, thunderstruck. She had never remotely taken into account the material prospect of a début amongst his relations—she supposed she had never really taken him seriously enough. And now she recoiled in frightened self-mistrust.

" Why not ? " said Mr. Eccles.

" She wouldn't want to see me, would she ? "

" Of course she would. In fact I'm sure she'd be most interested."

Then she was to be taken up and shown off like some doubtful horse or ox on approval ? She could see that Mr. Eccles, for all he inferred to the contrary, was desperately anxious to get an outside opinion on her.

" If you wore that dark hat and coat of yours," said Mr. Eccles, " you'd make a great impression, I'm sure."

That, she also saw, was a shy hint as regards impressing the aristocracy of Chiswick. He had praised the sober style of that dark hat and coat before. " All right," she wanted to say, " I know how to dress myself—thank you." But of course she did not say it.

" But I thought we were going to keep it a Secret," she said instead.

" Yes, we *Were*," said Mr. Eccles. " But we can't go on like that for ever, can we ? If we're going to be married you'll have to meet them."

" But when did you think, then," said Ella, making herself ask him what she had never dared ask him before, " that we would be married exactly ? "

" Oh, in two or three months," said Mr. Eccles, and caused the whole of Regent's Park to recede from Ella in surprise and confusion.

" Two or three months ? "

" Yes. We could do it before if we could get things in order."

Two or three months ! With the warily manœuvring, cautiously advancing Mr. Eccles, she had thought of this consummation in terms of years—of tens of years ! And here he had brought it down to a matter of weeks—eight weeks or less ! Eight weeks only in which to make up her mind, when she thought she had the greater part of eternity.

" You see that's why I wanted to talk about it," said Mr. Eccles, all of whose doubts now seemed to have fled. " I want to get the Ring some time next week."

The Ring ! The Ring, and after eight weeks, enslavement for life—a life of Sundays in which she walked respectably round Regent's Park with this rather elderly, rather good-looking, arch, often irritable, self-conscious bowler-hatted maniac who had never rightly understood a single thought going on in her head ! How could she decide such a thing in eight weeks ? No—she had decided already—she could not go through with it.

" And then you'll be really mine," said Mr. Eccles. " You needn't think I'm going to let you go."

" Aren't you ? " said Ella, faintly. How was she going to tell him ? Was ever anyone more complacent purblind, and in-

accessible ?  Could she write him a letter ?  Yes—that was an
idea.  She would write him a letter.

" Doesn't the lake look lovely ? " said Mr. Eccles, for by
now they had walked right round into view of the lake.  " I
shall never forget this lake."

" Won't you ? "

" No.  That was where we walked when we first *Knew*," said
Mr. Eccles, giving her another nudge, while Ella concentrated
gropingly on a Letter.  A postman alone could curb this prodigious man.

## CHAPTER XXII

ELLA had an aunt, on her father's side, who dwelt at
Clapham.  This was a cheerful woman, early widowed and in
" a good way " comparatively, with a small house of her
own and a back garden.  In the summer Ella would often spend
her whole afternoons and evenings off in this garden, thinking
of it as a refuge of laziness and peace, but in the siege of winter
she seldom got over there.  When she did she was made warmly
welcome, given muffins or hot toast in an indescribably cosy
tea, and, made achingly to sense the innumerable amenities and
minute blisses of an independent income, however small.  But
the hour came to go, and she was back in the bleakness and
slavery of the week.

Needless to say, Ella Loved her Aunt (she would have Loved
her in any case because she was her Aunt, but she loved her
over and above this) and her Aunt loved her.  In fact Ella was
known to be her aunt's " Favourite," whatever that might
mean.  She was a younger woman than Ella's mother, and for
that reason Ella was sometimes able to confide in her certain
matters which she was not fully able to confide to the latter.
In fact Ella had often thought of confiding properly in her
aunt about Mr. Eccles.

This did not mean, of course, that Ella Loved her Aunt
more than she Loved her Mother, for in Ella's sternly conven-

tional hierarchy of Love, it would be a crime of the first water to place one's Aunt in the same category as one's Mother, who took precedence over all others, including even Father, if you had one. And Ella, in her orthodoxy, did not regard this as a purely personal classification, but one that applied to all families all over the world.

It was next Thursday that Ella decided to make a long-deferred journey over to Clapham to see this Aunt Winnie, having written her a letter the week before announcing her intention. After her last Sunday with Mr. Eccles, she really felt she could go on no longer without advice, and she fully intended, if she could lead the conversation round that way and take the plunge, to come out with the whole story, and throw herself upon her Aunt's verdict—perhaps requisitioning her aid in the composition of that Letter, which she had no idea how to begin, but which she still felt was her only rock to cling to in that submerging flood of indefatigability which was Mr. Eccles.

But this was not to be. For no sooner had Ella, on her arrival at her aunt's house, been welcomed and kissed in the hall way, than she was swept into the sitting-room and acquainted with the fact that instead of having her life clarified this afternoon, it was to be further confused by what her aunt with warm and innocent pleasure described as a Bit of Good News for her.

At first Ella thought that this might really be a bit of good news, though she could not conceive from what source good news could befall her; but it soon turned out to be about as middling a piece of news as she had ever heard. What it amounted to was that there was a *Chance*, said Aunt Winnie.

" Oh yes ? " said Ella, looking politely bright-eyed and avid for further enlightenment.

A real *Chance*, said Aunt Winnie, and where did Ella think *she* might be packing off to before long ? " Where ? " said Ella, a remote glaze already stealing into her eyes at the thought of her involvement with Mr. Eccles in relation to all this. " *India !* " said Aunt Winnie, " What do you think of that ? "

" *India !* " said Ella. " Good Lord ! "

" And what do you think as ? "

" What ? " said Ella.

" It's as a nursemaid," said Aunt Winnie, and then she got down to details. Ella hardly listened to these, so confused and nettled was she, but it transpired (as might be imagined) that a Mrs. So-on-and-so-forth, who in turn was an old friend of Mrs. So-on-and-so-forth, whom Aunt Winnie had been housekeeper for, twenty years ago, and so on and so forth—Ella couldn't quite gather who was who, but anyway what this Mrs. So-on-and-so-forth wanted was a Really Reliable Girl. There were two sweet little children—a boy and a girl—and in this case they wouldn't require looking after so much as so on and so forth. It was not so much a question of Experience, as Reliability and Honesty. Well, naturally, Mrs. So-on-and-so-forth had mentioned the matter to Mrs. So-on-and-so-forth, and somehow Aunt Winnie had got in on it, being by now as thick as thieves with both the Mrs. So-on-and-so-forths, and having suggested Ella as a candidate. In this scheme Mrs. So-on-and-so-forth had apparently shown boundless interest and hopefulness, having the greatest reasons to trust Aunt Winnie's recommendation on account of yet another (and rather vital) *Miss* So-on-and-so-forth, who, by a weird coincidence knew both Mrs. So-on-and-so-forth and Aunt Winnie years before the War, though they hadn't known it, and so on and so forth. Well, what it boiled down to was that Mrs. S.O.A.S.F. was most anxious to *See* Ella, and if she but fulfilled the favourable impression already created for her (and how could she do otherwise ?) the thing was as good as in the bag. The salary was thirty shillings and they left for India in six weeks.

" Now isn't *that* a piece of good news ? " said Aunt Winnie, when she had finished.

" Yes," said Ella. " That's wonderful." For to throw cold water upon the burning secret endeavours of her Aunt Winnie and a united front of amiable Mrs. So-on-and-so-forths at the same time, was more than she could find in her heart to do.

" Look at the salary," said Aunt Winnie. " And you always said you'd love to look after children—didn't you ? "

" Yes," said Ella. " I did." And this was the truth. To have something to do with " kids " had naturally been her passionate ambition ever since she had had to work for her living.

" And *India*, too," said Aunt Winnie. " What an adventure ! "

" Yes, it would be," said Ella. " Do you really think there's a Chance ? "

She said this half hoping that there was yet some snag which might release her from the dilemma with which fate seemed to have conspired wickedly to confront her. India ! India at any other time—but India, of all things, at this time ! Six weeks in which to go to India, and eight weeks in which to marry Mr. Eccles ! It was utterly beyond her to explain Mr. Eccles to her aunt now, and yet if she did not explain him how was she to stop active preparations for India going ahead ?

" Of *course* there's a Chance," said Aunt Winnie. " If you write the right sort of letter, and go along in the right way there shouldn't be the slightest doubt."

Then she had got to write a letter and go along ? This was awful.

" When should I do that ? " asked Ella.

" As soon as possible I should think And then you can go along next week. You've only got to show how willing you are," said Aunt Winnie.

" And then perhaps," said Aunt Winnie, " you'll be able to say good-bye to that dreadful public-house of yours. I never liked you being there."

Ella saw that now Aunt Winnie's optimism had cast " The Midnight Bell " into history, she was prepared rebelliously to view it in its blackest light, whereas before she had unreservedly accepted Ella's " nice situation." Which was silly, and likely to make them both look fools if India failed.

Shortly afterwards Aunt Winnie began to get tea ready, and they moved on to other subjects parenthetically for a little ; but Ella's afternoon was devastated. There is nothing in the world so confusing, vexing, and perplexing as having tea with an Aunt who is convinced in all her senses that one is going to India, whereas one knows in actual fact that one is engaged to be married to a gentleman in Chiswick ; and Ella's aunt could naturally not leave the theme alone for long. Ella was to do this, and to do that, not to Dwell too much on the fact that she had been a barmaid, not to stress " The Midnight Bell " as a pub, but rather as a Sort of Hotel, in which she had Helped, to

" wear that dark coat and hat " (these seemed to have made a
terrific impression !), to Mention this, and Leave Out that, and
all the rest of it.

" Well, it's ever so kind of you, Aunt Winnie," said Ella,
as she kissed her good-bye in the hallway on her departure,
" And I hope something comes of it."

" Yes. I thought you'd be pleased," said Aunt Winnie. " It's
a chance in a thousand."

And as Ella made her way reflectively homeward she found
that some of Aunt Winnie's enthusiasm had infected her, and
that the idea after all was not so inconceivable. In fact, putting
Mr. Eccles aside for a moment, the notion, in its very wildness,
strangeness, and novelty, had an extraordinary appeal to her
in her present mood. What if she ran away from Mr. Eccles
and began a new life in India ! And looking after kids—had
that not at one time been the highest peak of her desire in her
life of compelled service ? And *India !* India—for one who had
looked upon the Euston Road and the endless washing of
glasses and pulling of beer for men as her blind and never-
varying station in life. Where and what was India ?—she didn't
know much about it—except that it was that big red bit that
came down to a point. They had Coolies there or something,
didn't they ? And Curry, of course. And then there was Caste,
wasn't there ? She didn't quite know what Caste was, but they
had it in India—together with Sahibs, and Tiffin, and Rajahs
and Hindus and Fakirs and Heaven knew what—a whole different world of picturesque and intriguing paraphernalia in a
remote, sun-baked clime. And reached over hundreds of miles
of enchanted sea. That, as compared to the fog and rain of
London ! Suppose India suited her and she had been fated for
India all along ? Suppose adventure and romance were coming
into her life at last ? But she was going too fast. To begin with
Aunt Winnie was known to be a huge optimist in matters of
this kind, and Ella could not see what anybody would want to
take *her* to India for. Possibly it would all turn out in nothing.
And then what about Mr. Eccles ? This notion could only be
harboured on the assumption that she was going coolly to jilt
Mr. Eccles, and how could she do that ? And should she
tell Mr. Eccles about India, or keep India up her sleeve ? She

rather thought the latter. Then, if it came to a question of jilting Mr. Eccles, she would have India to fall back upon. In fact India might even justify her in the jilting of Mr. Eccles, and it might be a good idea to refrain from fully deciding about him until India had been substantiated. Then she might jilt India—she did not know. It was rather mean, to play a double game like this, but as far as Mr. Eccles was concerned she had an irresistible feeling of being justified in considering her own welfare before his, since he had not really any feeling for her as a human being, and had landed her into this engagement with him by gradual assumptions which had never, at any given moment, exacted her full consent. Besides, it was quite impossible to conceive of a state of affairs in which Mr. Eccles endured any really heart-broken suffering over her. That, probably, was one of the main reasons why she so often felt she did not like him enough to marry him.

Well, whatever else it was, India was at any rate another diversion and excitement in her life. She would write to-night if she could to Mrs. Whatever-her-name was (her Aunt had given her a card, which was in her bag) and ask for an interview next week. It would have to be in the afternoon, of course, and if Mr. Eccles was wanting to take her to tea that day, she would have to resort to falsehood. She was skating on pretty thin ice, wasn't she ?

She did not, however, make any attempt to write any such letter that night, for on arriving at " The Midnight Bell " there was a letter awaiting her. This was from her mother, begging her to go over to Pimlico to-morrow afternoon if she could manage it, as her stepfather, Mr. Prosser, lay dangerously ill. The wheels of fate were indeed speeding up.

## CHAPTER XXIII

THERE were three or four different Ellas battling for supre-
macy in the Ella that hastily left her work and hurried out
to board a bus to Victoria next afternoon, and her mind
was in a fever of speculation.

She had hardly slept last night, and having had no further
word from her mother, she had no means of guessing what
developments there had been since last night or how " ill "
her stepfather actually was. Naturally her first concern was
for the sick man—or at any rate that was what she stoutly and
resolutely held to amid the innumerable, irrelevant, base,
rebellious, unscrupulous, egoistic thoughts and impulses
springing up on all sides from her subconscious mind. And in a
way she was sincere. Death is the only common foe which
unites all parties and sinks all differences in a blind contest
against its onslaught, and so far as deeds alone were concerned
Ella was ready enough to show the genuineness of her feeling
for the victim. In fact, it would hardly be an exaggeration
to say that Ella would have willingly given her life for her
stepfather if it could have been done—so deeply ingrained is the
instinct in live people to battle against the mystery, pathos, and
irredeemability of this event. Then how was this feeling to be
reconciled with her other feelings—her past hatred of the fiend
in human shape, of the " wicked " man—her resentment of his
whole existence, her real longing to have him out of the way ?
If he died, of course, then all his sins would be forgiven—in
fact his sins were forgiven already. But suppose he didn't die ?
Would his sins be forgiven then ? Therefore, could she say that
she had truly forgiven his sins now and desired nothing but to
preserve his life ? Ella succeeded in doing so, but at the cost
of her integrity—such being the penalty paid by orthodox souls
like hers in moments of testing reality.

Then again, if she was to regard herself as mentally battling
for and selflessly concentrating upon the unhappy man, why
was it that she found her mind continually wandering away
into criminal speculations as to the possible result of the event

of his death upon herself and her mother ? India, for instance. What effect would Mr. Prosser's death have upon India ? And India was only the beginning for it might have the profoundest effect in every imaginable way upon her mother and herself. For had it not always been tacitly understood between them that in the event of Mr. Prosser's death, in the event (in their shy and respectful parlance) of Anything Happening to him, there was a " little something coming " ? How much this exactly little something coming amounted to Ella did not know, but in his savage way Mr. Prosser had always been a saving man, and it was known that from his better days he had at one time put by a sum in Post Office Savings amounting, she believed, to not less than three hundred pounds. How much of this astounding sum had been drawn upon in his latter days of ignominious employment she did not know, but she knew that it had been his bitter and semi-fanatical endeavour to keep it intact for illness and old age, and that there had often been quarrels between her mother and himself on account of his refusal to provide her with necessities when the money was there. While sympathizing with her mother Ella had in this single instance also a certain sympathy for Mr. Prosser, as she was a great saver herself, seldom failing to put by something like three shillings weekly from her own meagre earnings, and having now accumulated the sum of seven pounds, which all the pressure in the world would not induce her to touch.

Three hundred pounds—however you might reproach yourself, it simply was not a sum which could float into your orbit and exert no magnetic power. Ella did her utmost to forget about it, but the effort was beyond her strength. What could you do with three hundred pounds ? What could you not do with three hundred pounds ? With such a capital Ella could foresee happiness, health, freedom, a cottage, fresh air—everything she had dreamed about for her mother and herself. It was a sum which, in its proportional hugeness to Ella, had no defined limits, though she had at the same time a perfectly practical knowledge of the prime objects upon which she would expend it and eke it out. Besides that, the moral reinforcement of three hundred pounds, the temporary freedom from the gnawing pains of penury ! Would she want to go on working at " The Midnight Bell " if she and her mother had three hundred pounds ? Would she (and here was the point) want to marry Mr. Eccles if she and her mother had those three hundred pounds ? It was impossible to say. Three hundred pounds lifted her whole existence on to a plane so giddy that she dared not examine the view.

But she must not think like that, she told herself again and again in the bus going to Victoria. It was tempting Providence, among other things. " *Tempting Providence.*" What was this ? Ella all at once realized that by using that expression mentally she had hopelessly caught herself out. While her stepfather lay dangerously ill—and possibly in agony—she was blaming herself, not for her vulture-like contemplation of his savings, but for tempting the Providence which might put those savings into her hands ! She could not credit her own baseness, and marvelled at the contradictions in human nature.

Her heart beat faster as she neared the house, and climbed the dark, hollow stairway to the stricken abode.

The door to the kitchen she found ajar, and putting her head timidly around, she was smitten in a moment by the breathless quiet of critical illness—an atmosphere which seemed in some way to reproach her, to be, as it were, one up on her, in that those who were living in it had all the medical technique and latest vital information in their hands, had put all the furniture in different places for good reasons, and had been conducting all the ardours of the crisis on their own initiative and without aid from her.

Also there was no sign of her mother in the kitchen, but instead a young lady whom she at once recognized as the Floor Above (in other words the Top Floor) who was washing up. This young lady (whom Ella afterwards ascertained had rendered assiduous and invaluable assistance) was about thirty-seven years of age, and had not previously been on friendly terms either with the Prossers or any of the other floors—this on account of the frightful way she painted her face, and smuggled gentlemen up to her room when others had gone to bed, leading them warily down again by candle-light and bolting the door on them in the early hours of the morning—a furtive sound by night, bringing a keen sense of further and subtle degradation to all those who, sufficiently downcast merely by the day-time circumstances of this lowly lodging-house, might be awake and listening in those zero hours. But Poverty strikes in a thousand underhand ways. Moreover, she had been no friend of Mr. Prosser himself, who had been known publicly to storm at her and Show her Up (as the phrasf was) from his landing, although, oddly enough, he had himsele acquired the sinister reputation of having been Seen with her in a public-house not far away, and even of having been in the early days one of the actual smuggled concupiscent gentlemen in the nightly Takings-Place Above—but this was gossip. Anyway, here she was, making herself useful, and, as Ella was to discover soon, being intensely sentimental about the whole thing, and frantically Helping everybody on all sides, in that rather maudlin and too highly charged emotional manner common to those of her loveless calling when they are given the opportunity to prove their worth by participating in the affairs of those whose instinct it is to despise them.

Directly she saw Ella, she smiled and put her hand to her lips, to enforce quiet, and explained that Mrs. Prosser was at this moment lying down on the sofa in the next room trying to get a little sleep, as she had been up two nights without a wink. Ella then asked about the patient, and so as her mother should not be disturbed, a whispering conversation was held in the kitchen for something like ten minutes. Ella learned that her stepfather had been taken ill with great pain three nights ago, and had since sunk into a coma. The Takings-Place Above (this was how Ella, who did not know her name, could only think of the woman) had done everything she possibly could to Help, to be of Assistance, to Do what she Could, but they had had a bad time of it. There was every reason to Hope, of course (one had to Hope, didn't one?), but the doctor had been rather despondent, and the Takings-Place Above Knew how Ella must be Feeling. All this while Ella gazed in a rather fascinated way at the Takings-Place Above's longish nose, pasty face, and rather dirty neck, and wondered what the smuggled gentlemen saw in her. Finally Ella learned again that everything had been done that possibly could have been done by solicitous nursing, and that her mother was Solid Gold. Solid Gold, if ever anyone was. Ella had previously thought of her mother in numerous lights, as a trustworthy and lovable woman, but never exactly as Solid Gold. She nodded her head appreciatively, however.

At this moment Solid Gold herself appeared, not having been lying down at all—this being simply another sentimental fiction created by the Takings-Place Above in her anxiety to have everybody Lying Down while she Helped—but in the sick room and wondering why Ella had not arrived. They then all went into the sitting-room, and Ella was given further news of the history and circumstances of the illness, the Takings-Place Above providing the more graphic and dramatic details, and every now and again adjuring Mrs. Prosser to Take it Easy and to Lie Down. But this Mrs. Prosser would not do.

" She's Solid Gold, isn't she ? " said the Takings-Place Above, looking at her smilingly and appraisingly. . . . And there was a silence in which both she and Ella gazed at Mrs. Prosser, who had all the confused air of one who had perforce to be gracious under the compliment, but didn't quite know whether it was the proper thing to stand there being called Solid Gold (or indeed to be assisted at all) by one with a reputation which would bear so little looking into by respectable people.

It was then suggested that Ella should go in and see the sick man, and this she did. But she did not stay for long, as he was breathing heavily in sleep or unconsciousness and there could be no question of recognition. Ella's heart was indeed touched as she saw the deathly white, and at this moment not ignoble countenance of the bitter man she had known, grappling with this sudden reality, which dissolved all the other painful realities of his querulous being, and left her soul free of all feelings save one of wishing him well in whatever contest that intent look and steady breathing implied.

When she came out the Takings-Place Above already had tea in preparation, and was all for Leaving them. In addition to Lying Down, and Taking it Easy, and being Helped, there was a vitally important sentimental rule that people in these circumstances should, periodically and with great ostentation, be Left.

" Oh, must you go ? " said Ella, politely, but the Takings-

Place Above was adamant. No, she would Leave them. She Knew what they were Feeling, and she would Leave them. And Leave them she did—suggesting, without definitely stating, that a proper obedience to the regulations here necessitated our dear old friend the Good Cry, than which there was Nothing that did you more Good in the World, but which she was too tactful to stay and witness.

" She's been very helpful," said Ella's mother, when she had gone, and her expression and tone betrayed the reservation in her appreciation of this socially dubious and emotionally rather importunate lady who had stepped into their lives in so strange a way, and at so strange a time.

Ella was glad to be sitting down alone with her mother, and asked her what she really thought of the case.

" I don't really think there's much hope," said Mrs. Prosser, in a voice which shook slightly, and added that the doctor had said that he might go on in this way for a week or a fortnight.

Ella looked at her mother as she brought out the word " hope " and could not help wondering for a moment whether that queer shake in the voice would have been very different if she had been using the word " fear " instead, and whether her mother was also susceptible to such uncontrollable thoughts as had beset herself coming along in the bus. Remembering her mother's terrible life with the man in the next room, she could not honestly see how it could be otherwise. But she hastily crushed the thought, as one which, even if it existed underground must never gain conscious recognition in either of their souls.

" I've been through his papers to-day," said Mrs. Prosser a little later.

" Oh yes ? " said Ella.

" You knew there was a Little Something Coming," said Ella's mother, again with a slight quaver in her voice. " Didn't you ? " . . .

" Yes," said Ella. " I did know there was a little something . . as a matter of fact. . . ."

" It's something like five hundred pounds," said Mrs. Prosser. " He had a lot put by."

Five hundred pounds ! Before she could control herself,

her heart was seized and lifted up in lyrical exultation and surprise at this news, and she had the greatest difficulty in preserving a steady voice.

" Really," she said quietly. " All that ? . . ."

" M'm," said her mother, and Ella wondered whether it was in human nature to maintain indefinitely this funereal and disinterested posture in the vicinity of so vast and universe-transforming a sum. She herself could scarcely keep a straight face—being beset, in the conflict of her natural emotions with her sense of right and decency, by something uncommonly like a desire to giggle in a silly way.

" When's the doctor coming again ? " she asked, to get away from her thoughts.

" He said he'd look in again to-night," said Mrs. Prosser. " Of course he *may* get better."

" Well—let's hope he will," said Ella, using the same sort of hydraulic pressure as she applied when calling Mr. Eccles " Ernest."

" Yes," said Mrs. Prosser. " We can only do our best."

Ella decided that she must be the wickedest young woman in the world, and consoled herself with the certain knowledge that her mother would indeed do her best—would in fact, slave her life out in order to achieve a recovery, and that therefore any vile thoughts on either of their parts were of no account. A little later she went in again to see the sick man, and in repentance held his limp hand which lay over the sheet. Again she was moved by his tragedy and pathetic helplessness—both rendered more poignant by the fact that he was unwanted and she came out with a refreshed impulse to selflessness in a sorrowing and helpless world.

There was little else she could do, and the time soon came to return to work. She would come over to-morrow afternoon and her mother would send her a message if there was any change. She left her mother with the greatest reluctance, as she had never seen her look so ill and worn in her life before.

When all this was over, she reflected in the bus going home, she would really have to see that her mother got out of the fog and smoke for a real holiday. A real long holiday. Which brought her back (how could it do otherwise ?) to the five hundred pounds. Which brought her back to the future in general. Which in turn brought her back to Mr. Eccles—and to India— in fact the entire family of perplexities in whose ever-present and tireless company her thoughtful life in London was lived. Sometimes she wished she could give up thinking altogether.

## CHAPTER XXIV

A T this point it should be stated that Mr. Eccles had a Tooth in his head. This was a large one right in the centre of the upper front row, and gained eminence in his mouth less from its size than from its crooked tendencies, inasmuch as it came pointedly forth and hung down over the next tooth on the left-hand side as though anxious to conceal the defaults of its partner and to take all the dental glory to itself. Ella had noticed it the first time she had seen Mr. Eccles. Not that this defect reached the proportions of being a blemish upon Mr. Eccles' appearance as a whole. One did not say to oneself for instance, as one watched Mr. Eccles smiling, " Ah, yes—a nice-looking man—but he has a funny tooth." No, no—nothing as bad as that. It was a question rather of " Ah, yes—a nice-looking man —*and* he has a funny tooth." The tooth was a curious addition, rather than an identifiable exception, to the youthful comeliness of the rather elderly man.   Nevertheless it was capable of exercising a partially hypnotic effect upon those who looked at it for too long, and at moments made him look rather like a tiger.

Ella had always done her utmost to ignore or forget this tooth, but sometimes it got the upper hand of her. And never had this been so much so as when, three or four days later, she sat opposite Mr. Eccles in Lyons'.

This was the first afternoon she had not spent in Pimlico since the news of her stepfather's illness. On that front there had been no change; he lay and breathed in the same way; and with the extraordinary adaptability with which people in forty-eight hours can become hardened and cold concerning what were formerly the most agonizing states of suspense, she had practically swallowed the whole Pimlico catastrophe (including the victim's pain from hour to hour), and had allotted this afternoon to expenditure of energy on another front— that of Mr. Eccles, whom she had not seen for nearly a week.

They had just been for another walk in Regent's Park, and had come into this small Lyons' in Baker Street to have a cup of tea before she returned to her work. This had become an almost established routine with them by now, and Ella had noticed that he never took her to the theatre nowadays. In fact, although she had got the impression that he was so rich and generous, and that she was going to have such a splashing time with him, when you came to think about it he had only taken her to the theatre once ever since she had known him. They had twice gone to the pictures—that was all. Such were the steadying influences of familiarity. She wondered if she would ever go to the theatre if she was married to him.

Having been duly solemn for about two minutes concerning her relative's illness, Mr. Eccles was in a jolly, smiling mood this afternoon; consequently the Tooth was being given a more pronounced airing than usual, which was probably responsible for augmenting Ella's hypnosis concerning it. She could hardly listen to him, as he talked across the marble-topped table, so fascinated, so intrigued, so impressed, was she by her fresh realization of this Tooth's size and angle in regard to its relations. Not that he was talking about anything important. He had been going on for a long while about one of his Funny Little Habits. She was stalely familiar with the Funny Little Habit Series, the discussion of each Funny Little Habit form- ing, as it were, exercises in the Short Elementary Course in Ecclesry he was giving her. There was his Funny Little Habit of Getting his Own Way, there was his Funny Little Habit of Speaking the Truth, there was his Funny Little Habit of Return- ing other people's rudeness with Interest ; there were his Funny Little Habits of Summing People up on the Quiet, of Making Decisions Quickly, of Knowing his Own Mind, of Gently but Firmly putting others in their Place, of not Saying much but thinking a Lot, and so on indefinitely.

The Funny Little Habit under immediate scrutiny was his
Funny Little Habit of being Rather Careful in his Choice of
Words—in other words his objection to swearing.

" I mean to say it's not Necessary, is it ? " he was saying.

" No . . . " said Ella, tooth-gazing.

" I do think it's so unnecessary to be *Unnecessary*," said Mr.
Eccles, getting into slight tautological difficulties. " You know
what I mean—don't you ? "

" Yes. I do." She wondered if it would have been any better
if it had come down straight. Even then it would have wanted
the point filed off to get into line with the rest.

" I mean to say if you've got to use expletives why not use
just ordinary, decent, everyday words ? "

" Yes. Why not ? " (His other teeth of course were in
excellent condition for his age.)

" I always think it was such a good idea," said Mr. Eccles,—
" a fellow I read about in a book. Instead of saying ' Damn '
and ' Blast ' and all the rest, whenever he was annoyed he used
to say ' *Mice and Mumps—Mice and Mumps !* ' "

" Oh yes ? " (Couldn't a dentist break it off halfway down,
and then crown it ?)

" Humorous idea—but it always appealed to me. Got it
off his chest, and hadn't said anything he regretted."

" No." (Or he might have it yanked out altogether. But
the gap would be worse.)

" ' *My giddy forefathers* ' is enough for me."

" Yes. Same for me." (Unless the teeth on each side grew
inwards so as to cover it up. She believed they sometimes did
that.)

" But all these—Bees," said Mr. Eccles. " They get on my
nerves. . . . I can't stand Bees, can you ? "

" No. I don't like them." (From her experience in the bar
she could herself have included a large variety of initials rivalling
or reducing to naught the mild scandal of Bees, but she was not
so unmaidenly as to tell him so.)

" Dees are bad enough," said Mr. Eccles. " But *Bees*. . . ."

" Yes. It's very unnecessary." (He might wear a Plate of
course, but she didn't think she could stand that.)

" And then all this Dragging in of the Deity," said Mr.

Eccles. " Why does everybody Drag in the Deity every time they open their mouths ? "

" I don't know, I'm sure," said Ella, feeling that he was rather exaggerating the average man's resort to this form of appeal.

" Neither do I," said Mr. Eccles. " Not that I'm a Religious man."

" No," said Ella, non-committally.

" But I think there's something *There*, don't you ? "

" Yes. I suppose there is."

" I mean there must be something *There*, mustn't there," said Mr. Eccles, painfully unable to specify exactly Where, and leaving Ella rather doubtful as to how she was to show her comprehension.

" Yes," she said.

" A Great First Cause," tried Mr. Eccles. "—which we Obey."

" Yes."

" A Spirit of Good."

" Yes."

" Something which Looks On."

" Yes."

" And Guides."

" Yes."

" In fact I suppose you would really say that I *am* a religious man—though I don't show it on the surface."

" Oh yes."

" And I certainly believe in going to Church."

" Oh—do you ? " (Good Lord, was he going to turn Religious on her now ?)

" And I believe in the Power of Prayer."

" Do you ? "

" Yes—don't you ? "

" I don't really know," said Ella. . . .

" Ah—but you Must—you Must," said Mr. Eccles with sudden extemporized Chadbandian fervour. " You must let me Help you."

This was frightful. If he was going to superadd Religion to all the other mental thumbscrews and tortures he had at his disposal in the dungeon of his shameless and enwrapping personality, she really could not bear it. Not that Ella Minded religion, in the ordinary way. Her sole reflection on the matter was that there was just as much religion in Some people as there was in Others—if you knew what she meant. But Religion and Mr. Eccles simply did not go.

" You must try," said Mr. Eccles. " It all Comes—if you Try."

" Does it ? "

" Will you Try, for my sake ? "

" Yes. I must," said Ella, and decided, this time she believed for good and all, that she could not marry this monster. And was there the same obligation to marry him now, if there was five hundred pounds coming her way ? Or, if she must not be so wicked as to take that into account, what about India ?

(She had written to India, that was to say to Mrs. Thingyma-jig, only yesterday, as a matter of fact, and she was expecting an answer to-morrow.)

" It's so easy when you Start," said Mr. Eccles. " To get in touch with the Spirit of Peace upon the Waters. . . ." And Mr. Eccles looked at her in a steady, perturbing way, as though here and now he was getting in touch with the Spirit of Peace upon the Waters, amid all the spoon-clinking, order-calling, and china-clanking of the crowded restaurant.

" Is it ? " she said.

" Ah," said Mr. Eccles with a smile of sickly winsomeness. " I see that you will have to let me take charge of your spiritual as well as your bodily welfare ! "

And the smile, of course, revealed the Tooth which had now got beyond the passive hypnotic stage, and was nearly driving her mad.

" Though I don't know," added Mr. Eccles with his head on one side, " that Little Ladies need bother their little heads too much about such grave matters."

What a fool, and what a Tooth ! And how she would like to shake up his complacency ! In his bland egoism he had shown the minimum of interest in the happenings over at Pimlico, and she wondered what he would think now if he knew how those happenings were likely to change the whole course of events ?

And what would he think if he knew about India? Well, let him go on dwelling a little longer in his toothy paradise. It was strange, how the combined action of Pimlico and India should have brought to the fore and enabled her at last fully to indulge her previously concealed dislike of a mere tooth, but she was now finding that these two localities had strange and magical influences in all directions.

"They're more worried," said Mr. Eccles, "with High Heels than Heaven—eh?"

"I suppose they are," said Ella, smiling. Let him go on. Let him go on. . . .

"I say—I should make an awfully good Preacher, shouldn't I?" said Mr. Eccles, and started on another tack.

## CHAPTER XXV

"5 Amprey Gardens,
N.W.3.

"Mrs. Sanderson-Chantry thanks Miss Dawson for her letter, and would be obliged if she would call to talk the matter over at the above address between 2 and 3.15 on Friday afternoon.

"E. SANDERSON-CHANTRY."

ELLA could not help feeling a little chilled, indeed a little snubbed, by this briefly scribbled postcard which came two mornings later. After all the fuss and carrying on between the several Mrs. So-on-and-so-forths, she had somehow been led to anticipate a warmer and more welcomingly confiding acknowledgment of her letter. And what a funny way of putting things, in the third person and present tense like that, as though relating a story, or like a broadcasting announcer describing a sort of athletic event in progress, with themselves as the chief combatants. And no "yours faithfully"

or " yours truly " or anything—no human note at all.  Just E.
(what did E. stand for ?) Sanderson-Chantry—as much as to
say that was enough for anybody.  But she supposed this was
the way " Ladies " were compelled by their own rigid laws to
conduct matters—" Ladies " having a whole host of ascetic
rituals unfathomable by the uninitiated—and so she would not
let herself become despondent.

Again, it was very awkward—the way in which 2 to 3.15
had been regally and arbitrarily fixed upon as the time for her
call, as unless she took an aeroplane it was physically impossible
to get up to Hampstead by 3.15 on a Friday, when she didn't
finish her work in " The Midnight Bell " till three, and had to
dress and all.  But " Ladies," who toiled not nor spun, nor
did any work save the work of working others, were notoriously
incapable of understanding what it meant really to be a working
person.

However, quashing these unfruitful grumblings at the gods,
and feverishly utilizing the half hour she had off for lunch for
the purposes of washing, dressing and making herself seemly
in the critical eyes of " Ladies "—Ella contrived to leave " The
Midnight Bell " at two minutes past three in full war array—
if war array was the right expression to use in describing her
intensely studied moderation as regards clothes, cosmetics, and
demeanour, in trying to look like a natural-born genius as a
nurse-maid for children in India.

It is in nearly all cases impossible for servants, or wage-
slaves of any kind, to seek happier conditions of slavery free of
charge, and the heavy tax of fourpence (eightpence there and
back) was exacted by the Underground Railway on her way to
N.W.3.  But Ella (seriously as this cut into her weekly earnings
—which, if she was to Put anything By amounted only to six
shillings weekly, and her clothes had to come out of that)
regarded this blindly as an Investment, and made no demur.

But even when she had arrived at Hampstead, and asked the
way shyly from passer-by to passer-by, she had enormous
trouble in locating Amprey Gardens, which was reached up
hill and down dale, that was to say up all the wrong hills and
down all the futile dales, in the mazy northern suburb.  But
at last she found herself getting warmer, and amongst the Am-

preys, and her heart beat faster as she saw " Amprey Gardens " itself written up in a superior road with trees and houses lying back from the pavement in spruce front gardens.

She found Number Five, but was now in such a state of fright that she had to walk on a little way to collect herself—an affliction of the nerves common to wage-slaves, with only their labour power to sell, and the consciousness of their insignificance and powerlessness before their aloof and comfortable masters.

However, at last her footsteps were scrunching up the gravel path, and she was standing in the porch listening to the lingering tinkle of the bell at the back of the still house.

A silent, beastly moment, if ever there was one, and not much improved by the opening of the door—this by a fellow wage-slave, dressed in the neat insignia of wage-slavery, a cap and apron, but not very friendly or understanding in her manners. Hidden rivalry and circumspection, rather than fellow-feeling, most often exists between wage-slave and wage-slave in circumstances such as these, possibly because of their sensitiveness to the dangerous surplus of willing wage-slaves on the market, and possibly because certain fortunate wage-slaves come to acquire some of the aloof and clannish airs of their lords above.

It was half a minute before a coolly stared-at Ella could make her rights and business clear, and then she was reluctantly and silently escorted into a drawing-room on the left of the hallway, and surlily left.

The door was not quite closed on her, and as she looked around; marvelling at the pictures and ornaments of the chintzy room, she could hear and sense the life of the house around her.

This consisted of a succession of curious and rather violent Bumps from above, betokening the presence of a Man in the house—the dim clatter of washing-up in the basement, and the sound of doors being opened and closed furtively. She had evidently caused rather a crisis in a minor and mysterious way.

Finally a door burst open somewhere; heavy footsteps ran thumping down the stairs, and a Man's raised voice was heard shouting " Rosie! Rosie! . . . Will you keep this *door* shut! " and a door was slammed.

The next moment Ella's own door was flung with desperate

anger open, and she found herself glaring terror-stricken into the outraged eyes of a tall, good-looking gentleman with a moustache.

" Oh—I'm sorry," said the tall good-looking gentleman, and had shut the door on her and vanished completely in a flash.

Rather a funny way of meeting a tall good-looking gentleman with a moustache, she reflected. . . . The Master she presumed. She wished the Mistress would come, as this suspense was getting on her nerves.

About five minutes later the Mistress appeared, with apologies for the delay. Also with a large brown dog preceding her. Which dog at once began to bark the house down, and to spring lickingly upon Ella in a very insecure and dubiously welcoming way. " *Down*, Buster, *Down* ! " cried its mistress—a tall, hatchet-faced, lady-like lady with grey hair. " *Down* ! . . . Bustah ! . . . Bustah ! . . ."

" He's always like this," she explained, but it wasn't much consolation to hear that.

It was quite a minute or two before the animal was under any form of control, and then they began to discuss the matter in hand. But somehow the life had been taken out of their powers of concentration by the dog, who was grasped firmly but still rebellious, and they could not get down to the thing with very great intimacy or seriousness.

However, in the cool and indifferent manner of her class, Mrs. Sanderson-Chantry described the various advantages (" *Bustah* !—Don't ! ") and disadvantages of the post, mentioned Ella's aunt (" *Don't*, Bustah ! ") sketched the salary and the sort of duties which Ella hypothetically would be called upon (" Bustah ! Will you *stop* ! ") to undertake, and so led gracefully on to the snag, which was that there was Another Girl (" Bustah ! ") whom Mrs. Sanderson-Chantry had as good as engaged as far back as three weeks ago, before she had even heard of Ella—only this Girl hadn't yet been able to decide whether or not she could come. Mrs. Sanderson-Chantry had always Wanted this girl, and she couldn't very well let her down if she still wanted to come—weally, could she ? Mrs. Sanderson-Chantry spoke in rather an affected voice, but Ella decided that

she was a Very Nice woman at heart. It is to the advantage of
wage-slaves wistfully to form an early opinion that their pros-
pective masters and mistresses are Very Nice, and they generally
manage to subdue and shape their subconscious impressions
to this gratifying conclusion.

" So you see it's weally wather impossible—Bustah ! *Bustah* !
Lie down Bustah !—impossible," went on Mrs. Sanderson-
Chantry, " to make a Weal Decision at the moment. Lie *down*,
will you !"

" Did you know when you might be knowing, Madam ? "
said Ella. She was having a certain amount of difficulty in
bringing out her " Madams," having had no practice with this
lately—her service at " The Midnight Bell " requiring only the
familiar " Guv'nor " or " Mrs." to the powers that were. But
she well knew that it was a very different proposition when you
were on parade before a Real Lady like this, and she brought
the word out with due solemnity every time she spoke.

" Oh—I should think in a few days at the most. I'm going to
write to her again to-night as a matter of fact."

" Then perhaps you could let me know, Madam, when you
hear."

" Oh yes, of course I will. *Bustah* ! Bad dog ! Personally I
don't *think*," said Mrs. Sanderson-Chantry, " I don't *think* that
she's really *likely* to come. And *then*, of course. . . ."

Ella was extremely anxious to hear the end of this trailing
sentence, since it sounded very much as though in that event
she could look upon herself as practically as good as engaged
—but she was not destined to hear this. For at this moment the
dog Buster having espied, or imagined that it had espied, a
tradesman entering the precincts, wrenched itself free from the
grasp of its mistress, and with wild and deafening barks went
rushing and slithering over to the window.

" Bustah ! *Bustah* ! Come here, Bustah ! *Bustah* ! Come here !
Bustah ! *Bustah* !" cried Mrs. Sanderson-Chantry, adding her
own ear-splitting yells to the din and tumult already caused by
the dog, and Ella felt that the atmosphere was no longer really
ripe for pressing home any further enquiries, and signified by
her look that she was ready to go.

The dog had now rushed out of the door, with Mrs.

Sanderson-Chantry in hot pursuit. And with Ella following, and with Mrs. Sanderson-Chantry screaming " Bustah ! Bustah ! Will you come here ! Will you stop that noise ! Bustah ! Bus*TAH* ! "—interspersed with a few polite repetitions of the fact that she would write to Ella, and that she was glad to have seen her, and did she know her way back all right—Ella took her leave, not feeling that she had made a very profound impression upon the Sanderson-Chantry household. " Bustah ! . . . Bustah ! " were the last dim cries she heard as she turned around the corner.

However, she had all the elation of one who has got over an interview, a light, hilarious feeling, rather like coming out of school, and on reflection she decided that it had all been Very Satisfactory. She was a Nice Lady, a Very Nice Lady, really, and she was sure the gentleman was nice too, only she happened to have caught him in a temper. He was probably having his afternoon nap. Yes—they were both nice, and she could see herself being very happy with them. And it did look as though she was approved of, if only that Other girl didn't decide to go after all.

She shot down the flying suspicion that this Other girl was a pure romantic fiction created by Mrs. Sanderson-Chantry in order to have a graceful line of escape, and again reassured herself that it was all Very Satisfactory. She would Love to be with them. Wage-slaves, as we have seen, are constrained to go on reassuring themselves like this.

But they cannot keep the flag of their spirits flying all the time, and in the train going back, and having a sudden reminiscent vision of the hostile maid, the Sanderson-Chantrys, and Bustah " Oh, if only I had some *money* ! " Ella said tensely to herself, thus revealing her underlying impressions of the interview.

## CHAPTER XXVI

" **O**F course," said Master Eric, who after a period of dis-
interest had condescendingly decided to help her again
in the bar this morning. " If you can get the balls into
the Anchor Position, you can go on scoring indefinitely."

He was discussing Billiards—in which evidently he was an
adept. She had to admit, sacrilege as it was, that she was getting
a little tired of this little boy. Oh no, that was going too far—
she would say rather that children were naturally a little " wearing " when you had troubles on your mind. And she didn't
think she had ever had quite so many little troubles and perplexities as at the moment.

To begin with, her stepfather had lain in a critical condition
for well over a week now, and there had even been talk of his
recovery. Not very serious talk, but enough to justify redoubled energy in nursing (her mother would kill herself nursing him if she was not careful), and to throw everyone into a
state of confusion and suspense. Ella did her utmost not to
think about that five hundred pounds, but now that it had
shown these minute symptoms of withdrawing itself from her
orbit she found herself thinking about it more and more. That
the hellishly sinful words " Buck up " had ever entered her mind
in connection with her thoughts concerning the ill man was one
of the dark disgraces of her inner soul. All the same in that
inner soul she knew perfectly well that she wished he *would*
Buck Up, and she was verging upon the consoling but disin-
genuous theory frequently adopted by people in like circumstances, that it would be Best for him.

Then there was India. She had had not a word from India,
though four or five days had passed, and she was beginning to
think that they were never going to write, and had decided
against her. Finally, there was Mr. Eccles, to whom (in putting
off meeting him) she had lied on that day she went up to Hampstead, and who had half-suspected this, and was also beginning
to get a little angry and jealous over her enforced and frequent
visits to Pimlico.

With all these things on her mind she felt justified in finding Master Eric a little " wearing," though of course she would never be so Unkind as to show it. Though she had been feigning a certain knowledge of Billiards, she hadn't the remotest conception what the Anchor Position was, and replied " Oh yes, that must be very clever."

" It's not a question of being *clever*," said Master Eric. " Anybody can do it. *I* could do it."

" Oh yes."

" You've only got to get the balls into the right position."

" M'm. That's the thing to do."

" How would *you*, for instance," asked Master Eric, " set about getting the balls into the Anchor Position ? "

" Well, I really don't know."

" I suppose you know what the Anchor Position *is* ? "

" Well—I don't think I do, really."

" But I thought you said you understood Billiards ? "

" Well, so I do. I've played it once or twice."

" And yet you don't know what the Anchor Position is ? "

" No. I'm afraid I don't."

" Do you know *anything* about Billiards ? "

" Yes. I've said I did."

" Do you know what a Nursery Cannon is, for instance ? "

" Well—let me see now. . . ."

" It's nothing to do with *Children's* Nurseries, if that's what you think," said Master Eric, quite unfairly attributing this fanciful conception to her, and then unjustly scorning her for it.

" No. I didn't think it would be."

" Then what *is* a Nursery Cannon ? "

Ella was anxiously hunting round in her mind for another evasive answer to this, when the situation was saved by the appearance of Bob, who had come to open the house (it had just struck eleven), and who told Master Eric that he was wanted by the Mrs. upstairs. Master Eric had therefore perforce to go, not without the threat that he would " come back and ask her later." But anyway the proper atmosphere for tying Ella up had gone for the moment, as the little beast was never able to show off in front of Bob, who could wipe the floor with him on Billiards, Football, Wireless, Chemistry or anything.

About a quarter of an hour later there were five or six customers in the bar, including a stout red-faced, middle-aged gentleman in pince-nez and a bowler hat, whom she had never seen
in the house before. But he was talking, in a rather aggressive
and haughty voice, to one of the other customers, and she had
decided that she liked neither the sound nor the look of him,
and hoped that he would not develop into a permanent customer.

Her surprise and resentment, therefore, was all the greater,
when in passing his area of the bar to fetch a bottle, she heard a
stentorian " Excuse me," and, turning, saw him staring imper-
tinently at her.

" Yes ? " she said, pretending that she thought he wanted
to be served or something.

" Are you the famous ' Ella ' ? " said the stout, red-faced
gentleman, so that everybody could hear, and Ella's heart
missed a beat.

" Yes," she said, enquiringly. " That's right."

" Ah—I thought there was no mistake," he said. " You and
I have a mutual friend, I think."

" Have we ? " said Ella, the blood rushing up to her cheeks
as she realized what was coming. " I don't think so."

" Oh yes, we have. You think again," said the stout red-
faced gentleman, looking at her in a patronizing, appraising and
confidential manner which made her want to run out of the
bar.

" No. I don't know what you mean," she said.

" Don't you really ? Surely you do. And very good taste
brother Eccles has, I must say."

Ella was so infuriated she could not trust herself to speak,
and just gazed at him distraught. And broadcasting it in his
horrible voice in front of the whole bar like this ! By the grace
of God Bob was not in the vicinity at the moment, but he might
come into earshot at any moment, and *then* what was she going
to do !

" And she blushes very nicely, too, doesn't she ? " said the
red-faced gentleman, turning to the customer standing next to
him, who had perceived Ella's embarrassment, and was looking
rather a fool himself.

"I think," said Ella, "that you must be making some mistake."

"Oh no, there's no mistake, believe me. I've been told all about it."

"Well—I—"

"We've got to look into our old friends' little indiscretions, you know," continued the red-faced gentleman, "just to see that they're not being led on."

This was too much for Ella, and she cast all courtesy and restraint to a customer to the winds.

"Well," she said, "I don't think there's any need to shout out about it all over the place—is there?"

"Oh! So she's a little Spitfire, too!" cried the red-faced gentleman, but Ella had now left him, and was pretending to busy herself with some bottles in a cupboard beneath the surface of the bar.

Well! Of all the cheek! Of all the blooming nerve! Of all the cool calculating impudence! Her resentment was concentrated not so much upon the present offender, as upon the absent Mr. Eccles, for his underhand and unforgivable action in putting her in such a position. So he was sending Spies now, to come in and look her over! She had not the slightest doubt that she had been talked over and over with this red-faced man, who was apparently an old friend, and that Mr. Eccles had slyly sent him in to form a second opinion. Otherwise why should he as a stranger have gone out of his way to come to "The Midnight Bell"? The whole thing was as clear as day, and never, never had she been so angry. Well, he had overreached himself this time, and wouldn't she just let him Have it! Let him wait till she saw him to-morrow! She didn't care a hang for his beastly money, and she would let him have it as he had never had it before from anyone, with his beastly Religion and gossiping!

The whole of this episode was over in two or three minutes (the red-faced gentleman, also furious because she was not going to play, leaving a few minutes afterwards with a very sarcastic "Good Morning, Madam," and an exaggerated raising of his hat)—but the memory of it stayed goadingly with Ella all day. A thousand schemes for revenge upon and retaliatory humiliation of Mr. Eccles went through her brain, but it was not until the evening that fate seemed to play into her hands, and oddly enough through the instrumentality of Bob.

It was getting on for closing time in the crowded bar when Bob, who, she noticed, had been in very good spirits all the evening (there was no mood of Bob's she did not notice)—asked her if she would like to come to the pictures and tea with him to-morrow afternoon.

"You're free all right to-morrow afternoon, aren't you?" asked Bob.

"I should say I *am*," said Ella, and indeed, she was so over-come and delighted at the rare prospect, that for a moment or two she quite forgot that she was engaged to meet Mr. Eccles at the usual time and place to-morrow afternoon. When she remembered this she at first had a great shock, for she realized that it was too late to get a letter to him in time, and she could not find it in her heart, richly as they might deserve it, to let anyone down like that. On the other hand she equally could not find it in her heart to relinquish this precious opportunity to know Bob better (she had half a mind to confide some of her perplexities to Bob)—and she at last alighted upon the reckless expedient which alone would meet the case—she would send Mr. Eccles a telegram.

A telegram! She had once sent one for the Governor, but never one on her own behalf, and she was appalled by her own temerity and extravagance. But no sooner had the idea got hold of her, than she was intoxicated by its potentialities and nothing else would do. You could be as curt and excuseless as you cared in a telegram, and she could not help feeling that it would Show him as nothing else might. It wouldn't have occurred to him that barmaids could send telegrams as well as anybody else, would it?—and what would haughty Sisters-in-Law think of telegrams from despised underdogs arriving at the house in the morning? In fact the more she thought about it the more she revelled in the luxurious thought, and she began to frame the brief words she would use.

She slept badly that night, staying awake into the small hours, thinking about her telegram, and sensing the silent proximity of the telegraphically innocent and sleeping Bob in the next room. At a quarter to three she heard him get up for a drink of water from his jug (a habit of his with which she was familiar in the dark quarters of the night, but her secret knowledge of which was never likely to be mentioned or come to light), and it seemed at least an hour after that before she dropped off herself.

In the morning she hastily slipped out just before the house opened, and despatched the wire.

" DON'T MEET TO-DAY AFRAID ENGAGED."

was what it rather crudely ended up as, for although she had innumerable other abrupt and wilfully mystifying alternatives, she had not definitely fixed upon any single one, and she was in such a hurry that she got in a panic and wrote down the first thing that occurred to her.

The morning dragged by slowly enough, and yet was insidiously pervaded by the excitement and pleasure of the afternoon jaunt ahead (though Bob, of course, had said nothing more about it, as it was his pose to appear blasé in matters such as this ); and at three o'clock she hastened up to her room to get ready.

She dressed herself with a care and attention verging upon, but not overstepping, the ostentatious boundaries of the " Nines," and decided that she looked rather nice. In fact the fantastically hopeful notion actually entered her head that perhaps she was quite an attractive girl after all, and hadn't realized it. For after all there was Mr. Eccles, who had said that she was beautiful, and here was Bob taking her out (and did men " take you out " unless they thought you were "attractive" ?), and even that red-faced Horror had said that he admired Mr. Eccles' good taste. In which case perhaps Bob himself might be coming to " see " something in her ! What a thought ! No more Mr. Eccles, no more India, no more vulture-like craving for dying people's money—no more puzzling doubts or anything—just supreme and everlasting happiness ! For of course she would throw over the whole world for Bob. But this was nonsense, and that was Bob calling her from below. It would never do to make him impatient by keeping him waiting.

They were in great spirits as they set off, and although they
were pressed for time and could not see the second feature film
all through, a keenly enjoyable afternoon was spent.  Madame
Tussauds was the cinema Bob had chosen, as being the nearest
and most luxurious, and after the pictures they went to tea at a
little restaurant over the road.  No Lyons' or A.B.C.'s for Bob,
whom Ella reproached for being so extravagant.  But she could
not help taking a certain pride in the thought that Bob could do
things in style as well as Mr. Eccles, and she wished Mr. Eccles
could see them now.

Over tea Ella summoned up all her courage, and half for the
sake of confiding in someone, and half to see what effect it would
have on Bob, shyly announced that he might be Losing her before long, and told him about India.  This she did with a certain
naïve satisfaction in the mysteriousness and impressiveness of
foreign travel and India in connection with herself, and treated
the matter rather as though it was very nearly decided.  Bob
showed the liveliest, and, as usual, scrupulously courteous
surprise and incredulity, but alas, his heart was not touched
at the thought of her departure, and any lingering foolish hope
that he might be beginning to " see " something in her, was
dispelled.  But this was stale news, and as usual she did not let
it interfere with her pleasure in his company, or her general
delight in an intimate and charming winter's afternoon.

Another surprise awaited her directly they got back.  She
went up hastily to dress in her room, and was staggered to find
the brown envelope of a telegram propped up against an orna-
ment on the mantelpiece.  That it was a reply from the man she
had deserted this afternoon she instantly realized, and as she
tore it open she marvelled at the quickness and force of his
return blow.

" WHY ME NOT MEET WRITE PLEASE."

Ella was at first inclined to smile at the inverted, indeed the
rather pigeon-English, manner of this message with its twisted
" why me not meet ? "—rather as though Mr. Eccles had
mysteriously decided to adopt a disguise, and with his hands
crossed and his eyes screwed up was telegraphing from a hiding-

place in Chinatown. But she soon saw that there was nothing
to laugh at, and that she had received something uncommonly
like an ultimatum. There was something querulous, rather
than pathetic, in the " why me not meet ? " and peremptory in
the " write please," which informed her that he somehow knew
she was up to something and was not going to stand any nonsense. And why had he sent a wire, when a letter would have
served the purpose ? Just to show her that he could send wires
as well as herself. There was going to be trouble next time they
met.

But if he had one upon her, he also did not know that she
had one upon him in that disgraceful happening in the bar
yesterday morning, and she was not afraid of him. In fact she
would rather welcome a battle.

Besides she had India and other things up her sleeve now.
With those behind her, Mr. Eccles was not the same formidable
man.

Unless, of course, all those things failed her. Then where
would she be ?

## CHAPTER XXVII

ON Monday the most sinister and outlandish thing happened
in the universe—the day failed to dawn. Between half-past
six and seven, when Ella usually turned on her pillow and
thought of rising, it might have been between half-past two and
three in the morning, for all the light that showed through the
blind. Baffled and perturbed, she rose and looked out of the
window, to discover that the whole invisible world was wrapped
in a dense black-brown fog. Relieved in some measure by her
previous experiences of this vile but scientifically explicable
London phenomenon, she hastened to light the gas, and busy
herself with dressing. But there is nothing in the world so
depressing, so insidiously fear-inspiring, as gas-light at a time
of day at which gas-light is not proper, and she felt hopeless.
Besides which, the air was damp and freezing cold. She heard
Bob's alarm clock going off in the next room and a little later
his footsteps across the room as he went to shut the window and

make his own discovery of the gloom-stricken and afflicted day.

Things were no better when she got downstairs. It was colder than ever, and she had to switch on weirdly unfamiliar lights wherever she went in the blackness and frigid silence surrounding everything.

" Letter 'ere for you, Ella," said the Governor, up early, and puddling about without his collar, and blowing steam into the frozen air. " Nice sort of a day—ain't it ? "

" Ta, Governor. Yes—ain't it awful ? "

From India !—there was no mistaking that handwriting. She had pictured herself receiving this letter a hundred times already, but never with her teeth practically chattering with cold in the unearthly illuminations of a dense fog. And what news did it bear ? She put it on a shelf as she went on with her work, as she had to wait till the Governor was out of the way before she opened it. Was sunny India destined to be her salvation from fogs and the bleak cold monotony of London ? Or was it all off, and had she to continue her dreary life without the inspiration even of this hopeful excitement ? She would know in a minute.

At last the Governor disappeared and she tore it open.

" 5 Amprey Gardens,
N.W.3.

" Mrs. Sanderson-Chantry regrets not having been able to write before and wishes to say that she is now suited. She hopes Miss Dawson has been put to no inconvenience.

" E. SANDERSON-CHANTRY."

So it was all off. . . . Oh well that was that. She must take it bravely. And with distant memories of " Bustah ! Bustah ! " and the hostile maid, and the stormy man, perhaps it was just as well.

But she wished she hadn't got the news in this dreadful fog. And again she could not help feeling snubbed by the brief and cruelly impersonal wording of the note. They didn't seem to think you had any feelings or longings—those above. They didn't treat you as a human being. Besides it was never nice, to learn that somebody else had been preferred to you, and to be coolly told so—with the underlying implication that you were not quite a first-rate article, and might as well know it. Whatever the circumstances, no one likes to think they are a second-rate article.

And what a score for Mr. Eccles—though of course he would never know he had scored. She had only that enigmatic five hundred pounds to fortify her in her contest with him now, and it looked as though she had been getting above herself.

India was Off—that was the burden that lay on her soul all the long dark day. She wished she had not told Bob about it, as she now had to tell him that it was Off. He was sympathetic, but had his own thoughts to attend to, and she could see he had no true comprehension of the desolation of a fog-ridden world in which India was Off.

The fog improved not at all as the day wore on, and at eleven o'clock, when the house was opened and the people came in, the struggling electric light was burning everywhere, and it was neither day nor night. Rather it seemed, as you saw one wretched customer coming in after another from the abysses of mystery outside, that the gods had at last convicted human nature of its crimes and had thrown them all into a vast cold dungeon away from the light of day for ever.

A frightening thought. She wondered whether Bob ever had such thoughts as these. As he moved near her, in his strong yet modest way, he seemed constitutionally unassailable by fear. She was afraid she would not be able to keep her desolate longing for Bob at bay, if this fog went on. His nearness, his strength, his quietness, and the gentle look in his dark eyes, were disturbing her nervous system. In the terror and coldness of the dungeon you so desired to cling to someone you loved—and the passionate desire to take Bob out into a passage there and then, and to cling, for strength and consolation of her misery and weakness, to the desperately attractive man, made her heart sink achingly.

But she frequently had attacks of Bob when the weather was bad. In the afternoon the fog lightened a little to the colour of curry—the curry she would have had if she had gone to India—which was Off—but at night it was as black as ever. A black day and night.

## CHAPTER XXVIII

HER plan was to keep calm. She had one up on him, and
if there was going to be any trouble she at any rate was not
going to make a fool of herself. This was her decision as
she left the house at five past three, and walked along to meet
Mr. Eccles at Great Portland Street Station at a quarter past.

She had not seen him for nearly two weeks since their peculiarly unfriendly interchange of telegrams. She had written
him a brief note saying that she would " explain " when she
saw him next (though she had no idea how she was going to
" explain " without quarrelling with him), and she had had a
briefer letter back saying that he was confined to the house
with a chill, and was staying indoors till the weather was better.
But, shortly after the fog, came snow, and after the snow, mud
and rain, and then more snow, and it was days after dreary days
before she got another note fixing a meeting.

In those intervening days she had had time to cool down
from her first rage and resentment at him for her humiliation
at the hands of his red-faced friend ; and in her general gloom,
in no way lightened by sundry trips in the foul weather over to
Pimlico (where enigmatically and maddeningly still no Change
had occurred, the wretched suffering man still mulishly refusing
to do what benign sophistry urged was Best for him) she almost
felt she could marry Mr. Eccles out of hand. If only to solve her
puzzles, and get away for good and all from the slow, mournful
influence of Bob. For she had never anticipated this long
stretch of bad weather, and Bob was getting on her nerves—
at times to a pitch which she felt she could not stand.

So she had got to be wise and cool, and perhaps marry a nice
gentleman with money.

She was there before the time, but he was standing there
waiting for her. He was looking depressingly like himself—
she had somehow hoped that he would have changed for the
better in the long interval—and there was the same quizzing,
although now perhaps slightly aggressive, look in his eye, as
he stood watching her as she came up, and then raised his hat.

" I'm not late, am I ? " she said.

" No. You're not late," said Mr. Eccles, and looked up at the sky. " I believe it's going to rain."

" Oh—I think it'll hold off," said Ella. " Where are we going ? " And they decided to walk down Great Portland Street in the direction of the Corner House where they would have tea.

" How's your cold ? " said Ella, politely and ingratiatingly as they set off. " I was very sorry to hear you'd been bad."

" I think it *is* going to rain," said Mr. Eccles, looking up again at the sky, but with an innocence of eye which did not divert the mind from the fact that he had purposely and pointedly (though she could not quite see the point) ignored her polite question. Oh—how well she knew his ways and could read his soul ! Quite apart from his grudge about the broken appointment, which he was dying to get off his chest, she could see that this was one of his yellow days and he was all out to take it out of her in any case. But she had decided to keep calm and so gain the advantage.

" Oh—I don't think it is, is it ? " she said with studied and model restraint.

" Yes, it is," said Mr. Eccles, and promptly began to put up his umbrella.

Now if there was one thing which Ella detested more than another in Mr. Eccles it was his umbrella—or rather it was not the umbrella she objected to so much, as having to walk along with him when he had it up. For although she would often have much preferred to walk outside of it in the rain, he was unable, in chivalry, to keep it all to himself, and included her rather grudgingly by slanting it over in her direction. This had the objectionable result (described already) that the tip of the furthest spoke kept on coming plomp down on to the top of her head, every half-dozen paces or so, with a sort of methodical springy poke which she could not mention in view of the fact that she was accepting his umbrella hospitality, but which nearly drove her out of her senses, as well as making her feel that it might at any moment go into her eye and put it out. She had had bitter experience of this umbrella from Mr. Eccles, who was a very keen umbrellaist at the smallest drop of rain, and she could not feel that it was going to help her to keep her temper now.

However, up it went, and they had hardly gone twenty paces before she felt the first tentative little plomp on her head —the first drop as it were, in the shower of plomps which she knew was about to descend upon her.

" Well," she said, " you haven't told me about your cold yet."

" Haven't I ? " he said. " You seem very interested about my cold." (Plomp.)

What a thing to say ! He evidently was spoiling for a row, but she was going sweetly to keep her temper.

" Of course I am," she said, " is there anything the matter ? "

" No. What should be the matter ? "

" Oh, I thought there might be."

" I was wondering, as a matter of fact," he said, " about your telegram. What happened ? Had someone died ? "

She saw that this telegram, which she had failed to explain by letter, was piquing his curiosity dreadfully, and that he resented her having any concern, apart from him, which could warrant the extravagance.

" No," she said, " no one died."

" Really ? " He spoke as though someone certainly ought to have died in atonement for the outrage upon his appointment with her.

" No. It was nothing at all bad. I just couldn't come."

" Couldn't you have sent a letter ? " (Plomp.)

" Yes, I suppose I might. But it'd have meant going out and posting it late at night."

" You seem to have a wonderful lot of money to throw away, with a telegram whenever you feel like it," he said, absolutely abandoning himself to his livery spleen. " I didn't know you were as rich as all that."

Oh—the meanness of that !—with its betrayal of his inner jealous knowledge of her poverty as the power he tyrannically held over her, of his miserly fear of having that power reduced by the minutest symptom of economic liberty—he, with all his riches, and she with her wretched little shilling on a telegram !

"Oh—" she said, "one's got to be extravagant sometimes you know."

"Has one?" he said. "I hope that's not going to be your attitude in the happy domestic future." And she saw him grinning in a green way as he walked along. She had forgotten, of course, that they were supposed to be Engaged! Remembering that, she saw his point of view a little more, but it was hard to subdue her rising temper. (Plomp.)

"What *did* happen, then?" he said, and she wondered what on earth she was going to say, as she had unwisely prepared nothing in all the time since she had last seen him.

"Oh—I had to go out. . . ."

"Oh yes? Who with?"

"Well—it was with Bob, as a matter of fact."

"*Who*?"

"Bob."

"*Who*?" (Plomp.)

"Bob."

"You don't mean the *waiter*, do you?"

"Yes. What's wrong?"

"Well, this is *Funny*," said Mr. Eccles, completely giving way. "I didn't imagine I was going to have a *waiter* as a rival. This is really amusing."

"Well, there's nothing amusing in being a waiter."

"I'm sure there isn't," said Mr. Eccles, who was too choking with rage to think of anything better for the moment.

"I don't know what's wrong with you."

"So you put me off and upset my plans just because you thought you'd go out with the waiter. Really. Are you sure it wasn't the pantry boy?"

Ella felt she could hit him in the face for this, remembering Bob's charming impulse to take her out.

"There's no need to talk like that," she said. "Bob's just as good as anybody."

"I may tell you that you upset all our arrangements at home," said Mr. Eccles parenthetically, "and that I had to have bread and cheese for lunch that day."

Dear me, thought Ella sarcastically, that was too bad.

"Well I'm sorry," she said, "if you were thrown out.

But I was feeling fed up with you at the time." It was coming out now—not quite as dramatically as she had hoped.

" *You*—fed up—with *Me* ? " said Mr. Eccles, in laboured tones of exasperated incredulity at this hellish affront to his majesty.

" Yes, I was."

" Really," said Mr. Eccles. " I think you forget our Positions." (Plomp.)

" What Positions ? "

" *Our* Positions," said Mr. Eccles not quite daring to say monetary and social Positions, which was what he meant.

" I don't see any difference in our positions."

" Don't you ? I don't suppose you would." (Plomp.)

" Just because you're well off, you're not God Almighty, you know."

" There's no Need—" began Mr. Eccles.

" All right. I know ! There's no need to drag in the deity. Say it." Her blood was up now, and it was going to be a good old row. In addition to which it was coming on to rain rather hard. She wished more than ever that she did not have to share his umbrella, as it was extremely awkward to conduct a row with anybody while you were hunched up against them in the wet and they were poking the top of your head all the time.

" Well," said Mr. Eccles. " We can at least keep our talk decent." (Plomp-plomp.)

" I'm afraid you're rather ashamed of my company, aren't you ? " she said.

" Well, as you seem to prefer the company of *waiters* to my own, I'm afraid I am."

" You seem to forget that Bob's my friend."

" I can see that. I'm sure you have everything in common." (Plomp.)

" And anyway," said Ella. " Even *Bob's* better than *Spies*."

This was rather unfortunately put, seeming to allow, as it did, that Bob himself was pretty far down in the depths, but was at least one shade higher than Spies. But she was getting so confused and bothered with trying to shorten her neck to escape the plomps that this was all she could think of to convey to him her advantage over him concerning the red-faced gentle- man.

" What *do* you mean ? "

" You know what I mean."

" I'm sure I don't. . . ."

" He came into the bar to look me over."

" Who ? "

" You know all right."

" I'm sure I don't. . . ."

" Oh yes you do."

" *When* did he come in ? "

" So you *do* know then ? "

" I'm sure I don't know what you mean—at all." (Plomp.)

" Well—I'm not going to be discussed and spied upon—as though you were buying a horse. I've got some feelings you know."

" So you don't *like* my *oldest* friends to whom I *happen* to mention you *casually* in *passing*? " said Mr. Eccles, attacking her, and defending himself, in the same sentence, and at this he brought down the umbrella upon her head with such a savage and furious jab that he nearly had her hat off.

" Here ! Look out ! " said Ella.

" What ? "

" Your umbrella."

" I'm very sorry, I'm sure," said Mr. Eccles sarcastically.

" If that's your oldest friend, I can only say I don't like his manners, that's all," said Ella.

" Well, if you prefer your public-house friends to mine—there's nothing more to be said."

" You're doing it again," said Ella.

" What ? "

" Can't you hold your umbrella higher ? "

" You're losing your temper, aren't you ? "

" Well—I don't want my eye put out."

" Really, this is the Limit ! " said Mr. Eccles. " I've a good mind to leave you stone dead."

" All right. There's no need to Shout."

" I wasn't Shouting."

" Yes, you were."

" I wasn't."

" You were."

" *You* were Shouting, you mean," said Mr. Eccles.

" There you go again."

" Where ? "

" Shall *I* hold it ? "

" *Shouting*, indeed! My patience isn't eternal, you know."

" Well, you can always stop it if you want to. *I* shouldn't regret it."

" Oh, wouldn't you ! "

" Why should I ? "

" Oh—wouldn't you ! . . ."

" Why ? "

" You've got an eye on the main chance all right. Don't think I don't understand the situation."

But this was more than flesh and blood could stand. As another plomp was just about to descend she dodged from under his angry and hateful umbrella, and walked away up Great Portland Street.

For a few moments she walked at an even pace, giving him an opportunity to follow her. But it came on to pelt, and she had to run nearly all the way home to " The Midnight Bell."


## CHAPTER XXIX

CHRISTMAS ! . . . You could hardly believe it in such murky weather. . . .

For a long while Ella had known that this uncanny festival, so insincerely stimulated and out of keeping with a harsh commercial era, had been on the way ; but it had never dawned upon her that London was about suddenly to enter, as it were, the foggy yet festooned Christmas tunnel, until she came down one morning and found that the Governor and his wife, unknown to everybody, had decorated the bar !

After that she had no difficulty in realizing the event, for the bars were crowded morning and night. London Spent at this time of year, and there was a great deal of noise and excitement. Afterwards London repented having Spent, got thoroughly scared, and contrastingly left you high and dry and desolate in the New Year. They had no consideration for your emotions.

Not a word from her strange, strange lover. Or rather ex-lover, she had to presume, since it was over a week since she had left him in the street. If he had loved her truly, surely he would have written to her, and not have let a few bitter words stand in the way of the bright future he had planned. And, with her expert knowledge of Mr. Eccles' psychological processes, she still felt she would hear from him—probably just before Christmas Day. And what then ? Patch it up and marry him ? In this dreary season, with India Off, and nothing On, and still no Change in her stepfather, and Bob sending her into a decline, she so felt the world falling away from her, that she again believed she could marry him in sheer despair. She, of course, could never write to him. Lacking unconditional withdrawal, she could never forgive him that remark about having an eye to the main chance. At least technically she could never forgive him. Actually she could, because it was so uncommonly near the flat truth ! But the preservation of her human dignity would never allow her to tell him that, if they reached eighty years of age together in blissful married life.

" It's perfectly simple," said Master Eric. " It's Latin."
" Is it ? " said Ella. As this morning was Christmas Eve, and she had three times the work on her hands cleaning out and preparing the bar, she intensely wished that Master Eric would go and " Help " somebody else. But he had chosen to come inside the bar with her this morning, and had been swanking about his Christmas presents and getting in her way for fully half an hour. But she was irritable this morning, as it was another grey and bitterly cold day, with the tips of her fingers freezing, and, as usual, she detested the gloomy necessity of burning electric light in the morning.

She suspected, too, that this weather was at last beginning

to tell even on Master Eric's nerves, for he had been unusually impatient with her stupidity this morning, restlessly hovering around her in his ennui, and taking her up and ragging her on every point.

"Amo, I love—Amas, thou lovest," said Master Eric. "Amat, he loves. Go on—say that. Amo, amas, amat."

"Amo, amas, amat," said Ella. "Will that do?"

"Yes. That's right. Now say a different verb. Not amo, but Iamano. Go on. Just the same as the other. Iamano—"

"Iamano," said Ella, and saw the catch just in time. "No, I won't say that."

"Why not?"

"It's a catch. You want me to say I *am* an ass."

"No, I don't. I just want you to decline the verb. Go on. Iamano—"

"No. I saw that one."

"Well try this one, then," said Master Eric, "if you can't do Latin. It's a riddle. Just give me the answer."

> "Adam and Eve and Kick me
> Went down to the river to bathe
> Adam and Eve were drowned
> Who do you think was saved?"

Ella knew this one, too, though it was Pinch Me in her own version. She did not answer.

"Go on," said Master Eric. "Who?"

She mumbled something, and the next moment Master Eric had come up to her, seizing both her arms in his fierce young grasp, and was getting ready to kick her. "What did you say?" he said, now in a high state of excitement. "What did you say?"

"I didn't say anything. Look out, you're hurting. Leave go, Eric."

"Yes, you did. You said Kick Me!" cried Master Eric, quite beside himself. "You said Kick Me! All right—I'll Kick you!"

"Here, leave go! You're hurting!" cried Ella, in real alarm and confusion, for the little boy, in that hysteria which sometimes seizes the young when they cannot get what they want, was strugglingly driving her back all along the bar, wildly kicking at her and pulling at her dress. "I'll Kick you! I'll Kick you!" he yelled, and "Stop it! Don't be rough!" cried Ella receiving two fiercely painful hacks on the shin. At this a whiskey bottle fell over in the skirmish and she really began to get desperate for the child seemed to have gone mad. But all at once he was seized away from her by a stronger grasp, and she heard a smart report. This was the sound of the palm of Bob's hand over his head.

He had smacked his head, and now he was bundling him out of the bar!

A piercing yell arose; there was further skirmishing, another report (louder this time), sustained murderous yelling—and then the inner door was closed, and Bob was coming back to her.

"Did he hurt you?" said Bob, a little shaky himself.

"Oh, Bob," cried Ella, gazing at him. "You shouldn't have smacked his head."

But there was, in her heart, a kind of surging gratitude for his instantaneous chivalry in protecting her, and an adoring admiration of his strength and manly firmness, which showed in his eyes.

"Never mind about his head," said Bob. "Has he hurt you?"

"Yes—he kicked me ever so hard," she said. "And look at my dress."

"Yes. I saw him," said Bob, and "Here, let me," as she started to tie the bow of her jumper, which Master Eric had torn asunder.

"He's been working up for that a long time—" said Bob, but all Ella knew was that he was near and touching her as he tied the bow, and she felt that she would not mind being assaulted by all the children in London if only such a sequel awaited her each time.

"But, Bob, should you have smacked his head?" she said, thinking of the possible consequences.

"I'll smack it again when I see him," said Bob. "Just listen to him—the little beast."

For all this time the sound of screaming had not ceased for a moment from upstairs, where apparently someone was trying to console him. Although he was a " kid," she saw now that he *was* rather a little beast, and that a kind of submerged snobbish hatred and scorn of her which the child had mysteriously harboured ever since he had been in the house, had at last reached its climax in the disaster of a few minutes ago.

" But Bob, there'll be trouble, won't there ? " said Ella, " we'll have to explain."

" Who cares ? " said Bob, and a few minutes later the house opened, and they had perforce to put the matter on one side.

But an assault of any kind upsets the nervous system, and she took alarm later in the morning, as she saw nothing of Master Eric, whom she was now desperately anxious to Forgive (she couldn't stand the thought of head-smackings and being on terms like that with anybody), and who had possibly told all sorts of fairy tales to his seniors.

" The Governor wants a word with you," said the Governor's Wife's Sister (the tyrant of " The Midnight Bell " whom Bob and Ella both detested), during the morning. This she said forebodingly in passing, while Ella was hard at work, and Ella's heart sank.

" Does he ? Where is he ? "

" He's out now. He won't be back till this evening. You hurt the kid bad you know."

" *I* didn't hit him," said Ella, but the hateful woman had gone.

Here was a nice thing to have happened on Christmas Eve ! Had a crime more dreadful than she had imagined been committed ? After all, the kid's head had been sharply struck, and it would be a fine thing if she ended up with getting the sack or something ! Oh, why should *this* be inflicted on her, on top of all her troubles !

Ella was so tired with the Christmas rush that she lay down in her bedroom that afternoon. At four o'clock she thought she heard the Governor come in, and went out on to the landing to try and get a word with him at once. But, after tense listening to footsteps, and doors opening and shutting, on the landing below, she found it was not, after all, the man who so ominously wanted a Word with her, and she went back to do some sewing in her bleak room, in even more agonized suspense as to what sort of Word it was to be.

Nor had the Governor returned, or had she seen anything more of Master Eric by the time the house opened in the evening—an opening which was rendered even more desolate by the fact that Bob had the evening off and so was not there to support her. Moreover she had the knowledge that in two days' time Bob was going away for a week's holiday, which had been long due to him, but which she could not help grudging him, as she would be so lonely at so unpleasant a time of year.

It was about ten minutes after opening, and with only a few customers in the house, that Ella looked along the bar and could hardly believe her eyes. Was that not the Takings-Place Above rather self-consciously standing there? At the moment Ella was busy uncorking a bottle for a rather involved order from three gentlemen, and before going along in that direction, she had time in which to ponder the significance of this visitation. Had something happened, had there been a turn for the Worse, to bring the Takings-Place Above all the way from Pimlico with the news? What else? Ella had a vision of being compelled to leave her work and rushing over to her mother to attend a death-bed—in which case it would not be such an unexciting Christmas after all.

In getting another bottle she had to pass the Takings-Place Above, and she smiled and said " Good evening."

" Good evening," said the Takings-Place Above, smiling back in a strange, awkward way. Yes, Ella decided as she went on with her work, if she was not mistaken that was a death-bed smile, and she could hardly contain herself in her impatience to get to the woman. But two other men entered and brusquely ordered drinks and cigarettes, and it was three or four minutes before she faced her with a " Fancy seeing you."

The Takings-Place Above said " M'm " and again smiled queerly. " Can I have a small Johnny Walker ? " she added.

" Small Johnny Walker ? " said Ella, and went to get it for

her. This did not seem exactly in the death-bed spirit. Unless, of course, she wanted to fortify herself before proclaiming the evil news—that was to say the perfectly glorious news, for Ella had by now given up telling lies to herself in this matter.

" Soda ? " said Ella, holding the glass under the syphon.

" Yes, please," said the Takings-Place Above, still reticent.

There was a throaty hiss from the syphon, and Ella proffered the glass. Then, the Takings-Place Above, who had a feeling for dramatic effect, spoke.

" He's Better," said the Takings-Place Above, her face alight with the gleaming joy of the messenger.

## CHAPTER XXX

AND he was Better—more than Better—in fact, so far as Ella could see, the unpleasant man was in bouncing health, apart from being in bed. The Takings-Place Above at once launched out into lavish and luxuriously dramatic descriptions of the Turn, which had miraculously taken place last night in fulfilment of the Takings-Place Above's premonitions, prophecies, Strange Feelings, and Always Having Said so, etc., and now his temperature had fallen practically to normal, he was sitting up and taking nourishment, and the Doctor had pronounced him out of all danger only that afternoon. In fact, the patient was comparatively in such boisterous health that among other things he had actually spoken quite sharply to Ella's mother over a question of a pillow which wasn't to his liking ! And the Takings-Place Above had remarked humorously to her mother (who was Solid Gold, if ever anyone was) that it would be nice to hear him Ticking her Off Again, and she would have to Spoil him now ! It was all a Miracle really. So delighted had the Takings-Place Above been that she had been unable to resist coming over here to tell Ella. She had thought of her here, poor girl, worrying herself sick at Christmas Time, and not knowing What might have Happened.  And so she thought she would bring her over a little Christmas present in the form of this heartening news.  Freedom from this terrible worry would do her more good than all the Christmas presents in the world, and this should be the jolliest Christmas she had ever had.  The Takings-Place Above Knew what it Meant, and Understood what it Was.

In fact the Takings-Place Above plainly felt justified in indulging in a sort of vicarious celebration of Ella's emancipation from weeks of stark terror, ordered another whiskey (a large one), and began to get rather drunk.  The strain of listening to this emotional and dubious woman, combined with the necessity of pumping up courteous and seemingly enthusiastic answers, of having, in order to save her face, to play up to the farcical rôle of hysterical relief thrust upon her, was nearly more than Ella could stand.  The news itself was heartbreaking enough, but this blithe, self-indulgent hypocrisy into the bargain was really the last straw.


About twenty minutes later, and while she was still talking to the woman (for in politeness and seemliness she had to return to her at the conclusion of each order), Master Eric, apparently urged on by the Governor from the door within, stepped up to her, and with a grave yet fiery glance, delivered himself of an apology in which he had evidently been instructed.

" I've come to say," he said, meeting a rather frightened Ella's eyes, " that I apologize for Kicking you this morning." And he immediately walked away again.

" Why—what a lovely kid ! " exclaimed the Takings-Place Above, at once alive to the opportunity for sentimental participation in a reconciliation.  " Has 'e been Naughty ? "

" Yes.  He was rather," said Ella, who was not displeased. (It was better than getting the sack, anyway.)

" Did 'e Kick you ? " asked the Takings-Place Above, enchanted by the idea.

" Yes.  He did."

" Oo—the naughty boy !  And now 'e came to Apologize ! Ain't that lovely ?  I love kids, don't you ? "

" Yes.  I do."

" I mean I'd love to have a child, wouldn't you ? "

"Yes.  Of course they're a trouble at times."

" Yes, but it'd be worth it," said the Takings-Place Above,
and added warmly, " just to see that he didn't make the mistakes
you'd made yourself."

" Yes," said Ella, secretly thinking that if one actually was
crusading only against Mistakes, a more simple, effective, and
certain method would be for the Takings-Place Above not to
have a child at all.  But of this she showed nothing.

As the house filled up with people, Ella had an excuse to
absent herself more and more from this corner of the bar.
But the Takings-Place Above lingered on and on, eventually
establishing a connection with a stout middle-aged gentleman,
who paid for her drinks and sat down with her.

At a late hour she left the place with him, doubtless, Ella
reflected, to return with him to where she had come from—
the room above her mother in Pimlico—and to add yet another
scandal to those already existing there.  A shady ending to the
somewhat fulsome benevolence of the impulse which originally
brought her over to " The Midnight Bell."  Thus did this
murky bee of London go round dispensing and gathering her
over-sweet honey from place to place over the town.

Ella lay awake hour upon hour that night.  Before going to
bed she had slipped into Bob's room and put his Christmas
present from her upon his pillow.  This was a silk handkerchief,
wrapped around a box of twenty cigarettes.  This had been
planned months ago, when she had bought the handkerchief
at a sale.  She had thrown in the cigarettes in case his " lordship " (she could still with amused and loving deprecation think
of him as his " lordship "—it somehow summed up his transparent charm for her) did not like the handkerchief, and because
cigarettes were always safe.

He was in very late that night.  She never dared to think
where he was or what he was up to out late at night.  But to-
night he was so late that she got frightened, and did think, and
of course decided miserably that it was Girls.  But at last he

came in, and she listened breathlessly in the darkness for his pause in undressing when he saw the present, and thought or imagined that she heard it.  But in a few minutes, she heard him opening his window, as he always did last thing, and she knew that his light was out and that he was as good as asleep. So much for Christmas presents.  And, alas, it was beyond reasonable expectation to imagine that a silk handkerchief wrapped around a box of twenty Players could make a man love you.

Two hours later she was still awake and it was raining in the dark of Christmas Day.  It poured down gently with a steady level of dripping murmur on the roof—like something wishing to instil in her, in the quiet blackness of the night, a sense of the hidden but ever present realities of her lonely and meaningless struggle in the world of London—of the endless procession of solitary nights after senseless working days—of the endless procession of meagre triumphs and frustrations in connection with the disinterested agents of her fate—Mr. Eccles, her stepfather, Master Eric, India, Christmas, Bob, the Governor.  And though months had passed, with all these playing their stimulating or wearying parts, where was she now ?  In her cave, at night, with the rain coming down on the roof.  And on Christmas Day—like the last Christmas Day, and the next.  And still she could not sleep and still the rain came down.  She heard Bob get up and close his window.

## CHAPTER XXXI

THEY had a splendid Christmas Day at " The Midnight Bell."  A terrific midday dinner for all of them in the Governor's room, and in the evening they were allowed to wear the caps from their crackers in the bar !

And, just as Ella had foreseen, by the Christmas Day Post a letter from Mr. Eccles !  In the interval between dinner and tea, which on this astounding day was also taken in the Governor's room, by invitation, she took the opportunity to study this in her bed-room.

                    " 178 Mervyn Avenue,
                            Chiswick, W.4.

" Dear ' Ella ',

(*Still inverted commas, she noted, but perhaps that was because he was angry with her, and she would not become truly Ella until she had been forgiven.*)

" It will be Christmas Day to-morrow, and I am not the man to harbour anything—least of all a grudge. I never was—funny, but there you are." (*A little subsidiary exercise in the Short Elementary Course in Mr. Eccles, this, in spite of the tenderness of the situation.*) " Besides, I now see that I was as fully as much in the wrong as you over that little ' flare-up ' we had that day—you look *so* pretty when you are in a ' pet ' by the way !—in fact, I was more in the wrong, as I know I have a most provoking way with me sometimes when I am angry—friends have told me so." (*More of the Short Course !*) " I am truly and sincerely sorry if I said anything ' unforgivable ' and am sure you will realize that it was not meant.

" The truth is, my dear, that I get attacks of ' the blues ' at times, and then I am very crotchety. My doctor would tell you it is liver !—such a commonplace complaint ! ! But if I am ever to be your ' hubby ' (and we must really weigh up the ' pros ' and ' cons ' of the situation when we next meet) you will have to know my moods when they come along and just tease me out of them like the sly little puss you are ! A clever woman can do so much if she makes a study of her ' man,' and thank Heavens whatever else you can say about me, I have a great sense of humour, and am always the first to laugh at myself.

" What wretched weather we are having. Hardly ' seasonable,' is it ? I always feel that at Christmas time the house-tops should be covered with snow as we see in the Christmas cards. But the good, old-fashioned Christmas seems gone forever in this mechanical age !

" Well, I feel sure that you will take this in the spirit in which it is written and accept my apology if I hurt you. When shall

we meet ?  Remember that I still want to bring you over here
to introduce you to my sister-in-law (I am sure, you will like
each other) and then the die will be cast !  You must not be
frightened at the ' ordeal ' as we will have a talk about it first.

"Shall it be next Wednesday ?  We have your Christmas
present to think about.  I saw some nice fur coats in a window
the other day.  Expensive—but they looked so cosy for this
weather !  I can hardly wait to see you again—as you are always
in my thoughts—perhaps more than you know or I would care
to tell you !  Just at the moment, I could hug you and squeeze
you till you cried for mercy !  So write your toodlums a nice
loving letter with a great big kiss, and let us forget the past and
look to the future.

" Your
" ERNEST."

*Toodlums !*  What a man !  But she supposed he had made
amends in his own impervious, ostrich-like way.  And was he
really going to buy her a fur coat ?  That would be nice, of
course.  But what great big kisses her suddenly and idiotically
self-styled " toodlums " would expect in sweet payment for this
she dared not think !  The trouble with the man simply was that
he was an idiot—as far as amorous advances went, practically a
cretin.  But she supposed that that was not his fault, and that
he was well-meaning, and loved her.

She had no idea how she was going to answer this.  She
would have, she imagined, to make it up, and then all the
wearing problem would begin again—with Mr. Eccles continuing to make an ass of himself, and her unhappy mother
continuing to make hints, and she herself unable to make any
decision reinforced by her heart.  She found now that she had
subconsciously rather enjoyed her brief vacation from him.

Fur coats, indeed !  It sounded most proud and sinful.  It was
awful to think of the things she would be forsaking if she took
the opportunity (and it might never come again) of turning
him down at this juncture.  As she served that night in the
crowded bar, and laughingly rebuked the insincere compliments
of the men (they all said she looked " beautiful " in her cracker
cap) she wondered what they would all think if they knew tnat

there was a gentleman with a rich private income behind her, who really did think she was beautiful, and was prepared to support his opinion with fur coats and legality. It was not a chance which came the way of many barmaids, and there were few who would not rush at it.

Thus the strange and unforeseeable pattern of yet another Christmas Day was lived through. On the next day, Boxing Day—the last stretch in the hateful Christmas tunnel—Ella thought a great deal more about Mr. Eccles, but still had made no attempt to reply to his letter. She somehow excused and felt that he would understand her procrastination on the score of the prevailing irregularity of the Christmas posts, though actually she knew there was one which would reach him to-morrow. She even felt justified in delaying making any decision about Mr. Eccles, for in the Christmas tunnel you felt that all matters were as though suspended, and you could not properly resume your existence and pick up the threads until you came out into the clear mental daylight of Thursday. (After that there was another little tunnel of festivity ahead, in the New Year, but that was not a Severn tunnel, like Christmas.)

On Boxing Day Bob went off for his holiday—without saying good-bye—and she was rather hurt—though it was in the afternoon when she was over at Pimlico, where the fiend had made further miraculous and merciless leaps forward, but her mother was nearly dead with fatigue, overstrained nerves, and overdue rest. Ella gave her her usual ten shillings.

It was rotten—not having Bob to listen to in the next room that night—creepy somehow. The wind howled round the dark house, there was more rain, and she wondered what on earth he was doing with himself on such a stormy night. He was supposed to have gone to Brighton, but she dared not think about that. Anyway it would only be a week—a week went soon enough—sadly soon for the released toiler, and she would have him back fresh for the New Year.

The next day she could still not make up her mind as to the form of her reply to Mr. Eccles, and she took a walk by herself in Regent's Park to think about it. She rather thought she would make it evasive for the time being, until she had taken some advice. Why not confide in Bob when he came back?

It seemed a funny choice, but Bob was young and alone understood her general outlook on life. She had no other young friends. Yes—she would confide in Bob. As she could make nothing else of him, she could at least make a friend of him, and not be silly about him any more. She was going to train herself in not being silly about him any more while he was away. And when he came back they were going to be great friends. That would be a happy evening.

It was with these resolutions that she came down to her evening duties.

It was about five minutes after opening, and she was standing alone wiping glasses in the bar (for the man taking Bob's place was not coming until to-morrow), when Freda, the barmaid round in the public bar, who did not sleep in, and whom Ella did not know very well or like particularly, came round into Ella's province to fetch a bottle.

" Have you heard about Bob ? " she said, as she delved in a cupboard.

" What ? " said Ella, her heart pounding.

" He's gone," said Freda.

" Gone ?   I know he's gone."

" No.  Gone for good," said Freda, and having found what she wanted, went out of sight. A customer entered and ordered a bitter.

" A trifle milder to-night," said the customer.

" Yes.  It is," said Ella, but she had no idea what she was saying.


## CHAPTER XXXII

HE had broken her heart—that was all she knew about it. She had got all the details there were from the Governor and the Mrs., but they were both really as mystified as herself. However, a change of waiters meant nothing to them.

He had come in during the afternoon and said that he was
going back to sea—he had always wanted to do this, and a
chance had come which he felt he could not pass by. It was
" lucky " (said the Governor and the Mrs.) coming at this
time, as they had a new man to hand and would be put to no
inconvenience in the transition. And packed up and gone to
sea he had, all in the space of an hour or so. " He left a special
message for *you*," the Mrs. said. " He sent his love and said he
was sorry he couldn't see you." And " He was a nice boy," said
the Governor, " we'll all miss him, I'm sure." " Yes," said the
Mrs. " and good-looking, too. . . ."

A special message ! What was the good of that, after cruelly
breaking her heart ? How could the Bob she knew have been
so thoughtless, so heartless, as to play this trick on her behind
her back ? To run off while she was not looking, without a
word, without warning, without an attempt to confide in his
companion in slavery. After all their fun, conspiracy, and
intimacy in the bar, after the Christmas present she had given
him, after their going to the pictures together, after all those
nights she had listened to him in his room, after everything.
It was too hard. She would never trust in anybody again.
Was no one to be trusted ? And he had sent her his " love."
What did that mean ? She cherished it, although it meant
nothing.

Most poignant disaster of all, they had put her into his room.
A considerate thought of the Mrs. as it was actually the better
room of the two. And how could she explain to the Mrs. that
she adored the vanished waiter, and could not bear being put in
his room ? The New man would have her old room. His name
was John, and she had met him—a measly, weedy, would-be
vulgar little man with a thin nose and a tiny grey moustache—
but she had to be nice to him as he found his way about.

She had to move in next day. She did it in the afternoon.
She had to light the gas (the gas he had so many times lighted !)
as it was so dark. It was about a quarter of an hour before she
went downstairs for her evening's work, and she stood there,
looking at the vacant, wall-papered cell of the departed spirit.

He had obviously gone in a hurry, for he had left, again with unbearable poignance, many little things behind. . . . A half-used bottle of ink; some old razor blades; and some books and papers. A second-hand copy of Macaulay's History of England, a little green Volume One of Gibbon's Roman Empire, and some old numbers of John O'London's Weekly. Ella had always known that Bob was a great reader, and she had often wondered why he had wanted to stuff his head with such dry things, while secretly admiring him profoundly, and being in a manner proud of him, for his excursions into learned realms beyond her comprehension. He had once told her with naïve pride that there were seven volumes of these Gibbons in all, and he was getting them one by one. But she had never seen another, and now he had left it behind. Why had he forsaken these tokens of some secret ambition to study and improve himself? She picked up the Macaulay, and glanced through its mysterious pages. She saw from the condition of the pages that he had not read it all through, and in a manner which struck her as curiously touching, he had in parts underlined the small print in pencil. Here, for instance: " *Yet it was plain that no confidence could be placed in the King. Nothing but the want of an army had prevented him from entirely subverting the old constitution of the realm.*" Why had her dear, dear, Bob, who had vanished forever, been so anxious secretly to call attention with his delighted pencil to the truth that no confidence could be placed in the King at this period? And later: " *The discipline of the navy was of a piece throughout. . . . It was idle to expect that old sailors, familiar with the hurricanes of the tropics and with the icebergs of the Arctic Circle would pay prompt and respectful obedience to a chief who knew no more of winds and waves than could be learned in a gilded barge between Whitehall stairs and Hampton Court.*" That must have appealed to his strange, charming, reticent soul as a sailor. Where was he now—on the high seas, battling with the winds and waves in the dark? Seeing and touching these relics of the inner life of an aspiring, striving and departed presence, she forgave him all his guilt in forsaking her, and was aware only of a gentle pity for the frustration of all souls, including her own, under the dark firmament.

But now she had to unpack, and make his cold cave her own.

To use his jug and basin, to open and shut his window, to draw his curtains, to make all the little sounds she had heard him making, as though by a process of metamorphosis she was him, and was hearing herself from the next room! It was almost more than she could bring herself to do. Never would this cave cease in her mind to be Bob's cave, and she a nymph compelled sorrowfully to inhabit it, reminded ever and again of what had gone.

And that letter still to be written! In her present mood the mere thought of that man made her ill. Why not have done with him? How, with the dear memory of Bob in her mind, could she submit to his vile, moustached embraces—his Squeezes, and Teasings, and sly little Pussings? And he was so certain of himself in his financial power over her. She was to write to her Toodlums with a great big kiss! Oh—how she would love to put him in his place! Toodlums! She would give him toodlums!

On a sudden impulse she fetched pen and paper.

" Dear Mr. Eccles,
    " Thank you for your letter, but after all this time I have been thinking it all out and have decided that we would never be suited to each other. I am sorry if you have been put to any inconvenience, but we are not in the same class, and I do not love you enough, and you must not write any more as I should not answer. I thank you very much indeed for the kind interest you have shown in me, but this is final I am afraid. Thanking you again.
                              " Yours regretfully,
                                    " ELLA."

She wrote this straight off, without any attention to punctuation or style, and she stamped and addressed the envelope when she was down in the bar and had begun her evening duties. But she did not post it.

She had her mother to consider, and she doubted if she would have the cheek to post a letter like that.

## CHAPTER XXXIII

IT is a sad pass when a solitary young woman in London is so low in spirits and miserable in her thoughts that she decides she must buy herself some sweets and go by herself to the pictures and sit in the gloom, to hide from the roaring world, and try to divert her mind from its aching preoccupations by looking at the shadows. You will sometimes see such lonely figures, eating their sweets and gazing gravely at the screen in the flickering darkness of picture theatres, and it may well be that they are merely other Ellas, with just such problems and sorrows in their grey lives as hers.

It is the sweets which give the tragedy to the spectacle. To have reached such an age, to have fought so strenuously all along the line of life, and yet to have come to a stage of hopelessness and isolation wherein the sole remaining consolation is to be found in sweets! Yet this was Ella's predicament the next afternoon.

It was raining. She could not stay in her room or she would go mad; she could not bear the thought of going over to Pimlico to her people. She had to have something to buck her up, and all she could think of was the pictures and some sweets. She decided to be extravagant and go to the Capitol, to which she had never been, and she bought four ounces of Italian Cream (for which she had a passion dating from childhood) on the way.

It was a tremendous extravagance, as she knew you could not get into the Capitol under one-and-six, but she was beyond caring about extravagance, and she had to have some distraction.

In her bag she still had her unposted letter to Mr. Eccles. That was why she dreaded going to Pimlico so much; for there she would be plied with further wretchedly hopeful questions about the Gentleman, and pressure might be put upon her which would cloud her judgment. She had to decide this matter by herself, but she still had no idea whether she was going to post the letter or not, or what she was going to do if she did not.   Perhaps she would decide in the Cinema.

She had no sooner entered the imposing, lavishly mirrored portals of the Capitol than she had a feeling that her impulse to entertain herself had been a mistaken one.  She bought her one-and-sixpenny seat, getting the impression that the uniformed staff and invisible dispenser of tickets at the office would have preferred her to have spent even more than that, and she was taken to a seat in the first six rows.  Here she was with a few odd people and children, and she tried to concentrate upon the show and enjoy her Italian Cream.

But although this was very nice, she had to be careful not to make herself sick, and she soon found her mind wandering and her heart sinking.  It sank in sudden unexpected lurches, which left a slow ache behind.  When it sank like this, it did it either for no reason at all, or at some little memory or thought of Bob—of Bob now on the high seas, of Bob smacking Eric's head, of Bob sending his "love," or Bob taking her to the pictures himself, and to tea afterwards, in those warm friendly days when she had no idea of the desolation that was to befall —of Bob this and Bob that—Bob all the time.  It was no good. He had struck, as it were, a blow upon her soul which had been transmitted to her physical being—a feeling which she could definitely locate in the region of her diaphragm, and which nothing could alleviate.

Moreover she had come in in the middle of a picture, and the children behind her kept on kicking her in the back.  Each time those sudden love-sick lurches came, she felt she could barely keep still, but must get up and walk away somewhere— but where?  However, she manfully stuck it out for an hour and a quarter.  Then, after a succession of lurches increasing in pain and frequency, as though the ship of her lovelorn condi- tion had entered even rougher water, together with a cold feeling all over her body, she sprang impulsively from her seat and left the theatre.

But you cannot walk away from sorrow like that.  And in any case there is nothing in the world more dreary, damping, and obscurely perturbing than to come out of a cinema in the after- noon to a noisy world.  And she did not want any tea, or know where she was going.  And it was bitterly cold again, with the wind in the east. She walked into Lower Regent Street and up towards Piccadilly.

And in the murky dusk of evening, it was a turbulent and terrifying spectacle which met her eyes and smote her ears. She had never seen so many desperate buses, and blocked cars, and swarming people, in her life. In all the teeming, roaring, grinding, belching, hooting, anxious-faced world of cement and wheels around her it really seemed as though things had gone too far. It seemed as though some climax had just been reached, that civilization was riding for a fall, that these days were certainly the last days of London, and that other dusks must soon gleam upon the broken chaos which must replace it.

And what place had she in it all? And where was she going now? Back to " The Midnight Bell " to talk to Bob? No—no Bob ever again. The horrible New man—John—instead. At this thought her heart sank down again ; she felt she was being drowned in the flood of passing people and savage traffic ; and her soul cried out for aid in its darkness. Oddly enough it came.

" Ella ! " came a voice from behind her, and she turned and was staring at Bob.


## CHAPTER XXXIV

FOR a moment they simply stared at each other, in the stream of people passing them each way, she looking with fright into his dark eyes, and he looking down at her with a sort of diffident concern and suspense.

" Well, you, of all people. . . ." he said. . . .

" But, Bob, I thought you was gone to sea," she said.

She could say nothing else, seeing this strange, lovely and comforting ghost from a lost world.

" No. I don't go till next week," said Bob. " Well, this is fine. What're you doing down here? "

" I've been to the pictures," she said, like a scared child

answering examination questions—so impressed, so awed was she by his presence.

" Well, let's go and have some tea," he said, taking her arm, and leading her away stupefied. " You've got time, haven't you ? "

" Yes. There's plenty of time."

" I know the times all right," said Bob, " I've cut it short enough plenty of times."

" So have I," said Ella, but she felt a bitter pang at this reference to their old companionship, in the fetters from which he was now mysteriously free, but to which she was still bound in loneliness.

" You've got more than half an hour," he said. They were now in Piccadilly itself, and she had no idea where he was leading her.

" But, Bob, why did you leave so sudden ? " she said.

" Oh, I don't know," he said. " I was waiting for the chance you know. An' it just come along."

" But you ought to have let me know, Bob. I was ever so hurt."

" Were you ? I'm sorry Ella. I hoped you would be in that day. I was going to write to you in any case."

" Oh, Bob, you weren't ! "

" Yes, I was, Ella. Honest." And he seemed so sincere and friendly as he looked down on her, that she almost believed him.

" I wouldn't forget you," said Bob. " Let's go down here." And he led her into the doorway of a little lunch-and-tea restaurant which was reached down some dark stairs.

There was only one other customer in the dimly-lit, fancifully decorated little dive, and they sat at a small table covered with a red, checkered cloth. They were served by a lady-like looking person in green. The one other customer left, and she was alone with Bob. So in these strange surroundings, and at so strange a time of day, she had been destined to spend her last moments with the man she loved.

" But where are you *going*, Bob ? " she said, as they waited for their tea.

" Me ? " said Bob, " I'm going to Iceland first of all." And he smiled at the oddity of his destination. "We're sailing Wednesday."

"*Iceland*, Bob? What a funny place."

"Yes. I have been to most places, but I never been up there. But it'll all be new. I was very lucky to get it."

"Of course I suppose I've never really thought of you as a sailor, Bob."

"No?" said Bob, and their tea came. "You be mother," he said, and she poured it out.

"But when did you decide, Bob?"

"Oh, I don't know. It's been on my mind a long time. I wasn't doing much good here."

"Weren't you?"

"No. It wasn't leading anywhere. And maybe I wasn't cut out to be a landsman."

"Weren't you?" And as she stared at him it seemed that there was some truth in this, for he seemed now, to her fond eyes, like some creature that belonged neither to land nor sea, but to some beautiful and remote plane above mortality.

"Is that clock right?" she said. "I mustn't be late."

"No. It's fast. You've got ten minutes or more."

Ten more minutes, and she was never to see him again. A feeling of coldness came over her, and her hand trembled as she lifted her cup to drink. Friendly and sympathetic as he was, he had no idea of her state. How could he? She suddenly remembered how the Mrs. had once remarked that "the girls would all be after Bob," and she saw how perfectly true this was. Any girl with eyes in her head would be after him. How then had she, a plain insignificant girl without any of the resources of others, ever dared hope to that she might make an impression upon so unique and shining a being?

"Then what are you doing with yourself at the moment, Bob?"

"Oh. I'm making do. It's only a few days now."

She did not press her questions, as it was too painful. But she could not help wondering about the whereabouts and present mode of life of this unusual character wandering alone about London, and loved so dearly by her.

"You left all your books behind."

"Did I ? I believe I did."

"Don't you want them ? "

"No—I don't want them."

"Not all your wonderful History books ? "

"No. I don't want them. You have them as a present from me."

"Thanks, Bob. I'm in your room now, you know."

"Oh—are you ? I'm glad of that. You always wanted that room, didn't you."

"Did I ? I used to hear you moving about at night."

"Did you ? I used to hear you sometimes."

"They've got the new man in my room, now."

She knew she was exacerbating and tearing at her wound, but she could not stop herself. She had never had any idea that she loved him like this. As she looked at him now, in these last few moments, it seemed that he was transfigured with almost unholy attractiveness—physical attractiveness—that was the point—sheer physical attractiveness. It was at that moment, perhaps, that she made up her mind about Mr. Eccles. For she had a glimpse, forsaken as she was, of something in Bob and in the depths of her own being which put Mr. Eccles on a level of sacrilege to which she could not, with her youth still on her, descend.

"Have they ? " said Bob. "What's he like ? "

"Oh, he's all right. Not as nice as you."

"Well—I'm glad of that."

"Nor as nice looking."

"Well—that's good too."

"Oh, Bob, you shouldn't have gone and done it," she said, her heart at last speaking.

"I'm sorry, Ella. But there've got to be changes everywhere, haven't there."

She could stand this no longer. "Come on, Bob," she said. "Let's go." And she rose.

It was darker and colder than ever outside, and they had to walk into Regent Street, where he was going to see her on to her bus. He took her arm as they walked along, and they had very little to say. She was only just keeping her teeth from chattering and she had an extraordinary feeling as though he was leading her along in the crowd not to her bus but to her execution, silently sympathetic with her bravery, himself moved by her ordeal. Perhaps he knew after all. And, indeed, it was a form of execution, for her farewell to him was going into the darkness for ever from the shining yet unattainable world she had glimpsed.

" Will you write, Bob ? " she said.

" Yes. I'll write. If you'll answer."

" Oh—I'll answer all right," said Ella. " And talking of writing—" she added, and opened her bag and looked for her letter to Mr. Eccles.

" Yes ? " said Bob.

" You might post this for me, Bob," she said, and she felt she formally handed him the tribute of her love.

Bob looked at the address. " Mr. Eccles—eh ? " he said. " Is he still as mad about you ? "

" Maybe he is. I don't know."

" You just haven't any use for him ? "

" No. He was too old, after all, Bob. And I am young, aren't I ? "

" Of course you are."

" And he was ever so silly, too. Look, Bob, that's my bus if I run for it."

" Yes, it is. Perhaps you'd better. . . . "

They began to run. " All right, Bob. Don't you worry. You write. And don't forget to post that letter."

" No. I won't. . . Well, good-bye, Ella." The bus had stopped and the people were getting off and on.

" Good-bye, Bob. . . You must kiss me, you know, as it's good-bye for good."

And with an effrontery which she marvelled at afterwards, she put up her face, and kissed him.

" Good-bye, Ella."

" Good-bye, Bob."

With these words in her ears, she was climbing the steps of the bus, which was already snarling away, and she did not look back to see him wave.

It was a rather pale, but as ever neat and spruce Ella, who

came down to the bar that evening to begin her work, and no one would have suspected her of being any less cheerful than usual, as the customers came in and ordered their drinks. It was " Good evening, Miss " or " Good evening, Ella," and " Good evening, Sir " or " Good evening, Mr. Er—" just as usual. They all came in telling her how cold it was, and she agreed, shudderingly clasping her hands and smiling.

Not that her customers ever suspected her of having any private worries—or even of any private thoughts. And not that they would have been impressed by them if they did. They would have known unconsciously that the vast total burden of life in London is distributed upon all pretty indiscriminately— is shouldered by each in his own way —and that " worries " were nothing unusual on this planet, in a girl behind the bar or anywhere else. They had enough " worries " themselves.

At about nine o'clock, however, under the stimulus of a few drinks, the burden of life, for them at any rate, grew rather lighter, and as usual they became a little " fresh," and she was made the butt of their friendly irony and arrogance. As usual she was up to them, and was seldom at a loss for a reply to throw back over her shoulder as she got them their drinks.

If anything had happened to Ella, then, which made her a different Ella to the Ella who had served in the same bar, months back, when Mr. Eccles had not appeared on the scene, and she was calmly living her daily life with Bob as an eternal fixture, it was not observable by the gentlemen, or the Governor, or the Mrs., or any of the staff.

And, indeed, what had taken place in those dull months ? Nothing, really, whatever—nothing out of the common lot of any girl in London, if you came to think about it. She had had an elderly admirer, (what girl has not been in such a dilemma at some time or another ?) about whom she had not been able fully to make up her mind. Nothing in that. A connection of hers had been ill—a stepfather whom she disliked, and there had been domestic troubles. Nothing in that. She had been depressed by the fogs and the cold—who had not ? She had looked for another job, but it hadn't come to anything—an ordinary enough occurrence. She had had what the gentlemen in the bar would have called a slight " crush " on the waiter. But that was not the first time a girl had a " crush " on a man she worked with. You soon get over that. No—seen from an outsider's point of view she was lucky if she had nothing more to grumble about, and the gentlemen committed no error in tact in joking with her and teasing her just as usual.

And on no occasion did she give the smallest suspicion that she required special treatment—and indeed it never flashed across her mind that she did. She was too busy, among other things. A little while before closing time the crowded bar became rather more hilarious than usual, owing to the rambling absurdities of an exceptionally intoxicated little man, who had been drinking himself to stupefaction under Ella's chiding yet friendly eyes. He liked Ella, he said. And she was a damned clever girl, too. " *Exactly*," he said when she said anything. She was clever. Ella had often found that it was not difficult to acquire a reputation for cleverness with those who were drunk, for she had only to say the most commonplace things, for which they in their fuddled and groping minds had been long searching, and, lo, they were proclaimed with vinous rapture as shrewd, cutting, universal, solemn, awe-inspiring verities. Thus to-night she had happened to remark that too many cooks sometimes spoiled the broth. " *Exactly !* " said the bemused man, and later became so silly that he was led away amid laughter, still protesting that she was Clever.

Then came closing time, and the new man, in stentorian tones, amazing in so small a man, began to call " *All out !* " " All right, but you'll have to hurry," she whispered conspiratorially, as she always did, to her favourites who begged for a last drink. And " Good-night, Sir ! " she cried, " Good-night," and wiped the bar and tidied up roughly (ready for next morning) in the same old way. And she felt the draught coming in from the opened doors, as she always did.

" Good-night, Ella ! " " Good-night, Sir ! " " Good-night." And at last they had all gone, as they always did, and the doors were being bolted in silence.

" Cheery lot to-night," said the Governor, coming through the bar, and " Yes," said Ella, though she really thought they were just about the same as ever. This was one of the Governor's pet sayings at the end of the day, and she always answered agreeably in the same way—a sort of blessing, as the house settled down in a peaceful hush to its normal and anticipated repose.

But at about half-past ten that night, John, the new waiter at "The Midnight Bell," coming up tired to bed after a hard day's work in the job he had taken on, listened, and heard the barmaid weeping.

THE END